Many Blessin
in this and Eve
Season.

Clark

One Season Of Lovely

Faye Clark

Copyright © 2006 by Faye Clark

ISBN 0-7414-3066-5

Published by:

INFIℳITY
PUBLISHING.COM

1094 New DeHaven Street, Suite 100
West Conshohocken, PA 19428-2713
Info@buybooksontheweb.com
www.buybooksontheweb.com
Toll-free (877) BUY BOOK
Local Phone (610) 941-9999
Fax (610) 941-9959

Printed in the United States of America

Printed on Recycled Paper

Published July 2006

Dear Reader,

One Season of Lovely is a fictional depiction of the lives and relationships of one family, living in a small non-existent farming town called *Lovely,* Kentucky. For me, writing the book gave opportunity to create and intertwine various characterizations and plots, respectively. It has also allowed me to informally address both the importance of nurturing healthy relationships, and what can happen when we don't.

An old African proverb says; *the destruction of a nation begins in the homes of its people.* Trust, loyalty and communication are only a few of the traits missing in the relationships portrayed within these pages. Within *Lovely's* community, and due to a systematic obliteration of their livelihoods, the inhabitants often perceive difficult circumstances as inevitable and not changeable. Greed, envy, prejudices and fear bring about more of the same. And everyone suffers.

But through a show of love and collaborative efforts to preserve and not to destroy, comes *hope.* With the revelation of past histories comes a removal of fear and shame, and thus greater appreciation for, and determination to exercise, all freedoms. They express their freedom of speech. They are freed from intimidation and certainly free to pursue life, liberty *and* happiness.

In this book, it is important that the characters remember their histories so that past degradations are not repeated. With renewed faith and trust, their legacies can be protected and they can greet their futures with the greatest expectancy. For as they come to realize, life is truly a gift, and living it to its fullest is the greatest show of appreciation.

I hope you enjoy the book!

Sincerely,

Faye Clark

First, honoring and being ever thankful to My Lord and Savior for His Word, His Grace and His Promise. To Kenneth and Cedric (the DeWayne's), to Eva Iula, and my loving family and friends: I am humbly grateful for all your love, encouragement and support. Thank you, for believing in me!

Prologue

LaRetha Greer loved the cold season. It was the first week of November and frigid temperatures in *Lovely*, Kentucky were already becoming close to unbearable. It had snowed for a week now, and her food supply was diminishing. Since the grocery store was at least four miles away – four *country* miles – and with recent predictions of another snow storm, already preceded with an icy rain, she needed to make this trip as quickly as possible.

With the old Chevy truck warmed up for the trip, she revved the engine, marveling at how chilled she had gotten just walking those few feet from the house. A southern city girl for most of her life, she'd been thankful to return and find her father's place in such good condition. And so far, this country living was as easy and therapeutic as she'd expected when she had defied all warnings and sold her Atlanta home to move here.

She did miss living in Atlanta - missed seeing old friends and familiar faces. But here, she was adapting amazingly well, especially considering she hadn't experienced this lifestyle in over thirty years. So *no*, she hadn't regretted her decision even once. Not even on days like this one.

This farm was once Vernell Watson's pride and joy. And it wasn't until *Watson,* as everyone called her father, had suddenly become ill that it had seen its first season without at least ten acres of it being planted and harvested, and grazed. Back then, and for as far as the eyes could see, there would be rows and rows of vegetables; corn, tomatoes, peas, cabbages, potatoes and the like. Along with melons and fruit, and fig trees that grew all the way across the pasture to the main road. And, back then, anyone needing a day's pay could earn it on a farm like this one. There was always plenty of work to do.

Because so many people had relied on her father's generosity and employment, when it was first said that he'd died, few had wanted to believe it was true. The man had been perceived as *invincible*. But, it was true. He had quickly succumbed to his illness.

When she'd found out, it was almost too late. And then, he was gone, leaving behind a substantial inheritance that included his house, this truck, and over one hundred acres of beautiful country land with all of its possibilities. And so, being his only blood descendant, here she was.

Considering her father's remarriage over twenty-six years ago, and his two grown adopted sons, LaRetha was surprised that he'd left her this entire estate. And that his wife, Cecelia, hadn't challenged the Will, but just took what she said rightfully belonged to her; money from their bank accounts, benefits from a substantial insurance policy and all her personal belongings, and left town for good. But Thomas and Andrew had long been gone since leaving for college. They were raising families of their own, now. Had she stayed on, Cecelia would have been alone. She had decided to move back to her family home in New Jersey, instead.

Understandable, LaRetha had thought. This place was a far cry from New Jersey, she imagined. And practically everyone she knew had warned her not to get too attached to it, or the lifestyle, saying she wouldn't be out here for very long - assuming she preferred a faster life and sunny weather to the isolation and snow storms. She didn't. Even the tough but understanding MacDonald Henry, better known in the newspaper publishing world as Mac Henry, or *Mac* to her, had given the whole endeavor six months, tops.

You just need a little time to grieve, he'd told her over a year ago, convinced that she would miss the quick city pace she was flourishing in as an emerging journalism professional, and return. They were all still waiting for her to come to her senses.

Well, little did they know, she thought. Enthusiastically, she had come here to write, and with plans to keep the place up. To refocus her life. She had no desire to farm, but was enjoying owning her own piece of the country. There was plenty of time to decide what to do with it.

She also had family here. Although estranged from her father somehow, there was the possibility that they might want to become acquainted. Right now, however, she was enjoying the fact that, if nothing else, life in *Lovely* was peaceful.

Besides, Atlanta wasn't *that* far away. She could see her mother and her son Germaine, at any time. And, when she decided to venture that way again, she could also spend time with her best friend, *wanna-be love interest,* Kellen Kincaid.

But after divorcing her husband of over twenty years, unlike Kellen, she was in no hurry to get involved. Her divorce from Gerald had been both trying and emotionally draining, albeit completely necessary. Luckily, she'd been prepared when the time came. And the emotional separation wasn't so difficult at first, considering he was already gone in her mind, anyway. And because she'd always handled their household finances anyway, that part of single living was a piece of cake.

She thought she'd done pretty well; picking up the pieces of her heart and moving on - not allowing herself time to grieve the loss for very long. She had worked hard to close that chapter of her life, while still trying to be there for everyone else. But this time around, she had made herself the priority, doing what truly made her happy. Even if no one else agreed with the way she'd chosen to do it.

But just when she knew she had a handle on things, a year after the divorce, her father had passed away. Buried emotions that she had avoided confronting had surfaced. And the compounded grief had been a lot to bear. To make matters worse, soon after that came the added distress of losing all contact with Germaine. And all she could wonder at the time was *'what could possibly happen next?'*

Her losses and grief were three-fold; first Gerald, then her father and *then* the loss of a once close relationship with her son. And surprisingly, each of them had affected her the same. Always the tough daughter of a likewise tough single mother, she knew all about forging ahead, even when you couldn't quite see the way. But, unlike in the past when she'd quickly gotten through those unexpected hitches, this time around it just wasn't so easy to bounce back.

According to her co-worker and good friend, Constance, who knew just how frugal she could be with a dollar, she supposedly had it 'made in the shade' now, referring to her financial situation. Having enough money certainly helped. But LaRetha always knew that it would take something more than a good-sized bank account and sound investments to bring joy back into her soul.

Everyone thought they had the solution; *LaRetha just needed a good man*, they said. But right now, she needed something far greater than anything a new man could provide. What she needed, and longed for, was a *renewed spirit*. And she planned to find it here in *Lovely*.

She hadn't lived here since she was two years old and her mother and *Watson* were together. Her visits with him over the years that followed still held fond memories - comforting ones - anytime she missed her father.

Sure, the town had changed over time. And she had always heard that you couldn't go back again. But, it was her anticipation of change that had summoned her here. Either way, she figured, even if moving was a *bad* decision, with her know-how and determination, there would always be other options to explore.

This unanticipated opportunity had been timely, nevertheless. As though by premonition, and despite her husband's doubtfulness, she had already chucked her *9 to 5* corporate job to work for Mac full time at the *ATL Weekly News Reporter*. And then made the decision to freelance instead.

And now, all those questionable decisions made perfect sense. She could work from home, writing for more publications. And travel only when necessary. Having already received a few local awards for her stories on urban lifestyles, she now had bigger goals - for national recognition. And having already established herself as an accomplished journalist, even in *Lovely,* she could achieve this.

She was happy with her life. It was just too bad that her ex-husband resented her so much for it. She had tried to be fair; sharing with him the profits from the sale of their home, even after it was awarded to her in the divorce. He had hardly been grateful. Still, that hadn't deterred her. She figured she had worried enough over *him.*

Besides, like Constance said, and due to great planning and a lot of discipline on her part, her finances were good. There was the annuity that she'd contributed to for retirement and for her son's college future. It had grown substantially over the years. She only hoped he would come to his senses soon and use it.

After selling the house, she and Germaine had moved into a condominium in Dunwoody – one that she'd purchased in a distress sale. Her decision to live there while renovating it had saved her *bundles*. Now, with other changes in the area, it rented for more than twice its monthly note. And when you included the value of the farmhouse and land, and the benefits she'd received from an insurance policy that her mother had insisted she keep up out of concern that her father's wife might not be so responsible, her financial position was *excellent.*

Cecelia had refused her offer to pay her father's burial expenses, insisting instead that she was entitled to it all. This did nothing to soften her mother's impression of the woman, however.

LaRetha slowed at the fork, examining her options, before taking the westward road, which was wider and easier to travel, and considering that it was the only one with streetlights.

There won't be any traffic jams out here, she thought with a smile. She rarely saw her closest neighbors, who lived over two miles away. But that was the point, after all. As for now, her only problem was with dodging hanging limbs and potholes.

No one passed her as she drove through dull terrain that was so captivating in warmer seasons. On those days, its velvety summer-green carpeting would encircle thick trees that went on for miles and miles, and mountainous treetops would appear to rise and fall to meet the most beautiful clear blue summer sky. The only pending peril in these surroundings, however, were on days like this one, when deceptively clear but icy roads might be easy to slide across and down the sides into deep ditches that ran parallel.

She drove very carefully because according to old tales, it wasn't unusual for abandoned vehicles to surface along the embankments once the snow cleared. And according to *Watson,* there had been a time or two back in the day when the occupants had been found frozen to death inside of them. She used to wonder why, if that was the case, no one ever bothered to erect safety barriers alongside the road to remedy the problem. But, so it was with old folktales, she guessed. Those things just weren't to be messed with.

Shuddering, she turned up the heat and then the radio. Only the weather station played clearly, giving the same forecast from this morning.

Ice and snow was expected for another week. Power outages were occurring. Drive as little as possible. Prepare to be snowed-in for a few days.

Finally reaching the main road, and then the store, she smiled victoriously.   Parking was easy, as always. As would be the conversation. Today, however, she just wanted to hurry back to her warm fireplace, a good meal and several hours of work at her computer. Besides, Kellen would have called or sent an e-mail, by now. And she always looked forward to hearing from him.

Several locals greeted her as she went inside, their large pack-ages giving little hope that anything would be left on the shelves. Bundled tightly, with list in hand, she nodded a greeting to the storeowner as she grabbed a cart and headed for the heating section.

Kerosene for her emergency heater, *matches, candles, extra batteries.* Another flashlight wouldn't hurt, either. She dropped a pair of gloves into her cart.

'*...expecting six to eight inches by tomorrow morning,'* the weather announcer was saying over store speakers that blared inside. This one would last for a while. Yesterday had been much warmer. But then, Georgia weather had been similarly sporadic. One day would be sunny and warm, the next, schools and businesses would close due to cold weather and frozen pipes. Except out here, the power outages seemed to last forever.

Still, the view never failed to mesmerize her. Despite what her mother said about growing up here, living out-of-the-way and being snowed in like this wasn't so bad, she thought. For a lot of folks like her, this was the attraction. For others, however, it was their very reason for leaving.

"You're still up there at the Watson place, *ain't ya?*"

The old man grinned at her from behind the counter before giving his tobacco a few quick chews to keep the juice from spilling out of his mouth.

Mr. Bailey. Faded, oversized overalls fell from his very slim shoulders as if from a clothes hanger, and appeared long overdue for washing. His entire body appeared to be covered in a light coat of soot. He had opened and closed this store almost every weekday, like clockwork, ever since she was a child. And he always had the most interesting stories to tell.

He noticed her inadvertent scrutiny of him, and smiled, glancing down at himself.

"Had to help a *feller* with his heater before coming in this morning. 'Ain't much reason round here to be *dressin' up,* though. Thing is to jus' keep warm."

"It sure is," she said, offering a repentant smile as she started down another aisle. The store was practically empty for the moment. Best she took advantage of it.

She could see the man stretching his thin body upward, before leaning back against an old red soda cooler and propping his foot on something behind the counter. He was giving her a considerably long look. Apparently, their conversation wasn't over.

"You know, your daddy sure is missed in this town. It's been two years and I still can't believe he's gone. Why, he was even *younger'n* me and as tough as any of us. *Shoot, he was just like one 'a us.*"

This comment got her attention. She stopped and looked intently at the old man, seeing his tobacco-browned lips spread flat into a thin smile at the intended complement.

"So, you knew my father well?"

Of course he did, she thought. This was *Lovely,* after all.

Her question appeared to puzzle him at first. Then he nodded.

"Oh, yeah," he waved a thin veined hand in the air as if swatting a fly. He flashed a perfect row of white teeth that seemed out of place on his dingy, wrinkled countenance.

"We used to hunt and fish, together, all the time," he said. "Good man, he was. He talked about you all the time, *Lo-retta.*"

LaRetha, she thought. *Laretta is my mother's name.* She didn't correct him, being anxious to finish and get home before the temperature fell.

"A sad thing, his dying like *ke-hat! Lovely* ain't the same without him. Poor man must'a worked hisself to death. Never did know how to slow down. But, that'll be the death of most of us, I reckon."

A good man. She thought, swallowing.

"A *real* good man," he added as if reading her thoughts.

Sure he was, she thought, the words *just like one of us,* still ringing in her mind. She didn't need to ask what that meant. A fair complexioned man, *Watson* could never have been mistaken for white, but in those days a generation before when everything was a matter of race, he was accepted by the locals as a man with authority, simply because he came close.

Tall, at *6'3"*, with a medium build and hazel eyes that she'd always felt were looking straight through her, he'd had a very charming even-toothed smile and slick black hair that curled whenever he would sweat or after he'd bathed or gotten caught in the rain. Like all the other men in his family, he was considered very handsome. And except that her eyes were a dark brown, their resemblance was such that, despite her long absence, people around town always knew instantly that she was his daughter.

At *5'8"*, she took after her father in stature and complexion, but everything else was *Laretta;* particularly her eyes and enviably full lips, and her rounded figure. Like Laretta, who was beautifully dark and petite, she was shapely in all the right places, she was told. Still she was always known as *Watson's* child. Few people in town had ever bothered to remember or call her by her married name. Not that it mattered, now.

Unlike her mother, *Watson* had lived in *Lovely* all of his life. A firm, religious man like his father before him, he'd been considered hard but fair. Aside from running the farm, he had also been an activist, of sorts. Vocal about local farm and community matters, he'd openly opposed injustices against minority farmers like himself. He was known to work hard at everything that he did, and without complaining. Not even, according to Cecelia, when people had expected way too much from him.

With an imposing presence, he'd been one of the more outspoken landowners when local fires had threatened to consume the poorer farms in their small town. The economy was suffering. And several of them, particularly the minority farmers, were being strong-armed into selling for next to nothing after having their crops and livestock destroyed. There were suspicions of who was responsible. But initially, because of threats and very little representation where it counted, few had openly complained; out of fear for themselves and their families.

But, after a time, when it was clear that any help coming to their town to assist the local farm owners wasn't coming to them, they had organized. Several boycotts had followed. And despite pleadings by local government that violence be avoided at all cost, it had frighteningly prevailed for a time on both sides. According to her mother and father, it had been a difficult, ruthless time.

Out of necessity, *Watson* and other farmers had led the effort to fight back. They listened to and initiated complaints and petitions, while supporting one another's efforts to hold on to their legacies. They would defeat this, they'd said, as long as they stuck together and protected one another.

And now that the battle had crossed color lines, and several fire-starting culprits were identified, there had begun an effort to restore peace. And to rebuild what had been destroyed. Each family helped the other, regardless of race; aiding in restoring burned properties, and housing and feeding those displaced families in the interim.

The town still belonged to them, except now, they had a say in it. Nothing like this had ever occurred in this small nondescript town of *Lovely*. Residents slowly began to regain their pride and confidence, and everyone was making an effort.

However, as popular and revered as *Watson* had been with other farmers, he was quite the opposite to those who had stood the most to gain from their losses. That had put him in danger, to say the least. Efforts by prospectors to court him into encouraging other farmers to sell were unsuccessful. He had believed that to do so would be to contribute to their poverty. It would alter the economic and social dynamics of their small town, and certainly not to their benefit in the long run. *Farming was what they knew,* he'd said. And farmers were who they were.

Those efforts to revitalize their businesses and the town had paid off. All of the farmers were getting the respect that they said they both demanded and deserved from their government. Town meetings were no longer off limits to them. Finally, their concerns were being seriously considered. It didn't happen overnight, he'd said. But, for this to occur at a time when greedy financiers had maintained that *colored* men should stick to farming and leave big business to them, well that had been nothing less than remarkable.

The town was beautiful now, with its restored brick structures and colorful landscaping. Clearly, the hope and pride of those same visionaries was manifested into the lives of their children, influencing them to contribute to what might otherwise have become a tourist attraction. Or worse, a kind of industrial wonderland with hardly a memory of its rich history and many great traditions, on all sides.

Watson had played a big part in it. Fearless, she thought he was. Praying, he'd said, until getting his answers. Still, there had also come the burden of leadership. There were always those people who had benefited, but who would still accuse him of being selfish and manipulative when he'd suggested compromise rather than confrontation. And others on both sides of the color line, who, despite their own consistent and peaceful interactions, had resented his standing for *coloreds* and then re-marrying *white*.

Bringing the woman and her two young sons from a previous marriage out to the farm to live was more than a little risky in those days. But, he had never backed down. Not even when angry locals had come to their door.

LaRetha could clearly remember that one summer when she had visited the farm. A group of men had driven out to their house. They needed to *talk* to him.

"Take the children into the bedroom and close the door!" He'd shouted and Cecelia complied, hurrying her, Thomas and Andrew into a very dark corner of the boys' bedroom. Frightened at his sudden outburst, they had all huddled together and waited. And she remembered that Cecelia had prayed the entire time.

There were noises - loud voices. And she could hear *Watson* daring even the *first* one to step onto his front porch. He knew his rights, he'd said. He could be heard hurrying throughout the house. And still more voices telling him to *come outside right now to talk.*

A hall closet opened and slammed closed. The front screen door opened and shut with a bang. Seconds later, there were gunshots. More loud voices. More gun shots - but closer, this time. Someone and *Watson* were shooting.

It seemed an eternity, waiting in that bedroom. But finally those engines had started and the cars had left as quickly as they had come. It was years before she knew the reason. As it turned out, several of her father's friends and supporters had heard that there might be trouble and had come in large numbers to help. Once they were surrounded, these unwelcome guests had felt encouraged to leave.

Watson had come a short time later, gathering them together and hugging each of them until they were duly comforted before sending them to bed. In the kitchen, he had consoled his tearful wife, assuring her there was no need to worry. Then, he had risen very early the next morning and gone into town to initiate a few talks of his own. That incident was never repeated.

He was a Christian man, he'd said in anguish. *Who had the right to dictate over his home or his family? What right did they have to assert their opinions in this manner? His family was his business.*

By this time, *Lovely* had begun to experience the changes that came with greater acceptance and understanding of racial differences – acceptance being the key, and not *tolerance,* she believed. Like her parents, LaRetha felt that it was *behavior* that should or shouldn't be tolerated – and not people, who should be *accepted.* By then, it was expected that the racial climate in this town would continue to get better, and not worse.

She often wondered if Thomas and Andrew still remembered, or even thought about those times, much. With only a few farms left and even fewer that actually operated, life here was different, now. Large companies did finally come, but after collaborative planning. There was still some consternation over the pollutants that disturbed the water and soil – important concerns. But now, with increased acceptance, more access to information and greater opportunities, Lovely's land and business owners, including minorities, were thriving as never before.

The population had greatly increased, as had the number of churches, retail shops, restaurants, libraries and family entertainment venues. Several colleges had extended their curriculum to this area, enticing more young people to remain after graduation and others to come in from different cities. *Lovely* was thriving. And it was truly a town to be proud of.

Getting her mother to see this was impossible, however. She despised everything that *Lovely* stood for, and didn't mind saying so. She simply hadn't shared her husband's enthusiasm for staying and making a difference. According to her, very little had truly changed; the system of separation hadn't dissipated but merely shifted, becoming more indirect but just as deadly.

According to Laretta, *Watson* and those men had accomplished much. Not because of any perceived advantages, but because they would never take *no* for an answer. Despite his charisma and leadership abilities, she said, it was never that her father had held some special formula for success. It was simply the fear of a *crazy* man who came from a *crazy* family that had borne that local respect.

Watson had been LaRetha's everything. Her relationship with her father had always been wonderfully close. But their bond was later tested when she'd defied warnings and married a man that neither of her parents had approved of. If those two had agreed on nothing else, they'd both felt Gerald Greer had nothing to offer her aside from a lifetime of heartache. One look at his bright yellow souped-up Honda, his colorful clothing, high-boxed haircut and diamond-studded ear lobe, and her father had summed him up in a sentence.

He's entirely too slick for you, he said. Never pretentious or one to spare feelings when sharing a little wisdom would be more beneficial, like her mother, *Watson* had made his low expectations of his future son-in-law, *quite clear*.

LaRetha hadn't understood their contempt for her fiancé. Gerald's slick, sarcastic demeanor could be expected of any young black man trying to defeat the obstacles of a poor upbringing in one of Atlanta's toughest housing projects. For her, that tough and flashy exterior had been a great part of his charm.

More than that, she'd admired his determination to redirect his life – to not end up like his brother Graham, who was by then incarcerated. Or his friends who'd all lived dangerously and met what he'd called their 'expected ends'. With positive influences, which she preferred to call 'divine interventions', he had worked hard and finished high school, earned a college degree, and then became employed at a major architectural firm, where he still earned a substantial income. Now, with a company-paid-for master's degree, he was a top engineer. For that, she'd defended, he was to be *commended,* not criticized.

But country manners preceding, her father had insisted that her future lay in marrying a man with *substance* and strong spiritual beliefs, which Gerald did not appear to have. And knowing this, while harboring a bit of anger against his own absentee father, Gerald had made no secret of disliking her father for it, in return.

They had done well, financially. With a dual degree in business and journalism, and a set of goals of her own, LaRetha had been easily promoted in her management positions. So, it had been risky, deciding that once Germaine was older and more independent of her schedule, she could finally pursue the writing career that she'd always wanted. And she had.

Gerald hadn't been enthused about the loss in income. He would have to make changes, as well, particularly to curtail his lavish spending habits. But, it was what she'd needed. And this was *her* time, she'd insisted. He hadn't argued.

But her mother remained unimpressed, pointing out that he drove a Cadillac while she drove a standard car. That he dressed far too flashy and expensively to have a wife who was content with wearing clothing that she would only purchase on sale.

"Nobody can live up to your parents' expectations. If I'm not hearing it from her, I'm getting it from him," Gerald had once said. And sadly, he'd been right about that. She believed that her parents' distrust had led him to try less with his own child – the grandson they had adored so much. Germaine had become *her* child and *their* grandson. And most likely, the child had always known it.

But like his own father, *Watson* had always been strict and no-nonsense when raising her, and then Cecelia's two sons from a previous marriage, whom he'd later adopted. His father had been the same, except *Watson* was kinder. Laughed more. Talked more. He was a loving family man and friend. But Gerald could see none of that. It wouldn't be until after Germaine was born that the two men would finally declare a truce.

Cecelia's boys were young when they came to *Lovely;* Thomas was thirteen and Andrew was ten. LaRetha was about *twelve* at the time, and was therefore considered the middle child. And she and the boys had been as close as she could have imagined them being.

Even now, LaRetha considered the difficulty they must have faced – having been uprooted and brought to a place that was so different from their previous life up north - a place where interracial marriages were unheard of at that time. But, there had been no divisions in her father's house. They were all *family,* and that was never questioned.

Still, LaRetha figured her assumptions was correct, because as soon as they were old enough, both sons had applied to different colleges up north, leaving *Lovely* far behind. Returning, for a time, only on special holidays. And then finally for their father's funeral.

If *Watson* had taught any of them anything, it was about hard work and fortitude. It was never doubtful that all of them would be successful; Thomas was a *CPA* with his own accounting firm and Andrew, a scientist in aeronautic research. She had also done well.

And while they hadn't kept in close touch over the years, they'd all been genuinely happy to see one another at the funeral, each promising to never allow so much time to pass before talking, again. Then, they had all moved on with their lives. And, she'd sadly suspected, they would probably not visit again, except for another funeral.

"Why did you leave my daddy?" Fourteen years old, LaRetha had faced off with her mother at their kitchen table when she mentioned that *Watson* and Cecelia wanted her to visit on the upcoming Labor Day weekend. By now, she understood that, although no one would take responsibility or cast blame, her parents' separation had been *somebody's* decision.

"Your daddy and I were just too different, LaRetha. You'll under- stand when you're older."

"No. I won't!" She'd cried, storming from the dinner table to go to her room, where she could be angry, alone.

It was unfair that her father would live with another family on *their* farm in Kentucky, when he could have been with them. She had never heard *Watson* and Laretta so much as argue when he'd visited. So, why couldn't they stay married? *Why couldn't the three of them be together?*

It was a long while before LaRetha finally realized that he was never coming to live with them in Atlanta. Nor would they ever return to the farm. Her father was remarrying and she would only see him on those special visits, usually during summer breaks.

Cecelia couldn't have been more different from Laretta, and not just outwardly. City bred and easy mannered, she was of medium height and build. Average looking she guessed, with long brown hair and hazel eyes like her father's. And, unlike her mother, who was a successful real estate broker and independent divorcee', Cecelia was quite contented with living on the farm and being a homemaker, having readily accepted the lifestyle and dedicated herself to taking care of *Watson* and the children.

Even aside from the racial differences, it was an unusual union, to say the least. Something strangely like *city north* meets *farm south*. But, they had all gradually fallen in sync. And for her and Cecelia, there was found a common interest.

A former writer *slash* actress from some off-off-off Broadway stage, Cecelia had shared with LaRetha her passion for literature, which somehow ignited something in her, bringing her own talent for writing to surface. This quickly became her primary reason for visiting so often, and for staying as long as she had, her occasional visits extending to two whole months, one summer.

But, even as a child she had been conscious of her mother's feelings and never shared this enthusiasm with Laretta, who'd still believed she had needed coaxing. Cecelia had understood the risks as well, because she'd never mentioned it to Laretta. It became their little secret.

"I really don't think she's all that fond of black folks," her mother had commented once when driving her out to stay at the farm while she visited her ailing parents for a week.

"Talking 'bout they met when he visited an old school buddy upstate and fell in love *instantly,"* Laretta had said, in angst. "She's just some city slick hussy looking for a sugar daddy! And your father is just too *country* to see the truth."

LaRetha had sat in the passenger's seat, allowing her mother to vent, recognizing it for the hurt and regret that it was.

"She's probably been disowned for some reason," her mother continued. "It's mighty funny her people don't even visit. They probably don't even know he's a Negro!"

At the time, LaRetha couldn't imagine *anyone* not knowing who her father was. Still, Laretta had always insisted that there was something amiss. *She is an actress, after all,* she would say. LaRetha had almost understood her mother's misgivings. But, moving away had been her idea, her child-mind had reasoned. So, wouldn't that make this her fault?

As happy as her mother had become with her life in Atlanta, LaRetha recognized her unspoken *what if's.* What if she'd stayed with *Watson?* What if she hadn't made so many mistakes as a teenager? What if she had supported his efforts more? What if?

Her mother didn't deny being a difficult adolescent. For her, *Lovely* had been much too small, and being an only child, she had looked for excitement wherever she could find it. Along with the usual infractions of skipping school, she had been a sort of *wild child,* popular with the wrong crowds, openly defying her parents and staying out late. She'd been quite a challenge for the parents who'd prayed for a child and had gotten one in their late thirties. And who frankly didn't know what to do with her.

But, she had finally found her right road. Her parents had never stopped praying for her. Never gave up on her. And after experiencing her share of trouble, she had finally understood what they had between them and what they were offering to her. She had tried to make up for the pain she'd caused them, devoting herself to caring for them in their last years, and making certain that they had wanted for nothing.

And as different as the two women were, in LaRetha's mind, there was never a competition between them. Laretta was her mother, *hands down;* her blood, her bearer and provider. And Cecelia, more like a very close friend. She'd known that she could go to her mother for her care, for practical advice and certainly in times of trouble. And then to Cecelia when she'd wanted to be creative. They would bake cookies and make handmade dolls, and talk about writers and authors and faraway places. Both women had taught her to strive for her dreams, and she had needed them both.

LaRetha wondered how her son was doing. He and his uncles had gotten along well on that day of her father's funeral, when they'd seen one another for the first time since he'd grown up. They had teased him about being taller than them, marveling at his maturity. By the end of the day, both had invited him upstate for summer visits. Except he hadn't yet followed up.

Germaine had fallen in love. And not long after the funeral, he'd moved out of their condo to live with his girl, *Tori,* and at a time when she had preferred that he would concentrate on his future. Taking the jeep that she and his father had given him at high school graduation, he'd emptied his bank account and moved with the girl to live with relatives of hers. They hadn't spoken, since.

Finding his note, stating how much he loved and appreciated her, but that he needed to be on his own for a time, had been heart breaking. And after hearing from him only indirectly for the next year, mostly through Kellen, who was a friend to them both, she had finally gotten irritated with the entire situation and asked him to relay a message to Germaine.

"This is absolutely ridiculous! I'm not taking any more messages. He's going to have to talk to me, *directly.* He has my address, my phone numbers and my e-mail address. Tell him I said to *use* them."

He hadn't sent word, after that. And everyday, she denied her own disappointment, filling the time with her other interests. But, sometimes, many times, she ached to take it all back. *Any* word from him was better than none.

But like his father, her son had moved on with his life, so her only choice was to do the same. One day he would realize that she was still here for him, and come around. She hadn't been *all wrong* as a mother, had she?

This loss had led to her decision to move. And despite her initial concerns, once her mind was made up, everything had seemed to fall right into place. And now, for the first time, she could say that she was divorced, accomplished *and* happy.

Now, there was no need to pretend to anyone, particularly her mother and Kellen, that getting the divorce hadn't hurt. *Terribly.* Or that she wasn't somewhat concerned about her future. She could enjoy her life one day at a time, without having to explain anything to anybody. The pain she felt would ease, eventually. In the meantime, she was here to stay.

It was getting late and her cart was completely filled now, mostly with items *not* on her list. Naturally, everyone in the short line at the checkout counter had similar purchases. Conversation flowed around her about the anticipated storm, a dispute over somebody's property lines, and someone's daughter having another baby. She laughed to herself, thinking how these were things that would've driven Kellen crazy.

Kellen Kincaid was most certainly *citified*. Handsome and smart, he was also very much in love with her. Still, there was no way he would ever have moved out here, under *any* circumstances. He thought she had lost her mind to even consider it. Presently, he was embarking on his own little campaign to get her back to Atlanta, and to him.

"How is it that you can complain about Germaine just up and running away when you're doing the same thing?" He had asked.

As the much older brother of her son's best friend, Kadero, Kellen was also her best friend. Except he thought he knew better than her what she needed, which was *him*. And he'd been totally perplexed that she had disagreed with all his theories on why she shouldn't move.

"Who said I was running away, Kellen? Maybe there's something there for me. You're always saying that change is necessary and good for everybody. Well, now is the time for you to prove that you mean it. I would appreciate your support."

Kellen's concerns were appreciated, but she'd long recognized his phobias about losing *family*. And to him, that's what she and Germaine were. Just two years before, his mother had moved out of state, closer to his father's job, leaving Kadero in the care of his older, independent brother. At least until he'd graduated high school in another two years.

To her, that was a most unselfish sacrifice that Kellen had made, adjusting his lifestyle to accommodate a younger brother who, as a teenager, definitely needed guidance. But he had managed, receiving sufficient support checks from their parents each month. And working odd jobs to tide him over after a lay-off, before getting hired as a full time staff reporter by Mac Henry.

They had met when she was married to Gerald. He would come by to drop his brother off to visit Germaine, and had therefore become a friend to her son. She remembered being impressed with his reliability, and his concerns that they didn't impose. Even her mother had found him charismatic.

"Is he coming around for Germaine or for *you?*" Laretta had questioned. The divorce was final by that time. And his visits had noticeably increased.

At the time, she had welcomed this, considering Gerald's sporadic visits with Germaine. Undoubtedly attractive, Kellen had been charming and easy to get to know. But she hadn't entertained any chemistry. It was much later that they had explored other possibilities between them.

Unexpectedly, they had become serious. So serious that moving away had been just the thing she'd needed to clear her head *and* heart of him. She'd needed to reevaluate her life and this relationship. To consider where this was going and whether or not she wanted it to, and certainly to give him enough time and space to do the same.

Finally, the front of the checkout line! Once outside again, she loaded her items inside the truck. The temperature had severely dropped. Most of the roads would be closed, soon.

Carefully avoiding dangling limbs and power lines on the way home, she finally sighed with relief as she turned into her driveway.

1

The house was cozy and warm when she returned. A big house, traditionally styled for that part of the country, she figured it was just right for her. It still had the same type of white wood siding and green shutters as when it was built. The floor plan was circular, with just a few, very large rooms. She had added a master bathroom, and enclosed a side porch to make a sunroom which, aside from the kitchen, was her favorite room in the house. Outside, a separate two-car garage was just twenty paces away. A large red barn stood a few hundred feet from there. Once filled with farming equipment, it hadn't been used in years.

Watson was young when he'd built this house for him and her mother. He had wanted to remain on the farm, near his parents. That house still stood about a quarter mile down the road. And aside from her wide front porch with wood railings, and the sunroom, this house was exactly the same as theirs.

Aside from the challenge of finding local contractors to do the work, remodeling this house had been easy. A fireplace had replaced an old wood heater in the master bedroom. Old painted-over paneling was replaced with sheetrock and painted a variation of soft, complementary colors. Hardwood floors were stripped, buffed and shined. And large storm windows replaced old paned ones, allowing in enough light that she didn't need electricity, most days.

Her kitchen was completely changed; a light yellow coat of paint replaced dated wallpaper patterns. And white cabinets with glass doors left no traces of the old maple ones. There were all new appliances, and attractive granite countertops were wide enough for all her appliances and gadgets - a luxury she didn't have at the condo. She particularly loved the view outside the bay window in the bright eat-in area.

Next spring, the window boxes would sprout large blossoms and the hedges would regain their color. She would sit on the front porch swing, reading and working on her laptop, or just talking with Kellen on the phone. His calls often made her wish he was here. But to say so, she feared, would change everything.

Putting the groceries away, LaRetha recalled many mornings when *Watson* and Thomas would return from early chores, and the family would sit down together to a hearty breakfast of homemade biscuits, country fried ham and red-eye gravy, cheese grits and scrambled eggs. Coffee, juice or milk would be poured to their liking.

It was always a welcomed sight in comparison to the lighter, healthier fare that Laretta preferred on rushed weekday mornings; fruit and cereal or fruity oatmeal, and every now and then, pancakes. She had never warmed to those microwaveable turkey sausages. They tasted nothing like her father's home-raised pork, she would complain.

"Look *child*, we don't live on a farm, and last time I looked, we weren't raising no hogs, *so eat!*" Laretta would exclaim, before telling her that the meal she turned her nose up at today, would be one that she prayed for, tomorrow.

I doubt it, she would think glumly, chewing slowly, trying to give her taste buds time to adjust and her mother time to leave the room before she tossed it into the trash. She was happy when they'd finally hired Marilee. The kitchen table had become a much more inviting place.

She warmed her hands by the fireplace before sitting at her laptop computer to check her e-mail. Laretta had written her. Not surprisingly, she had just closed on the sale of another high-end property. They had celebrated many large commission checks back in the day - usually with their traditional apple cider and carrot cake. Their biggest celebration, however, had been over LaRetha's divorce.

And now, with Gerald out of the picture, Laretta had her opinions about Kellen. He had arranged a small farewell dinner at her condo for their mutual friends and the office staff before she'd moved, and her mother had spent much of the time observing them.

"Be careful with that one," she'd said and LaRetha had shrugged off.

Despite being a divorcee' and raising a son, and standing completely on her own two feet by then, her mother and her friend Constance, still couldn't accept that she was capable of taking care of herself – a common misconception about divorced women, she soon learned. It irritated her that she was forever required to prove herself independent. Supposedly, she was now susceptible to every possible con that a man could invent. This, coming from divorced women.

Younger men just can't be counted on, Laretta had asserted.

Not to worry, she'd said, telling her that Kellen was just a friend. But her mother had seen something more.

"Your mother's pretty *cool,*" he'd said after Laretta had gone. "You two seem close."

"She's *priceless,*" she'd said. "I'm glad we have the relationship that we do."

"You should be. She's a wonderful lady."

But now, Kellen and her mother were siding together, sharing an opinion about *Lovely.* With her mother trying to talk her out of it, Kellen had added to the pressure by showing up on moving day and playfully boycotting with small picket signs that he'd wielded to passers-by who gave puzzled and amused looks.

"You're giving up everything you've worked for to live out in the wilderness, alone? What if you don't feel the same way when you get there? Are you going to just move back to Atlanta?"

"I won't know that until I get there, will I? Besides, even if it's only temporary, I'm willing to as least give it a try."

"What if it *is* temporary? *What then?*"

She had stopped loading the car to give him the attention he'd wanted. Hugging him tightly, she had kissed him goodbye, one last time.

"I'll cross that bridge, if and when I get to it," she'd said. Closing her trunk, he had hugged her, again. They'd said another goodbye.

Even now, he disagreed that her decision was a selfless one, feeling she was doing this for all the wrong reasons. That this was her way of shutting him and everyone else out of her life.

"The *problem* is that I'm finally doing something for myself, and not everybody else. I've given my *20* years of service, Kellen. I've worn all the hats. My family has moved on, and so will I."

He still frowned, shaking his head.

"Just try and look at it the way I do. It's a rare opportunity, and I'm taking advantage of it. I'm comfortable with my decision, Kellen."

"But, am I *crowding* you?" He had pressed. "Just say so, and I'll… give you space. I would hate for you to regret this, later. I care about you, so I have to ask."

"This is nothing about you," she'd said, untruthfully. "Just promise you'll come and visit me, sometime."

"*Visit you?* Sure, until you meet somebody more to your liking."

Kellen feared losing her. He already knew her misgivings about their age difference – nine years to be exact. But, instead of mentioning this, he had warned her of the dangers, asking who she'd call if something happened. But she wouldn't need *rescuing,* she had laughed.

"I won't be in any danger," she said, thinking of the mace she'd bought, and the heavier protection lying at the bottom of her garment bag. She was going to be fine. "But, if I ever am, I'll call you right after I call the police. *Best of friends,* remember?" She'd teased. That had made him smile.

Scanning her e-mail now, she saw nothing from him, so she signed off. A meal would be good right now, she thought. Deciding on a tuna sandwich and diet soda, she carried them into the living room so she could watch the news channel. Two inches of snow had fallen since morning but more was expected. Her phone rang. She looked at the caller ID.

It was Jake Foreman. An old friend of her father's who had sold his *You Pick It & Buy It* orchard, some years ago. He'd said he was getting too old to run the place. But she figured he missed farming because he was always riding through.

"Just calling to check on you, *Miss Watson.* This storm is picking up pretty good, right now. So, if you need anything, I could run some supplies out there to you. But I'd have to come now, if I'm coming."

The name is *Greer,* she wanted to say. The man had stopped by three times, already. And neither time had she needed anything. But she thought it was very considerate of him to be concerned.

"Hello, Mr. Foreman," she said, smiling into the telephone. "Thanks, but I am completely stocked and prepared to wait this thing out, even if it takes a couple of weeks."

"Well, from what they've predicted so far, it just might," he laughed. "But, think about my offer. By the way, you might know Janice Harvey? She's about your age. Well, she has a sister who's just moved back into town. *Laura Harvey.*"

"*Okay,*" she said, although she didn't.

"She's looking for a place to live, so I thought you might need a roommate. I don't want to get in your business, you understand? But, it'd be a whole sight safer for you out here, don't you think?"

Did I ask for a roommate? She thought with irritation.

"Thank you, but I'm not looking for a roommate, right now."

"She might be good company," he persisted.

"I don't think so. But, thank you," she said, as pleasantly as she could.

Thank you but no thank you! She thought. She didn't even need to think about it. She truly doubted she'd change her mind.

"Okay," he said. "Just keep it in mind. I know her folks. Good people, the *Harvey's.*"

"I'm sure," she said. "Thank you, anyway. And thanks for calling. I appreciate your concern."

They said goodbye and hang up.

A roommate? Not in this lifetime! She had grown accustomed to having her privacy and the idea of being snowed in with some stranger who probably didn't clean behind herself and who'd be all into her business, just didn't appeal to her. She would move back to Atlanta, first.

The wind was picking up and a final check of the premises was in order, she figured. Wrapping up tightly, she ventured out into the freezing weather. Passing the garage, she looked inside. The shiny chrome wheels on her SUV seemed much too flashy and out of place in their new surroundings. There was nothing like having an old Chevy truck with snow chains that could truly handle its weight out here, especially in this weather.

After finding everything in place, she trekked back to the house through the deep snow, taking the long way around for exercise.

And now, flipping channels with her remote, she could see the sun setting through the parted living room curtains.

Surely Kellen is home by now, she thought. She typed an e-mail.

Hi, Kellen!
Sorry I missed you. The snowstorm is on, but I'm ready
for it. Hate I missed you. I have to finish an article for
Mr. H by morning. Think about me while you party the
night away, *okay?* Let's talk tomorrow, if you're not busy.
***Missing you,* LaRetha.**

After clicking *Send,* she was able to finish editing not one, but three articles that night, and forwarded one to Mac Henry. The others would go to different magazines for their upcoming holiday issues. Pleased that she was ahead of schedule, as usual, she saved the files to a disk before shutting down the computer.

Where could Kellen be at this hour? She wondered. *Probably on a date.*

But she had always known that he would meet someone, eventually. Only she hadn't expected to feel so envious.

She remembered how Germaine had noticed them growing closer after the divorce, and even closer after moving to the condo.

"Are you two dating, Mom?" Germaine had asked.

"No. What made you think that?"

"Because he can't move without your advice, and you can't move without his opinion." Something Laretta had said, no doubt.

But she imagined that it had appeared that way. And oddly, he hadn't had a problem with their being in a relationship. Apparently, those two had already discussed it before Kellen had even approached the subject, which made her feel like a child needing parental consent to date. And from her *son,* of all people.

But Germaine was the reason they had come together – their common link. And he was close to them both. With a year gone by since the divorce, her son didn't feel she should be alone.

"You two kind of act alike," he once said.

"Because we're older than you - *alike*," she had laughed.

They did have a few things in common, like interests in writing, and other art forms. He was athletic and she was always trying to be. And then, there were the boys; Germaine and Kadero, who were always *unintentionally* throwing them together.

If she had to describe Kellen, she would say that he was probably the most positive fixture in her life. Being newly single, she had sometimes sought an ear, and his support had been invaluable. Except after a while, her feelings for him were noticeably starting to change, and she hadn't needed the distraction, at the time.

It was during the summer of Germaine's eighteenth birthday party. Still living in the family house after the divorce, she'd taken up the *'For Sale'* sign, just for the day.

Kellen had been far too handsome in jeans and a dark green t-shirt that molded well to his perfectly muscular physique and brought out the best hues of his ebony skin. He had greeted her with raised brows as she'd ushered him and Kadero inside.

She had taken greater pains with her appearance as well; dressing stylishly casual in a flowing red blouse and black fitted jeans. She even wore a little makeup, which was something she'd rarely done.

Aside from celebrating Germaine's birthday, Kadero had officially announced that he would be enlisting into the military, right after graduation. So, this event had a dual purpose, of sorts. But it wouldn't have happened without Kellen's help.

She had just flown in the evening before from a weekend long trip to Florida with her mother, and spent a long night finishing a piece about a group of senior citizens that was investing their time and talents into the youth in their community in order to prevent takeover by drugs and gangs. It was a profoundly immersing assignment that would bring excellent pay and accolades. Still, she'd been worn out.

Even in her exhaustion, she'd known better than to expect her *ex* to come through with the party he'd promised to give Germaine at his townhouse. His space wouldn't permit it, anyway. So, she'd struggled to make good on that promise, instead. Only, the guest list had doubled and it was more than she'd had time to prepare for.

With invitations mailed and Germaine extending a few more over the phone, there would be no time for the respite that she so desperately needed. And when Kellen called to ask what to bring, he had heard her distress.

Don't worry, I'll help with everything, he'd said. And she was greatly relieved. He had proven true to his word, doing everything from hanging patio and pool decorations and shopping with the food list, to helping Germaine and Kadero to set up tables and chairs in the backyard.

The barbecue and pool party was a tremendous success. Germaine was happy with everything – the decorations, the music and the food.

If only Gerald cared enough to be here, she remembered thinking, just before deciding that if he wouldn't participate in their son's last celebration before he was to leave for college, it was his stupidity and loss. Upset at the time that he couldn't drop by just anytime he chose, having tried and found the locks changed, he wasn't likely to show.

He was trying to punish her, she thought, when in actuality he was hurting Germaine. And although he'd said nothing, their son had been clearly disappointed.

But afterward, his hugs and *thanks you's* had all made the whole endeavor well worth the hard work. With the guests finally gone, he'd asked to hang out with Kadero and their friends. She hadn't the heart to insist they stay for clean up. She and Kellen had been left with the mess.

"Great party," he'd said, finishing off the last slice of lemon cake and smiling that million-dollar smile at her.

"Yes, it was," she had said, fatigue finally settling into every part of her weary body, it seemed.

"You look tired. Do you need help with this? I can stay a while longer," he'd said, the anticipation in his voice being not too discreet.

"Thanks, but I think I can handle it," she'd said, falling into a chair, unable to move another muscle.

He had patted her tired shoulders, telling her to leave everything. That he would come back early the next day to help. And again, he had kept his promise, cleaning the cluttered patio as she cleaned, inside.

Like Germaine, he hadn't once asked where Gerald was. Had probably already known. Apparently, her son had shared many details about his father with Kadero that he hadn't shared with her, his devotion to them both causing him to turn to his best friend, instead. Kadero had, in turn, told them to his big brother.

Their son understood that the divorce was not his fault. That it was neither his responsibility to hold their marriage together, nor to protect her. Besides, he was as much a victim of having a poor father as she was of having an unfaithful husband. The fault was *Gerald's.* And hers, she thought, for not seeing the forest for the trees.

A younger version of his father, Germaine was tall, medium built and also handsome. He put people at ease with his ready smile and his ability to talk to anyone about anything had made him very popular with both teachers and students at his school, where he had played on the basketball team since middle school, and always kept an *A* average.

So, it wasn't surprising when the phone had begun ringing constantly and that most of the calls were from girls. That had led to the hardest part of raising her son – the laying down of those strict rules which he very grudgingly realized were permanent and non-negotiable.

They were attending one of Kadero's basketball awards banquets when the question first came up.

"Who's the little girl hanging on Germaine's arm? You met her yet?" Kellen had asked.

"*Nope*," she'd replied, shrugging her shoulders. "Not yet. Why?"

"It seems serious." He grinned.

"How so?" She'd been puzzled.

"Well, because she hasn't left his side, once. She's *cute*. Your boy's got good taste. A chip off the old block, I guess," he said, smiling charmingly.

She had laughed at this. He'd never mentioned Gerald before. She took it as a compliment.

"Well, whoever she is, let's hope it's only temporary. That boy is going to college if it *kills* me."

Except his expression said he wasn't so convinced, and she'd decided right then to be more attentive to what was happening with her son. Sure enough, the two teenagers were sticking together like glue. She learned that afternoon that Tori was officially his girlfriend.

Tori Burgess was cute and petite, with a small round face, big expressive eyes and curly black shoulder length hair. She was soft-spoken and quick to smile. And judging by the tight clothing that this child wore on her womanish body, it was easy to see why her son was so smitten.

That's the style these days, her friend Constance had said, brushing off her concerns.

"Style or not, no daughter of mine would leave the house dressed like that. I can appreciate the snug pants – we did that. But, low cut, falling out of the top of their blouses, and pants so low in back you can just about see her *crack?* I don't think so! Life is *not* a music video. And what happened to leaving something to the imagination?"

"They ain't doing that, now." As usual, this mother of two small boys appeared unconcerned.

"Well, *I'm* doing that and I'm grown. Shorter skirts are one thing, but low-rider pants and visible thongs on high school girls? I don't think so!"

Maybe she was old fashioned. And looking back she could also see how she might have handled that situation differently. But admittedly, at the time, her greatest concern had been that her son wouldn't fulfill his dreams of college and professional ball. And those were not just his dreams, but *their* dreams.

But her good intentions had led to the rift that now existed between them. *Had she known this would happen, would she have done things differently?* She often asked herself. But she didn't think so. Germaine was staying out too late, sometimes calling from a friend's house to say he was sleeping over. She had known Kellen wouldn't contribute to his disobedience. Still, he'd missed curfews, consistently. And ignored any rules she'd set for him.

When she'd figured out that he was sneaking out to meet the girl and covering up the fact, she'd been unsure of how to handle this with him. Her son was becoming a man. She called Gerald.

"You really should do something, Gerald. *Talk* to him," she had complained.

"Why? Germaine knows how to handle himself. Besides, we can't watch him all the time."

She'd felt Gerald was venting his concerns at having been caught up with, not Germaine's. This annoyed her even more.

"That girl is barely seventeen, and Germaine is not even close to being responsible enough to have a family, but that's where it's headed."

"We don't know that, so don't assume it. As usual, you're getting all worked up for nothing."

Gerald wouldn't be of any help. He only dealt with problems when he absolutely had to. Besides, he had a reason to keep silent; *too many skeletons of his own.* So, while realizing it might be interpreted as meddling, she decided to contact the girl's parents.

But, what was she going to say to them? *'Look, I think you have a wonderful daughter, but I just don't think she's right for my son? She's way too advanced for him?* He was still dependant upon *her,* for goodness sakes!

The word from Kadero, by way of his older brother, was that the girl was nice and really cared a lot for Germaine. But that she was usually involved in lengthy relationships with older guys. She was also said to be a constant runaway. That had worried her. Because judging from the look in her son's eyes, it had occurred to her that he wasn't far from running with her. *Little did she know at the time!*

After worrying for a few weeks, and watching her son's grades plummet and his secrecy worsen, she'd decided to call Tori's mother and find out if she even knew that her daughter was seeing Germaine. And to enlist her help in getting involved, before it got any more serious.

"*Yes,*" Mrs. Burgess said once she had introduced herself as the mother of a young man Tori was seeing.

"I know she's dating a nice boy from her school. I thought it was good for her, considering the year she's been through, with those mean rumors circulating, and all. She really needs good friends, right now."

"Yes, well I'm concerned. He and Tori seem to be getting serious, rather fast."

"Oh, *really?*" Mrs. Burgess sounded even less concerned than Gerald had.

"Yes, they're spending a lot of time together and it's affecting his grades. If this continues, he might even lose a college scholarship."

Silence.

"I'm not saying Tori would cause that. That's his responsibility to care about. He knows what he has to lose. Still, I'm concerned that he might miss this opportunity. He *needs* this scholarship. And he's worked really hard to get it."

"I'm *sure,*" the woman said in a surly voice. She continued.

"I know you must have similar concerns for your daughter. I just thought that maybe together we could influence them to really think about whatever's going on here. Get them to just stop and think about their futures. To make better decisions than they're probably making, right now."

"I don't know what it is that you're so sure is happening..."

"Well, Mrs. Burgess, my son is spending every free minute with Tori. And that might be okay if everything else wasn't suffering. He's never failed his classes, before."

"Look, if you called here to accuse my daughter of something, or to start up some more rumors about Tori, then..."

"*No!* I'm not. I'm just a concerned parent. That's all."

"*Uh huh,*" she retorted, defensively.

"And I'm concerned about both of them. I'm not saying that she's a bad person."

"Well, I wish your son luck in life, Mrs. Greer. But, whatever concerns you have should be taken up with him, *not with me, and definitely not with my daughter,*" the woman replied, angrily. "Now, I don't deny that Tori's had some problems, but does that make her a bad person?" Oddly, the woman's voice was beginning to sound a bit more reasonable.

"Of course not." She said, hoping they were finally heading toward a truce.

"Well, as far as I'm concerned, my daughter has *been* raised and knows right from wrong. She hasn't always done the right things, but that doesn't mean she'll always do wrong, either."

"I agree. Neither of them will."

"Frankly, I'm offended that you would even call me about this. My daughter can't ruin your son's future. I raised a *good* girl. What you just told me sounds like *your* problem. You need to talk to your son!"

The woman's irritation had returned, but LaRetha wasn't giving up so easily. She cared about Germaine's future, even if this woman cared little about her daughter's.

"I'm sorry you have that attitude about it. Tori *is* your daughter. But, Germaine is my son. I'm only trying to keep him from making a decision that he'll regret. He needs to go to school."

"Well, I don't worry about Tori like that."

Which is exactly the problem, LaRetha thought.

"It's too bad that you're not concerned," she said, instead. "Apparently, this has been a complete waste of time."

"*Apparently.*"

"You have a good day, Mrs. Burgess."

Silence.

"*Mrs. Greer?*"

LaRetha waited, holding the phone and hoping for a positive response, finally.

"Like I said, I wish your son luck. But, as far as my daughter is concerned, what they decide to do is *their* decision to live with."

LaRetha hang up, frustrated that the woman had no intentions of even speaking with Tori. Like Gerald, it appeared she would only concern herself *after the fact,* if at all. Well, she wasn't waiting that long.

But what more could she do? That call was her last option. More than that, she had probably just alienated her son even more by trying to save him.

Maybe she should take Gerald's advice and just let it all fizzle out, she had decided. The less fuss the better. She decided to change her approach.

Aside from a little unruliness in class and a few missed class assignments, Germaine had never been in any real trouble. He'd always been respectful of her and his father. And she could have easily dictated her decision and forced him to concede. But at the price of losing his trust, and she hadn't wanted to do that.

So, because of this, she'd finally decided to give him the benefit of the doubt and to trust him, convincing herself that it was okay to do so.

No longer looking at the clock when he came in a little late, she had also stopped asking questions. They would discuss only what he volunteered. She let go of the stress that this was causing her, choosing to smile and hug and encourage him more often, instead.

Germaine had noticed the change, and he began talking to her, again. She worried still, but knew that to show it would only drive him away. What she hadn't realized, though, was that in spite of this positive change, the train wreck that she'd feared would come was just about to hit. And there was absolutely nothing that she could do about it.

"*How could you, Mama?* Tori is a nice girl. How could you call Mrs. Burgess and say those things?"

He had faced her squarely as she prepared their dinner. She could see his disappointment but, she wouldn't back down. Now that he was willing to listen, she would get right to the point.

"Germaine, I know you care a lot about her, but you're moving way too fast. You're both so young, with your whole future ahead of you. Why not take it slow?"

"*Slow?* You called her mother and told her you didn't want me to see her again, because you wanted me to take it *slow?*"

His inquiring eyes were almost intimidating. But, she'd stood her ground.

"I never said that, Germaine. I'm concerned that you've lost interest in everything. Everything *except* Tori, that is. What about your schoolwork? And the scholarships?"

"What about 'em?" His tone was biting and it made her angry.

"Boy, don't get smart with me. The way you and that girl are going, you'll be lucky to finish high school without getting her in trouble."

"If you mean *pregnant,* that won't hardly happen."

"You can say that. But you and I both know better."

"You've just met her. How would you know?" He'd asked, as if he were the one talking to a child.

"I'm just concerned, Germaine," she sighed. "All this talk about older boys and running away – it's just too much."

"*For who?*" He asked, his voice raising an octave. "I don't care what people say. She's a good person and she's nice to *me.* That's what matters. "

I'll just bet, she thought, disdainfully.

"Mama, you had no right."

"*Wrong.* I had every right. And I'm telling you that you need to stop and focus on more important things, like graduation and college – things that are important to your future. Don't lose everything you've worked for because of something that might not even last! "

"*Our* relationship will last. But you talk like all we're about is *sex.*"

"I don't know that, but you do. Listen Germaine, you don't have to give up on your dreams. You can be in love *and* go to college…"

"I know this."

"Then act like you do. And don't even *think* about having un-protected sex, either. I can't make you refrain from it, but at least be smart about it."

"I think I've already had this conversation with Dad. Besides, I never said I wasn't going to college. You are just assuming…"

"So why are you failing in school? And after all your hard work!"

He'd shrugged. He was shutting down.

"Why not just slow it down, a bit?" She'd continued, calmly this time. "Get your grades back up. See what college has to offer before turning it down. If your relationship is what you say it is, then surely it can survive that."

Her son studied her face as if considering this. She waited.

"I know you're concerned, Mama. But just 'cause you and Daddy didn't work out, you shouldn't be so protective of me."

"This has *nothing* to do with me and him. I just want you to have a *good* life. But, with no college education..."

"I know! I won't have a future. So you've told me."

"Then, why aren't you listening to me?" She had demanded, exasperated.

"Mama, you worry too much. And, Tori doesn't need people treating her like some kind of weirdo just because she's made a few mistakes. No wonder her mom's mad. You wouldn't want anybody judging me like that."

"That's too bad. Somebody's got to show some concern."

"You offended her mother."

"Her mother offended *me*."

"I apologized for you," he sighed. "I knew you were just worried and upset."

"Don't ever do that again!" She retorted in anger. "I meant every word I said to that woman."

"But that wasn't right. I would have talked to you, first."

"I tried that, but you wouldn't talk to me, remember?"

She wasn't about to let this kid run guilt trips on her. As far as she was concerned, she probably hadn't said enough.

"Germaine, you just want to do as you please, and you're not old enough, or responsible enough for that. And I don't deserve this attitude you're giving me. I love you and like it or not, I did what I felt I had to do."

He opened the refrigerator to get a soda, and looked at her.

"Maybe you don't deserve it, but look at Daddy. He can't say anything. He's got women crawling out of the woodwork. But I guess you always knew that," he said, sarcastically.

She'd struck him before she knew it, and seeing the distraught look on his face, she had regretted it, immediately. She hadn't touched him since swatting his diapered behind as a child. And from the expression on his face, she knew it would be a long time before he forgave her.

But Germaine had pushed the wrong button this time, openly disrespecting her, and she wasn't having it. As much as she'd hated what she'd done, LaRetha had been tempted to *kick* him out, for that remark.

"I don't need any observations about what your father is or isn't doing. You *will* be respectful of me and him, do you understand?"

He had looked confused, as if he was wondering why she even cared what he said about Gerald. Not understanding that she only wanted for him what she'd had with her own father, even if Gerald wasn't making that easy. Besides, how could she explain that acknowledging his father's numerous indiscretions felt too much like acknowledging some failure of her own.

Germaine left home that evening, not returning until well after midnight. She'd already called Kadero to find out if he was there. Kellen answered, saying that he was.

"He'll be home once he cools off," he'd told her before she even mentioned their disagreement. She didn't mention the slap, not wanting to embarrass Germaine.

"I know. Thanks, Kellen."

He did finally come in, and she was waiting up for him. They went into the den to talk.

"First of all, Germaine, I want to say I shouldn't have hit you. I'm sorry for that. I want to help you, not hurt you."

He'd nodded.

"But, as your mother, I have a right *and* a responsibility to tell you when I think something's not good for you. This isn't just about Tori. You're moving so *fast*. Just totally losing sight of what's most important, right now. And I don't understand why that is."

"I probably could accept the relationship if you were following up on your plans for school," she'd continued. "But, you're not, and that concerns me."

"I'm sorry, Mama. I respect you, and I'm sorry we've argued over this. I'm going to college. I just need to get there my own way. "

"Okay, well, if you lose those scholarships, you'll have to. Don't sabotage what you've already worked for. This is a one-time deal, Germaine. Don't screw it up."

"But, she needs me, right now. She's having some problems at home, and…"

"You are not responsible for that girl," she'd said, incredulously, although relieved that he was opening up to her. "If she needs help with something, then we can try and help her. But, you can't take responsibility for her problems."

Germaine stood up, nodding.

"Don't worry, Mama. I understand. It'll be alright, I promise." Then he had hugged her, goodnight.

She prayed that night for things to get better between them. And for a brief while, they had. Then, less than three months after his high school graduation, she'd found the note. He was gone. There was no mention of Tori, but she already knew.

She couldn't count the nights she had sat up worrying and waiting for him to call or to show up. Several weeks passed and he'd finally sent a message through Kellen and Kadero. *He and Tori were fine*. He had a job and they were looking for an apartment.

Once again, Kellen's friendship had gotten her through, and she was grateful. She had never expected what happened next between them. But looking back at the circumstances, she could almost forgive herself. She'd been alone for the first time in her life. Worse, she was feeling very lonely. And Kellen had been there; caring for her, consoling her, and relating to her pain all too well.

That was a beautiful, romantic September night. A perfect moon had brightened the nighttime sky. She was happily renovating her condo during that time but looking for something else to busy her, on that day. Kellen had called early that morning, asking if she wanted to spend the day together. This would be their first official date, and with Germaine having left by then, she couldn't find a reason not to.

Despite it being a little cool out, it was a pleasant walk back to her place from dinner, after spending the day at a fall festival being held at a nearby park. And also perfect, in fact, for people in love - which she quickly acknowledged to herself that she and Kellen were not.

She'd often wondered why he was making so much time for her, thinking he should have wanted to be with someone closer to his own age - certainly with someone without 'ex-husband and grown son' drama. When she'd asked him why he'd called, he had simply taken a deep breath, exhaled and then replied, *because I love you.*

What? You're crazy! Taken aback, she could only laugh.

He'd smiled, doing a wounded little skip-dance away from her and back, again.

"Don't look so surprised. It's not a wishy-washy, *oh baby, I can't live unless I'm breathing your air,* kind of love. I love who you are."

She could only laugh, feeling unusually speechless.

"I can't explain it other than to say that you are my best friend. You and Germaine are *family* to us. You're like important pieces that were missing in my life. Kadero feels the same way."

His voice had dwindled for a moment, and then continued as they walked together.

"And I know what you're going to say even before you say it – *I'm younger than you.* I know this," he'd said. "But, not so much that it matters. We're both adults. And I've been on my own for a long time."

She nodded and he continued.

"You've been good to Kadero and me, without even noticing you were being that way. That's just how *real* you are," he'd said with so much emotion that it left her speechless.

She'd never imagined it went that deep. Still, he went on, reminiscing about days gone by. Like the day their apartment had been ransacked. Still married to her absentee husband at the time, she'd had plans to travel and welcomed him and Kadero to stay over with Germaine.

Then, Kellen mentioned the time she'd loaned them their new truck to move into another apartment. "Not many folks would do that," he said.

"No sweat. It was Gerald's truck," she had laughed, deviously.

"A brand *new* truck," he'd reminded her. "Then, you sent us hot chicken soup when I had the flu. I mean I could go on and on."

"Please don't." She remembered feeling oddly bashful. "None of that was anything worth mentioning, again. That's what friends do for one another."

To her embarrassment, he continued.

"The first time I came to your house, you had this big friendly smile and I couldn't stop thinking about you," he continued. "You were so *down to earth*. That surprised me. Judging from where you lived and everything you seemed to have, and truthfully, the way you look, I had expected you to be a bit standoffish. You were nothing that I'd expected from somebody living the good life."

That good life had turned out to be anything but, she had thought.

"I admit I was *shook,"* he'd laughed. But, I respect the marriage thing, and besides, I figured it was a crush and wouldn't last, anyway. So, I planned just to ride it out. Just being a part of your family, of you and Germaine, was enough for me. Like recently, when Kadero was going through that tough time with our folks. You helped me stay grounded in a lot of ways. That helped me to be there for him."

"I would have done it for anybody. It was nothing big."

"But it was. You told me things that kept me on the right path."

Like what?" She honestly didn't remember.

"Like, *don't make the same mistake that I made with Germaine. Explain the pros and cons, but let Kadero make his own decision,"* he recanted. "You said that's how kids learn to live with their own consequences. Your relationship will be better for it. That's what you said."

Now, she remembered.

"Even when you know something, hearing it can sometimes make it clearer. When I finally told Kadero what you said, he said that you were amazingly beautiful and *wise*."

"Enough with the flattery. Besides, when you get this old, you'd better be wise," she'd laughed, dismissing the rest of his compliment.

"It's not that, at all," he said with a seriousness that caught her off guard. "You're hardly *old*. Being *fine* doesn't hurt, either," he'd said. She remembered feeling butterflies flutter inside her stomach.

At that moment, he stopped walking and pulled her closer to him by her waist.

"There's something I've been meaning to do. I hope you won't mind."

Uncertain of what was happening at the moment, she didn't resist him. Standing a few inches taller than her even in high heels, and smelling like good dinner wine and musk oil scents, Kellen had surprised her by slowly and carefully leaning forward to give her a kiss.

After having time to think about it, she'd decided that it had been *perfect*. Just long enough and warm enough to cause her toes to tingle in a way she'd forgotten they could. Afterward, they had walked in silence, both probably disbelieving that it had finally happened.

"Well, maybe it *is* sexual," he'd admitted. "I hope you're not offended."

"I already figured as much. But so you'll know, I'm not looking for sex outside of marriage, and I'm definitely not looking for marriage."

He had contemplated this, giving her a questioning look that said he didn't quite believe her.

"I value our friendship, Kellen. And I care a lot about you. But, right now, I need more than just a casual, sexual relationship. So, I think I'll just wait for marriage."

"*Really?*" He didn't sound convinced. "But, we're both adults, LaRetha. I mean, I respect what you're saying. But, wanting to be loved is nothing shameful. And I would love to wake up to you tomorrow morning after a night of fulfilling *both* our needs."

She had blushed, involuntarily. She was the older one. *So why was she feeling like a schoolgirl, all of a sudden?*

"Don't look so surprised. You had to know it was coming."

"I can't commit to you, Kellen. I'm barely divorced."

"But you are."

"I am what?" She'd asked.

"*Divorced.*"

He had leaned toward her again, and their kiss belied her sentiments. This preceded hand-holding, and a slightly hurried and affectionate walk back home.

"I'm not pressuring you for a commitment," he'd whispered when they were back at her place. "I just want to be with you, and make you happy. You deserve that."

Now, she knew a line when she heard one. But never from him, and never with so much intensity. And certainly not when she'd felt so vulnerable. So, despite knowing it was the absolute wrong decision to make, she had justified it. No ties and no commitments, they had agreed, although she believed that Kellen would have agreed to just about anything at the time. She also knew that, whether she *did* or *didn't*, they would still remain friends.

She had foolishly tried to turn off her conscious. Having a love affair was no big deal, these days, she'd told herself. She was *grown*. So was he. Why shouldn't they? She considered her recent promise to herself.

But maybe they could be together for this one night. Then they could decide on tomorrow which way this would go. Then she'd thought about how this went so totally against everything she believed in, and how much guilt she could expect feeling, on the next day. And now, she couldn't believe how easily she'd relented.

It seemed almost like yesterday. She had relived every moment, over and over. The condo had cooled in their absence, and Kellen had tended the fire in the living room while she had poured glasses for them. They had sipped a smooth red wine and progressed slowly.

But, this is wrong! She'd thought, unable to shake an image of one particular childhood bible class where she'd been taught that *'opening the door just a little to sin would certainly lead to no good end'*. She was playing with fire, for sure. *Eternal hellfire.* And nothing was worse than that.

But, foolishly, she had turned off her mind, thinking that, just for a minute, she wouldn't worry about anything. She had dropped her defenses, and then felt suddenly shy with him.

What if she didn't measure up to his expectations? Would he compare her to another lover? How would she compare?

But, he hadn't given her much time to think about that. And despite the numerous warning signals that were exploding inside her head, she'd allowed him to stay, telling herself that it was foolish to worry.

And so, closing her mind to everything else, she had spent that entire night with him. And despite her initial nervousness, Kellen had made her feel as if she was the most beautiful woman in the world. She was satisfied. And he had fallen in love.

Waking up in his arms, LaRetha had felt more content than she had in years. She'd felt safe. *This man was good for her.* And considering his maturity, age would probably never be an issue between them, she'd thought. But days later, she had taken a less idealistic look at their relationship and realized that she couldn't fall in love with Kellen. She wouldn't encourage him to, either. She would simply enjoy his companionship, *outside* of the bedroom, just as she had in the past. And nothing more would, or should, be expected of her.

Kellen was at a different time in his life. Never married, with no children yet, nor any long-term relationships under his belt that she knew of. And aside from caring for his brother, he'd never had anyone to think of beside himself. The thought of having him awaken one morning and decide that they really had nothing in common was very real to her. As was her fear that she might do the same.

Such a huge mistake she'd made! After praying for forgiveness for doing such an impetuous thing, and feeling awful about not being able, or rather, *willing* to give him the type of relationship that he wanted, without further explanation she had refused to spend another night with him.

Angry by then, Kellen said it was unfair of her. He *loved* her, and would never hurt her, he'd said. Why was she pulling away from him like this? *He was not Gerald!*

It just wasn't in her plans. And despite her son's prior stamp of approval, she had wanted to set a better example for him. How could she tell him not to get involved in the wrong type of relationship when she was doing it herself? *And with a friend of his, at that!*

She'd heard of all the stereotypes about supposed love-starved divorcees, acting out from sexual repression. There weren't any such ideologies describing men that she was aware of. Gerald hadn't been a husband to her for some time, and she was sure he hadn't lost any time acting on *his* sexual desires.

Still, for her, continuing this intimate relationship with Kellen would be too much like starting from the very beginning, over *20* years before - with a young *Gerald.* She had lived and learned so much, since that time in her life. It would be too difficult a task. And she doubted that the relationship would even last long enough to make it worth the effort.

She'd gone on with her life as planned, throwing herself into her work to forget her disappointment at losing something so special when she'd only just found it. Frustrated, Kellen had said he would give her time.

Time. She'd lost a lot of that, she'd felt. She was only just beginning to enjoy that newfound freedom that he took for granted. After awhile, with him persisting and her resisting, she was no longer apologetic about her decision. They had agreed on 'no strings', after all.

Kellen was young, she thought. He would get past it, in time. Besides, wasn't it just as Gerald had always said? That a man's ideal woman was always the one he *didn't* get? Although he'd said it antagonistically, after living with him for a while, she could believe it.

But Kellen disagreed, saying *she* was his ideal woman, and he was certain that he could prove to be her ideal man. He had argued strongly, leaving her few excuses, until she'd refused to discuss it, again.

Yes, if anything, what she had needed was more time.

Just four months later, *Watson* died. LaRetha had called Germaine and told him about his grandfather. And as usual, Kellen could be counted on.

The day of his wake was one of mixed emotions. Kellen drove Germaine to her house. Her son attempted a smile when he saw her. He accepted her embrace. After that, he was quiet for much of the time.

"Where have you been, Germaine?" She'd asked quietly when Kellen was out of earshot.

"I've been here and there," he'd said, giving a lukewarm response.

"How is everything going? Are you doing okay?"

"I'm fine," he said.

"We really need to talk."

"Yeah. I know. But, if it's okay, Grandma asked me to ride with her to Kentucky. She said she was coming here, first."

"I know that. And it's fine," she'd said, hiding her disappointment. "So, what is this really about, Germaine? You've been gone for months, and you have nothing to say about it?"

"What do you want me to say, Mama?"

"How about something like, *I'm sorry for leaving like that.* Something to that effect, for starters."

By that time, her mother was coming inside. Seeing her grandson, she had exclaimed for joy. All other matters were forgotten.

It was raining heavily and Kellen had insisted on driving her. Laretta followed them closely. After checking into a hotel in town, they had gone directly to the funeral home. Gerald was there. Looking disturbingly attractive and well dressed in a dark gray suit, he seemed a bit disassociated from what was going on.

She'd suppressed a familiar twinge of resentment that once again, he wasn't truly there for her and Germaine, as he should have been. She had noticed from the scent of his coat as he hugged her that he was smoking, again. Well, she'd thought, at least he'd had the decency to come, alone.

The Community Baptist Church at Lovely, was a large building, filled to capacity for her father's homegoing. Cecelia and the boys had attended, together. Everything was in order and beautifully arranged. She'd cried quietly through both the wake on Friday, and Saturday's funeral. So did Germaine and her mother.

As she'd expected, Gerald hadn't shed a tear, but just treated it as personal time with his son. This irritated her. She caught his sideways glance at Kellen, but felt no need to explain. He had always known they were friends. But his eyes said that he suspected something more. He and Kellen ignored one another the entire time, which suited her fine.

Sadly, she saw no sign of her father's brothers or sisters, anywhere. Clearly, their estrangement crossed all lines, including death.

It was then that she wished she'd gotten to know them. Funerals had a way of doing that, she figured. Of making you face your differences with people and vow to change them. She would consider changing this, if only for Germaine.

The service was touching, although not too sad, as her father had requested. And she would never forget the beautiful floral arrangements that had filled the front of the church and adorned her father's expensive casket; nor the songs, the eulogy and all the warm comments from friends. There was little talk of the illness that had broken her father's strong body. The entire family had wept at the burial site, including Germaine. He had no grandfather, now.

Afterwards, Laretta had understandably declined Cecelia's offer to come back with them to the family house. After expressing her condolences to the family at the burial site, she had driven back to the hotel alone, while she, Kellen and Germaine, minus Gerald, who had already disappeared, had spent most of the evening at the farm. They'd barely had time to become reacquainted before being overtaken by visitors bringing food, money and cards of sympathy.

Cecelia had been wonderful about everything. Clearly sorrowful, she'd smiled through it all with only a telltale tear or two escaping her aging face, from time to time. Although overcast, that day was unusually warm for fall, so while people mingled at the house, LaRetha had spent time walking over the land with Thomas, who talked about his life after college.

Married with two children and yet another one on the way, he seemed very happy. Oddly, his family hadn't come. She didn't know what to think of this. Most people would want their wife and children to see how and where they had grown up, wouldn't they? But, she didn't question it.

Although his shyness still remained, Andrew had quickly embraced her and Germaine. And for a split second, it was as if nothing had changed between them. As if time and circumstance hadn't brought separation, and all of them were staying there at the farm still, with *Watson*. She could see them remembering, as well.

After Saturday's funeral, no one bothered her back at the hotel, except when Kellen asked if she wanted to get out for some fresh air. She'd declined, deciding to shower and turn in early, instead.

She joined Germaine, Laretta and Kellen for an early Sunday morning breakfast, where she convinced Germaine to drive back to the farm with her once again, to say final goodbyes. It was the perfect opportunity to put him on the spot, she'd figured. And she could tell that he knew it.

"Well, aren't you ready to talk to me, yet?" She asked on the way there, when they were alone.

"I didn't do it to hurt you, Mama…"

"But, you did."

"I'm sorry. But Tori and me are doing fine. We both work. We pay our own rent. We're doing alright."

"I'm sure that you are," she replied. "But, you know how disappointed I am about your passing up those scholarships. But, it was your decision to make. I can only give advice. And you can take it, if you want it."

He had nodded. She'd felt no relief.

"Just promise that you'll keep in touch - with me or with *somebody*. Call if you need something. If you can't get me, call your grandmother. Or Kellen. I'm not trying to ruin your life. I just need to know that you're alright."

She left it at that and he appeared greatly relieved. She could tell that he was doing well. She wouldn't push for what she wanted, or for something that he wasn't ready to accept. Germaine would just have to learn some things the hard way, she'd figured. Maybe then he would understand just how great a life he had.

At Cecelia's insistence, Germaine and his uncles had loaded their car with several containers of food and cards of condolences, brought by sympathizers. She and her stepmother had stolen a moment to talk.

"Cecelia, being out here brings back so many great memories. And you are as thoughtful and helpful, as ever. My father always loved that about you." LaRetha was having difficulty saying that her father *loved* Cecelia. She always had.

"And I loved your father, obviously. I left so much to come here. My home and my family. Everything I knew in life. What's funny is that I never thought I was missing out on anything. This farm was the best thing that could have happened to me, or to my sons, at the time."

LaRetha had nodded.

"I just want to thank you for always being a real sister to them. They always looked forward to your visits and they talked about you all the time when you were gone. You made their living here much easier than it could have been."

"I didn't do anything special. I've always loved my brothers. I just hate that we've lost so much time, together. We should all keep in touch. Visit from time to time."

"You're very right. You know, I can see the same things in Germaine that I saw in you as a child. You've raised him into a beautiful young man. Let's do keep in touch and get together again, soon. Look through a few scrapbooks - under happier circumstances, of course." She wiped away a tear.

"We will. We're still a family."

They were silent, as they walked further away from the others.

"Your father loved you so much. And he didn't really dislike Gerald. He was just overly protective." Cecelia said. "I'm glad they finally resolved their differences."

"I am too, although as you might have guessed, Gerald is well out of the picture now. We're divorced."

"I'm sorry."

"Well, I'm not sorry. My father was a good judge of character."

"Sometimes, but he wasn't right about everything, you know?" She smiled. "You and Gerald were young and in love. No one could predict the future. We older ones tend to forget our own mistakes, sometimes. I'm just glad you followed *your* heart. You have a wonderful son, and those memories will always be with you."

Cecelia was right. Parents didn't have all the answers. Like her, Germaine should be allowed to make his own decisions now, and she should accept them without casting guilt or blame. She was sure that her stepmother spoke from experience; from some hurt in her own life, considering her own family had never made an appearance.

"Thanks, Cecelia. I know that *Watson* really loved all of us. My mother too, in his way. And I mean no disrespect by saying that," she'd hurriedly added.

The woman had blushed without denial. She understood.

"But clearly your marriage was a happy one. That's what's important," she'd told Cecelia, who smiled with tear-filled eyes. "And you were always very good to me."

Cecelia had hugged her with gratitude.

"What will you do from here, Cecelia? Do you plan to stay on?" She couldn't imagine the woman changing her life, now. But, how would she survive out here, alone?

"I don't think that I will, LaRetha. I really want to talk to you about that. What your father didn't leave to me will go to you, of course. But, this isn't the time to discuss it, I don't think. We can talk about all that once we meet for the reading of the Will."

She'd nodded. That would be in three weeks. After exchanging phone numbers, hugging everyone goodbye and making promises to call one another, she and Kellen had driven back to the hotel to meet Laretta, who'd been waiting impatiently.

Now, she could remember waving to Cecelia and her brothers, who stood hugging one another in the grassy front yard, and waving back, as they had driven out of sight. At the end of the driveway, she had instinctively looked through the back window. And just for a split second, everything was just as it had been, twenty-seven long years long ago when her mother had picked her up in a sporty red Pontiac and they had driven away, with her waving back at them through the dust they'd left behind.

Driving back to the hotel, Germaine had noticed her distress. She wiped her eyes and blew her nose into a tissue.

"Don't worry. You'll see them again, soon. I'm sure of it."

But, he didn't understand. She would miss them all. But more than that, it was the childhood she'd missed with her father that grieved her the most, at that moment. She had visited him often over the years, taking Germaine so that he would know and understand where he came from. Her father had appreciated that. Still, she mourned for the times that would never be, again.

Once they'd crossed the Georgia state line, Germaine had called her cell phone to say he was going to his father's house. Gerald would take him home.

"Fine," she said, not angry this time. "I love you, son."

"Love you too, Ma," he said, enthusiastically, and her heart lifted.

Immediately afterward, Kellen invited her to his place. But she needed to go home first. She had quickly unpacked the car, showered and changed into jeans and a sweater, before driving over. She hadn't wanted to be alone, anyway.

Dinner was delicious. Baked salmon wasn't so difficult, he said. Afterward, they'd gone into the living room and talked – for hours. And she didn't remember ever finding him more handsome or charismatic than on that evening. She had even wondered how it might be if things were more serious between them.

But, Kellen had skillfully avoided all discussion of their night together, or any future they might have. Instead, he'd made her laugh and succeeded at bringing her out of her cheerless, somber mood. It would be a long time before they would ever discuss that passionate night, again. Although she could tell that he wanted to.

Soon after that night, Kellen's employer had closed its doors, and she had recommended that with his degree in English, he might consider writing for the paper. He'd considered it, managed to get an appointment with Mac Henry, and was hired immediately. Being no pushover, Mr. Henry had been very impressed with him. He was *in*.

They'd said that they would celebrate as soon as she returned from a vacation that she and Laretta were planning. Then, while he worked in the newsroom, she had traveled for her stories. They'd settled into a smooth routine, seldom seeing one another for days, due to hectic schedules. But, on those very special evenings that they did, they would meet for dinner and movies and have picnics in the park. He would keep her informed about office matters and she would share her knowledge of the journalism trade. And, they became comfortable.

"I was thinking about coming to *Lovely,* for a visit," he told her over the phone.

"Why don't you?" She asked. Kellen had just told her that he missed his *family*, meaning her and Germaine. She realized that she'd been missing him, too.

"Why should I? If you wanted me, you never would have left me."

She heard sadness in his voice. So strong, yet so easily hurt.

"I never said I didn't want you and I wasn't leaving *you*."

"Oh, now, that you're hundreds of miles away, you can admit that?"

"How do *you* feel about us?" She asked after a brief pause.

"I guess that answer would depend on who I'm talking to, right now. Is it LaRetha, my very best friend..?"

She sensed more anguish.

"...or *LaRetha Love*, that passionate female I was with for one very special night, just months before she up and moved away, on me? Just when I thought nothing could separate us, you found a way to do it. Silly me, I never saw it coming."

There were those abandonment issues, again. His being twice wounded and feeling helpless at thinking he had lost her, quite possibly for good.

But, surely he must know how very important he was to her by now? He was her *rock*. A sure shoulder to lean on. Funny, he was still so unsure of where he stood with her. But then, she had left, after all.

"How many women have you been with since me, Kellen?"

"If I had asked you that, you would've hung up on me."

"Probably," she laughed. "But, I'm asking you. How many?"

"*A couple.*"

"And did you break up with any of them just because you didn't agree with some of their choices?"

"First of all, I never broke up with you because we could never pull it, together, you left here so fast. Secondly, none of *them* were very smart so we never talked about *choices*."

She laughed that Monday morning as she sat at her kitchen table, chatting and cutting coupons, and wondering why he wasn't at the office. But he would tell her if he wanted her to know.

"Well, smart isn't everything, I guess. That just might be the type of woman you need," she teased. "Somebody you can handle and tell what to do."

"Smart is *everything*. And are you implying that I'm inexperienced with women? Particularly strong *intelligent* women? I'm offended," he said, sounding anything *but*.

"Well, am I wrong?"

He laughed, and she was glad he was humoring her. She needed the company.

"After that night we spent together, what do *you* think?"

She heard the cockiness, and frowned.

"You are so smart-mouthed," she said, softly.

Silence, on both ends.

"I miss you, LaRetha."

"Humph!"

"One day, you'll admit it, too. Until then, I'll keep this conversation short so you'll miss me enough to bring your fine self back home."

She smiled. He never liked to end on a sour note.

"But, I *am* home. And I miss you. And I wish you would visit. But, if you won't, then..."

"Then, what?"

"I guess I'll just have to wait until you miss *me*, enough."

"Woman, if you only knew. Okay. Bye, baby. Talk to you, soon.

2

"You're only going to be even lonelier out there," Constance had told her back in Atlanta when they'd met for a going-away lunch. "Isolating yourself won't help anything. I can't believe you're even considering it."

"I've heard all that, before. But if I don't go, the place will only go to ruin. You should see it. It's beautiful land."

"Forgive me if I don't get so turned on by some little white shack surrounded by flat lands with no traffic lights," her friend interrupted. "I can't survive without my smog breakfast and stress for lunch. Besides, you could probably die a lonely death out there and nobody would ever know about it."

"*Are you done?*" This sister sure knew how to turn sweet tea, *sugarless.*

"*No.* Stay here. You've always got me. And that fine Kellen Kincaid who's always hanging around. *You* have got a *great* life. You finally got rid of the old ball and chain," at which LaRetha laughed, "and now you want to *move?* Shoot, if it was me, I wouldn't change one thing about it."

LaRetha knew Constance's fondness for Kellen – hers and a few other women in the office. She had promised to keep the other prowling lionesses away from him in her absence, however. LaRetha had smiled, thinking how that probably wouldn't work for very long.

"You have a good job. A beautiful place," Constance had continued, referring to her condo, which had blossomed into a prime piece of property with all the recent changes.

"*And*," she had continued, "unlike most of us, you probably have enough money to tide you over for a long, long time. You could sell that property for a mint and never have to go that way, again. Besides, you don't have to quit the paper. Just take a break. Get your head together. Then, make that decision."

Maybe she was right. But, LaRetha didn't need noise and crime or an easy life, *per se.* She needed to challenge herself with something that might revive in her all those things she'd gradually tucked away over the years but hadn't realized it. She needed this.

"Besides," Constance had continued. "I know there ain't no men out there. I would hate to come visit and find you married to some old *rifle totin' Joe,* who sits in a truck all day, spitting tobacco juice every time he opens his mouth to boss you around."

She had smirked, brushing the thought aside at the time. But now, whenever it occurred to her, she would think of Mr. Bailey at the grocery store and marvel at the similarity.

"I'll still travel and meet people. That's how I've always socialized, anyway. Besides, I'm not looking to fall in love, anytime soon." LaRetha shrugged and Constance sighed, shaking her head.

"I have a lot of work to do with you," her friend said.

"Don't bother. I won't change my mind. Like it or not, I'm moving to *Lovely*."

Constance had good intentions, but they were nothing alike. Right now, she wasn't worried about her love life. And she wasn't planning on hanging out with her in nightclubs or at singles' events with the anticipation of meeting someone who would most likely have already dated every eligible woman in the room. She just wasn't interested in the hassle of trying to find out who was real and who wasn't. When the time came for her to get involved with someone, she would. In the meantime... life was just simpler this way.

The snow was coming down in white sheets, now. And the sky was almost impossible to see. Recent weather reports stated this would be their worst snowstorm, in years. Her doors and windows were secured, and despite the heat being on for now, the electricity probably wouldn't last for much longer.

After carefully placing flashlights, candles and matches throughout the house, she got more firewood from the back porch. It would be much too cold, later on.

The television played as she sat daydreaming about how different it would be if Kellen were here. Admittedly, there was no one else she would rather be with at the moment. But, that wasn't likely to happen, she thought. She went to shower and dress for bed.

Turning up the volume on the television set, she snuggled between red flannel sheets and against matching pillows that cradled her softly like a baby. She sighed in her comfort.

Travel will be dangerous for the next few days, the weatherman reported. *Stay inside, if at all possible.*

No Problem! She rubbed her cold feet together.

Next, they said, *tips for keeping warm when he electricity went out.*

Well, she was a few steps ahead of them, and hoped everybody else was, too. This was going to be a rough one.

After a time, hunger pains began setting in. Restlessly, she dragged herself out of her comfort and went into the kitchen to finish unpacking the last grocery bag, then decided to heat a couple of pop tarts.

The phone rang. She grabbed it with her one free hand.

"It's me, again," a familiar voice said, cheerily.

"What's up?" she responded.

"If only you and I were."

"How's the weather?"

"Warm for this time of year. But with Thanksgiving just around the corner, it's sure to change by then."

"It's snowing in sheets out here," she boasted, chomping on a hot tart.

"I know. I'm catching it on the weather channel. I've been worried about you."

"Don't be. I'm a big girl."

"So you pretend. Just remember, it's okay to change your mind."

She paused, then pursued.

"I called yesterday. You weren't in. Out on a date?" She asked.

Pause.

"You would think that, wouldn't you?" He finally said.

She decided not to ask, again.

"Check your e-mail. I'm sending you a picture of my front yard. You won't believe it. You really should plan to come out here sometime."

"*Hah!* I guess you want it all, don't you? The country air, the city man, and the crazy isolated lifestyle. And just what am I supposed to do while you're a-*plantin'* and a-*fixin',* and a-carrying on?"

"You'd keep me company, what else?" She asked, smiling into the phone.

He quietly contemplated this.

"You didn't have to go all the way out there for that. I still don't understand..."

"I'm sorry about that."

"I can tell. I'm sorry LaRetha, but I can't pretend this doesn't matter to me. You thought we were getting too close, huh? Well, just because you left temptation behind, that doesn't mean that temptation is going to leave you."

Huh? She thought.

"What'll you do when you're tempted by something out there?"

Kellen wanted her to feel guilty. She didn't.

"Before I forget," he said, changing tracks, suddenly. "I got a call last night from some guy. He sweet-talked the secretary into giving him my cell phone number. She's *fired,* tomorrow," he said, only half kidding.

"He said his name was Watson, I think. Yeah. *Therell Watson.* He's a relative, I guess. He says he just heard that your father died, so he can't be too close to the family. Anyway, he wanted your number, but I asked for his, instead. He didn't leave it though. He said he'd call back."

"*Therell Watson?*" She'd never heard the name in her life. "How did he know to call you?"

"I really don't know. I didn't think to ask at the time."

"Well, what *do* you know about the man?" His lack of information was beginning to irritate her.

"We didn't talk for long. Just long enough for him to hit me with some fast questions about you. Sounds like he's planning a visit."

"Well, I doubt if he'll make it out here in this weather."

She tossed a plastic grocery bags into the garbage, holding the phone tightly to her ear as she carried her plate of pop tarts, a bottle of water and a small bag of grapes into her bedroom. She plopped down on the comfortable bed in front of the television.

"Well, be careful. We really don't know what his intentions are."

"Thanks. I haven't heard from anybody, yet. But, I will be on the lookout."

"You might even want to ask the police to patrol the area. They should, from time to time, anyway."

They were both silent. She took the opportunity to chomp on a grape. Kellen blew a long breath of exasperation.

"You still don't miss me, LaRetha?"

"I missed you as soon as I crossed the state line."

Silence.

"I heard from Germaine, recently." He waited.

"That's good."

"Don't act like you don't care. It's killing you to know what's going on with him."

"Sure it is. But, I guess somebody will let me know if something happens to him, or if they see him on the news. Otherwise, I'll just assume that he's happy and healthy. That's good enough for me."

"He'll come around, eventually."

"*Humph!* Anyway, how's Kadero?"

"Fine. Still training. Coming home for a minute, early next year."

"I miss him, too."

"Me too. But, we keep in touch as much as possible."

"Good. That's wonderful."

"Germaine says Gerald asked about you, recently."

"Oh, well." Again, her son was keeping in touch with everyone but her. Disappointing. But, what could she do about it?

"Your son loves you, LaRetha."

"And I will always love my son, no matter how much like his father he is. As for Gerald, that is *so* over. I don't miss him, at all."

"Really? But, you did say you regretted the divorce, once."

She frowned as she tried to remember.

"What I *said* was I regretted having to *get* a divorce. I wondered how I didn't see it coming. But I've never regretted divorcing that man for a minute. By the time I finally did it, it was long overdue."

"Oh." He sounded relieved and she wondered how long that subject had been weighing on him. "So, are you still feeling safe out there in the woods?"

"Oh, so what is this, now? Some guy calls and I'm supposed to pack it up and run for the city?"

"Might be a smart thing to do."

"So, who are you seeing, now?" She asked, chomping into the phone.

"Come home and find out."

"Sounds like it's time to say goodnight. *Goodnight,* Kellen."

"Goodnight, LaRetha. Sleep tight. And call me, tomorrow."

"Sure thing."

They hang up.

It was really dark out, now, and the lights had already flickered, once. She thought about her caller. This *Therell* guy was probably just an estranged family member, looking for long lost relatives. But, how did he know about *Kellen?* And, if he found Kellen, he would easily find her, as well. *And for what?*

The wind was up, now. Peering out, there was nothing that she could see. And no sound of traffic, close or distant. She sighed, almost wishing she'd never talked to Kellen, tonight. His concerns certainly wouldn't help her to sleep.

This is what you came for, girl. You wanted solitude and you got it.

The ringing phone startled her awake. It was still dark, outside. The wind whistled around the corner of the house where her bedroom was located making a wistful sound that had lured her to sleep.

That would be Kellen, again, she thought, looking at the clock. *11:15pm.* He would want to know if she was still okay. She answered.

"Hello, *sweetheart*," she said with playful rudeness, like she always did when she awakened him. It never seemed to affect him.

There was no answer.

"Hello?"

Still no response. She stiffened. Kellen would never play around on the phone this way. She hang up the receiver. A few minutes passed. It rang again. She turned the answering machine on. The caller hang up.

She couldn't sleep at all now, for wondering who it might have been. *Probably a wrong number,* she thought. Turning over, she buried her head deep into her pillow. Sleep claimed her, once again.

Again, the phone rang. Turning over to pick up, she held the phone to her ear and waited. No one spoke, but the breathing was audible, just faintly. She slammed the receiver down.

Shaken now, and even though it was well after *2am,* she called Kellen. He answered on the fourth ring.

"What's up?" He Asked, obviously awakening from a deep sleep.

"It's me. *LaRetha.* " She whispered.

"What's wrong?" He sounded alert, now.

"I just got a couple of calls and no one answered when I picked up."

"Oh," he said, sighing with relief. "Happens to me all the time."

"Not out here. Not since I've been here. Do you think it could've been *Therell?"*

"*Could be.* It sounds like they gave you quite a scare. Have you checked your windows and doors?"

"You know I have. It's just strange that I would get a prank call, now," she said.

"It's probably nothing. Maybe a problem with the lines or something."

"*Come on,* Kellen." She didn't want to be humored. She wanted answers.

"I wish I could be there. I can think of a lot for us to do on a night like this. We wouldn't even notice the storm. Or the phone."

She was silent. He wasn't thinking about her current concern, at all.

"Look," he said. "Forget this madness. How about you come back to Atlanta, at least until this bad weather ends? You can stay at my place. Work from here, and everything. I won't pressure you, at all. Hey, I'll even cook for you. How about it?"

He was saying he wouldn't pressure her for sex, but she knew better.

"I think you're trying to make an offer I can't refuse. But, you know I can't leave right now. Besides, you how I love a challenge."

"Don't I challenge you enough? You know I try."

"That, you do," she said, laughing softly.

They talked for a few minutes more. Feeling better, she apologized for bothering him, promised to get some sleep, and said goodnight.

Her real protection was right where she'd left it – inside her night stand drawer. Kellen didn't know she'd bought it before moving. Or about the .*38* revolver that had once belonged to her father, and that Cecelia had left, unloaded, inside a kitchen drawer. That one, she kept in what appeared to be a fake drawer in her living room table.

Kellen hadn't been raised with guns, the way she had. She had been taught to shoot hunting rifles when her father had first begun taking her out with him and the boys. They had also taught her gun safety. It was all a part of surviving on a farm.

But, Kellen would never understand. After losing a childhood friend in a robbery, and almost losing a cousin in a carjacking, he despised guns, and distrusted anyone who used them.

Despite his many opinions, however, she *was* here alone, with only herself to rely on. She was daring, but not stupid, she thought. And she didn't plan on being surprised by anyone and not being able to get to one of them or the other. She checked her nightstand to make certain that hers was still loaded, and placed it back inside the drawer with the safety on.

Sleeping by the dim glow of the nightlight shining from her bathroom, she drifted off, again. But again, her slumber was disturbed. This time by a sudden noise.

Thud. She sat up, startled and uncertain if she'd actually heard the sound, at all. But then, there it was again.

I know what I heard, she assured herself. That noise had come from the far end of the house. Flicking off the lamp, she sat in total darkness, wondering what to do now.

The doors were locked - she was sure of it. And the wind was up and quite possibly the cause. Still, she wouldn't rest until she knew where it was coming from.

Apprehensive, she got a flashlight out of the bottom nightstand drawer. Then, believing that she should be *better safe than sorry,* she retrieved the automatic from the nightstand. Flipping off the hall switch, she proceeded toward the kitchen in the dark.

It could be nothing, she told herself. *Maybe just an animal or a fallen limb. I really shouldn't let a noise frighten me like this.*

There was a tree standing very close to the house. A few of its limbs stretched over the roof, on one side. Still, with the flashlight in one hand and gun in the other, she moved quietly through her kitchen to peer out onto the back porch, into the direction that the sound must have come.

This feels nothing like hunting, she thought, as she slid quietly alongside the wall for cover, her gun hand poised for a quick response. Stopping suddenly, she listened. Still nothing. But, she would wait.

Thud.

This time, it was closer and much louder, and it sounded almost as if someone was beating a heavy stick of wood against the side of the house. Shaken, she began to talk herself out of her fears. It had come from outside the back porch. She stopped again, to listen.

Was that the sound of her kitchen doorknob turning? That would mean that the culprit was on the back porch.

"Who's there?" She called out, sounding much braver than she felt.

Nothing.

"I asked *who's there*. Answer or I'll shoot!" She raised her hand and poised her gun to do that, stilling that hand with the other to keep it from shaking.

Still nothing.

Minutes passed, with panic holding her captive until she was finally able to move toward the back door and re-check the locks and the latch. Peering out into the darkness beyond the porch, she flipped the switch suddenly, throwing light out onto the snow.

Better I see them before they see me, she thought. Still, nothing was moving, so she hurried back to her bedroom, locking the door behind her before sliding between the covers, once again. Propping against the pillows, she sat upright with the gun still in one hand and flashlight in the other. And that's where she stayed until the sun came up and the phone awakened her.

She looked at the alarm clock. *7:55 am.* Both the gun and flashlight had fallen onto the comforter. She quickly picked up the receiver, not speaking. *It could be another prankster,* she thought.

"Hello. Is this *LaRetha Green?*"

The voice was deep. The speech was slow, almost slurred. Much like that of most men from the area. She didn't speak, but waited.

"*Hello?* Well, if it is, then I have the right number," he continued. "Sorry about last night. My phone wasn't charged. It kept cutting me off. *Hello?*"

So, he was last night's caller? Still, she said nothing.

"Is anyone there? This is *Therell* Watson."

Her breath caught. *Therell?* And where was he calling from, exactly? Outside her house? She peeped out of her bedroom window, before realizing that he was waiting for a response.

"I don't know a *Therell* Watson," she said, angry that she had been frightened.

"Well, *hello,*" he said. "I thought I'd been disconnected, again. I'm sorry to call so early in the day, but I'm in town for just a short time and hoped to catch you before I left. And the reason you don't know me is because we've never met. I used to live here. I didn't visit the farm, back then, but I knew all about you."

"Okay. So maybe I should know you. And you're calling now, *because...?*"

"I wondered if I could come out there and talk to you."

"What about?" She asked with intentional rudeness. She wasn't inviting trouble.

"Well," the voice replied. "Some business matters. I think it would be better for me to explain that when we meet."

"How did you know where to reach me? Or about my friend in Atlanta?"

He chuckled.

"I talked to Cecelia, recently. She told me about *Watson's* passing. She told me that Mr. Kincaid was a close friend of yours and that you two worked together. So, I called your office."

Humph!

"She said to tell you, hello. She warned me that you might not know me. But, this is very important. Do you think we could get together sometime this week to talk?"

Considering this remark, she felt compelled to say *no*.

"Haven't you noticed the weather? I can't come to you, and I doubt you'll make it out here, anytime soon."

She wouldn't decline outright, she decided. This might be important, after all. Still, considering those weird phone calls he'd just owned up to, this could all be some kind of a hoax, as well.

"I'm used to this climate. I thought maybe we could meet some time soon, if that's alright with you. Just name the day and time, and I'll be there." The drawl continued.

"Well," she replied, reluctantly. "I guess Thursday is good for me."

That would give her a little time to check this guy out before he arrived. Although she doubted he would get there on Thursday, or any other day this week, for that matter. This weather wouldn't permit it.

"Thank you, LaRetha. I promise not to take up much of your time."

"Do you know how to get here, Mr. Watson?"

"*Course* I do. And please, call me *Therell*."

His voice was strong. Kind, almost. And she didn't trust it for a minute.

"Is there any way that I can contact you, before then? In case something comes up?"

In case I change my mind.

"Well, I'm in Room 124 at the Comfort Ease Motor Inn, right now. I can give you my cell number, too."

"Fine," she said, scribbling it on a pad. "And how about we make that an early visit? Like Thursday, noon?"

In daylight, she thought.

"Sure, LaRetha. See you then."

The man's voice sounded strained, as if he didn't care for being dictated to. Well, she didn't like any of this. Besides, if he knew as much about Kentucky climates as he claimed, he should have known better than to visit *Lovely* in this weather.

Hanging up, LaRetha silently reprimanding herself for taking such a risk. She knew nothing about this *Therell Watson*, and considering her scare just last night, she wasn't looking forward to his visit, either. Something in her trusted instincts told her that this whole thing smelled of trouble.

Figuring she had disturbed Kellen enough, she dialed Laretta, instead. Except her mother didn't answer, and LaRetha remembered a real estate conference in Florida. *Most likely a vacation,* she thought, enviously. She could just imagine Laretta enjoying a beach side hotel and the luxuries that warmer climates provided, as she endured such harsh temperatures as these.

After dressing warmly, she headed outside to see if she could determine what had caused last night's disturbance. Oddly, neither a limb nor a power line had fallen. Nothing was out of place. Venturing into the garage, she quickly flipped the inside light switch. Nothing.

Turning off the light, she went back outside, feeling as puzzled as before. Something had turned her doorknob, last night. And it sure wasn't the wind.

Breakfast was light – one whole grain waffle with syrup and a scrambled egg. Settling down with her plate and a glass of grapefruit juice, she turned on the television. Still bad weather for the next two days, they said.

Old Therell might not make it out here, after all. She had a feeling that was best. For her, anyway.

The hours went quickly, with her writing keeping her occupied. And then, Thursday arrived. By *11:01am,* the house was cleaned from top to bottom. And frankly, she was bored out of her mind and certainly tired of waiting and wondering what to expect. Finally, it was less than a half hour before her guest was scheduled to arrive.

Telling herself she'd done the right thing by inviting him to come, she waited in the living room, but was becoming a bit uneasy, now. But, Therell claimed to know Cecelia. And, according to Kellen, he was a relative. So, he couldn't be that dangerous.

Relax, she told herself, before deciding to do something to occupy her time until he arrived. A batch of frozen cinnamon rolls were browning well when the doorbell rang. Straightening her simple attire of faded jeans and bright yellow sweater, she checked her appearance in the hall mirror, practicing a very serious expression.

Good enough, she thought, and went to the door.

The bell rang again, and she looked out of the top glass. It was difficult to see the face of the man standing sideways, looking away from the house and over the property. She could only determine that he was just over six feet tall, and was wearing a thick scarf and hat, and a brown suede coat. And even from where she stood, she could see a family resemblance.

Relaxing a bit, LaRetha opened the door and he turned around and smiled.

"*Therell Watson*. We spoke on the phone."

Looking at him, face on, there was no doubt that this man was a relative. Taking a deep breath, she unlocked the storm door to allow him inside. Standing in the foyer, his brilliant smile beamed with confidence.

Easily slipping out of his coat, he handed it and his hat to her. His hair was just like *Watson's,* she noticed - thick, black untamable curly hair.

Standing voluminously inside the doorway, he allowed her to direct him into the living room, and waited as she locked the door behind him.

"I would have known you anywhere," he said, smiling, with his booming voice feeling the room. "You look just like *Vernell*. They told me in town you would be easy to recognize considering you're his spitting image. They didn't lie."

She gave him a brief smile and offered him a seat.

"Thanks. This place wasn't as hard to get to as I'd thought. My tires were bad, so the old man at the hardware store rented me his truck to get out here. These tough winters haven't changed very much, have they?"

"Not since I was a child. I doubt they ever will."

"You've done some updating, I see."

"*Some*. It didn't need much. When were you out here, last?"

"Not since I was a kid, living with my aunt and uncle. And then I only walked over the property. Don't think I've ever been inside. That's probably why you don't remember much about me."

"You do have an advantage. I have to admit I don't remember you, or even hearing your name before. But, before you tell me, I have coffee if you'd like some."

"Great! *Black,* please. And anything else you've got that's edible around here. That hotel food's not nearly what it should be, and a lot of the restaurants are closed, today."

"So you're hungry," she said, rather than asked. She hadn't planned to *cook,* she thought sullenly.

"I sure am. And something in your oven smells good. But, don't let me put you out. I can always get something at a convenience store, back in town."

She almost settled for that, but could hear Laretta's voice chiding her girl-child for not using the good manners she was raised with.

"Not a problem. I think I can warm something up for you. Would a sandwich, do?"

"That would be fine, with a little something to drink. With the coffee, I mean." He smiled, again.

"Sure. It'll just take a few minutes. Make yourself comfortable. News is on, right now." Handing him the television remote, she went into the kitchen.

In less than twenty minutes, she had prepared a hot turkey and cheese sandwich with lettuce and tomato on rye bread, and heated a good portion of oven-baked beans, adding a sizeable portion of potato salad, as well. With a full plate on the table, along with two glasses of fruit punch, and a steaming cup of black coffee for him, she announced that the food was ready.

"Where can I wash up?"

She directed him to the guest bath and was putting the last cinnamon roll on a plate when he returned. Sitting down at the table, he bowed his head to say grace before digging in.

LaRetha couldn't help but notice as he ate that he was more than a little bit like her father's family. There was that same thick build, and that same slump in his shoulders that all the Watson men were subject to have. Only Therell was slightly taller than her father. And her father never wore a mustache.

From the looks of his clothing; that thick designer sweater with fashionable jeans, heavy Timberland boots and an expensive gold watch that gleamed from his wrist, this man was no pauper. There was no wedding ring either, she noticed. And his nails were immaculately manicured, so he certainly was no farmer. She wondered where he had been all those years and why no one had ever mentioned him. Not even her mother.

She allowed him a few bites and sips of coffee, before putting down her glass.

"You said you were just settling in when you called the other day. You here on business?"

He looked up, spreading his mouth into a smile.

"Somewhat. Travel is part of my work. And growing up in the country kind of stuck with me through college. Now, I work with a company that's contracting with the government to aid farm owners around the country. I go where they send me. I happened to be sent to this area. Or, rather, close enough where I could come out for a couple of days and still call it work." He smiled again.

She nodded, biting into a warm cinnamon roll as he took another bite of the turkey sandwich.

"This is good, LaRetha. Thanks."

"Glad you like it," she said, nodding. "So how do you know Cecelia?"

He chuckled a bit, finishing the last bite of his sandwich and wiping his mouth with a napkin before replying.

"No," he said. "I'm not related to Cecelia. Not by any blood lines, anyway. However, her sons *are* my stepbrothers."

She looked puzzled for a moment.

"In case you haven't figured it out yet, you are my *sister*, LaRetha. I'm *Watson's* son." After hesitating, he added, *"I'm your brother."*

"Really?" She said, almost choking on the roll. A swallow of cola cleared it up. He nodded, briskly brushing his hands together, before taking a roll from the plate and chewing as nonchalantly as if he had just told her that spring was really coming again, next year.

"And who is your *mother?*"

"Aurelia Moss. I'm about three years older than you. I went to live with our grandparents when I was little. Then my mother moved away. After the Watson's died, I lived with our father's brother, *Verilous,* and his family. I hardly saw you or him, after that. But, I am Vernell's son. Can't you see the resemblance?"

"Really?" She asked again, neglecting to answer the question. "Where have you been all this time? And, forgive my asking, but why hasn't anyone mentioned you, before?"

"Well, *Watson* didn't raise me. I was sort of the *family's* child," he said, sounding more than a little resentful. "I believe it was a mutual decision that he and my mother never married. Only, that left me with a young mother who couldn't provide for me, and a father who could, but who wanted nothing to do with me. Clearly, I wasn't planned."

"But, if you were raised here in town, wouldn't I have at least known you *existed?*"

"Not necessarily. Folks were good at keeping secrets, back then. Besides, *Watson* and the brother who raised me weren't exactly on good terms.

"And, why was that?" She asked, suspiciously.

"It's a long story, I'm sure. All I can tell you is that, in spite of that situation, the family's been really good to me. They raised me until I left for college, and still supported me until I graduated. And truthfully, with *Watson's* help, I've never wanted for anything. He made certain of that. Even when he wouldn't have anything to do with me, he still felt obligated to see that I had everything I needed, *and* some."

She remembered the *old* way, when neighbors were as dependable as family. She also knew of the uncle that neither her mother nor father had thought much of. He and *Watson* had sort of lost touch over the years - apparently, after some very heated disagreements that were never explained to her.

"How wonderful for you," she said, with unintended sarcasm.

"It was. I always see the family when I come out like this. I plan to visit *Verry* and Aunt Nell later on, today. I imagine you talk to them quite often?"

She could tell by the way he asked that he didn't imagine anything of the sort.

"Not yet. I plan to do that very soon."

He was quiet, as though pondering the thought.

"How long have you been back here, LaRetha?"

"Just over a year. I moved here permanently in early spring, last year."

He nodded.

"So, let's just say that what you're saying about us being related is true," she implored. "Obviously, I can't dispute what I know nothing about. But, why are you here, today? Whatever brought you out here in this weather must be very important."

"Why would you want to dispute it?" He asked, defensively. "The truth is the truth. As for why I'm here, I'll just get right to the point."

"Okay." She said. *Finally,* she thought.

He eyed her placidly, observing her easy demeanor. This seemed to relax him. She remained unmoved.

"You know, I used to envy all of you when I was a kid."

"All of *who?*"

"You and *Watson,* and the other children. You all had so much. You had this place, big as it is. And a nice secure life. More than that, you had a name that everyone respected."

"And you had none of that, even being raised as a Watson?"

"Well, some. But, I think it was very different. Nell used to talk about how it was out here. How *Watson* lived for this land. And how he never would've left it, except in death."

"*True.* My father never lived any place else," she said, thinking, *tell me something I don't know.* She wondered what she owed him for her own pain.

He stood looking out of the living room window as if remembering. Wishing.

"You like it out here, don't you?"

"Always have. Even as a kid. I just never thought...well. I just never imagined that I would..." She stopped.

"What? *Own* it?" He asked. "*Watson* worked hard on this place. I remember tall corn stalks that used to line up so evenly out there on the land." He was pointing, defining with his hands.

"Everything was always planted and harvested, right on schedule, each and every year. I believe he would have done it all by himself, if he had to. He never missed a beat, that *Watson.* People say he worked himself to death. But I think it was his inability to work that killed him."

What could he possibly know about her father's dying? She wondered. *He didn't even know he was dead, until now!* She resented his comment.

"You told my friend that you didn't know he had died. Why didn't someone tell you?" *Since you know him so well.*

"Like I said, *Watson* didn't raise me. We had no relationship. There was no reason for anyone to tell me about a man I hardly knew."

"Even if he was your real father? I think I would've wanted to know."

He didn't respond.

"Tell me about your mother," she said.

"Well, I have pictures of her and her family. I haven't heard from my mother since I was a boy. I don't even know where she is, right now. Just that she's still alive, somewhere."

You found me, but you can't even find your own mother?

"That's unfortunate," she said.

"I was telling you why I came out here, wasn't I?"

"Haven't you, already?"

"Not exactly. Well, as I said, when my mother moved away, she left me with *Watson's* family. I'm told that she wanted nothing more than for me to have a name - my father's name. So, before she left, she had him sign a document stating that I was his son."

"And where is it?" She asked, skeptically. He didn't miss the insinuation.

"I have it. I always knew who my father actually was, but it wasn't until he died that I learned this document existed. So, I'm sure you can imagine my excitement when I realized he had claimed me, after all. To find out now, even at this age, that my father had finally *acknowledged* me is a feeling I can't begin to explain."

"You only found that out, recently?" She repeated.

"I did. It was in a box with some old papers of my father's. My *adoptive* father, that is. And considering that this letter exists, this *proof,* I'm here now to get what's rightfully mine." His expression was solemn, changing as quickly as it had when he'd smiled.

Okay, so here's the scam, she thought.

"And what do you think that is?" She asked calmly.

"*Bottom line?* I was told that this entire estate was left to you, when truth is, it was left to his *oldest living child.* Blood related. That terminology was written to exclude Cecelia's boys, I'm sure."

"So, considering that I'm older than you, and that he's acknowledged me in a legal, notarized document, signed by him, my mother and a witness just a year after you were born, that could only refer to *me,* and not to you."

Finally, the true Therell was surfacing, she thought, smarting at the haughtiness in his tone. But, he didn't know her very well. She might be new in *Lovely,* but she wasn't new in the world. And she had absolutely no intentions of falling for any phony document scams. Certainly not when her livelihood was at stake.

"First of all, that's not entirely what the Will required. It referred to an only *blood related* child, not *oldest living.* And as far as I'm concerned, nothing to the contrary has been proven just yet."

He scowled.

"Where is this *document?*" She asked again, feeling secure with an upper hand.

"My attorney has it, but it'll be available to you," he replied, more stolidly. "And to your attorney, of course."

"And why do you think that *Watson* would sign this document, but not mention you in his Will?"

"I can't say why he did that. But, he provided for me because I was his son. His *only* son."

The man was facing her squarely, eyeing her determinedly. She saw that this would only get more unpleasant. She should end this, now.

"Okay, I'll have my attorney look it over as soon as you get it to me."

Therell smiled victoriously, and she felt the need to explain herself.

"There's nothing that I can tell you, at the moment. And I don't mean this disrespectfully, but what you're saying is just not something that my father would do." Therell frowned and she continued.

"*Watson* was a *thorough* man – a *family* man. And I can't imagine him having a son living right here in *Lovely, Kentucky,* a son that he was providing for, but that he wouldn't want in his life. Or mine. Or that he would exclude in his Will that way. It makes no sense to me."

"I can't explain that," he retorted. "But facts are facts. This is the truth, believe it or not."

"I guess you can prove that he provided for you?"

"Everyone knows it. The family raised me but he supported me."

"*Hmmm,*" she responded. "But, why has no one come forward, before now? And why not when he was alive?"

Therell faced her with creased brow. His eyes glistened now. Still, she persisted.

"Well, I'm sure you understand that until I see this document, I can't even speak to you intelligently about any of this."

"But, you do see the family resemblance? Even if you didn't know me, everyone else did. I was never a secret."

"But, this is my first time hearing any of this. Until an hour ago, you were a perfect stranger to me," she said. "I need something more."

"And *then* what?" He asked with a smirk.

"Well, you must understand *my* position. Once it's clear to me that what you're saying is true, I will most certainly do what's right *and* fair, for the both of us."

He scoffed, and suddenly stood on his feet, looking at her as though in disbelief. She couldn't tell if it was an act, or if he was just now realizing that he hadn't exactly gotten what he'd come for.

She remained unmoved, but wondered how much time it would take to get to the drawer in the living room table. She would do whatever she had to, to get him out of her house and off of her property.

Anxious to be rid of him now, she slowly stood, too. Walking ahead of him to get his hat and coat. He put them on, his eyes never leaving her face. Clearly he was trying to read her, but her face remained expressionless.

Buttoning his coat and putting his scarf around his neck, he attempted a smile, which she didn't return.

"I'm not here to hurt you, LaRetha, or to rob you of anything. I know that what I just told you is surprising. But, what's done is done, and it was neither of our doing. But, by the same token, what's fair *is* fair. Part, if not all of this property and everything on it is my birthright, and I intend on getting what's mine. Just as you would, if the shoe were on the other foot."

"I'm sorry Therell, but I don't think you know me well enough to assume what I would do in this, or any other situation."

"*No?* Well, it's not hard to figure out. And I want you to know that I'm going to do whatever is necessary."

She heard the biting tone, but felt that the man did protest too much, which made her all the more doubtful.

Why hadn't he brought a copy of this determining document? And why was he trying to intimidate her?

"You don't have to make threats. It's possible that we don't even have a problem here. Surely, this can be easily confirmed. Especially in a town as small as *Lovely.*"

"*Sometimes.* Just remember. Only the courts have to be convinced. *The courts,* LaRetha!"

His voice was again challenging, and filled with animosity, now. She considered their isolation, and her safety, or lack of it. And her scare from the other night.

"Then we have no worries, do we?" Then, she smiled. And while her tone was friendly, she felt anything *but*. She opened the front door for him.

"But, until we resolve this, I think it would be a good idea for you to deal directly with my attorney. I'll have him to call you, or your attorney can contact me if you wish. But, until this is resolved, please don't come here, again."

He considered this, nodded, and walked through the doorway. She closed the storm door, silently locking it, relieved that he was finally leaving. After walking a few steps and standing up to his calves in snow, Therell stopped and turned to face her. Snow fell heavily on his wide hat.

"You know, I had hoped we could talk about this, civilly."

"I think we just did."

He nodded.

"Good day, LaRetha. It's been a pleasure meeting you."

"Goodbye, Therell."

Sure it has, she thought, closing the door, and watching through the living room window until the taillights of the red truck had disappeared.

Recanting their conversation, she decided that Therell Watson was either a swindler or a disgruntled relative, out to get something for nothing. And that would mean that he was out to get her, as well.

Surely her father hadn't done what this man was implying? And that was to leave behind a Will that was deliberately obscure in its language. He must have known that any son of his would not be overlooked in the matter, and that it would lead to certain dispute.

But if what this man had said was correct, this was exactly what he had done. And, her beliefs that her father had been appropriately concerned and considerate of her in his will would be misplaced. He would have been just the opposite. And that just wasn't her father; the family man she'd known all her life.

Therell Watson was an imposing figure, in size and personality. Just like her father. But then, so was she. And until he proved that he was who he said he was, she wasn't backing down.

The man must be lying, she thought as she washed and rinsed his coffee cup. He could be an imposter. Someone hired by somebody, based on his appearance. But truth was, he looked a lot like her father. Even had some of his mannerisms. Still it made no sense that her father would put her in this situation. That he would leave her to fight for this land, as it appeared that he had. But this was different. This time the enemy was quite possibly her family.

It was all a lie! She didn't know who Therell Watson really was, but she would get to the bottom of this. Feeling suddenly overwhelmed with anger, she impulsively tossed his cup into the garbage pail, vowing that those lying lips would never touch it, again.

3

Kellen was astounded when he heard her news on Friday evening. She had anticipated an even greater insistence on his part that she move back to Atlanta. She wasn't disappointed.

"So, *now* will you consider selling the place and moving back home to Atlanta, where you belong?"

"I don't know yet. Either way, there are things to work out." She said, lying back on down filled bed pillows, wishing he was closer.

"So, why don't you believe him? Doesn't he *look* like family?"

There was that sarcasm. He had never truly admitted to his prejudice about what he termed the *white* genes that her family possessed, but it showed, nevertheless. He liked her looks, but resented her genetics. *Such hypocrisy.*

"Not really." She responded with an equal amount of sarcasm.

"*Not really,* meaning he does, but that he'll have to prove it, regardless?"

"Something like that."

"I thought you were going to be fair?"

"That's not being fair? I'm giving him the benefit of the doubt. What would you do?"

"*Uh huh,*" he replied.

"He's the one with something to prove, not me. *If* he's really got that kind of proof, then why didn't he bring it with him?"

"Good question. Have you asked Laretta about it?"

"She's traveling, so I haven't caught up with her, yet. Hopefully she'll call back, soon. There's a lot about this whole thing that just doesn't sit right with me. And if anybody can clear this up, she can."

"Hmmm," he responded. "So, what's next?"

"Make a few calls and get some answers. Find a good attorney and get that in motion. After that, I'll just wait and see what happens."

"Well, if he is related, would having a brother be so bad?"

"Not at all, if he's a *nice* brother. I kind of like the idea of having someone to help me do something with the place. But, to tell you the truth, I think he's more concerned about *ownership,* than having a relationship. If he has his way, I'll be renting from *him,* soon. If he can prove this document is *legit,* I might end up with nothing!"

"*Slow down.* Nothing's been proven, yet. The least you should get is *half."*

"I agree, but stranger things have happened. I'm not worried, though. I'm seeing an attorney first thing, next week."

"Good. I wouldn't prolong this. These family disputes can get real ugly, really fast. Desperate people do desperate things, and Therell sounds desperate to me."

"It's already ugly, if you ask me. But I'm as determined to keep this place as he is to take it. He doesn't want to mess with me."

"Not if he knows what I know," he kidded, humoring her.

They talked more about Therell and the things he'd told her about himself, before ending their conversation with her promising to see him during the upcoming Thanksgiving holidays. That satisfied him for the moment. They said goodnight.

By Monday, the weather was letting up. Ice was melting and the roads in town were mostly clear. Anxious about her upcoming research and bored at the same time, LaRetha decided to begin her search for information. She searched under *genealogy.*

There had to be a way for her to get more of this man's history, she thought. Finding little that was interesting, or that she had the patience to explore, she finally decided to call her boss at the newspaper. Mac Henry answered on the second ring, sounding characteristically upbeat.

"Good morning, my little *runaway.* I have your article. It's great. Send me more."

"I'm glad you like it."

Mac was a good mentor. He had run the paper for over twenty years. It was his life, and he respected anyone who shared his fondness for the craft. Not to mention, he paid her very generously.

"You just keep writing like this. Look, I have a tip that there was a newsworthy incident not far from where you live."

"What type of incident?"

"Well, it appears that one of your local farmers was burned out about a week ago. I want that story. Send me something. I prefer an impartial perspective, but I know how you country folks only talk to your own. And nobody out there knows you're really *Hadira Jones* anyway, do they? "

"None of these *country folks* really care," she responded, cynically.

She said she would see what she could find out, while changing her mind about asking him to help research Therell Watson's background. Yet, she was puzzled. Somebody was recently burned out? Why hadn't she heard about it? Why wasn't it in Sunday's paper?

Maybe it was as simple as a kerosene fire. Those happened easily in these aging wooden buildings, when people carelessly started fires for heat. But, Mac Henry seemed to think there was more to the story. And maybe there was.

Taking a note pad, she scribbled some notes. That took her mind off Therell for a while. The local paper wasn't online, so she'd have to go into town for one. But, what better excuse was there to travel after being shut away for several days?

Therell had said he gave assistance to local farms. She wondered what kind of help and which farms. She doubted *Watson* ever got that kind of assistance. But times had changed. Or so she hoped.

On this side of town, there was her farm, and a horse farm down the road a few miles. Another farmer sold produce to several of the stores in town. The last landowner had erected chicken houses on his property. That one wasn't hard to find, considering the smell.

Looking out of her window, she decided to go outside and have another look around. Dressed warmly in thermal underwear, a thick brown sweater, jeans and boots, she put on a heavy wool coat and hat and wrapped in a scarf before venturing outside with flashlight in hand. As an afterthought, she put her father's old gun in her pocket. There was always the possibility that she might need it. Therell was still out there somewhere, after all.

The view was simply *breathtaking*. Tall, thick trees were stiff with ice and grounded in huge banks of snow. Power lines were covered with thick icicles that hang low enough to convince you that you could touch them when you really couldn't. And the smell in the air was so fresh and clean she could almost taste it. She wriggled her nose.

But she couldn't get Therell out of her mind. *Was she wrong for not trusting him?* For not wanting to share the farm? But, until evidence stated differently, *she* was her father's only living birth child. Laretta still hadn't called, but there was someone else who would know.

Finding everything in its place, she went back inside, to her bedroom to get her address book. She easily found the number she was looking for.

So that we can always keep in touch, the woman had said, before leaving *Lovely* for the last time, the day of the reading of her father's Will. Well, she sighed. If ever she needed to contact Cecelia, it was now.

The phone rang for a long time before a young man answered. She could hear what sounded like loud rap music in the background, and tried speaking over it.

"Hello. This is LaRetha Greer. *Is Cecelia Watson in?*"

The music was turned down.

"No, she's not. Is there something I can help you with?" The young man sounded like someone in Germaine's age group.

"This is LaRetha Greer. Can you tell me when you expect her?"

"She hasn't lived here in months. I'm renting the place, now. But I can give her a message."

"Can I get her number, please? It's very important. This is her stepdaughter."

"*LaRetha Greer,* you say? Well, that would make you my aunt. I'm *Jason,* Thomas' oldest son. I'm living here while I go to college. I would give you her number, but somebody's been calling a lot lately, asking for it. She told me not to, and she's paying the phone bill, you know? She'd rather I just take messages."

"That wasn't me. This is my first time calling. And it's very urgent."

"Oh, no! That caller was a man," he explained. "I don't think she wants to talk to him, though."

A man? She immediately figured it was Therell.

"Well, please tell her that I called, and that I need to speak with her, right away. It's an extremely important family matter. Okay?"

"Sure, Aunt LaRetha. Hey, how's Germaine? My dad says he's really cool. I can't wait to meet him. Look, I'm sorry about your father. About *Grandpa.*"

She smiled at his attempt to catch up on years of family matters in one conversation. It was too bad he'd never met his grandfather.

"Thank you. Here's the number." After giving it to him, she added, "And if anyone else asks, I never called, okay?"

"Sure thing. It was great talking with you."

"Same here. Tell everyone, *hello* for me."

"Sure thing. Bye, Aunt LaRetha."

"Take care, Jason. Good luck with school."

She was finally able to drive into town, but the trip wasn't nearly long enough. The town had suddenly come alive. People were coming and going as though in a hurry to get back to their usual routines. And kids were moving playfully about the sidewalks near their parents' establishments as schools were closed until the power could be fully restored.

She followed the directions she'd gotten online, and drove to the opposite side of town, pulling onto the parking pad of a white, ranch style office building. She parked right beside the sign that read; *Law Offices – Billard, Hanes & Davis.*

Inside was very pleasant. A woman sitting behind a sliding glass window was on the phone. Hanging up, she slid the glass back and eyed LaRetha casually, before speaking.

"Yes, how may I help you?" She stood to file a folder in the cabinet behind her. Short and heavyset, tanned with stylish white hair, her face was friendly. Appearing to be only in her late fifties maybe, she seemed full of vitality, moving easily to accomplish her tasks. LaRetha felt she could probably get the information she needed from her.

"Hi, I'm LaRetha Greer. I tried to call but I couldn't get through. I'm here to make an appointment to see an attorney about a land ownership situation. Is anyone available this morning, by any chance?"

The woman studied her face for a moment. Her expression suddenly changed.

"I apologize for the telephone inconvenience. Our lines are only back up, just now. You're *Vernell Watson's* daughter, aren't you?"

"Yes, I am" she said, smiling.

"Well, *hello,*" she smiled brightly. "I'm *Marva Hanken.* I knew both your parents. I didn't know your mother that well. I'm a bit older. It's an *inheritance* problem, you say?"

"Yes. Is anyone available?" LaRetha realized she would have to get past Marva to accomplish anything.

"Mr. Davis has been handling most of the civil cases, but he's out at the moment. *Bob Billard* is here, though. He handles *criminal* cases."

"Then, I would prefer Mr. Davis, if you don't mind."

"Okay. But he's not due back until tomorrow. But, Bob Billard can hear your concerns, and if he agrees that you have a case and if you still prefer Douglas Davis after that, he can refer you. How about that? Might save you some time?" She urged.

"Well, alright. If you don't think it would be a problem."

"Not at all. Were you referred to Mr. Davis?"

"No. It's just that this is a *civil* case. Not a criminal one."

"Right, I understand."

"But, your suggestion is fine. I'd like to see Mr. Billard, then."

"Not a problem. He's here now, and he's available. I'll just let him know you're here. You can fill these out and take them in with you," she said, handing her a plastic clipboard with several forms on it.

She retreated to the reception area; a very nicely furnished room with white walls and teal green carpeting. Matching sofa cushions and coordinating valances looped over partly open blinds. Tables with glass tops gleamed spotlessly. Soft music played from small speakers, overhead. It was all very relaxing.

Done with completing the forms, she waited patiently, nodding and humming to a jazz rendition of a Toni Braxton song. She was thumbing through a magazine when she heard her name being called. Glancing up, she looked into the face of a big burly man with lively, bright blue eyes that scrutinized her as he smiled. He extended his hand in greeting.

"Miss Watson? *Bob Billard.* I'm very pleased to meet you. I knew your father well. We used to hang out together in fishing holes, as children. So, naturally I would love to help you with your situation. Please, step into my office."

She shook his outstretched hand and walked in the direction he was pointing. His office was extremely large. Furnished in everything *maple,* it had its own private bathroom, and a nice sized deck extending from beyond double doors with nice velvet drapes. The building was much larger than it first appeared.

"Have a seat."

She did, waiting as he slowly eased his bulky body into a wide blue leather chair behind his desk, as if concerned that he hadn't enough room, although there was plenty. Once comfortable, he slid forward to lean his elbows onto the desktop and look over her forms.

"So, how may I help you? You say this is an inheritance problem?"

"Yes. Well, I'm living at the Watson farm. I inherited it from my father, *Vernell Watson?"*

The man nodded.

"Well, last week I had a visit from a man who claims that he's my father's oldest child. Only he didn't come just to get acquainted. He wants my inheritance."

The man nodded, his brows creased. "What exactly did he tell you about himself? And please, take your time."

"He claims to have a document proving that he is the legitimate heir to everything my father has left me. So, obviously I'm concerned. That farm is all I have, now. So, I'm here because, at his recommendation, I'll need an attorney to help me with this."

She continued, recanting everything about Therell's call and visit. Mr. Billard listened until she finished.

"Therell Watson says that what I own rightfully belongs to him. And now, he's threatening legal action that I'm not certain he can take. But that does nothing to ease the aggravation."

"*Hmmm.* Well, this is going to require a review of the Will and this proof that he says he has. Depending on its wording, he might need to further prove his claim. That he is either the oldest living blood heir or that he was legally adopted. And then the Will must provide for that. Otherwise, I'm not certain that he has a claim, at all."

She breathed a sigh of relief.

"However, we don't want to *assume* anything, just yet. First, we need copies of these documents. We'll know where to go from there. But, I must warn you. This might not be too difficult for him to prove. You have to consider what you would be prepared to do, if he really is your brother."

"I understand. I just need to know, for sure. This isn't *just* about the land, but the possibility that someone's trying to take advantage, here."

"I see." He contemplated this. "Well, have you spoken with your father's people about this? The ones he says raised him? Surely they can bring some clarity to this."

"Not yet." She hadn't exactly been in touch with them, or they with her. It didn't seem right that this would be the first thing that she would contact them about. But, she would do what was necessary.

"I see," he repeated, frowning again.

She wasn't sure that he did. Something in his demeanor told her that he wasn't convinced that her concerns were valid.

"Well, there are a lot of ways to prove paternity, even after the father is deceased. One way would require exhuming the body, which is the most extreme way. The easiest way would be to prove it by record."

The first option was naturally unappealing to her. She certainly didn't plan to take it that far.

"Still, this could all be premature and unnecessary. *But first things, first.* I know some of your people, personally. Tell you what. I'll look into the matter, find out what I can and get back to you in a few days. We'll know where to go by then, for sure." He smiled.

"Okay. So, does this mean you're taking the case? What is your fee?"

He shook his meaty head and smiled.

"Not to worry, yet. I wouldn't accept your money unless I was absolutely certain that I needed to. This matter might be easily resolved. Someone around town should be able to shed light on this situation."

He handed her a business card.

"Keep this, call me anytime. And if this man so much as looks at you wrong, let me know. This doesn't have to get complicated. We just don't want to make any assumptions, you understand?"

"I understand. But I have to say, I would prefer to approach my family about this, before you do. I haven't talked to them and I know how offended I was when Therell even mentioned an attorney without giving me time to even digest this and work something out with him. I'm only here because he's made it clear that I need to be. Otherwise…"

"I understand. And I appreciate your forethought, Mrs. Greer. But I assure you that I won't take any liberties that I shouldn't."

Still, she was doubtful. *But what choice did she have?* It never hurt to have capable people on your side, she thought.

"Alright," she said. Relieved, she stood to leave, thinking that Kellen gave good advice.

She thanked him and said a friendly goodbye to Marva. Then, she drove in the direction of the shopping plaza. A new discount linen store had just opened, and she felt like spending a little money. She made a maximum withdrawal at the ATM and didn't leave the store until she was down to her last five dollars in cash.

Kellen wasn't in when she called him later than evening, but he called back at about midnight, figuring she wouldn't sleep until she heard from him, she guessed. He was right. She couldn't.

"Hey," she said, softly, happy to hear a calm voice of reasoning.

"*Hey, yourself.*" He sounded surprised at her relaxed tone. "What's happening in *Nowhere Land?*"

She told him about Billard, and how he considered it a simple matter.

"*Good*. Who is he? Some stud who thinks that taking the case is going to score points with you in other areas? I could tell him otherwise."

"His name is *Bob Billard,*" she retorted. "And he's as old as *Methuselah,* but nice as pie. He hasn't even charged me anything, yet. Says he wants to be sure it's necessary, first."

"Well, sounds like you have it under control out there," he said.

"*Working* on it," she said, proudly.

"So," he said, "Thanksgiving is just over a month away. My brother won't be home. I think it's because of a woman. He just doesn't want to hurt my feelings."

"Could be. But what about you and your woman?"

"Well, the one I had is over. *Done.* I called it off."

"Why?" She asked, anticipating that he might say because of her.

"*Too high maintenance.* Besides, you know I never liked long distance relationships, anyway. It's much too cold for that."

"*Humph!* Well, I'm sure she's all tore up about it." She said.

"Hah! Truth is you've spoiled me, LaRetha. I don't fall for every short skirt I see, anymore. I need *substance.* Think I'll ever find it, again?"

"Sure you will. Question is, will you know it when you see it?" She teased.

"I would, but would *you?*"

"Sure. Why else would I bother being a friend to such a picky man?"

"Yeah, right, *picky.* But, you changed the subject. What about Thanksgiving? Going anywhere? *Expecting guests?*"

"You know, Kellen…"

"Okay, here it comes," he said, in a low voice.

"I wasn't dodging your question," she lied. "I haven't made plans yet, but last year was nice, even if you and Germaine didn't come around. I think this year will be special, too."

"Yeah, right. You'll spend it all alone without any of the people who care about you. I tried to understand, last year. But surely you can make an exception, just this once? Your mother wanted me to ask. And Germaine isn't exactly a total lost cause, you know?"

"It sure seems like it."

"You know better. He's missing you and he wants to see you, but he thinks you won't accept his living with that girl. You should tell him this, personally."

"Let's not talk about Germaine, right now. If you don't mind."

"*Sorry.* I just wanted you to know how he felt."

"Thanks, but he'll tell me himself, when he's ready."

"Okay, then. What about me?" He exhaled with exasperation.

"I would love to have everybody here, this year."

"By the way, I heard from another of your family members. You won't believe it. But it was *Gerald!*"

"Gerald? What did he want?"

"He said he just wanted to know how you were, but we didn't vibe too well. He won't be calling me, again."

"What happened?"

"I just told him he was stupid for losing you and to stop bugging me, basically."

She considered this and laughed.

"*Forget* Gerald," she finally said. "He didn't care how I was when we were married. He's got no claims on me, anymore."

"Well, somebody needs to tell him that."

"I have. He's just…"

"A *jerk,*" he said, indifferently.

"Well, *so as a man thinketh, he is.* Gerald will always be tormented. He just can't imagine anyone having a good life without him, although that would be just about *everybody!*"

"Doesn't sound as if you have any regrets."

"*None, whatsoever.* The last time I caught him in something he went to a hotel and called me, apologizing. Never mind he'd been working with the woman. He probably got her the job."

"Did you forgive him?"

"Does it look like I did? I told him I wanted a divorce."

"*Wow.* And what did he say?"

"He cried like a baby, then he told some woman in the room to turn down the television."

Kellen had heard this story before, but laughed as he always did.

"I would never do that to you, you know?"

"You're so right, you wouldn't. I don't live in dreamland, anymore, sweetheart. It takes a whole lot more to fool this old goat."

"Don't say that."

"Okay, so I'm not a goat."

He laughed again.

Having Kellen as a friend was therapeutic for her. She hoped he wasn't tired of her confiding in him.

"So, tell me what's going on at the office," she said.

He described some incident with Mac Henry, and her mind wandered back to Gerald, finding it odd that he was concerned about her. *The nerve!*

She remembered the indiscretions, and how that first realization had truly rocked her world. She remembered the shame of it all. How she had foolishly blamed herself, and even tried to change those things he'd begun to criticize about her.

She'd wasted so much valuable time, wondering what she was or wasn't doing in their marriage. Until finally accepting that there was nothing she could do to salvage the situation. *Gerald* was the one with the problem, and not her. And he simply wasn't willing.

But, in spite of the disrespect, and the anguish, *life goes on,* she thought. She had finally realized that this man she'd married did not define her. He never had. No one did. *He was not her Maker.* And what he didn't make, he couldn't break. That included her *spirit.*

By the time she had started the divorce proceedings, he was staying away from home for days at a time, anyway. They weren't even speaking to one another. She had avoided him at all cost, thinking that this was her chance at a brand new life and she wasn't going to be talked out of that. It had surprised him that his opinions no longer mattered to her.

Then suddenly he was always around; complimenting her, helping out around the house, talking with Germaine about sports and school, and simply testing her will. But she'd stood her ground, in spite of the disappointed look in her son's eyes. She knew that look, and understood his feelings.

Why couldn't they all stay together? It was the same question she'd had for her own mother, at one time. But, she had already told herself that if she was to survive this, she would have to meet her challenges *head on.* And she had, despite feeling sadder than she ever had in her life.

Gerald had taken his time getting all of his things out of the house, apparently hoping she would change her mind. It had been stressful those last two months they'd lived together. But, she'd prayed her way through it, knowing she was doing the best thing.

Still, he hadn't understood the urgency. At least they didn't have *financial* issues, he'd exclaimed one day. They still had time to reconsider, he'd said. Germaine had left the room, sensing the explosion that was about to occur.

As if she *wanted* to be in a dead-end relationship, she had responded. *As if just having the name Mrs. Gerald Greer was some sort of an honor in itself!*

"You know, you really need to grow up," she'd told him. "You're setting a really poor example for Germaine. Is this what you want to teach him about being a man, and respecting a wife?"

"Whatever has happened between us, LaRetha, I have always done right by our son. He doesn't want me to leave, *you do!* What do I need to do? What do you want? Do you want me to leave my job after all the years I put into it? If that's what it takes, I'll do it,"

"It's too late for all that, now. Why don't you just admit that you've let this family down? There's nothing left to fight for, Gerald. You know that better than I do."

"You're not being reasonable," he'd persisted. "People get through this type of thing, everyday. We've worked so hard for everything…"

"You're right, they do. And more power to 'em! But I've been more than reasonable. I was loyal even when you were lying to me. But, I can't live my life like that anymore. *I won't!*"

"And please don't make this about your job," she'd continued. "*You* are the problem, not that job. You still don't think you've done anything wrong. You won't go to church. You won't get counseling. Marriage takes *two*. And I've been alone in this one, long enough."

Kellen was calling her name, now. He was still waiting on the phone for her response.

"Sorry," she said. "I guess I drifted for a moment."

"I was telling you about my new job offer. But, it's late, so I guess I'll just say goodnight."

"Oh? Tell me."

He'd just interviewed in Ohio, he said. A friend of a business associate needed a manager for their accounts department. He'd met with the owner and gotten the job that same evening.

"And you're just now telling me this? I'm so happy for you! Are you ready for the move?" She asked, trying to hide her disappointment at the thought of him being even further away, but knowing that she had no room to complain.

"Of course. It's a huge adjustment. But *hey*, if you can adjust to the wilderness, I should at least give this a shot," he laughed.

He was going on with his life, which was best for them both. She said she wished him everything that made him happy.

"There's nothing holding me here, I don't guess."

"Well, you know where I'll be," she kidded, barely able to hide the sadness in her voice. "Even when you've married and started a family of your own, I'll still be your *best* friend, for as long as you want me to, anyway."

He chuckled sadly, and her heart ached. She said she would let him sleep, now. Hanging up, she tried to do the same, but thoughts of Kellen going to Ohio and forgetting all about her were plaguing. Finally, she got up and sat at her computer. Ignoring her gut feeling that this could be a huge mistake, she threw caution to the wind.

You've Got Mail, it read. She clicked onto *Compose.*

Kellen,
Consider this; FIVE GLORIOUS DAYS/NITES in
'Nowhere Land' with me (as friends). Think about it
and let me know, okay? We can plan for Christmas, later.
U-no-who!

I really should think about this, she thought. Clicking on *Save Draft,* she decided to sleep on it and send it in the morning if she still felt the same way.

She went to bed with happy thoughts about having Kellen there. He might like it well enough to stay…

Get real! She told herself. It just wasn't going to happen. But, it was okay to dream.

4

She was showering when Bob Billard left a message on her voice mail the next morning. She should come in as soon as possible. He thought they should go ahead and begin preparing a case.

He must have found something, she thought, calling back right away. Marva answered in a friendly voice, and booked an appointment for them. Tomorrow morning, *10am*.

She breathed relief, before going outside to start her car engine and allowing it to idle. The Chevy hadn't started for two days. After changing its battery, she found out that wasn't the problem.

"It's your transmission," said Hogan from *Hogan's Garage*, who came in a tow truck, ready to haul it into town. He puffed on a cigarette while she contemplated this.

She'd had enough experience with hiring mechanics. A non-suspecting woman could easily get the biggest bill for the smallest repair.

"Are you sure? I wouldn't want to go to that expense then find out it was something as simple as a *starter bendix*."

He looked at her with surprise.

Yes, I know what that is, she thought. Gerald and Germaine had tinkered around with cars enough for her to pick up on a few things. She gave him a knowing look.

"It could be that simple. Let me haul it in. Check it out. I'll call you, afterwards."

"Thanks, but be sure to talk to me before you make any repairs. If they're *too* expensive, I might just wait until after the holidays."

His glance went from her face to the house, then the stretch of land around it, and she could almost read his mind. This was all *inheritance,* and she could definitely afford to repair it.

"I'll have to get that engine worked on soon, too," she added, hoping that would convince him to go easy on her, this time around. "It's knocking a bit."

The man's face lit up and he smiled, his gray cigarette ashes hanging but never falling.

"Sure ma'am. I'll just need forty bucks for the haul. Then you pay for the estimate when you come in. If we fix it, I'll deduct the estimate from any repairs we make."

She nodded, and placed *four* ten dollar bills into his greasy palm. By the looks of him and the equally dingy face of the little boy he had in the truck with him, he could really use the money. So she doled out an extra *ten.*

"For your son. He's working too, isn't he?"

The man looked surprised and then smiled again. "Thanks, ma'am," he said, gratefully.

She watched as the truck was pulled away, sliding vigorously across the drive as if trying to loosen its restraints. She put Hogan's business card in her jeans' pocket and went inside.

She would start that story for Mac Henry, today. So far, she hadn't written anything, wanting to get a clear angle before putting it on paper. But, she always made her deadlines. Besides, if he was so impatient, she thought, he could just fly up here and write the story himself.

She finished another holiday piece for a women's magazine, before starting a list of personal priorities for the remainder of the year. She hesitated at calling them *resolutions,* simply because she'd never kept any of those.

Looking at the bright side of things, the farm was hers, for now. Still, she wondered what she would do with it if she kept it, or if she didn't. She thought about Billard and what he might have found. She needed to find out whatever she could about the Watson family tree, she thought, realizing she was looking forward to the research. There were so many things about this town and her family that she had yet to learn, but was excited about discovering.

Thoughts of Therell Watson sobered her a bit. The man could pose a real problem for her. But, she had until tomorrow to either worry about it, or to trust that the best thing would occur in this situation. She decided to trust.

Sitting down to begin writing the ideas she had finally formulated, she let her fingers take control, starting with what she knew about the town, itself:

The term, *Lovely,* is not just an expression or a description of something or someone which might be pleasing to the eye. It also describes a southern place, mountainous country, miles and miles north of Atlanta, Georgia. It describes a small rural town where African-Americans, Caucasians and Latinos, young and old, farmers, academicians and industrialists, all represent family and friend to one another, and nothing far different to any outsider. It is a town where three blankets of snow can freeze the unprepared, while simultaneously providing a reason to offer warmth to the coldest heart. It is where the locals are presently concerning themselves with helping one another through damaging rain and snow storms, volunteering their time and working tirelessly side by side to return the town to normalcy, after which they quickly celebrate their victories, until the next one. It is a place where, whether you were born here or are just visiting, you always feel relatively protected and cared for. It is a Utopia of sorts – a world within another much more unpredictable, frightening and threatening one. You were always safe in *Lovely*, Kentucky. That is, until recent fires....

She stopped there. The thought of fires took her back to years before, when her father had shared stories about the town and the difficulties it had faced.

But did she want to share that? Did she have enough information to do so? Just how personal would she be willing to get with these people whom she hardly knew, but could imagine wouldn't want to relive any of that, again?

Mac Henry was right. It would be difficult to talk about the town from a totally neutral perspective. Then she decided to start with only general facts.

But once engrossed in the story, she wandered into more descriptive prose about the town and it's history. Afterward, she formulated a story outline about the town's history of arsons. Writing this piece could be either very rewarding or extremely invasive, she thought. She would have to be careful. She decided that, after her trip to Bob Billard's office tomorrow, she would go to the library to see what else she could come up with.

There was nothing interesting in her e-mail, she thought, until one particular subject line caught her eye.

Hey Beautiful, Most Lovely. It was from Kellen. Her anticipation grew as she opened the mail.

Hey Beautiful, Most Lovely.
I enjoyed our conversation last night. I miss you, so much.
I need to confess, though. I have a holiday invite from a
friend. A woman. I didn't want to say so. If you turned me
down, I wanted it to be for your reasons, not mine. But why
did I even worry? You want to move on in life. My feelings
aren't yours. I realize now that you weren't joking about
never coming back.
So, following your suggestion, I've made plans to go to

**Cincinnati. I met her after my job interview. She's very
nice. She knows about our friendship. Forgive me for lying.
And if you change your mind about Thanksgiving, PLEASE
give me a Heads Up! You're always Tops on my list. I'll be
there in a flash. In the meantime, and as you often say, life
must go on. I had only hoped it would be with you.**
   Love Always,
   Kellen Kincaid (Just look at the Mess We've Made!)

She groaned and her heart sank. *Why had she been so slow and
silly about inviting him?* Oh well, she thought, he must really like
this woman, for him to even mention her. And now, like the other
men in her life, he was *so going* that he was already *gone*. And it was
all her doing.

She couldn't very well send that E-mail, now. He would think
she was playing games or teasing him. Disappointed, she saved his
letter. Despite the surprising news, reading it made her feel closer to
him, somehow. Signing off, she busied herself by unloading the bags
of new linen that she had left in the middle of the floor.

I might send it later, she thought. But, deep in her heart, she
knew that she wouldn't.

Bob Billard looked serious when she walked into his office.

"*You've got problems,*" he said, once she sat down. "That document Therell Watson told you about is exactly as he says. It says here
that *Vernell Watson is the birth father of Therell Watson.* Your
father's signature is right here," he said, pointing to a place on a
faxed sheet of paper. "Aurelia Moss signed just below it. And, it's
witnessed."

She looked at the sheet that he was holding in front of her. He
was right. At the bottom of the copy was her father's and Aurelia's
signatures, and that of an attorney who had witnessed it all.

"This verifies that Therell Watson is your brother. And depending on how that Will reads, he's probably entitled to *half* of the farm
if not more. *See here....*"

She continued to examine this fax copy of a weathered certifi-
cate that was both signed and notarized, and stating exactly what the
man had claimed. It was all right there in faded but legible ink.
Watson had signed it, stating that this young man was his son. And a
woman's signature stated that she was his mother.

"That's your copy to keep. It was prepared by a personal friend
of mine. She says she remembers your father, the boy and his mother
coming to her to have it done. How she can remember all that, with
her old self, I don't know," he laughed. "But, she is living proof that
this is real."

"But, how can you be so certain that those signatures are authentic? That it was actually my father who showed up and signed this? And looking at this fax, it appears to be an old document, but that could have been contrived as well," the journalist in her remarked.

"And here, it shows that it was signed in *1969*. Where has it been all this time? And why didn't someone bring it, or Therell, to my attention before now? *Before* my father's death? "

The man frowned as she shook her head, folded the paper and put it inside her purse.

"I don't believe that *Watson* would keep such a secret. His stand on family issues was no secret in this town. How could he have done that while abandoning that same responsibility? *Why would he?*"

She thought about it further, and shook her head, again.

"You have to be realistic here, Miss Greer. That was a long time ago. Anything could have been going on at the time…"

"Still, my father suffered through a lot of situations back then; racism, threats and even hostility from being in an interracial marriage and raising another man's children. And now I'm to think that he refused to raise his own *son?* I don't believe that. "

Billard shifted roughly in his seat. She ignored his agitation.

"I'm sorry, Mr. Billard, but this is a total contradiction of everything he ever believed in, and taught his family. So, forgive me if I'm a little bit skeptical. I just don't trust it."

The man reached into his pocket, searching for something; a lighter for his cigar.

"I understand your concerns, but remember, that was your *father's* land, first. *He* worked that place and kept it up. He cared about that land and I agree that he wouldn't have signed such a document if there wasn't some truth to it," he added in a surly voice.

"Well, I don't know how well you knew him, Mr. Billard. But I knew him well. And *this* was simply not his style."

"Well, apparently he had good reason. And if you didn't know Therell even existed, then there was obviously some lack of communication between you, somewhere. People used to keep these secrets all the time, honey. Your father would be no different than a lot of *colored…*"

"*Excuse me!*"

She stiffened in her anger against his words. If she wasn't mistaken, he was about to make an insinuation that she wasn't trying to hear.

"All men, and that includes *African American men,* do not abandon their families, *Mr. Billard.* My father's second wife had a white husband who abandoned her. So, apparently my father took responsibility for a lot of things having nothing to do with his *color.*"

"I didn't mean it that way. What I'm saying is…"

"I've heard enough of what you have to say." She said to the red-faced man. She stood up, clutching her purse. Ready to storm out of his office.

Billard stood as well, shaking his head. Raising his hand to stop her.

"*Miss Greer*, this is a *legitimate* document, do you hear?" He was angry and flustered, and beet red by now. "And that's proof enough to me. This document and the testimonies of your family members will be enough to call for a re-evaluation of that Will. Get used to the idea. You don't own it all. You never did. So, you might as well plan on sharing it. That's only fair."

He threw his hands up as though fully exasperated with her. Well, he didn't know the meaning of the word *fair*, yet, she thought.

"I'll decide what I think is fair, Mr. Billard," she responded, coolly.

If he wanted a fight, she would sure give him one! Nobody was taking away what she had given up her entire life for. Not Therell. And definitely not *Bob Billard!*

"This still has to be heard in a court of law." She added, gathering her coat and scarf and walking to the door.

"Right, but if you knew the law…"

"Maybe I don't, entirely. But I'll see Therell in court before I let him or anyone else take my land away."

She turned to leave.

"Just talk to the family." His voice was calmer, now. "That's only fair. Before you go ruffling everybody's feathers around here."

There he goes again, talking about fair, she thought. She stopped at the doorway to face him, defiant and angry.

"I won't need your help any further. You can bill me for what I owe you. You have my address. *Good day, Mr. Billard.*"

She stormed out of the office and past Marva's surprised eyes, feeling 'angrier than a wet hen', as her mother would have termed it. And when was she coming home, anyway?

The nerve of that big bully telling me who worked for what, and who deserves it!

She fumed as she started her car. Enraged, she stomped the accelerator, unintentionally spinning her tires as she left the graveled drive. She was anxious to get home, and to finally talk to one person who, if anyone, would know the truth.

Laretta answered her phone this time.

"I've been calling you for days," LaRetha scolded.

"My business trip was great! But, I can tell by your voice that something's wrong. What is it?" Laretta sounded concerned.

"Well, I hate to make this your welcome home. I know you needed that rest."

"Oh, don't worry about it. I'm back and ready for about anything."

"Well..." LaRetha began to tell her mother what had happened since she'd been gone.

"*Therell Watson?* He came to see you?"

"Yes. Do you know him?"

"Yes, I know him, the *rascal*. I knew his mother, too. But as far as I know, *Watson* never confirmed he was that boy's father. That family of his kept that going. I'm interested in seeing this document, though. If he signed it, it must be true. I just don't believe it."

"Why has no one ever mentioned the words *Therell Watson* to me? I can't believe I might have had a brother in this town, all this time, and no one said anything. Not even you."

"If I'd ever believed it, I would have. I always suspected it was something they did just to get money out of *Watson*. And it worked."

"*Really?*" LaRetha couldn't say more.

"Your father and Aurelia dated before we were engaged. So, when she said he was her baby's father, like everybody else in his family, he sent money to help take care of him. If you ask me, I think they used the boy as some sort of *cash cow*. He was well cared for, and so were they."

"My father must have been very generous."

"Well, she got pregnant and decided that out of all her boyfriends, he was the baby's father. And this without a blood test. He was the best prospect she had. It almost caused me not to marry your father. But, he said he would do what was right, anyway. Therell lived with your grandparents, and when they died, your uncle and Nell took him in. *Watson* had no part in those decisions. That much I do know."

"Even though Therell was supposedly his child to raise, *they* decided to do it?"

"Not as a favor to him. But people didn't ask many questions, back then. Not like now. We didn't have homeless folks in *Lovely*. People helped one another. They would take in other people's children when the family couldn't raise them, even if they weren't related. That's just how it was. But, your uncle and Nell don't deserve any awards for it. People carried your uncle a lot of times."

"The boy was raised right across town," Laretta continued. "But they never brought him around. And they never cared about any relationship, then. They just took the money and *ran*. We didn't see or hear from any of them, because that check was always in the mail. But now, *Watson's* gone and they see something else they want. Now, that's not right."

"Well, I think I can understand how he feels," LaRetha mused. "Never being acknowledged by a man he thinks fathered him and left him behind to raise a family that wasn't even his own? If it were me, even if I didn't really *want* the land, I think I might come after it, too."

"So, go on and give it to him, then," her mother replied, with finality.

Hardly!" She exclaimed. "Regardless of that fact, I've put a lot of time and money into this property. And there's still no guarantee that these signatures are even legitimate. I won't be suckered in that easily. He'll have to prove it to me."

"*Thatagirl!*"

"Do you think *Uncle Verry* and Nell would talk to me about it? Let me know where they stand?"

"Well, that goes without saying. They'll say he was entitled. That would give it back to them and that's about the only way they'll get it. And they've always wanted it, *bad*. You have to be very careful about this, LaRetha. About approaching them. This could get *tricky*."

"I know."

"I had my issues with these folks, especially with his brother. But that doesn't mean that you have to. There is no question that you're Vernell Watson's child, and that entitles you to everything that you've inherited. I married him, Aurelia didn't. But then I know your giving heart..."

"Therell's paternity still needs to be proven. I just don't want to alienate them..."

"But, you will. Still, do what you have to do. You have a lot to lose, right now. You would want them on your side, just don't expect it. He's their *son*. And when it comes to doing dirt, these folks do stick together."

"I can imagine."

"And whatever you do," she continued, "remember that there's a lot more to *Lovely* than meets the eye," her mother said. "Lots of secrets. Lots of little indignities that people won't ever talk about. It's not always the simple life folks think it is."

"I know. I'll give them the benefit of the doubt before I decide what to do. And this time, I'm getting a *real* attorney."

"Good thinking."

As angry as she was with Billard, he was right about one thing. There was no way to approach this without talking with the family. Her uncle and aunt lived close to town, and according to the phone book, still owned a television sales and repair shop, there. Handling this from a distance wouldn't be to her advantage. She needed to meet with them.

LaRetha drove a few miles into town. Slowly circling the block, she considered that they might not want to see her. *Well,* she thought, *they would just have to tell her that!*

Parking was easy. She walked up the sidewalk, searching for the store, and finally saw a sign that read *Watson's Television Sales & Repair- Just Bring It, We Fix It!*

A bell rang as she entered and sidestepped a tall stack of boxes teetering dangerously near the door. The store was large and bright, and very clean, but filled with televisions and electronic equipment. Aside from a woman talking on the phone, it was unoccupied. The woman smiled at her.

"I'll just be a moment, dear. Look around," she barely stopped chatting to say.

She hadn't come to look around, but she did, as the woman muttered *uh huh's,* and *yeah girls,* into the phone. Even with her back turned, LaRetha could feel her scrutiny, until she hang up.

"Don't tell me. *LaRetha Greer?* You've finally come out of those woods to meet your folks?" Smiling, the woman came around the counter, and reached out to share a hug with LaRetha.

"*Aunt Arnelle?* Yes, I have. I know this visit is long overdue."

Nodding, the woman laughed haughtily, standing back to give her a once over.

"But call me *Nell.* Everyone does. Your uncle's going to be so surprised to see you, here. We kept saying we would come out to visit, but we didn't want to impose. Grief can be a funny thing, you know? I figured you'd come around on your own once you were ready. And here you are."

Releasing her, Nell continued to smile, endearingly.

"So, how have you been? Getting used to this crazy weather? We've been concerned about you being out there at that big old place, by yourself. Old man Foreman told us you were making out just fine, out there. He's a mess, isn't he?"

"He's very kind. Everything at the farm has been fine. Luckily, I was prepared for the worst with this last storm. It didn't last nearly as long as I'd expected."

"You sound disappointed. Honey, the rest of us worried that it *would* last."

They shared a laugh.

"I guess you're here to see *Verry?* He should be back momentarily. He went to deliver a set down the street. He was going to walk it over with his hand truck."

She nodded.

"So, how's your mother? I haven't seen her since she left here. You were a baby, then."

"She's doing very well. She's still in Atlanta."

"*Did she ever remarry?*" Her voice lightened, as if she was asking something secretive. Something that she had wondered about for a long time. Clearly, ambition carried less weight with Aunt Nell than tying the knot. *Well she certainly won't approve of me,* LaRetha thought, still smiling.

"Never did. I'm not sure she ever will. But, you never know about those things."

"Shame, it didn't work out with her and your father. We had our differences, me and her. But at least she was one of *us.* Know what I mean?"

LaRetha was about to say that she didn't, but hadn't time to respond because her uncle whisked in at that very moment. He stood staring at her and smiling as though he'd been told she was there and was excited to see her. She blushed under his smiling gaze.

"*LaRetha?* My gracious, girl. I wondered when I'd get to see you, again. I haven't since you were a little girl. How are you?"

She gasped as he hugged her tightly.

"I've been meaning to come out there to the farm and check on you, but everything's so busy. With folks needing this and that, I haven't had time to follow up. They forget I'm just the *TV* man. Not the plumber, roofer, heating and air man, you see," he said, laughing.

The stout man moved and spoke quickly, walking behind the counter and hardly taking his eyes off her.

"You certainly do look like *Watson.* Not a lot of Laretta in you, except for the eyes and the shape of your face. That's *her.* Everything else, height and all, is *Watson.* So, I hear you married and had a son?"

"I'm divorced, but I do have a son. Germaine is *nineteen,* and he lives in Atlanta." Try as she might, she couldn't elaborate on the subject.

The door opened and the usual bell sounded.

"*Hey, Levi!* Don't tell me it's busted, again!"

LaRetha looked up to see a young man standing behind her, staring from her to her uncle, then back at her, again. She gave him an inquiring look and looked at her uncle before realizing that he had come in to get a close look at her. She smiled. *Some things remained the same, wherever you lived.*

"Levi, that's my niece, LaRetha. But, don't get excited. I think her son's about your age."

Everyone laughed. As Levi began talking to Nell, her uncle came around the counter, gently guiding her by the arm to the door, while looking over at the two, deep in discussion.

"*Uncle Verilous...*"

"Call me *Verry.* Everybody else in the family does," he smiled. Standing close to him now, she could smell a mixture of faint cigar smoke in the fresh air.

"Okay, *Uncle Verry.* I really need to talk to you. Do you think you could make time to meet with me, soon?"

"Well, I could come out to your place," he said. "Let's see. Tonight is choir rehearsal night. But I don't think they'll miss this old frog too much. We've been singing the same songs for the longest, anyway. Who needs more practice?"

"*You do*," the woman interrupted, having overheard every word. He laughed boisterously.

"Oh, LaRetha, you did meet my wife, *Nell?*"

"Of course she did," her aunt said. "What do you think we were doing while you were taking your time getting back here?"

He nudged her elbow and they stepped outside the doorway, now.

"What time should I be there?" He stooped to pick up a torn receipt from the otherwise meticulous sidewalk and tossed it into a nearby trash barrel.

"When do you close, here?"

"About *five*. So, how about, say, *six-thirty?* It'll give me time to close my register and lock up, take Nell home, clean up a bit, and just enough time to get to your place. Sound good?"

"Sounds perfect," she smiled. "Aunt Nell is invited, of course."

"*Nah*," he whispered, smiling gleefully in his deviousness. "One of us needs to be at church, tonight. She can tell me what I missed. No need in both of us being lost, on Sunday."

"Okay, well, maybe next time. See you at the house, *Uncle Verry.*"

"That you will. Be careful on those slick roads. They can fool you."

"I will. Thanks. I'll see you at dinner, tonight." She gave a wave, goodbye, before crossing the street to get to her car.

Putting her business concerns aside for a minute, she realized she had been missing out on more important things.

Now why didn't I do that a long time ago? This had been a good first meeting. Hopefully, tonight would be productive, as well.

Recalling that many people her uncle's age were either very weight conscious or required to eat right for health reasons, to be on the safe side, LaRetha prepared something light and simple. They would have garden salads with a vinaigrette dressing, two succulently baked Cornish hens, greens and a creamed corn casserole, with wheat rolls. There was sweet and unsweetened tea, and diet soda to drink. The creamy chocolate and vanilla crème cake would be optional, she thought. *But, who was she kidding?*

Her bell rang at exactly *6:30pm*. She answered, accepting another brief hug before ushering her uncle inside and taking his coat.

"Good, you got here safely."

"Oh girl, I've plowed most of the roads around here. Can't *nothin'* about this land fool me," he said, releasing a new coat and a rather worn looking hat into her possession.

"Have a seat. Make yourself at home. "

"Mind if I look around? Haven't been out here for many years, now."

"Sure. You never visited?" She asked as he peeped around the corner.

"Once upon a time," he said, from the hallway. He was back in a few minutes. "It's too bad, but me and your father had a falling out and just never resolved it. I can hardly remember why we even argued, to tell you the truth. But, your daddy was as stubborn as I was relentless. We just couldn't work it out, between us."

He re-emerged and joined her in the kitchen, smiling his broad smile.

"I see you're really fixing up the place. Amazing what a little color and carpeting can do."

"Well, it wasn't quite that simple, but it does make a difference."

"I'm sure it wasn't," he said, contemplating. "But, maintaining property this large can get to be very expensive."

She nodded.

"Well, the table's set. You hungry?"

"All the time. Let's eat," he said.

As he said grace, she thought of her father. How she wished he was there. *Uncle Verry* interrupted her thoughts.

"Your father did more with this place than I ever could. Or ever wanted to. I just wanted to get out. Be my own man, you understand," he said rather than asked.

"Sugar or sugarless?" She asked as she poured their tea. He nodded toward the sugarless pitcher while preparing his plate.

"How long have you had the store?" She asked.

Her father had mentioned years before that *Verry* had finally realized he was nobody's farmer. He'd chosen electronics, instead.

"About twenty some years, now. I was always tinkering with old TV sets and things. The first owner retired and Nell suggested that we buy it. I took a little electronics class over at the school and found out I had a talent for it. Bought it, and it's about the best thing I ever did, I suppose."

He ate a forkful. Closed his eyes as if savoring the taste. Opening them again, he smiled.

"This is spectacular, *baby girl*. I didn't know they cooked like this in Atlanta. You really put your foot in this," he teased.

She smiled, thinking that was exactly what Germaine might have said. Tasting her own food, she thought he was absolutely right.

"So, tell me about yourself, Miss LaRetha. What have you been doing in the last thirty years I haven't seen you?"

She talked about growing up in Atlanta, marrying and about Germaine. Her former job and her writing career. He was especially interested to know that she was a journalist.

"Well, great. It's good to know you take your business seriously, like that. I can't say I have the smarts for it." He ate a forkful of greens. "*Pork?*" He asked.

"Smoked turkey wings. Tastes almost the same."

"Yes, that's what Nell uses. She sure does."

She smiled. It was good that he was so proud of his wife.

"I tell you what. If you ever decide you need to work here locally, I can always put in a word for you at the paper. I've been knowing old John over there all my life. He'll be sure to help you out. Course, it might not pay as much as you get in Atlanta."

"That would be nice," she said. "A little extra money never hurts."

"That's exactly right." He smiled as he poured a second glass of unsweetened iced tea.

"You can really cook. My girls could learn something from you. They're grown women with children and can't hardly boil water," he laughed.

"Well, my son's a pretty good cook, too. I think it's important that he can take care of himself. Besides, I'm sure your daughters aren't as bad as all that," she laughed.

"Oh yes, they are," he said, eating another bite and grinning, causing her to laugh out loud.

He talked as she cleared the table and they went back into the living room.

"That was a *good* dinner. I enjoyed every bite. I'm surprised some man hasn't tried to snag you, already." He patted his full stomach.

"I don't get out much, to tell you the truth. I've been so involved with my writing and fixing this place up. Just working through some things…"

"The best way to get over something is to get involved in something else. Tell you what, come to the church this Sunday and I'll make sure you meet everybody there. It'll save you from having to meet them on your own."

"Okay. Thanks, Uncle Verilous. I get to my mother's church, every now and then. But, I'll definitely come by."

"*Verry,* remember. Everybody calls me *Verry.*"

"*Uncle Verry.* I appreciate the invitation. I'll do that real soon."

"*Excellent.* Now, you said you had something to talk about. Have we covered it, yet?"

"No. That's another thing. I think you can probably help me, but just tell me if you can't."

"Of course. What is it?" He asked.

"I wanted to ask you about a visitor I had. The man you raised? *Therell Watson?*"

He frowned.

"Oh, yeah? When did you talk to him?" He asked, seemingly surprised at hearing the man's name.

"Just last week. He told me all about you and Aunt Nell. About how you raised him."

"Of course," he said. "My folks raised him after his mother ran off and left him. So, what'd he say? Is he still here in town?"

"I don't think so. But, I'm just concerned about something he said. He told me he was *Watson's* son. Is that true?"

There, she thought. She'd said it. Her uncle's face was unreadable. Then he shrugged.

"It's odd that he would come all the way out here and not stop by."

Yeah. Odd, she thought. *Almost unlikely.* But why was he changing the subject?

"I'm just surprised he even cares about this old land. But that doesn't mean he's not entitled to some of it."

One hundred plus acres and he doesn't care about it?

"It's just strange that no one has ever mentioned him to me in all these years," she said. "Especially if *Watson* was providing for him."

"It happens. Your father got Aurelia pregnant and didn't want to marry her. And that's it."

"So, why did you and Aunt Nell take him? Why didn't he go with his mother's family?"

"She couldn't care for him very well. So, after she moved away and my folks passed on, Nell and I took him in."

"I can't believe my father would keep this from me. Therell's not much older than I am…"

"Your father always claimed him," he interjected. "He never once denied the boy. He and Aurelia made an agreement and *that was that.* Nell and I were raising him before our own children were ever born. That's how committed we were to doing the right thing by our family."

Still uncertain, she realized she might be asking questions that he'd prefer she didn't.

"But, why would he never even mention Therell? And why would he leave so much to question with that Will?"

Her uncle didn't respond.

"And *Cecelia!* Wouldn't she have mentioned it? Surely she knew something about all this."

"They've got some kind of agreement between them, that *Moss* woman and your father. So, what Therell said is true. Your father had *four* children that he legally cared for. You and Cecelia's *two*. And he would be the fourth. The oldest living child."

That phrase rang terribly familiar to her.

"What about blood tests?" She persisted. "Were any ever taken?"

"Well, nothing can be proven about those, considering the doctor took all the records and burned them in the same fire that killed him. He set that fire himself, the *crazy loon.*"

"That's terrible. What led him to do that?"

"Personal and financial problems is all we could guess." Her uncle shrugged. "Happened a long time ago."

She shook her head. The more explanations she got, the less sense any of this made. But, she'd heard enough. There was more to this story than was being said. But, her uncle's position was clear, and discussing it further might be a huge mistake. But he wasn't done.

"Your father left this place to his oldest child, which makes this a hard situation, to say the least. But, then again, it's just like him to leave a mess for everybody else to work out, is all I can say."

"Really?" She said, not correcting him and trying not to sound as offended as she was. Brother or not, the man was out of line. The *Watson* she'd known wasn't as irresponsible as all that.

Her uncle stood and stretched a little.

"I hope I answered your questions," he said, and she nodded. "And thank you, for the meal and the conversation," he added. "We'll need to do this at the house, sometime."

"Thank you for coming," she said, momentarily putting other thoughts out of her mind. He had on his coat and was at the door, then turned to her.

"If you ask me, you'll find it easier to try and work it out with him. You might even be able to sell him your share, if you wanted to."

"I wasn't planning on selling. I came to stay, *Uncle Verry.*"

"Oh? Well, in that case, just try for a reasonable division before he tries to take it all. And he could very likely do it. All I can tell you is the truth as I see it, LaRetha. I don't know how you do things in *Atlanta,* but family folks resolve things more easily out here. Do you have an attorney?"

"Well, at Therell's suggestion, I've spoken to someone," she said, figuring he might know as much, already. "I'm just considering my options." She stopped at saying an attorney might not be necessary.

"Who is it? Maybe I can talk to him."

She considered this, before deciding to withhold that information, for now. Billard was out of the picture, anyway. Who she'd spoken with since then was her business, she figured. *Never let your left hand know...*

"Well, I haven't exactly retained anyone. I mean, proving the authenticity of a document can't be that difficult," she said. "Hopefully, we'll resolve this, soon."

He frowned and she knew she'd started something with this conversation. They had gotten off to such a good start. But, this could divide them before they had a chance to even get to know one another.

Then, she also remembered how much her mother distrusted these people. She had probably said too much, already.

"That would be best," he finally said.

"There's something else that I wanted to ask you about," she quickly said. "I understand there have been a few fires set in town, just recently. Do you know what caused them?" She asked. That brought a glimpse of suspicion into his eyes.

"No, but that's got nothing to do with any of us. It's just been small stuff; a couple of barns and an old shop, out at the Richards place. I'm thinking the man probably just got desperate for money and set it, himself," he laughed, shaking his head. "Times are particularly hard on all of us, right now."

"That happens a lot around here? Then, I wonder why it's making national news?"

"Is it? Well, a few people got hurt. One was a federal agent, I hear. I don't know the details, but it'll all come out sooner or later. Just be watchful out here. I don't think you have anything to worry about, but just keep your eyes peeled. And definitely call if you need something."

He stopped to write his home, shop and cell phone numbers on a piece of paper.

Handing it to her, he took her hand and patted it.

"Thank you, for the visit," she said, sincerely. "I appreciate your coming over."

He studied her face for a moment. "You're one of us, LaRetha. We're all family, here. Don't you ever question it." His face became oddly sad as he turned away.

"Of course," she responded, feeling somewhat puzzled.

She watched him drive away in his company van and thought about her father, again. She didn't close the door until he was long out of sight.

Kellen's called several times a day, over the next four days. And each message sounded more frustrated than the last.

Why hadn't he heard from her? She could at least let him know how she was doing.

She didn't respond – didn't know how to say goodbye, again. So what, if she was being inconsiderate? He was moving in his own direction, without her, now.

She hadn't heard from Therell since his first visit or from her uncle since their dinner, together. But other things concerned her today. When researching *Lovely's* history, she'd read that the mission in town had only a small staff and few volunteers. With the Thanksgiving holidays coming up, they could use extra volunteers.

It was a small, overcrowded building, and it took a while to find the right office to sign up. She asked for *Miss Canter*, the mission director, and was told she'd just missed her but that she could wait for her in the sitting area or have a look around. She decided to walk around instead. Another employee directed her to the kitchen where the others were.

Once there, a girl named Monica asked if she would fill in for another volunteer who was being detained. She was happy to, she said. She rolled up her sleeves and dove in.

The other volunteers were friendly and high spirited as they went about checking their inventory, organizing boxes of recently donated canned goods and storing them in the limited space they had. Only one van was unloaded, they said, and it was early still - well before noon. LaRetha was there for over an hour before Miss Canter arrived, announcing there was another van and even more boxes to unload.

Judging by her name, LaRetha had expected someone older. But Vera Canter was about her age. She also looked more like an athletic advertisement than a center director with thick, braided hair, and dressed comfortably in a gray and yellow jogging suit and sneakers. Everyone greeted her happily.

"*Ahhh,* new people. Great! Welcome, all of you. I'm Vera Canter, Mission Director. We really appreciate all the help. Could someone help grab boxes out of the van, for me?" She asked.

Grabbing her coat, LaRetha and a few others followed the woman outside to a service van, where they carried boxes inside. Soon, there were so many people helping that they were getting into each other's way, until deciding to form a line from the van to the building and to hand-off each box.

Before long, all the boxes were emptied and neatly stacked for an arranged pick-up. Turkeys and loaves of bread were stored in the freezer and pantry. Cans of vegetables neatly lined the many shelves. Centerpieces were dusted and stored for later use. Tablecloths were washed and refolded. Plastic utensils and plates were all accounted for and put away, as well.

"Some of this work may seem premature," Vera announced to her line. "But we had a big response to our request for donations this year. With a small staff and growing demands it's been hard to keep up, but we have. Every year we get more and more people in here, but we've never had to turn anyone away. And with the weather being so unpredictable," she said, running her fingers through her stylish braids, "we should do as much as we can, while we can."

Several people agreed with her as they continued to work.

"How many do you think you'll accommodate this year?" LaRetha asked.

"A couple thousand, easily. And miraculously, our dear head chef, Mr. Hurt over here will make it happen." She briefly hugged a shy looking but smiling man standing close to her and he waved to them, duly pleased at being recognized.

"He's our miracle worker, always managing to stretch the food and feed everybody without anyone going away hungry, in spite of fewer donations over the past two years."

The group applauded him and turned back to working on decorations, talking animatedly while holiday music played softly over an intercom.

When everyone began to leave, Vera came over. Removing one rubber glove, she extended a hand to her.

"I feel we've met before. I'm *Vera Canter*, the director here for eight years, now. That's mostly because no one else wants the job, but it is a job, so what can I say?" She smiled warmly.

"I'm LaRetha Greer. I recently moved back to *Lovely*."

"That's right. I knew you were a Watson, just not which one. I know your folks. I go to church with the Watsons."

"Oh, really?"

"Yes, *Verilous* and Nell, and them. So, you say you've moved back here? Usually I know these things, but I've been so busy…"

"Oh yes. I'm *Vernell's* daughter. I inherited the farm when my father died. I've decided to stay for awhile."

The woman nodded, studying her closely.

"Yes, I do remember you. And thanks for everything. We appreciate our volunteers. Please come back, anytime."

"Well," LaRetha said, "if we're done, I have some errands to run."

"Sure. And since you're new here, if you're not busy on Saturday, we'll begin decorating for Thanksgiving out at the church. Are you familiar with *Joyful Missionary Baptist?*"

"Of course. That was my mother's church back in the day. When she married, she started attending Community Baptist with my father. But I remember both churches. My uncle invited me to come to *Joyful Baptist Church*, this week. What time are you decorating on Saturday?"

"Between *nine and four*, is fine. We provide lunch at *12:30*. Dress casually. We also have a play on Sunday night. You might enjoy it."

LaRetha remembered that these people spent a lot of time at their jobs and at church. And truthfully, she missed not having been in a while.

"I'll be there. And I'll see you, then."

On the way home, she decided to stop at the auto shop and see about the repairs on the truck. She hadn't heard a word since the repairman had towed it. Surely he knew something by now. She saw that it was on a raised ramp, so was hopeful that he'd found the problem.

She went inside the small unkempt office. It was empty and no one seemed to notice her standing there, so she walked past the 'No Customers Allowed Past This Point' sign, and approached the man she recalled as *Hogan,* who looked as if he'd hardly bathed or changed clothes since she'd last seen him.

She tapped him on the shoulder and he turned around. Seeing her, he grinned, flashing a perfect set of teeth. She figured he and Mr. Bailey must have the same dentist.

"Miss Watson? Yes, I was gonna call you, today. You needed a bit of work on that transmission, and a new set of brakes, too."

Needed?

"So you have my estimate for the work?" She asked.

"Oh no, ma'am. The work is done," he said, beaming happily. "You can take the truck, today."

"But we agreed that you wouldn't do anything unless you spoke to me, first. Isn't that what we agreed on?" She asked, struggling to speak calmly.

In spite of the cheery holiday music playing outside over street intercoms, she wasn't feeling so festive, right now. She'd expected that one big perk to country living was that she could *stop* getting hustled.

"Well, I guess we did, didn't we?" He smiled sheepishly, his big green eyes amazingly clear behind an oil-smeared face.

"So, what is this, then?" She demanded, waving toward the truck, attracting the attention of the other mechanics, who stopped working to listen.

Well, if they had never witnessed a scene before, they were about to, now.

"*Ma'am,* I remember, now. We were going to tell you, but with the holidays coming up, we went ahead and did it for you. If you like, you can pay half now and the rest, later. Or, you can pay it all. However you want to do that is alright with me. It was our mistake, after all."

Nothing doing, she thought. *An agreement was an agreement.*

"Look, mister. I'm not trying to cause problems for you..." The other mechanics seemed relieved and went back to their work. "...but an agreement is an agreement, and you distinctly agreed to talk to me before getting me into debt with you. Now, you want me to pay for work I didn't authorize. Is that reasonable, to you?"

"Well, it needed fixing, and it's not a big bill, I don't suppose. Let's see..."

He wiped his hands and ruffled through a large stack of invoices on a nearby desk. It appeared that he was scamming quite a few folks, she thought. *Well, she wasn't biting.*

"*Here.* We had to break down the transmission to find the problem, and ended up rebuilding it. And that comes to *four hundred fifty-five dollars,* including the estimate."

"*Rebuilt it?* But, I didn't ask you to do all that and I don't intend to pay you one dime on this bill. I've paid you for towing, and I'm paying for the estimate. And that's all! So, it looks like you just worked yourself out of four hundred-fifty five dollars. *Let my truck down, now.*"

She began to write a check and the man's face darkened, causing his green eyes to stand out on his countenance even more.

"Ma'am, our policy is to never release an automobile until we are paid in full. I'm willing to accept half, today and the rest, later."

"I *am* paying in full. For what I authorized. *Towing and an estimate.* I never consented to anything else. That arrangement was never made, to my knowledge."

She stood watching him defiantly, trying to hold her temper, while he stared at her as though she was out of her mind.

"*Business is business,* ma'am. And we have to be paid before we can release the truck."

Looking down now, he scrubbed his feet across the concrete floor of the shop, looking harmless but being anything but, she thought.

"Look, I might not be from around here… I intend to get my truck back, today. You won't get away with this," she said with frustration.

Walking out of earshot, she dialed her cell phone. She hated asking favors, but right now she had very little choice. And her uncle was the only person she knew to call.

He answered and she explained the situation. He would come right over, he said. And he did.

"*Old Sal,*" he said, greeting the younger man, who laughed and shook his hand. "Why is my niece calling me out here, at this time of day? You know I've got a business to run."

Both men laughed and kidded for a few minutes, and she waited patiently for her uncle to get to the point. He finally did.

"Now look, Sal. You know you can't be fixing nobody's cars without permission, and holding them like this. It's just not legal. Now, you said you would call her, first. She paid you for the tow. All she really owes you for is the estimate."

The man smiled sheepishly, slowly shaking his head in disagreement.

"Now, if you went ahead and repaired the truck, and it's running alright, then she might go ahead and pay you. This is a more than reasonable charge for all that work. But, you know you can't refuse to give her the truck."

The man didn't budge.

"Tell you what. Just charge her the estimate and bill her for the rest."

"She can pay the estimate. But, to get that truck, she's gotta pay the estimate and at least half for parts and labor," Hogan responded. "We had to break down that whole transmission to find the problem. It made no sense not to fix it. Who's *payin'* for that?"

"But, I never got an estimate," she retorted. "And I never approved the work. You agreed to call me, first. Now, I'll go ahead and pay for the estimate, but not the entire bill. It's the principal of the thing, *Mr. Sal.*"

The man frowned. Obviously Sal Hogan wasn't his name.

"If you had called me as agreed, we wouldn't be having this conversation. But, you didn't. So, the loss is yours, not mine!"

"Come on, now Sal, What's the cost of the estimate?" Her uncle asked.

"*One twenty-five,*" he said, with no enthusiasm.

"I'll pay that. That's all I agreed to pay." She took out her checkbook and began to write.

"You can bill her," he said to the man. "*Right,* LaRetha?" Her uncle asked. But Hogan shook his head. And she wasn't satisfied.

"*No.* We settle up right now. *Here,*" she said, handing Hogan the check. He looked at it, and frowned.

"Ma'am, we ain't trying to cheat you or *nuthin'.* But that's just not satisfactory."

Her uncle looked at the check, and gave her a helpless look before taking her aside.

"Now LaRetha, I know these fellows. They don't do everything by the book, but they're more than fair. That work would've cost four times as much at another shop. Just pay something now, if you can. Or tell him when you will."

She frowned.

"Don't look so worried. He'll guarantee the work. But it's important to keep good business relationships in a town like this. Never know when you might need 'em, especially on these roads. So how about paying what you can and giving him the rest when you have it?"

"Oh, I have it, and I've just about *had* it."

She took the check from her uncle and tore it up, rewriting one check for *two hundred dollars.* Her uncle took it and looked at it.

"*Now, LaRetha.*"

"Contrary to popular belief, I am *not* made of money. That's almost half. He took the risk and now he'll have to wait on the rest. That's more than fair, where I'm concerned."

Taking a look at the check, the man's expression fell. Her uncle could do what he wanted to keep *good relationships*. He wasn't her!

"Let her down, *Robey*," Hogan told one of his workers. They all watched silently as the truck was lowered, looking as if someone was taking away their last meal ticket. Hogan quickly wrote her a receipt and handed it to her, not meeting her gaze.

"We'll bill you for the rest, Mrs. Greer."

"I'm sure. Have a good day."

Her uncle walked her to the truck where she got in and started the engine. It purred like a kitten and she couldn't hide her delight. Her uncle shook his head with amusement.

"You'll have to learn these people around here, LaRetha. They're just having hard times, you know? We all have them." He looked as if she had let him down, somehow.

"I do know hard times! And I appreciate the work. And the rate he charged. But I also value good business ethics. I think I was more than generous, considering the circumstances."

"You have to understand the hard work involved."

"I know a little about mechanics, too. But, thank you for coming and helping me to resolve this. He wasn't giving up the truck at all, until you came."

He uncle smiled, looking duly pacified.

"Well, don't forget about Sunday morning service. And dinner at the house, afterward."

"Sure. Sounds great."

"Tell you what. I drove in with Nell, today. So, if you park the truck on the street and leave the keys under the mat, I can drive it out to you when I close, and you can take me back home."

Judging from the way he was admiring the truck, she could tell that it meant something to him.

"Why don't you just take it home with you? I'll get it later. I hardly ever drive it, anyway," she said. *Well, I don't,* she thought. "That is, if you don't mind," she said.

"I sure can," he said, smiling broadly. "I'll park it right in my driveway. Just let me know when you want me to bring it back to you."

"Keep it awhile. Let me know if it's straightened out. With the weather breaking, I won't need it for a while, anyway."

She left the truck at the store and walked back to her car feeling oddly relieved. Her uncle seemed to want nothing more than for her to feel a part of this town and his family. Maybe her coming here was the opportunity he needed to finally make peace over the differences he'd had with her father. Being around him sure felt a lot like having *Watson* around.

Heading home, LaRetha was happy that Verilous had come to her aide. Satisfied that she'd made her point with the mechanic, she was also glad that she hadn't totally embarrassed her uncle.

5

It was the Saturday before Thanksgiving. She planned to help out at church, and treat herself to a nice dinner some place, afterward. The parking lot was full, so she parked and walked to the fellowship hall.

She easily found Vera, who was again wearing trendy athletic wear and sneakers. Busy organizing the people, as usual, she waved, and pointed her toward an adjoining room. There, she found a large group sitting about, waiting on instruction. She sat at a table of friendly looking people.

Shortly afterward, a man and woman who introduced themselves as Henry and Viola Scott divided them into groups for various assignments. She was appointed to hanging garland and ribbons, and to wrapping presents to be placed under the tree as a surprise for the Sunday School classes. She got involved, meeting a lot of people in the process. Many of them were curious about her, but their questions weren't annoying at all. For the first time in a long time, she was having fun.

Before everyone left, Vera announced that LaRetha was a returning member and that she was going to join them for Sunday Services. She told them she was looking forward to it and she was; seeing folks she hadn't seen in years and others she'd never met, meeting their families, reestablishing herself in this town. All of the things she had been avoiding but now looked forward to.

As safe and as comfortable as it was inside her little renovated cocoon, volunteering was helping her to come out of her shell, a bit, she guessed. Everybody needed change from time to time. This would be her first evening for change.

Dinner at a small family restaurant in town proved interesting. There she met the owners, a very friendly couple who encouraged her to come by anytime. As delicious as the food was, that offer would not be wasted.

The sun was setting when she got home and she was glad she'd thought to leave the lights on inside. After closing the garage door, she entered through the kitchen, carrying a take-out plate and a large paper bag full of extra ribbons and garland that she had promised to arrange. It was all to make her feel a part, she knew. She certainly didn't mind.

Placing everything on the kitchen table, she walked through the living room into the foyer to hang her coat and remove her boots and gloves. Once there, she turned and stopped.

Something was different and very wrong. But, looking around the room, she couldn't figure out what it was. Slowly and quietly, she backed into the foyer where she put her coat on, again. Then, she quietly checked her surroundings, once more. The television and stereo systems were all in tact. Her shelves were still neatly arranged. Her center table was unmoved. Yet, something was out of order.

Then she knew. That morning she had left the overhead light on in the hall and in the living room. The hall light was completely off, and the living room was almost dark. Someone had turned the dimmer switch.

Maybe the light's just blown, she thought. But, twisting the dimmer knob, the lights were up again.

Someone was in the house!

A sudden fear overtook her. She had always felt prepared for something like this, but now it was actually occurring, and she wasn't sure of what to do. Most likely, if someone was in here, they would know she was home, already. The very thought made her shudder.

Maybe she could make it back to the garage without incident, she thought. But first, she needed to get to that coffee table drawer. It often stuck, but if she moved quietly enough, she could get to the gun, inside.

But, what if she didn't make it? If the person was in the hallway, they might have fewer steps to get to her than it would take for her to get to the drawer. But, if they were outside, she might have a fighting chance. She had to take that chance.

In the short time that she'd stood there, the sun had gone down. And suddenly, every second counted. She took a deep breath, realizing that she was sweating and that she could even hear her heartbeat.

She slowly crept over to the table, kneeling carefully so she wouldn't make a sound. It was when she reached for the drawer that she heard the back door suddenly being kicked open.

LaRetha screamed as she jerked anxiously at the drawer, which thankfully, gave way the first time. She retrieved her father's gun. Removing the safety, she aimed at the kitchen doorway.

Slowly, she kneeled in the corner beside the sofa, as she watched a shadow approach, looming larger than life in the kitchen doorway. Desperately wanting to make a run for the front door, she stopped when she saw the full body of a man dressed in dark clothing. His face wasn't visible, but the dim kitchen light from behind him illuminated his outline. He wasn't so very large, but he appeared to be masked and wearing gloves. And he was just standing there, staring back at her.

Holding her weapon on him, she tried not to appear frightened as she quietly prayed she wouldn't have to shoot.

"What do you want?" She demanded, feeling faint with her hands shaking, uncontrollably. *"Stay away from me!"*

He said nothing, but moved toward her amazingly fast, as if trying to get to her before she could fire at him. But he had greatly underestimated her presence of mind. LaRetha aimed and fired the handgun. He kept coming, so she kept firing until it was empty and her intruder had fallen to the floor. There was a deafening silence, now.

LaRetha had somehow managed to make the *9-1-1* call, and now, police cars were everywhere, along with an ambulance and the coroner, who took the man's body away. Visibly shaken, she was driven into town to give a statement. She called her uncle from there. Once again, he was there without hesitation, and stayed the entire time that she was being questioned, before finally being allowed to drive her home.

Her intruder was easily identified as *Paul Straiter,* a homeless man, born in *Lovely,* who had wandered there from *Atlanta,* one officer said, with emphasis. *As if that would mean something to her,* she thought.

Fortunately, the man wasn't dead, but close to it, they said, his survival thus far being nothing short of a miracle. When questioned, she explained that she didn't know the man. Had never seen him before. Nor did she remember how many times she had shot him. She had only fired the gun to disable him, she told them.

What had prompted him to charge at her that way? They asked. She said she didn't know. The same questions were being asked, over and over.

How did she know that he was in the house? Why did she have a gun? How many times did she shoot? Did she know the man? Did she see a weapon? What did he say to her? Why was she living out there alone, anyway?

And suddenly, *she* felt like the intruder. Irritated and upset by now, she responded.

"I *told* you, he kicked my back door in, and he came into my house and rushed at me. I thought he was going to kill me, so I wasn't taking any chances."

"*Yes*, I have a gun," she said. "It belonged to my father. His wife Cecelia left it in the house and I kept it, *just in case*. And, obviously, that was the best thing I could've done."

To her relief, they finally said she was free to go, recommending that she remain in town pending their investigation. She left feeling greatly relieved.

"How're you holding up?" Her uncle asked on the ride home, his face showing concern.

"Fine, under the circumstances. I just can't believe this happened. I had just left the church, I stopped for dinner in town, and now *this!* Now, I'm under suspicion for attempted murder."

"You were defending yourself," he said with exasperation. "There probably won't be any charges filed against you. But maybe you should hire an attorney, anyway," he said, quietly.

"I agree. It never hurts to be prepared."

They rode quietly for a while.

"It's a good thing you kept your father's gun," he mused.

"Yes, it was," she responded with relief. *At least he wasn't blaming her for that.*

"I can only imagine where I'd be right now if I hadn't. I'm glad that Cecelia left it behind."

Her uncle nodded and they made the rest of the trip in silence. It was well after *eleven,* when she returned home from the station. The mess there indicated that her house had been searched.

Stealing away for a moment, she checked her nightstand drawer and was surprised to find that the other gun was still tucked away, underneath a stack of paperback books. Surprisingly, it hadn't been found.

With *Watson's* gun having been confiscated as evidence, she hadn't volunteered this second gun, thinking how, at the rate things were going; she might very well need it.

Uncle Verry continued to be a help to her by calling a carpenter friend to repair her back door. The man arrived within the hour, repairing the doorframe and replacing the splintered door and knob, making certain that it was secure before he left. She clutched the keys he gave her as she paid him, thanking him for coming out so late, and on such short notice.

Her uncle invited her back to his house for the night. She declined, saying she would be fine.

"*Call me, LaRetha,*" her uncle said. "I know you're determined to stay on out here, but as you can see, it's not necessarily the best thing. People wander in from the highway, looking for shelter, mostly. Your place isn't that far from there. And by it being so isolated, this could easily happen, again."

"But they said he was a *local.*"

"He was a vagrant. There's no telling how long he'd been watching the place. He's been arrested for robbery more than a few times."

Thanks for the warning, she thought.

"Here," he said, reaching inside of his coat and placing something in her hand. "This one's registered to me. Use it only if necessary. I couldn't in good conscious leave you alone out here, without one. Not after this."

"Thanks, *Uncle Verry.* I'll be sure to give it back as soon as I replace the other one," she said, thinking it was better that he didn't know she had another one, either.

Had she imagined that strange look he gave her? Or was that a look of concern? Was he expecting a breakdown of some kind? She was too angry - too much in shock, for that.

She shivered as she said goodbye, not really wanting to be left alone. But she couldn't inconvenience his family, and only wanted to sleep in her own bed, tonight. Still, she felt solace in knowing that her uncle wouldn't be very far away.

What do I do now? She asked herself, before remembering the bloodstains that were drying on her beige carpet. Finding a bucket, brush and plastic gloves in the laundry room, she scrubbed the floor with a diluted cleaning solution, changed the water and scrubbed again, until those stains were no longer visible. A deep cleaning should finish the job, she thought, wearily.

It was very late, now. Still, she phoned and left a message for her mother to please call her, as soon as possible. There was no need to try Kellen. That was officially over. Besides, he was probably in Ohio, already. Or preparing to go.

At that moment, she envied his girlfriend for all the affection and protection he was wasting on *whoever she was,* that rightfully belonged to her at a time like this. But their relationship was forever changed, now. And she'd been the one who'd wanted it.

Her double-stuffed down comforter didn't feel so comforting, tonight. A police car would patrol the area for a few days, and the thought of that extra gun helped, if only a little. And now, the house was silent, once again, as though nothing out of the ordinary had ever occurred.

Both the living room and bedroom television sets were playing, but did little to keep her company, or to still her trembling body. Trying the radio, instead, she still felt uneasy. Finally giving up on sleeping, she sat up to watch a DVD, hoping the comedy would somehow distract her from her foreboding thoughts. It proved to be more annoying than anything.

She was just too alert. Too aware of every little sound, like every tick of her wall clock in the living room and each time ice fell in the icemaker. She imagined the doorknob turning, and hearing it being kicked in, again. She decided that she would stay awake all night, if that's what it took. And with her gun in her lap, she dared anyone else to come.

Her uncle phoned early the next morning. Paul Straiter was still alive, but, barely. He also had an attorney in mind for her. *Billard, Hanes & Davis,* he said. She was about to refuse when he told her the particular attorney's name; *Douglas Davis* - Billard's law partner. The man she'd intended to speak with, before. But now, she doubted he would even consider her case, or that she should consider hiring him.

Still tired, and not wanting to make another hasty decision, she graciously accepted the information and thanked him for it. She doubted she would call. But considering how few lawyers there were in this town, she would keep her options open.

She prayed for direction. After trying a few firms and learning that they were all either backed up with cases or didn't handle this type, she responded to an irrational urge to call Davis' office. It made no sense to her, and it was risky, to say the least. Still, she felt compelled to try, again.

This is crazy! She thought. She had all but called Billard a racist, and stormed out of his office and parking lot like a wild woman. Now, she was going to call for help?

But, after a time, she decided that if they went for it, then so would she. Besides, what did she have to lose? She dialed Marva, again.

"Yes," the woman said, sounding genuinely friendly. "*Miss Greer,* it's good to hear from you. I heard about that shooting last night. How're you doing?"

"I'm okay, thanks for asking. Just happy to be alive. Right now I'm in a dilemma because no one that I've called locally can assist me. I haven't been charged with anything, but I think I'll need legal counsel, just in case."

"Yes, dear," the woman said, sympathetically. She took a deep breath before plunging.

"Well, I was referred by my uncle to your *Mr. Davis.* I remember your mentioning him, before. But under the circumstances, or rather, after what happened the last time I was there…"

"*Worry no more*, Mrs. Greer. Our attorneys have served most of the people in this county, under good circumstances and bad. Besides, Mr. Billard is out of town for a couple of weeks, advising a client. And it wouldn't hurt for you just to meet with Mr. Davis."

This is true, she thought, relieved, thankful for the great timing.

"So, when would you like to come in?"

She scheduled a time, and thanked Marva for her assistance. Sparing her uncle the sordid details, she gave him the day and time. She could meet him at his shop and they could drive over together, he said. She thanked him, breathing much easier when she hang up.

Laretta phoned her back at *9:30 am.*

"*LaRetha Greer!* What is this about a *shooting?*"

After first scolding her mother for taking so long to return her calls lately, she explained the entire ordeal, in detail.

"I can't believe this. How are you doing? Are you okay? What's going to happen, now? Are you going to trial? Do you have representation?"

Laretta's questions were coming faster than she could answer them.

"Hold on, and I'll tell you." She mentioned her upcoming meeting with Douglas Davis. *No,* she hadn't met him, yet. But, she said, her chances with him were as good as with anyone else in this town. Besides, everyone else she'd called was occupied.

"I need to come out there. I'm taking the first flight out."

"*No.* Don't leave your work, just yet. Let me find out what's going to happen, so we'll know the best time for you to come. I'll give you Douglas Davis' phone number and address. Keep in contact with him after tomorrow if you can't reach me."

Laretta wrote down the information.

"Now, what if I can't reach either of you?"

LaRetha wasn't quite ready to reveal that her uncle was helping her. But Laretta needed an answer, or she would be there before the sun went down, if she could.

"I'll have someone call you. Don't worry. It looks like the man is going to pull out, okay, so there might not be any charges. But, I'll make sure of that and keep you posted."

Laretta sighed.

"And how are you doing? It's hard for us women living alone," her mother sympathized. "You know, we always prepare for things like this, but we never expect, or at least we *hope* we never have to face it. I applaud you for your bravery, baby. I don't know *what* I might have done."

"I only did what I had to. I can't say I'm proud of it. I'm just going to try and stay busy so I won't think about it," she said, telling her mother about her volunteer work prior to the incident.

"But tell me, where did you get a *gun?*" Laretta had finally thought to ask. She told her about *Watson's* gun, but not her own. And not about the one her uncle had given her.

"Well, you know I never liked guns, but I suppose it's a good thing you had one. Your father did something right, teaching you to shoot."

"That was for hunting. I never thought I'd use one for this. I just wanted to scare the man. He *forced* me to shoot him. It was…frightening. I just hope he survives." She blew her nose and sniffled.

They were silent.

"Are you sure you don't want me to come? It sounds like you could really use some support while all this is going on."

"Please just stay put. If it gets bad, I'll call you first. You know that."

LaRetha had never liked being fussed over. If she fell, she would pick herself up and go on. If she was sick, she would administer her own medications, *thank you very much*. Her son's stubbornness had come naturally. Why then, did she have the hardest time of anyone, dealing with him? She asked herself.

The story was covered on local news. She couldn't avoid watching it. Paul Straiter was still in intensive care, and his chances of a full recovery were still undeterminable. She had refused interviews with outside media, as had her uncle and, so far, practically everyone in town. With the recent fires occurring, no one wanted the extra attention or further interruptions in their own daily routines. Certainly not for the prying eyes and noses of *outsiders*. For that, she was thankful.

Surprisingly, Mac Henry hadn't phoned, again. And right now, there were bigger worries than sending a story. According to *Uncle Verry* on the drive to the attorney's office, Douglas Davis was *the man*. Billard was semi-retired, he said. And their third partner, old man Hanes, hadn't hit a lick at a snake in years.

Davis normally handled civil cases, he said, but he'd said he'd look into this, for them. Her uncle's certainty was comforting. They needed the best, and Davis, to him, was certainly that.

Like an obedient child, she followed him into the same building as before, but to see Mr. Davis this time. When she saw her, Marva clucked her tongue, in either sympathy or disapproval. LaRetha couldn't tell which, until the woman spoke.

"*Poor thing*. You are a brave one. Your stay here has just been plagued with problems. I guess you wonder if coming here was even worth the trouble, huh?'

LaRetha gave her a polite smile, but Marva was waiting for an answer.

"Well, I hate that it happened," LaRetha defended. "But I've never been one to scare easily. A chip off the old block, I guess."

The woman glanced at her uncle doubtfully, before saying they could wait in the reception area. Less than fifteen minutes passed before Douglas Davis emerged.

It surprised her to see that he was much younger than Billard, and a black man; tall and muscular, cinnamon brown with dark brown close cut wavy hair. Just *fine,* she thought, and eking confidence. And, considering the expensive blue suit and Rolex watch he was wearing, he was also very high maintenance.

Just like Gerald, she thought. But, in line with his apparent sophistication, he had a slightly crooked smile that was endearing, as it showed off a sort of rugged charm. And he smelled *divine.*

He shook her uncle's hand, smiling and exchanging pleasantries. She waited until Davis introduced himself to her and did the same. They were ushered into his office as he instructed Marva to hold all calls and closed the door. And right away, it was evident why her uncle had so much faith in this man.

Her concentration on his striking physical traits was broken as he began to ask questions about the incident, about her life, and regarding the time she'd spent out on the farm. *Had anything like this ever occurred before that night?*

He listened intently, and she noticed how his eyes would wander around the room as he spoke, as if to put her at ease. *Or probably thinking about some other case,* she thought.

To recapture his attention, she became more descriptive of the incident, trying to impress upon him that this was not something to be treated lightly. A man's life was hanging in limbo, and her future was at stake, as well. He must have detected her concern because he leaned forward, appearing to listen a bit more intently.

After describing the details of the situation, and answering questions fired at her, one after the other, she felt more at ease. She kept up without any interference from her uncle, never flinching as this man studied her face, as if trying to determine if she was being honest. He made notes as she talked.

She must have been convincing, she thought, because Mr. Davis finally nodded, then handed her the usual forms to fill out.

"Right now, Miss Greer, it appears that you're in the clear. No charges have been made against you. It sounds pretty clear-cut, so I would say you have very little to worry about. Most likely it'll be considered a case of *self defense,* and closed."

She nodded, breathing relief. Her uncle patted her hand.

"*However,* I can appreciate your concern. If and when charges are filed, I will gladly represent you."

"Thank you. And your fee won't be a problem. Should I pay it, now?" She asked, anxiously. He smiled.

"Not just yet. Let's see what happens. I'm almost certain there won't be a need for it. I'll do some checking, and if I have to represent you, I'll let you know. You can pay the fee, then," he said with smiling finality.

They left the office with LaRetha feeling much more at ease than she had, going in.

"How is it that a man like Douglas Davis would end up working in the same office with a man like *Bob Billard?*"

Her uncle looked over at her, as he rode with her back into town.

"So, you've met Billard, already?"

"When I told you I'd already talked to a couple of people, he was one of them. But, it didn't go very well, so I didn't want to mention it, unless I had to."

"Doesn't matter. But, it's a good thing you didn't hire him," Her uncle said, looking slightly amused.

"Why is that?"

"Because everybody knows your father hated Bob Billard's *guts!*"

Early morning found LaRetha sitting in her darkened living room, staring at the blank television screen, feeling as if her entire world was unraveling and trying to figure out how to get it all back together, again.

It was Tuesday before Thanksgiving. She hadn't attended service, as planned. Considering it was only three days after the shooting, she hardly wanted to reenter *Lovely's* religious community with this hanging over her head.

She wished she could call Kellen. But, he was making crucial decisions, right now. She had no right to interfere with that. Her mother was always busy at this time of year. And Constance would only say *I told you so,* if she called her, as she had.

What would her father do? She asked herself. It didn't take long for her to figure it out. Sobbing into her hands, she gave a long, fervent prayer; for herself, her family and for *Straiter's* recovery, for answers where Therell and this land was concerned, and certainly for a restored peace of mind.

Afterward, feeling all cried out and more certain now that all her questions would soon be answered, she decided to spend the rest of the day engaging in anything that would take her mind off her troubles. She decided to pamper herself, as the women's magazine she wrote for said she should do when under duress. After almost an hour of exercise, she soaked her tired body in a hot tub of fragrant bubbles and beads, and started reading a book.

At early evening, she was lying on her sofa, reading an inspirational novel by lamplight when headlights beamed through her living room window. There were several of them, she noticed. And she was ill prepared to receive guests.

Turning on the overhead lights, she rushed into her bedroom, changing from her sweatpants and shirt into more appropriate attire. A beige sweater and brown pants would work just fine. She slipped her feet into a thick pair of socks and low heeled brown boots, and had just enough time to splash water on her face before the doorbell rang.

With the porch light already on, she opened the front door. To her surprise, at least twenty or more people were standing there and spilling over onto the front lawn, and they all were smiling. Many of them were carrying what appeared to be containers of food. Beyond them, she could see at least a dozen cars, all parked uniformly along the length of her driveway. And backing up the crowd was *Vera!* Waving and smiling.

"Hello, Miss Watson," someone called out. "We're here from *Joyful Baptist Church.* Happy Thanksgiving!"

Astonished, she ushered them inside and into the kitchen and dining rooms, where they unloaded their packages. She'd never imagined having so many people there, at once. Nor, so much food.

There was a huge fried turkey, greens and potato salad, corn muffins, several desserts and several liters of soda. Someone had even brought a stack of *God Loves You Because...* greeting cards, made by the children in their Sunday School class the week before.

Flabbergasted, she could say very little as they greeted her with hugs and introduced themselves, one by one.

"Now, we know you were probably going to cook for the holidays," a woman who had introduced herself as Minister Leah Harvey, told her.

"But, considering all that's happened, we've decided that you shouldn't have to worry with that. Consider this our official welcome home gift to you."

"Thank you, so much." LaRetha was practically speechless.

"No thanks, necessary. We consider you one of our own. Your folks grew up in our church. And aside from those fat little ponytails you used to wear, you haven't changed much, and neither has your membership with us."

Feeling overwhelmed, LaRetha thanked the woman, again.

"We're so sorry about your incident," she continued. "We've been praying for you, and for your return to church for services soon, too."

"I know. I had planned to come..."

"We understand. But, until then, we wanted you to know that we're here for you."

LaRetha had been strong up to that point, but this time holding back the emotions was difficult. After telling everyone to make themselves at home, she excused herself, going into the bathroom to regain her composure. She quickly emerged, finding the group deep in conversation, discussing something that had come up in their evening study class. Vera took the opportunity to pull her into the kitchen.

"Look, if we're imposing, I can easily show everybody out. We wouldn't be offended. We understand."

"No, I'm just glad you're here." She smiled and Vera gave her a hug. "Thank you for being so thoughtful."

The woman searched her face, doubtfully. Satisfied she was sincere, she smiled, also.

"Okay, then. Just remember, no speeches are necessary. We're here for *you*, not the other way around. "

They rejoined the group.

"Miss Watson, after we heard about your intruder, everyone was worried about you," the minister said. "We didn't come to stay long. We just wanted to show our support."

The group agreed.

"I can't believe that you would do all of this for me. It's been so long since I've lived here. I'm not sure that I remember most of you," she said, apologetically. "I haven't been to *Joyful Baptist* in so long."

"That's alright, darling," an older woman cooed. "We know you're a good person from a good family, who just got caught in an unfortunate situation. It's too bad about that *Paul Straiter*, but just remember that *you* were the victim, not him. This was bound to happen to someone who made the choices he did. Sooner or later."

"What we're saying is, please don't personalize this whole thing." One of the youth ministers said, nodding sympathetically. "We're all subject to this type of crime. We really have to be thankful that it wasn't any worse. We'll pray for his recovery, and his salvation. And we'll be praying for you, as well. That was a lot to have to go through."

Others nodded and agreed.

"Thanks for saying that. I've been wondering what I should have done differently," she said, surprising herself with her straightforwardness. "How this whole thing might have been avoided." She quickly wiped away an unexpected tear. Minister Harvey gave her a hug and she felt greatly comforted.

"Maybe it couldn't have been. Maybe this was in the Creator's plan for *him*, " another woman they called Miss Jonnie said. "God can use anything for good."

The others agreed.

"Come, everyone," Minister Harvey said. "Before we go, let's join hands and say a prayer for *Sister Watson.* That she be delivered from any guilt, fear or shame. That whatever joy and peace she has lost, be restored. That her hurts and wounds, be healed."

Guilt, fear and shame, LaRetha thought. This was exactly what she was feeling. The woman minister prayed amidst *'amen'* and *'yes, yes'.*

Afterward, she offered to serve them some of the desserts that they had brought and, surprisingly, everyone accepted. She, Vera and a friendly woman named Liz, went into the kitchen to prepare everything, then passed hot cocoa and slices of cake to everyone. The group of them stood around, eating and drinking in the kitchen and dining room, despite her saying not to worry about the living room carpeting. *Thank goodness that bloodstain came up,* she thought, guiltily.

The conversation turned to church events they thought might interest her. Someone asked about her work, then said that she was fortunate to be able to work from home. She hadn't thought about it much lately, but she truly was. Then, the conversation turned to her plans about *Lovely.* She said she would remain on the farm, which surprised some of them.

"We don't have many people coming back from the city. At least, not for long. But we're glad you're here. Everything will work out for the best. You'll see. Just don't get discouraged," Lorenzo Preston, a young man with a friendly smile told her.

She graciously accepted their encouragement. Then, the eldest man of the group spoke.

"I think we've inconvenienced *Sister Watson* long enough. Let's all say goodnight. We hope to see you on next Sunday!"

"Certainly. I plan to be there. Thank you all for coming. It has meant a lot to me, having you here and having your support."

"Well, we were thinking," Vera said, "if you find you need some company or want to spend time in town for awhile, there are several of us who can put you up – me, for one. I live alone, too. And, I make a pretty good roommate," she kidded.

Vera was trying to make it an easy decision for her. Others laughed as she continued.

"Liz here has a basement apartment, and she's offering space." The woman smiled from behind small black-framed glasses.

"I couldn't ask that, or inconvenience any of you. This was more than enough." *And it was,* she thought.

"You didn't ask," Vera said. "We volunteered. Besides, I would welcome the company. And you can work with no interruptions."

"Thank you for the offer, but..." she said, and the woman looked dismayed, sensing what was coming, she supposed. "And I mean that, sincerely. But, I don't expect to run into another *Paul Straiter* anytime soon. So, I'm fine for right now. But, if something changes, I will certainly call somebody, *quick/*"

They laughed and after leaving a church directory for her, they all said goodnight, leaving only Vera, who said she would stay and help clean up. There was very little to clean, but LaRetha could tell that she was in no hurry to leave and simply wanted to talk. And she could use the company.

Vera cleared the living room of the few paper items as LaRetha vacuumed the crumbs left behind. Then, they decided to cut the turkey so it would fit into the refrigerator, eating as they worked.

"People here are so kind. I mean, there are nice people in Atlanta, for sure. But folks here are treating me like I've never left," she said.

"Well, most of us haven't lived anyplace else," Vera said. "I would love to travel more, maybe live in a large city for a while. But there's so much *need* here. So many homeless and hungry people now, even in this small town. A lot of them are from other cities. They feel safer on these streets than wherever they're from. Others were born here, and never recovered from losing their homes or their heads of household."

She nodded biting into a delicious slice of turkey.

"And our young people! Runaways, mostly," Vera continued. "Some have homes, but they're not welcome there. They want understanding, more than anything else. I've had a few close calls, dealing with that particular bunch. But, the thing is, once you're able to really get through that tough exterior, they become more of a blessing to you than you could ever be to them."

"I believe it," LaRetha said, thinking about Germaine. Hoping he was well and wishing for the *ten thousandth* time that he would make some attempt to get in touch with her.

"We just have to learn to *listen* to them," she told Vera. "It's different for kids now. They have so many opportunities, but far more challenges and temptations than we had to deal with, I think."

"I think you're right. Spoken like a woman with a child of her own."

"Oh, sure. You want your child to have everything that's good in life, but you can't always be the one to lead them to it. You just have to pray for them, keep the lines of communication open, be steadfast but listen to their concerns. I think they always tell us what they're thinking, one way or another."

"That's a *discernment* thing that parents own, I guess," Vera said, quietly checking out their handiwork, looking satisfied.

"This place looks really nice," she said. "You've done wonders with it. I visited here with my father when I was a child. He and *Watson* were good friends. I remember your brothers were always talking about what they were going to be when they grew up. I think Thomas was going to be a doctor, and Andrew wanted to be a 'big time movie producer' as he put it," she laughed. "How are they doing, these days?"

"Well," LaRetha replied, "Thomas is a CPA with his own firm, and Andrew is a space scientist of some sort. Last time I saw them was at *Watson's* funeral."

"Yes, I was sorry to hear about your father. It all happened so suddenly," she mused.

"Did you see him when he was ill?" LaRetha questioned.

"No. I didn't get the opportunity. But, I've known your family since *forever.* I used to date your cousin. *Verry's* son. *Paul?* He married a woman from California, didn't he?"

LaRetha hesitated to tell Vera that she probably knew more about her family than she did. She had heard about *Uncle Verry's* oldest son, who ironically had the same name as her recent intruder. But, having never spent time with them, she hesitated at saying much about him.

"I haven't had a chance to talk with everybody. But my uncle was over for dinner, recently. Maybe I'll see them over the holidays. I can tell Paul you said, *hello*." She teased.

"Never mind that." Vera vehemently shook her head. "That was way back in high school. I rarely ever think about him."

I'll just bet, LaRetha thought, laughing mischievously. Vera probably knew everyone and everything about this town. She would be the perfect person to answer her questions regarding the recent farm fires, and about Paul Straiter's history.

"I was only kidding. But, I think I'll come by the mission again, soon. Volunteer a bit," she told Vera. "Need anyone this week?"

"Of course," Vera said, emphatically. "Come anytime. We're open everyday until *six,* except Sundays. There's a shelter in town that provides Sunday meals. I have to have *some* time for myself."

"I'll bet. I can come for a few hours on Wednesday and maybe even help out Thursday, with Thanksgiving dinner."

"*Wonderful,*" she responded, walking with LaRetha to the foyer to retrieve her coat. "And remember LaRetha, you don't have to get through this alone. We're your family. We're not perfect people, but we do try to take care of one another. This church has helped me through numerous situations. So, never think twice about asking for support."

"Thank you, I won't. Hopefully, *Straiter* will be alright, too. I've covered a lot of stories, never thinking I'd find myself in the middle of one. And certainly not one like this."

The woman frowned. Nodded.

"Just remember, we're only a call away. And we all plan to look out for you, from now on. Like it or not," she said, giving LaRetha a hug before she opened the front door.

"But that really won't be necessary," A deep, familiar voice replied.

Both she and Vera turned to see who was speaking. It only took a second for her to realize that the figure standing just outside her front door was *Kellen Kincaid*.

Vera stepped back, looking surprised and raising an eyebrow as LaRetha exclaimed her surprise, allowing him inside.

"*Kellen?* What brings you here?" she asked, accepting a tight hug from him, before backing away to give him room to remove his coat.

"You, of course!" He laughed. And he looked great!

"*Vera*, this is Kellen Kincaid, a dear friend from Atlanta. Kellen, this is Vera Canter, a new friend from *Lovely*," she smiled.

They exchanged pleasantries as Vera stepped outside.

"Wait, Vera. I'll walk you out." LaRetha said, making a face at a smiling Kellen as she grabbed her coat.

"So, Kellen's a close friend?" Vera asked as they walked to her car.

"A family friend. An *unexpected* friend, as a matter of fact."

"Well, I can see that all our concerns were for *naught*," she said with a raised eyebrow.

"No, they weren't. I'm very glad you came. I'll have to find a way to thank everybody for their trouble."

"I'm glad, too. I've been praying for new friends, myself. I work too much and play too little. Maybe we can hang out, sometime."

"That would be nice, Vera."

"Hey, and don't worry, girl. I'm nobody's gossip, so your secret is safe with me," she laughed, and LaRetha felt relieved.

"He's just a *friend,*" she repeated, laughing.

"*Uh huh*. I hear you. Well, call me sometime. Take care," Vera said, giving a mischievous wink before closing her car door and starting it up.

LaRetha waved as she drove away, before going back to her anxiously awaiting guest. Standing tall and looking even more handsome now than she remembered, he looked oddly out of place out here. *Wonderfully* odd. She willingly accepted his strong embrace.

"Oh, that feels good," he said. "I missed you."

"I missed you too. What brought you all this way? I thought you might be with your little *chippie* in Ohio, or someplace by now."

"And you thought wrong, as usual. Luckily I called your mother."

"I didn't know you had her number."

"Sure. I used to talk to Germaine over there, all the time."

"Really?" She hadn't known about that.

"Well, not lately. But, you know your mother. She is a talker."

"Yep! She is. Everybody has that number, anyway. To Laretta, everybody's a sales lead," she laughed.

"Why didn't you call? You know I would have been here in a heartbeat."

"I didn't want you to feel you had to come and babysit me."

"But, I thought we told each other *everything*." His forehead creased. His eyes searched her face, questioningly.

"I do believe that during our last conversation, you mentioned a certain job opportunity and a new girlfriend. I didn't want to interfere with your plans."

"I'm angry with you about that. I thought best friends shared everything. We're *best of friends*, remember? Has that changed?"

She sighed, pulling him over to the sofa to sit down beside her.

"I don't need a lecture, right now. Just give me a big hug and tell me I'll survive this. That this crazy feeling of *helplessness* won't last forever."

He pulled back from her, studying her face. Apparently surprised at seeing her so vulnerable.

"So, you've missed me, and you're glad that I came?"

"*Of course*. Did you think that I'd kick you out?"

"By the way you've been avoiding my calls, I didn't know what to expect. I just never know with you."

"Well, know this. Your showing up here is like an answer to my prayers. I could use a real friend, right now. So, thank you," she said, kissing him softly on the cheek, "for coming."

"So, I guess you won't mind my bunking on your sofa for a few nights?" He asked, his eyes twinkling.

"You can sleep on my sofa for as long as you like," she smiled.

Kellen's words were assuring, his hugs comforting and assurances that everything *would* be alright, were just what the doctor ordered. And she couldn't help but think the entire time how Gerald would have never done anything like this. If anything he would've rolled his eyes and told her to just *get over it.*

They must have been extremely tired, because they both dozed off, snuggling there on the sofa, embracing. He awakened first, nudging her awake. She opened her eyes to see him smiling lovingly. She straightened.

"You were snoring like a bull," he teased. "You were shaking the house and everything."

"I never snore." She sat upright. "Besides, don't bulls *snort*?"

"You were doing some of that too," he laughed.

"What time is it?"

"*Late.*"

"Are you hungry?"

"*Am I?* I smelled that hot cocoa and cake when I came in. What took you so long to ask?"

She made a face. "Well, if you want to get comfortable, you can. Maybe get out of that suit…"

"I'll have to get my bags," he said, hesitating.

"Sure. I'll show you to the guest room. You'll have your pick from two of them."

"Okay. I'll get my stuff and then I'll get *comfortable,* as you say. Just whip up something good in that kitchen of yours. I could eat a horse."

Saving the turkey for Thanksgiving, she prepared baked lemon-herb chicken, which was becoming her favorite. Kellen loved mashed potatoes and gravy with practically everything, so she prepared that with peas, stewed squash and hot buttered rolls.

He finally joined her in the kitchen, looking great in gray sweat pants and a matching long-sleeved t-shirt that accentuated his muscular shoulders and chest.

"You've been working out," she said. He flexed his pecs, play-fully, and she had to admit the man looked *marvelous.*

Careful, girl! She thought, grimacing.

After seating her, he sat down across from her. Looking her over from head to toe as she gave him an incredulous gaze, he nodded.

"You look *good,* woman. Country air is agreeing with you."

"Thanks, same to you. Knowing how much you hate to cook, I expected you'd be starving in Atlanta. Clearly, that's not the case."

"Not as long as they sell that fattening fast food," he said, flexing his toned body.

"Don't I know it? *Double burgers, triple burgers,* and probably even *quadruple burgers.*"

"Don't forget the *shakes,*" he teased. "But no, I've been working out, a lot. I had to do something to keep from going crazy without you."

He dug into his food and didn't sit back again, until he'd finished.

"That was really, really good," he complimented, looking satisfied. "But you haven't eaten much."

"I had cake and cocoa just before you came. I'm full."

He nodded. "So, who's Vera?"

"She heads the mission in town where I've been volunteering. She brought a church group over, earlier, to pray with me over the incident. That's where all these desserts came from," she motioned toward the fully covered counter behind him.

"I wondered if you were eating like that everyday."

"*Humph.* I know I've gained a couple of pounds…"

"In all the right places, baby. Don't even worry about it." He winked and she was flattered.

Sill, those extra four pounds she'd gained over the last two months were *doomed for deletion,* she thought. Maybe he could help her to develop a workout routine.

"Let me help you with these dishes." He stood and began clearing the table.

"Let me help *you* with the dishes," she teased, joining him. "And you can tell me about your new job, your new everything."

It turned out that he was starting the Ohio job in mid-January. The company was small but well established, he said. The salary was pretty good and they would pay his relocation costs. They had already provided a listing of apartment homes near the office. He would check them out after the holidays, he said.

When she asked what he would be doing, he proudly stated that he would supervise a staff of four and manage the company's accounts. And she was proud of him.

"I knew things would work out for you, Kellen. You have a lot to offer the right employer. I know Mac is going to miss you."

"Of course, he will. And thanks, baby." He gave her a hug.

They finished clearing everything away and she turned the light off before joining him in the living room. He pointed her to a chair. Standing over her, he began massaging her shoulders.

"And just what do you think you're doing?"

"Just relax, will you?"

Sliding her sweater down a bit, he began kneading her right shoulder muscles with strong hands. She closed her eyes.

"How's that?" He asked, working his fingers with great expertise.

"You aren't trying to *seduce* me are you, Mr. Kincaid?"

"*Me?*" He feigned surprise. "Certainly not." They were quiet again, relishing the moment. "So, tell me everything." He worked on the other side.

His hands were soothing, and she felt her tensions begin to ease. Trying hard to focus, she began to tell him all the events of that fateful day, from beginning to end.

She also told him about meeting her aunt and uncle, and inviting him to dinner. About the shooting and how helpful *Verry* had been. He laughed when she told him about the car repair incident.

"But, about that intruder. Why do you think he chose this house? Don't you think you're in danger with everybody knowing you're out here, alone? That could easily happen again."

"Okay, here we go."

He stopped working, turning to face her.

"LaRetha, if things had happened differently, we wouldn't be together, right now. I'd be helping them plan your *funeral.* Why put yourself in that position? Why put any of us in this position?"

"*Kellen*" she started, moving from her chair. "If you came here to make me think about moving, you've wasted a trip. I plan to stick this out. So, if you can't support that then maybe you shouldn't be here."

"Oh, *really?*" He took a deep breath, and she didn't care that he was annoyed. "I came here to support you, LaRetha. But I won't pretend this isn't dangerous. Don't hate me for caring."

He stood up and she felt apologetic, but said nothing.

"I have never felt so wrong for feeling so right about another person. Even *Mac* says..."

"*Mac?* What exactly did you tell *Mac Henry?*"

"He knows we were seeing each other. That's not a crime, is it?'

"I never said... You told him *what*, exactly?"

He said nothing. Looked at her sadly. "So, I should've kept my feelings to myself, is that it?"

"The man signs my paychecks. He has no business knowing who I do and don't see or... *sleep* with. It's bad enough that I have to be concerned about what they'll think at the church, now that Vera knows you're here. But *Mac,* too?"

He turned to her. Searched her face with angry eyes.

"Well, if you're feeling that bad about it, if you're *that* embarrassed about sleeping with me, then *maybe* you shouldn't have done it." His words were angry. And they cut deep.

"Kellen, I didn't mean..."

"Could you just show me where I'll be sleeping?" He interrupted.

She said nothing, deciding to get him settled to a bedroom before things really got out of hand.

"*Right*. A good night's sleep would do us both some good."

"*Good night*, LaRetha."

LaRetha lay awake for a long time, regretting her remark, and hating the way she'd offended this man who had come so far, possibly delaying his business plans, although he would never say so. Here for one good hour and already they weren't speaking.

He was probably lying in the next room, thinking what a huge mistake he'd made to even come. And, his words still rang true. But, she was a grown woman. She'd made a mistake in judgment and repented. Still, she truly needed to stop harboring this guilt.

Separation had made it easy for her to put Kellen and everything else out of her mind. But now, here he was again; invading her space, her mind and her heart, all at once, and all over again. Well, she couldn't change the past. The question was, what did she plan to do, now?

He was asleep when she peeped inside. The ceiling light in the hallway allowed her to see in, its yellow glow falling hazily upon his face. He was sleeping in cotton pajamas, lying face up and sprawled out massively over the regular sized bed that looked smaller with him on it. His eyes were closed, and it appeared as if he was barely breathing. She saw that his feet touched the end of the bed. And the smell of his clean, musk cologne permeated the air. She slowly inhaled.

Looking at him like this, she realized that she *could* love him. He was just so direct, so *in your face* about everything, and she just didn't have any answers for him, right now. Kellen played for keeps. Only, she had been there and done that, before. And until now, she'd been sure that they just weren't looking for the same things.

But now, here he was, in *her* environment, ready to declare his undying love, and at a time when she felt so emotionally needy. And now, it wasn't quite so easy to just pull away.

Why had he even come?

A pancake and egg breakfast was warming on the stove when Kellen finally emerged from the shower the next morning, smelling and looking squeaky clean in burgundy sweats and a white tank shirt, and wrapped in a thick blue and burgundy robe. White socks covered his feet. No shoes.

"*Man,* it's cold out here," he said, bearing an imperfect white-toothed smile. She felt gratefully forgiven.

"It is not *cold!* The heat's on. Why are you shivering?"

"Just looking outside makes me cold. Funny, home isn't that far away and it was nothing like this. Just a little chilly."

"You can start a fire in the living room, if you want."

"Anything to stop shaking like a scared rabbit." He followed her onto the back porch for firewood. And soon after, a fire blazed brightly in the living room. She said she was impressed.

"Oh yeah. I use the fireplace at my townhouse all the time," he said, reaching for a plate. She wouldn't have time to set the table.

"When did you buy a townhouse?" She joined him, and he waited until she said grace, then dug in.

"Didn't I tell you? First of the year. I moved a few miles further out from the city. But, it's on the bus line, near Stonecrest Mall and everything. It's pretty cool."

"How could you not tell me that?"

"Thought I did," he shrugged.

"No you didn't think that. I'm surprised at you."

"Guess I'm picking up your bad habits."

She smarted at this.

"Okay. I had hoped to surprise you, so I kept it a secret," he admitted. "But, you never came home. I'm subleasing it when I go to Ohio. College kids. For a while, anyway. Until I see how the job goes," he said, between bites.

She nodded, feeling sorry that she had disappointed him. He had gotten this place, probably hoping to impress her enough to get her to stay whenever she'd visited. Only she never had. *How sad.*

"So, I guess this Ohio girlfriend was happy to hear that you're moving in her direction? Is she the reason?"

He stopped chewing, his inquiring eyes searching her face.

"No. That would never work. She has nothing to do with it. She doesn't even know that I took the job."

She considered this.

"What happened between you two? Really."

"She expects too much. Asks for too much. I started feeling like an *ATM.*"

She laughed.

"Is she pretty?"

"*Yep.* And *that's* the trap. I like a confident woman, but not one so self-absorbed. And especially not one who sees me as a personal bank."

"Meaning, you can better handle a low maintenance frump like me."

"*You? Frumpy?* Never. But, you aren't just pretty, you're *beautiful,*" he said in an alluring voice, sending chills over her that she ignored and hoped he couldn't see. "And you know it took all the willpower I had to stay out of your room last night, don't you?" He said, teasingly.

Me too, she thought but knew better than to say.

"So, for that, you owe me."

He got up and pulled her to him. Hugged her, tightly. She sighed, before gently pulling away. He looked exasperated.

"So, should I have come, LaRetha? I feel like you don't want me here. Like you don't trust me, or maybe you don't trust yourself."

"I'm just not ready to pick up where we left off. So, if that's going to be a problem, then maybe you should just go before we both say or do something to cost us our friendship. I don't want to risk doing that."

"I know you didn't invite me here, LaRetha. But, I don't want to leave you, yet. I like being here with you, this way. And as mad as you make me, sometimes, I can't stop coming back to you."

She nodded, knowing the feeling all too well.

"Our friendship won't ever change," he said. "But, I won't lie about not wanting more from you. A deeper commitment, a promise, or... *something.* What do you call that? *Love?*"

"A *glutton for punishment,* maybe?" She laughed, painfully.

"That's me," he said, nodding guiltily, and being quite accustomed to her bluntness. "Truth is, I'm concerned about you. Besides, I still think we have something to fight for, don't you?"

"I don't know, Kellen. But, whatever happens, I do love the fact that you're at least willing to try. And I love it how you're not afraid to throw caution to the wind and go after whatever you want. I'm trying to be that way, again. It's just not easy when so much is spinning out of your control, you know?"

"But, that's the purpose of it. To throw away caution and allow whatever happens to work itself out. To let go of feeling you have to control it. Besides, I'm here, now. You're not alone, anymore. Just lean on me, okay?"

Right, she thought. *Lean on you.* One of her expectations when moving here was that she would never have to count on anyone, ever again. To never be hurt again by doing so. She had hoped to release all the pain that feeling hurt and abandoned by those closest to her had brought, and to make sure it could never happen, again.

Kellen was making this virtually impossible. And for now, she truly didn't care. Right now, and like him, she was just happy that they were talking, again.

The snow and wind had picked up, again. The fire was roaring and they were trying to break a tied score in a card game when the phone rang. She answered it.

"Hey, LaRetha. You doing okay, out there?"

"Yes, I am, *Uncle Verry.* Thanks for asking," she said, looking at Kellen, who nodded. "What's going on?" She asked.

"I just thought I'd call to tell you the news before you heard it somewhere else."

"Why, what's happening?" She gushed.

"Paul Straiter *died* last night."

"*Oh!*" She gasped, dropping the cordless phone onto the floor. Kellen picked it up and offered it to her, but she couldn't take it.

"Hello. This is Kellen Kincaid. I'm a friend of your niece's. I'm visiting for a few days. Is something wrong?"

Kellen listened intently as her uncle spoke to him.

"Yes, I'll make certain she's there. *10am.*" He hung up.

By now, LaRetha was coming undone, her hands covering her face as she sat horrified. He came to her side, pulled her to him.

"I *killed* him. They told me he might live, but he's dead and I killed him."

"No. No, baby. You didn't. Your uncle just explained that the man died from... other causes."

"How is that so? I shot him, in cold blood," she sobbed. "The poor man didn't have a chance. He tried to stop me from shooting him, but he couldn't. I shot him so many times..." She was almost hysterical now, but couldn't control it.

"No. Listen to me, LaRetha. He died, but not from gunshot wounds. They found him dead in his hospital room. *Somebody had smothered him with a pillow.*"

Douglas Davis' voice mail was on, so she left a message that she needed to talk with him, as soon as possible. Then, they spent the day before Thanksgiving not talking about it. She would find Kellen watching her sadly when he thought she didn't notice. He wouldn't allow her to do anything for him the entire day, but catered to her, instead.

"Let's go out and get some air," he finally said, trying to get her out of her mood. "I'll drive. You can show me the sights."

They rode quietly for over an hour, listening to his jazz CD's, talking about music and nothing of much importance before he suggested they get ice cream cones.

"I know your tropical *butt* ain't trying to eat ice cream in this cold weather," she laughed.

"That's the best time," he said, before driving to the window and ordering double scoops for both of them. He finished his and the rest of hers. Afterward, covering her hand with his, he gave her an endearing smile, and she was glad that he was here. As it turned out, he had known better than she, what she needed right now.

The found the house well lit, warm and inviting when they returned. Settling on the sofa to watch a movie, he polished off a huge bowl of popcorn with a soda, as she sipped from a glass of iced tea. The movie ended.

"Well, it's late. I guess I'll turn in," she finally said.

"Are you sure? We could sit up and talk."

"Thanks, but I'm sure." She nodded, before turning to him. "How long are you planning to stay, Kellen? I know you have to get back home and prepare for your move and everything."

"*I'll go when I'm good and ready, woman,*" he teased. Then more seriously, he lovingly pulled her close. "Let's take this one day at a time. Right now, you're much more important. But, you already know this."

"I'm sorry about Thanksgiving. I know you hadn't planned on spending it this way."

"I came for *you*, not just for Thanksgiving. Besides, I wouldn't have done anything but sit around eating fried chicken and mashed potatoes in front of the stupid television set. I would rather be with *you*, eating in front of the stupid television set. But you know this, already."

"*Oh, no!*" She remembered.

"What? What is it?"

"I promised Vera I would volunteer at the mission, today. And tomorrow for Thanksgiving. I was going to help..."

Kellen sighed with relief.

"LaRetha, I honestly don't believe they're going to hold it against you, under the circumstances."

"You're right," she relaxed. "What was I thinking?"

"You just need to calm down. Stop worrying. Get some sleep. Things will be clearer in the morning, I promise you."

"Thank you, Kellen. For being here. For keeping your head while I slowly lose my mind."

He laughed.

"Whatever you lose, I'm here to help you find. Just *chill* for a minute, okay?"

Chill, she thought. That's exactly what she needed to do. Paul Straiter was dead, and she couldn't afford to lose her head about it. Someone had suffocated the man in his hospital bed, and she had no idea, who or why. Or, if they were coming after her, next. The thought alarmed her.

Suddenly she wanted Kellen close. To have him beside her tonight, just holding her. Only, she couldn't handle any of the confusion it would cause, between them. Nor could she be sure of her own actions, if they did.

"Kellen. I…" She couldn't say the words. He was right. She wasn't sure that she could even trust herself.

She couldn't explain it, but everything in her *being* told her that something unexplainable was happening around her, and that it went much deeper than she'd first thought. She needed to focus. And confusing issues with Kellen was not the way to do it.

No, she decided. It was much better that she slept alone.

"What is it?"

She shook her head. "Goodnight."

He hugged her. Kissed her softly. "Goodnight, baby. And don't worry. Everything's going to be fine."

LaRetha closed her bedroom door, not quite believing the change in Kellen. She had known he was capable of it, but just never expected it. But, after Gerald, she unfortunately didn't expect much of anything from anyone, anymore.

But, she *liked* this. His being here almost made up for the fact that everything else in her life was so undetermined, at the moment. Here she was, possibly facing criminal charges, and in a situation no one could have told her even six months ago could occur. And in light of all that, here *he* was; ever the stable and immovable ally, no matter how hard she tried to shake him. He was her rock, and she had to admit, she needed him.

It was Thanksgiving morning, and after a restless night's sleep, she and Kellen drove to her uncle's store. Douglas Davis had returned her call and said that, although no charges were being filed against her yet, he still had a few more questions. They would need to be prepared.

Uncle Verry was waiting for them, easily sliding into the backseat of Kellen's mid-sized rental car before he could turn off the engine. LaRetha introduced them. The two men exchanged greetings.

"I don't understand, *Uncle Verry*. Why would someone kill this man? I thought he was a drifter or something like that."

"So did I. Question is, why would anyone even bother with him, much less try to kill him? For someone to risk getting past the nurses and guards, and then to sneak back out again, he must have had some serious enemies."

"Apparently," she added.

LaRetha sat quietly while her uncle directed Kellen to the law offices. Once parked, Kellen got out and waited as the two of them spoke quietly, before joining him.

"Am I a suspect for last night's murder, *Uncle Verry?* Truthfully, now. I want to know what to expect when I get inside this man's office, so don't try and protect my feelings."

"No. From what I gather, you aren't. Besides, you had an alibi last night, didn't you?"

Yes, she did, she sighed, as he glanced at Kellen, giving him a friendly nod. And depending on the time the man was killed, Vera and her church members could also verify her whereabouts, she said. She only hoped it wouldn't come to that.

Marva was out for the holidays, so Douglas Davis stood waiting in the reception area. Crisply dressed in a dark suit and burgundy shirt with a matching tie, he made a striking impression. He greeted them, before seeing them into his office and urging them to sit down.

"I'm not sure that I need to be in here." Kellen hesitated

"Please, stay," she said.

"As long at the lady has no problems with it, neither do I. Please sit down, *Mr..?*"

"*Kincaid*," he reached over to shake Douglas' hand. "*Kellen Kincaid.* I'm LaRetha's friend, visiting from Atlanta for the holiday."

"Mr. Kincaid. Please have a seat. This should be brief."

"Thank you for seeing us, today. Being it's Thanksgiving and all." She said, sincerely.

"Nooo problem, Miss Greer," he said absently, as he shuffled a few papers before finding the one he wanted.

He tapped the page as he sat studying the three of them. LaRetha waited from a middle chair, as her uncle sat nearest the window with its open blinds. Kellen, seated closest to the door, eyed the man as suspiciously as he was, them. Finally, the man spoke.

"Well, it appears that we have lost our suspect. They found him late last night, *asphyxiated* - smothered by a pillow in his hospital bed. Question is, who would do this and why?" He looked at each of them, curiously.

"My question, exactly," she offered. The two other men agreed.

"Well, Miss Greer, I've spoken with the police. They won't bother you any more than necessary. They understand the circumstances of that incident at your house, and they had already decided to put it to rest, when this happened."

"As it turns out," he continued, "Paul Straiter was seen hitchhiking here from Atlanta, just the day before this happened. You are from Atlanta, aren't you?"

"Yes, but I don't know anything about this man. I've been here since spring of last year, and I've never seen him around."

"We're both from Atlanta," Kellen interrupted. Everyone looked at him. "Sorry."

"No problem," the man said, smiling a bit. "He arrived the night before he broke into your home. So, the obvious question is, why did he come, who sent him, and what was he looking for at *your* house?"

"You think his breaking into my house has something to do with his murder at the hospital?"

"It's possible. If he was just some hungry drifter, why would anyone want him dead? That makes little sense to *me*," Douglas said.

LaRetha contemplated this.

"Seems he has no family here anymore," he continued. "So why come back? *Lovely* has far less to offer the homeless by way of accommodations than Atlanta does. So, what was his reason, and what, if anything is the connection?"

She saw where he was going with this, and the thought frightened her. She needed to make him understand. To make him see whatever he needed to, in order to trust her. To see it from her point of view. Otherwise, her chances of beating this were shot.

"I'm sorry to ask this, but could I speak with Mr. Davis, alone?" She asked her uncle and Kellen. They barely hesitated in responding to her request.

"Sure," her uncle said.

"We're right outside if you need us," Kellen said, more to Douglas, it appeared, than to her. The man sat back in his chair, watching Kellen with interested eyes. The door closed behind them, and she began.

"I asked them to leave because I have something to ask you."

"I'm listening." He said, casually meeting her gaze before looking away.

"This is purely confidential, am I right? Off the record?"

"I'm *your* representative, Miss Greer. Nothing gets past me without your prior knowledge. So, what did you need to ask?" His gorgeous brown eyes squinted, his gaze steady upon her face.

"I think there might be, or rather there *could* be some connection between this man, and a few other strange things that have occurred around my home."

"How so?" He waited. She couldn't help thinking about how someone might easily get lost in those big brown, inquiring eyes. She refocused.

"I spoke with Mr. Billard a few weeks ago. It was about the claim my... that *Therell Watson* is making on my inheritance. I'm sure he told you about that?"

"I am aware of it. But, what do you think the connection is?" He asked, sounding as though he'd already considered the same thing.

"I don't know. Maybe this *Straiter* guy was sent to my house for a reason. To scare me, maybe. Or maybe even to get rid of me. I've met my *supposed* brother. He seems like he could be capable of this type of thing."

"Of *murder,* you mean?" He frowned.

"I wouldn't say *murder.* I *would* say sending someone to my house to scare me. Just before he called the first time, I heard strange noises outside my house, and then someone turned my doorknob. He called and hang up without saying anything, then called back the next day, and apologized. He said his phone had been giving him trouble. But, it's possible that he was calling from outside the house the entire time. And that he was trying to intimidate me, so I would be more apt to accept his proposal. It was all kind of scary."

"Maybe there *was* a problem with his phone."

"*Maybe.* But it's still snowing, and I haven't heard those noises, since."

He sat back, looking out of the window, stroking his moustache. Then he looked at her as if he'd had some sudden epiphany, and then looked away, again.

"I haven't heard from Therell since he came to my home, threatening to take my farm. He has an attorney, and I know that he and Mr. Billard have corresponded, but I haven't personally heard anything."

"So, a long lost relative shows up, angry about you having inherited the place. Then, soon afterward, a drifter appears. You figure the relative sent the drifter?"

"Isn't it possible?" She asked.

"Anything is," he said. "But, might I give you a word of warning? That old man you brought in here today practically raised Therell Watson. But, I figure you know all about that because you asked him to leave the room."

"I asked *them,* and that was because I didn't know how you would react to it..."

"Or how he might react to you, when you mentioned Therell's name in connection with these crimes. Remember, I've lived here all my life, Miss..."

"Please call me LaRetha," she interrupted.

Of course, LaRetha. I'm a native of this town and I've represented most of these people in one case or another. This is why they trust me. So, as I was saying, be very careful expressing those viewpoints to anyone around here. I see on your inquiry that you're a news reporter, so then you know like I do how important it is that we get the facts, first?"

"I freelance, and I do know. I just want to get to the bottom of this. I mean, what's going to happen, now? I'm very upset about *Straiter.* I'm sorry that my shooting him has led to his death..."

"But we don't know that. He could have been targeted for reasons unknown at this time, LaRetha. Don't... you can't blame yourself because we don't know, yet."

"I know that I thought this man was going to kill me. I know that all these things that are happening can't be entirely coincidental. I'm not trying to make out like some victim, but I am concerned. How do I even know it's all going to be over when this case is?"

"Let's just take it one day at a time," he said, nodding sympathetically. "In the meantime, I wouldn't discuss this with *anyone.* Let's not complicate matters with conjecture and have it come back on us. Your case isn't over, yet."

"I know."

He proceeded to speak legalese about a possible hearing, and then his expectations that there would be no charges, and that the old case would be closed for good.

"I'll call you no later than Monday if I need anything further from you. In the meantime, will you be on the farm, alone? Or will Mr. Kincaid be here for a while?"

His eyes fell to the V-neckline of her gray sweater. Even Kellen had raised an eyebrow when he first saw her that morning. Douglas Davis looked away, again.

"I don't plan to relocate, but you'll know if that changes. Kellen will be here for a couple more days, I guess. He has his work to get back to."

"Which is?"

"Is he a suspect, Mr. Davis?"

"Please, call me *Douglas.*"

"Is he?"

"Not if he was with you all night."

"He was."

"Then, *no.* Not that I'm aware of," he said, stacking papers on his desk and standing to walk with her out of the office. "But let me know if and when he decides to leave. I don't think he'll have any questions to answer. It's just easier this way."

"Thank you," she said, standing and reaching out to shake his hand. He accepted the handshake.

"Take care, LaRetha. "I mean it." He walked out to meet the others, smiling as he faced the two men.

"Take care of our lady here, *fellas,*" he said with concern in his voice. "I'll be in touch."

"Thank you, Douglas," her uncle said, shaking his hand. "You come on out to the house if you get hungry. Nell's got the table spread. They're holding dinner. And don't forget about Saturday."

"That's very thoughtful of you, Mr. Watson. But, I have plans for tonight. You all enjoy your holiday."

On the ride home, she was let in on the newest plan. She and Kellen would join her uncle at his house for Thanksgiving dinner. They normally ate around *three,* and there was no need for them to bring anything.

"I don't know..." she started. She wasn't sure that she was ready to deal with the entire family. Especially with Therell being at odds with her, right then. There was so much to sort out.

"Well, just think about it. And LaRetha, I haven't heard from Therell. I wouldn't put you in that position," he said, solemnly.

So he did understand, she thought.

"Not that I think this has anything to do with *him,*" he continued. "It doesn't sound like him, at all. He blows a lot of hot air, but he's harmless."

He had guessed her reason for talking privately with Douglas, and felt the need to reassure her about his adopted son. Understandable, she thought.

"I don't want you feeling unnecessarily fearful of your own folks."

My folks. She still couldn't consider Therell Watson that way, regardless of what her uncle said.

"And, I'm concerned about you being out there, LaRetha. I was just telling Kellen here how everything's busy right now. You might decide that being out there alone is a bit much for you. Don't hesitate to call us. I've talked to Nell and she feels the same way. Call us, visit us, come stay with us, anytime. You hear me?"

"I hear you. And thank you, so much. And for going to see Davis with us. I feel better knowing all the support I have. You two, the church..."

"Yeah, Nell and I were sorry we couldn't come out the other night. I hope all went well."

"It did. They're all so thoughtful. We prayed together and they brought desserts so we ate a little. It really has made a difference. Then Kellen surprised me by coming. I couldn't feel more blessed."

"Wonderful. And our dinner offer still stands, in case you change your mind. If nothing else, you could just come by and meet everybody. It's rare that all my kids are in town at the same time. But everybody came this year," he said, proudly.

"How many do you have?" Kellen asked.

"Well, eight in all. By birth and adoption," he added. "We're all concerned."

Not all, she thought, considering Therell was one of the eight.

"You don't think it's over, do you?" She asked. His face tightened, and he looked sad.

"Never is, until it's over. I don't want to alarm you, but drifters have friends, too. And sometimes, people they owe and do favors for. So, I wouldn't take any unnecessary chances."

Favors, she thought. Like a favor for *Therell Watson.*

"Thanks, *Uncle Verry,*" she told him, sincerely. They dropped him off at the store, and drove home, in silence.

"LaRetha, can you come in the living room for a minute?"

While Kellen was parking the car, she had gone inside, and now she lay across her bed feeling more tired than she had in a while. She heard him come in and go into his bedroom, then call to her from the hallway. Reluctantly, she got up to join him on the sofa.

Tired, baby?" He pulled her down onto his lap, nuzzling his face against hers. He felt and smelled so nice.

"*Mmmm.* You smell great," she said.

"So do you." He smelled her skin. Kissed her.

"What did you call me for?" She asked.

"For this. What else?" He kissed her, again. Her expression said she wasn't amused, although she was.

"Do you really want to go to my uncle's for dinner?" She asked.

"Only if you want to. Or, if you prefer to go alone, I understand."

"No. Let's stay in, tonight. We can visit another time, maybe."

"I was hoping you would say that."

A short time later, the phone rang. This time it was Nell.

"Just calling to find out if we can share our turkey with two *lovebirds,*" the woman said, snickering mischievously at her own joke.

"Thank you, Nell. I appreciate the invitation. But I think I prefer to stay home, tonight. I do want to come over and meet everyone before they leave. Can we make that another time?"

"*Of course.* This would be a bit much, I guess. But, look. We always have a holiday gathering every Saturday after Thanksgiving. For our *out-of-towners.* There's never anything to do in town, so we bring the town to us. How about it? We usually start around *seven.*"

"*Saturday at seven?*" She looked at Kellen. He shrugged. "That's a perfect idea. How can we help?"

"By showing up, is all. We do the rest."

"Thanks, Aunt Nell. And have a wonderfully blessed Thanksgiving. We'll see you then."

"We'll see them for *what?*" Kellen asked when she hang up the phone. She told him about the party. His face brightened. Clearly, her humdrum existence was beginning to wear on him.

"So, what to do, Mr. Kincaid?"

"How about showing me around the farm?"

"In the snow?" She asked. "*You?*"

"Best time. I've only been out here once, and I didn't see much."
She remembered the funeral.

"I want to see the barn and all the things you used to describe
when you talked about this place. Besides, I miss going to the gym."

"I don't," she grumbled.

"A little fresh air never hurts," he said.

She waited for him at the front door and they spent the next two
hours walking over the land. He listened intently as she described
the flower garden and shrubbery that would blossom in spring. She
showed him the barn and described what used to be in there.

Becoming adventurous, she drove them a few miles out to her
grandparents' old house. The weather had killed the brush, so they
could get through. Still, she warned that they should proceed with
caution, not that she had to.

Although old, gray and dilapidated now, it was still standing. She
pointed out an old covered well in back, where water for drinking
and bathing was once drawn, and then to where her father's mother
would sit and churn butter on the porch.

He laughed as she described the way baby chicks once ran
around in back, where the children would toss seed for their food.
Pointed out the place where the cows and pigs were once slaugh-
tered, and then where an old smokehouse used to be, where meat
was salted and hung up. He listened as she explained, nodding a few
times, saying he could almost see it.

Later, they drove back to her house. Changing clothes in her
room, she realized her phone hadn't rung in almost two days.
Normally she would have talked to her mother, by now. She sat
down and dialed. Laretta answered on the second ring.

"Hello, sweetie. *Happy Thanksgiving.* Did Kellen ever make it
over there? Tell him I said, hello," She said and asked, at once.

"Why am I not surprised that you knew this?" She asked, and her
mother chuckled into the phone. *How sneaky!* She thought. And so
like her mother.

She was coming to *Lovely* for a week at Christmas, *so make
room,* Laretta warned. A male friend had invited her up to Cincinnati,
and she would visit her, right afterward. Then she asked how the
case was going, and would there be a hearing?

No, she responded, telling her that Douglas Davis was confident
that no charges would be filed against her. Laretta was in her car, on
the way to close on a house, she said. So, with Kellen waiting in the
other room with popcorn and drinks, she didn't get into details about
her visitors, her uncle or the invitation he'd extended. They both said
quick *I love you's,* and *talk to you later,* before hanging up.

"I just talked to my mother. She says hello," she said, accusingly.

"Good." He smiled.

Then, getting up to turn off the stereo, and coming back over to her, he sat beside her. Taking her hand, he kissed it softly before facing her. She could see something different in his face. He was totally relaxed and watching her intently.

"What's this?"

"LaRetha, I think it's past time that we have a serious talk. There's something I need to tell you. *Tonight.*"

"And what is that?"

"I love you."

"You've told me that. You already know how I feel."

"Do you really love me? You've said it before, but not once since I've been here."

"I thought I had."

"Don't pull that forgetful act on me. You know you haven't."

"You know how I feel about you, Kellen. Or you wouldn't be here."

"I know that and I *am* here. And I want to say something."

"I'm waiting," she said.

Reaching into the pocket of his sweat pants, Kellen retrieved a small box. She inhaled, holding her breath for a long moment.

"LaRetha, I told you over and over again how I feel about you. Now I want to show you. So, don't say a word, just open this."

She accepted the small blue velvet box with slightly trembling hands. Slowly she opened it, and gasped.

"How *beautiful!*"

"Just like you," he said. "You are my exquisite and unique treasure, and I want to have you and love you for the rest of my life."

She slowly shook her head. He stilled her with a touch.

"I'm not asking for a decision, today. Not now or tomorrow, even. This ring signifies what I just told you and all I would like to be, in your life. But, I only want a commitment when you're ready to give it."

"So, why such an expensive ring, if it's only for friendship?"

"Because, a little motivation never hurts," he said, laughing a bit.

She stared at the ring, moving it ever so slightly to watch the diamonds flicker brightly around a large center stone. He took it from her hand and slid it onto her ring finger.

"This is just... It must have cost so much."

"So, what do you say?"

"I'm not sure what to say," she said.

Saying nothing, he easily removed the ring and placed it on a finger on her right hand.

"Wear it here, for now. When you change it over to your left hand, you and I both will know that you're ready to seal this deal."

"But, that could be awhile. Or..."

"*Look,* woman. I know how difficult it is to get you to commit to anything, right now. So, I thought I'd try this."

"But, what about my farm? And your job in Cincinnati?" She asked, feeling flustered. "It's way too early for this."

"Mere details, my lady. And look. It fits perfectly."

He pulled her close and she easily went into him arms. This time she kissed him, first.

"So what does *this* mean?" He asked, expectantly.

"This *means* that I appreciate your being so thoughtful. You know you're making this very difficult for me," she said.

"Well, that's my intention. I wouldn't want you to be blindsided by other things."

"Meaning what? What *things?*" She asked.

"*Never mind.*"

"No. What things, Kellen?" She asked defiantly.

"You think I don't know he's interested in you? I saw the way he looked at you. It's as clear as the nose on my face."

"Who? What are you talking about?" She asked, puzzled.

"You *know* what I'm talking about."

She pondered this for a moment.

"Do you mean *Davis? Douglas Davis?*"

"Stop playing. You knew this, so stop acting so surprised."

"But, I am surprised. That man has no interest in me. He could be married, for all I know."

"I don't think so. Douglas Davis has been locked away in this town since forever. Probably hasn't seen anything like you in his whole life."

"Oh, and you have?" She asked, sassily.

"I did meet you first." He planted a kiss on her cheek.

She nudged him playfully in his side. "I can't believe you. You didn't just give me a ring because of him, did you?"

"What?" He asked. "No way, baby. Surely you know I had that when I got here."

"But would you have given it to me?"

"Sure," he shrugged. "Why not?"

Why not. She got up from the sofa.

"*Enough about Douglas Davis.* He's my *attorney,* nothing else. You know I don't play those kinds of games. If I was involved with him or anyone else, I would've told you the minute you got here."

"Sure." He didn't seem convinced.

"Kellen, I've always been honest with you. I don't know any more about Douglas Davis than you do."

"Well, I had to ask. I never know what's going on with you anymore, LaRetha."

"Sometimes, I don't either," she said. "But, I know *that's* not happening. Not with me."

"Well," he said, "this is the Thanksgiving holiday, isn't it? Where's the *bird?* And all that other stuff you fix every year that Germaine was always boasting about?"

She smiled. *Germaine.*

"Have you heard from him?" She finally asked, hopefully. Feeling suddenly bashful under his sympathetic gaze.

"He said he would call. I'm working on him."

"Well, I appreciate it. He's trying so hard to prove that he's an adult that he's overlooking the most important things. Even when my parents disapproved of Gerald, I didn't throw them to the wind when we got married. They were still there for me, and for Germaine."

"I didn't know that your parents disapproved of Gerald."

"I'm surprised my mother never told you."

"She's never mentioned him to me. All she worries about is her precious LaRetha and her *bad-boy grandson.*

"Is he keeping in touch with her?"

"I don't know. Wouldn't she tell you if he were?"

"Well, those grandparent and grandchild relationships can be strange. But Laretta can only keep a secret for so long before she spills it and demands that all sides make up. She would've told me."

"Alright then. Now I know who to call when you give *me* trouble."

"Don't even think about it. Ready for dinner?"

"Sure. A man could get real fat living out here."

In no time, the table was adorned with an intimate holiday setting of candles flickering atop a white linen tablecloth. There was a lot of food, but considering his appetite, maybe not enough, she thought. They sat down to eat the fried turkey with dressing and gravy, greens and macaroni and cheese. Everything the church had brought over, and cranberry sauce on the side.

"Tired of *Lovely's* excitement, yet?" She asked.

"Not *yet,*" he said, and she figured that he was bored, already.

"Well, don't let me keep you," she sniffed.

"You brought me here. Why wouldn't you keep me?" He leaned over to press his lips against hers, stroking her face with his fingers. And for a moment, they revisited the passion from before, when they had gone beyond the boundaries of friendship. Stopping, she took a deep breath. Slowly exhaled.

But he tightened his hold, gently nudging her face upward as one hand explored the low neckline of her sweater.

"*Kellen!*" She gently pulled away. "Don't start."

He sighed with exasperation.

"You know, you women kill me with that. Like you're so rational and reasonable that you *never* lose your head when it comes to sex. You act like you don't want it, too. And we both know better."

He shook his head with incredulity to make his point. She gave him a long look, refusing to explore the issue.

"Okay, point taken. This is torture, but we'll do it your way, for now," he conceded. "I'm hungry. Let's eat."

6

Kellen suggested that they go sledding on a nearby slope that she hadn't noticed before. He recruited her into helping make a sled of plywood and odd sized pieces of scrap wood, and afterward, volunteered to try it first. One piece fell off, but he managed to make it all the way down to the bottom of the slick icy slope, where he turned and grinned, quickly giving her a thumbs-up.

She wasn't so sure how much fun this was going to be, considering they had to use sticks to brace them on the tedious walk *up* the slope in order to slide back down. But, it was great exercise, and Kellen made it interesting.

Back inside, they toasted marshmallows on extended wire hangers over the open fireplace. Sitting on a plush throw rug and telling ghost stories, they stuffed themselves with the marshmallows and what he called 'cheap soda'. The conversation and laughs felt good, and she secretly wished it didn't have to end.

Kellen always could read her moods.

"How about we do a little shopping, tomorrow? We can leave out early in the morning, and check out the malls."

"There aren't any malls out here, Kellen. But we can drive over to Louisville…"

"Well, what *do* you have?" And she sensed he didn't care for a long drive.

"Lots of new outlets. I've only been to the linen store."

"I can tell," he said, referring to what he laughingly called her 'furniture store showroom'. She swatted him with a pillow.

It was decided. And being the first one up the next morning, she had showered and dressed and finished making breakfast before he emerged from his bedroom, greeting her with his usual warm hug and kiss before they sat down to eat. She could see that he was as excited about their outing as she.

Although local weather reports didn't recommend travel, having new tires on her SUV made the drive around *Lovely* an easy one. They started with her usual store, then ventured into a men's clothing store, where he bought dress pants and nice shirts, saying his old ones would never do for his new job. She didn't comment on what it was costing, but she did wonder how he could afford so much. But, Kellen acted as if the bill was not an unusual one for him.

They finally decided that shopping might take awhile, so after loading the car, they headed to a local doughnut shop for a break.

"LaRetha Watson!"

A man waved as he drove past. Parking at the corner, he put a few coins in the meter before hurrying over. Sharply dressed in a soft brown leather jacket, brown pants and matching boots, he came closer. Instantly, LaRetha saw that he was someone she should know.

"LaRetha Watson?"

"That's me," she said.

"Right. I'm *Paul* Watson. Nell and *Verry's* son. I got into town early yesterday. How are you, cousin? It's good to finally meet you," he said, smiling broadly and hugging her, tightly.

"I'm fine," she said when she was finally able to breathe, again. "And same here."

She introduced Kellen. The two men exchanged greetings, and considering his stocky, muscular body, his short curly black hair and big smiling eyes, there was no doubt that he as indeed *Verry's* son.

"So, you're here for the weekend?"

"Yes, with my wife Valerie, and our two boys. I surprised everybody by actually coming, this year. We'll be here until Sunday evening. Everybody's here this year."

"That's great," she said.

"We live in *LA,* and with our busy schedules, it's just hard to get away. That's Valerie's home, so it's been much more practical to spend holidays with her folks, and come here in summer when travel is better. But, my folks weren't hearing it, this year," he said, laughing a lot like his father.

"Well, I'm glad you could make it," she said.

"Not very much has changed about this town since I left over thirteen years ago. But, I knew you right off, LaRetha. You still look a lot like your baby pictures."

"I sure hope not." She kidded, and they laughed. "We're going into the donut shop. Do you want to join us?"

"Sure. I could use a cup of hot coffee. I had forgotten just how cold this place is, in winter. I've been spoiled in that California climate."

"It is cold. LaRetha is used to it now, I guess," Kellen joked, as Paul walked a few steps ahead and held the door.

"What'll you have?" The young counter girl asked, smiling at them from behind the counter.

"What do you want, sweetheart?" Kellen asked, hugging her close. The girl raised an eyebrow and LaRetha glowed inside.

"One *glazed* with a cup of hot cocoa for me."

"And you?" The girl asked Paul.

"Sounds good. How about you, Kellen?"

"Same thing. Make that *three*."

Kellen suggested they get a table while he waited for the food. Paul pulled out a chair for her, and she noticed the confused looks a couple seated nearby were casting in their direction. She smiled and greeted them, and they did the same. She had forgotten how much attention strangers could get in *Lovely*. They were probably noticing the similarities in her features and Paul's. He greeted them as well.

"My father told me about your break in. We've always had drifters coming through town, but usually in better climate. And I don't recall much of that in this area, before. Too bad for him, though. Do you know why he was there? I heard he sometimes drifted to Atlanta."

She smarted at this.

"No. I don't know too many white, male homeless people on a personal basis," she retorted. "As long as I lived in Atlanta, I never had anything like this happen. But here, where you would least expect it, I've already been threatened with lawsuits, almost was assaulted and had to shoot a man who died of mysterious circumstances. *Me* of all people."

She noticed Kellen frowning at Paul as he approached with their tray, obviously having overheard. Disbursing the food, he sat down.

"I didn't mean it the way it sounded. It's just odd that a person would break *in* when you came home, instead of running in the opposite direction. What was he after, I wonder?"

"It could have been as simple as the man wanting money from her," Kellen interjected.

"We don't know yet," she said. "But we're checking into it."

"Good. And you're doing alright?"

"*Fine*. I hate to sound unfeeling, but at least I know I don't have to worry about him coming back. I'm just concerned about the way he was killed, and why anybody would want him dead."

"I know. It's something to think about, huh?" Paul drank from his steaming cup of cocoa.

"It gave us all a scare, but it's over now," Kellen said, clasping his hand over hers. She smiled at him, with gratitude.

"Let's hope so," Paul said, frowning.

"I know you're just here from LA, Paul, but what's going on with the recent fires in town?" She inquired.

Paul hesitated, before slowly shaking his head, as if dismissing the thought.

"I don't know. My father seems to think it's all just some prank, or somebody's attempt to get some insurance money."

"But, wasn't somebody killed in one of the fires?"

"Yes, some federal guy who was snooping around, although nobody seems to know why he was even out there, in the first place. Those folks haven't farmed that land in years. They're talking about selling."

"*Hmmm*. It's ironic, isn't it? All these things happening around the same time? Do you know if they have any suspects?"

"I don't think there's any connection, LaRetha," he quickly said. "It's not unusual for somebody to get careless with their heater, around here. You might even want to check your heating system, soon. And I know just the person to do it. My dad fixes everything."

"Thanks, but that's not necessary," she laughed, remembering his father's comments about being considered an *everything man,* of sorts. "I'm okay for now."

"Okay, then."

"So, what do you do for a living, Paul?" Kellen asked, and she was happy someone had changed the subject.

"I write for television shows. *Taylor, Todd & Tadd* and *The Big Badder Squad.* Shows like that," he said.

Reaching into his pocket, he found a business card. Writing his number on the back, he handed it to LaRetha, who read it and handed it to Kellen. He looked at it and gave it back to her.

"Your father never told me that," LaRetha exclaimed. "That's a coincidence. I'm a writer, too. Mostly freelance. We both are. I guess it runs in the family, huh?"

"My dad rarely mentions it to anybody. He didn't think it was real work for a man. When I left for college, he wanted me to stay and help him out with the farm, but I couldn't. Neither could my brother Dave. He's living in San Francisco and that's a whole other story. Dad's kind of disappointed in me, in spite of my six figure salary, *five thousand square foot* home and private schools for my two kids. He's just set in his ways, I guess."

"So, how did you get into that?" Kellen asked.

"Through a college contact. The wife of a professor friend does the same thing. He always appreciated my writing, so he got her to turn me on to a few people. I did a few things here and there before I got a break. I interviewed and within a month I was hired."

"You make it sound so easy," she said.

"Not really. There was a lot of down time in between those jobs. Fortunately, I have a very understanding and supportive wife. I tell her all the time that she doesn't even have to work now. But, she doesn't want to hear me. Valerie's got this *independent* attitude, you know."

"*Go on, Valerie!*" She said, playfully cheering with a napkin, making him laugh.

"Pops thought I was crazy, going out there to school. But, staying here meant depending on him, and that just didn't appeal to me. I never really had the tenacity for farm living or electronics, anyway. So, I'm glad this worked out. He's slowly coming around, though. I've finally convinced him that I never deserted him. We both just did what we had to do."

She understood. More than he would ever know.

"Those are some great shows, too," Kellen added. "*Classy!* Especially the *Big Badder Squad.*"

"Thanks, man." Paul appeared duly complimented.

"Think there's room for another writer?" Kellen asked. "I write some, too. And that might be just the thing," Kellen said and she winced.

"Are you planning to move to California anytime soon? 'Cause that's what it would take."

"I've never considered it before… But hey, it's a thought," Kellen said, ignoring the frown on her face.

"Let me know and I'll see what I can do. Can't make any promises. I don't call those kinds of shots. But, if you know you have what it takes, then it's a worthwhile risk. For me, it was, anyway. And if they can take me, they'll take anybody." He laughed. LaRetha smiled, halfheartedly.

"I'm sure you're very good," she said.

"So they say," he said, with very little modesty, which caused them all to laugh.

Paul finished his doughnut, hurriedly wiped his mouth on a red paper napkin and stood up.

"I hate to run, but I'm late meeting *Pops*. Listen, it's been a long time since we've all seen one another, and most of us haven't met you, LaRetha. Did you know about the party at my folks' place, tomorrow night? You both should come."

"Yes, your mother invited us."

"Okay. *Saturday*, then. It's always a big deal. Everybody in town usually comes. There's always great food, music and great company. It should be fun."

"We'll be there." She said, hugging her cousin goodbye. He quickly shook hands with Kellen.

"*Later*, man," Kellen said. And Paul left.

Noticing her wry expression, Kellen sat down his nearly empty cup.

"Did I do something wrong?" His eyes flashed with annoyance as he sat back in his chair.

"Did you really have to ask him about a job the first time you met him? Couldn't that wait until Saturday night? You know, after you've worked you way up to it?" She asked with attitude and irritation.

"I know you're not upset with me about that, LaRetha."

"I just wish you hadn't come across like you needed something from him. I'm just beginning to know them. I wouldn't even ask them for anything, just yet."

"I wasn't *begging*, LaRetha. That's *business*. I did what he's already done to get his own job. *I asked.*"

She felt his wrath, and was ready to respond with her own.

"I just think that, with the invitation and all, it might have been better to get to know him, first. He might have made the offer to you."

Kellen pushed back from the table and looked at her long and hard, and almost expressionless.

"*You know what, LaRetha?* I don't think he believes I'm some desperate person. And I can't believe that you were even embarrassed at my bringing it up. If anything, *you* could have plugged me a little. Or at least, shown some enthusiasm on my behalf."

She finished her drink and reached for her purse.

"I just think you could have been more subtle. These people aren't Hollywood scouts, Kellen. And this *isn't* Atlanta. They're my family! If you'd said you wanted another job, I could have put a word in for you. But, silly me, I thought you had one. *My bad!*"

He squinted at her, his eyes reddening. His face tightened.

"LaRetha...." He balled his fist and shook it in the air. She gave him a look that said, *I dare you.* "I won't even say it. I'm ready to go."

"So am I."

She was done with arguing, anyway.

Putting on her coat, she walked out as Kellen held her door. They walked to her car in silence.

LaRetha hated that they had fought, but she also didn't like feeling used, or that Kellen's behavior might have suggested as much to Paul. He should have discussed it with her first, she thought.

She could already hear what her mother would say. *What did I tell you, girl?*

Starting the car, Kellen's eyes avoided hers as she sat facing him.

"Kellen, I don't want to fight."

"*We won't!,*" He turned the steering wheel and slowly backed from the parking space and drove toward the interstate. She guessed the shopping spree was over.

The quiet drive home bothered her. She had never seen him this angry. Maybe she had used the wrong approach, she thought. But he needed to know her feelings. Still, was it worth them being angry at one another?

"*I'm sorry* that we disagree," she finally said. He didn't respond. "I just wish you had considered my feelings. It's just…"

"I know what it is, LaRetha. You've let these people and this place change you, and your feelings about me. We never used to disagree. And we didn't need *rules*. You used to trust me. But now, I can't say or do anything right. I don't understand it."

"*I* haven't changed, Kellen. Our relationship has. Before, we were just very good friends. But, we crossed that line a while ago. We've got a new situation, now. And, everything won't be so easily resolved."

"You think I don't know this? Look, I'm trying to be what I think you want, LaRetha…"

"But, that's just it. You don't have to *try*. Be the same Kellen Kincaid I knew in Atlanta. *That's* what I want. And it's not me that's changed, it's the circumstances."

He was quiet for a moment. Took her hand.

"So you *do* want me?" He asked. She couldn't answer. After reading her expression, he smiled. Nodding, he said nothing for a while.

"I didn't try to embarrass you back there, LaRetha. But, I don't think I should feel bad about it, either. Paul will help me out, or he won't. Either way, I'll never mention it, again. Whatever makes you happy, okay?" His face was solemn, now.

LaRetha couldn't tell if their fight was ending or just beginning. Settling back into her leather seat, she hummed to the radio, hating the fact that they had fought about this. She so wished that things were different and that Germaine was here for the holidays.

"Let's go get a Christmas tree," Kellen said. It was dark out, aside from the glow of the porch lights.

"Right now?"

She was sitting comfortably on a chair in the living room, dressed in a loose fitting beige sweater and jeans, and studying her fingernails as she painted them glittery beige.

"Sure. It's early, still. Only eight-thirty. You remember how late we used to stay up, in Atlanta? Besides, something has got to be open in this ghost town."

"*Careful,* with that 'ghost town'," she said playfully. "Everything shuts down around six. But, I'm sure the tree lots are still open. You can go on, if you like. I have to finish my hands and my toes," she added, nasally.

"You're kidding me, right? You would send me out there with the lions, tigers and bears, just to get *you* a Christmas tree while you paint your fingers and *toes?* I am so disappointed!" He grabbed her chin and kissed her flatly on the lips.

"Don't be. I do it all the time. There's nothing scary out there."

"So you say," he teased, as he put on his shoes and coat. "I've only been here for three days, and I'm scared, already."

She couldn't help thinking he had good reason to be.

"*Sorry.* But as you can see, my nails are still wet."

"*Excuses.* Well, is there any particular kind of tree you want?"

"Tall. *Real* tall. I have plenty of ornaments around here, some-where. In the attic, I think."

"Forget it. I'll buy some more. I'm not scrambling around in your old dusty attic."

"I was hoping you'd say that."

"So, where is this tree lot?" He asked with feigned impatience. Smiling, she directed him back toward town where most of the lots were on the same road.

"Be back in a minute."

He got his coat and she felt the cold air rushing in as he left. She imagined he would have cabin fever, right about now. With him gone, though, the house was disturbingly quiet.

Her phone rang.

"It's me, sweetheart. Miss me yet?"

"Kellen! You haven't even turned the corner, yet."

"But, you do, don't you?"

"You know I do," she whispered, playing along.

"Call you when I get there."

Hanging up, she was happy that their fight had officially ended. She didn't want to lose Kellen. The more time they spent together, the more she could admit to having deep feelings for him. The thought that he was envious of Douglas Davis amused her. Granted the man was fine. *Real fine,* when she thought about it. But Kellen could hold his own with her. He just needed to know that.

She would miss him when he was gone. The way he smiled at her so seductively from across the breakfast table each morning, and how he sang so loudly and out of key in the shower. She would especially miss having someone take charge and do things around the place the way he did, and without acting as if she owed him something for it. Once she summed it all up, she was really happy that he was here. And despite their disagreement, he appeared to be happy, to.

Another hour passed before he called again, describing just about every type of tree on the lot. Finally selecting one, he said he was on his way back. Advising him to be careful, she waited. A familiar knot coiled in the pit of her stomach as she remembered all those stories of people dying on the road - their cars found in ditches once the snow melted.

What a terrible fate that would be for Kellen! But, he was a safe driver who never took chances on the road. Still she sat waiting, and looking out of the living room window until he returned.

"What took you so long? Town is just eight miles away. You were gone for over two hours."

"*Worried?*" He asked smiling deviously as he brought the huge tree inside, and stood it against one corner in the living room.

"No. Just making sure my other man got out of here in time."

"He'd better be out of here in time, if he knows what's good for him," he snarled, taking off his coat and gloves, and sitting down to loosen the straps on his boots.

"Not too many people out, tonight." He fell clumsily on the sofa beside her and kissed her, sideways.

"I'm not surprised, " she said, lying back against her sofa pillows and watching him. "Most of them are probably at home finishing off their turkeys and yam."

"*Yam?* Do people still say *yams?*"

"*Funny.* Well, *your* yams will be ready, shortly. Are you hungry?"

"All the time. But, I know that country folks eat on time, hungry or not," he teased.

"*Shush!* If I didn't feed you, you'd really complain."

He followed her into the hall bathroom where she went to wash her hands. Standing behind her in the mirror, he appeared to be checking the two of them out as a couple. He stood over her by at least four inches, and his well-toned body had obviously been getting a good workout at the gym. But, she wasn't bad herself, she thought. Kellen pulled her hair back and planted several kisses on her neck.

"You're beautiful. Why don't you know how beautiful you are?"

"*Humph!* So then, do you think you even deserve me?" She teased, dancing in the mirror.

"I doubt it," he said, leaving the bathroom, smiling mischievously at her reflection.

"I'll take that as a compliment, *thank you very much!* She called out to his receding back.

He was rambling around in his bedroom, singing to himself, and it occurred to her that one thing was for certain – Kellen loved her. And she could finally admit that she was slowly falling in love with him, too.

Playfully, she held her hand up in the mirror, watching the ring as it twinkled and reflected in her eyes.

"*Vanity is a sin"* he called out from the hallway as he passed by. "I'm setting the table. I can't wait for you to stop making out with yourself. A man could starve to death."

He did just that, and by the time she got there, their plates were filled and he'd even prepared more tea.

"Your secret is out. You set a better table than I do," she teased. "How long was I in there?"

"For almost half an hour. Don't you know that a single man is usually a hungry man? Women these days still don't know what their grandmama's knew. But thankfully, I can do this for myself. And I don't have to deal with the drama queens who would do it for me."

She sat down with him and he bowed his head as she said *grace*. She figured this was a sign that they were making progress, and sipped her tea before continuing the conversation.

"You talk like a *woman hater*." She watched as he began to eat.

"Not at all. I just *hate* dealing with a possessive *woman*. And that's something that you are not. As a matter of fact, I'm starting to rethink that philosophy."

"*Hmm*," she muttered, her mouth full.

Even with hardly an appetite, the food was great, once again. Then, she remembered *Straiter*, and a lot of mixed feelings began to arise. There was the possibility that she might be charged for his death. And, despite what Douglas Davis said, that possibility was very real to her.

Then, there was the anticipation of the party on tomorrow night. Not to mention the fact that she had an extremely desirable man bumping around in her kitchen right now who had serious ideas about how they should fill the rest of their evening. Admittedly, the more her problems compounded, the more she craved the intimacy. And the harder it was to keep turning him away.

All these thoughts and feelings had her mind reeling. There were some things about being married that, admittedly, she did miss. She prayed for strength.

"What're you wearing Saturday?" She asked Kellen after dinner, as he looked through her CD collection, tossing more of them in the 'don't like' pile than in the 'do like'.

"Do I look like I want to talk about my wardrobe? I am *not* one of your girlfriends," he kidded, putting on an R&B Classics CD. "Let's dance. You probably need the practice. I don't want you embarrassing me at the party."

She hit his shoulder playfully. "As *if*. Don't get left behind when I do my turn, like *this*," she said, doing an awkward twirl and stopping in a silly ballet-like pose. He shook his head, covering his laughing mouth with his hands.

"What you got? Let me see?" She challenged in boxer-like fashion.

He read a CD cover and selected a Grover Washington, Jr. song.

"*Mister Magic?* I thought I lost that when I moved."

"No, but let's see if you've still got it."

He swirled her and they danced together rather awkwardly, at first. Until, exasperated, he leaned her back and looked down into her face. "Would you let me lead, *please?"*

She did and found that he did a rather nice job, as he turned her, leading this time.

"You've been practicing. So that's what you do when I go to bed?" She exclaimed, impressed that he moved so smoothly.

"Nope. I used to help out at my aunt's dance school. *Hated it!* But it does come in handy when I'm trying to impress the ladies. Are you impressed?"

"Always," she said, breaking away and into a funky chicken, the dip and the slide.

"*Oh, man.* Don't ask me to dance with you at the party, okay?"

"Just don't complain if you have to stand in line."

Later that evening, the phone rang. *Uncle Verry.* They had way too much food, and wouldn't she and Kellen come over? Everyone was there and anxious to see her.

She looked at the clock and grimaced. It was already *9:00pm.*

"Well, if it's not too late."

"Not at all," he said, sounding pleased.

It took Kellen all of fifteen minutes to change clothes, and to wait for her by the door. He helped her into her coat, and out to his car which was waiting in front with its engine running.

Approaching the wide, brick three-level home, Kellen whistled. Settled in the middle of a big beautiful corner lot, this house was four times the size of hers, at least.

And Therell complained about a lackluster upbringing? She thought with disbelief.

Several cars were parked along the driveway, and the outside of the house was grandly decorated with white lights and huge red ribbons.

A young girl opened the door with a smile, and as they entered, they both instinctively inhaled, embracing the aroma of food, cinnamon and other spices. And if the outside of the house was spectacular, the inside was no disappointment.

The house was exquisitely furnished and decorated for the holidays. Extra loud voices were coming from the den, and she could see that *Uncle Verry* was standing right in the middle.

He beckoned for them to come inside. They were greeted with *hellos* and hugs.

"Everybody, this is my niece, LaRetha. She's cousin to most of you. She has recently moved back here from Atlanta - hopefully, to stay. This good-looking young man is her friend, Kellen Kincaid, also from Atlanta. And you two, *this is everybody*. Make yourselves at home."

With few places left to sit, Kellen found a place on a floor cushion with several people playing video games on a huge flat television screen mounted on one wall. He motioned for her to sit beside him. She begged off, watching from a bar stool and admiring the way he'd just fallen in with them, so easily.

This was a very nice room. Big and marvelously decorated with two large brown leather sectionals that faced the television screen and that was filled to capacity with people. Contemporary furnishings were scattered about. Pictures, plaques and trophies were tastefully mounted and displayed behind lighted glass cabinets. Track lighting threw an alluring glow over the room.

Most appealing were the large windows that parted to expose acres of backyard, also decorated with white lights that made the snowy view beyond the house appear beautifully serene and undisturbed.

Wanting to see more of the house, she wandered toward the kitchen where there were more voices. She admired the huge country kitchen from the doorway, along with its long countertops and center bar where brass pans hang overhead.

Hand painted ceramic tile accentuated the walls and coordinated with burgundy mini-blinds. Best of all, there were even more windows here – an entire wall of them – extending from the countertop to the ceiling. She imagined it made for a very pretty sight, mornings.

Nell and four other women were working at the island, not noticing her at first.

"Hello, everybody," LaRetha said, greeting them. Everyone looked up. Nell immediately broke into a smile.

"*Girrrl!* Come on in here. I was just telling everybody that you were coming. I knew your uncle wouldn't let you miss this chance to meet everybody." Her aunt walked around the island from where she had been pouring vegetables from a glass bowl into a plastic container, and gave her an endearing hug. "How are you, *sweetie?*"

Nell looked absolutely stunning in a pale green sweater and skirt at just the right length to make her appear taller than 5'4", as did her matching suede high-heeled boots.

"I'm just fine. And you?" She asked, returning the gesture.

"Wonderful, dear. You and your friend just missed dinner. He is here, isn't he?"

"Yes, he's here," she said, smiling. "That's okay about dinner. We've eaten. We just came to say hello to everybody."

"You look *fantastic!*" Her aunt stood back, admiring her lavender beaded sweater over black pants and silver belt. "Like a *teenager*. What's your secret?"

"Looks to me like you already know," she complimented. "And those *shoes!* I've never seen a pair quite like those."

"Well, if y'all are through admiring one another," one of the other women interrupted, "we'd like to meet our cousin, too."

"LaRetha, these two ladies," Nell pointed at the two women who were sitting at a table and writing names on a list of some kind, "are *Verry's* sisters, Carole and Rita. His brother John couldn't come. He's overseas. And *this* dear young lady sitting at the bar would be my second oldest daughter, *Bernice.*"

Getting up to hug her, Bernice smiled, looking every bit like her mother in height and stature. LaRetha thought she was very pretty.

"Hello, LaRetha. I've heard so much about you. You're just like *Watson,* just like they said," she said, matter-of-factly.

"Thank you. It's good to finally meet everybody."

"And I'm kinda clean too, don't you think?" Bernice began modeling her tight jeans and matching jeweled jacket. Possibly no older than thirty, she was obviously full of energy. And between her and her mother, she clearly had the stronger personality.

"That is simply *gawgeous,* and it fits you so well," LaRetha said admiringly, with an exaggerated southern accent. They all laughed.

"You haven't met *Valerie,* Paul's wife. He told us he ran into you guys in town, today."

"He did. And he's so nice. So much like his dad," she said. They agreed. "Hi, Valerie," she said to the friendly faced woman standing beside Bernice. "It's nice to meet you."

If anyone, Valerie was the gorgeous one. A model type, she was tall and slim with naturally long brown hair, dark eyes and exotic features that made it hard to distinguish her nationality, at first. She was about Bernice's age, as well. She stopped putting food into plastic containers to speak to her.

"So, you've met my husband? He's a character, *huh?*"

Definitely one a' us, she thought, recalling the grocer's comments.

"He's the spitting image of *Uncle Verry.* I would have known him anywhere, I think."

"He used to be *mean,*" Bernice interjected. "I guess married life has mellowed him out, a bit. We actually had a conversation today without him disagreeing with me."

"Well, I'm still waiting for that one," Valerie said, to their amusement. Clearly she loved her husband, but found pleasure in affectionately pointing out his shortcomings, as did his sister.

"If you've met Paul, then you know that he and Valerie live in *L.A.,*" Nell quipped, proudly. "He's a writer and she's a program manager at a radio station," she said, proudly.

"Bernice lives in Tennessee. All my other offspring are congregating in the den, I guess. Where is *Jasmine?*" she asked Bernice and Valerie. "I haven't seen her since this afternoon."

"Who knows?" Bernice shrugged, concentrating on trying to get just one more bowl into the full refrigerator.

"Those two are my only girls, the rest are boys. Everybody's here this year, thank goodness. That hasn't happened for over five years. Here, have a seat on this stool and talk to us. How's everything out there on the farm?"

"Well, I'm sure you all heard about my intruder."

"I did, you poor thing," Bernice cooed. "I heard he didn't make it. Somebody suffocated him at the hospital? It was on the news for a whole day."

Valerie shook her head and frowned at Bernice, and then continued with her work.

"I'm avoiding listening to news reports for a while," LaRetha said, trying to smile. Bernice gave her a sympathetic look.

"I sure don't blame you," Valerie said. "I don't know if I could even sleep at night behind all that. You're still planning to stay out there all by yourself?"

They all stopped working to listen to her reply.

"Well, I don't have any plans to move just yet." No one responded. She figured they were in disbelief. *Well, so was she.*

Everyone appeared to contemplate her response. She remembered Laretta's warning. *These people work together,* she had said. She needed to be careful when talking about the farm, she realized. Her problems with Therell were yet to be resolved.

Needing a diversion, she asked for the bathroom and was directed down the hall by Bernice. She returned to find that the work there was finished, and everyone had gone into the den. Bernice saw her coming and steered her into the living room, instead.

"How do you stand it out there, all by yourself?" She asked, and right away, LaRetha could tell that she was also the most inquisitive one. Or maybe just the one designated to get answers.

"Well, I'm not exactly *alone,*" she responded, slowly, wondering where this was going. "I have a friend visiting with me, for right now."

"Oh, yes. I saw your *friend.* And he *is* fine. That's reason enough to never want to leave the house."

She couldn't help but laugh at the comment.

"Well, I don't know about all that. He's a good man. He's just trying to help me get through this."

"I'll just bet," her cousin teased. "Don't look at me like that," she said, nudging her side. "We're country, but we know where children come from. I hear you're divorced. I am, too. I've got three kids and up to my ears in debt. But anything's better than keeping a sorry man or depending on my folks, you know?"

She nodded. *Yes, she did know.*

"Now, *Jasmine!* That's a different story. She's so high maintenance, she can't get enough help. She's got a business and everything, but still can't get enough money. Not to mention that big mortgage and car payment she's got, and the liposuction she had done, last year. Girl, I think if a man pinched her hard enough, she'd pull slap apart."

LaRetha frowned, nodding thoughtfully. Keenly aware of the sibling rivalry that must exist between them.

"Well, lots of people are doing it."

"*She* shouldn't have," the woman added, nonchalantly.

"Let's go into the den with the others," she finally said. There were still people she wanted to meet.

Making a face Bernice conceded and led the way, clearly disappointed at missing an opportunity to further pry into her business, and to tell everyone else's. The others were already there, sitting on their bar stools and watching the television screen.

"Your friend is in here getting the *crap* beat out of him by those kids with that video game," her uncle said. "I never could maneuver those joyful sticks or whatever they call 'em. Too much like work, to me."

Everyone laughed.

"Oh, LaRetha, forgive us," he said. "We didn't introduce you to the boys, and they don't have manners enough to do it, themselves."

"Hey," one young man of about *twenty-five* said, standing to wave from where he sat near his father on the opposite sofa. He looked like both her uncle and Nell. "I'm *Manny*. I'm the youngest son," the cute, curly haired boy said. "That over there is Marvin," he said, pointing to a slightly older young man, who nodded. "Jarvin is his twin, but he just left. You've met Paul," he said. "Those two little boys are *his*."

Paul waved from the floor where he was helping two very small boys assemble a train set.

"And those other kids, they all belong to Bernice," he said, laughing.

"They do not," Bernice quipped. "Only three of them. The other four are Aunt Carole's nieces and nephews on her husband's side.

"Oh," Manny continued. "You'll meet Big Dave. He ate too much so we probably won't see him for awhile."

"Behave yourself," his mother rebuked. "So," she continued. "That's about everybody. Now, Paul tells us you're a writer, too, Kellen?"

He hesitated and she could feel his need to look at her for approval, except he didn't. She looked away, enjoying the fact that he was squirming.

"Well, that was my career. I'm starting another job, next month."

"Oh?" Nell looked at him, questioningly. He didn't elaborate.

LaRetha figured that now, any speculation about whether or not he was here to stay was satisfied.

They stayed for another half hour, making small talk and getting acquainted. Finally, she nudged Kellen to say she was ready to leave. Several people expressed their disappointment.

"We'll come back, tomorrow," she said, before saying goodnight and walking with her uncle to the door. Kellen offered to drive the car around. "Thanks for inviting us. It was great meeting everybody."

"I talked to Douglas Davis earlier, today," he said, walking her to the car. "It'll be after the holidays before he can tell us anything. But, I agree with him that you have nothing to worry about."

"I hope not. But I won't rest until its official," she said, feeling suddenly uncomfortable at discussing it at the moment.

Douglas should have called her with this, himself. She got inside the car as her uncle held the door.

"Everything will be just fine," *Uncle Verry* told her. "You all have a safe trip home. And call us if you need *anything,"* he said with emphasis.

He watched as they drove away. Overall, she felt good about the visit, but found it odd, and a good thing, that no one had mentioned Therell, even once. *Was he still in town?* And if not, did he leave before or after Paul Straiter was killed.

She decided to worry about it later. Kellen was here, and it was still a holiday. And she was determined to enjoy it.

They spent Saturday morning decorating the Christmas tree, before going out into the freezing cold and shoveling the drive and sidewalk - trying to work off some of the stuffiness from their holiday meals.

Later, as Kellen watched television, dozing off from time to time, she worked on her story about the town and local perception of the cause of the fires. But she wouldn't send it yet, she thought. There was more to this story than they were telling her.

Yawning, she finally decided to call it quits. With Kellen here, she was sleeping easier and concentrating on her dilemma less, considering he was doing all he could think of to distract her.

But what if it did happen, again? And what if Kellen couldn't protect her or himself? Or she couldn't defend herself, the next time? Everyone was convinced that she'd been lucky that last time, and she supposed she was. But, that did nothing to ease her concerns.

A feeling of panic overtook her. Fearful and anxious now, she looked for her protection – the guns. She was relieved when she found them where she had left them. She awakened Kellen, insisting he come outside.

"For *what?"* He asked, groggily.

"Come on. I'll be out back."

It was a while before he emerged, looking startled when he found her. Stared at her as if she was out of her mind.

Why did she feel the urge for gun practice all of a sudden? He asked. What was the purpose?

"My uncle gave me a gun after that last incident, and I have one of my own. Come on. Use this one," she said, handing him her gun. "It's just target practice. You might need it if a bear ever came out of those woods. You ever shot one, before?" She asked.

"Never in my life, *Annie Oakley*. But, I get the feeling I'd better learn if I expect to survive out here with you."

She showed him how to load his gun, and where the safety was. Then she watched as he fired his first shot at the cans lined up on the tree stumps. It was a lousy one. She told him so.

"You think I don't know that?" He said, missing another can with three more attempts.

"Here. Look through here, and aim," she said, adjusting the gun upward. He shot and missed twice more before she took her turn. She hit twice out of the next four shots.

"Just how much *ammo* do you have?" He asked, wryly.

"Enough. Now, *concentrate.*"

He was finally able to zoom in on a can and hit it. She said he was getting the hang of it. He shrugged.

"I'm not much of a shooter. Now, Kadero, he loves them. If ever there's a revolution, I'm hanging out with him!"

She agreed. With his interest in *shoot 'em up* video games, and his rifle magazine collection, Kadero's decision to go into the military had come as no real surprise to any of them.

"But, I'll be ready for whatever. Anything, to be able to protect you," he smiled, winking.

Still, she sensed his resentment. But, he didn't understand. He had never been the victim of a violent crime. Had never come face to face with a man like *Straiter,* and had never experienced the panic she'd felt when she thought she wouldn't get to that gun in time.

And now, her life was forever changed with the realization that she had rendered a man helpless enough to be murdered at a time when he was supposed to be recuperating. And that she might be even more unsafe if anyone wanted to avenge his death with her.

Douglas Davis had asked about Kellen's plans. *Was it possible that he suspected him? Or even her?* It was entirely possible, she decided. But, Kellen was with her all night, and if Douglas ever knew Kellen for himself, he would see that he was one of the most levelheaded people she knew. Certainly not one who was capable of taking a life.

Death by asphyxiation. It took a heart of cement to kill a person that way. Something she couldn't even imagine of Kellen. She would make certain that Davis understood this. Kellen was here for her, after all. She owed him as much.

After their practice, she put the guns away, intentionally not revealing their locations to Kellen, who appeared to have no interest in knowing. She told him she was going to take a walk and would be back, shortly.

"Annie, don't forget your gun," he said, only half kidding, from where he sat at her laptop computer, logging onto the internet. She didn't find it funny at all. Protecting herself was no joke. Not out here. He could laugh all he wanted.

"Oh, yeah? Well, just call me if *you* need protection."

Annoyed and exasperated, LaRetha made her way through the snow to the barn and went inside. The icy cold cement floor was damp. She put old remnants of hay in a pile and sat down, putting her head in her hands.

She had hoped that seeing the family last night would help her to figure things out. But, she still couldn't shake that ton of bricks looming overhead. And seeing them, noting their concerns, had done something to alter her perspective, forcing her to confront a reality that would never depart from her.

Paul Straiter was dead. And Kellen wasn't just visiting for the holidays. She could soon face murder charges, and in spite of their friendly reception of her, with all the confusion about land ownership she had the feeling some of them might not mind so much. Most certainly not *Therell Watson.*

Despite her uncle's belief that she owed Therell something, and knowing that she didn't feel the same, he was being more than helpful, right now. And she was certain that Therell Watson wanted this property no less today than he had when he'd come by with threats to take it away.

But where was he now? Why had no one mentioned him last night? Certainly not to spare her feelings. She could just feel the man watching from the wings, waiting for an opportunity to pounce.

Stop it! She told herself. She wouldn't make herself crazy over this. This land was still hers, and she had a great attorney who would make sure that it remained that way. And as long as she kept her wits about her, she could most definitely rise above this, too.

Thoughts of Kellen's proposal made her heart sink. Turning the beautiful cluster of diamonds on her finger, she had to wonder what it truly meant to him. And how he could even afford it. He'd been offended at the donut shop, concerned that she saw him as some sort of *opportunist.* She didn't. But one could never be too careful.

"What should I do? She wanted to scream through the open doors up into the heavens. *Is there even a place in heaven for someone like me? For a believer with blood on her hands?* She wondered. Because, no matter what anyone said, it still felt like cold-blooded murder to her.

Maybe she had been kidding herself, thinking that living a chaste existence out here on this isolated farm would make her life any different from before. Life in Atlanta was never as difficult as this.

Where are you Watson, now that I need you?

Was he looking over her like people said the spirit of loving relatives did? Did he know that she was in this mess? More than anything, why had he put her in this position, to begin with?

Had her father truly been a *good* man? Or, had he, for some reason, set her up to fight some ridiculous and endless battle against people he had supposedly despised, and they, him? How could he have forgotten that he had an older child – a son - if he'd indeed had one? And why had he never mentioned him?

There were so many questions she wished she could ask him, but never would. And Cecelia still hadn't returned her call. Jason had said that someone else was calling for her. A man, he'd said. But Therell claimed he had talked to Cecelia already, while Jason had said he never gave the caller her number. Maybe it wasn't Therell calling her, after all.

She thought of her uncle and smiled. He seemed so happy that she was here. But, could his anger possibly run so deep that he resented her as much as he had her father, but was hiding the fact?

No, she thought. He was doing more to help her than she could ask of anyone whom she barely knew, even a relative. And even if his motives weren't entirely unselfish, it was what he *did* that counted at this point.

Besides, without his help, she'd be in this alone. Despite whatever differences he'd had with her father, he was including her now, and trying to look out for her. And for that reason alone, she should trust him.

The party! It was tonight. Kellen hadn't said anything more about it, but judging by the way he was contentedly lying around the house, she knew he was thrilled about having something to dress up for.

Never one to wear out a welcome, she wasn't exactly looking forward to it, and would have passed it up had he not been there. But, in spite of the intense trepidation she felt inside, or her mother's warning, she couldn't alienate her people, now. Not when they were doing so much to include her.

She bolted the barn door back into place, and made the trek back across the yard to the house. Kellen was dozing on the sofa, so she changed clothes in her bedroom. She started to awaken him, but stopped, He was sleeping so soundly. Stooping, she kneeled beside him to see him, up close. She could see every pore, every angle of his smooth, handsome face.

How lucky I am that he cares about me, she thought. Women were always drawn to Kellen, and for whatever reason, he was drawn to her. He was resilient and devoted to her, and he had a great big heart. And despite their differences, she was glad he was here, still a part of her life.

Unable to resist, she leaned in to kiss him softly on the cheek, trying not to stir him. She yelped as he surprised her by throwing an arm around her neck and pulling her in for a deeper kiss on the lips.

"I could never sleep without you here," he murmured.

Sliding over, he allowed her room to lie beside him.

"Are you okay?" He asked, as she snuggled in and he wrapped his strong arms around her.

"*Fine,*" she responded, turning to face him. "But, I want to say something, and please don't take this the wrong way."

"What is it?"

"Well, first of all, you know how glad I am that you came here. But, I feel so bad about keeping you. You don't have to stay, Kellen. You should go home and get ready for your new job. I'll be fine."

She didn't feel fine, but she couldn't ask him to stay until this was resolved. Who knew when that would be? He had his own life.

He sat up, reached for her right hand. Rubbing the diamond ring, he looked into her eyes.

"This ring hasn't moved, yet. But, I'm a patient man."

"Kellen?" She sighed.

"What, baby? And don't say it again, because unless you really want me to go, I'm not leaving. Not until you feel better, and this mess is over and done."

She nodded.

"Besides, I know what's important in life. So until I know that you are really okay, I'm *staying.* I would never forgive myself if anything ever happened to you."

"You are not responsible for me."

"Yes, I am. And you for me. *Got it?*"

"Kellen?"

"What?"

"Did I ever say I loved you?"

"No, you didn't."

"*Liar.*"

"Say it, again."

"*Again* means repeat. So I did say it."

"I want to hear it again." He demanded and cocked his head to one side, waiting.

"I love you in a lot of ways," she said softly, kissing his cheek.

Dropping his head sheepishly, he finally looked up and into her adoring eyes and smiled.

"I know."

What was she going to wear? Searching through her full closet, she wished she'd taken time to shop for clothing. Her career had taken her many places, but the outfits were usually the same; mixed and matched conservative pieces in neutral colors. Mostly jackets, long blouses over tank tops and skirts, and button downs. Aside from that one big splurge on a shopping spree right after her divorce, much to her mother's delight, she hadn't bought much for herself. But, looking inside her closet now, she couldn't see where that money had gone.

There has to be something here. Pulling out a few items that still had price tags, she narrowed her search down to three outfits; an off-white calf-length dress with intricately woven lace sleeves, a slinky black dress that went everywhere, and a red pantsuit made of soft wool.

She decided that the pants suit looked more festive. Trying it on, she liked the way the jacket hugged her waist and the pants fit her hips not too tightly, but just so. A sheer cream-colored blouse would go perfectly underneath this jacket, she thought. A pair of red and gold heels would finish the look, perfectly.

She set her hair on mid sized rollers, covering it with a silk cap before showering. Her favorite scented lotion, powder and perfume came on afterward, before she sat down at her dressing table to rummage through her minimal supply of make-up.

First skin moisturizer and then foundation. Eyeliner and mascara, a glittery beige eye shadow just lightly over her lids, a touch of natural toned rouge and a matching shade of lipstick completed her look.

Uncurling her hair, she separated and twisted it around her fingers before pinning it up loosely with decorative hairpins and a small barrette, leaving a few tendrils in front to frame her face. Finished now, she sat back to eye her handiwork, and was pleased. The transformation was nothing short of remarkable.

Searching through her jewelry collection, she couldn't help but notice her ring, glimmering in the dimly lit mirror. And suddenly, she decided that if things continued the way they were going, it might not stay on that hand for long.

As usual, he finished dressing first. Standing tall, broad and fit in a black Armani suit, his thin-striped white silk shirt appearing vibrant against his smooth dark complexion. His jaw dropped when she came out of the bedroom.

"You look *beautiful*, LaRetha. More beautiful than I've ever seen you."

"Thank you, but I couldn't very well put you to shame in that suit, could I?" She asked, blushing as he continued to stare. "You look quite handsome yourself, baby," she added, giving him a peck on the cheek.

He twirled her in the floor, still admiring her.

"I hope you don't plan to do this all night," she teased, "It's making me dizzy," she feigned a swoon, finally resting in his arms.

"Not all night. Just for part of it." He kissed her, lovingly. "Be glad that most of the people there will be your relatives, otherwise I'd have to keep you here, at home."

"Hah! Just try it. I don't dress up to sit home and watch the walls."

"Let's go. Before I change my mind," he said, seriously.

Helping her into her coat and allowing her to do the same for him, he led her to the car. And then they drove away, both of them feeling like royalty, going to the ball.

If they had expected a *small* gathering, they were wrong. The festivities were in full swing when they arrived. A line of cars was coming in behind them, and pretty soon, parking would be impossible.

Soulful holiday music played loudly as they approached the house. People were coming and going through the front and side doors. Inside, Christmas lights decorated huge garlands and small trees, and mistletoe hang overhead.

Narrow cafeteria styled tables lined the hallway all the way to the kitchen. Covered with fancy white linen and candle arrangements, they held all types of succulent looking dishes. And everything smelled *delicious*. She exchanged surprised looks with an already smiling Kellen.

Kissing her cheek, he went into the den, while she opted to go into the kitchen, instead. Certain that she would find someone in there to talk to. Valerie was in there alone, and looking quite content.

"Hey, LaRetha. You look fabulous!" She said as LaRetha sat on a stool, across from her.

"Thanks! So do you," she told the beautiful young woman whose fitted black pantsuit and sparkling pink top became her, emphasizing her shapely figure.

"Doesn't she look nice?" Valerie asked Bernice as she walked in, dragging a man who was trying desperately not to spill his punch. He protested as she insisted he follow.

"Hey, LaRetha. Come into the den, when you can," she said. "We're dancing in there." She left with her captive in tow.

"Bernice is the only person our age that I know of, who always insists on dancing at *every* get-together," Valerie laughed.

"She does seem to like having fun. But, I would think you and Paul might get out a lot, living in *L.A.*"

"We do, but it's usually business..."

Suddenly, she as snatched away from the conversation and stood facing her uncle who was standing with arms opened wide, smiling from ear to ear.

"Hey, *baby girl.*" He gave her a big hug. "Glad you could come. Fix yourself a plate and join us in the den. You too, Valerie. You've been quiet all day. We're watching Paul's Thanksgiving video. You'll like it," he beamed, not noticing the frown on Valerie's face.

"*Again?*" She complained as soon as he disappeared, seeming very annoyed. "I didn't come to do Thanksgiving dinner over and over again, did you?"

"Well, it's his party. What can you say?" LaRetha kidded.

"He's been playing that thing all day. They know exactly what's coming up and when. I say when it gets to that point, it's time to show another video." She frowned.

Something was itching Valerie, and LaRetha wasn't really interested in finding out what that was, at the moment. She walked around to taste the deviled eggs Valerie was putting on a platter.

"Obviously, my uncle is very proud of his family, and that includes *you,*" she chided the suddenly disgruntled woman, playfully bumping her shoulder.

"*Humph!*" Valerie responded, but smiled.

"*Hmmm,* these are good!" She took another devilled egg to go.

"Well, I'd better go and grab my date, wherever he is. Catch you later." She was all too happy to leave Valerie in the kitchen, understanding now why she was in there alone.

Her cousin Paul appeared to be in opposite spirits than his wife, moving about and joking with everyone who wasn't otherwise engaged in conversation. He waved her over, introducing her to several old classmates of his. She could tell he was in the midst of showing off, and made a hasty exit to a bathroom in back of the house, where it was quieter.

It was also cooler there. She took her time, stopping to touch up her make-up before exiting the large powder room that led to an even larger bath. Walking down the long hallway, just out of the loudness of the speakers positioned at the front of the house, she could hear voices coming from a room that must have been a bedroom. She started to hurry past, but something compelled her to stop and listen.

Two people, a man and a woman, were in the midst of a heated conversation. Not wanting to be caught eavesdropping, she began a slow pace as she passed, listening intently. The woman was angry about some promise that wasn't kept. And the man was explaining. She couldn't identify either voice, although the both of them were trying but failing miserably at whispering, obviously being too angry to pull it off.

"*But, you promised me…*" The woman was angry, now.

"I know what I told you, but it's just not happening, yet. Give me some time." He was whispering, but speaking hurriedly, as if concerned about someone catching them there.

"*How much time?* It's been months, and nothing's happening. And that is *not* what you promised." The woman's voice faded in and out of audibility as if she was pacing the floor.

"Just take it easy, will you? It's gonna happen." The man was annoyed, it seemed.

"Look, this will have to be done, soon. We only have until the end of the year. Are we going to make it?"

"*We'll make it,*" he said through his teeth, it sounded.

"Well, you just make sure the others know that."

"I'm handling this. *You* deal with *them,*" he said.

The conversation seemed to be wrapping up, so LaRetha hastened back down the hallway, just turning the corner before hearing the bedroom door open.

The music was off, now. Finding Kellen in the den, she sat besides him. Giving her a smile, he put his arms around her shoulders and they sat listening with the others as her uncle explained the video that played on the television screen.

She could see what Valerie had meant. But, by the looks of this place, the man had obviously come a long way in life. He had a right to be proud.

"We love all our family and we're thankful for every one of you coming here. Sometimes, we just need to take time for the really important things. Nothing replaces *family,*" he said, smiling in her direction. Surprised, she returned the gesture.

He talked on, and she thought about Therell. And considering the conversation she'd just overheard in the back room, she couldn't help being uncomfortable with the possibility that his was one of the voices she'd heard. That he *was* there, and that, based on the deadline being discussed, she might soon be confronted for an answer she couldn't give.

"What my father is trying to say is, *enjoy yourselves,* everybody," Bernice piped in. Her father pinched her playfully on the arm

"*Here, here!*" Someone else said, just as music began to play, again.

The *DJ* was nowhere to be seen, but music played in each room at the front of the house. And just when she thought she might hear again, the volume went up. Then as if on cue, furniture was being pushed back against walls and the quick change was amazing. Now, the floor was open for dancing.

She retreated to a seat at the far side of the room, well out of the way. The volume was louder, now. And a few couples were finding their way into the floor to dance.

It had been years since she'd attended a function like this, and that was either for work, or with Gerald; friendly get-togethers, business dinners, awards banquets and luncheons. But, this family gathering was becoming more and more *club-like*.

"You wanna dance?" A young man asked, his eyes shining a bit too brightly, in her opinion. Somewhere, somebody was pouring alcohol.

"No thanks," she said, feeling a hunger pain and weaving her way through a small group gathered near the doorway to get to a food table that was being kept replenished. *Valerie!* She thought.

On a clear plastic plate, she piled wings with celery and dressing, before testing a bit of punch. Finding it safe, she poured a cup. She went back toward the kitchen, trying not to bump into other people moving about, on the way. Now she understood why Valerie was in there.

But, Valerie was gone. Her uncle and Nell were there, instead. Standing over the sink, their backs to her, they were in deep conversation, and sounded very concerned about something. Her instincts told her she might want to know what that was. She approached them and said, *hello*.

They didn't hear her, at first.

"I don't know why he's being so stubborn about this," Aunt Nell was saying under her breath.

"I know. She just needs to get acquainted. He shouldn't be here. He'll just mess it…" he looked up to see her standing in the doorway.

"*Hey, LaRetha*," her uncle said, a little hesitantly.

"I didn't think you heard me speak to you. This food is great," she said, going in. "You do this every year?"

"Sure do," Nell said, glancing at her husband. "Glad you're enjoying yourself."

"Is everything alright? Can I get you anything?"

"I'm fine. I came to see if I could help Valerie with anything," she said.

"Everything is under control, I think," Nell said. "Go ahead and enjoy your family and friends."

"Sure thing."

She left them to find Kellen. She finally did, but didn't like what she found.

"What's wrong?" he asked his eyes a bit too glassy, his head bobbing to the beat of the music. He must have been drinking. She was the designated driver, she supposed. She pulled him aside to talk, privately.

"Kellen, I think something's going on. We might need to just say goodnight and go home."

"Why? What happened?" His face showed disappointment.

"Suddenly I'm seeing Therell all over the place, and I'm just not too cool with that."

"Where? Is he here?" His face registered concern. Maybe she was getting through to him.

"No! Not that I know of. I mean, I don't know. There was a rather heated conversation down the hall. And then my uncle and Nell were in conversation. Something about *him* being here when he shouldn't be. That *him* could only be Therell, and he's the last person I want to see, tonight. So, let's just say our good-byes, okay?"

But, the look in Kellen's eyes told her that it wasn't okay. He wasn't moving toward his coat, either.

"But, I don't understand. You knew all along that these were his people, and they know all about your land troubles. So, why worry about that? Especially, when you don't even know if he's here?"

"Well, I don't plan to be around if he is." She reached between a few coats to pull out her own. "I don't want to discuss land and lawsuits, tonight. We've said our *hellos,* and met everybody. Let's just go. It really wasn't a good idea to come in the first place," she said. But, he stood motionless.

"Look, you know what's going on. How would you feel?" She asked.

He looked puzzled and shrugged, which made her angry.

"I shouldn't have to explain this to you, Kellen. You're my guest, I'm not comfortable and I want to leave. What part of *let's go*, don't you *get?*"

His eyes changed from a faint, watery glow to a glower, as he stood facing her, almost defiantly. She couldn't believe that he was going to be indignant about this. Well, so was she.

"I'm leaving, and I'm taking my car. I'll say my good-byes, and you can come or you can stay, whatever *you* feel more comfortable doing."

"We went through all this trouble to get here and you just want to leave. Just like that?" He wasn't even looking for his coat.

"Just like that! We've been here for over an hour. That's long enough for me," she said, sliding her arm into her coat, this time without his assistance.

"Well, I'll see you at the house. I'll get a lift."

She stood, watching, in disbelief, as he turned away and walked back toward the den.

"Kellen!"

He kept walking, as she stood in the semi-darkness, doing a slow burn. She could imagine her face was as red as her suit, as she told herself to calm down.

But how could she explain leaving if her date was still here, having the time of his stupid life? If she said she was ill, they would wonder why he didn't seem to care. If she said it was an emergency of some kind, they would expect him to go with her, or might even volunteer to drive her. She sighed, having no choice but to go back into the den as if nothing was going on. And to come up with another plan.

He'll see me back at the house, alright, she thought, hanging up her coat.

"Is everything okay?" a gorgeous young woman that she hadn't noticed before asked as she sauntered past.

"*Fine.* Everything's fine," she said, and the woman disappeared as quickly as she had surfaced. LaRetha followed in the direction Kellen had gone, quietly seething.

Shrugging, she found another table of food. Frustration always increased her appetite, and if she continued hanging around Kellen, she figured it was just a matter of time before she added a couple hundred pounds.

But, whoever had prepared this spread was to be commended. These were not the usual party favors; sliced seasoned roast beef, fried chicken and shrimp, spicy turkey meatballs with pasta, crispy fried fish nuggets and several variations of hot wings. Various side dishes filled the next table, and another was covered with desserts. A small corner table held ice, wine and liquors she hadn't heard of. She would need to stay away from that one, she thought. Tasting the food, she murmured her satisfaction. She added more to her plate.

Satisfied that she had sampled almost everything, she accepted a cup of punch from a friendly man who had just poured two for himself and his smiling date. Finding a comfortable bar stool in the corner of the den and the hallway, she sat eating contentedly while watching the others.

I might as well enjoy this, she thought, taking a drink of punch. Kellen was talking with several women, now. Each of them seeming far too interested in what he had to say. It was way past time for him to tear himself away and remember whom he'd come here with, she thought, smarting from his abandonment.

As the evening wore on, she soon forgot about what she had overheard and concentrated on enjoying the people. She sought out conversations with people in the crowd, and was surprised to learn that many of them already knew her as a member of this family; and about her coming to live in *Lovely,* again.

There was talk of children and grandchildren, in-laws, class reunions and wedding anniversaries. *Time had surely flown by,* she agreed. She graciously accepted invitations, gave out her home phone number, receiving several in return. Thankfully, no one even mentioned the shooting.

By now, the holiday music was straight *hip hop.* The beat thumped loudly from overhead and she was getting sure signs of a headache coming on. Maybe she was just becoming some old *fuddy duddy,* she thought. Too much solitude could do that to a person. This hadn't been her scene for some time.

But she was here, now. And this was her family's party. It really wouldn't hurt to *try* and enjoy it, she thought.

But thoughts of Therell and the possibility of running into him were pressing her skull like the constant beat that flowed all around her. She already had more than her share of trouble with the verdict on the shooting being up in the air.

She tried to relax and enjoy watching the older people dominating the dance floor, but she could only enjoy it for a moment before she got that old foreboding feeling, again. Right now, she wanted nothing more than to go home and crawl into her own bed.

But, that wasn't fair to Kellen. And why was she letting Therell intimidate her? That farm and everything on it was *hers*. And, considering her present annoyance with Kellen, she couldn't help but think that he really wouldn't want to show up, right now!

According to her watch, it was *11:55*. And the atmosphere was changed. The children were quickly ushered out and the music had quickly advanced to an edgier style. People were coupling off to dance. And Kellen was making his way over, attempting an apologetic smile, which she duly ignored.

He had almost reached her when someone came over and introduced himself to her as a family friend and asked her to dance. She declined, but could still see Kellen frowning in her direction as he approached. He made his way over, holding a full cup of something thick, dark and unrecognizable. He noticed her frown.

"Bernice said it's made from plums." He held it up for her to see.
Plum wine?

"You really need to be careful with that," she warned.

"Have you changed your mind about dancing?" He asked.

"Oh, are you finally *asking?* I think I'm getting a headache. Maybe later," she begged off.

She didn't want to dance with anyone, or to engage in polite conversation with Kellen. She wanted to leave.

Nodding, he walked away, his wounds quickly forgotten as a young girl asked him to dance.

Just as I thought. She should have insisted on their leaving just now, she thought. But, her aunt and uncle had obviously gone through a lot of trouble to arrange this. And everyone seemed to be having so much fun. Besides, there was nothing better to do at home. And this was rather interesting to watch.

"*LaRetha Greer?* Well, hello. I'm glad to see you out and about," she heard a deep voice say. She turned around to see a familiar face.

Douglas Davis! The man was standing there, smiling down at her and looking nothing like the firm legal professional she'd come to know. Tonight, he was nothing less than gorgeous in a deep berry colored sweater and black pants. And he smelled marvelous, as usual. She met his gaze and smiled.

"Hello, Douglas. I didn't know you were here," she said.

"I just got here. Your uncle absolutely insisted that I drop by, so I did. I thought I might run into you." He smiled and she blushed.

"*Right*. Well, Kellen's here, too. Out there," she said, waving an indifferent hand toward the dance floor. Douglas frowned.

"He's a brave one, leaving you over here unguarded with all these loose cannons running around," he laughed, while unabashedly looking her up and down. "As lovely as you're looking tonight, somebody could snatch you away."

"Thank you, for the compliment," she said.

A safe, fast tune was playing, and as usual, Bernice was herding people onto the dance floor, threatening those who wouldn't oblige her with bodily harm.

"That Bernice doesn't play when it comes to her fun and games, does she?" he stated, jovially, showing off two dimples she hadn't noticed before.

"You're right about that. I caught a headache a while ago, and she's still going strong."

"Can I get you something? An aspirin, maybe? Or, we can go into the living room where it's quieter. It's rather warm in here."

Just what the doctor ordered, she thought, following him as he made a path in the crowd, while feeling the pressure in her head lessen with every step.

He led her to a chair in the near empty living room and went to find aspirin, returning to find her pressing her temples on either side to ease the pain. After taking two of the pills he offered, she sat quietly, waiting for the throbbing to stop. Finally, it eased.

"Thank you, Douglas, for the suggestion and the aspirin," she said. "I feel better, already."

Douglas sat next to her, watching her with concerned eyes.

"Too much to drink?" He asked.

"Not me. Too much to eat, maybe," she responded. He laughed.

"It's good that you don't drink. Very good," he responded.

The beat of the music slowed, and with the relief from her pain came a sudden awareness of her environment. Aromatic candles burned and the fireplace flickered, making the atmosphere feel far too romantic. And sitting this close to Douglas under dimmed lighting seemed much too intimate. She moved further down on the sofa.

But she needn't have worried, because a couple asked to borrow him for a moment and instantly pulled him away. Her own date was still not lacking dance partners. She also noticed that he had been twirling the same woman for some time. It was the woman from the foyer.

Humph! She thought. Not one to be made a fool of, especially not at her own uncle's house, she figured it was about time to cut in. She headed in their direction, but Douglas was coming back. He stopped her.

"Leaving so soon?"

"Not yet."

"Then you must dance with me, at least once," he said, surprising her by pulling her with him, leaving her no chance to argue.

"I'm sorry, Douglas. It's this headache, you know?"

"*Come on.* One won't hurt."

Refusing to take *no* for an answer, he led her to the center of the room. And as if on cue, a slower jazz tune began to play. He casually took her hand into his, placing his other one lightly at her waist. And after a moment, she decided it was okay. Her headache was gone. And for a moment, they were practically floating, it seemed. She just hoped that her inattentive date was taking it all in.

After a while, she looked up to see that her dance partner was smiling down at her.

"You dance very well, Douglas. Do you go out, often?" She asked.

"Hardly ever," he responded.

She was glad to hear this, thinking how much she would hate to think that he was out partying a lot, when he should have been concentrating on her legal matters.

"But, you're pretty good, yourself. Do *you* go out often?" He asked.

"Hardly ever," she repeated. "Not for a really long time. But, this is nice. I've enjoyed meeting everybody."

"Well, at the risk of sounding redundant, I have to say that you look *fantastic*, tonight," Douglas said, leaning in close to her ear. "I almost didn't recognize you out of your farming clothes," he said, grinning.

"*Oh really?* Well, I almost didn't recognize you out of that stiff business suit."

"*Touché!*" He laughed. "I see your date is fully enjoying himself," he commented more soberly.

"Isn't he though?" She tried to sound nonchalant, while finding the fact neither amusing, nor one that she would discuss. "So, you're here alone, tonight? No date?"

She found it hard to believe, but Douglas nodded, turning her slightly without missing a step. It appeared that everyone was doing the same *two-step*, and she figured the late evening and the drinks were wearing on them.

Watching him dance, she found it odd that a man like him would be alone during the holidays, even in this tiny little town. *Especially*, in *Lovely*. There had to be at least twenty other single women in this room alone, that were obviously *looking*. Except, he did say he'd had plans for Thanksgiving dinner. But that wasn't her business, either.

He moved a bit closer. *Careful,* she thought. She didn't want to appear inappropriately interested in the man. And she certainly didn't want people to think that she was spreading herself around, although he didn't seem the least bit concerned.

The song ended and she quickly excused herself, taking the opportunity to find the bathroom. Coming out of it was Bernice.

"Having fun, LaRetha?" The woman smiled at her mischievously.

"It's very nice. Thanks for inviting us."

"I see you've run into Douglas. I'm surprised to see him. And Kellen seems to be having a good time. I wouldn't leave him for too long if I were you. But that's just me."

I hadn't planned to, she thought, as the woman retreated down the hallway. Douglas met her coming back. And his presence made her suddenly uneasy. She turned her wristband to look at her watch.

"Have you seen Kellen? I'm about ready to go, now," she murmured, making light of an openly disturbing situation. She knew where he was. All she had to do was look for his dance partner's tight green dress and big alluring smile.

Douglas shrugged, obviously unconcerned about Kellen's whereabouts. His eyes settling on her ring.

"Are you and Kellen engaged, LaRetha?" He asked, puzzled.

"I just asked if you'd seen him. It's not like we're late for a wedding."

He laughed, but was only distracted for a moment.

"So, is your friend leaving after this weekend?" He asked, watching her closely.

"Is this a personal question or a professional one?" She asked.

"Everything that we discuss tonight is off the record. So, don't worry about that," he said, drinking from a half-full cup of fruit punch and popping a salted walnut into his mouth.

"I'm not sure. He said he'd stay as long as I needed him to."

"Why would you need him to?" He asked in such a way, she almost thought she hadn't heard him right. *How was this any of his business?*

"What?" She asked.

"I asked you," he said a bit louder, "why you felt you needed him to? You don't feel threatened or anything like that, do you?"

"No, but better safe than sorry. Until we can figure out why that man was in my house, and why he was killed, I feel much better having Kellen here. I know it might sound silly..."

"*Not at all.* I understand. You're a woman living alone. And after what you've been through, you should be concerned. Just remember that I'm here if you need me. Call me anytime, for any reason. Okay?"

Surprised, she looked into his big brown pools of intensity, and wondered if it was the atmosphere messing with her normally clear head, or if she was really feeling as if she could fall right into them. Suddenly, someone accidentally bumped her arm. She looked around to see that it truly was no accident. It was Kellen.

"You pushin' up on my girl, Davis?"

His speech was clear but his eyes were strange. And, he was quite serious. His jacket was off now and he was sweating through his shirt, which was partially unbuttoned. And all she could think of was that she wished he would just go away. But her moment with Douglas was ended, which was probably a good thing, she realized. Kellen's mission had been accomplished.

"Excuse me, I see someone I need to talk to for a moment. Enjoy your evening," Douglas said to her and Kellen.

"*Remember what I said,*" he said more closely to her ear as he walked away, clearly not caring if Kellen overheard.

She remained where she was, looking at Kellen, hoping he could see her anger and disappointment in him.

"Are you ready to leave, now?" She asked, looking at his slightly disheveled appearance. "I think we've both had enough for the night. Let's go while you can still walk."

She could smell alcohol on his breath as he stood close to her, and his body heat as sweat beaded on his forehead. His eyes softened, and she hoped that he was finally seeing the sense in what she was saying. She started to relax. Kellen would do the right thing. They would leave now.

But, she was mistaken, for his look suddenly became hostile, again. The change was unsettling and she felt uncomfortable under his mocking gaze.

"What's your hurry, *beautiful?* I saw you and the lawyer looking all comfortable over here in your quiet little corner. If you like, I can give you a little more time. Maybe he can make you a proposition you can't refuse, since I can't."

"You are being really silly, right now." She sighed. "But, if you can tear yourself away from *Luscious* long enough, I'll drive you home."

He said nothing.

"Let's *go*, Kellen!" She hissed, not really caring that her voice was loud, now. Or that people were watching. He was embarrassing the both of them, anyway, she figured.

"No!" He said with finality, before walking away.

LaRetha steamed. She didn't like this man very much, right now. This game was so familiar. He was trying to punish her for not being intimate with him, and for holding another man's attention, despite his own actions. Well, she thought, he would suffer before she did!

It was *1:25 am*, now. All the conservative folks had gone, and her uncle and Nell had turned in for the night. Liquor was poured openly, now. And the younger men were becoming considerably bolder about asking the women to dance.

Fine for them, she thought. She was about to retreat into the kitchen, and asked herself why she didn't just leave Kellen here. But she had a feeling she would regret that decision. She couldn't stop him from drinking, but she could at least keep him from crashing on her uncle's sofa. *Or some place worse,* considering his dance partner for most of the night. She would see him home, she decided. After that, she didn't care what he did!

She looked at the time, again. She wanted to relax, but couldn't. Her thoughts went immediately to Douglas, and she felt a pang of guilt. Apparently, neither she nor Kellen were thinking rationally tonight.

"Jasmine! Where in the world have you been?" Bernice was asking.

She turned around just as a strikingly attractive woman entered the den. Tall and slender, round faced with very smooth clear skin, Jasmine wore a flaming red razor cut hairstyle in a thick mane of hair that reached just to her shoulders. Even in the dim lighting, she looked fabulous in a tailored gray pantsuit that was similar to LaRetha's outfit, and very high heels. She appeared cool and confident, greeting several people with hugs and kisses.

LaRetha watched curiously from a distance. *So, this was Jasmine!* She had certainly made herself scarce over the past couple of days, she thought, finding the woman's late entrance to the event somewhat interesting.

Like everyone else there, LaRetha looked on with both admiration and amusement as her cousins carried on a Watson Family dance contest, which she declined to participate in, finding it much more fun to watch.

How nice it must be to have so many brothers and sisters, she thought. Particularly ones who cared so much for one another.

She wondered what Thomas and Andrew were doing right now and hated that she hadn't contacted them before the holidays. Then, she thought about her baby, Germaine. She sighed. Prayed that he was well.

As for Kellen, she'd had just about *enough.* Fully annoyed now, she walked toward them. *He was leaving if she had to drag him home by his shirt collar.*

Seeing her approach, the woman touched his arm, nodding in her direction. Spotting her as she came their way, Kellen smiled at her, and the woman quickly walked in the opposite direction.

Tramp! She thought.

"I know, I know," he said, nodding and raising his hands, defensively. "You're ready to leave. Right after I find the men's room. I'll meet you at the front door. *Five minutes.* I promise."

Not giving her time to respond, he quickly headed down the back hallway. She closed her eyes a moment and sighed heavily. She hadn't planned on being anybody's keeper, tonight.

He was finally being reasonable, she thought. Maybe it was a good thing that they had come after all, she thought. Now, she knew the right answer to his proposal.

Kellen loved her, but that wasn't enough. Love alone wouldn't keep them together. For her, *respect and consideration* were just as important. And it was evident to everyone present tonight, Douglas in particular, that this much was sadly lacking.

But Kellen's rude display might have been to get her attention. That woman who'd been cornering him all night couldn't have meant anything. He was simply showing off. But all that she could be certain of was what she knew right now. And right now, it didn't appear that this would work out between them.

She managed to get past Douglas without interrupting his conversation. They would talk again when they met to discuss her case. Going to the Watson women, minus Jasmine, who had disappeared as suddenly as she had appeared, she said goodnight. Bernice hugged her before leaving her with Valerie and a friend.

After a few minutes, she began to wonder what was keeping Kellen. They had a lot to talk about, and tonight might be their last opportunity.

Pop.

They all stopped talking and listened. Even the men were quiet, looking questioningly in the direction of the hallway.

Pop, pop.

There it was, again. There was no mistaking it, now. It was the exact sound that she had heard all afternoon when she and Kellen had engaged in target practice.

Valerie looked as stricken as she was feeling. Hastily following her, LaRetha raced toward the back of the house in the direction of the noise. A small crowd of people was hanging back at the end of the long wide hallway. She got there just in time to hear Bernice scream and to see her fall down. Someone was trying to revive her as Paul yelled for someone to call *911.* Jasmine was standing just inside a bedroom doorway, looking on as if in shock.

Feeling the need to push through, LaRetha made her way to the center of the crowd.

"Somebody's been shot," a man called out.

Someone was lying on the floor, and the knot in the pit of her stomach told her she really didn't want to find out who that was. But, she had to.

Pushing past a few more people, she strained to see what was happening. And right there, lying in a pool of blood in the middle of the hallway was *Therell Watson.* And standing over him, looking dazed and bewildered, stood Kellen. And he was holding a gun in his hand.

7

Everything after that seemed to happen in a blur, as if it wasn't real. But, it was soon a known fact. *Therell Watson was dead.* And Kellen had been arrested for his murder.

LaRetha remembered calling out to Kellen, who never looked in her direction. Nor did he move when her uncle burst through the crowd, dressed in pajamas and a robe, and grabbed the gun from his hands. Handling it with a towel that someone gave him.

He didn't struggle when he was pulled away by someone she didn't know from the place where Therell was lying face up on the floor with thick dark blood pouring from his chest, and a hidden place in back of his head. There was on his forehead, one small, neatly rounded hole that trickled one drop of blood onto his face.

Maybe it was the horror of it, the terror of seeing yet another man lying in blood, right in front of her, that caused her to freeze up. Because suddenly, it wasn't Therell but *Paul Straiter* lying on the floor with the bullet-ridden body. But then, she realized that was not the case. Lying there with his eyes open, appearing to look right at her, was the one man she had tried to avoid seeing tonight, and whom she had never figured on seeing like this.

It was definitely Therell. She only saw him for a moment, before hearing someone, who must have been her, screaming. Right before she fainted.

LaRetha awakened on a bedroom sofa, with Valerie fanning her, attempting to revive her. Sitting up, she learned that most of the people had been moved to another area of the house. Valerie's face showed concern as she slowly regained her senses.

"What happened?"

"The police have Kellen. They took him into town. I'm sure they plan to keep him. There's nothing you can do for him, tonight. Do you have a way home?"

Coupled with concern, she heard sensibility in the young woman's voice. And she was right. Going home was the best thing for her to do at the moment.

She found out that the ambulance had been there and gone, taking Therell's body away. The man was undoubtedly *dead*. Everyone was to stay until after the police had questioned them all. They spoke with her as soon as they saw her up, again.

But, she'd had nothing different to tell them. She hadn't seen anything, just heard the shots. *Yes*, Kellen had come with her. He'd been right where she could see him, practically all night. *No*, she hadn't seen any struggle between the men – hadn't known they had even encountered one another, considering Therell hadn't been visible, all night. And *no*, Kellen didn't own a gun.

Once again, it was recommended that she remain in town for further questioning. *As if she planned to leave now*, she thought. Finally, with almost everyone else having gone already, someone volunteered to drive her home in her car. She left without speaking with her family, not wanting to upset them any further. Certain they wouldn't want to talk to her right now, anyway.

She barely remembered the ride home. Thanking the driver for his trouble, she assured him that she would be fine getting inside, by herself. Parking in her driveway, he handed her the keys before getting into a car with someone who had followed them. She hadn't even noticed, until then.

Finally home, sitting on the sofa, she realized that her head hurt, even worse. Her body ached, feeling stiff and sore. And all that she could think about was Kellen.

Kellen. She couldn't stop the tears that flowed down her face, searing a path through makeup that felt like mud on her face, now. She immediately went to wash it off, and to remove the clothing that was sticking heavily to her body. Pinning her hair, she ran a tub of very hot water.

Throwing in scented salts, and slowly lowering herself into the tub, she finally allowed shuddering sobs of frustration to surface. She couldn't believe this mess they were in. First, she was under suspicion for contributing to a murder. And now Kellen would be convicted of committing one, and worse, for murdering *Therell Watson*, the man who had claimed to be her brother.

Playing the week's events a thousand times over in her mind, she tried to figure out any possible incident that could have led to such a thing. What possible connection could there have been between those two? She couldn't think of any.

She sat in the tub until the water was much too cool, before getting out. Wrapping in a thick white terrycloth bathrobe, she realized that the hot bath hadn't quite done the trick. The dirt was still there. It was permanently irremovable, it seemed. What had occurred on this night had been yet another nightmare. *But, how had this happened?*

She recalled everything from the first day Kellen had showed up on her doorstep, until now. Even last night, when her family was all together at her uncle's house. Nothing out of the ordinary came to mind.

But then, there was this stupid party and Kellen's refusal to leave. There was the woman from the foyer who had somehow become his eager dance partner for most of the night. Then, there was Douglas Davis, who had been great to her, even after Kellen had been rude to him. And the man had been more than clear about his interest in her.

Then, she remembered Kellen's promise to finally leave, then hearing the gunfire and seeing the man lying dead on the floor with Kellen standing over him, holding a gun.

Finally summoning enough energy to search for an aspirin, she looked in the medicine cabinet. Unaware of how long she'd stood there, before finally sitting on the edge of the tub, her body wracking with sobs. She awakened on the floor some time later. It was daylight now and she still had a throbbing headache.

Managing to wash down three aspirins with water cupped in her hands, she forced herself to look through red, swollen eyes at her reflection. She looked as tired and distraught as she felt. And, to her dismay, she realized that she was looking at the reflection of the murderous girlfriend of a killer.

Slamming her fists angrily against the mirror, she tried unsuccessfully to break it - to destroy the image of this person that was so responsible for everything that had happened. If only she had left the party when she first started to, and if only Kellen had gone with her. If only she'd never come here. *If only....*

Her phone began to ring, constantly. She didn't answer. There was no one she wanted to talk to and nothing that she wanted to hear, right now. She'd told the police everything she knew, particularly about Kellen's reason for coming to town. She couldn't go through another interrogation.

No, she'd said emphatically. Kellen didn't know Therell prior to this incident. Neither of them had even known for sure that the man was in town, much less in the same house. She had spoken with him only once, and Kellen, *never,* as far as she knew. And, she was certain that, had Kellen known that the man was anywhere around, he would have told her.

"Kellen wouldn't just shoot someone," she'd said. He never carried a gun. *He doesn't even own one,* she'd insisted.

She closed her eyes right now, quietly berating herself. Her own stubbornness had led to this. If she'd just stayed in Atlanta...

Therell had been at that house, all along. Either he'd come in when she wasn't looking, or maybe he'd been there the entire time. And, he was probably the man she'd heard arguing with that woman. And then, considering her absenteeism for most of the night, Jasmine was quite possibly that woman.

Her aunt and uncle had known this. But, from what she'd overheard, they hadn't been expecting him, either. But, why had he been hiding? Because of her? Or maybe he just hadn't gone in for parties, either.

Therell had come across as a man with a terrible temperament. Still, as perturbed as she was by the man's presence, she wouldn't have wanted him *dead*. And Kellen knew that. She'd had enough of the violence. Had he been *that* intoxicated? And, where had that gun even come from?

A sudden thought jerked her into realization. She ran to her bedroom to check the nightstand drawer. Her gun was still there. Remembering, she started into the living room to look for her uncle's gun, praying that she'd find it. Jerking on the drawer handle, it resisted at first. But, with a harder pull, the drawer came open. She reached inside. *Nothing.*

She got down on her hands and knees, reaching as far inside as she could, thinking that it could have slipped down, somehow. But, it hadn't, because it wasn't there.

Out of bed and dressed very early the next morning, LaRetha was trying to wash down a blueberry muffin with a cup of hot black coffee when her doorbell rang. Her first reaction was to ignore it. To pretend she wasn't home. Her next thought was that she should answer because it might be something important.

The ringing persisted until she peered out of the window to see who it was. Looking into the friendliest face she could imagine seeing right now, she hurriedly opened the door.

Douglas' head jerked up as the door opened, and in less than a second he was inside, his arms catching her as she fell into them. He led her to the sofa to sit down, waiting patiently as she sobbed quietly into a tissue.

"Drink this," he finally said, after leaving her side long enough to prepare her a fresh cup of coffee. She accepted it, finally having run out of tears.

"You've had a tough time."

"Right now I have a worse headache than before. I'm still waiting for my aspirin to take effect."

"Poor thing," he said, smiling sympathetically.

"I can't believe any of this, Douglas. I can't imagine what caused this. Kellen didn't have anything against Therell. He's never even met the man..."

"As far as you know," he said, softly.

As far as I know? She stopped for a moment to think about that. But, when would Kellen have even had the opportunity? They'd been together practically every minute since he'd arrived, until the party. She said this. Douglas said nothing, although he appeared to be contemplating this.

"I don't see a connection. Kellen's not a violent person. And we only talked about Therell a couple of times. He wouldn't intentionally do something like this. Especially not to someone in my family."

She suddenly thought about the irony. Now that the man was no longer a threat, she could refer to him as *family*. It occurred to her that Douglas was probably thinking the same.

"I believe anybody is capable of anything, when provoked," he said.

She, of all people, could give testimony to that, she thought. Kellen was capable, and clearly he had.

"No," she said, shaking her head. Douglas sighed.

"I tell you woman, every time I think we've got a handle on this thing, something new occurs. Just be prepared for more questioning. They'll need to know what it was that these two people had in common. What might have been going on, if anything, that concerned the three of you. As for now, I don't understand this, either."

She nodded, blowing her nose, again.

"LaRetha, I've been waiting to talk with you. I ran into your uncle the other day, and I asked him to have you contact me. When I tried to reach you, you didn't answer and you never returned my call," he said. "I left a couple of messages."

She remembered her uncle mentioning talking with Douglas, but he'd said nothing to her about calling him. And she had checked all her messages. There were none from him.

Kellen! She didn't respond.

"Therell's attorney has requested a private meeting with the two of us. From what I was told, they wanted to come to some sort of agreement that might prevent a court hearing over this land matter."

She put her cup down and looked at him. Puzzled.

"I intended to present the results of the handwriting evaluation that's being done, once I get them. I should have had that by now, but it is the holidays."

She said nothing.

"I was going to recommend that you consider going. It wouldn't have hurt, and it would at least have opened up communication between you."

So, did he believe Therell was her brother, too? Having counted on his full support, she didn't even want to think about that.

"*Really?* Well, it's a bit late for that now, isn't it? And why didn't you tell me this, before? Like last night?"

"The truth is, when I finally saw you at the party, I couldn't find the right opportunity. I didn't want to spoil your evening. You seemed to be having such a nice time."

Thanks a lot! That knowledge might have saved her a whole lot of duress, she thought.

"How's that headache, now?" His voice softened, again.

He put his hand on her arm, but somehow it was disturbing. She put the coffee cup and saucer back on the table.

"I appreciate your coming out here, Douglas. Unless there's something in particular that we need to discuss..."

"No. I just wanted to make certain that you were alright," he said, standing and looking around. "So much is happening that I'm not sure it's a good idea for you to remain out here, alone."

"And just where do you suggest I go?"

"I don't guess I could suggest a relative's place at this point. But, *Lovely* has a few nice hotels that could accommodate you for a time. At least until this is over. Or for as long as you decide to stay."

"Well, you're right about the relatives. I definitely wouldn't be welcome at my uncle's place right now. As for a hotel, I don't think so. I would be miserable the entire time, and I'm not about to exhaust my bank account on what could be an endless situation."

"So, what did you have in mind?"

"I plan to stay right here, is what I have in mind."

"That... I couldn't allow it. It's too dangerous, LaRetha. There's no reason for you to end up like... your... relative. We don't know what's going on, other than the fact that there've been two murders since..." His voice dwindled and she didn't have to guess why.

"Since I came here, you mean? Since Kellen arrived? You think he had something to do with *Straiter's* murder at the hospital, don't you?"

Douglas' silence answered her question.

"Well, if you thought that, then why would you be concerned about my safety? He's in jail, and couldn't possibly hurt me, even if he wanted to, and he doesn't. Besides, if that was the case, he could have done it long before now."

"You never know who's in bed with whom, in these type matters." After seeing her shocked face, he added, "It's a figure of speech."

"I know he didn't shoot Therell intentionally. It's just not possible, and it makes no sense. What reason would he have? And, aside from that, why would he intentionally kill a man, right in front of all those witnesses? That house was filled with people - *Therell's* people. That wouldn't take much planning *or* conspiring, would it?"

Along with her anger, she could feel the journalist in her taking over, once again.

"Well, from what's been said to me so far, and not by my asking, your boyfriend came here after you refused to move back with him to Atlanta, am I correct?"

"No. You're *not* correct." She faced him, angrily. "Kellen had just taken a job in Ohio when he came here. It doesn't begin until the first of the year, and that's why he could spend this time with me. *Any more questions?*"

"But, how did he feel about your living here in *Lovely,* like this? Alone, I mean? Did he ever offer to move here with you?"

"No. Like everybody else I've talked to lately, he wasn't crazy about the idea. He wanted me to go back with him, at first. But then he took the job. We never discussed it after that."

"*Never?* Not even with him moving away, for good?"

"No, not since he got the offer. I told you that."

"*Hmmm,*" he said. He walked over, closing the distance between them. Taking her hand, he looked into her eyes.

"LaRetha, I know we don't know each other, well. But, I have to ask you something. How much do you trust this man?"

She glared at him. Got up and walked away from him.

"How well did you know him before he came here?" He persisted. "How long were you involved with him? And who else do you know that knows this man you've been living with?"

"Kellen and I were not *strangers,* Douglas. And I don't like where this is going. I totally resent what you're implying."

"I'm just telling you what you need to expect to hear from the police. I'm on your side. I just need to understand this. Is it possible that he was the one who wanted to scare you? To maybe get you to move back to Atlanta? He might have done it for the right reasons, maybe. To protect you. But, is it possible?"

"That's ridiculous!"

"But, it's possible. It's also very obvious that he was the one holding the gun, last night. Nobody else. We both agree on that, don't we?"

"I don't appreciate you jumping to conclusions about Kellen. He couldn't have cared less about Therell, or my problems with the man. He must have had good reason for what he did."

"Okay. A witness overheard the two of you disagreeing rather heatedly last night, and told this to the police. They said you wanted to leave, but he refused."

A witness? Of course! The woman Kellen had danced with for most of the night.

"Who was she? What's her name?"

"I never said it was a *she,*" the man said, looking as if he felt he was onto something. "Who did you think I was talking about?"

"I remember someone being around when Kellen and I talked. But, it wasn't *heated*. We just disagreed."

"Apparently so."

"It *is* so. We had a harmless disagreement. Neither of us was angry about it. You should know that. You were there. Did I seem angry to you?"

He shrugged, watching her intently. She squinted, seeing now that he wasn't fully convinced.

"Douglas, I hardly see how his wanting to stay longer at the party even led to ... what happened."

"Some people might not agree. Some might say that he stayed for a reason. Maybe for a reason you don't even know, yet."

It then occurred to her that she should be careful about what she told this man. *Suddenly*, Douglas felt less like a helpful friend, and more like the enemy, and she wanted him out of her home.

"I think you should leave."

"I'm going. I didn't come out here to upset you. Just to get you to see what you might not want to. I know you two were practically engaged." His eyes fell upon her right hand and the beautiful diamond ring that she still hadn't removed.

"I know you might feel your world is shattered, LaRetha. That's totally understandable. But don't close your mind to the truth - the *whole* truth. Maybe there are things you're either overlooking or just refusing to see. So, if you think of anything, or whenever you decide you want to talk about this, you should give me a call first. *Before* you talk to the police. I can help you..."

"Douglas, I have nothing else to say to you about this. And don't worry about representing Kellen or me. I'll find another attorney." She didn't look at his face, but felt his stare as he stood hovering over her.

"You're sure about that?" He finally asked, his composure having altered a bit.

"*Positive*," she said, feeling far less certain than she sounded.

"Fine, then."

He walked to the door with a confident stride, but she could tell that she had disappointed him, and possibly hurt his feelings. She was sorry for that, and might have apologized, but for her own pain.

"There's something you need to realize, though," he finally said, turning from the door to face her. "You're going to need to have people on your side, now more than ever. You can't go through all of this alone. I realize I've upset you, and I apologize, because that wasn't my intention. But, once you've calmed down and given this some thought, you should call me."

She turned abruptly to carry her cup into the kitchen, and to get away from his commanding tone. He might be right, she thought. But, she just didn't want to hear this, right now. He followed, never missing a beat in what he was saying to her.

"Because once the police come probing, it's possible they might begin to blame *you* for some of this. Them, along with your family and everyone else in this town. You're going to realize that I'm right."

"So, unless you're planning to run away from this thing, you're going to need someone on your side... on *Kellen's* side. Someone who genuinely wants to help. Someone who knows these people and who can mediate for you. That's how it works here in *Lovely.*"

She said nothing as she stood facing him with arms folded, refusing to meet his gaze.

"Now, I don't pretend to be a friend of Kellen's. But, I can help you. So, think about that and get back to me. You know how to find me. I'm more than willing to help."

She watched as he put his coat on, preparing to brace the winter cold, outside.

"And why are you so *willing?*"

"I've told you why." He stopped and looked at her.

"No. I mean, how do I know that Kellen can trust you?"

"Because you can. Besides, consider your options. Would you prefer a court appointed attorney in a court that might already be biased? Or an outside attorney who wouldn't begin to know how to communicate with the people who actually knew this man? If you ever want to see your friend, your *lover*, or whatever he is to you, get out of jail, then you'll stop being so stubborn and call me."

Hearing his anger, she gave him a haughty stare. Douglas could be right all day long, but she had no intention of saying so. What right did he have to march in here and tell her what she ought to do? There were other attorneys in the world, besides him. Besides that blowhard *Billard*. Besides any of them.

"I'm not here to hurt you, LaRetha. I don't play games with other people's lives. And truthfully, something about this whole situation simply isn't right, and that bothers me. But, I came here still, because whether you're willing to admit it or not, you need me." He reached for the doorknob.

She knew this. Not only would she need proper representation for herself and for Kellen, but she would also need him as an ally. Knowing how difficult it had been for outsiders to come in when her father was alive, she knew that little had changed. Finding an out-of-town attorney might result in alienating the entire community, and that was the last thing she needed, right now.

She did want to see Kellen released. So, if it meant hiring this man who, just last night had appeared her knight in shining armor, but this morning seemed questionable in his intentions, then that's what she had to do. Until something else opened up, anyway. Kellen's life depended on it.

Douglas' eyes were softer, now. He came over and gently took her hand.

"Don't push me away, LaRetha. I know that wasn't you standing there, holding that gun. We just have to make certain that everyone else knows that, too. That they don't believe your fiancé was acting on your behalf. Trust me enough to let me help you."

She said nothing.

"Think about it. I'll be in touch." He released her hand and let himself out.

That they don't believe your fiancé was acting on your behalf. The words resonated in her mind, and she couldn't believe that it had never occurred to her that someone might even think it.

She decided to call her mother. But first, she needed to speak with her uncle. She had to face him and the others, sooner or later.

His family probably surrounded him, right now. They would provide him with the support that he undoubtedly needed. Still, he might want to hear from her, too. He might even expect to, she reasoned. The sooner she stepped up to the plate, the better, she decided. She picked up the phone and dialed.

"Hello?" It was Nell's voice. Suddenly, LaRetha was teary, again. Trying not to sound as nervous and upset as she was, she began to speak.

"Hello, *Aunt Nell?* This is LaRetha. I was calling to see how everybody was doing, and to say how sorry I am about what happened last night. I don't begin to know how or why it happened, but I do plan to find out."

Nothing.

"How is everyone? Is my uncle doing alright, Nell?"

There. She had said what she had practiced over and over in her mind. But, so far, there was only silence. She waited a moment.

"I wanted to call and to..."

"I can't believe you're calling here." The voice was cold and callous. And she could feel the woman's pain. Therell was her *son,* after all.

"Nell..."

"My husband doesn't want to talk to you, and he doesn't need to. I don't know what kind of life you led in Atlanta, but it seems to me you've been nothing but trouble since you came to this town."

LaRetha swallowed. Couldn't speak.

"You must have brought every murderer in Atlanta, up here. And all the time pretending you came with good intentions. I'm beginning to wonder what's really going on, LaRetha. Why are you really here? And, just what were you running from when you came?"

LaRetha felt her heart sinking. Nell blamed her, all right.

"That's so unfair..," she started.

"*Unfair?* We took you into our home, treated you like the family we thought you were, although your father hated us for years, and for no good reason. And now, you come here and act on that hate, and you have the audacity to *call* here? After what happened last night?"

LaRetha was too devastated to speak for a moment, but quickly gathered her wits. She couldn't leave it like this.

"I don't know what happened last night, Nell," she responded, unable to resist sounding a little defensive, "or why, but..."

"Isn't it obvious?" The woman interrupted, sounding tearful. "Your uncle has been destroyed by this. You know how much he cared for Therell, yet you allowed this to happen. And for what? What was your part in all of this, really?"

"You're blaming me?" LaRetha exclaimed. "I don't know how or when the two of them ever met. And from what my uncle said, I didn't expect him to even be there. That's why I'm calling you. To see if we can figure this out."

Nell said nothing. She felt devastated.

"You'd rather blame me, and for something that you know I had no part in."

"Sure, I blame you. We all do. And why not? If you hadn't come here, none of the mess that's been going on these past weeks would have happened. Therell would still be alive. Paul Straiter, rest his soul, would be alive, too. And no telling who else, weeks from now. Now, correct me if I'm wrong."

She was speechless. How could she convince Nell that she was wrong, when just a while ago she had been thinking the very same thing?

"Well, it seems you have your mind made up, and it's so unfair. You have to know that I've never meant to cause this family any harm. Your family is my family, too. I'm as angry and shocked as you are. I never wanted this to happen. If I had even thought..."

Silence.

"Nell, this farm doesn't mean that much to me where I would want to see anyone die, just to have it. But, you have to blame someone, and I guess I'm the perfect target, aren't I? But the truth remains to be told. And I *will* get to the truth!"

"Well," the woman interrupted, again. "I guess you are the perfect target because as far as I'm concerned, the *truth* is evident. And rather than call here, intruding on our time of grief, let me make a suggestion to you. I speak on behalf of the entire Watson family when I say that I would suggest you make arrangements to live *elsewhere.*"

LaRetha's hand flew to her mouth as she subdued a sob. Nell couldn't be serious. But, she was still on the phone, which meant she might still be able to get through to her. If anyone needed to make her position clear, she did. Even if she had to be argumentative, to do it.

"You can't tell me where to live, Nell. I own this farm. And you have *no right* to judge me, like this. You gave the party, not me. And *you* invited us, *personally*. Obviously, this wasn't intentional, but if I were to be so unfair, I could ask what your part was in all this? What was Therell doing there when my uncle said he wouldn't be? And what were his intentions toward Kellen *and* me?"

Nell said nothing. She continued.

"I met Therell, *up close and personal*. It's entirely possible that this was purely an act of self defense!"

LaRetha was immediately sorry – for striking back and for opening up this possibility without having facts, just yet. She had intended to wait until the truth was unveiled, preferably by Douglas. But, Nell had pushed the wrong buttons at the wrong time.

Still, she knew that Therell was important to these people. And now he was dead. Worse, she'd said that he had caused it himself, a sentiment she really didn't need to share, right now. They would only take that one way. That she was just trying to save her lover's skin.

"*What?* You've got some nerve. I've said all I intend to say about this. Don't mind me while I hang this phone up in your face," the woman said, angrily.

"*Likewise*," LaRetha muttered, hanging up after hearing a loud click, from the other end.

Now she was truly upset. Douglas had been exactly right. If Nell had anything to say about it, no one in the family would want anything else to do with her.

Evidently, as difficult a person as Therell might have been, there were still a lot of people here who cared about him, blood related or not. These were people who had lived with and loved him all those years she'd lived in Atlanta with her mother. She couldn't compete with or compensate for that.

She had been so mistaken to believe they would ever regard her as true family. Despite what her uncle felt, to them she was *Watson's* daughter and would always and forever be the *outsider*. Especially now.

She needed her mother, right now. Sitting at the kitchen table with a cordless phone in her hands, she remembered something Laretta had always told her when she was a child. That no matter how bad things got, keep your chin up. They could always be worse.

She'd never fully appreciated the statement until now. Just when she'd thought things were as bad as they could get, *now this*. And, judging from the way things were going with Nell, and with Douglas, something even worse could be in store. She needed to prepare for it.

She signed onto her computer and sent her mother a short note:

Mama,
I couldn't reach you by phone. Something absolutely
awful has happened. Kellen is in deep trouble. Call me.
I need to hear from you, *ASAP!*
Love, LaRetha.

She wondered how Kellen was doing. He hadn't called. And
Tuesday, visiting day, was two days away. *How would she survive*
until then?

She tried to phone him at the jail, but was told that he couldn't
receive outside calls until Tuesday. She hang up, disappointed.

The entire day seemed long and lonely, and sleep didn't come
for hours, that night. At one point, she had awakened, thinking she
had heard Kellen coming in. But, it was only the wind blowing
brushes against her window.

The following morning wasn't any easier. Even eating was difficult, and after a few bites she tossed her food into the trash. To make
matters worse, the incident was all over the news. Kellen was being
profiled from his home in Atlanta. There was a quick shot of the
office, and her name was mentioned as his *girlfriend,* first cousin to
the deceased. There were no leads on the cause of this tragic event.
No one at the party knew anything, they said.

But somebody knew, she thought. And as upset as she was, she
intended to find out who that was. Although it wasn't her job to
prove it, she had to make sure everyone knew that Kellen was no
murderer. Except, they didn't seem to care about that. He had clearly
shot the man, so as far as they were concerned, and in spite of any
hope that Douglas might possibly want to give her, they had their
man. *Case closed.*

There's a lot more to Lovely than meets the eye. Lots of secrets.
Lots of little indignities that people won't ever talk about. It's not the
easy life folks think...

She remembered Laretta's words. *Tell me about it,* she thought.

It was Monday morning and she would be able to talk to Kellen,
soon. To get some answers. In the meantime, she would busy
herself, straightening the guest room he'd used. The police hadn't
searched the house, as she'd expected. Kellen had left such a clutter.
And she had nothing better to do, after all.

Douglas was convinced that there were things she didn't know
about Kellen, like why he was really there and how well he might
have known Therell. Looking at the scattering of clothing and bags
that he had left there, she figured if any of this was true, then there

must be a clue in here, somewhere. It wouldn't be strange or unusual for her fingerprints to be found in this room. Just the same, she put on a pair of elastic gloves.

His pants pockets gave her nothing, the same as his shirts, which were already neatly folded and placed at the end of the bed, ready to go back into his tote bags when the time came. She opened the bags and emptied the contents on the bed, only to find... nothing. No notes, no receipts. No letters or anything of the kind.

She shook his jackets. Nothing there, either. She went through the dresser drawers. *Nothing.* Then she noticed a cloth wallet lying on the floor near the bed. It must have fallen from his jacket pocket, she thought. She figured she might as well check it too.

She opened the wallet, finding nothing but food and gas receipts. Carefully unfolding each one, she read the addresses on them, looking for a sign that Kellen had stopped someplace out of the ordinary on his way there. They were all in line, accounting for the direction he said he'd come.

Shaking the wallet, another slip of paper fell out. She replaced the receipts before picking it up and opening it. It was a twice-folded sheet from a small yellow note pad, and the message on it was written in pencil. *30 more days!* The words were written dark and underlined.

Why did that sound so familiar to her? She had heard this very thing just recently. But, this was evidence, wasn't it? Someone had written this to Kellen, giving him a deadline of some sort. She shuddered to think what for.

But, this could have come from anyone, at anyplace and time. And it could be about anything. Maybe his new job. But that was more than thirty days away, wasn't it? And clearly he had posed a question, if the note was in his possession? Looking at the darkened exclamation mark, she sensed that this was quite possibly no friendly note.

She changed the bed sheets and remade the bed, neatly stacking his clothing and bags, nearby. Carrying the note into the kitchen, she dropped it into a plastic sandwich bag and sealed it before removing her gloves. Whatever the reason for the note was, the writer's prints would very likely still be on it. It was worth checking out.

She would see Kellen in the morning. She would ask him about the note, then. It wouldn't hurt to call Douglas and tell him what she had found, she thought, before deciding against it. Could she trust him, yet? Besides, he hadn't yet taken the case. So this time, she would proceed more carefully.

Finally, it was *7:30 am,* on Tuesday morning. She had been up for hours. She would see Kellen, today. She thought about what Douglas had said the last time they had talked. She was grateful that he'd agreed to talk with Kellen. And yes, she did need him. Probably far more than even he realized.

His office wasn't open yet, but she could still call and leave a message. That would be better than having to talk to Marva, anyway. There was no doubt that the woman felt as the others did - that all of this was totally her fault.

She dialed and waited for the voice mail, then selected his extension. Hearing his voice soothed her, for some reason. She waited patiently for the beep, before speaking.

"Mr. Davis, this is LaRetha Greer. I need to talk with you this morning. Please call me as soon as you are available, and let me know if you can meet me out here at the farm, say, some time today? I know this is short notice, but please call me and confirm. Thank you."

She remembered to leave her number before hanging up. Then she concentrated on drinking her morning coffee. Her request wasn't so unusual, she thought. She would treat it as a personal visit. Besides, with all the speculation that she was sure was going on, he might appreciate the discretion.

She finally checked her phone messages. Constance had called from Atlanta, leaving a message, sounding desperate as she pleaded with her to call her back, *ASAP.*

Mac Henry had called several times over the last couple of days. He wanted to speak to her, *immediately.* She knew what that meant. Her suspicions were confirmed when she read her E-mail:

Hello, LG;
There appears to be a story in your town that you haven't
mentioned. Sorry about your man, Kellen. Call me about it,
ASAP! We have to discuss. I need to know your angle on
the other stories we've discussed, and this one. Can you
handle it?
MH

He'll get an angle, alright, she thought, indignantly. And the fact that he'd mentioned Kellen's situation so casually as if it were unimportant, was offensive. Kellen had just been in the wrong place at the wrong time. Therell had caused this, she was sure. Not the other way around. Still, there was the matter of her uncle's missing gun.

She waited as long as she could for Douglas to return her call. It was after *nine o'clock,* and still nothing. He was probably just getting into his office, or headed to court, she thought. The man did have a practice. And a life, she reasoned.

The phone rang, and seeing her mother's number on the Caller I.D, she quickly picked up. It was Marilee, calling for Laretta. Her mother had gotten her e-mail, and was busy tying up loose ends at her office. *She would arrive at the airport this morning, and would LaRetha drive over and pick her up?*

LaRetha thanked Marilee for the call, wondering as she hang up why Laretta didn't rent a car and drive from the airport, like she usually did. But, her coming here meant a lot, considering the way she felt about *Lovely*. And the fact that she'd been so against her moving here in the first place. Either way it went, Laretta was coming, and *Lovely* was in for a real shake-up. If nothing else, it would certainly prove to be interesting

8

As usual, Laretta looked like a million dollars, stepping through the doorway of the airport, a few steps ahead of her daughter. Recalling her mother's arrogance at times, LaRetha had already told herself not to become annoyed at anything her mother did or said. And, if she really got on her nerves, to send her packing on the first plane out of Kentucky.

"I had almost forgotten this place," her mother said, stopping to inhale in the biting cold air, as a kind baggage man loaded her things into the trunk of LaRetha's car, waiting at the curb. "*I tried to, anyway.*"

She turned to face LaRetha and smiled, her lovely ebony face illuminating against the falling snow and the bluish-white fur collar of her coat. The woman had style, no doubt about that, LaRetha thought. Returning the gesture, she added a hug. After paying the baggage man, she got into the car.

"You're looking much better, now. Taking care of yourself. I guess there's nothing else out here to do?" Her mother asked, as they drove off.

"That's why I came here, after all. And, how are you, Mama?"

She was happy to have Laretta there. Her mother loved to talk, and talking was what she needed, right now.

"Fine, as always. Business is great. Life is great. I just bought another investment property and I already have a buyer."

She nodded, while carefully guiding the SUV through recently salted streets.

"From the looks of this town, I can understand your being troubled. It hasn't changed much since I left. It's kind of dreary, still. But I thought you would've been back in Atlanta by now, fully recovered and doing something more constructive than this with your life..."

"This *is* my life, Mama. Only, right now it's not looking so good."

"Let's wait and talk about it at the house, alright?"

Laretta must have sensed her hesitation. Relieved, she concentrated on the road. With most of the debris cleared out of the streets and the sky a lovely blue again, she could almost feel the anticipation of spring in the air. She let her window down a bit. *Inhaled.*

Her mother did the same, her expensive perfume wafting past LaRetha's nose, reminding her of mornings when her mother would drive her to school, as a child. That fragrance represented security. The closeness they'd always shared when the two of them only had one another. Her mother's preference in some things hadn't changed very much, it seemed.

"When have you heard from Germaine?" Laretta asked.

"I *haven't.*"

"I could just whip his *butt,*" her mother exclaimed. "That makes no sense, whatsoever."

"Don't worry about it, Mama. From what I hear, he's doing fine. That's all I can ask."

"Well. Guess who just bought a house from one of my agents? Your *ex!* He's friends with Pinky's husband. They sold him some rental property," she said, eyeing LaRetha closely as if waiting for a negative response.

"*Fine!* I hope you and your agent earned a nice hefty fee from the stingy rascal."

"It didn't cost him very much. It might take some time but with a lot of hard work and about thirty thousand dollars, he can make something of it, I guess. He's just trying to do what you did. I wouldn't have bought that one, but that's him."

LaRetha smiled. Gerald was making bad investments. She felt redeemed in an odd sort of way.

"Oh, and 'the family' sends their *hello.*"

LaRetha knew that 'the family' was the team at her mother's real estate office.

"Great. How's everybody? Is Lynn still making a thousand sales a month?" She joked.

"I wouldn't tell her, but I still can't figure out how somebody who hates to get out of bed everyday can sell so many houses," her mother laughed. "But, I'm certainly not complaining."

Certainly not, LaRetha thought, remembering how those commission checks had paid a lot of bills and even bought her first ten-speed bicycle.

"I'm sure you're doing just as well. She had to learn it from somebody."

"Well, yes, I'm doing quite well. But, you know we do have our share of drama," she laughed.

Laretta looked out of the window as they drove silently the rest of the way, and LaRetha used the time to think about how her mother had actually come. Obviously, she was worried. And, as it had always stood, when you messed with Laretta's child, you messed with her.

Finally, they were parked in her driveway. She helped her mother carry the bags inside.

"*Nice digs.* You've done great things to this old place, I see. It's hardly the place I used to live in. The outside is deceiving, though," Laretta said, sitting down and kicking off her shoes.

LaRetha had expected this. Her mother was accustomed to maid service and housekeepers. *Well, she was neither one.* And once these bags were parked, Laretta would be on her own.

"They do have wheels, darling," she said, and LaRetha politely ignored.

Laretta followed her and the trail of luggage down the hallway, and around to the guest room.

"*Not bad at all,*" she said, referring to the remodeling and décor.

LaRetha's extra efforts to fix the place up had paid off. Matching comforters, rugs, curtains and valances graced each bedroom; a deep red, beige and gold for her bedroom, blue and beige for the bedroom Kellen had used, and burgundy and a very pale yellow for the one her mother would use. It was the smallest room, but adequately furnished.

"I think I'll take a shower."

"Check out the one in my room. I had it added on."

She did.

"*I like!* But I won't put you out. I'll use the other one."

LaRetha shrugged and left her to prepare brunch. Laretta finally emerged, looking elegantly comfortable in a yellow sweater and matching pants. Totally without makeup now, she still looked as young as her, LaRetha thought. Beautiful, smart and wealthy she was, all the things that attracted men, particularly younger men who, coincidentally, her mother preferred to date right now.

"LaRetha Watson Greer, is that an *engagement ring?*"

Her mother came over and looked at the ring on her right hand.

"Not exactly. It was supposed to be, but…"

Her mother eyed her curiously.

"I haven't accepted any proposals. You would be the first to know."

"*Uh huh.*"

"Speaking of men, how're things with that *Bill,* guy?"

She poured lemonade into glasses and they sat down to veal cutlets sautéed in lemon and garlic sauce, boiled buttered potatoes and her favorite vegetable, string beans. She only put bread on her plate since her mother rarely ate it. Laretta inhaled, her expression showing appreciation. They both said grace.

"I guess he's doing fine, wherever he is."

"Well. He didn't last for very long."

"Girl, he got on my nerves." She bit into a potato. "This is very good, by the way." She took another bite. LaRetha leaned forward to eat and listen. She always did love her mother's stories.

"I told that man that if he didn't leave on his own, I was going to have the sanitation department come and toss him out! He never wanted to bathe. Wouldn't pick up after himself..," she said, and LaRetha settled back in her chair, anticipating a punch line that never failed to come. "...talking 'bout *that's what the maid is here for, ain't it?*" Laretta mimicked.

LaRetha laughed.

"He tried to work poor Marilee to death! I told him, 'oh, but, you're not the one paying her salary, and I'm not paying her to come in here and scrape your dirt off of my expensive furniture. Now, get your naaaassssty, so and so on-up-*outta* here!"

"How did he take it?" She asked through her laughter before trying the beans. She was enjoying this heart to heart sisterly conversation, realizing just how much she missed it.

"Not well. I couldn't believe him. Good looking, making a ton of money in banking, and just would not bathe. I miss him, but I'm not trying to catch *nuthin'* out here." She bit into her veal.

They laughed well into late afternoon, with Laretta rehashing old rumors, and sharing new ones. She planned to retire in two years and was trying to decide where to vacation for a few months, afterwards. With her assets all fully paid for, income from several rental properties, and a nice hefty retirement account, she didn't plan to sit down for a minute.

LaRetha could see that her mother was waiting for her to explain her concerns, and appreciated this. She felt bad about not seeing Kellen, certain that he was wondering why she hadn't come. She needed to explain everything to her mother. Maybe she would accompany her.

"Mama, *Kellen shot someone,*" she said, unable to contain her distress.

"*What? Who did he shoot?*" Laretta stared in disbelief.

Composing herself, she took a deep breath, exhaling just as the phone rang. It was Douglas. He was back in town, he said. He'd gotten her message and wanted to meet with her, as well.

She explained that her mother was visiting, and that she had hoped to see Kellen some time, that afternoon. He insisted that she wait until they talked. A friend who worked at the jail had informed him that Kellen was being far less than a model inmate. He didn't go into details, but said it might be better if she gave it at least another day.

She felt terrible, abandoning him. But Douglas wouldn't hear of it. And he didn't think Kellen was ready to see her, either. It was *2:00 pm*, and he wanted to know what time they could meet.

"Well, my mother's here, now. And I wouldn't want to leave her, alone."

"Fine. Meet me at *Gino P's* in two hours, and bring her along if she wants to come. They have excellent food there. And I would love to meet her."

He gave her the directions. Hanging up, she repeated this to Laretta, who looked pleased at the invitation.

"So, this is about... *the shooting?*" She asked carefully, as if just saying the words might upset her.

"Yes. Douglas is an attorney. He's going to help Kellen. I hope," she said.

"Would you mind telling *me* what happened?"

LaRetha nodded, and began to tell her mother everything from the day Kellen had surprisingly arrived, to the night of the party, and then her last conversation with Douglas. Laretta said very little, but listened intently until she finished before commenting.

"I'm just...*dumbfounded.* These can't all be coincidences. I'll admit, when you first mentioned your intruder and what happened that day, I figured it was just a sign that you didn't need to be out here, living all alone like this."

"I know," she said, sullenly.

"But now," Laretta continued, "I'm starting to smell a conspiracy. I think you and Kellen both have been set up in the worst way. And I hope this attorney person you seem to trust so much is worth it, because you're going to need all the help you can get. I'll be here for as long as I can, but he was right. Kellen will need local representation."

She agreed, before mentioning that they had only a little time to dress before meeting with Douglas. It was too bad that the circumstances weren't more social, she thought. Seeing her distress, Laretta gave her a hug.

"I'm sorry about *Therell.* But, your worrying over it won't change anything. We'll get through this."

LaRetha nodded, blowing her nose as her mother retired to her bedroom.

She could hear Laretta rambling around in the guest room, undoubtedly looking for something stylish to wear to this mystery restaurant. Despite the problems at hand, LaRetha knew that she should dress to impress, considering that Douglas always took great pains with his appearance.

Looking at the ring on her finger, she decided it was silly to continue wearing it. Besides, she didn't want to have to answer questions that she couldn't, just yet. And Douglas would surely notice. She dropped it into a small drawer in her jewelry box and closed it.

After a quick shower, a little makeup, and a steam curl to her hair, she was pleased with the results. From her closet she selected a black and white flowing knee-length skirt and silky black blouse. A silver looped belt fit her trim waist perfectly. Lastly, sheer black hose and black leather boots. She would wear a long coat, tonight.

Diamonds were a bit much, she figured, selecting sterling silver jewelry, instead. Gerald did have good taste in birthday gifts once, she thought.

"You look very nice, honey," her mother complimented, looking fabulous herself, when they prepared to leave. "This man must be something special."

Laretta's own dark green wool coat contrasted nicely with her matching sweater and skirt. Wearing boots as well, the only sensible choice in this icy cold climate, she looked even more like her sister than her mother. Those good genes were a blessing to them both, LaRetha thought, as they pulled the SUV out of the driveway and headed toward the interstate that led to the other side of town.

Surprisingly, the restaurant parking lot was full. There was valet parking, and when they entered, they found the place buzzing noisily with a clientele that she hadn't before seen in *Lovely*. There appeared to be singles, couples, and groups of professional people that looked *thirty* and over. This had to be the after-hours professional crowd.

She and Laretta were quickly led to the dining room, just past the bar that was practically invisible behind the wall of people seated there on stools. LaRetha imagined that this had to be a pretty common spot for socializing. *Why hadn't she been here, before?*

"Goodness!" Laretta said. She seemed both annoyed and intrigued by the noisy din of the restaurant. "I haven't been out and around this much activity in a while, now."

"I would've thought that was all you were doing in Atlanta, these days." LaRetha sipped from her water glass, looking appreciatively around the room.

"*Noooo,*" her mother responded, reprovingly. "Aside from a business lunch here or there, I don't bother. I have entirely too much work to do, and too many folks to manage. I meet enough people through my work. Mostly referrals, you know," she added, proudly. "But what about you? Surely you and Kellen went out a few times."

"Not like this. But, now that I know it's here…," she said, finishing with a shrug.

She glanced over her mother's shoulder in the direction of a rather handsome, well-dressed man, standing in the doorway. His eyes searched the room and then landed on hers. He smiled and LaRetha smiled briefly in return, before averting her eyes back to her mother's knowing face.

"*Uh huh,*" Laretta said, without turning to look. They both laughed.

The waiter came by and was duly instructed by Laretta to please show Mr. Douglas Davis to their table once he arrived, as if she was the one who had arranged this dinner. They ordered their salads and after biting into a warm buttered roll, LaRetha decided to just relax. She watched the other activities in the room. The food came and her mother began to eat.

"We don't want to look *greedy,* Mama," she groaned, as soon as the waiter disappeared.

"Girl, *please.* I'm famished. Besides, these men know what time it is," she said, with a youthful toss of her head. LaRetha smiled, thinking that having her mother here just might be enjoyable, after all. "He should have been here, by now."

Laretta rarely ever waited for anyone to show up to eat. If you were late, you just had to catch up, she always said. LaRetha still disagreed.

Douglas was just over thirty minutes late, and arrived to find the both of them finishing their salads and receiving their main courses from the waiter. LaRetha smiled with embarrassment. He looked amused.

"I apologize, ladies," he said, as he comfortably accepted the chair that the waiter was drawing back for him. "A meeting ran over. I couldn't get through when I dialed the restaurant, and I couldn't find your cell phone number, anywhere," he explained, smiling apologetically at LaRetha, his brown eyes twinkling.

"That's okay. I forgot to bring it. Douglas, this is my mother, Laretta Watson. Mother, my attorney, *Douglas Davis.*"

Laretta accepted Douglas' extended hand in greeting with an endearing smile, before giving her a quick look that said that he'd met with her approval. Dressed very nicely in a dark gray coat, a light gray ribbed sweater and dark gray pants, he looked marvelous. *And that cologne!* He removed his wool scarf and laid it over his chair before sitting down, and the scent floating past her nose was *divine.*

A waiter quickly appeared to take his order; a house salad, Cornish hen, broccoli casserole and tea to drink, he said, declining the waiter's suggestion of the house steak, instead.

A health conscious man, was he? She liked him more, already.

"We hated to start without you, but it didn't look like you were coming," Laretta said, not too apologetically.

"No problem, ladies. I appreciate your meeting with me on such short notice."

They nodded, appreciatively.

"First of all, let me preface our conversation by saying that any and all investigations regarding *Paul Straiter's* shooting have come to an end. No charges will be filed against you, LaRetha. The case is considered a matter of *self-defense,* and is officially *closed."*

She and Laretta whooped for joy, and several people turned to look. Instinctively reaching for Douglas' hand, she brought it to her face, squeezing it and seemingly catching him off guard. She hardly noticed.

"Thank you, so much, Douglas. I needed some good news."

She released his hand.

"Well," he said, smiling, "it was clearly a case of breaking and entering and attempted assault. It's being considered self-defense. You really had very little to worry about. It's just that I couldn't make any promises."

"I understand, and I appreciate the professional way you've handled all of this. Thank you. *Thank heavens!"*

"You are quite welcome," he said, smiling. "But, I'm just the messenger."

"So, kiss the judge for me, won't you?" They both laughed.

"Okay. Next time I see him."

"*So,* you're an attorney here in *Lovely,* are you?" Laretta wasted no time asking questions as the waiter removed her salad bowl. "I'm from here. Do I know your people?"

"I'm not sure. My father was Douglas Davis, Junior. I'm the third. He passed away five years ago. My mother died when I was twelve, and her people moved away, right afterward. You might have known them, though. *Douglas and Marissa Davis?"*

"Marissa? I only knew one Marissa, and she left high school early to get married. I never knew what happened to her, after that. *Marissa Shelton?"*

Douglas nodded. "Yes, that was her maiden name. Then you did know her."

"Yes! Beautiful girl! I remember her from elementary school on up to tenth grade. As I recall, that marriage caused quite a stir."

"It did." He smiled, nodding, again. "My father was in his twenties, and my mother was considered too young to marry by some people. But, according to the law, they could and they did. Most people thought she must have been pregnant. They still believe I'm a few years older than I really am. But, she wasn't. She was simply in love."

Laretta nodded, frowning slightly. Remembering.

"I'm sorry to hear that she passed away. She couldn't have been more than..."

"*Twenty-nine.* It was hard on my father, but he managed to raise my little sister Candace, and me, alone. He never remarried. He just fell into his practice and that filled his time, I guess. My sister's in Chicago, now. We both went to law school. And both still practicing."

"Wonderful. I'm sure your mother would have been very proud. Surely, your father was."

"Thank you. I hope so," he said, sounding sincerely grateful.

LaRetha was quiet for a moment, digesting all she'd just heard. Aside from his sister in Chicago, Douglas was practically alone, too. Like her, he was managing to carve out a life of sorts from what remained here in town for him. Why then, didn't people think she could do the same?

"Well, have you heard anything new?" She asked. She saw no point in delaying bad news.

"Just that Kellen will be charged with first degree murder, unless something that's overwhelmingly believable surfaces. It's questionable whether or not the two men didn't know one another prior to the incident. But I wouldn't want to elaborate on that without more facts. Have you thought of anything new, yet?"

She frowned, noticing her mother's raised eyebrow, as well.

"No, nothing," she said sadly, remembering the note she'd found in Kellen's bags, but saying nothing. "And, frankly," she added, "it's hard to believe. I just hope I can find out more when I visit him, tomorrow."

Douglas nodded, digging into his salad as though he was starved. LaRetha watched him silently as she ate her dinner, thinking how a man with such an appetite might probably be just as insatiable in other ways. She tossed that image aside.

"I'm still in shock because I didn't know Therell was at the party, or even in the house. Nobody mentioned him, all night. I'm just wondering what was really going on."

"You should have expected him, LaRetha. *Really*," Laretta stated."

"No, not *really*. When *Uncle Verry* invited me over on Friday night, he assured me the man wouldn't be there. He said it outright without me even asking, that he wouldn't put me in that situation. So, why would I expect anything different? According to him, when I told him about Therell's visit, he didn't even know the man was in town."

Douglas' brows furrowed. He didn't reply.

"This is all much too strange for me," Laretta said. "Now Douglas, I have no earthly idea what's happening around here. But it's probably got everything to do with that property that LaRetha is living on. That *Verilous* and his family have always felt it belonged to them and not to her father, all along. There's a lot of bad history about that situation. Those two fell out right after we married. I don't think they ever got along after that."

Even LaRetha listened to this. She'd never been told.

"Now," she continued, "I believe they're trying to do to LaRetha what they couldn't do to her father. He was born and raised out here. He knew these folks and how to handle them. But she's new to the place and they plan to take full advantage of the fact. That's what *I* think, and nobody can tell me different. The problem is that whatever their plan was it backfired and cost them one of their own."

Douglas listened with interest, saying nothing, just yet.

"I know these folks," she continued, and Douglas nodded. "They don't forgive or forget. They don't see their wrongdoing. And right now, they want blood from somebody, and that would be either her or Kellen, or *both*. My question is what can we do about it?"

Douglas placed his glass on the table, using a napkin to wipe his mouth before speaking.

"I know some of that land's history, but it seems to me you have a lot more information that we should discuss, further. That would really help Mr. Kincaid's case."

Laretta looked to LaRetha, who interjected.

"So, are you representing him? If not, we probably shouldn't discuss this any further."

Laretta nodded her agreement. LaRetha knew that her mother would have plenty to say about her opinion of this man's abilities, later on.

"I will if he wants me to. I charge a retainer..."

"How much?" LaRetha quickly asked.

"Fifteen hundred for this case. One-fifty an hour once that is exhausted."

"Not a problem," Laretta said. "I can handle the bill until he gets out. Then, he can owe me. Tell him that. He knows who I am."

"You don't have to..." LaRetha started. Laretta raised her hand.

"I know you can afford to do it, LaRetha, but I insist on it. It's not for him, anyway. Helping him is just my way of letting that family know that we don't play like that. We can discuss it later, but unless he objects, I won't change my mind."

"What if we lose his case? Can you afford to risk it?" Douglas asked, and his question caused LaRetha to raise an eyebrow. She left him to Laretta to handle.

"If I couldn't do something, Mr. Davis, I would simply say so. I wouldn't misrepresent myself. I just hope you can say the same, or Kellen will have to arrange for other representation. I know how this town works. So, please don't waste our time on this if you already know it's some sort of conflict of interest for you, or if you don't believe he's innocent. I'm not lining anybody's pockets with his blood or my money."

LaRetha drew a sharp breath at this. Her mother was testing Douglas, but she found this approach to be a bit extreme. But then, he was an attorney and shouldn't be ruffled by her mother's brutal honesty. Or so she hoped, for Kellen's sake.

Douglas laid his fork down and waited until his meal was in front of him and the waiter was politely dismissed, before speaking.

"I appreciate your concern, Mrs. Watson. I don't know Kellen Kincaid, personally, but I know this town and the people. I believe you when you say the history of that property might explain a lot, and that it could possibly lead to the truth, or least a motive. However, all I know so far is what I saw at that party. And I saw Kellen Kincaid with my own eyes, standing over Therell Watson with that gun in his hands."

"The thing that puzzles me about it most," he continued, "is that he didn't seem remotely aware of what he was doing, or even that he was holding the gun. He wasn't even excited about the fact that the man was lying in a pool of blood, right in front of him. Even when he was arrested, he seemed... not so much intoxicated like I thought at first, but *dazed*. I want to know why. And, I want to know if he even knows why. There are a lot of unanswered questions here."

Laretta nodded, still waiting for an answer. He continued.

"So, you see, I can't say whether he's innocent of first degree murder, or guilty. What I *can* say is that I have no reason or motive to misrepresent Mr. Kincaid. I have no present ties or loyalties, or business relationships with your family. And I don't need the money, so that's not my motivation, either. I'm simply offering to help the man because he's your daughter's friend, and because she had already come to me for representation, prior to this incident."

Laretta nodded. LaRetha listened on.

"So, in answer to your question, if you want a capable, reliable and certainly straightforward representative for your friend, you're looking at him. Or, you can certainly take your chances, elsewhere. Either way, I don't mind helping your daughter as much as I can."

Laretta looked from one to the other of them for a moment, her eyes resting on LaRetha, who nodded. She finally nodded.

"I believe what Douglas is saying," LaRetha said. "I don't see any reason not to hire someone who's able and willing to help. But, it's Kellen's decision. And if he approves, then so do I."

The other two nodded at this, and they all returned to enjoying their meal and to more pleasant conversation.

"That was truly enjoyable," her mother said, as they left the restaurant.

"Yes, it was," LaRetha agreed.

"Good food, excellent company. We must do this again, some-time," Douglas said, flashing that wonderful smile, his eyes twinkling in the lamplight.

"At least once more before I leave," her mother said, smiling, accepting his extended hand and a gentle shake.

The valet arrived with LaRetha's car. Douglas first opened the door for her mother, who got in gracefully, then walked with her to the driver's side, pulling her back with a loose grip on her elbow.

"I meant what I said LaRetha. I'll help you any way that I can. Not just for his sake. I want to see you through this. I'm here for whatever you need."

She blushed, hoping he didn't notice in the cold air that pinched her cheeks. She smiled from behind her hat and scarf, and pulled her long coat more closely around her.

"I appreciate that, Douglas. I'll call you as soon as I've talked to Kellen, and hopefully we can get to the truth of this matter."

"So, you still believe he's innocent? I can understand if you're unsure and just doing this as a friend. Out of obligation?" His eyes searched her face.

"I *know* that Kellen didn't intentionally murder Therell. Something isn't right about this whole situation. Hopefully, we'll find out what that is."

He nodded, and gave her a slight hug.

"Take care." He stepped away from the car. "Call if you need me."

"Goodbye. Thank you, Douglas. For everything."

He turned toward the parking attendant who had just brought his car around. Joining her mother, she found her car sufficiently warmed up for them. From her rear view mirror, she could see Douglas' black Range Rover pulling away from the curb and heading down the street. She drove in the opposite direction.

"Okay. *Now,* I understand. You have *two men* vying for you; one is in jail and the other is his attorney. *How ironic."* Laretta sniffed, checking her makeup in the mirror.

"Douglas is just trying to help. I wouldn't call that *vying."*

"Then what would you call it? The man so much as said he was going to help, whether I liked it or not. And he is some fine piece of work, that Douglas. But what happens when Kellen gets out? What *then?"*

"Mama, I just met the man, and already you've got us dating, engaged and getting married. *I am not looking for a husband.* Okay?"

"Uh huh!" Laretta looked annoyed. "Maybe you should be."

It was visiting hours at the jail. She waited in the lobby until she was directed to another room by a tall, thin expressionless guard. She sat between two other people at the one long table and glass partition that divided the room.

Kellen arrived a few minutes later and the sight of him caused her heart to sink. In rumpled clothing, he was unshaven, with a huge welt on his forehead. He looked as if he hadn't slept since before he'd been arrested. He avoided her eyes as he picked up his phone to talk to her.

"How are you doing, Kellen?" She asked into her phone

"Good as can be expected," he said, flatly. Shrugged his shoulders.

Are you sleeping? You look tired."

"I wasn't expecting visitors," he retorted, seeming irritated that she hadn't come before now. She ignored that.

"Tell me what happened. Why did you shoot Therell? Or did you shoot him?"

"You were there. You probably saw more than I did."

"Where is my gun? It's missing and I know that you took it."

"I don't know what you're talking about. And I don't appreciate being accused of something I didn't do." He looked around. "You shouldn't even be here, LaRetha. If you want any chance at keeping peace with that family of yours, you might want to act like you don't know me."

"What's that supposed to mean?" she asked. He didn't respond. "I came here to help, Kellen. But for that to happen, you'll have to *talk* to me. Do you even remember what happened that night? You were drinking a lot..."

"I wasn't *drunk*. I remember it, clearly. I just had a drink or two..."

"A drink? Or two? You were *drunk*."

"Okay, I might have had too much. I'm used to drinking a lot more and not getting so messed up. I talked to a few people..." His voice tapered off as if there were some he would rather not mention. She remembered. She would get to that later.

"What else?"

"I remember most of it. I remember us going in separate directions when we got there. I stood around, talked to a few people, for a while. Then, when we were ready to leave, I asked somebody where the bathroom was. One of *Verry's* daughters pointed me to one in the back of the house..."

"Who?"

"Bernice, I think. Anyway, when I came out, I ran into this dude who said he needed to talk to me, privately. I saw the family resemblance. But I knew something was up because he kept looking around like he didn't want anybody to see us. So, I said *no*."

"Did he identify himself? Did you know him, already?"

"I never saw him before. I just know that he wouldn't take no for an answer. When I tried to leave, he shoved me into the bathroom and locked the door. Then he started talking all crazy. He said something disrespectful, so I tried to hit him, except he dodged the punch."

"He was talking about how you and me had better get out of town. It made me mad, so I went after him. We wrestled for about a minute. I got him down and hit him a few times. I stepped around him to try and get out of the room..."

"And that was *Therell?*"

"In the flesh," he said, with sarcasm.

"You're sure you've never seen him, around? Some people think that you had."

Kellen silently shook his head. "*Never.*"

Although relieved, she wasn't quite convinced. But, he wanted to talk, so she listened.

"Anyway, you were waiting for me. I just wanted to find you and go. But, before I could turn around, he had come up from behind me and pointed something that felt like a gun in my back. I was drinking, but I wasn't too drunk to know this cat meant business, so I cooperated."

"So, I did what he said. I went into this room next to the bathroom and I sat down like he told me. That's when he said his name. He said he was your brother. Then, I knew what it was about. He said he wanted to make some sort of deal with me."

"He talked. I listened. But, all I really wanted to do was to get that gun away from him. He asked me something and I told him to get out of my face. Then he hit me. I wrestled with him and I finally got hold of it. He was down already, so I held it on him while I tried to get out of there. I made it as far as the hallway. That's when he came at me, again."

"He was strong. And he said I wasn't leaving until I gave him an answer. But, from the things he said and the way he lunged at me... that crazed look in his eyes... I felt like the man would kill me if he could."

"I warned him. I told him I would shoot if he didn't back off. But he kept coming, talking about breaking my neck or something like that. And all I could think about was getting him off me. Before I knew it, he was on the floor and I was standing there with his gun in my hands. He was dead. *I'd shot him.*"

He paused, as if thinking about this for the first time. She shook her head. *How terrible.*

"All I could hear was screaming. And well, you know the rest. I was arrested, and now I'm here. That's it. That's what happened."

"But, that was self-defense!"

"So you say, and so I believe. Now, to prove it."

She nodded, realizing the true complexity of the situation.

"Did anybody see any of this, or hear what was happening?"

He shook his head.

"If they did, I didn't see them. It's like everybody just disappeared. And now I have to prove I didn't intend to kill this man. I did shoot him, so I'm done for, either way," he said, matter-of-factly.

"Not necessarily. I know somebody who's willing to help you, Kellen. And you don't even have to pay him until you're released. When you're able to pay," she explained.

"Let me guess. *Douglas?*" He said, sarcastically. His eyes dulled over, and she could sense his hopelessness. She sighed.

"I don't know anybody else in this town. I think he'll do a thorough job. And you can trust him. *I* trust him. He's willing to help. I think you should let him."

He stared at her as though disbelieving what he was hearing.

"From what I'm seeing, nobody else in this town would be impartial enough," she continued. "Nell and the family are blaming both of us, as if I would ask you here to get rid of the man. I told her it must have been self-defense. That really made her mad. She acts as if we planned it all, from Paul Straiter to this."

"They claim that we're both just troublemakers," she said. "Just upsetting the entire town with our ill intent. And they've made it clear that they want us both out of here, *for good!*"

"That's exactly how Therell came at me. Now do you see what I was up against?"

She nodded, considering this.

"Sorry to hear that, though. So much for a *family reunion*," he said sarcastically.

"And why does this amuse you?" She was getting angry, now. *You try and help somebody...*

Kellen was upset, but so was she. And now was not the time to fight.

"Laretta's in town," she said, subduing her anger.

"*Laretta?* Oh, this is bad, isn't it?"

He seemed embarrassed, and angry.

"She's here for support. She's offered to pay your bill until you can reimburse her." She saw no reason not to tell him this, thinking it might improve his stinking attitude.

"Did she? *Whoa!* I am appreciative. For real," he said, seriously. "Except, I don't like what you're recommending. Think about it, LaRetha. Do you honestly think I can trust Douglas Davis to keep me out of prison, when my going might be the best thing that could happen to him?"

"*Kellen!* The man *wants* to represent you. What's wrong with that?"

He gave her a hard look. Laughed briefly and sat forward.

"Because, Douglas Davis is *infatuated* with you, for one," he said, his voice was low and angry. "I'm not blind. Besides, this man knows these people. Didn't you see how friendly he was with your uncle? That man raised Therell. So, it's possible that the same deal they tried to offer me just might have been offered to him, too. Except *he* might've taken it."

"We don't know what's really going on here, LaRetha. I don't even know for sure how you feel about him. I just know I can't afford to risk it."

"He wouldn't dare try it. Why are you so distrustful?" She asked. There was the matter of a certain woman he'd spent most of his time with, that night, after all.

"I'm *realistic*. They won't take me down. Not them and not you!"

LaRetha's face burned in anger. Still, she could hear the fear in his voice. He felt betrayed by her. She had to convince him to put aside his pride and suspicions to get the help he needed. Both of their futures depended on it.

"What in the world are you talking about, Kellen? What do you mean, *take you down?* You know I would never turn on you. What would I stand to gain? You came here to help me. I'm just trying to do the same thing for you. Why won't you let me?"

He shook his head. Then, laughed, caustically.

"You are so smart, yet so blind. *The-man-was-at-their-party, LaRetha!* And he was *sweatin'* you the whole time, not caring what anybody thought about it. So, unless you invited him, they did. Do you trust that? Do you think that *I* should trust that?"

"He was only being polite and he never disrespected you. You were the busy one, so don't try and turn this into something that it wasn't. Nobody was doing anything to try and hurt *you.*"

His expression softened a bit. She sat back, sighing. He wasn't the only one tired and angry. Except now she was ready to do something, anything, to fix this, while he acted as if he had all the time in the world.

"You have to trust somebody, Kellen. Me, most of all! I wouldn't even recommend Douglas if I thought it would compromise your situation. I'm trying to get you out of here."

"Then, post bail for me," he said, sitting forward. "I have a court appointed attorney, but if I could just get out of here, I could find one on my own," he said, staring at her, blankly. She stared back at him.

"You said you wanted to help."

"How much is bail?"

"*Fifty thousand dollars.*"

"I'll see what I can do."

"You said you wanted to help." He repeated. "Will you?"

She nodded, but couldn't help visualizing a frightened Kellen running away, for good.

"I'll have to get back with you on that, Kellen. I'll see what I can do." She answered, although she wasn't so certain that what he was suggesting was sensible.

"What, so you have to consult with Davis, first? Get *his* opinion? I'm not worth the risk, but you want me to think that he is? Now, I understand."

"I won't fight you on this, Kellen. Let's try and stay on the same side."

"Sure. *Same side,*" he retorted, sourly.

"We need to think this through, and not make any rash decisions."

"Think it through? That's what brought me to this sorry town – *thinking!*" He said, loudly. "I thought I could help you by coming here. I thought we had a future, together. All I wanted was to make you happy, *thinking,*" he emphasized, "that I could do that for you."

She shook her head.

"And now, I'm having to *think* my way out of this place, when that's what got me here in the first place. *Thinking* that you needed me on your side. But you don't need me. Not anymore." He was belligerent, now.

"Kellen, you're wrong…"

"I'm not wrong. I came here to protect you, and I did, or at least I tried. So, as far as I'm concerned, there's nothing for you to *see* about? All you have to do is get me out of here."

Fighting an urge to lash back at him, she looked away, hoping to hide her hurt expression. So, he blamed her, too. Squaring her shoulders, she started to speak. He spoke, first.

"These people *hate* you, LaRetha," he said, his voice filled with malice. "And, they hate me for being here for you. They want you out of here and they wanted to use me to do it. So, didn't it occur to you that they might even send an attorney to help them do the job?"

Ignoring his comments, knowing they were made out of hurt emotions, she responded.

"Douglas has no reason to send you to prison. You're just being paranoid."

"Maybe," he rasped. "Maybe I am. But that don't mean it ain't happening, baby. I do know one thing. If you don't wise up soon, you're gonna see a whole lot more people suffer for your… *thinking!*"

She scowled at him, not believing the attitude he had with her.

"*Wake up, LaRetha!*" He whispered, vehemently. "They won't stop at me. Whatever's going on with your family is causing me to be in here, and here is where I'll stay until you give them what they want."

"And what might that be?" She asked, but he didn't answer. Clearly, the land had something to do with this, maybe everything. But, *Kellen* had shot Therell. Not her, and not the other way around. Shouldn't that be his first concern?

"What was it that Therell wanted you to do, Kellen?"

He didn't answer.

"So, you'd rather sit in here than help me to help you, and to help myself in the process? That's smart," she said, sitting back in her chair.

"I won't rot in here for your...sake," he said, sounding as if he would rather have said, *for your stupidity.*

That was the last straw for her.

"Say what you will, Kellen, but that wasn't me holding a gun in my hand, with a dead man lying on the floor! I came here to find out what happened and why you wouldn't leave when I asked you to. But the answer is clear - to me and to everybody else."

His eyes narrowed as if he would strike her if only he could. But, he could just *think* mad, she decided. She was his best hope, right now, so he would want to listen to her, and to be honest with her, as well.

"Was my wanting to stay at some stupid party a *crime,* LaRetha? Your folks invited the both of us, but that was my crime?"

"I won't talk in riddles with you, Kellen. I just want to know what Therell was offering you. And who that woman was that you couldn't tear yourself away from, all night? The one who told the police that we were arguing."

He said nothing.

"Why won't you tell me?"

"So, you're not bailing me out? Well, it's good to know where we stand. Thank you for coming, LaRetha. Don't bother to come back, again."

With that, he stood up and walked away, leaving her puzzled, and angry that she'd come in the first place.

Laretta had lunch ready when she got home. A tossed salad, ham sandwiches and tea.

"I called and made hair appointments for us, first thing tomorrow morning. Hope you don't have other plans."

"Cancel mine. I'm running errands in the morning, but I can drop you off," she said, thinking about her dwindling grocery supply. Turkey and dressing could go only so far.

"So, how did it go?" She asked LaRetha after they sat down and said grace.

"Not well. That man had the *nerve* to walk out on me. He refused my help, and Douglas' help. He won't even talk to me, now."

"Why? What did he say happened, that night?" Laretta frowned.

"He claims Therell cornered him at the party and made some nasty comments. That he refused to talk to him, so Therell pulled a gun and forced him into a back room. He wanted Kellen to agree to something that pertains to me and this land..."

"Didn't I tell you?" Her mother interrupted.

"But he refused to listen," she continued, "so Therell charged at him. They fought and he got the upper hand. He took the gun from Therell, and when he came at him, Kellen shot him. He says it was self-defense, and that is what it sounds like to me."

"So, did he admit that he already knew Therell like Douglas says?"

"He says he didn't."

"Yeah, *right,*" Laretta scoffed.

"I know. He claims he never saw him before that night. He wouldn't tell me the proposition Therell offered him, either. As it turns out, he doesn't quite trust Douglas *or* me, so he's just not talking."

"Nah, that story's just too clean for me," her mother mused, shaking her head.

"Me too. Why would anyone, including Therell, pull a gun on somebody he didn't even know? Why would he even approach a man who's clearly intoxicated at a party, right where people could see, and start an argument that might lead to a fight? Or worse, to *this?*"

"I don't know. But it looks like Therell got what he had planned for somebody else. I'm just concerned that he might've come there for *you.*"

The thought made her shudder. That's when she told her mother about the note she'd found in Kellen's wallet. She also remembered to show her the copy of the notarized document that Billard had given her. Reading it, Laretta sat down, giving her an incredulous look.

"How do you know these signatures are real?"

"I'm thinking they're not, but Douglas has someone working on that."

"Did you tell him about the note?" Laretta pressed.

"No. He's not Kellen's attorney, yet."

"Did you tell the police?"

"No, of course not."

"Somebody was pressuring Kellen. Did he say what the note was about?"

"I forgot to ask. But I'm thinking that, by the way Therell approached him that night, it must have come from him. I think Kellen is lying about not knowing him. And probably about other things, too," LaRetha said.

"Like what?"

"Like, why he even came here. And why he doesn't want Douglas representing him."

Her mother frowned at this.

"And now, he's angry because I won't bail him out of jail. He *must* be insane. As scared as he's looking, I just know he'll run."

"Yes, he would. Nobody wants to be tried for murder in a town like this."

"I also suspect that he doesn't want Douglas involved for a reason. Like he's afraid he might get too close to something."

"Makes sense to me," her mother said. "Why else would he refuse free and willing help? I wouldn't if I were jobless, broke, and in jail for murder."

LaRetha nodded. Her mother had a way of sifting through appearances to get to the truth.

"It's because he's lying to me. He could've had that note when he came here, and now he probably owes somebody something that he can't deliver. And that's why Therell pulled a gun on him, I'll bet."

To think she might have been living with her enemy all this time, thinking he was her protector. She shivered.

"My question is, when in the world did all of this happen? The man hardly left my side the entire time he was here."

"Maybe that was the job. I always say, never underestimate a man. If they want to hide something, they'll find a way. Believe me!"

"I know this. I am divorced, after all. But, what would Kellen stand to gain that would be worth a *murder* conviction? If it's the land..?"

"*If?* That's all it's ever been. Maybe he was planning to get you to sell. Marry you so he could control that decision. He latched onto you for some reason."

"You just don't understand our relationship," she defended, ignoring her mother's look of disbelief. "He would've told me something like that. Why not, if my selling would get me back to Atlanta, and keep the both of us out of danger, too?"

"Because, ain't no money in scaring away the prospect," her mother said, matter-of-factly. "He knew you well enough to know that you wouldn't have sold this place behind something like that."

"I think it's like he said. After I shot *Straiter,* he only came to protect me. But somebody got to him. *Therell* got to him. Asked him to do something he wouldn't do. And now, he's afraid to tell me because..."

"Because it might put you in more danger?" Her mother gave her a comforting hug.

"With your problems over now, why not just move back to Atlanta with me? At least until some of these questions are answered? Right now, we don't know who's been doing what, who with, or why. It's just not safe, here. It never was."

"I couldn't leave now. Kellen is in real trouble. And as long as Douglas is willing to represent him, then he's got a chance. I just have to get through to him, somehow."

"How about just temporarily? Until the smoke clears? Kellen couldn't protect you now, if he wanted to."

She nodded.

"That family is probably very angry and plotting revenge. It's just a matter of time before something else happens. There's nothing you can do, anyway. Not if he doesn't want your help."

"But there's something he's not saying. I think he wants the help."

"But, who's going to help *you*, LaRetha? Are you going to shoot another intruder? That man was killed in that hospital for a reason. Kellen's killed a man and the family wants nothing to do with you, now. You're on your own, out here."

She couldn't respond.

"Right now, you're letting your feelings about *Kellen,* that family, and whoever you need to prove yourself to, just totally cloud your vision. Use your common sense! Nothing good can come out of this, for you. *You could die out here, girl!"*

She knew her mother was right. But, she had to follow her instincts on this one.

"All I can say is, he must be some kind of lover!"

"*Mama!* Sex has nothing to do with this."

"I thought you came out here to find some peace? It's been anything *but* peaceful for you."

"I know. But, he doesn't have anyone. And as stupid as he's acting, I know he's scared to death. I can't leave him."

"*Shooot!"*

After seeing her pained expression, Laretta sat next to her. Sighing heavily, she shook her head. Maybe she did understand, after all.

"If you get killed, you'll *leave* him, true enough. You'll have no choice in the matter."

Clasping her hands together, she could only shake her head.

"Okay. *Alright.* You know I'm here for you, honey. I'll stay for a few more days. I don't think Kellen is anybody's cold-blooded murderer, either. Except, proving it won't be so easy," she sighed. "But I won't leave until I know it's okay."

"Thanks, Mama. That means a lot. I'll talk to Douglas tomorrow and see if he'll at least talk to Kellen. I'll know what to do, after that."

"That Douglas is a *fine* young man. Good looking, smart *and* rich. And you want the broke, incarcerated one," Laretta mused.

She watched her mother retreat down the hall to her bedroom, unable to disagree. This wasn't about who she wanted. There was a lot more to consider, and to be concerned about. And without communicating with Kellen, she would have no idea what was going on with him.

But, she was tired, so for now she would get some much-needed rest. This was going to be a long, uphill battle.

Lying in bed, she heard Laretta laughing at something on television from the living room, where she sat flipping channels. Her mother was nobody's fool and was seldom blinded by her emotions.

She, on the other hand, always wanted to think that things might get better, rather than worse. Only she didn't see that happening anytime soon. Not this time.

Laretta was eating cereal, and pouring over the guest list for her annual Christmas party.

"You should come this year," she told her.

LaRetha remembered those grand holiday events that her mother's office gave every year – one just before Christmas, the next just after the New Year. Usually held at some lavish hotel, they were pretty much the industry event of the year, with live entertainment, comedian hosts and exquisite catered meals. Not to mention expensive gifts and door prizes. She used to love to help plan for those. Only she wasn't in a festive mood and doubted she would be, by then.

"Think about it," Laretta said, before she could answer.

LaRetha ate in solitude as her mother placed business calls from the bedroom. Taking advantage of her moment alone, she reflected on Kellen's sudden appearance at her home.

Laretta didn't know about his mystery woman from Ohio. Or about the job he was to start soon, but probably wouldn't now, under the circumstances. But thinking back, that *job* business was beginning to sound a bit far-fetched. Just like his behavior at the party, and his little tantrum at the jail. This wasn't the Kellen that she knew. Was it possible that Douglas had a point? *How well did she really know Kellen, after all?*

Later, on the drive into town, she talked to her mother about her meeting with her uncle, and about how kind he and Nell had been, at first. She described the cousins she'd met on that Friday night, and then, Saturday night's party.

"You know what, LaRetha?" Her mother began, looking out of the passenger window as they rode through miles of country road. "There's a serious story behind this, and I'll bet that uncle of yours is right in the middle of it."

"Well, I wouldn't know. I'm not *allowed* to speak to him."

"*Forget Nell!* You can talk to him anytime you like. I can almost promise that he doesn't feel the way she does."

"You know what? I had completely forgotten that Douglas said Therell's attorneys had called, wanting to set up a meeting about the property."

"When was this?"

"That was before the shooting."

"*Hmmm,*" Laretta said. LaRetha could almost read her thoughts.

"Question is, knowing this, why would Therell risk a confrontation with Kellen? It makes no sense."

"It makes no sense, *yet,*" her mother quipped in. "*Not yet.* But you have a point. If there was going to be a meeting, all he had to do was wait on the outcome."

"*Unless,*" LaRetha said, "he was afraid of that outcome. Maybe he knew it wasn't going to go his way, so he was trying to seal a deal ahead of time. Protect his interests."

"Or rather, his *greed,*" her mother interjected.

"As for *Kellen,* I can't believe the way he's acting. He hasn't been the same since the day of the shooting."

"And how's he acting?" He mother asked, frowning.

"*Very disrespectfully!* He refused to leave the party when I asked, and spent the entire evening dancing circles around me with some other woman."

Laretta gave her a look of disbelief. She could just hear her wondering, *and you still want to help him?*

"Right now, he's acting so… I should have broken it off with him a long time ago. Then this wouldn't have happened."

"You wouldn't have done that," he mother replied.

"Yes, I would have. I never wanted a long distance relationship, with him or anybody. And I don't want the kind he does, anyway."

"Which is?"

She hesitated, knowing that her philosophy and her mother's were a bit different where this was concerned.

"Well, just any kind of relationship won't do, for me. I wasn't sleeping with Kellen, and it didn't sit well with him. At first, I thought that was why he acted so different at the party, but now I'm not so sure."

"He's been here all this time and you two aren't…*together?*"

"Right. I'm not saying we… It's just that I don't want a man who's intimate with other women. It would have to be *exclusive.* And that means marriage."

"But, he gave you the ring, didn't he? And you accepted?"

"He asked but I never accepted. But, that's another thing. How can you propose to me in the afternoon, and cheat on me that same night?"

"*Cheated,* huh? I feel you, girl. This dating thing is a no-winner. I'm starting to believe that everybody cheats."

"Well, my man is out there, somewhere. Except I'm not chasing him down. He'll be heaven sent, and we definitely won't have to go through anything like this. Not that I'm in any hurry."

Laretta was silent as she turned her SUV onto Main Street in the town square. It was early, but stores and shops were opening, and people were rushing to their various places of work.

"Nobody can help Kellen Kincaid until he starts telling the truth," she mused.

Her mother nodded, thoughtfully.

"I just can't stand all these *secrets*," she continued. "I'm a *news writer,* for goodness sakes! I'm supposed to know *everything* first," she exclaimed.

"None of us have that privilege."

"*Humph!* It's just dangerous, you know. Being kept from things you're better off knowing."

"You're right," her mother sighed. "You are so right, and let me be the first to apologize for that."

She looked away from the road, giving Laretta a questioning look.

"I need to explain something to you," Laretta added. "I sometimes forget that you're a grown woman and it's no longer my job to withhold things because I think they might worry or upset you. It's not fair or even smart at this point."

"Okay. So where is this going?"

"It's about time for me to grow up and stop trying to keep you a child, forever. To deal with things I've kept silent about for far too long."

"Okay. It sounds like we're about to have a heart-to-heart talk that's long overdue. So, I'm just going to park this car and you can start from the beginning," she said, pulling into a convenience store parking lot and finding a space.

She turned the key, shutting off the engine, and faced her mother.

"I'm all ears."

"Well," Laretta, started, taking a deep breath, "you've always known that I was never close to your father's family. I just never told you why."

"Why?"

"They thought that *I* was the reason that your father had nothing to do with them, after we married. But, *they* pushed him away, not me."

"How, Mama?"

"Well, it goes back to inheritance. That farm was left to all the children, except nobody else wanted the responsibility. They all moved. Found jobs. Started families. And when times were hard, they needed money."

"*Watson* was the only one of them who would work that land. Their folks wanted to keep it in the family, so he offered to buy them out and they all sold it to him. Every one of them did. Your father paid them very generously with money he borrowed against the property - money that he would have to repay. And nobody was complaining about it, *then.*"

LaRetha nodded, engrossed in the story, now.

"Well, it took years for him to pay off that debt. He took a gamble, but he did what he had to do, trying to keep it out of the hands of people who'd wanted to take it, all along."

LaRetha suddenly remembered the night visitors.

"The problem is, once they'd spent the money, they all wanted their land back."

"Okay. Now, it's making sense."

"Because it's the truth. When he refused to give it to them, your uncle got mad and accused him of stealing it from them. They were never reasonable folks, but just out for themselves, as usual. And their greediness and nastiness drove a wedge between me and your father."

"I never knew."

"I never wanted to drag you into it. But, you need to know these things, now. I've always detested everything that farm represented. This was the life *Watson* wanted, not me. Most of the time, I felt lonely and alienated. And eventually I began to hate living in that house you're in. It felt like a prison to me."

"So, after three years, I left your father. He didn't want me to go, but he loved the land too much to walk away. And I never expected him to. I knew he loved me, but he'd been entrusted with caring for it. For keeping it in the family. *His* family."

"So, being as headstrong as you know I can be, I moved on, hardly looking back. But, it appears that even with your father's death, those old squabbles still haven't been buried."

"I never looked at the farm as a prison," LaRetha told her.

"That can be any place, when you're unhappy. The biggest hurt came when Aurelia got pregnant. It was before we were engaged. His family was determined that he would marry her, and not me. I used to wonder why. At first, I thought it was because she was so pretty. But I think it's because they knew they could control her. It was all about the farm, the entire time. Had I known that…"

She shook her head sadly, and continued.

"I loved your father. They knew I didn't care about money or social position. They had nothing to string me along with. They wanted Aurelia, but she couldn't stand them. I don't think they ever knew that. *Watson* told me."

"He loved you," LaRetha said, wistfully. "And you were pretty, too. So, why wouldn't he prefer you?"

"He did. Only, back then, all I could be out here was *Watson's* wife. After a while, that just wasn't enough for me. I felt closed in. Like everybody was just waiting for me to prove that I was unfit for him – his being a *religious* man, and all. His family made me feel that way."

Laretta quietly felt her mother's hurt.

"There's something else I never told you. A few people knew it back in the day."

LaRetha waited.

"Before I met your father, I dated your *Uncle Verry.*"

"You *what?*" LaRetha said, with disbelief.

"It wasn't a relationship. It was before I even met your father, and very short termed. We saw a couple of movies together, that's all. It was never anything sexual, that's for sure. I never even kissed the man."

"But, one day, long after *Verry* was out of the picture, a mutual friend introduced me and *Watson,* and I just *fell.* It was obvious to me that they were brothers, except he was much more mature. A few people knew about me and *Verry.* I finally told you father, before we married. It didn't matter to him."

LaRetha stared at her in disbelief.

"So, was that the problem, then? My uncle wanted you for himself?"

"No. Although *Verry* used to compete with him in everything. But by the time we met, that relationship was inconsequential. Just something his family tried to use against me, whenever they could. *Verry* made sure of that."

"But why?" LaRetha asked as she listened to this painful recounting of memories best forgotten.

"Your uncle was the reason that I finally left town. He lied. Made accusations. Created problems between me and their family. I just couldn't do it, any more. Especially after that last thing he did."

"And what was that?" LaRetha questioned.

"I was nineteen. Married. You were still a baby. Your father was gone into town," Laretta continued. "*Verry* came to the house, looking for him. He hadn't done that in a while. So, even though I knew how that family felt about me, I never wanted to come between brothers. I told him that *Watson* was due back at any minute, and I asked if he wanted to wait."

"He wasn't in that house ten minutes before he started talking about how I had turned his brother against him. He insisted it was my fault that your father wanted nothing to do with him."

"I told him off, and I told him to get out of my house. I finally made him mad enough to leave. But not before he started ranting and raving about ruining my name and taking back what belonged to him."

"What did you do?" LaRetha asked.

"I threatened to tell *Watson,* and to shoot him myself, if he didn't leave. He was always afraid of your father. He left, but he said he was going to tell everybody that I had called him over when I knew *Watson* would be out of town, and tried to seduce him. Right in his own brother's house."

"No, he didn't!"

"He did that. And there are still people in that family and in this town that think I tried to pit them against one another in that way. That I married your father because his brother wouldn't have me. As if *he* would have been the better man," she sniffed. "The lies were unreal, but people around here believed it."

"That's too unbelievable!"

"I was young, but I knew that, in spite of all I had done to be a good wife to *Watson,* his brother's lies would change things between us, just as he intended. Your father tried to protect me, but the damage was done. I didn't feel that I could go to my folks. They had warned me not to get involved with that family, to begin with. I felt very alone."

"Finally, I got tired of defending myself. Of being whispered about and feeling like I had embarrassed your father with his family. I was sick of the whole town, by then. So, I left, taking you with me."

"I know now that your father couldn't have believed it. But back then, it was the one simple-minded thing he could do to destroy our marriage. But back then, I was young and I didn't know how to fight for my family. It seemed so major. Maybe today, it would've been a minor thing."

"Don't be so sure of that," her daughter said. "I do stories about people who've been slandered all the time. Some folks have the *nerve* to call it 'free speech'. But, it's a devastating thing, to that person and to their family. You can't just erase those lies once they're out there."

"It takes some mean dirty snake-in-the-grass to even say some of the things that I'd heard your uncle was saying," her mother said.

"I just can't believe that *Verry* would do that, and then come back to the house and look me in the eye, knowing he was the cause of our family breakup. And over a *lie!*" LaRetha marveled at this.

Laretta shook her head, as she relived the pain and humiliation of it all, even after trying so hard to forget.

"Maybe he's changed," she said. "That was a very long time ago, and back then, people questioned very little. We were told who to like, who to love, who to associate with. A lot of times we didn't ask questions, we just believed whatever we were told. I guess it was just a sign of the times."

"Like I said, things haven't changed much," LaRetha interjected. "It's like the power of the media. We say we love total strangers. We cry for people we've never met, and even hate them for no reasons, all because we're told to, and because of our need to feel that we *belong.* I've been surprised more than a few times when I've approached so-called *celebrities.* They're rarely what you expect."

"That's true, I'm sure. But, don't let this scare you. I still want you to leave this place, but I don't want you to run away from the problem like I did. You *own* that farm and you have every right to be here. Fight for it, then sell it, or do whatever you want. But it's your decision. Remember that."

"Yes, but isn't it a shame how this kind of destruction can start in our homes, with families fighting and dividing and hating one another out of jealousy and greed? Even worse, that we allow this? We even enable it, encouraging it to happen. Then we waste more time, casting blame. Either way, once we're divided, we all lose our power. Our strength as a community. But, isn't that the devourer's plan?"

Her mother was nodding.

"I'm just angry that *Watson* didn't stand up for you."

"He did. But he wasn't feeling the wrath like I was. He was a practical man, and I felt he had enough to worry about, with the farm and trying to make a life for us. What he did out here was pretty remarkable."

"But, to repeat the question you asked me earlier, *what about you?*"

"*Watson* never understood my frustrations at being regarded as some sort of unworthy, kept woman. He saw how hard I worked at being a good mother and companion to him. I worked hard on that farm, too. He was just proud that he could provide for us."

LaRetha nodded.

"Distance made the gossip less important. But still, it hurt that no one ever asked *me* what happened. My husband's brother said it, his wife supported his story, and a brother wouldn't lie to a brother about something like that, now would he?"

"That's just *crap*. Isn't it possible that people didn't believe him like you thought they did?"

"Many of them did. And they didn't hesitate to say so. I would easily fight somebody for offending me, back then. But, I had to raise you, and I didn't want you struggling with this all of your life. I could just see that there was something better out there, for us. And there was. So, for whatever reason, I know now that I made the right decision by moving away."

LaRetha was quiet. Struggling to understand.

"My only mistake was not making them tell the truth. Not thinking enough of myself and my own importance to demand it. And that's why, although I'm afraid for you. *Deathly afraid,* I admire your sticking by Kellen. My marriage was destroyed, but they had no right to interfere in your relationship."

LaRetha just sat there, trying to take it all in.

"I just can't believe you're talking about my *Uncle Verry.* He never mentioned any of this. He seemed so happy to see me. I don't get that."

"So much time has passed, and *Verilous* is probably just mellowing in his old age. You'd be surprised at what some of these old folks have done in their day," her mother laughed through her tears.

"But your father, now he was a gentleman. And I've learned that even though I really like my life in Atlanta, there's nothing like having a good man in your life. I would do things differently now, I think."

"Didn't he come looking for you? Or try to get you back?"

"He did. I just couldn't do it. I hated *Lovely,* by that time. And I hated that look of disappointment in your father's eyes. I didn't know if it was because of me, or his brother, or both of us. He always said he believed me. I hope that he did. But, I despised *Verry* for the pain he caused us. And as much as I hate the fact, I still do."

LaRetha closed her eyes, shaking her head in empathy.

"In time, I managed to forget. I'm still working hard on forgiving, for my own sake. I did what I thought was best for us both. And for you. And in the end, this little colored girl learned to love herself, and that was most important. I don't think I would have done that, here."

"You've always been a great mother. And a beautiful woman. My father was *lucky* to have you. *Very lucky.* And you were never to blame."

Laretta smiled gratefully, and LaRetha realized that as confident as her mother was, it was important for her to hear this.

"Well, it wasn't easy, back then - certainly not for strong-willed women like me. But we made strides. And starting a business back then wasn't easy for a woman, either. Certainly not a *black* woman."

"But, I was blessed. And happy that I was finally something other than somebody's *wife.* I was way ahead of my time because everybody else that I knew only wanted marriage and kids. I have learned since then that being a wife to the *right* man, to a *good* man, does have its merits. For some, that just might be enough."

"So, you never remarried *because..?*"

"My decision. I never found my soul mate. I've met nice men. Good looking, professional men. But it never happened for me. I never took the time, I guess. *A big sacrifice for a career.* But, I have been seeing someone off and on over the years. He's someone I admire and respect. Couldn't be with him if I didn't. We're just so comfortable, I guess. We're in no hurry."

LaRetha nodded.

"Truthfully, I never fell out of love with your father. But, I never interfered in their marriage. After eight years of separation, he had to go on with his life."

"So, the family never learned the truth? About you and *Verry?*"

"They knew the truth from the beginning. But they thought our separation would make it easier for them to control *Watson.* They found out it wasn't."

LaRetha considered this.

"The real confusion started when Cecelia moved out here. They assumed she had money, I guess. So they started asking him for loans, again."

"Who did?"

"*Verry,* mostly. The rest of them fell in at his suggestion. But *Watson* wasn't having it. Nothing they tried ever worked. He wasn't thinking about giving back that land."

"*Wow.*"

"Right. So, don't expect Nell or anyone else over there to be too forgiving about anything. They seem cool on the surface, but those folks have a lot of old grudges and unseen motives."

"And she had the *audacity* to blame me for all of this. Knowing all this."

"That's Nell," her mother said.

"But Mama, why didn't you tell me this before I left Atlanta? I sold everything and you said nothing. If I'd known, I could have at least made an *informed* decision. But now...well, I guess it's too late for *what if*."

"I am so sorry, LaRetha," she sniffed. "It was just so hard to dig all that back up, after finally learning to let it go," Laretta said, shaking her head, sorrowfully. "Never in a million years did I think you would stay here. I thought you'd be back home, by now."

"Well, leaving here is starting to sound pretty good," she replied.

"I wish you would consider it. But, don't lose what rightfully belongs to you."

"I just never expected any of this," LaRetha said.

"My only regret is that your father died without us being around. I never knew how sick he was. I would have been there."

"He's still here with us, Mama. *In spirit.* Don't blame him. I told Cecelia the same thing. She said he didn't want us to remember him like that. It was his decision."

Laretta nodded, accepting her daughter's pat on the hand, and feeling as if a huge burden had been lifted from her shoulders.

"So, you see. None of this is about you, or anything you've done. You're *Watson's* daughter. And mine. You were born from a loving marriage and there was never any shame in us. *Ever.* We married and we split up. But your father never stopped loving you."

"I know, Mama, but, what about Aurelia? Where is she, now?"

"I don't know. She was out of the picture long before we married. Now, I can't say what happened with whom, because I wasn't there. But we both know that if he'd really believed that boy was his, your father would've claimed him no matter what anyone said or thought about it."

"My point, *exactly,*" LaRetha exclaimed, feeling validated.

"I found out later on that *Verry* was raising him, which meant only one thing to me."

"What was that?"

"*You* figure it out."

9

Saturday's sunrise found LaRetha scrubbing her bathrooms. Keeping busy was keeping her mind off of things. Laretta was sorting new items that she'd bought from *Lila's Boutique* in town. She had run into an old friend from high school at the salon and accepted an invitation to an afternoon tea with her and a few more old friends. She was excited about going, but having a hard time choosing an outfit. LaRetha was glad she'd made plans.

The phone rang. It was Douglas. They exchanged cordial greetings. She told him what had transpired over the past two days, leaving out the details her mother had shared. He was annoyed by the way Kellen had treated her.

"I can't believe him," he said. "He should be glad you're still in his corner, is all I can say."

"True. But, I think I may know what's going on, here."

Just knowing her mother's secret had shed a different light on everything.

"What do you think is going on?" He asked.

"I can't be certain, but..."

"Let's talk in person," he said.

"Sure. I could come to your office, later today. Or, we could talk out here, at the farm."

Douglas hesitated.

"Maybe we should discuss this, more privately," he finally said. "Your mother is quite charming, and very easily the *eighth* wonder of the world, and I do mean that most respectfully. But what we discuss might only worry her more, don't you think?"

"Of course." She didn't, but then, she didn't know what he wanted to talk about, either.

"How about tomorrow evening at my place? Mrs. Starks is my cook and she makes a mean seafood platter. Shrimp, crab cakes and lobster. How about it?"

"Douglas…"

He said nothing and she could imagine him smiling into the phone. Dinner at his place sounded very appealing.

"Okay, that sounds nice. But as far as I know, Laretta only has plans for today. I really don't want to leave her, alone."

"You might be right." He sounded disappointed.

"So how's your schedule, this afternoon?" She asked.

"I'm free after about *eleven*," he said.

"Great. I'm driving her into town for a luncheon with some friends. We're leaving about that time. I could meet you after I drop her off."

"Great," he said. "I'll arrange for lunch at my house. Is that alright?"

"Just fine, Douglas. And thanks for your time."

"No problem." He gave her directions.

Deciding on the navy blue skirt suit took a few minutes. Then heels and a little jewelry. She held her hand out to admire the beautiful ring that Kellen had given her, before sliding it off her finger. She placed it inside her jewelry box, snapping the lid shut.

Checking her e-mail before she left, she learned that Mac Henry had sent payment for her last article by *priority mail*. It should arrive tomorrow, she thought, gleaming with satisfaction.

By *9:00am*, Laretta was sitting at the kitchen table, sipping hot coffee. From the looks of it, she'd already been outside. Her exercise habits hadn't yet rubbed off on her daughter.

"You look cheery, this morning. I made breakfast."

"Thanks, Mama. Been up long?" She asked as she uncovered her plate of bacon and eggs, and added strawberry jam.

"*Six-thirty.* It's a habit I can't break. 'Early to bed and early to rise'. That's me."

After breakfast, she told Laretta that she had some research to do after she dropped her off. She would explain later, if necessary.

They arrived at Laretta's friend's house at *11:30*. It was a beautiful beige stucco structure with very attractive dark wood designer framework around the outside windows and doors. Several cars were there, already. Laretta waved from inside the doorway. LaRetha pulled away from the curb feeling strangely excited about her visit with Douglas.

Following Douglas' directions, LaRetha's journey ended at the driveway of a large, two story brick home that was even more impressive than her uncle's place. Not what she had expected of a single man, wealthy or not. But who needed this much space? *He must be divorced,* she thought.

Mrs. Starks, an attractive, petite woman whose gray hair belied her age, smiled kindly as she ushered her inside. She followed the brisk walking woman through a huge open foyer with marble floors, into a bright and spacious living room. There she waited.

Looking up in amazement at high ceilings with large, lovely chandeliers, she admired the wood-sculptured wall panels and plush carpeting that complimented the colorful and very elegant over-sized contemporary furnishings. Now, she was starting to know who Douglas Davis was, and he was certainly no phony.

"*LaRetha!* Thank you for coming," the man said, greeting her with a quick embrace. He looked wonderful, as usual, in a tailored green suit and shirt of a lighter shade that brought out the brilliance of his brown eyes and cinnamon colored skin. She tried not to stare, although he was making no such effort.

"Thank you, for inviting me."

She allowed him to show her into an adjoining room where they relaxed behind a sliding door amongst even more beautiful contemporary decor.

"You really live here, Douglas?" She asked teasingly. He smiled.

"*Family home,*" he said, nodding. "Built and passed down from some hard working people. I'm here weekdays, and travel most weekends. Would you like something to drink?"

"Sure, thank you," she said. "Douglas, this view is *spectacular.*"

She walked over to a far wall to get a better look out of a tall ceiling- to-floor glass window, absorbing the scenery beyond the house that hadn't been visible from the front entrance. There was a large beautiful lake there. *Laretta would love this,* she thought.

"My father was an attorney but dabbled a bit in architecture. My mother had great decorating tastes, as well. I haven't done a whole lot, other than change a sofa here and table there. Everything else suited me, I guess."

"*Really?*" She exclaimed. "It's very nice," she said. Then, "Okay, now you have my undivided attention." She sat and crossed her long legs. "Where do we start? Food or conversation?"

"Would you like a drink, first?"

"Just soda, thank you. Do you have ginger ale?"

"I think I can accommodate you. I forgot that you didn't drink."

"Not routinely," she said, watching him go behind a hand carved oak and glass bar to pour soda into a frosted glass, before making a drink for himself.

"You look refreshed," he said, handing her the soda with a paper napkin. "It's good to see you smiling." He said, sitting down and observing her as she sipped from the cold glass.

"It's good to feel like it." She said, taking a sip. "This is good."

"Brunch is running a bit behind, I'm afraid. I had forgotten that Mrs. Starks was coming in late, this morning. She didn't have time to stop at the market, so seafood won't be practical in the time that we have. I apologize for that."

"That's no problem" she said, suppressing a rumble in her empty stomach.

"But we can talk while she prepares something else. She never says what it's going to be, but it's always very good. I hope you're not in a hurry."

"That sounds fine. I do love to eat, but I guess you can tell."

"I can tell you have nothing to worry about," he said, those marvelous eyes twinkling as he smiled. She felt flattered and self-conscious, at once, as he continued to check her out without modesty.

"So," he finally said. "What transpired with Kincaid? And what is it that you suspect is really going on?" He asked, breaking the spell of the moment.

"*Right,* I'll get straight to the point." She said, uncrossing her legs to adjust in her chair, and crossing them, again. He was watching her every move. And she did not mind at all.

"I didn't mean to rush you," he laughed, "I just know that you Watson women prefer *directness.*"

"True. Well, after talking with Kellen, and having time to think about it, I'm sure that, since he came here, he's been approached about my inheritance. I *believe...,*" she said, taking a deep breath, "...Kellen was being targeted to conspire against me, with a promise of something in return. He never told me this, but I think it's because he was concerned for my safety. For *both* our safety."

"And what do you think he was offered in return?" Douglas asked, squinting those big beautiful brown eyes a bit. Surprisingly, he didn't seem at all phased by the news. *Was everyone on to the truth except her?*

"Well, I don't know exactly."

"He didn't tell you?"

"No. Like I said, this is pure conjecture at the moment. But, I know that a gun I was given is missing, now. That concerns me."

"Did you ask him about it?" He inquired.

"He says he doesn't know where it is. It's registered to *Uncle Verry.* He left it with me after the incident with my intruder. I never returned it, and he never asked for it."

"*Hmmm.* That's interesting," Douglas said.

"I just don't want it turning up in the wrong place at the wrong time," she said. "Assuming it's not the one used in the shooting."

"No. That gun was registered to Therell," he said, and she was relieved.

"Douglas, Kellen is nobody's cold blooded killer. I think he's been pressured ever since he got here and that all this ties together with my other problems with Therell. I just don't know how, just yet."

"But, doesn't it concern you, all this secrecy he's keeping? He says he hasn't seen the gun, but it's missing. You think he's been approached, but he obviously won't confirm or deny the fact," Douglas said, thoughtfully. His eyes weren't mocking, but she felt foolish, all the same.

"He's still trying to protect me, except it could send him to prison."

"So, you're sure he reacted for your benefit, and not because of some lucrative deal gone bad?"

"That's just it. I don't think he's made any deals with anybody. Not one that they had anticipated, anyway. And he didn't tell me to protect me."

"And what does your mother think?" He asked.

So, she thought, he suspected these were Laretta's thoughts and not hers. She was slightly offended.

"My mother doesn't run my life, Douglas. She's here to lend her support, and that's it. I respect her opinion. But I assure you, I can assess a situation for myself, however bad it looks."

"*Point taken.* I didn't mean to imply that you couldn't do just that."

She sipped from her glass, averting her eyes from his scrutiny.

"But, about what you said earlier," he started, pouring himself another drink. "I've been wondering some of the same things. I know Kellen's type - city born and bred, ambitious, and maybe even a bit impulsive. But I couldn't imagine him chucking the fast life and leaving Atlanta, right when he's trying to convince his girl to move back? To marry him, even? It just seems a bit far-fetched."

She shrugged, having wondered the same thing.

"But, then I saw that huge rock on your finger. And I figured I was wrong. That it must be *love*. Pure and simple."

She thought about the ring safely shut away in her jewelry box at home and realized he'd already noticed it missing. She looked up to find him watching her intently –her and her now barren finger.

"Then," he continued, "I realized which hand it was on, and I knew there was still a chance."

"A chance for what?" She asked, sipping her soda, absentmindedly.

"For this," Douglas said, surprising her with how closely he was standing over her, all of a sudden. He easily took the glass from her hand, and placed it on the table. Carefully, he pulled her up from the chair to stand close to him. She was taken aback.

What is he doing? Her thoughts were reeling. But the answer was clear. He lifted her chin with one finger. He looked at her intently, and it caused her heart to flutter. Alarmed, she gently pulled away.

"This isn't right. This isn't why I came here," she explained, stepping away.

"Of course not. I invited *you*, didn't I?" He was totally unruffled.

Was this the reason for the invitation? She wondered. *Did he expect to seduce the woman while condemning the man to a life sentence? Had she already said too much?*

Clearly, Douglas Davis planned to get paid in more ways than one, she thought. And Kellen hadn't been far wrong.

Remembering her cause, she moved away, quickly and easily slipping out of his reach.

"I couldn't get involved with you, Douglas, you know that. And certainly not with Kellen being in jail on my account." She turned her back to him, afraid he could read her with those beautiful hypnotic eyes.

"*Says who?*" He asked, taking her arm, turning her around to face him, again. "How do you know that it's all on your account? Or that Kellen isn't getting just what he deserves?"

Suddenly, she wanted to distance herself from this man who had such a magnetic pull on her. But, he wouldn't allow it, moving closer, instead.

"We don't know what's happening with Kellen," he said. "And he doesn't want us to. He might already have representation, and might just be hiding the fact, probably to get you to post bail. He might've even gotten paid for some service he was providing. Before this, I mean."

She hadn't thought of that.

"Something has been bothering me about the way that whole thing went down, last Saturday. You remember, I told you that?"

She nodded, and he walked away from her, looking puzzled. He had her full attention, now.

"Well, I played it all over and over in my mind. I tried to figure out what it was that I was overlooking. Then, I remembered." He looked at her intently as he spoke. "Kellen danced with one woman all night. I noticed it, so I'm sure you did, too."

She didn't respond. He continued.

"This woman. She's a business associate of your cousin's. She works at Jasmine's public relations firm in Ohio."

"You're kidding me!" She said, incredulously. "A *PR* firm in Ohio?"

"Why? Do you know about her?"

"*Know about her?*" She inhaled to keep her composure. He waited.

"Kellen wrote me about a woman from Ohio that he'd been seeing but wasn't any longer. I don't doubt that she's one and the same. But, I got the impression that this contact was a *he*. Or maybe that's just what he wanted me to believe."

Douglas nodded, his expression knowing.

"When I visited him at the jail, he wouldn't say who the woman was, even after I asked. Or that she was a friend of Jasmine's. He hasn't said that he knew either of them, before the party. But I guess that was all a part of the lie."

Douglas was silent but looked concerned. She continued.

"And now, I see that she's not only still in the picture, but she's been right here in town when he was staying at the farm with me. Jasmine's friend is the very same woman he was going to spend the holiday with, I guarantee you!"

Douglas shook his head, his expression exhibiting surprise.

"I don't believe it. He took a job with my own cousin, and not one of them ever said a word. Not even about already knowing him, already, either that day or the day before."

"And neither did he," Douglas added, to which she nodded. She shook her head in disbelief, too distraught to pretend that she wasn't hurt by it all.

"I can't believe Kellen, or this family. I guess I've been deceived about a lot of things."

"We don't really know that he expected her to be there. Just that she was. Could be a coincidence."

"Please!" She said, angrily. For her, Kellen's behavior as of late was proof enough. She guessed now that if she had left the party without him, it would have suited him, just fine.

"My question is, what is their relationship, *really?*" She said. "And what is her involvement in all this? Or was she the real reason for his confrontation with Therell? She seemed his type," she said.

"And, what type is that?" Douglas asked quietly, looking intently into his glass, obviously preparing for her to make an even bigger fool of herself than she had by trusting Kellen, she thought. *She had to pull herself together.*

"Never mind that," she said, meeting his questioning gaze from where he sat on the arm of the sofa, looking dapper and a bit too satisfied at this discovery, for her tastes.

"I guess there's more to Kellen Kincaid that even you knew?" He asked. She smarted at this.

"And to think, I've been running around, trying to help that man. And now that I've refused to post his bail, I guess he doesn't need me. And that's why he sent me away." She exclaimed, incredulously.

Douglas face said that he was stunned that she would say as much. *Well, she was Laretta Watson's daughter,* she thought. And there was no point in hiding the obvious. Besides, he already knew what she was thinking, and obviously agreed.

"Well, now that you know, do you still care if he gets out or not?"

She eyed him quietly for a moment. "You would think not, wouldn't you?"

"I asked because I know that learning the truth can make a big difference. It changes your heart and your mind."

"I still don't think he meant to shoot Therell. Even if it was over another woman, it might easily have been in self defense."

Douglas shrugged. Raised his glass and took a sip.

"Kellen has been there for me through a lot of situations, long before I came here, and long before all this started. Besides, we weren't engaged. He had the right..."

"Yeah, *right* in front of your face," Douglas spoke, ruefully. "I would call that being a bit disrespectful, but that's just me."

She frowned. He was right, but so what? He wasn't her judge.

"I came here to ask for your help, and I have," she responded, calmly. "I know you have no reason to want to defend Kellen, and he is being rather uncooperative, right now. But, he's just scared. Would you at least talk to him about it?"

He appeared to think about this. Started to speak and appeared to change his mind.

"I've said what I came to say, Douglas. It's up to you. When can I expect your answer?"

She started for her purse, with plans to leave.

"Wait. We can still have lunch..," he said.

"I have to go. There's so much to do, right now."

'Well, I wouldn't be too concerned about helping Kellen. He seems to have enough of that."

Finishing his glass, he placed it on the bar. And she wondered if he didn't drink more often than he really should.

"Is that your answer?" She asked.

He shrugged, shook his head. Said nothing.

"Douglas, understand this. I think Kellen is just the beginning. Somebody is playing dangerous games, and my relatives are definitely involved. Therell was, and now Jasmine, and who knows who else?"

He nodded.

"Sure, I'm angry about it. But, we only have a little time left to figure this out. Less than *30 days,* to my understanding."

"What's the deal about *thirty days?*" He looked puzzled.

She reached into her purse and retrieved the small plastic bag containing the note she'd found. He read it and slowly whistled.

"You know this, and you still want to help with his defense?"

"I've explained that to you. I owe him the help."

"What if he's been lying about everything? What *then?*"

"That would be his cross to bear and mine, wouldn't it?"

He gave her a somber look before walking to the window. She followed. Unthinking, she reached out and touched his arm. He turned around, studied her – his seductive brown eyes drawing her into him. She took a step backward and looked away. He sighed.

"Are you sure about this, LaRetha? This could get very ugly, and far more dangerous. If he's willing to sit in jail, then maybe you should let him. There has to be a reason…"

"I wouldn't ask if I wasn't sure. Besides, he isn't willing to sit in jail. He asked me to bail him out, remember? Except I'm not going to."

"*I* certainly wouldn't. You don't want him running out on you, and I wouldn't put anything past him, right now."

She nodded.

"There are a lot of issues at work here, LaRetha. And I wouldn't risk being the one caught in Kincaid's crossfire. You've had a bad enough time, as it is. But, if it's really what you want… it's your money, after all."

"Don't worry. I said I'm not bailing him out."

He seemed convinced, and relieved.

"Good. There are worse places that he could be. Jail might be his only protection. Therell's family isn't too happy right now, and from what I remember about your uncle from back in the day, your friend's life might not be worth very much if he gets to him before this is resolved."

She must have looked horrified because he quickly took her hands into his.

"I didn't say that to scare you. But it is a real possibility. Besides, he can't leave town and where else can he go? That's safe, I mean?"

He was right, again. Until she knew the truth, she shouldn't put either of them at risk.

"So, okay. I will speak with him. Get a feel for whatever's going on. And, if we both agree on it after that, I'll take his case."

"*Thank you, Douglas.* And, we're still taking care of your fee. Just tell us when." She removed her hands from his grasp and walked toward the foyer.

"Like I said, it's your money, lady."

She felt like hugging him, but decided against it, feeling his presence all too strongly at the moment. She needed time to think. And she needed space.

"I have to go," she said. "Thank you, again. For the invitation and the advice. I needed this to get back on track, I think."

"You were never off track, I don't believe. You probably know a lot more than you realize." He walked a step ahead of her as she went into the foyer to retrieve her coat.

"Goodbye, Douglas," she said as she allowed him to help her into it. He walked with her outside, into the falling snow. Pulling the coat tighter around her, she got in her car. Looking back only once as she pulled away, she saw Douglas standing in the doorway, looking very concerned.

"So, did you run all your errands?" Laretta inquired.

"Truth is, I went to Douglas' place." There was no reason not to tell her mother, now.

"So, you do that often, at this time of day?" Her mother asked, sounding tickled, and more than a little bit mellow. *An afternoon tea, my eye,* LaRetha thought.

"*First time.* I didn't say anything, in case nothing came of it."

"Well, did it?"

She told her Douglas' decision to talk to Kellen, after all. Her mother didn't seem at all surprised.

"Well, he's doing it for you, anyway. Not Kellen."

"You know that for a fact, then, huh?" She responded with unintentional sarcasm. Her mother looked insulted.

"*Sorry,* Mama. It's just that I keep coming up with more questions and fewer answers. What I thought actually was, probably wasn't. I trusted somebody, after saying I never would, again. And now, I'm wondering what *really* happened. Do you know what I mean?"

"I think so, honey."

They were silent for a while. Then LaRetha wanted to brighten the mood.

"I meant to tell you before that I love that new cut," she said about her hair. "I didn't expect you to take so much of it, off."

Laretta's prior shoulder length locks were just below her ears now, in a full, blunt cut that truly became her, bringing attention to her gorgeous face and eyes. Its deep black coloring was highlighted with reddish tones.

"Cold weather or not, I needed a change. You like it, huh?"

She turned so that LaRetha could see it, better.

"*Cute!* You look way too young, now. And you're forcing me to resort to drastic measures, here. This battle is coming to *war!*" She teased, pulling her own very curly hair at its ends. Her mother laughed, thoroughly enjoying the teasing.

"Well, you always looked great with longer hair. You know how to style it. Me, I don't have the time or patience to work with it."

"Well, that style is really working for you," she complimented and her mother beamed.

Happy to be on one of her favorite subjects, Laretta led her to her suitcases to show off some of her more recent purchases, offering her a beautiful chocolate brown dress with long sheer sleeves and small red designs. There was a matching throw.

"My goodness! That is *nice!*" LaRetha was delighted.

"I was undecided about this one. But, I think it'll look great on you. For those special evenings with a certain special someone," she said, grinning.

"If I ever find another one," she replied, playing along. She truly doubted she and Kellen would see any more days, or evenings, like that.

"You already have, you just won't admit it," Laretta replied, pulling more evening wear out of her bags, handing them to her.

"Here," she said. "I got these at a steal. They're just a little *young* for me," she said, referring to a few skimpier ones. "And, since you have inherited my great genes in the figure department," she teased, "I thought I'd give them to you. Wear them with pride, girl!"

At Laretta's urging, LaRetha tried one on. She was amazed at the excellent fit. Taller than Laretta, but a little thinner, the light blue evening dress with glittery beading fit her perfectly.

"It's funny how we've always looked great in the same colors," Laretta mused. And, she was right. The dress looked as good on LaRetha as it must have on her.

Three more dresses followed. Beautiful and well fitting.

"But, they're so *expensive*."

"No, I got them at *seventy percent off!*"

"I'll wear them when it's warmer."

"Girl, I saw that beautiful black cashmere coat in your hall closet. *Wear them with that*. It's time you dressed with some style."

"I resent that," she laughed. But it was true. Being single had made her consider her wardrobe far more seriously. She was once a clotheshorse like her mother. But that was *BDG*. 'Before Drama with Gerald'.

"Now, you can be the sophisticated businesswoman by day and a beautiful, sexy vixen by night. *And I ain't mad at you*."

"Well, I still prefer the *demure* approach. I don't want to attract the wrong kind of man, with the wrong kind of vibe, you know?"

"Honey, even a *saved* man wants a sexy woman at home, don't kid yourself. Besides, you can be a knockout for him without looking like a tramp to everybody else. Just find out what he likes. *You know*," her mother did a little shimmy in the mirror, "put a *smile* on his face." And LaRetha laughed aloud.

"I'm glad we had this little *talk*," LaRetha teased. "But, right now, I need to get some work done. You're sure about the dresses?"

He mother picked one up and pretended to pack it away.

"Give me those!" She carried the load of them into her bedroom where she carefully hang them up. She looked forward to an opportunity to wear them.

Two hours later, she closed the laptop computer and went searching for Laretta, who was engrossed in a magazine. Looking up, she saw her and patted the seat next to her.

"Here. Sit down. What's the matter?"

Laretta could always read her moods, so there was no use denying this one.

"I still can't believe I *shot* a man. Right here..." her voice waned.

"I know how you must feel. It happened. But you didn't plan it, *he* did. Your life has to go on."

"I know."

"It's only natural that you would lose sleep over something like that. It's going to take time, that's all."

"You're right," LaRetha nodded. Still, as she showered later and got into bed, she considered the *30 days* and how little time was probably left. And what might happen when that time was up.

Feeling very tired, LaRetha tried to sleep, but it wouldn't come. She hadn't realized how taxing all this had been on her. She was used to a hectic pace, but this was an emotional journey that she hadn't anticipated. Douglas and her mother were supportive, which made it easier. Yet, she wanted nothing more than to awaken in the morning, with all of this being far behind her.

Laretta had always told her that she was strong - stronger than her, even. She didn't *feel* strong. Certainly not right now. But her mother always insisted.

"When you were little, it was *your* strength that kept *me* going," she used to tell her, from time to time. "*It's true,*" she would say. "I remember being in my bedroom, bawling my eyes out because I'd had a miserable day. I had been docked a day's pay on my plant job for being out sick, I had just gotten bad news from the doctor who said I needed to have emergency surgery. And then I'd had an equally upsetting conversation with your father. He was dating, again. And it tore me up."

"I was just miserable. There we were, in another new apartment amongst strangers, and I had nobody to talk to about it. I missed my family, but I thought they were hardly missing me. And, I missed your father, very much."

LaRetha would suppress sympathetic tears, as her mother remembered.

"Then, when I thought I was never going to stop crying, and you know that took some horrible day for me, you came strolling your little four-year-old self into my room, talking about you were hungry."

"I remember turning my back so you wouldn't see me crying like that. Then, you said it, again. When I didn't answer, you hauled off and punched me in my side, as hard as you could."

They both would laugh at this.

"I was so angry, I wanted to spank your behind, and I told you that. Then, you said something that made me straighten up. You said, *Well, I had to do something to make you stop feeling sorry. I'm hungry and can't nobody feed me but you. So get up and fix me some dinner!*"

LaRetha could never suppress a laugh whenever she'd heard this story, and neither could Laretta. Lying here now, laughing even in her pain, she realized for the millionth time just how fortunate she truly was.

First of all, for having a mother like Laretta. Some people found her a bit tactless. Others, like herself, appreciated her gentle spirit but firm honesty and her kind heart underneath it all.

And now, lying in her bed, she knew she needed to stop feeling sorry, and *get up and fix some dinner,* so to speak. She had to clean up her life, and rid herself of all the craziness. And to pray that she find a way to do it.

She switched off the lamp, remembering how, as bold as Gerald was about most things, he could never sleep in complete darkness. She also remembered asking how he was going to survive then, *in hell.* He had never forgotten it. Reminded her every time the thought upset him. She laughed again.

Pulling covers up to her chin, inhaling the light fragrant air from her shower, she smiled to herself.

It'll all be okay, very soon, she thought. And, within minutes, she was sound asleep.

10

Douglas Davis sat in his home study, still dressed from his morning workout, his gym bag on the floor beside him. He was concentrating on the wallpaper pattern, and thinking about the beautiful, sensual as all get out, *LaRetha Greer.*

LaRetha, La-Re-tha. He slowly repeated the word, rolling each syllable over his tongue, time and again. Almost like *Aretha.* A name he'd always thought was befitting of only a few women. But, hers did her little justice before actual introduction. Only when you met her did you realize how its uniqueness and breathiness fit her quite perfectly.

The woman had seemingly fluttered into his life, and her very presence made every pore of his body come alive. That dinner at the restaurant with her and her mother had told him a lot about her. She was classy, and seemed a bit conservative, although he couldn't figure how Kincaid had factored into that. She was definitely *centered,* self-directed and caring. Maybe too caring, considering the company she kept; her mother being the exception.

LaRetha was different from any woman he knew– especially at this age. *Free spirited, energetic, enthusiastic.* The woman seemed to treat life like some sort of adventure; always searching and never relenting in digging for truths.

Most women would have kicked Kincaid to the curb, by now. But, she was loyal; to him, to her mother, and apparently to everyone she loved. More than that, as adamant as she was about supporting Kincaid, she was nobody's fool. That woman could definitely take care of herself.

Tossing his bag back into the hall closet now, Douglas went downstairs and poured his second drink since she'd left some hours ago, as he pondered the entire situation with her and Kincaid, which was perplexing, to say the least.

During their first visit to his office, they had seemed your ordinary couple. Surprisingly, she had worn what appeared to be an engagement ring, but on her right hand. Still, he'd quickly dismissed any thoughts of a possible opportunity there, thinking she intended to marry the man. But then, there they were at the party. And now he knew differently.

Aside from Kincaid being a stupid jerk, he recognized the age difference, which was really the problem, as far as he could see. There were very different levels of maturity, at play here. That man just didn't appreciate her for the woman she was. And it didn't hurt that she was tall, curvy, and absolutely gorgeous! And with the clearest complexion he'd ever seen in his life.

The first time he'd met with her at his office, he had gotten lost just thinking about the possibilities that lay ahead for the two of them, while she'd spoken to him about a few things he still couldn't recall. He remembered the admiring way the young man had looked at her, before glaring at him, as he sat pretending that he wasn't captivated by this woman who hadn't even seemed to notice. But *Kincaid* had noticed, and it was clear from the beginning that he considered him a threat. And, he imagined, as it stood right now, he probably was.

He thought he'd made a fool of himself, from the way he'd practically fallen over her when they'd left the restaurant. But, she didn't seem to think so. On the contrary, she seemed pleased with him. But confusingly, nothing about today's meeting had indicated she was even remotely interested in him, in that way. She had pulled away from him, after all.

According to the information she'd provided on this form that he was holding, she was quite the professional; having a strong managerial background in government and corporate business, and with writing credits from several well-known publications. Living on that farm alone, and obviously happy to do so, it appeared that she was doing what she wanted in life.

But, he hadn't done too badly, himself, he thought. He never lacked for clients. He was highly recognized by his peers, even those much older and with far more experience in law. He had fallen into his father's footsteps, and had never taken the responsibility lightly. And, he would have never, ever, considered risking his reputation, at any cost. But, this time, there was something more at stake and he was willing to take the risk.

He remembered the first time their eyes had met. The way she'd looked at him. There had definitely been strong chemistry, although she was quick to look away, returning his gaze with one less inquiring than the first. But it was too late. The kindling had been ignited, already. And his heart's flame burned for her in a way that he'd never thought possible.

What did she see in this younger man, Kellen Kincaid? Tall, dark, with a build only slightly leaner than his own. *Okay,* so he could understand a physical attraction. He did look virile, as far as that went. But, he doubted Kincaid could provide her with what she truly needed, which was someone she would never have to take care of, think for, or clean up after, like she was trying to clean up after him, now.

As far as he was concerned, the man was guilty of *something.* But first degree murder? Highly unlikely. It was possible he'd come here with the wrong intentions. And what was most irritating was that nothing about his behavior, as she described it, implied any realm of remorse or concern for his actions, or for his future.

Kincaid was a *fool,* pure and simple. Whatever, if anything, he had been promised by Therell Watson couldn't have been worth losing the affections of a woman like LaRetha Greer. Beautiful, smart *and* resourceful, that woman was.

He made notes about their earlier discussion. Whether Kellen Kincaid ever got out of jail didn't mean a hill of beans to him. Still, the case was intriguing. Besides, those Watson folks were something else. Always in the news for something or other. For many years, back in the day, it was for fighting. That was that *Verilous,* character. Oddly though, after all those years of being cited for one thing or another, he'd managed to turn it around and began receiving commendations and awards from those same departments. That, again, was her *Uncle Verry.*

LaRetha couldn't know the history between her uncle and her father. Either that, or she'd managed to find a forgiveness that could only be commended after so many years of the *Hatfield and McCoy* type relationship those two households had fostered. But, old man *Verry* had stopped drinking, and it was years since he'd heard of him being arrested, so maybe his brawling days were over. He hoped so, for Kincaid's sake.

He remembered Therell Watson from elementary school on through high school. Always tall for his age, he was smart, athletic, and considered good looking by the girls. But, like his uncle, a bit untamed and unscrupulous. And, just like the young *Verilous,* he was known to get into more than a few brawls. Usually over a bad deed, or a girl, or something else he considered his territory.

Learning he'd made threats to LaRetha had come as no surprise. What *had* surprised him, though, was the way the man had presented himself so lowly in this matter when a little tact could have taken him so much further. If he'd done his homework, he would know how much this woman loved her family and that she would have embraced the idea of being closer to his side of it. She might have welcomed him as a brother, and *given* him what he wanted, if he'd been patient and a lot more respectful.

Therell Watson must have started something with Kellen Kincaid. Threatened and then assaulted him. He'd certainly had no intentions of meeting with them over this document matter, because most likely it was as phony as LaRetha had suspected. Just like him.

He knew that, to LaRetha, the idea of being hated and ill-treated over a family matter was far-fetched, but, that could be because she didn't fully know the history of this dispute, or the farm's value - sentimental or otherwise. And because she just wasn't made like that.

He wished he could in good conscious advise her to just *sell* the place. But they clearly had no real intentions of paying for it. Then again, he knew what her father had always said to his father, Douglas, Senior, who was also his legal advisor. If that property ever got back into those greedy people's hands, it would be sold or squandered away within a year.

Watson had fought tooth and nail to keep that land. And now, it appeared to have gone to the right person. He had known his daughter, well; fiery by nature, and just as stubborn as he had been. And, as was characteristic of a professional journalist, she was determined to get to the root of this family issue, not realizing that she was liable to stir up a bigger hornet's nest than even she could imagine.

But, somehow, LaRetha trusted him. And that complicated his situation, a bit. And then, there was the matter of Kincaid's Ohio girlfriend. He had no doubt that she was standing right smack in the middle of this. It simply amazed him how the woman had managed to infiltrate herself into LaRetha's life without her even knowing.

Kincaid was clearly involved with her. *Seriously engaged?* Douglas thought not. He had been all over that woman at the party, but why? What had that *trickster* promised him that he wasn't already privy to? What had they offered that drove him to the point of risking it all? *And, why had Jasmine brought her to town, knowing what had happened between him and that gold digger, just two summers ago?*

He scratched his head with his pen. LaRetha would eventually find out. He'd planned to tell her. But with all that was said here today, he just couldn't. Not just yet. And he didn't know why, except that, now that he'd found LaRetha Greer, he wasn't going to let her get away from him.

He would do what he had to, to keep her nearby, even if that meant fighting to save Kincaid's hide, and *then* telling her about him and Samira Neely. Anything to soften the blow and to get her away from Kincaid long enough to make something happen, for himself.

Sighing, he looked at his watch. He had a meeting at the jail in another hour. He didn't expect it to go too pleasantly at this point. Still, this was what he was being hired for.

He went to change clothes. Then, dropping a tape recorder, pad and pen into his briefcase, he put on his coat, waving to Mrs. Starks on his way out to his garage. He decided to drive his new Mercedes.

Oh, the lap of luxury, he thought. And he could easily share it with a woman like LaRetha, because he knew that she would never take it, or him, for granted. Besides, she had her own purse. So, she would neither rush to marry him, nor leave him for it. Not like some women. Not like *Samira.*

"I have to leave in a few days," Laretta said, and LaRetha dreaded it, instantly.

"Well, I knew this was coming," she sighed. "Is everything alright at the office?"

"Fine. You sure you won't come back with me?"

"I'm sure," LaRetha nodded.

"Okay. Your breakfast is on the stove."

"Thanks," she said, going into the kitchen with Laretta in tow. Thinking how she would surely miss not having to cook, mornings.

"Talked to Kellen, lately?"

"No," she said, flatly. "And I hadn't planned to. He can't get me out of the way fast enough. So he can just get whatever's coming to him."

Her mother frowned.

"But, what could that be? I thought about this all last night. You're still here, on the farm. And now the man who threatened you is dead. What could he stand to gain, now? Why refuse your help?"

"That's just it. I have no idea. Just a clue, but nothing clear cut."

"Well, I've thought about what you said, and I think you're right to some extent, LaRetha. Kellen is ambitious, but more than anything, he's in love with you. So, whatever it is that he doesn't want you to know about, even if he did stand to gain something from it, it's possible he felt he had no choice. But, that doesn't excuse his hostility, or his keeping secrets."

"I agree, but I'm not so sure about him wanting to protect me, anymore. And he didn't appear to be under any duress, to me. His attitude wasn't one of concern. It was just...*bad.*"

Her mother nodded.

"But, you know what, Mama? I think I owe *Mr. Bad Attitude* another visit. And this time, he's going to tell me the truth. I deserve to know, and I'm not going to be the only one who doesn't."

LaRetha waited at the table for him to come out and talk to her. Jasmine and the family had tried to use Kellen and she wanted to know how. From what she'd learned so far, anything was likely.

Kellen was too resourceful to be broke for very long. So, it was difficult for her to imagine that he would chuck away years of friendship with her and Germaine for ill-gained money. Or that he would propose marriage for the mere purpose of controlling her, and not for love. But, between Laretta and Douglas, these new revelations were bringing with them a *jolt* of reality that this was indeed the case. And she was being electrocuted.

Kellen finally emerged, looking less assured this time, but certainly healthier. He pursed his lips as if blowing a kiss and smiled before picking up the phone. She gave him an expressionless stare. *Was she supposed to be flattered?*

"You must really miss me. Why are you back here, LaRetha?"

Now, *this* was the Kellen she was coming to know - sarcastic and unappreciative.

"I just wanted to see how *Mr. Stupid* was doing. They treating you alright in here?"

"What if they weren't? What would you do about it?" He hissed, bruised by her intentional affront.

She stared at this man and wondered where she had missed the obvious. He wasn't going to make this easy for her. But, this wasn't entirely for his benefit. She would get what she came for.

"Who is the woman from the party, Kellen? The woman you danced with all night?"

"Why do you insist on doing this to yourself?" He asked, emotionlessly.

"What is it that I'm doing to myself by coming here, and trying to help you?"

He sat back in his chair, eyeing her as if annoyed, but she sensed something deeper. He had never been that good at hiding his feelings from her.

"You're trying to give me a hard time, but I think you're just full of hot air," she said. "Somebody's offered you some money, and you think that by sitting in here, you're guaranteed to get it. Am I right?"

He said nothing, his eyes resting on her lips as if remembering. She was immediately annoyed. Uncomfortable with her own thoughts.

"Talk to me, Kellen!" She said in frustration. He looked taken aback, but still said nothing.

"I can't believe I've laid awake nights, wondering how to get you out of here."

"Well, it certainly wasn't by bailing me out, was it?"

"And why should I? When you won't even talk to me? I may not be as street slick as you pretend to be, but I'm hardly the slowest person in *this* room."

"I agree. I think you're extremely smart. You know that."

"You lied to me about that girlfriend from Ohio. She was here all the time and you never said a word. You wanted me to leave that party so you could spend time with her? Am I right?"

"Okay, it's true. I danced with her," he said, shrugging an unsuccessful attempt to show indifference. "You were there too, remember? Did I look like I was trying to sneak and do anything? I was right where you could see me, if you'd been paying any attention."

He spoke matter-of-factly, and it only angered her, more. She sighed heavily. Adjusted her posture in the hard, uncomfortable chair.

"Okay, let's get down to it. Here's the situation. I'm at a point where I almost don't care if you never get out of this place. Maybe this is exactly where you belong – if not for your own protection, at least for mine. It seems to me that since you were put in here, nothing bad has happened to anybody else. Could that be the reason?"

His eyes glowered for a second, before returning to their previous disinterested state.

"I want to know who she is and why you spent so much time with her."

"Her name is Samira."

"Samira *what?*"

"*Samira Neely.* We met at your father's funeral. She introduced herself as a family friend, and gave her condolences. I gave her a business card and forgot about her. Then in September, she called to see how I was. She flew into town, we spent some time together. But, you knew I was seeing other people. So, what's my crime?"

"I don't care about that, anymore," she said. "So don't even worry about that. My question is why was she at my father's funeral? And *what* is she doing in *Lovely?*"

He sat forward, moving the phone closer to his mouth.

"She and Jasmine are best friends. That's probably why she was there. I really don't know. The last time I had talked to her was in Atlanta. I told her I was coming for the holidays. She said she might pass through, and she did. I didn't expect her to be at the party that night…"

"But you were hoping."

"I knew it was a possibility. She came over to speak to me and I talked to her. And yes, she was one of the reasons I wasn't ready to leave. And why does this surprise you?"

"*Finally, the truth!*" She said, her sudden outburst startled the guard, who appeared to have dozed off, standing up. He quickly composed himself.

"But tell me, how could you come here, and not tell me that you were dating my first cousin's best friend? That she was here to see

you and might be at my family's party? I would call that *trifling* of
you, but that would almost be a compliment."

Saying nothing, he looked at her with different eyes, but she was
too angry to care about having his respect, right now.

"I can't believe you would betray me like this. You came here
because of her. Am I right?"

"No, I didn't," he said, lowering his voice, "I came to be here for
you."

"Stop this. You're here because you lied. To me and a few other
people. But, I can tell you this, I'm only here out of concern for
myself and whoever else might get hurt by this and whatever it is
that you've gotten involved in. Unlike you, I'm going to do whatever
I can to prevent another senseless murder, my own being no
exception."

He looked serious for a moment, and she saw a glimpse of the
old, caring Kellen.

"LaRetha, I can only tell you to be careful. This thing isn't over..."

"What *thing?*"

"Look, I appreciate your coming, but I have an attorney. There's
nothing you can do, here."

"*Who*, Kellen? Who is your attorney?"

"I told you to leave it alone."

Suddenly, she stood up, catching him by surprise.

"Well, you know, it's your behind that's going to prison for life, *if
you're lucky*. But, call me when you're ready to tell the truth,
because that's the only way you're getting out of *here*."

With that, she slammed down her phone and left him sitting
there, open-mouthed and watching as the heavy door closed behind
her, locking with a loud clang. She left with no remorse and no
regrets. *He could rot,* for all she cared.

A week later, LaRetha was back at the jail. Kellen had called.

This had better not be for nothing, she thought.

But this time, he seemed genuinely glad to see her, despite
trying not to show it. But she was so tired, and thinking that she
probably should have worn *hip boots* just to wade through the mess
he was about to unload on her.

Just last night she had told Douglas about Kellen's call, and his
wanting to see her, again. He'd warned her not to expect too much.
She didn't.

Kellen sat down across from her, watching her intently and
saying nothing at first. She waited. This was his show, after all.

"Thanks, for coming. You look great. Losing weight, again?"

"Get to the point, Kellen. After the way you acted the other day, I am *too* annoyed with you right now," she said, calmly.

"First, I want to say I'm sorry."

You should be, she thought, saying nothing.

"I acted that way because I was hurt. I thought I couldn't trust you anymore, and you know you're all I have."

Although her heart did flutter a bit, she continued to watch him, solemnly. She sighed, heavily.

"So, what did you want to see me about?"

"I need your help, LaRetha. I need to get out of here."

"Oh, did your woman run out on you? Tell me about *Samira.*"

His expression went dull.

"Why didn't you tell me the truth about her? And what does she have to do with the property dispute with my family?"

"I already told you about that. I shouldn't have gone to that party. And I should've left when you wanted to. I'm sorry."

I'll bet you are!

"I was just mad at you for pulling away from me. I wanted you to see that if you didn't want me, somebody else did."

She knew this was partly true. But there was definitely a new game coming on, and she was ready for it.

"So, you proceeded to embarrass me in front of everyone? My family? My attorney?"

"You didn't appear to be missing me."

"Cut the hurt and abandoned act. I talked to Douglas for all of what, *twenty minutes?* But *you* ran off as soon as we got there."

He didn't respond. And something else occurred to her.

"So, when we went there on Friday night to meet the family, you already knew everybody?"

"No. Just Jasmine, and she wasn't there."

"But they knew about you, though?"

"It's possible. I had never seen any of them before."

"And you had never seen Therell before, either?"

"I answered that one, already."

He sat back in his chair. This clearly wasn't going the way he'd hoped. She persisted.

"Okay, so just tell me this. What kind of nonsense are you trying to pull, playing me against my family like this?" She asked, heatedly. "Getting involved with them and not telling me about it? Taking me to that party, knowing I didn't have a clue what was really going on with you and that woman?"

He said nothing.

"You've got some nerve to come here *uninvited,* to stay at my house and to even *propose* to me, knowing all of this. That is just beyond deceitful. And you know what? I don't know you, anymore. I just hope you get what you deserve." She stood to leave.

"LaRetha, don't leave. Please!" He pleaded, looking more vulnerable than he ever had. "I was wrong," he continued. "I was *stupid*. We both know that. And I understand your being mad at me, but I only came here out of concern for you."

"Why? What's going to happen to me? What do you know about it?"

"Nothing I hope. Nothing I would be involved in."

"Not *directly* anyway, huh? And I guess that exempts you from any responsibility?"

"You know how much I love you, LaRetha. I wouldn't come here for something like that. Besides, if I were that agreeable, Therell wouldn't be dead and I wouldn't be in here."

She smarted at this. Therell had threatened to hurt her, that night. That's why they'd fought. At least, that's what he wanted her to believe.

"Oh really? Well, you are here. And tell me this. What is it that's supposed to take place in *thirty days?*"

He was silent. Looked at her hard and sat back in his chair.

"How did you know about that?"

"You are in no position to keep secrets, so don't play with me."

"Who have you been talking to?"

"I'm talking to *you*, right now. Trying to get you to stop jerking me around, and tell me the truth. What was supposed to happen in thirty days, Kellen?"

He sat quietly, staring into space as though replaying something in his head. Wondering if he'd accidentally dropped the note, she figured.

"Look, I don't know what you had to drink at that party, but it should have worn off by now. Look at me!" She snapped.

"LaRetha, believe me," he said, lowering his voice into the phone and looking around the room. "I can't tell you from in here."

"Why not? Do you need more running room?"

"No, because I can't protect you if I tell you. I know you won't let the information rest, so I can't take that chance. I couldn't have that on my conscious."

"Oh, so I *am* safer with you in here? I'm really beginning not to have a problem with that. But, why is that so? Did you plan Therell's murder?"

"No." He closed his eyes, vehemently shaking his head. "But don't ask anything else. I have to go, now."

"Okay. Well, my hands are tied, but Douglas is still willing to talk to you. If you want his help, now is the time to say so. I won't ask you, again."

"Okay, listen. Tell him to come by. I'll talk to him. But, don't expect him to tell you anything, because I'm going to have to insist on keeping his confidence."

"So, you want the help?"

"Baby, I always did. I just didn't know how to get it without putting you at risk."

She shook her head, feeling oddly relieved, but wondering why she still couldn't shake that deep, disturbing feeling churning in her stomach.

"I'll tell him to pay you a visit."

"You do trust him, right?" He looked worried, and she felt relieved. Kellen was getting anxious now. His plans were all falling through. And he was alone. He would cooperate.

She nodded. He sat forward.

"Okay then. Just, until he tells you differently, don't come back here, LaRetha. You're not in any danger, right now. But if you keep coming back as if I'm telling you things, you might be. So, promise me."

His eyes were pleading, and she almost had compassion for him. But Kellen had lied and manipulated, and was probably very much involved with the people who had sent an intruder to her house and then murdered him. Therell's people. And *now* he warned her?

How could he have even put her in this position? *And why was everybody becoming a master at keeping secrets from her?*

She looked around the room. Seeing no one showing any unusual interest, she stood to leave.

"You'll see that I never let you down, LaRetha. We're still on the same side."

"That does remain to be seen. Goodbye, Kellen."

Once on her way home again, she let out a long exasperated sigh. She had been so terribly set up. So had Kellen. And if Therell and Jasmine were involved, then so were her uncle and Nell, and the rest of them.

But why would Therell even confront Kellen, when there was so much to lose?

With old questions being answered, new ones had surfaced. And there was still no end in sight.

She called Douglas as soon as she got in her car. *They needed to talk,* she told him.

"Okay, LaRetha. I'll do whatever I can," he said to her from across his desk, on that following afternoon.

"Thank you, Douglas." She handed him the check Laretta had left for his retainer, which he locked in a top drawer, before standing up and stretching.

"It's late and I'm hungry. Mrs. Starks has dinner waiting. *Won't you join me?*"

While tempted to say no, she consented, instead. Following him home in her car, she considered his cleverness. Douglas was determined to make this whole ordeal as personal with her as he could. And admittedly, she was enjoying the attention.

As for *Kellen,* now that Douglas had consented to help, she could only wonder if she was doing the right thing by asking. And if by hiring him, she wasn't somehow helping her enemies, as well. The only way to find out would be to stay close to him. She doubted he would mind.

They arrived to find his house warm and inviting. After washing up, she joined him in the dining room. The huge table that seated twelve had been set for two, and in grand style. Clearly, he'd expected her to come. He bowed his head as she said grace, joining in at *amen.* They prepared their plates.

She smiled at him from across his dining room table. "I do appreciate everything you're doing, Douglas. For being so helpful."

"I can't think of anything I'd rather do," he said, lightly, causing her to smile even broader.

With the housekeeper gone now, they had the house to themselves. Their solitude appeared to have been well planned. What else he had planned, she wasn't certain. But, she would keep a level head. There was no need to complicate matters, any further.

"This baked cod is delicious," she said, putting a hefty piece into her mouth, smiling happily.

"I hoped you would like it." He ate a bite. "You're right, it is. Remind me to give Mrs. Starks a raise."

"Consider yourself reminded. I say double her pay."

"Let's not get *crazy,"* he said with a morbid expression. She smiled, feeling duly humored.

They ate their dinner and food had never tasted so good; baked cod, squash casserole, a vegetable medley and delicious buttered rolls. Neither had strawberry cheesecake.

Afterward, he invited her into the den where he poured her the usual ginger ale. Handing the glass to her, his eyes were penetrating on hers - captivating. But considering the extra effort she'd put into her appearance, she'd expected that. She had even hoped for it.

She listened to the soft jazz music playing overhead. Reminiscent of the night of the party, it was a dangerous mix with the soft lighting. Sitting in a chair facing the fireplace, she decided it was time to discuss her reason for coming.

"I found out about the woman Kellen spent his time with at the party. Her name is *Samira Neely,"* she finally said.

Douglas studied her face, intently.

"He said he met her at *Watson's funeral,* of all places. And he's been in contact with her this entire time. He knew that she was Jasmine's friend. He even knew that she might come to the party, that night. And, *get this*...he says my aunt and uncle might have known about it, too. Except, when I introduced them, everybody acted as if they'd never even *heard* of Kellen. Can you believe that?"

"I figured as much," he said, softly, poking a fire that needed no attending.

"How so?"

She was standing close to him, now. Intrigued for a moment by the display on a far wall, where flickers from the fireplace were causing their shadows to engage in a very flirtatious dance. They were almost embracing. He must have noticed, because he turned to watch them, before moving away to retrieve his drink.

"If I'm going to represent Kellen, there's something you should know," he said, looking regretfully into her puzzled eyes. *"I know the woman."*

"You do? *How?*" She asked quietly. Apparently, Douglas was open for testimony. She would allow it.

"I used to see her. Two years ago, she came here with Jasmine to drop off an invitation to some exclusive yacht party that a client of hers was having in Georgia. Although Jasmine and I have never been friends, we used to travel in some of the same circles, so it wasn't so out of the ordinary."

She was stunned.

"We met again, at the party. We talked. I gave her a ride home, that evening. We started dating. I found her a bit rough around the edges, but interesting. And I hadn't dated for awhile, so I saw no reason…"

He stopped, seeing the horrified expression on her face. LaRetha looked into her glass, unable to hide her disappointment.

"I should have told you, before. I don't apologize for any of it, but I do regret it, now. And not because of Kellen's involvement with her. But because I wouldn't wish Samira Neely on my worse enemy."

Douglas poked at the fire, again. LaRetha didn't move. Finally, he turned to look into her eyes.

"How long did you date her?" She finally asked.

"Not long. Six months, at the most. Samira is a very misguided woman. But, one thing I know is that, if she's pursuing any man, there has to be some money involved. That's her *career*, you understand," he said rather than asked.

She considered this.

"So, when I saw her fawning all over Kincaid," he continued, looking away, again. "I figured there was something deeper going on, because he couldn't have very much of it. Or so I thought. Then, after the shooting, I realized that she must have been after something that *you* had. Particularly, since your folks were courting you way they were. They want that farm pretty badly. Always have."

"Sounds like you know her well," she said, not meaning to sound jealous, but it bothered her that this woman had been involved with practically every man that she was. *Intimately* involved. The thought baffled and amazed her.

"It was a *huge* mistake," he said. "I was foolish to think that I could just *go there*, and quit when I wanted. But, that came with a price."

"Why is that?" LaRetha thought about that magnificent face and body to match, and Douglas' own availability. It made little sense.

"Because, she's a manipulator. She lied, and she stole from me. She took important documents from my office, and denied knowing anything about it. But, I know this, and Jasmine had put her up to it."

"Well," she said, standing and walking away from him. "Looks like this Samira really gets around. She's doing something right, to hook both you and Kellen," she said, angrily.

"I wasn't *hooked*. I never loved her. It was all purely physical, and after a time, I learned that none of it had been worth it."

She wasn't impressed.

"I admit, I'm just as guilty. I was there, and it takes *two*. But, her betrayal was more than I could tolerate. Stealing information from my office and using it to benefit her friends and *patrons*, for lack of a nicer word, was totally inexcusable."

"How did she get into your office?" She steadied her voice, not wanting to reveal her true disappointment.

"Broke in, upstairs, when I was asleep. I didn't discover it until she was well out of town and just before the hearing was scheduled. She still denies it, despite mysteriously coming into enough money to buy a new Jaguar. Right after that, my client dropped his case and disappeared from sight. We lost a quarter million dollar settlement, at the very least."

Her eyes widened with interest.

"So you see, you weren't the first one hit broadsided. She and Jasmine are some team."

"So, if that's the case, why were you at the party?"

"You have to understand the social dynamics of this little town."

Humph, she thought.

"Everybody has to deal with everybody else here, on some level. We're not all alike, but we're all tied in together, which is necessary if we want to make sure that too much power doesn't fall into the wrong hands."

"Sounds like it already has."

"Well, I did go after revenge, but that's another story," he said.

Revenge? She wouldn't have thought him capable. But then, she hadn't known Kellen as well as she'd thought, either.

"Your folks know how I feel about them. Your father was the only one in the family that my father ever associated with. My pops and your uncle weren't too fond of one another. But, our differences were dividing us in ways this town could not afford. So, I've been trying to do exactly what you have, to bury those old hatchets so that we can agree long enough to make some *positive* things happen, here."

Good argument, Counselor, she thought.

"As for Saturday, your uncle invited me. Besides, he told me you would be there. I had hoped you would be there, *alone.*"

She really wasn't flattered, remembering how, at the first mention of the woman's name, he'd said nothing about knowing her. But, he *had* known her, in more ways than one. And he'd probably pursued Samira the same way he was pursuing her, now. As for the reason for their break up, this was only one side of the story.

"It's funny, but I noticed a few things at the party, too," she said. "Like the fact that I didn't see you talking to anyone in my family, and how you seemed so into me, right in front of everyone, including Kellen. That seems a lot like Samira's game to me. So, tell me, how are you involved in this? What do you really know about their little arrangement with Kellen, if that's what it is?"

"What are you implying?" He responded, heatedly.

"No more than you have. Kellen knew her, and *you* knew her. He slept with her and so did you. She pursued you and she pursued him. Both of you had intimate relationships with the woman. I'd just like to know the difference in her using *him*, and her using *you*," she said, gesturing with one hand to emphasize her point.

"As a matter of fact," she continued as he watched her with narrowed, angry eyes, "how can I be certain you're not still involved with Samira in some way? Maybe Kellen wasn't being as foolish as I thought when he refused your help."

"LaRetha, I apologize if this hurts you. I wasn't trying to deceive you. We hadn't agreed that I would work with Kellen, yet. Besides, I wasn't sure about her, then."

"And now?"

"She's definitely involved. I'm sure of that, now."

"*Uh huh.* Well, let's get something straight between us, Douglas. Regardless of how you do or don't feel about Kellen or me, I sure hope you're not helping him for the wrong reasons, because I won't just sit back and let you lay a murder rap on him. So, if this is part of some master plan or plot against either of us, it would be best if you bowed out, *right now.*"

She stood and walked toward the hallway, making it as far as the entranceway, before he caught up with her. The adage, *keep your enemies close,* came back to mind. Maybe that's what Douglas was doing by offering help to her.

"*LaRetha!* You can't believe that."

"I don't know you, Douglas. And I'm not sure that I want to on this level."

"So, you think less of me now? Because of a relationship I had with a woman before I ever met you?" He asked incredulously. "Before any of this ever happened?"

"You weren't honest with me. Now, I don't know if I can trust you."

"Boy, somebody really hurt you, didn't they?" He said, scornfully.

Douglas must have seen the loathing in her eyes at that moment. She grabbed her coat, putting it on as she hurried to the door, anxious to get away from this man whom she knew nothing about, really. But, who was seeing through her, so easily.

Grabbing her arm to spin her around, he stopped at the sight of her disappointed eyes.

"LaRetha, you have to believe me when I tell you I would never do anything to harm you. Or else, I can't…"

"*Oh well!* Do what you have to, Douglas. And I'll do the same." She was spitting mad, by now. *The nerve of him!*

"Don't do this, LaRetha. This is exactly what they want, which is why I never said anything. Without us standing together, Kincaid doesn't stand a chance. Asking me off this case could only serve to hurt him, and I know that's not what you want."

She looked at him, her heart slowly sinking. She didn't know why she was taking this so personally, other than the fact that she'd been lied to, enough.

Come here," he said, taking her hand and leading her back into the living room. Reluctantly, she sat down, again. "I can't let you leave this way. I was hesitant to tell you, at first. But, I couldn't allow my personal concerns to interfere with good judgment."

"This is looking more and more like a *family affair,* LaRetha. But, that doesn't make it any less dangerous. People are dead and others are being caught in the crossfire. And you could be in danger, too."

She could see that he was sorry for lying to her. But, she still couldn't trust him. Just like Samira, he seemed to be all in the middle and everywhere. *What else was he not telling her?*

"I'm not your enemy, LaRetha. You already know that. But, I'm just puzzled," he said. "You seem to have forgiven Kincaid for deceiving you. How is that?"

She wasn't sure of what he was asking. Was he concerned for her, or was he just curious to know how Kellen could be forgiven and he couldn't?

"I've told you, Kellen and I were very close friends."

"Were?"

"Think what you like about Kellen and me."

"You love him, don't you?"

Subconsciously, she rubbed the finger where his diamond once was. It still lay in the bottom of her jewelry box.

"I won't lie about caring about him. We have a history that's hard to walk away from. So, I guess we're still friends on that level."

"Say no more. I'm sorry for prying. It's none of my business, after all. Is it?" Douglas started. "Just know that Samira holds not one candle to you, lady. If he can't see that, it's his greatest loss."

"*Samira?* I have *no* insecurities where she's concerned," she said, causing him to raise an interested eyebrow. "I know some men will always have a *Samira* hanging around. And you're right. I *have* been hurt. I've been in that situation before and surely won't go back, again."

He nodded guiltily, watching as she walked over to the picture window. The sun was setting over the water. And it was all so beautiful.

"I promised Kellen that I wouldn't interfere if you represented him," she said. "There are things he doesn't want me to know, just yet. But, if this works out, if you decide to represent him, I'll leave keeping that to your judgment and hope I'm not making a mistake."

"Good then. I'll talk with him. Just like I said."

"Just assure me that you'll only keep that promise as long as my family isn't in any danger."

"Your mother, you mean?"

"Meaning my mother, my son, me and anyone in my family, including the part of it that dislikes me right now. I don't want this resolved by any more violence. Can you agree to those terms?"

"I promise I won't take any risks. I would never forgive myself."

Thank you for agreeing," she said, remembering that Kellen had said the same thing.

"I can agree to anything you want me to agree to, woman. *How about that?*" He asked, flirtingly.

She smiled. Looked away, before standing to leave. Putting his glass down, Douglas walked over to her. She watched him approach, and sighed.

Am I crazy? This man wants to get involved, and it was getting all too complicated. She raised a hand to stop him.

"Douglas! About this..."

"What about it?" He moved closer and gently touched her face.

"Let's not do this," she said, trying to move away. He didn't move, but only hugged her, gently. She closed her eyes and sighed. *Why did this feel so safe? And so meant to be?*

"Why can't we talk about this, LaRetha?"

"Not now. Not like this," she said, unable to deny the attraction, then finally managing to meet his gaze. "I'm not sure what's happening here Douglas, but I can't put Kellen at risk for my own selfish reasons. That's just not right."

"I understand," he said, reaching for her hand, clutching it in his. She closed her eyes and felt his lips brush softly against her cheek. "I know," he said, before gently pulling away. She was relieved.

"Don't think I'm being disrespectful of you or your relationship with Kincaid. But, you're clearly not taken, and until that happens, I'm not giving up on us."

"There *is* no us, Douglas," she responded, rather coyly. "We've just met."

"*Not yet*, you mean," he said, and she shivered under his gaze.

Punching him lightly on the arm, she waited as he opened the front door for her.

"Thanks again, Douglas. Kellen really needs your help," she said.

"Right, right," he said, looking deeply into her eyes. "So, am I in trouble?" He asked, as he put on his coat.

"Not at all. Not with me, anyway." She said, smiling.

"Kincaid had better know how lucky he is to have you on his side. For the first time, I wish I was the one in jail and you were trying to set *me* free," he teased.

"Douglas," she said. "I really must be going."

"But, it's early, still." He was wide-eyed at the possibilities, she guessed.

"Yes," she smiled. *Dangerously early,* she thought.

She walked swiftly down the driveway, slowing as he reached around her to open the car door. She slid in behind the steering wheel.

"You should've let me start your car up for you. It's cold out here."

"It's fine," she said. *I won't notice the cold. Believe me,* she thought.

"Are you sure I can't drive you? I could bring your car over in the morning?"

"No thanks," she said, starting the car. "Call me when you have something?"

"You know I will."

"Bye, Douglas."

"I prefer, *see you soon,*" he said. "And I'm glad you're still smiling."

So am I, she thought, as she drove out onto the street.

11

Despite LaRetha's concerns about road hazards, her mother had insisted on driving back to Atlanta. She missed her, already. And none of the town's colorfully lighted streets with garlands, candy striped street poles, Santa's elves and reindeer were managing to lift her dampened spirits.

Snap out of it, girl! She told herself. She had risked getting involved with Therell Watson, and the rest of her father's family, thinking her mother was just being unreasonable. And now she was feeling a kind of sadness that she couldn't seem to shake.

Maybe a few days in Atlanta was exactly what she needed.

Earlier, after leaving Douglas' house, she had stopped for gas at a convenience store in town, and was filling her tank when a white van passed by, then reversed. The driver's window came down, and someone waved to her. *Vera.*

"Hey! I thought that was you in there," Vera laughed, referring to the big coat and colorful knit scarf that was wrapped around her chin, but that still barely shielded her from the biting wind. LaRetha pulled the scarf underneath her chin.

"*Hi, Vera!* How've you been?" LaRetha was happy to see a friendly and familiar face, again.

"*Fine.* I'm really sorry about your cousin. And your friend, Kellen" she said with sincerity. LaRetha walked over to her window.

"Thanks. It's a lot to digest." she said and Vera nodded.

"How is Kellen, doing?"

"Well, he's in custody and not too happy about it. We're pretty sure that he'll get off once it's proven that it was self-defense."

Vera nodded again.

"Seems my troubles haven't ended yet," she said, trying to smile.

"They will. They don't last always, it just sometimes seems that way. I'm praying for you both, girl. Just hang in there."

Thanks, Vera." She breathed a sigh of relief.

"Listen, call me sometime. I'm pretty busy at the mission right now, but let's have lunch and talk sometime, soon," Vera said.

"That sounds like a great idea. I'm sorry I missed Thanksgiving preparations. I know I promised..."

"Don't even worry about that," Vera said, frowning away her concerns. "We understood. You have my number, don't you?"

"I sure do."

"*Use it, then,*" she said, smiling. "Call me, soon." Moving her truck forward to allow another car access to the tank, she waved. "I'll talk with you later," she yelled.

"Soon, Vera. Take care," she said, while thinking how she was the one needing to do that.

Watching the van pull away, LaRetha felt better, already. Vera was very thoughtful. And, much like Constance, she was very straightforward - a trait that she preferred in a close friend.

Apparently, the *entire* town didn't share the rest of the Watson family's sentiments, which meant Kellen still had a fighting chance. That was promising, at least.

Laretta rented a car to drive back to Atlanta for reasons her daughter didn't need to know, just yet. She dialed the number the minute LaRetha's car was out of sight. Not surprisingly, it hadn't changed.

He answered and she told him who she was and what she wanted him to do. As far as she was concerned, she said, what happened from here on out was going to be up to the two of them. Her daughter was in danger, her daughter's fiancé was in jail, and two people were dead. *Now, did he really want anything more on his conscious?*

Reluctantly, he told her to meet him at an old schoolyard in an hour. She remembered the place. It had long been boarded up, so they wouldn't be disturbed out there.

She reached inside her handbag for the tenth time. The mace was still there. She would try to reason with this man, but if he was anything like he was those years before, he might become belligerent. And she would be alone with him, after all. *Verry* was too old to even think of hurting her, she figured. But then, being *old* didn't mean that he was *weak.*

She arrived first and waited. He was late. She had told him she wouldn't wait, but decided to give it just another fifteen minutes. Fifteen became thirty. She waited, patiently.

At first, he wished he'd never answered the phone. Because on the other end was a voice he had hoped to never hear again, in life. *Laretta Watson* sounded much more mature, more confident. But, she was *still* Laretta, the *ex* sister-in-law he had wished out of all their lives for good. And the reason he'd lost his brother, forever.

Their conversation was short and to the point, and he couldn't help wondering how she looked, now. She was very pretty, back then; classy with a cute little figure and one of the best dressed girls in school. He'd heard that she hadn't changed much. Had she been a few shades lighter, who knows? But, unlike him, *Watson* hadn't been at all concerned about that type of thing. And even after he had told his older brother that he'd dated her, adding a few things that didn't happen, his brother had pursued the girl, anyway.

His stomach churned every time he thought about that one afternoon at the farm. She always knew that he'd disapproved of their marriage; of his jealousy that she was taking his brother and best friend away from him. But that day she'd let her guard down, inviting him inside to wait for his brother, saying he was less than a half hour away and wouldn't be long getting there.

Once inside, he'd seen the wonderful signs of family and warmth – all the things that *Watson* had done to the place. He remembered thinking how they had so much; the house, the farm, their father's blessing, and their obvious love for one another. And he'd been envious. She had offered him dinner. And that had made him mad.

This is my brother's house on my family's land. Just because Watson was the oldest, that didn't mean he should get everything! He remembered thinking.

It was his brother's fault for bringing her into their family in the first place. Just like it was his fault that they'd all sold their shares of land to him for the money.

He recalled how, knowing their financial straits and tiring of being asked to co-sign for loans, his brother had called a family meeting and made them all a very generous offer. But, they would only have a short time to decide.

Not wanting to disappoint their parents by selling elsewhere, and considering that they were the first generation to live off the farm and were struggling at finding good paying jobs, they had really needed that money. So, Watson had borrowed money to pay them, using some of the land as collateral. He would own it, continue to attend to the daily operations, pay off those loans, and keep the farm in the family.

But, in a big way, he had betrayed their trust, saying later that there would be no further negotiations where the land was concerned. That he'd never promised them any. And neither did that exchange lead to better communications between the two of them, or a rebuilding of trust, as he'd hoped. Instead, when he'd tried to talk to *Watson* about anything pertaining to their agreement, he'd refused to listen. Angry by then, he had relayed this to their siblings, and soon, the entire family was up in arms.

Admittedly, that money had made a lot of things possible; he'd paid off a few large debts, made a nice down payment on a brand new home and on the shop in town, and he was able to qualify for an open line of credit that kept the shop going, even when there was no profit. That money, along with the few hundred dollars that his brother had provided each month for Therell's care, had enabled him to care for his large family rather well. And although his sons and daughters knew about the buyout, they'd never known exactly how generous an offer their uncle had made. But then, why should his family appreciate *Watson* for what *he* had sacrificed for?

That day at the farm, he had been drinking. But he wasn't drunk. He had provoked that argument with Laretta, true enough. They had argued before. She'd told him off for some unkind thing he'd said. He had responded with another unkind remark. Then, *Watson* had intervened, and that was that. But, this time his brother was nowhere around. And Laretta wasn't backing down.

"This is why you and your brother don't get along, *Verilous Watson*. You show up here *drunk*, making demands and starting fights all the time. How can he take you seriously?"

He had smarted at this.

"You never come out here to work the farm or to help out with the place, big as it is," she'd exclaimed, "just to start trouble. I can tell you've been drinking, now. You just need to leave."

He'd told her what he was going to do. She was a *no good*, he'd said, dating him *and* his brother. She had responded with disbelief.

"There's never been anything between us and you know it. But if you weren't using that to start trouble, it'd just be something else. That's just the way you are!"

After she said a few other, much more unkind words, he did leave. And, he'd done what he'd said he would. He'd known there were people who would believe him over her. And that it was one sure way to hurt his brother. *So what,* if nothing had happened between them? He'd thought. *Watson* would never know that for sure.

And now, looking at his watch, he knew he would be late if he didn't leave, right away. He turned the key in his truck's ignition. It wouldn't start.

Must be the battery, he thought, as he raised the hood. It was. Laretta had said she wouldn't wait, and he didn't think he should aggravate the situation by not showing up. He understood her concern for LaRetha, and shared it. Only, there wasn't much else that he could do to convince the others that his niece meant them no harm. Or that, given a little more time, she just might come around.

That woman is as headstrong as her father was, they all said. And, they believed, given enough time, she would cause just as much trouble. But, he'd doubted that she had come to *Lovely* with any ulterior motives. She didn't seem the back-woodsy type to him, so it was possible that she wouldn't stay that long, anyway. He had advised them to just make her an offer on the place.

But that hadn't satisfied them. And now, their hasty actions were costing them all. Except that, for him, the cost had been much too high. He remembered his son and fought back tears of grief.

Sighing now, he realized that his truck wasn't going to start. And with everyone else gone into town to shop and to see a movie, his only other option was *Watson's* old truck.

It was right where he'd left it when he first drove it home from the shop. LaRetha hadn't asked for it and he hadn't mentioned it, either.

Should've been mine, anyway, he thought. Letting him keep it was the very least she could do, he figured, considering she had everything else. Besides, it looked very much at home in his driveway. And it was nice, having something of his brother's. Almost like he was still around.

He found the key on the full ring attached to his belt, opened the door and got in. The engine started easily, barely chortling as he administered a few pats to the accelerator until it idled smoothly and purred like a kitten. He smiled as he remembered riding in it, lots of times. Just him and *Watson.*

But no, that was another Chevy, almost forty years ago. He was starting to get a lot of things mixed up, these days. It was a very long time since he and his brother had ridden out together; drinking, hollering at girls and acting up. Making plans for the future. They were going to own this town. *Yes, that was a long time ago.*

Tears stung his eyes. He sure missed *Watson.* And seeing his brother's daughter out here, all grown up, had revived a lot of old memories and emotions. He wiped at his eyes to stop a bout of tears, figuring that old age was making him sensitive.

Revving the engine once more, he put the gear in reverse and made a semi-circle, before heading down the drive. Even the radio still worked, he discovered. Humming slightly off-key to a gospel song, he pulled into the street and drove toward the old schoolyard.

LaRetha considered her earlier conversation with Douglas. He had taken her concerns about his loyalty, to heart. And still, she could remember the touch of his hands on hers, and the feel of his lips on her cheek. And how *exquisitely* he'd smelled when he'd hugged her, close. She shivered.

Snap out of it, she thought. He was her attorney, and the worst thing that she could do right now, would be to get involved with him. Besides, there was a lot she didn't know about Douglas Davis.

He had finally told her about Samira, and how they'd been an item, once. She didn't doubt that he'd even fallen in love with her. Why else would it be so difficult for him to talk about? But, as happy as she was for his revelations, it only made her question him, more.

Just how freely did this man enter into and then leave relationships? Was he always this aggressive with the women he advised? And how could she be sure that he hadn't gone through half the women in her family, as well?

She knew about those men who, like some women, were just in love with the *idea* of being in love. The words *I love you,* only meant *I want to sleep with you,* and nothing more. Lust was as close to love that they would ever get, because to them, they were one and the same. She thought about Gerald and the fact that she really wasn't interested in getting suckered in by the town tramp because of *lust,* regardless of his position, here. And then be blamed for the privilege.

Still, she wondered what he would have done if she and Kellen hadn't gone to that party? Despite the problems he professed having with her family, or his supposed anger at Jasmine and Samira, he'd been there, that night. And it was a little hard to believe that he'd come just to see her.

He attributed his ties to her father's family to his community responsibility. But just how far did those ties extend? Would he sell Kellen short for their benefit? And did he stand to gain something if got Kellen convicted while seducing her, and then influenced her to sell?

Stranger things have happened, she thought. People here seemed liable to do about anything. Besides, every other man in her life had done an about face, and practically overnight. First Gerald, then Kellen. And now, possibly even *Douglas.*

I really don't know Douglas, she reminded herself. And in the short time since they'd met, he had moved in pretty fast. He could be a part of the whole plot and just playing with her emotions in order to blind her from his real intentions, she thought; distracting her with talk of a possible relationship between them.

It would be so typical for the enemy to send a man to her – their lonely, divorced cousin. And so silly of her to fall for it.

But that old devil must show himself. You just have to be willing to see him. Words of her father when he'd felt he was being deceived. Whenever things had seemed to fall apart, he would always trust his instincts. And she would do the same.

But, what was it that Douglas was showing her, that she just wasn't seeing? The man was always there, willing to help in any way possible, and even agreeing to at least talk to Kellen, while being honest from the start that he couldn't attest to his innocence.

What more could she ask? It wasn't as if they were in a relationship. He didn't owe her anything, nor Kellen, unless he took the case.

She checked her watch. It was early, still. She had planned to go to the library, and this afternoon had seemed the perfect time, but first things first. Looking into the mirror, she decided that Laretta was right about seeing a hairstylist. Since coming to *Lovely,* she'd been doing her own hair, and right now it showed. She pulled at the long strands that felt a bit dry to her touch, then reached for the phone to make an appointment.

Verry was nearing the schoolyard and thinking about the good times, *before* his brother's engagement to Laretta, when they had hung out like best buddies - mostly at the little 'juke joints' in town where they would have a drink or two. But that was *before* his brother had called himself *saved.*

Between school and working on the farm, *Watson* hadn't been one to date much, having easily accepted the grueling farming schedule that the rest of them had grumbled about. So it was only natural that he would take full responsibility for the place when their father had gotten too old to handle it.

Watson did have one other charge, however; to keep him out of trouble. And he remembered that there was always trouble. Always a fight or the threat of one. And always an argument with someone over something inconsequential. He had definitely been a hand full.

Once, the two older brothers of a girl he'd been seeing had cornered him. The girl was pregnant, they'd said none too kindly. *And what was he going to do about it?* Apparently, their little secret rendezvous' hadn't been a secret, after all.

What's that got to do with me? He had insisted. They had shown him just what, and he'd gone home aching, bloody and bruised. When he saw him, *Watson* wanted to find the boys and avenge what he considered a very unfair fight. Until their sister Carole had told him what it was about.

'You stupid idiot', his brother had yelled. *"You know that girl's daddy done already killed a man and she's already got one baby. Do you plan to take care of that one, too? How, when you won't work two days straight and can't even feed yourself?*

Watson and their father had gone to talk with the girl's parents and discovered that she was being sent away. Nothing was to be proven or expected. And, despite the embarrassment of it, he had gladly put it behind him.

Verry was nearing the school, now. And fond memories of the first day he'd set eyes on a very special girl came to mind.

Aurelia Moss. It was his junior year and she had returned as a senior. All the guys were watching her. Never one to leave an opening for the competition, he had sought her out at the end of the first day back at school and told her that she was the prettiest girl he'd ever seen. Before he left, she'd let him kiss her and he hadn't been able to think straight for weeks.

Back then, he remembered, there were little shacks all alongside this road. One of those had belonged to her grandmother, and that's where he would pick her up for dates.

Simply stunning, was the only way to describe her. Cocoa brown, tall and shapely, beautiful and unassuming, she'd been every bit her sadly alcoholic mother's daughter. There was that same long black hair that she would sometimes wear in small curls that fell past her shoulders. There were those same exotic facial features. The girl had big, beautiful doe-like eyes that slanted a bit in the corners. And she'd had the sweetest smile he'd ever seen.

Aurelia was *gorgeous,* but only vaguely aware of the effect she had on the boys who flocked around her, as girls from their high school had been unbelievably mean and had set out to make her life miserable. She'd been scorned for her mother's way of living; drinking, prostituting - everything that made the wholesome women in their town uneasy when it came to their own men. Teachers knew of her very poor life, but had shunned her as well. She had paid dearly for her mother's behavior.

But when she was sixteen, she and her two younger sisters were left in the care of the grandmother, who was almost blind and fast becoming dependant upon her granddaughters for everything. The woman was always wise to Aurelia. Just in no position to properly discipline her. By the time Aurelia had turned eighteen, the old lady had been moved to a nursing home, and she was left to care for the rest of them.

They had lived poorly, even with the money she'd earned working odd jobs to supplement the monthly government checks, and money given to her by her male friends. Times were hard on everyone then, but seemed especially unfortunate for her, he thought. It was a miracle that she'd finished school at all, because the ostracizing never ceased.

On top of her personal troubles, she'd been teased a lot. For being older than the other students. For 'thinking she was smart', and then for failing when she'd grown tired of it. For being pretty and then for the old clothes that she wore. For being liked by anybody, and then, just out of envy.

She had fought back, and therefore stayed in trouble. She had merely shrugged it all off, as if expecting that things might change for the better. Or that it never would. Which one, he couldn't be certain.

Like him, Aurelia was always a dreamer. They would share those dreams during hours they'd stolen away, undisturbed. She would be an actress one day. Or a fashion model. And she could have been, he'd said. Only, the options being presented to her in *Lovely* were hardly going to get her there.

They'd been so much alike; both of them feeling greatly misunderstood by the people around them; yet another reason he'd been so attracted to her. But word had gotten out that he had been seeing her. Nell questioned him and insisted that he break it off before everyone found out. But by then it was too late. Aurelia was pregnant.

But he was engaged to Nell, by then – a girl from the *right* side of the tracks, his mother used to say. Her parents were educators, an *honorable* profession, she'd said. Their father, however, felt it made little difference. His boys could make their own way. Besides, everyone else considered them all the same, he'd said. There was no need to further separate themselves.

Still, this new problem was not going away. And having been bailed out and chastised so many times for the numerous things he had done in mischief, *Verry* had wanted nothing more at that time than to win his big brother's approval, and their father's.

Feeling he had disappointed the family enough with his various offenses, he'd thought that having a child he couldn't support would only prove that he was as irresponsible and useless as they had always thought him to be. And once again, he would falter in comparison to his older brother. He also couldn't fathom the idea of the baby, *his baby,* not being born. Or of having strangers adopt and raise his child. He'd needed to come up with a plan, and quick.

She and the baby would need things that *he* couldn't yet provide, he'd told her one afternoon. But there was someone who could. Someone who would have the family's full support, and who would give her everything she wanted - once he accepted her. And *if* she was willing to go along. Feeling she had few other options, she had been.

By then, *Watson* had proposed to Laretta, but she was stalling. Ironically, her parents had strongly opposed her involvement with him and his family, and largely because of his little brother's reputation. So, desperately seeing this as his last opportunity, he'd sought his older brother out on a free afternoon and convinced him to go with him to have some fun. Although *farm* smart, his brother wasn't as experienced as he, with women. And his obvious frustration at having to wait for Laretta's answer had left him as vulnerable as he'd expected.

Watson never asked how he knew the girl. Like him, he'd kept their affair a secret, at first. However, once Aurelia told him about her *condition,* he'd quickly broken it off with Laretta, confusing her since she hadn't known about Aurelia at the time.

Then, just as suddenly, and when everything seemed to be going perfectly, *Watson* had refused to ever see Aurelia again, and soon began to court Laretta. Aurelia swore that she hadn't said a word about *them,* but he figured that she must have slipped and said something while unaware, because *somehow,* his brother had known.

When *Therell Vernell Watson* was born, there was no question in anyone else's mind who the father was. The family resemblance was there. And *Watson* had already taken full responsibility for what couldn't possibly have occurred in the time period Aurelia had given him.

And although his brother would have nothing to do with her, the family had accepted the girl. She was *Watson's* baby's mother, so she was provided with a nice, modestly furnished apartment that was large enough for her, the baby, and her two sisters. She was given a barely used car for driving the baby back and forth to doctor appointments, and a small allowance. It was understood that neither she nor this child would be denied anything. And it was only natural that they would all come to the hospital when the baby was born.

Verry figured that he might have congratulated his brother too boisterously. Or maybe he'd gotten a bit too caught up in the excitement of the impending birth, and appeared overly anxious. At the hospital, he had joked about finally becoming an uncle, while being only vaguely aware that his brother was saying very little, but sat watching him as if reading him, completely. As only he could.

The truth must have been in his own eyes, because after his initial excitement over seeing the child – his *first* child - and a healthy robust son at that, he'd hardly been able to contain his delight, or to meet his brother's knowing gaze.

It was too late to disguise it. It was mentioned that the infant had to be in the family, because he looked so much like childhood photos of *him.* And *Watson* had finally realized what he'd probably long suspected. He hadn't stayed at the hospital after that, but left him to be with his own son. And *Verry* believed that, on that day, his brother had been hurt more deeply than he'd ever thought possible.

He hadn't known that he would never see his brother's smile again. Or never get the anticipated pat on the back of his approval. That he would never regain his trust or respect. It all had seemed *fixable,* then. For him, the plan was infallible and *Watson's* 'just due' for all the pride and attention that the family and community always poured over his brother, but rarely toward himself.

But afterwards, *Watson* had wanted nothing more to do with him or Aurelia. While refusing to answer the family's questions about his decisions, *Watson* had continued to provide for the toddler, even after their parents had died and he and Nell took the boy in. And despite the obvious hurt and disappointment, and change of heart that no one understood but him and Aurelia, and that they couldn't or wouldn't talk about, his brother had never mentioned it to a soul. He took their secret to his grave.

LaRetha found a table at the busy library and began pouring over some old history books. She only found two that addressed local farm issues, and only one of them mentioned the fires occurring in the early *60's*. Nothing else stood out; just stories of the town's old families, a brief mention of Bob D. Billard as a prominent attorney-born from a long line of them, and a short mention of the older Douglas Davis as his legal assistant.

She skimmed through the books a little longer before selecting the ones she could check out. A rather skittish young man showed her to a room where she could look up very old newspaper articles. She printed several of them and put them inside her folder.

After locating a few other books on relative issues, and another on new business start-up, she went to the desk to check them out.

"Hello," she said with a smile. "I'd like to apply for a library card."

The woman behind the counter eyed her long and suspiciously. After a moment, she briskly handed her a form to complete.

"Complete it, bring it back and we'll make you one," she snapped.

There was no mistaking the hostility in her voice. Taken aback, LaRetha returned the woman's long gaze with a questioning one before carrying the forms to a nearby table to complete. Aware of the whispers and stares from the same woman and a young girl now sitting behind the counter, she angrily completed the form and carried it back to the desk.

After handing it over to the librarian, the woman took it, quickly handing it over to her assistant before walking away in an angry huff. The girl snickered as she began entering her information onto her computer.

"I didn't know there was a courtroom in this library," LaRetha said, as if truly stumped.

The girl gave her a puzzled look.

"*There must be*. You're holding court and finding people guilty," she said, snidely. "But, I guess being around these books all day must make you feel pretty smart!"

Clearly annoyed by her sarcasm, the girl frowned before divert-ing her eyes back to the computer screen.

The nerve of them, LaRetha thought as she left the library with her new card, and books in hand. *They don't know me!*

But, despite managing to skillfully dodge the press that kept her phone ringing off the hook, and then having posted several '*Absolutely No Trespassing*' sign at the edges of her property, some of them had managed to dig up stories about her and Kellen, and the entire *Watson* family, anyway. And even to create a few.

And while the family refused to comment, stories were running daily and in different variations, and she couldn't help but read them. A few of them noted her as uninvolved. Others named her as the *true* victim; a woman whose cousin had accosted her boyfriend, forcing him to shoot him. The more damaging ones referred to her as a person who was very likely more involved than they knew, and definitely someone to watch.

She was only mildly surprised at being portrayed as some evil, scheming big-city news reporter who had *allegedly* lured her lover here from Atlanta, then enticed him into defending her in an on-going family dispute. This dispute had quickly gotten out of hand, it read, leaving a cousin dead and her lover in jail, awaiting trial.

Who wouldn't find this stuff interesting? She asked herself, knowing she had a lot more of this garbage to look forward to. Her trade had taught her to never get emotionally involved with the subject, but what if *she* was that subject? How was she supposed to handle that?

She called Douglas to get his opinion.

"I wouldn't read too much into it. It's all hype and supposition that'll just be disproved by the trial later on... but you already know that, don't you?"

Suddenly, she'd felt silly for asking. She knew that her field of work was lucrative as much for the drama it created around these type incidents as it was for presenting the facts. The juicier the story, no matter how ridiculous, the more believable it would be. She refused to give an interview, feeling it wasn't time. Still, it wouldn't hurt to write a few pieces of her own in preparation for the day when the citizens of *Lovely,* and the rest of the interested world, would want to know the real truth.

Sighing, she decided not to cook tonight. Stopping at *Mr. Ba-con's Burger Box,* in town, she studied a greasy laminated menu before deciding on the *Mega-Burger Combo;* a quarter pound onion-burger on a huge toasted bun, with all the fixings. It came with a large order of scrumptious looking onion rings and a humongous thick, chocolate shake.

So much for that diet she was starting.

Verry was pleased that he was finally doing right by Laretta. Something had moved on his old evil heart over the years. His own anger and resentment aside, this seemed a most natural atonement.

In his heart, he knew that Laretta was no more responsible for what had happened between him and his brother than her daughter was for what had happened to Therell. He had always known it. That boy had always been overzealous. Except, this time when he'd warned him, his warnings had gone unheeded. And now, Therell was gone.

He was recalling things, now. And seeing Therell lying on the floor in a pool of blood had made him remember when he'd learned that his brother was sick. At first, pride wouldn't let him call or go to see him. But when he'd heard that he might not survive, *Verry* had put pride aside, and driven out to the farm.

He had waited in his truck until another visitor had gone, not caring that they would see him sitting there, before he'd knocked on the front door. Cecelia had allowed him in.

"*Hello brother,* he'd said after Cecelia had shown him to their bedroom, lingering nearby so she could hear. He couldn't blame her.

Watson's breathing was rasping and irregular, as was the rise and fall of his weak chest. He had never looked so small and frail, or helpless.

Surprisingly, there had been no *I.V.'s* or machines, at all. Just a very clean room with white linen and several bottles of medication neatly lined on an antique dresser. His brother had come home from the hospital to die.

"Are you okay, brother? Can I get you something?" Uncertain of what to say, or if he'd even heard him, he'd begun to chatter.

After a time, *Watson* had weakly turned his face toward him, his eyes tearing as they'd rested on his. Too weak to speak, his eyes had said something that *Verry* couldn't read. Blinking once, he'd closed them, his breathing clearing a bit as his chest rose and fell for some of the last few times of his life. *Verry* had broken down and cried.

"I know you're wondering why I came," he'd sobbed, sober for the first time in a long time. "But I didn't come to upset you. Just to talk, is all."

And talk, he did. About when they were children, and they would play outside in freshly plowed fields until long after nightfall, although they couldn't see two feet in front of them. About fishing in Magnus Pond without real bait. And about those school days, when they'd pulled the wool over many a principal's eyes, ditched classes and played pranks on teachers.

He'd talked about a lot of things. He'd even admitted the truth about Aurelia, and about what he had done to Laretta. He was so sorry, he'd said, weeping as he begged his brother's forgiveness.

He never knew if *Watson* had even recognized him, or if he'd cared about anything that he had said at that point. But, he had bared his soul, not wanting to waste one more day being separated from his beloved older brother. And it was all so little, and so very, very late.

The day of *Watson's* funeral had been his own day of reckoning. He couldn't bring himself to attend with the family. Not after all he'd put them through. Instead, he had stood far back on a hill that overlooked the burial plot, watching as the hearses arrived, grieving silently as they lowered the casket into the ground and eventually were gone again. And he'd wondered how in the world he'd allowed it to get so bad.

But, it was too late for regrets. *Watson was dead.* And the only thing he had accomplished with his hateful resentment and anger was to waste a lot of time that could have been better spent. Whatever his brother had done or didn't do, they should have moved past it. It was so easy to do, he'd realized. If only they'd made up their minds to do so.

He should have been more loving in his actions and much more responsible. Kinder to his brother and more understanding, he thought. It had never occurred to him before that his strong older brother had even required this.

He shouldn't have fought him on everything, but could have made his life much easier, instead. And he definitely could have strived for peace within the family instead of bringing confusion and shame, and blame. But, *sorry* now meant nothing, now. There was so much about *Watson* that he'd taken for granted, including his broken heart.

His brother had always tried to stand for what was right and truth – even *hard* truths. And he'd been exactly right about that land. *Watson* had known it would only have been a matter of time before all of it was sold to the first decent bidder. And when that was spent, each of them would've been right back where they'd started. Except then, their family legacy would have been gone.

So, he guessed that it made sense that *Watson* would leave the farm in the hands of the one person he must have trusted most in the world. And that was his daughter, LaRetha. But, knowing the troubles he'd had out there and the animosity that still existed within the family, he had also done what was akin to writing his own daughter's *death sentence.* And there appeared to be nothing that even he could do to stop it, now - except for this.

Watson had loved that child so much. He'd driven to Atlanta every month just to spend time with her and, as he'd feared, with Laretta. But then he knew all about a father's love.

He recalled when they had first taken Therell in. Finally, the boy was in his rightful place, although he'd never known it. It was years before he'd finally confessed the truth to his wife. But Nell already knew. After begging for and receiving her forgiveness, he'd wanted them to tell Therell, as well. But she'd disagreed. And he could find no easy way.

How do you tell your adopted son, who believes he is really your nephew, that he is your son, after all? That you've been lying on your brother, for all those years?

When Therell was *ten*, he had tried to tell him. But, by then, Aurelia was gone, *Watson* and Laretta had long split and he was remarried to Cecelia. There was no reason for this type of revelation. Never spoken, it was just simply understood between the brothers that his rightful father would raise the child. He never understood why *Watson* had continued with financial support, unless maybe he'd felt a little compassion over the land issue.

I should have stopped it before now. If Therell had known the truth, he might have chosen a different road in life. Maybe been less angry and more certain of who he was in the world. And today, he might still be alive.

But being so much like him; a womanizer and a fighter, always quick to anger and to threaten, his son had handled LaRetha just as foolishly as he had dealt with her mother. And the results were even more disastrous.

Maybe, starting today, they could declare a truce and come to some decision about how they could stop this terrible mess that he'd helped to start. He wouldn't worry about Nell and the rest. They had their own confessions to make.

There was a time when his wife would have gone along with anything he'd asked of her. But she had become a greedy woman, disinterested in the welfare of anyone other than herself and their children. She would oppose it. Just as she had when Paul Straiter was killed and he'd suggested they walk away empty handed, and just be thankful that they could.

He'd suggested it again before Therell had come back that last time. The idea of menacing his brother's daughter had worried him from the beginning. But he owed people and selling that land was the only way to pay them back, she'd said. He couldn't very well see his own family being put out of their home, could he?

Nell had even laughed in his face, saying he was too old to even think about going back into farming. There was nothing else for him, she said. If not running the shop, *what else did he plan to do?* And even that wouldn't very likely get them out of debt, in this lifetime.

He had never disliked her more than at that very moment. All he could think about was getting away from her and the whole group of them, taking with him those dreams of starting over. With his oldest son at his side, the possibilities to begin anew seemed endless.

But, being instinctive of his new plan, Nell had spoken with Therell. Poisoned him with her ideas and aspirations for the money the land would bring them all. They had begun speaking to him as though he was foolish, smiling secretly when they thought he wouldn't see. And suddenly *he* had become his older brother, and he was outnumbered.

He knew his family didn't understand why he hadn't been angrier with Kellen Kincaid about shooting Therell. Or why he hadn't taken up a weapon in revenge and arranged an *incident* to repay him for his deed. As wrong as it would have been, people still expected this of him. But the scripture, *vengeance is mine, saith the Lord,* consistently rang in his mind. He was definitely a changed man.

But, he was also an old man. And he had seen enough death and dying in this one lifetime. He didn't know Kellen Kincaid very well, but he did know his son. And this time, he wouldn't blame someone else. Therell had done a wrong thing and paid for it.

He had to do this, today. To make certain that LaRetha was safe again in this town, and most particularly, in her own home. That land, a sure blessing from a father who'd inherited it from his father before him, would stay in the family. And no one else would have to die for it. *Therell* had been enough.

He was nearing the top of Magnus Trace, a steep road that led to a short bridge that extended a quarter mile across a meadow. *Only a half-mile to go,* he thought, tensing a bit.

But what if Laretta was still very angry? Slander was no small deed. But, she had called him, hadn't she? And if he could help her to help her daughter, maybe by doing so, he could somehow make peace with his brother. And find a little for himself in the process.

Driving against strong winds in the snow, visibility was low. He noticed that the road topped off near an old oak tree, and he would need to slow down to safely make the last icy hill. He was running late, but could just make it. *He had to.* He was an old man, now, and quite certain that he didn't want to take so many things to his grave.

Feeling the truck slide to one side of the narrow road, he eased his foot off the accelerator and onto the brakes. There was no resistance to the pressure he applied there. He tried again. The truck didn't slow. Frantically, he pumped the brakes, panicking a bit. There was no slowing, still. His thoughts began to race.

Keep your head, he told himself, holding the steering wheel steady as he slowly pumped the brakes for resistance, but feeling a sudden pressure growing in his chest, instead. And he began to recall other things that he'd long forgotten about.

Like the time he'd messed with old crazy man Chloman's brakes, causing him to hit a tree and end up in the hospital. The man had never walked the same, again. Lucky he was, to even be alive to this day.

There was the nightclub brawl, where he'd hit a man over the head with a bottle, sending him to the hospital in need of over thirty stitches. He had talked to the man's woman for too long. It had angered old Stretch, a local welder who knew his reputation.

Woman stealer, he'd called him. And that had been enough to rile him.

He'd done a lot of people wrong. And his bad reputation had been rightfully earned. Only, back then he hadn't expected to live long enough to regret it.

But as it was now, his brakes were not working, and he was afraid. The truck was sliding. There were large limbs lying all over the road, only there weren't enough of them to slow him down.

Hasn't anybody come this way since the last snow? He wondered.

Swerving now, he thought about jumping out. But, that would be certain death. He was approaching the wooden bridge now, and by the way the truck was spiraling out of control, it was beginning to look more like the impending grave that it had been for more than a few unaware drivers.

And now, he remembered. The rope that usually closed this road had fallen away. Or maybe he'd driven over them in the snow. But everyone knew this road was closed off. It had been for years.

Now, he was hurting like crazy. Struggling with his coat, he tore his shirt open, so that he could breathe. His chest felt as though it was being squeezed so tight, it would burst. And he needed to talk to Laretta...

Unable to move his leg again, he did the only thing that he could. He crossed his arms to still the pain in his chest, and gave in to the slow lapse of time and movement. Flashing before him were both good times and bad ones. The fights, the lies and the disappointments he'd caused. He saw the faces of his mother and father, then his wife and children. And then, there was his oldest brother, smiling at him from his deathbed. And he saw himself hovering over him, crying for his forgiveness.

It was all there. All the terrible events of his miserable life.

Dear Lord, forgive me, he mouthed but couldn't say aloud.

A single tear fell from one eye as one last sharp pain cut through his chest. Then, he felt nothing as life slowly slip away. From a distance, *Verry* saw himself sitting *lifeless,* behind the wheel of his brother's truck, his expression strangely calm as it hit the wooden railings with a terrific force, breaking through the old splintering wood, before diving slowly over the side of the bridge.

12

Laretta arrived in Atlanta by nightfall, finding the house in immaculate condition and splendidly decorated, thanks to Marilee who had supervised the workers while she was gone.

Just two more weeks! And LaRetha would be here with the family and friends that loved her. Hopefully she would stay until after New Year's Day, for the annual celebration banquet.

Lounging in a favorite gown, she looked through a pile of mail, neatly stacked on her bedroom desk. Checking her Caller I.D. and seeing no names that required an immediate response, she called LaRetha. She got her voice mail.

Maybe she's out with Douglas, she figured. *Good for her.*

"I'm home, safe and sound. Talk with you later. Love you. Bye."

The girl knew how she hated talking to people first thing in the morning or after a long trip.

Her visit had been longer than she'd planned, but she had enjoyed the rest. She did work too hard, but what else was there? She would go into the office in the morning and see what was pending. Considering her competent group of agents, everything would undoubtedly be in order.

My poor little girl, she thought. LaRetha was having more than her share of difficulties, right now. But in spite of that, she looked *fantastic!* Far more vibrant and much happier than on her last visit there. And it probably had more to do with that *fine* attorney Douglas Davis, than Kellen, as LaRetha would have her to believe.

That Kellen was a real charmer; tall and handsome, with smooth ebony skin and rippling muscles that were tight and just right. And with an overt sensuality that she would have run from, were he pursuing her. She'd had her fill of *ladies men.*

But, even she had to admit there was something special going on between those two. He seemed to have come into her daughter's life at just the right time. And they had just *clicked,* somehow. So, despite her own misgivings, she had decidedly backed off, watching quietly from a distance. It did make for a better relationship with LaRetha.

When Kellen called to tell her that he wanted to surprise LaRetha with a visit, she had told him about the shooting. Now she wished she hadn't. But at the time, she'd hoped he might talk some sense into her, thinking that if anyone could do it, he could. How wrong she was!

And now, she was nearing the point of desperation to find someone who could get through to the girl. Then it occurred to her that this was a job for someone equally as headstrong and persuasive her daughter. And that would only be *Germaine.*

She hadn't wanted to hurt LaRetha's feelings by telling her, but her grandson had called two days before Thanksgiving; just before his mother's tragic incident with the intruder. *He just wanted to say he was okay,* he'd said. Everything was going well with him. But she could tell that he missed his mother.

"Call her! She's worried to death about you."

"I will. Soon."

"Why wait? What could possibly be more important?"

"She just doesn't understand me, that's all."

"Doesn't understand, or doesn't *agree?*" Laretta didn't mind letting her irritation show at this point. "Most people don't understand one another, child. But love is *unconditional.* We'll love you whether we agree with you or not."

"I know."

"Your mother's got enough on her hands without having to worry about whether her only son is dead or alive, or why you're so angry with her, because that's how she feels."

"I'm not *angry,*" he said, the little boy in him crying out for understanding. "I just didn't like the way she treated my girl. She didn't have to call her mama and all that."

"I'll bet she's got a laundry list of things you shouldn't have done, Germaine. And besides, everything ain't about you, baby. Remember what I told you; she divorced your father, not *you!*"

"She didn't ask me to go with her."

And there it was. He was feeling abandoned, just as his mother had when her father hadn't come back. She understood it, well.

"You had already moved out. Besides, you know you wouldn't have moved to that backward little town!"

"I might have."

"Even if your girlfriend couldn't go?" She'd asked while thinking, *uh huh*.

"She still should have asked me."

"Well, you shouldn't have left like you did. You're all your mother has, Germaine. And as grown as you think you are, she still worries about you and she always will, just like I do with her. You should've talked to her before you left."

"Daddy told me she's seeing some man now, and that she's probably going to get married again, soon."

"I see that your daddy still has a very active imagination."

He snickered in that lovable way that only he could.

"Child, just call her! Nobody can lie to you when you know something for yourself."

He still hadn't called and she doubted he knew about LaRetha's current troubles. The boy was as headstrong as his mother. Luckily, he was nothing like his father. Or worse, that great uncle on his grandfather's side who'd made everybody who ever loved him miserable, including Nell back in the day.

But LaRetha had done well, raising Germaine. As for *Verry,* she'd heard that he'd finally turned his life around, and that was good news because it meant that there was some small chance of getting him to understand her concerns, and to help.

In her opinion, LaRetha was far too concerned about how these people felt about her. They'd only accepted her in the first place because she looked more like *them* than her side of the family. She, on the other hand, had been shunned by them, mainly because of *Verilous.* She had coped with it before their marriage, believing *Watson* when he'd said their opinions didn't matter. And to her, none of it did. Until Aurelia got into the picture.

The last time she had seen Aurelia, she had looked as ripe as a melon - ready to have her baby at any given moment. There was no question that she was attractive. *Breathtaking* was no overstatement. But, she didn't seem to care about her beauty, just the things it brought her.

So, you're still going with *Watson?*"

The girl's question had come as a surprise. They were at a County Fair where she and her mother had a table set up to display the numerous handmade quilts that had been handed down through their family. At hearing the girl's question, her mother had stopped in her tracks. She'd stepped aside to allow them to talk. Watching and listening.

"You're the one who's pregnant. You tell *me* what he's doing." Her sarcasm was easy and obvious

Her mother had snorted in agreement. Aurelia appeared not to notice, but just smoothed her hands over the big yellow and white checked shift of a dress that did very little to conceal or to flatter her rounded condition. Laretta had felt both hurt and embarrassed to even be talking with this girl; her greatest competitor.

"Well, I ain't gonna marry him. I told him that."

Astonished at her revelation, Laretta couldn't comment, but felt as if her heart was crumbling, right there on the spot. Then, the girl had nonchalantly tossed her hair and walked on, followed by a younger sister who had looked at her with the same expressionless eyes.

"That girl won't ever amount to much," her mother had muttered, shaking her head, disapprovingly.

And at that moment, Laretta had a shocking realization. *Aurelia Moss was holding the key to her own future.* Her refusal to marry *Watson* had been his only reason for proposing marriage to her.

But, *Watson* denied ever proposing to the girl. He apologized for hurting her and for giving her cause to doubt him. And then, he had proposed to her, again.

But you have a child on the way, she'd reminded him, whereupon he'd shook his head, looked as if he wanted to tell her some important secret, but simply said that the boy would be cared for. That Aurelia was totally out of his life. They had no worries.

So, convinced that he wanted only her, she had married the love of her life, and just three years later, had left him. She had been very surprised to find that he had remarried, but not to Aurelia as she'd guessed. This was a woman that no one had ever heard of.

But, admittedly, Cecelia had done well by LaRetha, and that was all she could ask. LaRetha's fondness for Cecelia had done nothing to make her side of the fence less lonely. Still, she'd been successful, managing to have a good life- a *great* life - without him.

What had happened to Verilous? She wondered now, as she placed a bag of gifts near the tree in the den for Marilee to wrap. It had taken some effort to call him to begin with, and to tell him how this was their one big opportunity to rehash, forgive and to decide how they could all move forward. For *LaRetha's* benefit if not their own.

After hearing his voice again, she still couldn't stand anything about the man. But, he had to know what was going on. He was also very likely involved, which meant that he would know how to resolve it.

She considered calling first to give him a piece of her mind for not showing. But, there might be good reason, she figured. And he still might contact her. She would wait.

Turning in, she felt safe and comfortable in her bed, and very satisfied with her accomplishments – one of them being acquiring this beautiful home.

Built it from the ground up and decorated it myself, she would say to admirers as modestly as she was capable of doing. Like her, LaRetha had those same decorative talents. Only, no matter how nicely she remodeled that old farmhouse, it would always offer the same lack of promise as it had when she'd lived there.

Looking at her clock, she guessed that *Verry* hadn't yet made the decision to let bygones be bygones after all, even if he'd been the cause of it all.

Well, it seemed that everyone else was failing her. And at this point, there was probably only one other person in that town who might help her daughter to survive this. And that was *Douglas Davis.*

The office phone rang. Marva was at lunch, so Douglas answered. It was *Kellen Kincaid.* He asked if they could talk – pleaded almost. He could be there in an hour, he'd said. Kincaid sounded genuinely grateful when he thanked him.

LaRetha would be pleased, he thought, smiling to himself. And she had been right by distancing herself until all this was over. In spite of what he'd told her, Douglas couldn't be certain that his feelings for the woman wouldn't muddle his perspective, at some point. And the man did deserve a fair trial.

So, here he was, about to defend a man who was in no doubt, guilty. Just to impress a woman. However, it wasn't his job to judge, but to defend. And he would give Kellen Kincaid the best defense that Laretta Watson's money could buy. Because looking at the circumstances and knowing all the players personally, it was likely that the man would be convicted of something. If all else failed, he would at least make sure that the sentencing was as light as possible.

An attorney friend was on the phone now, telling him about a fatal truck accident that had taken the life of the one man in the middle of everything concerning him and LaRetha. *Verilous Watson was dead.*

This can't be happening, he thought, hanging up and dropping his head into his hands. His friend was convinced that it was an accident. What a terrible time this was turning out to be.

He didn't want to make this call, but he couldn't allow her to hear about it any other way. Right when things were looking up for her, just a little, her world would be turned upside down, once again. And, once again, he would be there for her.

She couldn't hear all that Douglas was saying through her own unrestrained outcry.

Just stay put, he was telling her. He was meeting with Kellen first, but he could be there in a couple of hours, *tops.* She had hung up in tears.

After hours of overnight searching, they had found him early that morning. Her father's dark blue truck was barely visible, he'd said. Buried by snow just off the side of the bridge, it was vertically lodged in the midst of a tall clump of trees and hidden from sight.

Apparently, her uncle had driven right past the signs and blockade indicating that the Magnus Trace Road was closed. It had been for many, many years. But he'd lived here all of his life. He would have known that.

No one knew where he might have been going, the radio announcer said, as he described the incident.

"Verilous Watson was a resident of Lovely all of his life. A family man, active in his community, he gave to numerous charities and children's funds over the years. He will be greatly missed by his family, his Joyful Baptist Church family, and his many, many friends."

She wondered what else could go wrong. His death was already ruled an accident. *But, how could they be certain?*

Surprisingly, her mother was already home when she called.

"He *what?*" Laretta sounded out of breath, and as totally taken aback as she.

"I don't understand this," LaRetha cried. "How did this happen, I wonder?"

"If they said it was an accident, it probably was. I'm sure it's got nothing to do with any of your problems, or Kellen's."

"We can't be sure of anything, Mama. That's the *only* thing that I'm sure about, right now. He was driving *Watson's* truck - the one that I loaned him. He's had it ever since I had it repaired. I told him he could drive it as long as he wanted to, and to let me know if it needed anything else. We never talked about it, after that. I just assumed he liked driving it."

"So, what are you thinking, sweetie?" Her mother finally asked, sounding worried.

"I have to know more about it. The road is all blocked off, now. The truck was towed. But, maybe Douglas can explain it when he gets here. He's coming over, later."

Laretta said she would call her, soon. She could come back to *Lovely*, in another week, if LaRetha could just hold on that long.

"Douglas tells me I should stay away from the family. That's not hard to do, at the moment. But, considering Kellen's other troubles, I'm concerned that they'll blame him, somehow."

"Even so, Kellen is in jail, which means you're in more danger than he is. Besides, Douglas might be right. What if you end up having a confrontation with Nell or one of the others? That would just make things worse, don't you think?"

"I know. I just wish I could pay my respects," she said, sadly.

"Paying respects is for the benefit of the family, LaRetha. Your uncle won't know the difference. They don't know what he did to our family, or care. And as far as I'm concerned, *Verilous* took that with him to his grave. He'll have to explain that one to his Maker. I'm more concerned about you."

"I know, Mama," she said.

"So, are you still coming for the holidays?"

"I plan to."

"LaRetha!"

"Okay, I'll be there. I *promise.*"

"*Wonderful!*" Laretta exclaimed. "That's what I was hoping for. I'll get Germaine to come by."

"That would be nice." But she couldn't get excited, just yet. She thought about her uncle and how frightening his last minutes of life must have been. Her heart went out to him.

"Just look out for yourself right now, LaRetha. And let me know what's going on with you. And please don't go anywhere without telling Douglas, or without calling me. Okay?"

"Thanks, Mama."

Laretta hang the office phone up in a daze. *Verilous Watson was dead?*

They had just talked on yesterday, and when he didn't show, the last thing she'd thought about was looking for him. She had gotten up this morning, fairly upset that he hadn't even bothered to call. Now, the man was gone and all hopes of getting him to do the right thing and help her daughter were gone, as well.

And poor LaRetha! Things just kept getting worse for her. And for Kellen! He may never get out of jail, now. With that family already grieving and up in arms, he was sure to have every charge thrown at him that was known to man. Such a terrible fate, but an expected one for *outsiders.*

She read over the sales contracts in front of her. She only had a few closings this week, and the next. But, she had to see about her daughter. Make sure she didn't end up like the others.

"Gladys?" She waved her into her office as she passed.

The woman approached her desk, smiling. Gladys knew all about her present concerns for LaRetha, and about her disdain for the place she had just returned from. Her smile fell when she saw the look on Laretta's face.

"Problems?"

"Yes. And the timing couldn't be worse. I need a favor."

She explained her need for help with the closings, which suited Gladys fine. The woman was married with three small children, had a brand new home and despite her income, was heavily in debt. She was always reliable.

"You'll be rewarded for this, I promise."

"Oh, I know it will. If there's anything I can say, it's that *Laretta Watson is truly a woman of her word.*"

She thanked Gladys, again. And now, to return calls from the stack of messages, left on her desk. But, there was one call she needed to make, first. She dialed long distance.

One look at the man, and Douglas felt something that he hadn't in a very long time. *Jealousy.*

Kincaid was tall, broad shouldered and very muscular. A few inches shorter than himself, he was enviably young with a boyish charm, and most likely, very popular with the ladies. With LaRetha, anyway.

She had a great deal of confidence in him, even in light of his current situation. And despite the regulation threads that he wore, Kellen Kincaid still looked like someone preparing for a modeling session, not one who could very likely be convicted of murder.

But that wasn't what bothered him, most. That would be the fact that, as much as he denied it, he was torn on his feelings about seeing him released. He had always been an ethical attorney, fighting to the last with all that he had to help his client to win. Everyone respected him for that.

But, this was different. This man was the one person standing between him and the future love of his life - a woman whom he felt had been heaven-sent to this town for one true purpose; to meet and to marry *him.*

He was jumping the gun, he knew. And he wouldn't dare say to her what he was thinking just now. He also believed in a fair fight. He would do his best job and what was meant to be would be, whether Kincaid did time or not. Until that time, there was work to do.

Kincaid pulled out a chair and sat down directly across from him. There was a guard at the door and no partitions in this room.

"Thanks for coming. How's everything? *How's LaRetha?*" He spoke hurriedly. Avoided eye contact. Slid down in his chair, and gave his head a youthful toss backward, sucking his teeth with hostility.

Douglas let a moment pass before speaking.

"I'm fine. LaRetha's fine. But how are you?"

Nodding, as though bobbing his head to some unheard music, the man raised his eyes and looked directly at Douglas.

"Good as can be expected. Look, I just want to know when you'll be able to get me out of this place. LaRetha seems to think it can be done, and that you're the man to do it."

"Winning on a self-defense plea is a possibility, but first things first. I need to hear everything that happened. Then, we dig for the evidence to prove it."

Taking the pad and pen from his briefcase, Douglas waited. Kincaid began to repeat the story that he must have told LaRetha.

"I didn't even know the man, so I didn't have any grudges against him, like people are saying," Kellen explained. "All I knew was that he said something about doing something to me and LaRetha. But, just think about it. Knowing that I wanted her back with me, how could I benefit by killing this man? Her relative, at that?"

Douglas said nothing.

"It didn't go down like that, man."

Douglas made a note.

"You already think I'm guilty, don't you? Well, I'm not surprised."

"Well, Mr. Kincaid, so far you haven't said anything to convince me that what I saw at that party wasn't what it appeared to be. You have to admit that your standing there, holding that gun over the man right after he'd been shot, tends to be a bit incriminating. What else am I supposed to think? Give me something to work with."

Kincaid's eyes appeared less sure while suspiciously sizing Douglas up as he leaned back in his chair.

"It's obvious that I shot him, but I was trying to get away from him. *He* attached *me*. Anybody out there could confirm that."

"Well, they haven't yet. No one's saying they saw or heard anything."

Kellen appeared to consider this.

"Did he ever say what he was proposing, exactly?" Douglas asked, making notes. Kellen shrugged.

"I never gave him the chance. But, what could it have been, other than for me to help him take LaRetha's inheritance?"

"Okay, now about the gun. The police have already verified that the gun you shot Therell with was registered to him. But, LaRetha's also missing one that her uncle loaned her. Can you tell me what happened to it?"

"I never touched any gun that her uncle gave her." He said.

Douglas straightened, giving him a sullen look. He could believe that story, were he not so trusting of LaRetha. And right now, he was *two minutes* away from walking out.

"*Look,* man. I don't know," Kincaid said. Then he nodded. "*Okay,*" he whispered. "I took a gun out of her drawer and carried it with me, inside my jacket pocket. I don't know where it is, though."

"How did you know where to find it?"

"Well… I found it when I was looking around, that afternoon. She had gone for a walk."

"Where is the jacket?"

"Like I said, I don't know. I was drinking. It got hot so I handed it to somebody who put it somewhere for me. I don't normally carry guns, so I forgot all about it until now."

"And you carried a gun to that party, *because..?*"

"Why do people carry guns, man?"

"This isn't a guessing game, Kincaid. Either you want your freedom, or you don't," Douglas said. "So, now that I have the story you told LaRetha, how about telling me the *real* reason you came to *Lovely?* Why you stayed, and why you were so cozy with Samira Neely at that party. And I still want to know why you felt you needed that gun."

The man snorted.

"Do you want me to represent you?"

"I'm here, ain't I?"

"Yes, you are," he said, ignoring the way the man's eyes narrowed in his direction. "And you'll be here until somebody gets you out, and I don't see anybody else trying."

Kellen nodded, sullenly.

"I'm only here today because LaRetha and her mother asked me to be. Now, do you want me to represent you or not?"

"*Alright.* Evidently, my woman has a lot of faith in you," he said ruefully and Douglas frowned. "So consider yourself hired. Now, just do the job."

Arrogant little maggot, Douglas thought.

"I'll take that as the best you can offer me," he said, instead, placing a contract and a pen in front of the man. He talked as his client signed each page and slid it back to him.

"*Now,* payment has already been arranged by your *woman's* family. You can thank her mother, later. Right now, we have to clear you of these charges."

"I'll begin by explaining attorney-client privilege," he continued. "Nothing that you say goes past me. Not even to LaRetha. So, I have to know *everything,* no matter how bad it might seem. Otherwise, I suggest you find another attorney. And this time, I mean it."

Kincaid nodded. Douglas dropped the signed papers into his briefcase and snapped it shut.

"*Cool.* I hear you," the young man said, and nodded again. Then he sat back as if relieved.

"She told you I didn't want you to discuss this with her, anymore?"

"She did," Douglas nodded. "Not that she had to."

"Okay then. Where do I start?"

"From the beginning, when you and LaRetha first met."

Douglas put a small tape recorder on the table in front of his client. He didn't want to miss the smallest detail.

Marva answered the last call before lunch. Billard was in court, and Davis was out seeing a client - she could only imagine which one. She'd been keeping up with the story on Kellen Kincaid in the news.

From what she'd read in the papers and overheard Billard saying on the phone, the man had killed his girlfriend's 'cousin but supposed brother' in a fight at the uncle's house. Now the uncle was dead, too. No one had verified any connections to the girlfriend having shot that intruder at her home, but it was certainly being implied. They hadn't seen this much action in *Lovely* since that same uncle was a boy, terrorizing the entire town, she thought. *Unbelievable.*

All guesses were that this had everything to do with that land she'd inherited and was trying to hold on to. With the brother gone, chances were she would keep it, now. *Unless* some other relative challenged the will on his behalf.

The phone rang, again.

Leave a message, she thought, clearing her desk for lunch and leaving her purse there before she made a trip to the restroom. Returning, she reached for her purse.

"Hello," a soft friendly voice said from behind her, startling her. She turned around.

"*Hello.* I didn't hear you come in. What brings you to town?" She asked, smiling, but wondering if she'd left that door unlocked. She hadn't done that since LaRetha Greer's home invasion, and Douglas' warning that she should.

"*Just visiting.* I came by to take Douglas to lunch. Is he in?"

Marva thought about his itinerary.

"He hasn't any luncheon scheduled, Miss Neely."

"I didn't schedule it," she said all too sweetly. "I just took a chance at coming by."

Samira Neely hadn't changed a bit. Pretty, petite, and very well dressed with long, wavy sandy hair, swirled neatly into a ball at the nape of her neck, today. Despite her attempts to appear friendly, however, she had always made Marva feel a tad uncomfortable.

Then, Marva remembered. Douglas had told her to never let this woman into his office under *any* circumstances, no matter what she said. That was a while ago, but he hadn't mentioned anything to the contrary, since. So, she had to do his bidding.

"Well, he's not in. He's with a client. I can give him a message."

"No. I'll just try back, later."

"It's easier to leave one. But, you know that, already," she said with a forced smile.

He'd simply said she had disappointed him. But Marva knew Samira had really hurt Douglas. Her normally calm and collected favorite attorney had fallen hard. She must have betrayed him in ways he couldn't divulge, other than to say that she was never, *ever* to be allowed on the premises.

Marva had laughed at the time, thinking it typical of a man to believe that a woman couldn't move on with her life once their relationship ended. But, there must have been something to what he'd said. The girl was here, wasn't she?

"I'm on my way out. You can write it here, before we go."

"No. But thanks, anyway." Samira walked to the door.

Scowling at Samira's turned back, she put on her coat and grabbed her purse, then waited to set the alarm. Whatever Samira had done to Douglas, the man wanted nothing to do with her, now. Unfortunately, it wasn't her job to tell her.

She knows what she did, the older woman thought.

Once in her car, she phoned Douglas. *No answer.* Leaving a message, she drove out of the parking lot behind a new silver Jaguar. She didn't doubt how Samira could afford it. What she wouldn't have given to be so beautiful at that age. She sighed. *Whoever had said youth was wasted on the young was exactly right.*

The car was sitting boldly in front of his house; a brand spanking new bright red Infiniti. Douglas inhaled and slowly exhaled. This was going to get *ugly*.

Getting out of his Range Rover, which he left in the circular driveway, he opted to leave his briefcase safely locked inside, until she had gone.

"Hello, Douglas." The voice was too syrupy sweet for the Jasmine Camille Watson he knew so well.

Her shapely legs made long strides in his direction, and now she was standing beside him, close enough to touch. Only he had no intention of greeting her with either a handshake or a hug. *She can just forget it,* he thought, choosing his house key from the others on his ring.

"What do you want, Jasmine?" He barely looked in her direction as he walked toward the house, anxious to be rid of her and not trying to hide it.

"I need your legal advice on some things." She was in true form with her perfectly groomed appearance and proper diction.

"If this is about Therell's death, or your father's, I'm afraid I'm not the person to talk to. I'm representing *Kellen Kincaid*."

The look on her pretty face was unmistakable. She was in disbelief. Or acting like it.

"You must be kidding me!" The gorgeous woman was dressed very nicely in an expensive gray coat with a long fur collar, concealing what he knew to be an hourglass figure. She took a step backward, one of her high heels scraping his recently cleared driveway.

"*Nope*," he said, with indifference. "So, be advised before you start talking."

He inserted the key but waited to turn the lock until she had gone. He didn't want her brushing past him to get inside, despite the cold weather. He heard her draw a deep breath, her fingers seeming to ball up as though wanting to hit him.

"I thought you were on *our* side! I saw you talking with that woman, but I had no idea!"

"Come off it, Jasmine. You had every idea, and that's the reason you're here. Let me guess. You want me to drop Kincaid as a client? Or, do you prefer I sabotage the case for a take of maybe a few thousand dollars and good standing with you and your family? If that's what you're thinking, *forget it!*"

She turned slightly red, lifting her chin in defiance.

"Can't I even come in out of the cold? I need to talk with you." Jasmine was anything but as humble as she was trying to sound, right now.

"Why? We can finish this little discussion, right here." He turned to face her fully.

"We were friends, once."

"*Yep.* Until you and your little partner in crime ripped me off. There's nothing you can say to get me to drop this case, Jasmine. I'm sorry about your father. *Terribly sorry.* I understand the wake is tomorrow night. And the funeral... well I hope it won't bother you if I attend both."

She gasped.

"Why would you want to, if you're defending the people who caused his death? I've never known you to be a *complete* hypocrite, Douglas." She was fuming, now. And he was getting cold.

"LaRetha had nothing to do with your father's death, and you know it. Besides, it would be hypocritical of me if I didn't come. I wanted to bring LaRetha."

"*You must be joking!*" In unmistakable anger, Jasmine stepped around to face him. Her fragrance brushed his nose.

Nice, he thought. Saying nothing, he raised an eyebrow of indifference to her.

"That woman had better stay as far away from us as she can, or I won't be responsible."

"Why are you so angry with her?"

She said nothing. It seemed to be getting colder and she didn't appear to be leaving anytime soon, so he opened the front door and went inside. She followed without invitation. Stopping in the foyer, Douglas pocketed his keys, subconsciously patting his pocket to make sure she hadn't stolen them, already.

"She didn't have anything to do with Therell's shooting, or your father's accident."

"What planet have you been living on, Douglas? That man is her *lover*, remember? Or maybe she's doing something that's causing you to forget?"

With that, she gave a sly, evil smile that was quickly erased by the annoyed look he gave her. Irritated, he straightened. You could never let Jasmine know when she was getting next to you.

"And, Nell," she continued, "she checked her caller ID just before they found Daddy. Somebody named *L. Watson* called him before he left that day. They had an Atlanta area code. Now, I don't know what name she goes by, but that can only be *LaRetha's* cell phone number."

He didn't respond.

"He talked to her just minutes before he took *her* truck out of the yard. So, he must have been on his way to see her. Only, he didn't make it very far. Can you explain that to me? Because somebody's definitely going to have to explain it to the police." She was speaking loudly. Challenging him as only Jasmine Watson could.

"Calm down, Jasmine." He walked into the living room and poured a drink, neglecting to offer one to her, feeling certain that his bad manners wouldn't go unnoticed. "Did you call the number?"

"No."

"Well, there you go," he said with unconcern. "I'm sure there are lots of *L. Watson's* in the Atlanta phone book, and quite a few who aren't. Besides, LaRetha's last name is *Greer.*"

"It *was* Greer. She may have changed it back after her divorce. Everybody around here knows her as *Watson*. She still answers to it."

"I know she didn't change it back. But, then, I guess I'm not the one to change *your* mind."

"Listen to me, Douglas. You obviously think a lot of LaRetha. I don't dislike the woman. I don't even know her. But, when I think of everything my father did to be nice to her and to make her feel at home... and now *this?* None of this would have happened if she weren't still hanging around here," the woman said, swinging around in her long thick coat to face him head on, now.

"If I were you," she hissed, "I'd make sure I knew what I was doing before I got involved with her, *or* that man she's sleeping with. She's nothing but trouble, just like Nell says her mother was. That's all she is, and that's all she's been since she got here."

He grimaced, giving her a hard stare. Then, sipping from his glass, prepared himself to wait out this emotional storm which had better end soon, before he kicked her out of his house.

"I *told* them," she sputtered, "I said we should just end this. Just do an *old fashioned*, and drive her out. But *no*, they wanted to do the sensible thing. And now, *look...*"

Angry now, he slammed his drink down on the bar, splashing some of it out of the glass. Jasmine drew a sharp breath. Her eyes were frightened.

"This *old fashioned* you're talking about had better not be what I think it is. What is it, exactly – this *old fashioned* that you intend to do on a woman you don't know and that you don't even *dislike?*"

Jasmine blushed in confusion at his sudden show of emotions.

"You've already tried to take her inheritance by scaring her out of her mind, hoping would leave town, running. Well, she hasn't yet. You're already blaming her boyfriend for defending himself against that *brother* of yours. And now, I see that your family is holding her responsible for your father's loss of memory and fatal heart attack. So, what in the world can this *old-fashioned* be, Jasmine? What can be any worse than what you've already managed to do? *Pray tell!*"

Jasmine's normally fair complexion was completely red, now. And she was speechless.

"Let me guess." He walked toward her. She didn't flinch although her eyes revealed her fear. "*It's all of the above!* Looks to me like you're already getting that *old fashioned* you want so badly. And why are you telling me this, anyway? I could use it against you in court, you know?"

Seeing her shocked expression, he didn't care that he was adding more fuel to the family fire. He settled down on a barstool and replenished his drink, hoping that her frustration with him would lead her to tell him more.

Jasmine recovered quickly. She walked hastily toward the door, waving an expensive handbag almost comically as she went. Quickly, she turned toward him, again.

"You've *changed*, Douglas. That's clear to me, now. But, you're no fool. You haven't been an attorney in this town for this long without knowing something about what I'm telling you. She can't stay here! She has to go, and you know it."

"Well, *you* haven't changed a bit! What your cousin does with her land is her decision. The way I see it, she's entitled to the same liberties as anyone else in this town, and that includes you! Her folks were born and raised here, just like yours and mine, and you don't even want to try and run *me* out." He stood and approached her.

"Who's trying to. You're just not looking at this the right way!"

"Oh, but I am," he said, sipping his cognac. "I haven't forgotten how you prostituted that little tramp Samira, to steal from me. Or that little scare you perpetrated at LaRetha's house...."

"I did no such thing!" She was livid, now, and he was enjoying this rare display. Jasmine never lost control.

"Sure you did! But, I don't intend to argue this with you. This entire conversation is inappropriate. I think you'd better leave."

She stood watching him, and he could see her hostile demeanor changing into a more relaxed state. He braced himself.

"So," she said, more softly, looking him over, biting her bottom lip rather seductively, "are you sure you want to handle it this way? Surely we can come to some type of agreement."

It was no secret that the usually aloof Jasmine Watson had always had an interest in him; one that only seemed to intensify upon his breakup with Samira. Except, as attractive as she was, he'd come to understand his father's adamant insistence that he and his sister never got involved with *those Watson kids.* And knowing what he did now, he wanted nothing to do with her or anyone on *that* side of the family. That much hadn't changed in the least.

She walked closer to him and again he could smell her enticing aroma. He looked at her intensely before sitting his drink down. Encouraged, she came close enough to tug at the lapel on his jacket. He could imagine she was thinking that if one trick didn't work, another would. *Well, not this time, and never with her!*

He lowered his head to her ear, as if to nuzzle it, but whispered into it, instead.

"Don't embarrass yourself, Jasmine. Please."

He turned his back to finish his drink and to distance himself from the numerous tempting but deadly possibilities. Behind him, the front door slammed and then reopened. He turned in time to see her reappear, looking flustered and very upset.

She raised her arm and a rock whizzed past his head, causing him to duck as it hit the wall, solidly, behind him and fell against something glass that sounded as if it broke.

"Jasmine!"

"You'll regret this Douglas Davis! I promise you that!"

"And you do keep your promises, don't you? Don't even *try* me, woman!"

His last words were drowned out by the slamming front door, and a few minutes later by her revving car engine, then the sound of squealing tires as she sped down the driveway. He went outside and looked around to make certain she hadn't damaged anything, particularly his car. Then, hoping the neighbors hadn't heard, he went back inside and locked the door.

Kellen lay inside his cell - fearful, yet strangely relieved. After two weeks in this hole and since LaRetha's refusal to bail him out, he'd finally realized that help wasn't coming. And, now that *Verry Watson* was dead, Douglas Davis was the only attorney who might be objective enough to do the job, even if his heart wasn't fully into it.

A little time and a lot of solitude had made this situation a whole lot clearer. It was a terrible thing, that he had hurt LaRetha like this.

Strange, how in the beginning that hadn't bothered him, but then nothing had prepared him for feeling like this. He'd gotten in too deep. And now, he was destined for prison, and possibly for life!

Samira! They'd met the way he'd told LaRetha. And he had thought it was an odd place to try and hit on somebody – at a funeral! Jasmine was there, saying very little. He and Samira had exchanged business cards, just the same. Then, being attentive to LaRetha and her grief, he'd walked away and forgotten them both. Until the day their company secretary had called. Their Public Relations firm had a managerial position open and *would he interview?*

If he'd been smart, he would have smelled a rat immediately, and said 'thanks, but no thanks'. He was making fair money at the time with Mac Henry – decent pay for decent hours worked. But then he'd foolishly decided that someone was just doing him a good turn. Besides, the compensation package they offered was unheard of, making it an opportunity he'd probably never have again, in life.

He had barely stopped to catch his breath, or to wonder how they'd known he would take a job, or relocate. They hadn't talked long enough at the funeral for them to even ask. But he knew they must have checked him out and figured he could use the money.

Once he was satisfied that the offer was real, he had hopped on a plane to Cincinnati the very next week. And despite the fact that he normally told LaRetha everything, somehow he'd known this was something that he shouldn't, just yet.

"The job is yours, but under certain conditions," the attractive red-headed CEO had said with a vague expression, after talking with him for less than an hour.

"And that is?" He'd asked, sitting with his legs crossed, confident that he was on top of his game, having given what he considered a very impressive interview, thus far.

"My assistant can explain that over dinner. You've met Samira."

He had returned to his hotel to shower and change, and found Samira already waiting when he'd stepped into the swank Italian restaurant. And that's where she had told him what was really going on.

A business proposition was made. And were he not so intrigued by the attentiveness of this beautiful woman, her fancy car and the gold card she had whipped out to pay for the pricy meal, he might have told her where to go with her offer, then gotten up and walked away.

Instead, with a full glass of wine and a head filled with dollar signs, he had listened intently. Not only would he get an advance, but the generous salary would afford him a car and a luxury apartment, nearby. He would only have to deal with LaRetha to get it, Samira said. Get her to agree to sell and they would handle the rest.

Twenty-five thousand dollars! Ten grand up front, the rest to be deposited into an escrow account until it was a done deal. And all he needed was some form of proof that she would sell to them to get it, or just to wait until they closed on the deal. *And* he had the next *30 days* to make it happen.

"Why is all of this necessary?" He'd asked. "Jasmine and LaRetha are cousins, so wouldn't it be easier to just talk to her about it?"

"I don't have all the details, but I'm told they don't expect her to be very cooperative, and they need to move on this, right now."

He thought about that, now. A fair, direct approach would have served them better. Therell's document had been their failure.

"They being *who?*"

"Jasmine and...them," the woman said, smiling.

"So, what's the rush? And what's in it for you? You don't care about this land, do you?"

She shook her lovely head, smiling over her lipstick stained glass.

"I just work for these people. Once you accept, my job is done."

"And if I don't?"

"Well then," she said, shrugging cutely, "this should no longer be of any concern to you."

"But how can you all be so sure I won't tell her about your offer, or *vice versa?* What's my protection in this?"

"How would telling LaRetha benefit either of you? If she finds out, she finds out. But, how would that put money in *your* pocket?"

What a cold bunch, he remembered thinking. But he wasn't fully convinced that this was a thing he could pull off.

"What if something goes wrong?"

"*Relax,* Mr. Kincaid," she'd laughed, pouring him more wine, filling his glass. "We have every faith in your abilities. All you have to do is just show her... the positive side. And it'll be a done deal."

Samira wouldn't reveal how much they were willing to pay LaRetha, but he had to assume it was a substantial amount. He'd been arrogant to think it would be an easy thing to do, and very wrong for wanting to do it. He should have called LaRetha and told her what they were planning. He could have protected her.

But instead, he'd said that he would sleep on it, *alone.* Despite her offer to keep him company back at his hotel. He called her the next morning.

"I've thought about it," he'd said. "I might be able to do this."

"That's great, Mr. Kincaid." The voice was light and satisfied. "We don't require a written contract. Our verbal agreement and that canceled advance check will suffice. Just remember that everything is riding on this. Your success will pay off, extremely well."

He should have known better. Instead, he'd nodded into the phone.

"We should celebrate," she'd said.

"I can't. I'm leaving town this afternoon. So, let's meet in the lobby of my hotel at check-out time."

"*Sure thing,*" she'd said with a slight laugh. "I'll take an early lunch and bring your check. You've made a smart decision. I've worked for this company for quite a few years. Their proposals are usually *win- win* for everyone concerned. And in this case, that especially applies to LaRetha."

He had flown back to Atlanta feeling very accomplished, and with a lot of things to consider. Already, he was ten thousand dollars richer with a great job offer pending and an exciting move ahead of him. Life didn't get much better. Or so he'd thought.

With the holidays coming up, finding a reason to visit her would be easy. Once there, he would convince her that she should sell while there were still offers on the table. The only problem was that LaRetha was just too insightful. He would need to be subtle but swift, and patient enough that she wouldn't catch on.

But, he really didn't make up his mind until he heard from Gerald Greer, later that week – a surprising thing, for sure. Sounding anxious, he wouldn't explain over the phone. But it had to be important; about either Germaine or LaRetha, considering they were all the two of them had in common. And knowing that he was seeing LaRetha, Gerald would certainly have no love for him, now.

"*What are your intentions toward my ex-wife?*"

He didn't think he'd heard Gerald right when they'd met after work at a bar, on the following day.

"What's it to you?" He'd asked, with little concern.

"I was wondering how serious you two were."

"Why do *you* care?"

Gerald was silent for a long time, the both of them drinking beer, on him. Then he'd made the offer. And then he was reminded of the way Gerald had been hopping around Jasmine and Samira at *Watson's* funeral and he realized that these people were leaving no stones unturned. They were desperate. And now, with that sizable advance already deposited in his bank account, so was he. He needed to know how involved Gerald Greer really was.

He'd listened and learned that Gerald was offering him, in full, what he already had in the bank. This, and the fact that he couldn't stand the man, had made the proposition entirely unattractive. And now, he needed to get him off his back without creating suspicion.

After his second drink at Gerald's expense, he'd quickly become argumentative, telling him exactly where he could go. Called him a few names. They had argued. Gerald had punched him squarely in the jaw, almost putting him on the floor, except he'd landed on his feet and returned the swing. They had been thrown out of the bar and finished their argument on the street.

"Don't be a fool, Kellen!" Gerald had said. "If LaRetha wanted you she wouldn't have left you. Be smart, man. What do you have to lose?" Gerald had huffed through bloody lips.

"*You're* the fool, Gerald. If you'd been man enough and taken care of home, all that would be yours, already. But, you walked out just when it would've paid off for you to stay. And now you want *me* to help you take it from her? What a joke!"

He'd straightened and laughed, walked away and left Gerald looking very perplexed. Yelling after him, the man had warned him not to tell LaRetha.

A bit bruised for his troubles, he'd gone home with mixed emotions. While he was thankful for such a lucky break, for the first time he'd felt guilty for even considering this deception of the best friend he'd had in the world.

But there was a lot of money in it for her; at least a half million dollars, he'd rationalized. And if he wasn't successful, then she'd lose nothing. But it was wrong, what he'd come here to do. Sizing up her situation, he'd known she wouldn't turn him away if he just showed up, one day. And knowing how shaken she'd been behind Therell's visit, he'd suspected that she would probably never be as vulnerable, again.

His call to Laretta had settled it. There had been an intruder. She was alone. He'd figured he was just what she'd needed.

He would go there and console her. Love her. Help her clear her head. *Shoot,* after talking with his boss, he'd thought he might even marry her. He was settled, industrious and could think of a million things to do with a half million dollars. And she, on the other hand, was beautiful, youthful and smart. Life could be worse.

But, that golden open-door of opportunity had turned out to be a gateway to *hell*. And if he looked at this thing the way that LaRetha might, he would say that he'd sold his soul for just a promise of fortune, and now he must deliver.

Even worse, if what Davis had told him about the circumstances surrounding *Verry's* death was true, in light of the fact that the man was driving LaRetha's old truck at the time, and that he was in here for shooting the man *Verry* had raised, *and* considering that everyone in *Lovely* thought LaRetha was his girlfriend *except* her, and probably figured she was involved, he could expect no less than a hanging judge on his case.

If he closed his eyes right now, he could picture her the last time he was with her – just radiant in that sexy red suit, long hair spiraling down over perfect shoulders, and long lashes fluttering with surprise when he had praised her, as always. She'd had his full attention. *Until Samira!*

What was he thinking? He asked himself. That he'd just mess around and make LaRetha jealous enough to take her feelings for him and his proposal, more seriously? But by the way this woman had attached herself to his side, openly flaunting in front of LaRetha, that wasn't even likely. And he'd been stupid enough to participate.

He'd never wanted Samira. That one night in Atlanta was just a *sex* thing. A celebration, she'd called it. But, seeing him at the party, she'd acted as if they were a couple. She'd been on a mission that night, and he'd fallen right into her trap. So caught up with avenging LaRetha's rejection, he had run headfirst into a whole string of deceptions, including a few of his own. He couldn't think of a time when his judgment had been worse. He had set out to teach LaRetha something that had been his own lesson to learn.

Two drinks! And he'd lost all inhibitions. It wasn't like him. Two were well below his tolerance level. But he'd been out of his head for a time. And not surprisingly, Samira had brought both of them!

LaRetha blamed him for this, but seeing her all cozied up with Douglas Davis, talking and laughing, well that couldn't be ignored. He'd seen the way Douglas was looking at her. The way he'd kept his head close to hers as if he would kiss her at any moment. They'd looked far too comfortable. And then, seeing them dancing together, well, that was enough to send him over the top!

Lawman was probably making his move right about now, and there was absolutely nothing that he could do about it. But, he couldn't blame LaRetha. Douglas had a lot going for himself. And, like her ex-husband, he had left that door wide open.

But, what he wouldn't give to do it over – and differently. He should never have gone to that party.

Like he'd told Douglas, there was no question in his mind that, if anyone, *his* was intended to be the dead body lying cold on that white tiled floor. He wasn't sure what the man believed, though. He hadn't batted an eye when he'd given his second version of what had happened; didn't seem at all surprised that he had come to *Lovely* with deception in his heart, and worse, against the same woman who was fighting for him, right now. And this concerned him, *a lot*.

Staring at a crack in the ceiling, Kellen wished he was home with her, cozying up in front of the fireplace, eating her delicious home cooking and drinking something good and intoxicating – and maybe even making love.

Ahhh, but for the twist of a woman's hips and a smile, he thought, amazed at his own misfortune. *Samira.* A *slick* if he ever met one, and too proud of it. But LaRetha? She was the real thing. There was nothing contrived or conspiring about this one. She was what and who she said she was, and made no apologies.

Not only did he long for her, he loved her – *truly* loved her. He could see that now. But, he'd been the worst kind of fool. And now he would never have a chance to prove it. Not unless a miracle occurred.

Laretta's phone rang. Marilee hadn't arrived yet, so she reached for it, only half awake and annoyed.

"Hello, Watson residence."

"Hello, Laretta. It's your ex-son in law. How are you?"

"What do you want, Gerald?" She asked rudely. He had to be up to no good, calling her.

"I know you're surprised to hear from me…"

Uh huh.

"…but I was wondering if we could meet sometime this afternoon, and talk? How about over lunch? On me? You name the place."

"Why would I want to do that?"

"It's about LaRetha. I'm concerned about her. How is she?"

"She's fine, under the circumstances. *Why?*"

He was trying way too hard to sound concerned. Gerald was definitely up to something.

"I would prefer to discuss this in person. You know if it wasn't important I wouldn't have bothered you."

She thought for a moment. What would be a safe, neutral place between them, where she could make a hasty exit when he started getting on her nerves?

"Okay. Downtown. *Shank's Seafood Buffet.* Eleven o'clock, before the lunch crowd shows."

"Fine. See you then."

Click.

Rude as ever, hanging up first, she thought, as she pulled the covers back over her head. She had another hour to sleep, and she needed every second of it.

LaRetha sat up in her bed, looking over yesterday's newspaper, for the second time. *Uncle Verry* was being buried, today, and she wasn't going. She had gone to the funeral home to view the body. Unable to bring herself to attend today, she'd sent flowers, instead.

When she'd asked Douglas if he would accompany her, he had hesitated, saying he didn't recommend that she go, but that he couldn't very well stop her. He suggested she didn't go alone.

Apparently, he felt there was a possibility that she might be targeted by both the family and the press. Some of them would blame her, if not all, she guessed. She had considered this, but it hadn't mattered so much.

Now, she felt that Douglas was probably right. But, she wasn't as concerned about the family as she was about saying goodbye to her uncle and gaining some closure for herself, and to all the animosity.

She'd done nothing wrong. Therell's story wasn't hard to figure out, considering his disposition, which she'd learned was well known. And her uncle's death had been an accident, brought on by his forgetfulness and sudden heart attack. She was grieving for him too, she thought. Surely they would see that!

But in spite of the numerous justifications she made, now that the time had come, she didn't feel in her heart that going was the right, or smart thing to do. This was *their* time to grieve, she decided.

Besides, in light of the things that her mother had said about the man, she probably shouldn't even want to go. Just a few months ago, she hadn't known any of these people. And now they had lost, not just one, but two family members within a week of each other. Her showing up today might be a bit much for them, and for her.

A stylish black knee length dress hang from a clothes hook behind her bedroom door. Other clothing items were on the bed, nearby. She'd thought that laying them out might make it easier for her to make up her mind to just get dressed and go. But, it hadn't.

Douglas was coming by - probably to talk her out of going. But, that wouldn't be necessary. Getting up from the bed, she put on a pair of blue khaki pants and a white sweater, slipped her feet into ankle socks and a pair of house shoes.

Douglas was right. She shouldn't go. Looking at the clock, she wiped away a tear, realizing the pain of goodbye, once again.

I'll see you in heaven, Uncle Verry. Rest in peace!

Douglas was relieved to see that LaRetha wasn't dressed to go to the funeral. He'd been practicing what to say to her on the way over, hoping to talk some sense into her and get her to think this through.

She allowed him inside, returning a brief hug as he sat with her in the living room.

"I've thought about it. As much as I want to go, I don't want to cause any more confusion. It might only upset the family. What do you think?"

"I agree," he said, sighing with relief. "Besides, I don't believe too many people will be expecting you."

She frowned, appearing to be saddened by this.

"I don't know why I'm so upset," she told him. "I found out that Therell was only doing what my uncle did to my family, for years. Still, I can't believe he's gone."

Douglas decided not to respond.

"He was so different from that when I met him. He wanted to make amends. But it looks like as soon as we came together, everything just went *wrong!*"

She stopped talking and he comforted her with a gentle hug, wanting to ease her mind. He wanted to say that everything would be okay. *But how,* when this thing was probably far from over? What comfort could he truly offer her?

"Douglas, did you ever find out about that handwriting on Therell's document? We haven't talked about that, since…"

"I sure did. It's not your father's signature."

She nodded her relief. Therell had lied, and so had her uncle. Her mother's supposition had been right on target.

"Why am I not surprised? That whole family has lied about everything. My uncle had to know, and so did Nell. And to think she blamed me for all of this."

"We think they knew. We don't know, yet. We're still trying to trace the owner of that signature."

She frowned.

"Jasmine paid me a visit, on yesterday," he said, intending to lend more support to her reasoning that she shouldn't go.

"She did?" She looked at him questioningly. "What did she have to say?"

She was watching him now as if expecting to hear something positive, and he immediately regretted saying anything. He couldn't disappoint her any further. He took a deep breath.

"I think she wanted me to represent them in a civil complaint. They probably want to place a hold on this property. Of course, I told her I couldn't."

"A *civil complaint?* Knowing that they lied about that document? I don't believe it!"

Her reaction surprised him. Apparently she didn't know the extent of her people's wrath. Well, she needed to understand that this was not just some small family matter, to them, only to her. And that was because *she* was the one holding the goods.

"She never said so, because I didn't give her the opportunity, but just be prepared for anything. They might try to charge you with some malicious involvement in both Therell and your uncle's deaths. They wouldn't win, of course. But, just be careful."

"Are you kidding?" She asked. He shook his head, *no.* "What *won't* they do?" She asked, heatedly.

"Absolutely nothing! But, you have nothing to fear because I'm on your side, and I can be quite a formidable foe." He tried to comfort her with a smile.

"*Well,* so can I," she said, appearing equally self-assured. "They don't know whose child I really am, do they? I report to a higher authority than them, so they'd better not underestimate *me!*"

"I don't doubt it." Despite her calm appearance, he could see that she was contemplating something.

"What is it, LaRetha?"

"Well," she said with a sad chuckle. "I was just thinking that I guess you won't be welcomed at the funeral, either."

"That's just too bad, I'm going anyway."

She nodded, sadly.

"But tell me this. Your cousin made reference to a call that your uncle got just before he left home on the day of the accident. It was from an *L. Watson*. That wasn't you, was it?"

"*What?* Okay..." she said, angrily, straightening and blowing her nose on a tissue. "So, tell me how I got into the middle of this one."

"Did you call him to ask him something or to get him to meet you some place?" Douglas didn't want to doubt her, but either she did or she didn't.

"I would have told you that. I never called my uncle, that day or any day since after the shooting. Even then, Nell wouldn't let me talk to him. She's made it clear that I'm no longer welcome on this farm, in this town, or on her precious little earth. So, how did I get into this? What are they implying?"

"It's nothing to worry about. They claim the call came from an Atlanta number. It's being suggested that he might have been led to that closed road by somebody intending to do him harm."

"And you thought that was *me?*"

"No, of course not! But, knowing how determined they are to place guilt on you *and* Kellen, I had to ask. They wouldn't give me the actual number, so I couldn't say. I told her you went by *Greer...* "

"Okay! That's it! I've heard enough. You can just tell Jasmine... *Better yet,* I shall tell her, myself," she said, marching defiantly down the hallway. "I'm going to that funeral, so don't you leave without me!"

Douglas raised a hand to stop her, but she was already out of sight.

Oh man! He thought, giving himself a mental kick in the head. *What have I gone and done, now?*

The church was filled beyond comfortable capacity, with almost as many people waiting to get inside when they arrived. She joined Douglas in a long line of stares and whispers, a few smiles and consoling pats on her hand. They walked around to view the body. To her, *Verilous* looked as if he was only asleep. Tears welled in her eyes.

An usher offered to seat them with the family. Graciously, she declined, finding space for them on a middle pew, instead. Douglas looked around, and then appeared satisfied. She wondered if he wasn't planning for a hasty departure, if necessary.

The service finally began. There was a hymn, and then *Verry* was eulogized by his childhood minister and friend, Reverend Edmund W. Dawes. The entire family was there, and she recognized quite a few faces from her uncle and aunt's holiday party. She also noticed Samira, sitting with Jasmine, Nell, Bernice, Valerie and the rest of them.

As the minister spoke, the family sobbed their grief, with the numerous grandchildren, nieces and nephews crying for their *Pa Pa*. And as angry as they were with her and as disappointed as she was with them, LaRetha regretted the circumstances preventing her from being able to console them.

All other hearts and minds must be clear, the minister was saying with a voice that rattled loudly from the pulpit. "Our time is but a minute away. *Verilous Watson* was at one time a very hard man. I remember a day when he felt he had gone as far down as he could go. He came to me, asking for help in working through his problems. He wanted to be a better husband," he said, "a better brother, father and friend."

They became close friends, he continued, and he discovered that *Verilous Watson* was never a bad man. That his greatest wrong was not that he didn't love people, but that he'd never known how to *receive* love - something he wouldn't learn until much later in life. And when he did, he'd also learned to be the man he believed his family and friends deserved.

Gratefully, the service was so far not a terribly sad one. After another hymn by one of the granddaughters, the eldest son, Paul, stood in the pulpit to speak. His eyes scanned the room, resting on her and Douglas for a moment, before he began.

"My father led a full life. He was a smart man, hardworking and a friend to many. He loved a lot of people, and he had a lot of people to love him. It just took a little longer for him to learn to love himself."

Here, here. The congregation moved and her pew rocked with their approval and their encouragement.

"It's true that he used to drink a lot back in the day..."

Well, well. The livened congregation was sympathetic.

"He would sometimes get into trouble. Sometimes quick to fight, he was considered a lot of things that I know he wasn't proud of, later in his life. But fortunately, for him and his children, he was married to a woman who loved him enough to help him through it. She forgave him. And she encouraged him to be better man."

Yes, yes.

"That's just a testament to me, and to my entire family that *love* can change anything!"

People testified to that truth, and it was a moment before the church was quiet, again.

"You know, love is a funny thing. There's no predicting who might be touched by it when you put it out there. *Love* changed my father," he continued, tearfully. "Love from his family, his church and pastor, and his community."

Yes it did. Yes, yes. The church became alive, again.

"I know that, sometimes, no matter who's being eulogized, people always try to say something good, even when there isn't much good to say."

That's right. Yes, yes.

"But, when it comes to *Verilous Onaldo Watson*, there are a lot of good things to say. Like how he raised a large family like ours, and even raised the family of others."

"*Amen*," someone, sounding like Nell, said.

"Like how he accepted the fact that everybody he loved wasn't going to love him. And how he took the disappointment and all the regret he had for the people he'd hurt as a young man, and used it for something positive, later on in his life."

"Tell the truth," a man said. LaRetha straightened. Douglas reached for her hand.

"We could talk about how he found salvation, and how it led him to give - to his community, where he was scout master when I was a scout, and to my basketball team when he was our coach, only because he believed in me, like he did all his children. My father became a leader in this church and a pillar of his community." Paul's voice lifted a bit. He appeared more sure of himself and more determined to have his father remembered in a positive way.

"And even when he tried to help people, they would still divide us and steal from us. But, he never held a grudge or said a harsh word, right up until the day he died..." His eyes rested on her and then Douglas.

No he didn't! She felt her face burn, but continued to meet his gaze. Somewhere, a camera flashed and someone was ushered out of the church. And she could see that, already, this was becoming a circus!

LaRetha could almost see the headlines blaming her for this one, too. She said a quick prayer that, in his grief, her cousin would not make a spectacle of this funeral, himself or of her.

As he continued, a few people were still looking in her direction. Douglas squeezed her hand. She glanced at him sideways, but he continued looking straight ahead. She drew in her breath, and he tightened his hold, even more.

Glancing around, she spotted Vera, who saw her and smiled, encouragingly. She gratefully returned the gesture, before looking ahead.

"We don't know why my father was going down that closed off road, where he died. We only know that the truth will stand and lies will fall. Doesn't matter if the lies go from here to *Atlanta*...."

Paul spoke adamantly, as if trying to summon support for his accusations. LaRetha gasped, feeling duly horrified. She was being convicted right here in church, and at her own uncle's funeral!

"...or *wherever*. The truth about my father's death will set us all free."

She could see Nell nodding and smiling through tears, giving full encouragement. And all she could think was, *and let the sideshow begin*.

"I hope you all will remember my father for the good man he came to be. Because for the last fifteen or twenty or more years, he did nothing but give...."

"*Here, here*," said a heavy set minister with a gray goatee.

Yeah, but you can't buy your way into heaven! She thought, allowing herself the luxury of being annoyed. Anything to lessen the disappointment she was feeling, right now.

Apparently, Paul was walking in his father's *old* footsteps; so easily placing blame everywhere but where it belonged. And right now, she hated she'd ever come. Or that she'd asked Douglas to come, as well. *What had she been thinking?*

Suddenly feeling very lonely, she dabbed her tissue at tears that were forming in her eyes. Those tears of anger and frustration that she'd shed for her own father and her uncle, were now for herself.

Paul ended his comments and Jasmine stood, before sitting down suddenly, her body wracking with sobs. Samira was there, comforting her and avoiding her eyes the entire time.

Then, Valerie stood to speak. Standing tall and erect, she walked gracefully into the pulpit. Saying nothing for a minute, but looking around, she paused when she saw the two of them sitting together.

Instinctively, LaRetha attempted to free her hand from Douglas', but his grip tightened. She sat still. After a brief pause, Valerie spoke.

"I didn't know *Uncle Verry* for as long as most of you," she slowly articulated. "But, I knew him well enough to know that..." her eyes wandered over and landed on them, again. LaRetha looked her squarely in the eyes. After hesitating as though losing her train of thought, she briefly hesitated, before continuing to speak.

"To know that..."

A few more people turned to see what the distraction might have been. Finally, she continued, as LaRetha ignored a few very curious stares. She remained motionless, thinking about how she might leave without causing further disruptions.

"Like my husband said, love is a powerful thing. This man showed us both love many times over the years, in many ways. He always treated me like a daughter. Through him, we learned that there's nothing in this world more important than our family. *Nothing!*"

"We've been through thick and thin," she said, smiling in LaRetha's direction, this time. "And I'm hoping," she continued, wiping away tears with a tissue, "that the same love *Verilous Watson* showed before he passed away will continue to be expressed by this family, in the years to come."

Yes, yes.

LaRetha slowly exhaled.

"*Verry* would be the first to say that all things happen for a reason."

That's right.

"We may not know the reason now, but he would say that it's not for us to blame. Instead, we should pray for one another, and encourage each other to be and to do the very best that we can - and to search ourselves, to repent, so we can be found without blemish."

Amen, amen, the congregation agreed.

"So, I pray for my family. That we stick together through this and that we continue to show love for one another. Otherwise, lives like *Verilous Watson's* will have been lived in vain."

Amen, sister. Amen.

"We should do that while we still have time," she said, nodding affirmatively. "*We love you and we'll miss you, Papa Watson. Rest in peace, until we meet again.*"

The room was quiet and Valerie tearfully found her seat after giving what LaRetha thought was a very brave message. It had never occurred to her that she, of all people, might view life this way. Douglas appeared to be moved too, and discreetly wiped at the corner of one eye.

Following comments were equally engrossing and people were becoming less interested in her presence there, it seemed. The important thing was that she *was* here, she reminded herself. And now, she was glad that she had come.

On the way out of the church, she leaned to Douglas's arm for a moment, to catch her breath. *Verilous* was gone, now. But life for the rest of them would go on. She needed to talk to her family and maybe work out their differences. Somehow, together they would remedy this. For *Watson,* for *Verry,* and for Therell.

She walked down the steps, and was stopped by an elderly couple who gave her comforting hugs. The tears in their eyes and their smiles, all said everything that they couldn't at the moment. She thanked them, sincerely. Starting for the car, she suddenly felt a hand grasp her arm and spin her around. It was Bernice.

"*You would come here after all that's happened?* You and your *lawyer…* would come here and pretend to grieve? Disrespecting this family and everybody who cares for this family?" Bernice was livid.

"You would actually show your face up here? I don't care if Douglas is on your side, it doesn't make you *right!* You've got some nerve!"

Surprised, LaRetha was momentarily at a loss for words. Looking into the woman's eyes, she had never seen such hatred. She shook her head, frantically. Instinctively reached out for the woman, who pushed her hand aside.

"So, you want to act innocent?" Bernice said, grabbing at her arm, instead, as if to shake her. She pulled away. "Knowing what happened? What your *boyfriend..*," she sputtered, "...what he did! *He killed our brother.* Just try and deny it."

Her tears were flying now. Nell and the others had been getting into the family limousine, but stopped to listen from a distance, her face showing evil satisfaction.

Several people were standing around, now. Some seemed surprised, others looked appalled. Well, she was angry now, as well. And *she* would have the last word, this time.

She turned to face Bernice, squarely. Someone gasped, anticipating a physical confrontation, no doubt. But what she had to say would hurt worse than that, she thought.

"Okay, so you want to do this *here*, Bernice? You're sure about that?" She had some suppressed anger too, she thought.

The woman said nothing, but stared at her with furious eyes, her nose flaring in anger on her pretty face.

"Well, here it is. What Kellen *did* was defend himself. Therell threatened him and then he pulled a gun on *him*. And if he hadn't defended himself, *he* would be dead right now. So just try and deny *that!* Tell me that Therell didn't plan to kill him. And act like you didn't know that it was going to happen!"

Bernice looked startled. Douglas started around the car toward them but she raised her hand to stop him. *She would handle this!*

She stepped closer to Bernice, and could see fear quickly surfacing in the woman's eyes. She continued.

"Why didn't you think I should come?" She asked, her voice steady, despite the tears streaming down her own face. "Because of his history with my father and the terrible things he used to say about my mother? I know about those things. Still, I appreciated him for the way he treated me. For trying so hard to turn things around. Whatever happened, he was still my *uncle,* and even you can't take that away."

Someone gasped and the woman was speechless and looked as if searching for the words to say. She didn't give her a chance.

"I came to pay my respects, just like everybody here, Bernice. And I couldn't care less what *you* or anybody else thinks about it."

She started off then turned back to the startled woman.

"But, you know what? In spite of the way you all have treated my family, and no less the way you've treated me, I don't hate you, Bernice. I don't hate anyone in this family. I'm praying for all of us. *Therell* shouldn't have happened. That intruder in my house shouldn't have happened. I wish my uncle was here, too. But, as much as I want to, I can't change that."

Bernice looked around and back at her.

"But, if we're *smart,*" LaRetha continued, "instead of waging family wars for the world to see, we would make sure nothing like this ever happens, again. None of them deserved to die. But, if we don't break this cycle of *whatever this is,* it'll probably happen again. The healing has got to start with us."

Bernice took a step backward and looked around as if seeking a way out.

"And I'm not saying this for my *boyfriend's* sake, as you call him, but for our children and for their futures. Not just yours and not mine."

Looking at the ground now, Bernice said nothing.

"My door is always open to you, Bernice. It's your decision."

My, my, someone said. And rather than hug her cousin as she would have preferred to do, she turned and with shoulders and head held high, walked toward the car. The group gathering behind her parted and allowed her through. Smiling triumphantly, Douglas opened her door and she got in.

"Can you believe that?" She asked as Douglas drove them away from the church.

"I don't guess you want to go to the cemetery?" He asked, seriously.

"No. Please drive me home as fast as you can, before I *scream.*"

He patted her hand, and increased his speed. And although the heat was on, she shuddered.

"Are you alright?" He gave her a worried look.

"I'll be fine. It's just that, with all the shooting and arguing, the deaths, Kellen's hearing, and now *this!* It's a bit much, right now."

"I know. I know it is," he said. "But, I think you gave everybody there something to think about. Well done. Your uncle would be proud. I know I am." He smiled at her.

"Thanks, Douglas. I'm just tired of being accused of doing things I would never do. It's *crazy,* the way they judge me and cast blame instead of trying to clean up this mess they've made. Wouldn't that be simpler?"

"Not for some people." Douglas shook his head.

"Well, like I said, thank you, for everything."

"That's not necessary. Now, let's get you home. It looks like it's going to storm," he said, turning his Range Rover in the direction of her house.

She sat far back into the leather seat, feeling greatly vindicated, although equally saddened that it had to happen this way. As for now, there was nothing left to do but wait and see what Douglas could do for Kellen.

13

Gerald waited at a table in the center of the restaurant. He had always liked attention, and he was getting plenty of it from a couple of very friendly waitresses whose eyes were openly drawn to his Rolex watch and diamond cufflinks.

But he wasn't *sloppy* in any sense of the word. His alligator shoes reflected the lights from overhead. He'd cut his hair differently and grown a mustache. And even he had to admit, *he had it going on.* Enough for this old broad to go back and tell her daughter what she was missing.

He had to admit that from where he sat watching her through the glass window as she approached the restaurant, *the woman looked good!* The restaurant wasn't yet half full, so she easily spotted him. He stood and greeted her. She ignored his effort and sat down.

"To what do I owe this invitation, Gerald? I don't have time for games, either." She sat down, placing her expensive purse in the chair beside her.

"A millionaire, and you still haven't bought lessons in *courtesy,* I see." He frowned, thinking that this might be more difficult than he had anticipated.

"I'm here out of curiosity, not courtesy! So let's not pretend to be friends. My loyalty is still with LaRetha, and I believe she's well rid of you. But, you know that. So, what's so important that you would treat *me* to lunch?"

A waitress came over and took her order for a glass of unsweetened tea, which was promptly delivered. Apparently, she didn't plan to stay, he thought. He ordered a soda and was considering an appetizer. Picking up his water glass he took a sip, while painfully aware by her look of disdain that none of his flashing assets - the jewelry, clothes and polite mannerisms - were impressing the old broad. He sat his glass down with impatience.

"I want to see LaRetha, again. To visit, that's all. I just want to make sure that she's alright. We may not be together, but I still care about her."

"*Uh huh.*" She sipped from her glass, her face reading that she truly doubted it. "*Why,* after all this time? You've both moved on with your lives. So why even go there, again, when you have so many unsuspecting prospects right here in Atlanta? Why not just leave her alone? Let her live her life."

He laughed, reminding himself that this was only a preliminary.

"Well, I didn't need your permission the first time, Laretta, and I don't need it now. I wanted to pay her a visit and I know you must talk to her, all the time."

"But why?"

"*Why?* Because I've heard they're having some serious problems out there."

"Oh, okay. Now I understand. Is it money that you need? A loan or something? The last time I saw you looking this flashy was when she threw you out and you had nowhere else to keep your clothes."

She laughed without smiling, her eyes taunting him, offensively. Her distrust was nothing new. But the rudeness, he couldn't tolerate.

"Look, I know you're supposed to have it going on, and everything. But, me and LaRetha, we were alright until you started trying to *fix* things." He said, angrily. He would give her a fight, alright.

"I took *good* care of LaRetha," he continued, angrily. "I gave her everything she ever wanted. I supported her dream to write, even when it didn't pay anything. I was there for her and you know it."

"Ordinarily, I wouldn't begin trying to speak for my daughter, but she's not here. *So, as I recall,*" she said, slowly and deliberately, "my daughter worked the whole time you were married, and *two* jobs when she started writing. You didn't do anything that she couldn't have done for herself, if she hadn't been raising Germaine when you didn't have time. Not to mention, raising you!"

He sputtered his intolerance. *What was it to her, anyway?*

"You thought you had LaRetha where you wanted her. You weren't doing her right and you know it. She just got tired of you and left. Face it, Gerald. Nobody divorced you from LaRetha but *you!*"

She finished her tea. Reached inside her purse to check her vibrating cell phone.

"This is going nowhere, and I have important business to take care of. But *here,*" she reached into her purse and retrieved a twenty dollar bill, which she threw on the table. "This should cover my tea. And while you're thinking about what I said, have a salad on me."

With that, she walked out, her stylishly groomed head held high and four-inch high heels clicking furiously on the floor. Enraged, he looked around to see who'd noticed, before picking up his menu and signaling to one of the waitresses.

Oh, this conversation is far from over, he thought, as the girl bounced over, her very long floating ponytail swinging behind her. He hadn't asked the golden question yet. *What was LaRetha planning to do with all that land?*

Well, at least the old bitter witch paid for my lunch, he thought. He placed his order.

With the *okay* from the police department, LaRetha's truck was moved to *Greenway Springs Salvage & Automotive.* She went to have a look.

Douglas caught up with her outside the shop as she was leaving. He had just dropped off some contracts to a client, he said. He'd seen the truck, earlier. Both agreed it was a terrible way to die.

"How about a cup of coffee before you go back home?" He offered.

She nodded. They walked to a corner diner, checking out the colorful storefront decorations along the way, and listening to soft holiday music that drifted from overhead speakers onto the sidewalks. But as he chatted, her thoughts were immersed in her uncle's plight, and her argument with Bernice at his funeral. She still felt badly about it all.

They sat down and a waitress took their orders for cappuccino.

"Douglas, I'm wondering more and more if those failing brakes weren't meant for *me.*"

"Your uncle was an old man LaRetha, and not in the best of health. Isn't it possible that his memory really did fail him and a heart attack caused him to go off that bridge?"

"But how do we prove that? They said the brakes failed."

"*We* don't have to prove a thing. Nobody's charging you with anything and speculation is not guilt. If they didn't know it before the funeral, they sure know it now." He smiled, and she nodded. She did feel better, having given Bernice a piece of her mind.

"Thanks, Douglas, for always being in my corner. I couldn't do this without you." She sipped her drink, the hot liquid soothing her as it slid down her throat.

"Yes, you could. But everybody can use a shoulder, every now and then. But, there's something else I wanted to mention. The police traced that call from your uncle's home to your mother's cell phone. Any reason she would have to contact him?"

"She's never mentioned any conversations with him. But I can ask her about that, tonight."

"Well, she might have already been questioned. But, do that and get back to me, won't you? Something may have upset him. Maybe she can shed some light on that for us."

He didn't need to elaborate. Like her, he probably figured that Laretta had called *Verry* to chastise him for what was happening. And knowing Laretta, she had made no bones about telling him exactly what she thought. But, even if that had upset him, it didn't explain his being out on that closed off road. Maybe Laretta could provide some answers.

Kellen's trial date would begin on the second week of the year, Douglas said. That's when he would begin to convince a jury that Kellen was innocent of first degree murder. He'd already subpoenaed people from the party for testimony, he said, including several family members. She wasn't certain what Kellen had told him, but whatever it was, it seemed to have left Douglas more confident than ever that he could get an acquittal.

Leaving money for their drinks, Douglas walked with her to her car and saw her safely inside. She hated leaving his good company, but knew he had work to do. Closing her door, he took her left hand into his, looked at her still barren finger and smiled.

"You know, I'm really proud of the way you're handling all this," he said. "At the way you handled yourself at the church. Your dedication to Kincaid. You've been a true friend to him. We should all be so lucky."

"Thank you. But, I really want to apologize to *you*."

"For what?" He looked puzzled.

"For asking you to take me to that funeral. And for putting you in the middle of my family squabbles. I had no right to make you choose between your business relationship with me and Kellen, and your relationship with my family. That was wrong, and I apologize."

"I didn't have to choose. I did what was right. You didn't need to go alone, and there was no way I was going to let you."

"*Precisely!* I knew that and I used that. It was wrong. You didn't owe me that. It has nothing to do with your representing Kellen. Besides, you're sticking your neck out enough for us."

"No harm done, LaRetha," he said. "And, I didn't lose any love at that funeral. They know what I do for a living. And they know now that you and I are good friends. They'll just have to get over it."

She started the engine and he backed away from the car.

"Thanks for the cappuccino and the conversation. Goodbye, Douglas."

"*Bye.* Just be careful out there on those wet roads," he said.

He waited for her to drive out ahead of him. She waved out of her window and he honked his horn as she turned left at the next light, and he continued straight toward his home.

Good friends. That's what he called the two of them, and she couldn't deny the fact that, once again and in spite of everything, someone had come into her life at just the right time.

But, Douglas wanted to be more than that, it seemed. And although the physical attraction was undeniable, she wasn't sure if she felt that way about him. The man had *everything* going for him. Still, she couldn't let her guard down. She also couldn't risk alienating him by leading him on when she wasn't sure of her own intentions.

Kellen had finally come to his senses and hired Douglas. But, he had his reservations. Maybe she should have them, as well. She worried.

But what did worrying help? According to one of her father's favorite scriptures, *if you pray, why worry, and if you worry, why pray?* She said a prayer of thanks for the help that she did have, asking for a quick resolution. Then, for patience, wisdom and guidance in doing her part in this master plan for them all.

Starting tonight, she told herself, she wouldn't worry, but allow herself to be contented and thankful in the moment; for life, for her loved ones, and for all of her blessings. Everything would work out, somehow. It always did.

The townspeople wanted Kellen's blood. They were standing on her front lawn, hundreds of them, demanding that she send him out to them. All of them looked long dead, staggering slowly as they came, and they were throwing fire bombs onto the house, saying they'd come to issue just punishment. Except Watson was standing in the doorway, holding them at bay with a shotgun.

Still, they came. He shot over their heads, but they kept coming. He couldn't stop them.

"I love you, LaRetha! I'm sorry! I love you!" Kellen was shouting wildly and at the top of his lungs as he scurried around her in the burning living room, looking for something to put into an open but empty suitcase.

"Kellen, you have to go. You don't have time..."

She reached out to pull at him and get him to hurry and leave, except his clothing was too hot to touch. She kept trying, but each time, she was burned. She looked up into his face. His skin was ashen and his eyes as red as fire. His face contorted. And now he was angry with her. Coming toward her and shouting.

"Where is it? I had it in my coat. What did you do with it? Where did you hide it? We'll need it if we're going to be married..."

LaRetha awakened, wrestling with her pillow, trying to dispel those images in her sleep. Until tonight, her nightmares had all been about Paul Straiter; seeing him fall and his blood trickling onto her floor, and then seeing him sleeping quietly in a hospital bed, until a pair of violent hands put a pillow over his face. He would kick and struggle until he could no longer breathe. This always awakened her.

But, this time, it was about Kellen. And she woke up with a pressing feeling that enough wasn't being done to prove his case. She had promised not to ask questions or to interfere. But that didn't mean she couldn't volunteer evidence on her own.

She sat up, feeling totally convinced that there was much work to be done. But, there was something of even greater importance to be concerned about. And that was, to take better care of herself.

It was just *5:45am* – too early to get up but she did so, anyway. After showering and getting dressed, she sat down to a breakfast of cold cereal and bananas, and began to plan.

Everything happening around her was connected, she was sure; Paul Straiter, Therell, and now her uncle's death. And there still remained the question of whether or not that truck had been tampered with.

Who would want to hurt her uncle, this late in his life? Hogan had fixed those breaks, but he'd been a friend of her uncle's. Those bad brakes had been meant for her. He would need to be questioned.

Finding a notebook, she turned to a clean page and began writing the names of everyone she'd met here and their occupations. Then, she drew lines between each of them and the people who'd introduced them to her.

She included her uncle, Nell, Therell, Jasmine, Bernice, Paul and Valerie, and even Samira. Then, the younger brothers; Manny, Marvin and Jarvin, and Big Dave. She listed her uncle's siblings; Dan, Carole, Rita and John. She even listed Mr. Hogan. And lastly, Douglas and Kellen.

Using red ink now, she linked non-relatives to the relatives who had introduced them to this scene. This connected Jasmine to Samira, Samira to Douglas, *and* Samira to Kellen.

Interesting, she thought. It was probably either Samira or Jasmine who had given Kellen that note. But when? She couldn't think of one solitary time when…

The night he bought the Christmas tree! Kellen was gone for over two hours, that night. Long enough to meet and talk with anyone. But who? Therell, maybe. Or maybe he'd seen Samira, that night. Someone would know, but who could she ask? Certainly not Nell. And Bernice was certainly out of the question. *Paul?* No, that would be much too complicated. But, there had to be someone.

Valerie! She thought. Making a note to pursue that avenue later, she stood and stretched, feeling amazed that she would feel so tired after just waking up.

But she had things to do. First, she needed to call her mother. With Christmas being just days away, she had last minute shopping to do – Laretta's favorite pastime. She looked forward to seeing everybody.

As she called to make reservations for the next day, she wondered if she shouldn't tell Douglas that she was leaving. But why risk having him tell her she should stay in town? She would call him once she got there. He could tell Kellen, if necessary.

She packed several bags for her week-long stay. Her flight was leaving early, which meant that she would arrive in Atlanta no later than *11:30am*, tomorrow. She would drive her car to the airport and leave it until she returned.

Laretta picked up on the second ring. She was coming to town, she told her. *Could she pick her up at Hartsfield?* Her mother was ecstatic. And with the holiday cheer going full force now, LaRetha made another list of everything she needed to do before leaving, then plans for things that she and her mother could do, and a list of things to buy for Christmas. At the top of that list, she wrote another task. She needed to do that right now.

She went to her bedroom nightstand and retrieved the gun she'd brought from Atlanta from the drawer. Inspecting it closely, she checked the safety and then bounced its weight against her hand. Despite her intentions to be safe, guns were the very cause of so much that was horrible in her life right now. Those shootings had led to her uncle's heart failure, she was sure of it. And no telling whose death in the future. She had to do this.

Unloading it, she laid it on the bed and looked at it. She knew this was a good decision. The police still had her father's gun, and her uncle's hadn't turned up, yet. And this one, well, it would be the last to go.

She closed her eyes. Letting go of her fears was hard. Believing that she would be protected, just because of her faith, was easier thought than done, but she would. She went to find a garbage bag.

It took forty-five minutes or so to drive out to the city dump, toss the bag filled with shredded papers, a few old magazines and the gun, tucked tightly away at the bottom, and to head back home, again. Taking the shortest route back, she checked her rear view mirror. No one had seen or followed her, it appeared. By the time she got home, she was already feeling relieved. That gun was history now, as was her use of them. And she would never buy another one, again.

And now, she could look forward to her trip to Atlanta. Maybe Douglas would visit for a day or two, she thought with a smile.

She would help him to make Kellen a free man, again. Until then, she resolved herself to enjoying as much of this holiday season as she possibly could.

Laretta was pleased that LaRetha had packed so many bags – a sure sign that she would stay for a while. They drove straight to her house, where Marilee greeted them at the door.

"Hello, LaRetha. Pleasant flight?"

"Yes. Thanks, Marilee. What's that wonderful smell?"

The woman smiled. Food was never wasted with this family.

"Breakfast pies. The kind you like, with sausage, eggs and cheese inside my homemade crusts. I saved you some from breakfast."

"Great. I'll put my things away and be right there. I just hope you made enough."

Marilee beamed, holding the door for her and her luggage. Laretta went upstairs, unusually chipper after having her sleep interrupted so early that morning. She would join her in the kitchen in ten minutes, she said.

By the time she did, LaRetha had already consumed one small pie and was working on her second.

"I miss this," she said, smiling at her mother, who nodded while still enjoying her first one.

"Yeah, but you'd better slow down. You're getting a bit *thick*, aren't you?"

"I can lose it when I'm ready," she smarted. "Besides, you're looking healthy, yourself." She knew that her mother was always conscious of weight; hers and everyone else's. But she intended to enjoy this meal, regardless.

"*Lovely* did it," Laretta said. "I usually can control my weight, but one trip to that town and *whew!*"

They laughed. Her mother was right. They agreed they would exercise every day that she was there.

"Its good having you here, sweetie," Laretta said. "You should consider staying until after the New Year."

"I can't," she responded. "But wouldn't that be a terrible thing; Kellen getting into trouble because I refused to leave, then my leaving now that he's in trouble?"

Laretta appeared to consider this. LaRetha waited for her to dispute that, but she didn't.

"I only meant for a visit. Everybody knows it's the holidays."

LaRetha nodded, her mind made up. Laretta could be grumpy about something else.

"You really shouldn't feel guilty about Kellen."

LaRetha gave her mother a look that said, *I don't*. But she did. She couldn't help it.

"He made his bed. Just be glad *you* didn't get caught lying in it."

She nodded as she chewed. *No use disputing the truth*, she thought. Kellen's intentions were highly questionable.

"You should stop blaming yourself for what other folks do, LaRetha. Those people lost that battle a long time ago. But just like back then, nobody wants to be held accountable. But that still doesn't make you responsible."

"Somebody sent that man to break into your house, the first time. And we still don't know what he was really there to do. Then, Kellen isn't there a week, and already he's in trouble. And even his motives are suspicious as all get out. But you didn't do that, either. He called me, talking about how concerned he was, and I agreed he should visit you. I didn't think it could hurt. *Little did I know!*"

"He would have come, regardless," she consoled. "For some reason or other."

"I *know*. That's what I'm telling you," her mother said. "These folks will use anybody, LaRetha. We don't know the motives, yet. I'm just thankful that whatever they had planned hasn't worked. I guess all your praying is paying off, girl," she smiled. "Just remember. You don't owe them or Kellen *anything*."

Motives. Kellen certainly had those. He'd probably been using her all along, and she'd been wide open for it, Getting him the job with Mac was her idea, sure enough. But it hadn't stopped there. Their little squabble about Paul wasn't far off base, either. And to think that he was already planning to work with the man's sister!

If nothing else, the man was *ambitious!* And he didn't mind using her family issues to get a leg up.

"I know, Mama. And I'm not being callous but I haven't come all this way to worry about my problems in *Lovely*. Or Kellen's. It's a holiday, and I plan to enjoy it as best I can."

"Good for you."

"So tell me. What's on the agenda for us?"

"I *like* this new girl," her mother teased. "First, we rest, then we shop, and then we see a movie while we plan what we'll do tomorrow. How about that?"

"Great. I have to see Mac Henry sometime tomorrow, and get a lead on some research I need to do. I've got to get more work done, but I've just been too distracted."

"Well, it's certainly understandable why you would be. Does Mac know about Kellen's situation?"

"Yep! He wanted me to help him break this story."

"You're kidding, aren't you?" Laretta frowned.

"Not at all. He's great at what he does, but the man has the compassion of a doormat. Somehow, he got wind of the fires down there *and* about Kellen. He's been trying to contact me, but I think he's asking a bit much."

"And he is! I mean, this is your *life*, for goodness sakes! Why would he even ask such a thing?"

"Inside scoop, what else? It's only business to him."

"But, it's so risky for you."

"It's very risky. I've been avoiding his calls to keep him from sending someone else. If anybody from Mac's office is going to tell this story, it's going to be me."

"But, look at what he's asking. How would it look if the defendant's girlfriend shows up in court to testify, wearing a press pass?"

"It would look as if I was manipulating the situation somehow, encouraging these terrible events, maybe even participating, just to get a story. Some people would do that, you know?" She had thought this through, after all.

"*Exactly!* So don't risk it. With you helping Kellen and having so much to lose, it would only cause you to get in your own way."

"It's called a clear conflict of interest. It's bad enough that people think I had something to do with *Uncle Verry's* death."

"What? How so?"

She told her mother about Bernice and her accusations.

"I can't believe you even went to that funeral, but go on."

"It's being implied that I lured him out there. But, Douglas says they traced the call back to you. Why didn't you tell me about that?"

"Oh, yes, the call. Truthfully, I'd put that completely out of my mind. I called *Verry* and told him I wanted to meet with him before I left town. I waited longer than I said I would, but he never showed. And the next day, you told me he was dead. That was the end of it."

"I thought so."

"I thought the man had lied to me. It never occurred to me that he was dead or that my call to him would be questioned."

"I thought the police might've contacted you about that call by now."

"*Please!* It'll be at least a year before those bumbling cops even think about tracing that call."

She nodded, making a mental note to mention this to Douglas.

"By the way, your *ex-husband* invited me to lunch the other day."

LaRetha stared at her, in surprise.

"That could only mean one of two things," LaRetha finally said. "Either he's had his soul saved and wants your forgiveness for being such a jerk son-in-law, or he wants to buy some property. Which was it?"

"Who knows? I met with him, but his appearance ticked me off so bad, I didn't let him say very much. So, I'm really not sure *what* he wanted."

"What was wrong with his appearance?"

"The usual; clothes too expensive, and tacky. Jewelry too darned flashy and his smile was way too friendly. You know I've never trusted him, and I told him that. I said my loyalties were still with you. That didn't set too well with him," she said, sitting back with such a satisfied look that LaRetha laugh.

"I wonder what he's up to."

"Well, for one, he wanted to know if he could visit you."

"*Ah huh?*" She made a face. "He wanted something other than that, I know."

"I think so, too."

"There's no telling with Gerald. I just wonder what that has to do with everything else. I guess I need to find him and find out."

"Just be careful. There's no telling what's going on with him, now."

The newsroom was buzzing with energy and activity, and instantly she missed her days working in-house. She learned that Constance was out of the office and left a note on her desk, asking her to call. They hadn't talked since she'd moved, but with Constance that wouldn't matter. They had that kind of friendship. Once they were together again, it would seem as if she'd never left.

Mac Henry was on the phone and waved her into his office, just as he ended his conversation. Quickly moving his robust 5'6" stature around his desk, he gave her a welcoming hug – his usual greeting.

"*Well,* if it isn't the little farm girl coming back to the city, and hopefully to stay. Tell me I'm right."

"Not quite. I'm just visiting. But, it's good to see you. This place is still a madhouse, huh? Have I missed much?"

"Of course you have," he said, studying her and smiling. "Like two deadlines, for starters. Luckily, I like you and those last stories you sent. They were very insightful. I had Cantrell make a few adjustments. One is being printed, tomorrow."

"*Cantrell!* Those are my stories. Why didn't you ask me to do it?"

"I tried. I called, you didn't answer. E-mailed, you didn't respond. I didn't have time to send a certified letter. If I didn't think I would have use for you in the near future..." he warned. She smirked at him. He always said it and never meant it. "So, what's new in *Lovely,* Kentucky?"

He leaned back in his wide leather chair, cradling the back of his head in his hands. She sighed, shaking her head.

"Well first, let me say that I appreciate your being so tolerant of my insubordination. There's so much that's new in *Lovely,* I don't know where to begin. And here?"

"I asked you. You're the reporter, aren't you?" He said, matter-of-factly. She was accustomed to his dry, direct wit.

"True," she said, undaunted. "I might be onto a few things."

"I guess I just haven't gotten that memo, yet," he said, rather surly.

"I'm still working on that one," she said, with indifference. "But you already know about Kellen, right? I can't believe any of that, myself."

"I did hear. I didn't think you'd call me first, and you didn't. I heard about your uncle, too."

"Of course you did. That's why you're the news man."

He shrugged off her attempts to be patronizing.

"I'll have something else for you, soon. I just wanted to drop in and wish you all a Merry Christmas."

"LaRetha, you know, you could just sell that place, move back here and start writing full time, again."

"I guess," she said, "but, Kellen needs me..."

"Looks like Kellen's gone and gotten himself into some mess that even you can't get him out of. He is a grown man, you know? It's alright to want to help him. Just make sure you know what you're getting yourself into."

What did he know about it? She wondered.

"Do you know why he was even there? What he was really after?" The big man inquired.

"What? You can't believe he was really there for *me*?" She asked, jokingly.

"I did, at first. But, now..."

"You sound like my mother. I do have concerns about that."

"You might want to listen to your Mama."

"I'll tell her you said hello. I've got to run, though," she said. "I'll write you as soon as I get something juicy."

"You'd better. Take care of yourself, LaRetha."

"I will. Enjoy your holiday."

She left as he answered another call. Driving downtown, she decided to take a tour of the city, just to reacquaint herself with what she'd left behind. Soon, she was headed in a familiar direction, figuring *why not?*

Turning the last corner into the subdivision and then onto her old street, she parked in a space just above the house. It was Friday morning and apparently someone was celebrating an early Christmas because that whole section of the street was lined with parked cars. *New neighbors,* she figured.

Sitting in the car, she looked at what used to be her home. Once trimmed in beige, it was pale green, now. *Nice touch,* she thought. Aside from seeing different cars in the driveway, everything else looked the same.

Several homes on the street had been sold, she noticed. Two years had made a big difference. She remembered how much they had loved living here. It was a great neighborhood, then. People were friendly and looked out for one another's properties and children, who had all played well together on this private street. And no one was ever offended when they were told what their child had been up to. It was expected. Then.

More than anything, she missed the way everyone would put up Christmas decorations at about the same time. Usually, two weeks before Christmas. White and colored lights would be strung outside every house by now. Santa and his reindeer would slide down that very roof, and an ethnic nativity scene would decorate their lawn. They would awaken early and have a huge breakfast, open presents and usually spend the day with her mother and various friends who had no other plans.

Usually on holidays there would be an unexpected presence or two at the dinner table. Birthdays were always full of surprises and their wedding anniversaries, especially nice. She smiled now as she remembered all the fun they once had.

But that was all just fond memories, pictures and videotape, now. Maybe now, she thought sadly, she could finally take them back out and look at them, again.

Gerald slowed as he passed the house and stopped. All this used to be his, he thought. And were it not for his own *stupidity*, he'd still be living here.

Life was good then, although it was certainly much simpler, right now. He had trimmed down his lavish lifestyle. And although he'd invested a bit over his head, with only a few more repairs to make on that house, he would have a nice bit of change coming in each month, he thought. He had finally begun doing what LaRetha had always asked; he was keeping the spending to a minimum, And the dating – well, that was another matter.

LaRetha. He hadn't seen or talked to her since *Watson's* funeral where, as soon as he saw her, he'd wondered how he'd ever let her go. She was *beautiful*. But aside from a giving him a lackluster smile and brief hug, she'd paid him no attention. And even that wouldn't have been so bad, if she hadn't been accompanied by the last person he'd expected to see her with. *Kellen Kincaid!* The man had looked at him as if *he* hadn't belonged there. Now, *that* had hurt.

He'd tried to ask Germaine about the two of them on the way back to Atlanta, but the boy closed up so tightly, he'd immediately changed the subject. He could almost read his son's thoughts; why did he care? He'd told himself over and over that he didn't; that he couldn't afford to. And besides, he could never go back.

He'd probably made a mistake, talking to her mother. She would surely discourage LaRetha from seeing him. But, with Kellen in jail and out of the way, this was the perfect opportunity to approach her. She might even be glad to see him, he thought.

So, he would visit, provide her with some much needed support - maybe even revive some of those old feelings. Nothing deep, though. He had one main goal right now. And he had to see it accomplished.

He could remember their first day moving into this house. And the first day they had met. At *nineteen,* she was quite a vision in tight faded jeans, a light blue suede sweater with silver closures on the front of it, and matching calf-high boots. Standing apart from her small crowd of friends, she'd had a smile so bright that he couldn't stop looking at her.

They were all stepping off the city bus, their arms loaded with books and shopping bags. She had turned to say goodbye to them and almost ran right into him. He had called out to her just in time.

After accepting her apology, he'd asked her name and offered to help carry her bags. After coaxing her into giving him her number, he had called her that night, and they had talked for hours. After that, they were practically inseparable. By the end of her junior year at college, he'd proposed. She accepted, and they were married a year later, just months after her graduation.

Despite the fits that her parents threw, his mother had loved and accepted her, treating LaRetha like a daughter until she died a few years later. His father, he hadn't seen since he was *six.* So, she was his family, and they were inseparable. They were always very close and in love. And that love had included Germaine when he was born.

But, as a friend once told him, Atlanta could be hard on a marriage. For them, it wasn't the money problems that his friends had, but the temptations of the thriving nightlife and other women, and her being all consumed with work, church, friends and all different the activities that she and Germaine were involved in.

She had tried to involve him, especially in church where she'd even started a home bible study group. Trying to bring the church to him, he guessed. But for him, it only gave him more free time to do whatever he pleased. And that attitude had cost him his family.

She must have known for some time, he figured. Those womanly instincts always knew. After a time, she'd quit asking about his day and questioning him about his whereabouts. He would only lie to her. She became disinterested in spending time with him. Then, just emotionally distant, looking at him with different, distrustful eyes. And eventually, they were very much like total strangers sharing a roof.

He'd done and said any and everything to rid himself of guilt - complaining about things around the house, criticizing her and throwing tantrums, just to keep her off balance. Just like his mother said his father had done. But that had only made matters worse. And rather than realize how much she needed him and what she stood to lose, she must have decided instead that she could make it just fine, without him. She was practically doing that, already.

Sure, he'd blamed *Watson* and Laretta. They had offered her refuge before she'd even asked for it. And then, there was something about that praying she did that had kept her strong and somehow had reversed everything he'd tried to do. Despite his belief that, given her faith, she would try to work it out before actually leaving. But she had divorced him without so much as a backwards glance, saying that not only *could* she do better, but that she deserved better, as well

And now, somebody on this block was playing loud music with a window open. There was laughter and conversation. Whatever kind of party that was, it was certainly no bible study group, he figured. The neighborhood was certainly changing.

He had messed up. He admitted it. He didn't even know why, because he'd had it all; the house, the career, the beautiful and loving wife, and a son with a promising athletic career, and who had loved him unconditionally. And every material thing he'd ever wanted.

It was his fault that Germaine had walked away from that scholarship. His fault that his son had left his mother's house the way that he had, because he had done the same thing. And, now it was his fault that his son's guilt and anger toward him was keeping him from talking to his mother.

He had never meant for Germaine to see. He'd never expected him to come over after spending an entire day together; shopping for accessories for his jeep and just spending time.

And evidently their day together had gone well because LaRetha had invited him to stay over for dinner. He could tell that she was happy about the time he was spending with his son. There was no confusion about their pending divorce. However, somewhere along the line, the boy had gotten his hopes up about their reconciling.

Thinking it was pizza delivery for his guest, he'd answered the door in his boxers and felt like the worst loser in the world when he saw who it was.

"What are you doing here, Germaine?" He had insisted with embarrassment as he felt compelled to let the boy inside.

Germaine had looked bewildered, at first. Then looking behind him, his smile had faded into an indescribable look of surprise and disappointment.

"Well, what is it? What do you need?" Gerald had demanded, assuming that the boy's mother had sent him.

But he'd quickly realized his mistake and could only drop his head in shame as Germaine looked from him to the woman sitting half-dressed on the bed in the adjoining room.

Although he didn't speak, he could almost hear his son asking, *why?* Hadn't that day meant anything to him? What were the man-to-man talks about? The sharing? It was all in his expression. Seeing that woman there, only partly wrapped in a thin robe and making no effort to cover herself, Germaine had become infuriated with him.

"Sorry to *interrupt*," he'd said, caustically. "I thought I'd introduce you to my girl. I guess it's bad timing, as usual."

"Wait a minute, son. Have a seat and I'll be out in just a minute," he'd said over his shoulder as he'd gone into the bedroom, closing the door and waving his company out of sight.

"Don't worry about it." Germaine had called out, turning to leave.

But he couldn't allow him to walk away this angry. He had to get through to him.

"Wait, Germaine! Hold up a minute!"

Quickly stepping into a pair of jeans, he had caught up with him at the parking lot. That's when he saw the girl with him. He reached for his son's arm to stop him.

"Man, get your hands off me!" Germaine said, sullenly.

"Wait!" He'd insisted.

"No, you wait!" Germaine's handsome young face twisted with disdain, looking so grown up, and so much like him. "My mother is starting to trust you again, and this is what you do?

"*Your mother and I are divorcing, son!* I'm sure she's seeing other people, too. There's nothing wrong with that!"

"Maybe so. But, you've always cheated on her. She was always sitting up, worrying about you. Waiting for you to come home..."

"This is why you couldn't make it to my basketball games, or to the track fields." Germaine struggled to remain composed. "Why you never showed up for anything I did. You chose *this* over me, and over my mom. I'm glad she's divorcing you! It took her long enough."

The girl was inside the jeep now, and Germaine looked anxious to get away from him, when just hours before he'd hated to see him leave.

"Germaine! Why do you think I'm living here? You *knew* this, already!"

"*Whatever!*"

He couldn't believe the boy's reaction. Hadn't seen him this upset in a long time. Grabbing this young man who stood almost at eye level with him, he had tried to embrace him. But the gesture was not returned and he could see all the progress they'd made that weekend just slipping away

"Let's talk about this. Meet with me tomorrow night for dinner. We'll go any place that you pick. It's my treat."

The brief glimmer of hope in his son's eyes was quickly lost. He stepped back and Germaine started the engine. Without another word, he drove away. It would be weeks before he would talk to him, again.

"Your son is mad at you?" Samira had asked when he'd returned to the apartment. She was wearing jeans and a blouse, now. That had annoyed him. Not wanting to show his pain, he'd just nodded.

"That's too bad."

"Well, he's just going to have to grow up and accept that parents have lives, too. *And now you get dressed?*"

Shortly afterward was *Watson's* funeral, and he could see that somebody else was playing husband *and* daddy, now.

Kellen Kincaid. And after all the times he'd welcomed this man into his home as a friend of Germaine's. He should have been smarter. Should've paid attention. Now, he wondered just how long it had been going on.

It looked as if LaRetha had played *him*. She must have counted on him giving her a reason to leave, considering what she had waiting for her on the sidelines. And now, he felt betrayed. Especially by Germaine, who obviously didn't have a problem with it, and that hurt, for sure. But, fortunately, he wouldn't have to worry about that, anymore. It seemed that LaRetha's little playmate would be on lock-down for a very long time.

But, all that was in the past. Early retirement wasn't that far off, now. And his aspirations of traveling extensively to African nations, to Europe and finally to the Caribbean, were getting closer to being realized.

He might even take Germaine, if he wanted to go. He had a lot of making up to do. Hopefully, he'd get a chance to do it. This, he would do. For Germaine.

He looked at his watch. *4:35pm.* And he had a flight to catch. First, he would pay her a visit. He would never forgive himself if he didn't. He owed her this much.

Preparing to leave, he instinctively looked back and noticed a driver parked at the curb. After a brief moment of recognition, he looked away.

Was that who he thought it was? Pretending to pick something up from the ground, he looked again. It *was!* Sitting just a few yards back, looking wistfully at their old house and seeming oblivious to anything around her, was the woman of the hour. He would know that long bushy hair, anywhere.

So much for that flight, he thought. *This was definitely meant to be.* If everything else went this smoothly, then pretty soon, all would be well.

Starting his car, he sat a long time, planning his next move. After a time, he slowly pulled away from the curb, watching from his side view mirror as she did the same.

With everything going so badly for her in *Lovely,* maybe she had already decided to move back here. She just might sell that property. She might even consider sailing around the country with him. Either way, he could only see this as a lucky break. Besides, that woman was living much too far away.

14

LaRetha thought she was seeing things. He was leaning against his car, and staring at the house they used to share.

Gerald. She almost drove away, except something about seeing him there captivated her. There was something very sad about the way he was looking at the house; as if he was remembering and regretting. He hadn't looked that vulnerable in a long time.

After a time he got into his car, where he sat for a few minutes before driving away. Certain that she hadn't been seen, and that he wouldn't recognize her mother's car, she slowly followed him to the traffic light at the end of the street.

She didn't know why she was doing this, other than feeling she needed to know where he was going and what he was up to. He was just three cars ahead of her now, making a left turn. Instinctively, she pursued him.

Finally, he pulled into the entrance of an expensive apartment complex. *Surely he didn't keep his old apartment,* she thought, remembering how he'd had to find a place in a hurry when they'd separated. Parking a building away, she watched as he unlocked the door and went inside. Driving past, she wrote down the building and apartment number, and then his tag number. If she ever needed to find him again, she could.

Most of that day was spent shopping with Laretta, and they didn't finish until evening. Back at the house again, she immediately dove into her bags, taking account of her purchases and wrapping them, before putting them underneath the tree.

She'd had little time to shop, and so easily decided on clothing for everyone, this year. Laretta would love the dress with a matching coat, shoes and purse. There were sports shirts and pants for Germaine, a sports cap and a few CD's that she thought he might like. She'd chosen a very nice cologne and tie for Douglas. And for herself, she'd bought several outfits and a comfortable pair of low heeled boots.

Feeling duly pampered now, she realized it was getting late and she still hadn't spoken with Valerie. She would call her as soon as they returned from their evening outing at her mother's church.

The event was every bit as interesting and inspiring as her mother had said it would be. There was a service being led by the youth department, followed by a beautiful reenactment of the birth of Baby Jesus.

In an adjacent building was a *Santa's Shop* where, inside, there were tables and tables of Christmas crafts and volunteer elves, making wooden toys. She and Laretta bought several, to be donated by the church to homeless children. A youth choir sang carols, and the tour ended with exhibits of various cultures celebrating the sacred birth.

Afterwards, she and Laretta enjoyed an excellent dinner at a nearby restaurant. The steak was tender and the hot buttered rolls seemed to melt in her mouth.

"See, this is why I can't hang out with you, Mama. You like to eat as much as I do. Now I really need to work out."

"And you can start in the morning. I've converted the basement into an exercise room. So, eat all the calories you're willing to work off."

"That would be *none.*" She laughed. "But I am taking my health more seriously now. I'm going to start first thing, tomorrow."

"*Sure you are,*" her mother teased.

"I saw Gerald this morning." LaRetha said as they waited for their desserts.

"Where? You didn't call him?" Laretta looked exasperated.

"*No way.* I rode through my old neighborhood and there he was. I followed him to an apartment about four blocks away. I guess it's a girlfriend's place or something."

"Well, did he say anything? Did he even see you?"

"*No.* And I didn't want him to."

"*Good.* That lunch meeting we had still concerns me."

"Don't worry about that. It's definitely a *done deal.*"

Her mother nodded and they dove into their apple pie.

Douglas looked at the caller I.D. *L. Watson*. Her message was
short and brief. She would be in Atlanta until after New Year's Day.
He should come and spend Christmas Day. Call her when he got in,
she said.

So, his girl was in Atlanta, he thought with dismay. Unable to
reach her for the entire day, he had already driven out to the farm,
just to make sure she was okay. There were lights on inside, but no
sign of her. He'd left a note inside her storm door. *CALL ME, DD.*

After listening to her message again, he dialed the number.

"Hello, Douglas. What's going on?"

She sounded in high spirits. *Was she moving away, after all?*

"So, you *are* in Atlanta. Just visiting for the holidays, I hope."

"Yes, just hanging out with Mama and getting some much
needed relaxation. Did you get my invitation?"

"I did. You're staying until after New Year's? I had hoped we
could celebrate together, here."

"We hadn't discussed it. I wanted you to join us for Christmas, if
you didn't have other plans, of course."

He considered this. There was so much work to do.

"How is Kellen's case coming along?"

"Pretty good, but question is, how're *you?*" He wasn't interested
in discussing Kincaid at the moment.

"I'm fine. I had a lot of shopping to do. I needed some things."

"Well, you never fooled me with that *low maintenance* act,
anyway," he said and they both laughed.

But, he rather liked that, he thought. A woman who cared about
looking great for her man. And this woman always looked great.

"What's new on the case?"

"Well, there are still a lot of people for me to interview, but
there's time. The hearing was postponed. So Kellen will be spending
a very merry Christmas on the inside."

"*Humph.* You don't sound too sympathetic."

"I sympathize," he said only half truthfully. "But, I figure there's
more here than meets the eye."

He wasn't sure how to feel about this guy, just yet. The jury was
still out on that one.

"As if what we already know isn't bad enough."

"Listen, I have to get to the barber's before he closes. Call me
tonight? I'll need to talk to your mother, if she's in."

She said that she would. He refrained from saying how much he
missed her and wanted her home. No use scaring the woman away.

Hanging up the receiver, he looked up from where he sat behind his desk and was startled to see someone standing in the
doorway.

How in the world did she get in, this time?

For a moment, Douglas ignored the woman, staring at the itinerary on his computer screen as he did a slow, silent boil. Samira strolled in and stood in the middle of the room, waiting on him to look up. He didn't.

But how could he possibly miss that long hair worn pinned up now, and those long lashes fluttering at him? Or the snug brown sweater worn with tight jeans and those very high heels? Were she anyone but Samira, he might have said she was simply *spectacular.* But this woman would get no compliments from him, ever again.

"Who let you in here, Samira? Or did you steal the keys?" He asked, giving her a stolid look.

"I didn't need a key. The door wasn't closed all the way. You should be more careful."

"You're lying. Since you were last here, that door is always locked."

"Here," she said, throwing a key on his desk.

"I'm not even going to ask how you got that." He was trying with little success to control the temper rising up inside of him. *She has the audacity to show up here, after what she did?*

"Sorry, but Marva got careless. I borrowed one from her desk drawer while she was in the bathroom. I had to be sure that I could see you."

"You know how I feel about you stealing from me. But be warned that if I find even one *shred* of paper missing..."

Turning off his computer, he stood up and walked to his office door, gesturing for her to follow him into the hallway.

"Can't we talk in here, Douglas?"

"*No.* In the front office."

He didn't trust her. Or himself with being alone in here, with her. Those memories of their tryst together weren't that far removed. *Save me from temptation,* he thought as he checked the offices and the hall closet. All were empty. Still, he was guarded.

"What are you *doing*, Douglas?"

He turned to see her standing in the hallway behind him, her coat off now and both hands on curvaceous hips, looking at him as if he'd lost his mind.

"Making sure we're alone, that's what!"

She threw her head back and laughed.

"Oh, so you think I wanted to corner you while somebody else ripped you off? You're crazy!"

She laughed again, and he continued his search. He knew the devil he was dealing with. Then, satisfied that the front door was locked this time, he sat with her in the reception area.

"Okay, Samira. I'll tell you what I told your little partner in crime, Jasmine. I represent Kincaid. If you have something to say that might help his case, then *spill it!* Otherwise, you should get out before I throw you out!"

A half hour later, they were sharing a pizza at the front desk, and drinking grape sodas that Marva had left for him in the refrigerator.

"I haven't stolen anything from you Douglas. I told you that you left those papers in a folder in my hotel room. You were drinking a lot and you forgot, that's all. Except, when you asked me about them, I went to look for them and they were gone. But, the maid didn't remember seeing them."

"Samira, my profession requires me to sniff out liars and perpetrators, and that's exactly what you are, right now. If there was a folder in your hotel room, *you* took it there. But, that's not why you're here, I'm sure. What did you come here for, this time? And what's it worth to you?"

"You've turned into some cold tuna fish, Douglas. There was a time…"

"*There was a time,*" he interrupted, "when I could turn my back while you were in the room. That time has come and gone. Now, I've ordered food for you, you've got your drink. I'm being as patient as I know how. I know this isn't a social visit, so what's on your mind?"

As Samira sat across the desk from him, flicking her long pink nails and watching him slyly, he remembered another reason that it hadn't worked out between them. The woman had no tact.

"Okay, okay. It's about your girlfriend," she finally said.

"What girlfriend is that?" He asked, looking at her with suspicious eyes. She laughed.

"I have some information that might be of interest to you, and importance to her."

"What *her* are you talking about?"

"You know what *her* I'm talking about. *LaRetha Watson.*"

"It's *Greer.*"

"Oh yeah? Well, *her.*"

"What is this information?"

The smug expression on her face fell, and she was suddenly serious. Douglas wondered what the game was, this time. But she looked frightened. He waited.

"This thing has gotten way out of hand, you know? It's not something I wanted to get involved in, but I had no choice. I owed some favors, and frankly, I needed the money."

"I'll just bet. Especially since you're always living beyond your means or depending on someone else's," he muttered, unforgivingly.

"*Anyway,*" she continued, "now, I find out I've been misled about a lot of things. And it looks like all the heavies are gonna walk on this one. Only, I can't let that happen because that means *I* could go to jail for *them.* Or worse, I could end up zipped up in a body bag, at the city morgue."

She waited for a response. He gave her a look that said, *and why should I care?*

"Who are these *heavies,* that you're talking about? Whoever they are, I already know why you were involved with them, but why are they involved with you?"

"*No.* Make me a deal, first. Promise me something. Or, I'm not going to talk."

Same old Samira, he thought. Always selling *something.*

"*A deal?* Let me get this straight. You expect me to think that if I don't promise you protection of some sort, that you're just going to let the bad guys get you? I don't believe that for a second."

"I need your help. And the only reason I'm here is because she needs my help, too, and I know that's the only way I'll get any help from you."

"What's going on now, Samira? Is Jasmine threatening to break your neck if you expose all her little trifling business deals? Is somebody threatening you if Kellen Kincaid walks, or if he doesn't?" He smirked.

"I *mean* it, Doug," the woman said, beginning to look very nervous, now. "This is some serious stuff that I've gotten into. You know about the shootings and that old man's death."

"That was an accident."

"Maybe."

"Okay, he said, "but I don't see what I can do..." He shook his head.

"Look," she said, raising her hand to stop him in mid-sentence. "I didn't come here to beg. I know my mistakes. And I know how much you must hate me, right now. So you don't have to remind me."

He was unmoved.

"I've done some terrible things, okay? But now, I want you to help me... for us to help one another. You're pretty well respected around here. They'll listen to you. And it might even help in Kellen's case. But, you have to promise to protect me."

"*Terrible* is right," he said, with an ill-humored expression. "You're lucky *I'm* not after you. But I knew it would all catch up to you one day. People like you never get enough. There's always that one last little con that you have to pull, and that's when you either get caught up with, or killed. So, what's it going to be for you? Who are you afraid of and why?"

He took a last swallow from his soda, leaned back in his chair and belched loudly, not caring that it was rude. This woman's middle name was *rude*.

"I *am* afraid, and you should be, too. For your girlfriend."

"What's going to happen to LaRetha?" He straightened in his chair, giving her a serious look. She crumbled. He didn't console her.

"They're going to get that land, one way or the other. She's got to work with them."

"No, she doesn't. It's hers and she can do whatever she likes with it. But what's going to happen, Samira? And don't lie to me."

She shook her head, the tears falling, now. Still, he had no sympathy.

"I'm sorry," he said, feeling anything *but*. "It doesn't look like I can help you. But I can promise you this. If something does happen to her, you'd better hope they get to you before I do."

She blinked but didn't respond.

"But, if you're really afraid and want somebody to cut you a deal, then maybe you should go to the police."

"I can't. I might go to jail."

"Well, I can't protect you from justice being served. Certainly not if you were involved in a murder." He watched her face, expecting a response and he got one. She quickly sobered.

"What if I was involved in *three?*"

LaRetha dialed, and after six or more rings, Valerie answered.

"*LaRetha?* What's going on? Is something wrong?"

Valerie sounded concerned, and she was relieved. At least *she* wasn't angry with her, too.

"*A lot*. If you're alone, I'd like to talk to you. Is this a good time?"

"Well, you're in luck. Paul's gone out to get dinner, but I'm expecting him back, any minute. Give me a clue what this is about."

"The *obvious*. I want you to know that I had nothing to do with *Verry's* death. Or Therell's."

"I know. I figured as much. Listen, give me your number and I'll call you back."

She did.

"I'm here, all night," LaRetha said, gratefully. "Or, if tomorrow is better for you, early morning is good for me. I'd really like to talk to you before I go back to *Lovely*."

"Where are you, now?"

"*Georgia*," she said, carefully. "Just for a minute. But, call that number, anytime."

"Sure. I'll get back with you no later than tomorrow morning."

They hang up, and LaRetha didn't know if she should be relieved or not. She did know that she was hungry and tired. A snack
would be good, she thought. Except, when she got downstairs, she
caught a whiff of something *wonderful*.

She uncovered the dishes on the stove and found fried whiting
and vegetables, mashed potatoes and cornbread muffins. Marilee
had planned ahead, once again.

Eating at her mother's kitchen table, she thought about the exercise room downstairs, resolving to use it. *First thing in the morning.*

Gerald paced the floor at his Atlanta townhouse with cell phone
in hand, trying to decide what to say when he called. *All that
worrying for nothing,* he thought, smiling to himself. The pieces
were falling into place, now. He was keeping his promise.

You're a fool, Gerald. You're crazy!

Kellen had laughed in his face. But *he* wasn't the one headed to
prison, right now. So who was really the fool?

That group of Jasmine's wanted results, *yesterday,* which made
them all the more dangerous. A couple of years had passed since
Watson died. And so far, no one had been successful at getting close
to that property.

He might have felt guilty about what he was going to do, but no
one had ever said *anything* about breaking and entering, and killing
people. He was just supposed to be a go-between, until this ordeal
was over. But now that her uncle was dead too, drastic measure
would be required. And as much as he hated walking away from the
prize, this was far more important. Except he really needed to do this
in a hurry.

This apartment would be the perfect place, he thought. It had
been provided for him, and had very little furniture. But, it was
everything that he needed, for the time being.

He couldn't believe his eyes when he'd seen her, today. Right
away, he'd counted his lucky stars that this job wouldn't be so hard
to carry out, after all. The little birdie had fallen right into his nest,
and just when he was about to pay her a visit.

He didn't know why she had followed him, but he had tailed her
to what had to be Laretta's little 'mansion on a hill'. Now, his plan
was set. He just had a couple of calls to make. Then all he had to do
was wait until morning.

Jasmine paced the floor, impatiently now. Gerald should have called a half hour ago. *This is ridiculous!* She fumed. Nobody was getting anything done, as it was. And time was too precious to waste.

Before, she had managed to stay in the background. But things were moving far too unpredictably for that, now. She had come to town for Therell's funeral. And just when they thought things couldn't get any worse, she'd lost her father. With the two burials being just a week apart, she couldn't think of leaving her mother, now.

Douglas could say what he wanted – LaRetha Greer was *bad news*. She had warned her father that getting too close to that woman would only complicate things. But he had worried about her from the beginning, saying they should at least *try* to discuss the matter with her, before doing anything.

Therell had put enough scare into her to send her running for help. Except she was supposed to have gone to Billard, but something had happened, there. And now she was being advised by Douglas. And there was no controlling him, or the outcome.

Her father had wanted to stop after Paul Straiter, despite having handpicked the man for the job. And he'd always been adamant about one thing; *under no circumstances would LaRetha be harmed.* He'd threatened the man's life to drive his point home.

But, unbeknownst to him, he'd been outvoted. Her father had owed people that she wished he didn't, and that meant that their family owed them, which made it a problem for them all. So, between her, Nell and Therell, they had agreed that there were some details he needn't know.

Straiter had seemed like the perfect candidate. Albeit a bit slow in the head, he had fit the profile perfectly; homeless, with no known family, and a long record of misdemeanors. And he hadn't asked for much in return – just a small trailer home to live in, and a little money to get him started. But, entrusting even this small thing to him had turned out to be a very bad move on their part

They thought they had considered all the dangers – even that she might have a gun. But, they'd never expected her to have a reason, or the presence of mind, to get to it and *use* it. Not only had the man stupidly kicked in her door and run *inside* after he'd made it out, he'd also given her an opportunity to shoot him. And now he was dead - an unfortunate end for being careless.

She wasn't too concerned when she heard he'd been shot, being certain at the time that it would be chalked up as a botched robbery attempt. But somebody in the group had been very concerned, and had decided to visit him at the hospital and quiet him, permanently.

With her father gone, his shop would probably close. He had always hoped that Therell would help their mother handle his affairs after he died, assuming that he would go first. But now, there was no one to help her run it. Getting his technicians to work without her father around was a real problem. Besides, a few of them disliked her mother, and Nell disliked running the store.

It was important to Jasmine that Nell would continue to live comfortably. Her father and Therell's insurance policies would help, tremendously. But with so many hands in the purse, and as generous as her mother was with her grandkids, that wouldn't last for very long, she thought. Luckily, the house and cars were paid for, now. That left everyday expenses and insurances. And her father's debt.

But why should they worry, when LaRetha certainly wasn't having to? They had thought for sure that she would sell the place after her boyfriend shot Therell and went to jail. But that hadn't happened, either. The woman hadn't even had the decency to make them an offer, after all that! LaRetha was just *immovable!* Just like *Watson* was. According to Nell, you'd think they were dealing directly with him, instead.

This had gone too far. She and Nell both wanted out. But first, she needed to see this resolved, to make sure that nothing else went wrong. Either that, or run the risk of becoming the next *Paul Straiter.*

Hiring Samira at the office, and then to handle certain details had been Therell's idea. He'd already backed her several times when she'd fallen short on cash, and had become a pretty good silent partner. So, she had gone along, certain that he and Samira were intimately involved, the entire time. Still, her brother was clearly not in love with the woman, so as far as she was concerned, she could have the job. As long as she was worth the money, and Therell stayed involved.

But this time, he'd crossed the line when he 'd suggested paying her an additional fee. Apparently, Samira was learning that she was far too useful to continue allowing people to use and manipulate her for chump change.

The girl was smart, and pretty to say the least. And until now, Jasmine had been successful at keeping her off-balance and second guessing herself. And because she had depended on her for practically everything, she'd been easy to control. But, with Therell gone, everything was changed. There had been a reconsideration of the fee that was promised. She hadn't told her, yet.

The truth was, Samira didn't need them as much as they needed her. She handled her administrative tasks well, but was even better at the other things that she did for them. And, Jasmine knew that she could trust her, if only to be deathly afraid of her. And despite growing concerns, that made it nearly impossible to find another *Samira* on such short notice.

Checking her watch for the one-hundredth time, she sighed with impatience. She didn't know what kind of architect this man was, but when it came to handling this matter, he was simply incompetent!

Jasmine suspected that Gerald's motives ran deeper than wanting the money. But he could chase after his ex-wife all he wanted, as long as he did what he'd agreed, and kept her family anonymous in the process. Once her father's job, it had now become hers to make sure that their names stayed out of all the mess they had gotten into.

If only her father was still here! He was their protector, at one time. He'd taken Therell's death so hard that she suspected what Douglas had implied; that grief was a major contributor to his accident. It had affected him mentally and physically. That loss, and the trouble the group was giving him was enough to give anyone a heart attack.

She remembered finding her father's gun in Kellen's coat, and recognizing its engravings. She had managed to put it back in his closet, where it belonged. Still, the fact that he would do something as silly as to give this woman or her boyfriend a gun had greatly concerned her. She had told her mother, who, in turn, had quickly told Billard. And it had hurt her to see her mother's disdain and disloyalty toward her father.

Has he lost his mind? The group had asked. They'd been concerned that something else would go wrong.

"My family wants out of this," she'd said at the meeting in Bob Billard's basement, just days before the accident. Her father had argued that she shouldn't say anything, but just to stick it out. She'd been frightened to death, but something had to be done.

"It doesn't work like that, Jasmine," the big red-faced man said. "It's too late to back out, now. You'll see this through. Your cousin will sell us that land, and you'll get your share of the money, like it or not. Donate it to charity if you want. But, everybody's getting what they came for."

The nerve of him! She'd thought. He wasn't a family member. He was just a business associate. An advisor. *A creditor.* And he was totally out of control, now.

None of them liked or trusted Billard. What had begun as a legitimate financial investment circle over twenty years before had become a group of elite arsonists and executioners. And her family was certainly guilty by association.

Her own guilt was almost unbearable at times. But, the alternative was even more frightening. Poverty was not a place they would visit again, her mother had said. And she was becoming even more frightening to her than Billard.

"I don't know what's going on here exactly," she'd said to Billard. "We agreed just to *talk* to LaRetha, and maybe shake her up a little bit. But nobody said anything about killing *anybody!*"

"Jasmine," Billard said, taking charge of the meeting, as usual. "I understand your concerns, but you're in no danger and you're not in this, alone. If we all stick together, we can get past this problem. Kincaid will be convicted, and LaRetha will have to leave. Besides, it's not like either of us ever pulled a trigger. So, if anyone needs to worry, it's not us."

Her father hadn't said much then, and it had angered her. But, during those last days, he had seemed very dispirited and almost despondent. She had even discovered him crying a time or two, but said nothing. Pretended she didn't see. But it had frightened her. She'd never seen him like that, in her entire life. It had hurt terribly to know that her father was no longer able to carry them through. And that he was going through something that he couldn't share.

Nell had become indifferent to him. Almost unkind. Except, she had been beside herself when she'd learned that Laretta Watson had phoned him on the day he'd died. There was mention of a past infidelity that Jasmine hadn't known about. It had taken some time to convince Nell that her father hadn't been seeing the woman in all that time. And that calling her about it might be a bad idea. It would only rub the woman the wrong way and bring negative attention to them all. They had enough problems with LaRetha. They didn't need her mother making things worse.

Somehow, Douglas had seen what was happening. For years, his father had distrusted hers. She'd heard that, as children, Douglas and his sister had been strictly forbidden from socializing with anybody in her family, *ever*. Or so Candace had shockingly revealed in a disagreement between the two of them in elementary school.

Now, and rightfully so, he had his own issues with them. And judging from their last encounter, he wasn't planning to look past any of them to consider getting close to her.

With the group's blessing, she had set him up with Samira. And the woman had done a remarkable job. Douglas had taken an immediate liking to Samira. And that had bothered her.

Admittedly, she'd been jealous and angry, just as she was when he'd told her that he was representing LaRetha's boyfriend. It made no sense that he would pass up an opportunity with her for someone with Samira's past, or to get mixed up with LaRetha when she clearly had a man. But he had.

Samira was becoming a complication. She wanted out and vowed to never show her face again if they'd just let her walk. She would even give up her share of the money, just to walk away. Besides, she'd said, she'd finished the job, hadn't she?

But, she was wasting her breath. Everyone was afraid right now, and no one was letting anybody out of anything.

"Tell them that and you'll regret it," she'd told her. "We're all at risk, Samira. Just sit tight and wait for further instructions. You'll get out of it when I do, *if* I do. That's the best that I can tell you, right now."

Jasmine checked her watch, again. Gerald still hadn't called to confirm arrangements for his arrival into town. This next step was crucial. He knew what to do. She only hoped he'd do it.

She had a plane to catch. Some things in Ohio needed to be handled, right away. She could fly out now, and be back here on tomorrow, before the Christmas rush, she thought.

There was just enough time to make it to the airport. She called for a taxi.

"*Eventful day?*" Laretta was home. Showered and changed into exercise clothing, she joined LaRetha in the kitchen.

Nodding, LaRetha filled another bowl with chocolate ice cream and handed it to her.

"We are a pitiful pair, eating all this fattening food and trying to run it off!" LaRetha exclaimed.

"You only live once. And you can't take it with you," Laretta said with a mouthful.

"Yes we can and we will, if we keep eating," she laughed. "Today was eventful. I finally got Valerie. She's going to call back tonight, or in the morning. Maybe then I can get some answers."

"Well! I guess you're right on the money with those instincts of yours. From the way you've described her, she doesn't sound like the type who would get involved in any land stealing schemes. Not like her in-laws and that hooker woman… *what's her name, again?*"

"*Samira Neely.*"

"Right. That type always follows the man and the money."

"She's certainly following all of my men," LaRetha mused.

"Oh? I know about Kellen. Who's the other one?"

She gave her mother a long look.

"*Douglas?* But she does get around, doesn't she? Is she after them intentionally, or do you two just have a lot in common?"

"I'm not sure, but I don't believe in coincidences. And I'm certainly not chasing after her leftovers," she said, rinsing her bowl and placing it on a nearby rack.

"Well, I can't wait to see you moving on with your life."

"You and me, both. I just can't believe all this is happening, just because I moved back to *Lovely.*"

"Says who?"

"I'm just saying that neither of those incidences could be mere coincidences, that's all"

"But, you keep saying this is all because of you, when it's not. Therell could have taken another approach, but he tried to bully you, instead. He was just too much like his daddy. He got himself killed. You didn't do that. And we know that Kellen didn't cause it either."

She shrugged and her mother continued.

"You would think they would be getting the message right about now that whatever goes around comes back around. And it *don't* take all day, either. Mess up at breakfast and you *will* be punished by dinner time, and your punishment will certainly fit your crime. What's that scripture about how, if you live by the sword you will surely *die* by it?"

LaRetha could only shake her head. Her mother's anger relieved her, in some way. Still, with so many fingers pointing in her direction it was hard not to blame herself. Nell blamed her, as did Bernice, and certainly Jasmine and the rest of them, by now. She knew she shouldn't worry about what they thought, but still, it concerned her. Things could have been so different.

Therell had been a bully, but that didn't change the facts where Kellen was concerned. But, she sighed, that wasn't something that she'd come to Atlanta to dwell on.

"Headed to the exercise room?" She asked Laretta, who was finishing with her ice cream.

She was, and after changing clothes, LaRetha joined her, choosing the treadmill as her mother perched on the seat of the exercise bike. They worked quietly for a few minutes.

"So, what do you plan to do when this is all over? You thought about that, yet?"

She nodded, stepping off the treadmill.

"*First*, I want to work things out with my son."

"Well, he did call, recently."

"*He did?*" She asked. "You never tell me what you need to."

Her mother gave her an apologetic look.

"Well, if you want his number, I have it. Remind me when we get upstairs. If he won't call you, then you have to call him because this had gone way past ridiculous."

"I agree," LaRetha nodded, already starting on the treadmill, again. Huffing in between words "And, in answer to your question, I also plan...*huff*...to...*huff*...*huff*.... do something good with the land. Then maybe I'll write a book about my father and the farm, the town and its troubles. Do some fundraisers for the mission and donate to other charities in the community. That would honor my father, I think," she said between huffs.

Man, I am so out of shape, she thought. Laretta stopped pedaling for a moment.

"Meaning, you plan to stay in that town?"

She shrugged. Her mother shook her head.

"Well, I'll be praying for you." She said, almost angrily. Then, unable to stand it any longer, she stopped pedaling and looked at her.

"*Look* child, I know you can't help acting like your father. He knew what he was doing too, leaving that farm to you. He knew you would fight as hard for it as he did."

Having no intention of arguing, LaRetha continued to walk the treadmill and said nothing,

"LaRetha, listen to me!"

She stepped of the machine and propped on it, giving her mother her undivided attention.

"Girl, you have so much going for you, but you can't see it for fighting for that farm. You're financially set, you own the farm and all that land and the condo here in Atlanta. You have your writing career, and now Douglas… If selling that land is the only way you'll ever have peace of mind to enjoy the rest of it, then I say do it!"

Nodding but saying nothing, she easily saw the concern in her mother's eyes. She wiped sweat from her brow and started walking on the machine, again.

"My father died on that land," she said. "I won't give it up."

"Well, owning land and living on it, are two different things. You can find another use for it that could settle this whole mess, once and for all."

"I'm considering that."

"Well, have you considered what you'll do if you can't get Kellen out of jail?" Her mother asked, indignantly. "What if he's *convicted?* What if it wasn't self-defense, after all? Have you considered that?"

"Mama, I don't know everything about this case. But, even if Kellen came to *Lovely* with wrong intentions, he only stayed to protect me. I know this because I know him that well."

"I just hope you're right about that man." Haughtily, Laretta grabbed her towel and left the room.

LaRetha didn't have time to worry about it because her cell phone rang. It was Valerie. Paul was gone for a few hours, she said. She could talk.

Now that she had her on the phone, LaRetha wasn't so certain about how to approach the matter. Then, she decided to just say it. Valerie knew enough to make this easy for her.

"I wanted to ask what you knew about the family's dispute over the farm. I know someone sent *Straiter* to scare me off. And now, we have two more deaths. Now, I don't want to believe that anybody would intentionally do anything else, but all things considered, I really need to be sure about what I'm dealing with, here."

Silence.

"I respect the fact that you are married to Paul, but I'm trying to save Kellen from a conviction he doesn't deserve, Valerie. You know my family better than I do. And you know what kind of temperament Therell had because even I knew it. So, if you can tell me anything about what was being planned and by who, it would help a great deal. It might even save lives. I won't lie and say I'm not concerned about my own."

"So, you want me to *snitch* on my husband's family?"

"No, I want you to tell the truth. To help save an innocent man. Nothing can bring Therell back, or my uncle. But that's no reason for

Kellen to go to prison or to get a death sentence over something he had nothing to do with."

"I understand your concern, LaRetha. But, I'd really rather not discuss this with you. Maybe I should talk to Douglas."

"Well, you could. But, I'm the one with the questions, not Douglas. He doesn't even know that I've called you."

"Oh? Well, I feel like I'm betraying Paul by even talking to you. I would have talked to Douglas before now, but I've finally regained my husband's trust, and I can't afford to jeopardize that, right now."

"You lost his trust?" She didn't know where the question would lead her, but certainly felt the need to ask.

"Yes I did."

"How so, if I might ask?" Obviously she wanted to tell it.

"By doing what people usually do when they lose someone's trust. I *cheated* on him."

LaRetha was silently surprised that Valerie would be so revealing.

"That must've been a while ago. You two seemed fine over the holidays."

"We were. Until he saw the man I'd cheated with at the party. *He hit the roof.* He wouldn't even talk to me after that, like *I* had invited him. No one should have invited him, but they did. And I was surprised he even came."

Okay, I'll bite, she thought. Clearly, this woman wanted to tell her something. So, while she was sharing...

"Anyone I know?"

"As a matter of fact, it is."

LaRetha remained silent. If Valerie wanted to tell her, she would.

"It was *Douglas Davis.*"

"Can't anybody keep their pants on, anymore? I don't believe this!" She yelled into the air.

Laretta came out of her bedroom to see what was going on.

"What in the world has gotten you so riled up?"

"Can you believe that Valerie just told me she's had an affair with *Douglas!*"

Her mother gave her an incredulous look, then shook her head and laughed.

"When?"

"Does it matter?" LaRetha was beside herself with anger.

"Well. A good looking, rich and single brother like that, running loose in little ole' *Lovely* Kentucky, can get with a woman any time of the day. Believe me."

"Why didn't he tell me? He told me about Samira. Why didn't he tell me about Valerie?"

"She is married to your cousin, isn't she? I'm surprised she told you at all. Unless, there was a reason for it."

"*Oh, there is a reason.* She wants me to stay away from him, that's her reason! And, I'm fully prepared to do it, too. I cannot believe that he managed to leave out that one little, minor detail about him and my cousin's *wife!* That dirty dog!"

"Calm down, LaRetha. The man never said he was a saint. He's a consenting adult, just like she is. It's not right, but it happens. Grow up!"

"*Grow up?* This man has been trying to get me into bed ever since we had dinner with him that night."

"*Trying? Hmmm,* good holding out, girl," her mother said, cynically. "Now, if you don't mind, I'm going back to bed. You could use a good night's sleep, too. So, come with me."

LaRetha gave her mother a dirty look, before obliging her, following her into her bedroom and noticing for the first time that the entire room had been remodeled. It looked much larger now – like something out of a magazine.

Nice, she thought about the bathroom, which was another wonder to look at. With medicine bottle in hand, Laretta went to her nightstand, wrote something on a pad and handed the torn sheet to LaRetha, who looked at it.

Germaine's phone number. She smiled, clutching it to her chest. *"Thank you, Mama."*

Then, Laretta pressed the bottle into her hand. *Sedatives.*

"Take two of those. Normally, I wouldn't do this, but if I plan to get any sleep, I have to make sure that you get some, too. You'll thank me in the morning."

"Sorry, if I alarmed you. It just surprised me."

"I know. Men are like that, aren't they? Just full of them."

"Full of *something*," she murmured. Her mother laughed.

"Goodnight. See you in the morning." She gave her a tight hug.

"Goodnight. And try to get some rest. Whatever's going on tonight will still be there tomorrow. *Trust me!*"

After reading the label on the bottle, LaRetha decided against taking any and dropped it into her makeup bag. Once she had collected her thoughts, she'd told Valerie that she would appreciate anything that she could tell her. And to call her, anytime. And this time, Valerie had agreed.

What are you doing to me, Douglas? LaRetha groaned. She turned over, buried her face in her pillow and tried to sleep.

It was early morning on Christmas Eve, and LaRetha sat on her bed, dialing the number her mother had given her. Saying a prayer, she waited as the phone rang. No one answered. She left a message.

"Hello, son. Merry Christmas. It's been too long since we've talked. I'm always happy to hear that you're doing well, but I'd rather hear it from you, instead."

Pause.

"I love you and I miss you. I'm in Atlanta for the holidays. I'm staying at Mother's, so let's get together for Christmas. Give me a call or a visit. I have gifts for you. And besides, I look forward to seeing you. Love you. Bye."

Hanging up, she sighed. Germaine had no idea of the depth of her love for him. She had always felt at home at her mother's house, and couldn't imagine what was keeping him away for so long.

Something had gone terribly wrong between them, somewhere along the line. It must have been something about the divorce. And Tori, of course. Or maybe Gerald had something to do with it. She couldn't imagine what it was. But maybe, this holiday, they could work things out. Get past it.

Douglas! This recent revelation had bowled her over. Her suspicions about him and other women in her family had been correct, but misplaced. Apparently, aside from his fondness for drink, he also had *women* issues.

Even worse, as much as he proclaimed to dislike her family, he obviously had no problem with the *females*. It also appeared that he had a penchant for dangerous women, or women in dangerous situations. She guessed that would include her.

But, her mother was right. They were all consenting adults. And once the trial was over, she was moving on, anyway. This man was putting too many skeletons in *her* closet.

Maybe it was her fault, developing a fondness for him without asking the truly important questions. Like, whether or not he'd had any prior sexual involvements with anyone in her family, or their friends or associates, that might interfere with or hinder any business or personal progress between them, she thought, haughtily.

But, she'd been so blinded by her need to have him on her side that she'd taken him solely on face value, and recommendation. Admittedly, his good looks and availability hadn't hurt.

In Laretta's eyes, Douglas could do no wrong. *He was a man, and what more did she expect?* Except he had done something very wrong. And she was just going to have to break it to her liberal and understanding mother that there would be no good looking, wealthy, attorney *son-in-law*. Laretta would be disappointed.

Was no one what they presented themselves to be? This man must have been just toying with her, trying to add her name to his little 'Bachelor Scoreboard', while keeping an inside scoop on Kellen so that he could destroy him. What better way to sabotage a case? It had been done to him once, and for some odd reason, that made some people feel entitled.

She couldn't complain that Douglas had a life before now. But, with so many single women in that town, why a married one? He didn't have to go *there.*

Besides, she could understand if he'd had a prior interest in Jasmine. *But Valerie?* What type of man would forego a relationship with her uncle's *single* daughter, for a fling with his son's *wife?* Didn't he care about anyone finding out? Valerie certainly didn't.

Apparently, he didn't care; about anyone's opinions of his representing her, or Kellen, or about anything. He was rich, single and successful, and he had the world by a shoestring. Problem was, he'd been stringing her along, as well.

She would tell him when she saw him, again. He needed to know that she wasn't going for it. She would squash this mess before it even started.

His work phone rang four times. Prepared to leave a message, she was startled when he picked up.

"Douglas…"

"*LaRetha!* Good thing you called. I have…"

"Yes, it is! Good thing is right," she interrupted. "I spoke with my cousin's wife, Valerie, last night. *Remember her?* She told me some very interesting things."

"What things? Listen, LaRetha," he said, without hesitating for an answer. "You've got to get back…"

Douglas was on a fast track, but they had issues to settle. He had said he wanted their relationship to go further, but how could that be when he hadn't been forthcoming about this?

"I told you I was here until after the New Year. Let's talk about whatever it is, after then."

"*What?* LaRetha, what are you talking about? Listen, you have to come home, to *Lovely,* right away. Some…"

"I can't believe you, Douglas. You should have told me."

"I should have told you what? Are you listening to me? You have to come…"

"I can't talk to you right now. Maybe I'll call you later." Sadly, she hang up on him.

LaRetha ignored the phone as it rang back. It was silent, then rang again. Luckily, she couldn't check her mother's voice mail, so she wasn't tempted to hear him out. The calls went on for a few minutes until she decided she didn't want to stay in the house, any longer.

It was unseasonably warm, today - already *68* degrees. A good morning for a drive, she figured. And a great day for getting Douglas Davis out of her system.

The car was still sitting in front of the house in the circular drive where she'd parked it, yesterday. Getting in, she started it up. Sitting there, she thought about her life; her career, her relationships with Gerald and Kellen, and with Douglas. Each one had started out good but ended terribly. She didn't know how or why it had come to this, but it was more than clear that the men's department was one she truly didn't need to shop in, anytime soon.

But, she'd prayed through it all, and figured that, for reasons she couldn't explain, much of it was meant to be. And now, it was time for a new start. For her to clear her head and her heart of all of them, she thought. She'd made a mistake even considering a compromise; she deserved an honest man, a spiritual man with ethics, a faithful man and certainly one who wouldn't end up in jail on murder charges.

Straightening the mirror, she caught a glimpse of movement in the rear window. Turning to look back, she was startled when the opposite door swung open and someone jumped into the passenger seat, slamming it closed.

Not even looking around, she instinctively tried to open her door and get out, but it was too late. They were already inside and pulling her back in, as well. She looked over in fear.

Gerald? She sighed with relief, and stared at him.

"What are you doing here?" She asked, trying to wrench her arm from his tight grasp. He didn't release her.

"Question is, what are *you* doing here? But then, you're not really here, are you? Let's go. *Drive.*"

"What are you talking about?"

"LaRetha, drive this car right now, *or else.*" He gave her a serious look that caused her to rethink jumping out of the car. She put the car into gear and slowly drove away from the house.

"Where are we going? I don't..." She started. She had left her coat and handbag inside the house. Hopefully, Marilee would realize it and know that something was wrong.

"Drive to the place you followed me to, yesterday. You know the way."

Her heart skipped in panic. *He'd seen her.* Worse, he planned to take her there, but for what?

"What is this about?" She asked as calmly as she could.

"You'll find out soon enough!"

They traveled the entire distance in silence and the apartment complex seemed much too close this time, her dread having caused the minutes to go by, very quickly. But, this man was her ex-husband. And she knew him better than this. Surely he wasn't capable of harming her?

"Gerald…" she said, as she parked the car.

"*Get out,*" he insisted, and she did. He nudged her toward the apartment door, following closely.

"What's going on, Gerald?" She asked, flatly. The timid role had never worked for her. Besides, he knew her better than that. "What is all of this about?"

"You tell me. You followed *me* yesterday, remember?" He unlocked the door, pushed it open for her to go inside.

LaRetha was surprised and concerned that the apartment was practically empty.

"Whose place is this? And why are we here? I would appreciate it if you would stop treating me like some kind of *kidnap victim,* and talk to me!" She insisted.

Haughtily, she looked up into the eyes of the man she had once loved with all of her heart, and who had made her so happy for the longest time. She'd never imagined that she would be just as glad to be away from him, one day. And this was obviously not a social visit.

"Sit down," he said, sounding more relaxed. "It's gonna be a long day."

15

Douglas slammed the phone down with irritation. *What was the matter with that woman?* Now, she wouldn't even pick up the phone. Who knew when she might hear his message and return his call. *And where was that cell phone number?* LaRetha needed to know that she was in real danger!

Driving through the town square early this morning, he had recalled his visit with Kellen, last night. The man had shed new light on a few other things for him – some of it shocking, to say the least. Like who had hired Paul Straiter, and why. And about the people who were backing the uncle, and Nell and Jasmine, financially. And that they weren't likely to back off, despite the recent tragedies.

Then, he'd heard the sirens. Saw the trucks passing him as he drove to the office. Impulsively, he had followed. He had scheduled an early meeting with Samira. She wanted to talk about things that she'd conveniently left out of their last conversation. The case was shaping up, finally and as he'd expected - almost at the last minute.

But, after hearing those sirens, a strange chill had come over him, and intuition told him this was no routine fire drill.

Samira can wait, he'd thought as he turned his car around. This could very possibly be another farm fire; another sad case of murder and arson. He had to see for himself. Seeing the direction that it was going in, a panic came over him. There were only three farms out that way. And one of them was *LaRetha's.*

It was as bad as he had expected, and worse. Fire trucks were everywhere, and other cars following like him were parked all along the main road, not being permitted to pass. He managed to get through by saying the house belonged to his client.

Where is the owner? People were asking in a panic. Seeing that her barn had been empty, he'd been relieved to say that she was out of town. He needed to tell her about this.

Driving back into town, he heard the phone ringing as he went inside his office. Thankfully, it was LaRetha. And although she'd been impossible and unwilling to listen, she was safe in Atlanta, and he was relieved.

And now, standing again on the icy snow in front of what used to be her house, he could see that although the firemen had worked throughout the morning to extinguish the flames, nothing was left. LaRetha would have to move. To start all over, again.

So why was he feeling relieved? Like her father, nothing short of an earthquake or forest fire would have gotten that woman to leave here, and this damage was akin to both. Still, she had put an incredible amount of work into turning that house into a small work of art. She would be heartbroken.

But, why was she so angry on the phone? Something about *Valerie?* LaRetha was so headstrong, sometimes. Still, she deserved better than this trouble that Kincaid had participated in. That man didn't deserve her. Better he kept sowing wild oats with the likes of Samira. LaRetha needed a man who would challenge her. To tell her she was wonderful, one minute, then to show her, the next. And Kincaid wasn't capable of the emotion, much less the honesty of the act.

So wrapped up in being there for everyone else, she had no idea of the effect she had on him. Or to what extent he would go, just to prove himself to her. Instead, she worried incessantly about... *him.*

LaRetha thought Kincaid had being framed, and was quite possibly right about that. But, considering the danger he had put her in, and the rewards he had stood to gain by abusing her trust in him, as far as he was concerned the man was right where he should be. And quite possibly for a very long time.

The scene in front of him was hopeless. Firemen, policemen and news reporters were everywhere. He drove back to his office. He would reschedule with Samira. Right now he had more pressing concerns. Everything that LaRetha had worked for was gone. And, if you asked him, in the tradition of *Lovely,* and what would happen to anyone who went against the grain, this was no accidental fire.

LaRetha sat down and watched as Gerald disappeared into the kitchen. She could hear him placing a call from his cell phone. At first glance, this place was a bit small for Gerald's tastes. But, obviously he had it for a purpose, whatever that was.

He returned, holding a can of soda in each hand and offering one to her. She didn't refuse it – there was no telling when her next meal might be. He seemed intent on detaining her for awhile.

They were silent. Her watch was ticking loudly, and she glanced at it. *10:14 am*. And nothing was stirring, anywhere. Finally, Gerald grabbed a chair, and she noticed as he walked how his body seemed to have stooped a bit since the last time she had seen him. It had only been three years, she thought.

He sat down, straddling the chair, his unwavering eyes traveling the length of her body, enveloping all of her within his gaze. They finally fell on her face, again. Once upon a time, he would have broken into a grin by now. But, that was *before*, she thought; before the divorce, before her father's death, before she had sold everything and moved, and before all the fighting and deaths, which could soon include her own.

But strangely, she sensed no danger. He was never a desperate man. But judging by his actions now, he just might be. She couldn't relax.

Time progressed and her watch continued to tick, with him watching her, and with her looking him solidly in his eyes. Finally, he spoke to her.

"Are you cold?"

She didn't respond. He got up to turn up the thermostat and then returned, posturing himself as before. Avoiding his gaze, she focused on a speck of pale green paint that had splotched the otherwise perfect whiteness of a window blind. She waited for him to state his purpose.

"So, you like living in *Lovely*?" He finally asked, as innocently as one child might have asked another.

Slowly, LaRetha nodded. She wouldn't speak until she had reason to, she thought. Not until he told her why she was here. And whatever else he could shed light on.

"I can't understand why. It's too country and way too secluded." He spoke slowly, as if time were of no consequence. This began to worry her. Although never desperate, *her* Gerald had always been in a hurry.

"You went there to start over, I guess. You haven't had a chance to do much of that though, have you?"

She almost heard sympathy in his voice, but still gave no response.

"Do you want to know why you're here?"

Still, she didn't move or speak.

"You're here," he said in a commanding tone, "because of business I haven't been able to finish when you *weren't* here. Know what I mean?"

She shivered.

"Here," he said quietly as he pulled his jacket from the back of a chair and gently wrapped it around her shoulders. He sat down, again.

"You are here for a lot of reasons, LaRetha, but mainly because there's no other way to do this."

Silence.

"I know you went to that place to be rid of me and your problems with Germaine…"

"Not true," she finally said. "I was already rid of you *before* I left Atlanta. And Germaine didn't cause me to move, either."

"Doesn't matter. You should have stayed *here*. We could have worked through it, together. Then it wouldn't have come to this. The others wouldn't have gotten to you or to Kellen."

"What *others*, Gerald?"

He continued, ignoring her question.

"See, you're just like your mother," he said, very defensively. "You never had any faith in me. Always suspicious and *accusing*. After all I did to make you happy, you never appreciated it. You always expected more. Now, why was that?"

She waited.

"I asked you a question!" He yelled, veins surfacing on his forehead. Deciding it was better not to provoke him, she finally spoke.

"I only wanted you to be a good husband and father," she said. "You keep blaming my mother. She had nothing to do with it. *You* were the one with all the *drama;* the women, the lies. You had no interest in me or Germaine. What did you think would happen? That wasn't the way I wanted to live. And I don't see my mother anywhere in that."

He shook his head. She shifted in her chair and he looked at her, then down at his hands as if wondering what to do with them.

What was he planning to do with her? Whatever he had in mind, she would have to keep him calm so that he could think it through.

"Mama never hated you. She just never trusted you. And she couldn't make me do anything that I didn't want to. You've got your divorce. All I want to know is *why am I here?*"

"I never stopped loving you, LaRetha."

"I know this," she said sarcastically, and he laughed.

"Same old LaRetha. But tell me, how long were you sleeping with Kellen Kincaid?"

She shook her head, refusing to answer.

"All that time and you were cheating on me," he said with a laugh, as if suddenly realizing that he'd been the victim of a very cruel joke.

"Don't put that on me, Gerald. I never cheated on you. But, what difference does that make, now? Why did you bring me here?"

"But, you had to be. You two got together as soon as I was out of the picture. He followed you all the way to Kentucky to get you to marry him. And you want me to think all that started *after* the divorce? Do I look stupid to you?"

She wanted to say *yes,* but decided against it.

"It's been *three years,* Gerald, and I don't care what you think. Why would I start lying, now? What difference would it make?"

"Maybe a big one."

Silence.

"Oh, so you don't have an answer, now?" He asked. "If you didn't divorce me for Kellen, then *why?*"

"*Because.* Gerald, you only see what you want to see. You never noticed how you were taking my life from me. My independence, my confidence..."

He looked surprised.

"My hope, our marriage, and our son," she continued. "Even when he left, you didn't even..." She stopped, fighting back her anger.

"You didn't even care," she continued. "You even blamed me for it. Why, when I've always encouraged a relationship between the two of you?"

"I wasn't trying to do that," he defended. "But, after the divorce, neither of you wanted me around. You didn't want to maintain a friendship. And Germaine never had time..."

"Why should we? You treated us that way, the entire time we were married. But then, you've got what you wanted. So, what's the problem, *now?*"

"I know that. I just don't mean to..."

"Then," she interrupted, "why am I here, if you don't *mean* to?"

He said nothing, but it didn't matter. She had already heard enough.

"I know what it was," he continued. "It was you, trying to be like your *mother.* You wanted everything that she had, except she told you that you didn't need me to get it. She was alone and she wanted you to be alone, too. But, you couldn't see that."

"That's a *lie,* and I despise you for it."

He shook his head, got up from his chair and walked over to a far wall.

"As for Germaine," she continued, "whatever you've said to him, it won't keep us apart for long. The truth will come out and my son and I will be *fine.*"

He looked at her intently.

"Are you ready to tell me why I'm here? And why *you're* so angry?" She asked.

He sat down again, staring at her, evilly. She couldn't read him, but knew she needed to stall him - distract him from whatever his plan was. She felt like venting, anyway. And what better time or reason was there than this?

"I can tell you why *I'm* angry," she said. "I was angry every time I found a woman's phone number or address in your pocket. Germaine knew about those affairs you had, didn't he? You weren't decent enough to be discreet. I left you because somebody had to teach our son *respect*."

He looked surprised, as if not expecting her to know these things.

"Now, I don't have to wonder if my husband is coming home at night. I don't cook and clean unless I want to. I come and go as I please, just like you do. I even work as I please. *What more could a girl want?*" She asked, sarcastically.

"I really hurt you, didn't I?"

His tone was dull. His gaze had slipped to the floor. She felt she was making progress.

"Germaine is alright," he said. "The last we talked, he was doing fine. He says he's starting college, soon."

"I'd rather hear it from him." She gave him a curt look.

"I'm sorry about what's been happening to you, LaRetha. I've heard a lot of things, and I was concerned. Like when your father died. If I had known, I might've been able to stop it. But, I didn't know."

"What are you talking about now, Gerald? What about my father?" She spoke more calmly than she was feeling, right now.

Again, he ignored her question.

"His death didn't have to happen." He threw his head back, eyes closed. Inhaled deeply.

"My father died from a lung disease," She stated.

Opening his eyes, he shook his head. She couldn't believe he would go as far as this. Standing now, she shouted at him.

"You'd better stop this, Gerald!" She shouted.

He shook his head, again. She hit him twice, using both hands. He grabbed at them, managing to hold her in his grasp.

"You know you're lying. *Tell me the truth!*"

She struggled against him, trying to free her hands to hit him, again.

"Stop it, LaRetha. If you'll just calm down, I'll tell you."

"No. I don't believe you. You're lying!" She screamed at him, hitting him one last time before crumpling into her chair, moaning tearlessly in her despair. He stood watching her as though helpless.

All she could think about now were the shootings and her uncle's death. To imagine that her father's death had been the beginning of it all was too much.

Finally, she straightened. He wouldn't break her this way. It simply wasn't true. He only wanted to upset her. He needed to, for some reason.

"Who are you saying killed my father?" She asked quietly.

He stood and walked over to her.

"All you need to know is if you stay on at that farm, you could be next. I wouldn't want to see that happen. I think you should just sell it and get the heck out of there. For your own sake."

"Why are you saying these things?" She asked, wiping her own tears and not in the least bit touched by his sudden show of concern. "Why are we here? *What do you want from me, Gerald?*"

"Like I said, if you'll calm down, I can tell you. Don't make this harder than it has to be. I'm trying to protect you. You've got to let me."

He moved toward her as if to touch her, but she recoiled, feeling nothing but disgust. Giving him a look that she hoped read exactly how she felt, she waited for the truth.

Laretta was almost at the mall when she discovered that she'd forgotten the *70%* off discount coupons that she would need to buy the last gift on her list – a beautiful African sculpture that Marilee would just love, considering her penchant for art. She had no choice but to turn her car around.

She parked in the circular drive, planning to run inside and back out, again. She noticed that the car she'd loaned to LaRetha was gone. But Marilee's was still there in the driveway, and the front door wasn't completely closed.

"Marilee?" Where was she?

She was off, today. But she might have come by early to pick up her Christmas present. But she never left the house open like this. Not even for a minute.

"Marilee? Are you in here?"

She passed through the foyer, but paused at the doorway. The house was unusually quiet. On a normal day, the woman would have the radio on the gospel music station, and you could hear her humming and rambling about, somewhere in the huge house. Today, there was nothing. No sign nor sound from her.

Placing her purse on the small table in the hallway, Laretta noticed LaRetha's coat and purse on a chair, there. Apparently, she hadn't left yet. But, the car was already gone, wasn't it?

She looked outside. It was. Maybe, Marilee was using it for some reason. But why? This made no sense.

"LaRetha?" She called out.

Going upstairs, she saw that her daughter was gone. Suddenly sensing danger, she held her keys tightly between her, ready to strike out, using them as a weapon, if necessary. She went back downstairs, picking up a vase from the hall table with her other hand as she proceeded to the kitchen.

Marilee?' She whispered. No response.

She walked through the kitchen to peer out of the window into the backyard. Her housekeeper was nowhere to be found. *Maybe she had missed a message from her.*

Just then, she heard a shuffling noise coming from just beyond the kitchen. Gripping her vase even tighter, she slowly walked toward the place it had come from. She reached for the doorknob, fully prepared to clobber anyone that she might surprise.

But, the surprise was hers, because as soon as she opened the door and switched on the light, a large bag of flour fell at her feet, startling her into a near scream. But that scream was stifled by the sight of Marilee lying on her side on the pantry floor, her mouth covered with tape, and both hands and feet bound, as well.

"*Marilee!* What happened?"

The woman struggled against the rope and she fumbled with it to untie her and waited for her to catch her breath.

"A man came in behind me and attacked me. He tied me up and left me in here."

"Are you hurt?"

"No, he didn't hurt me. He just told me to cooperate, or else."

"Who was it?" She asked as she dialed the phone.

"I don't know, but he knew my name."

"Where is LaRetha? Her coat and bag are here, but she's gone."

"I don't know. I heard a car leave after he locked me in here. It must have been hers. I didn't see another one."

"I'm calling the police."

She dialed as Marilee hurried from the pantry. Giving her name and address, she reported a possible burglary and a kidnapping. The dispatcher was sending the police, right away.

Barely fifteen minutes had passed before she heard sirens. Still, she waited inside until she heard them knock.

Finally, she thought with great relief as she unlocked the front door.

Jasmine heard about the fire as she was driving to her hair appointment. Immediately, she changed directions, calling Nell at home. They were meeting at Bob Billard's in an hour, her mother said. She would wait for her and they would go, together.

With the exception of Paul, the rest of her siblings were still in town. Their children were at Aunt Carole's house for a while. With the shop closed for two weeks, she had hoped her mother would finally get some rest. Nell seemed to be adjusting, having accepted her husband's failing health as the cause of his death, so she felt obligated to feel the same, although she wasn't truly convinced.

Pulling into her mother's driveway, she was dismayed to see her car missing from the garage, and another one waiting for her, instead. Billard had sent his driver for her. *As if we would try to leave town*, she thought.

"Good morning, Miss Jasmine," Charles said with his usual rasp. Never talking much louder than a whisper, and flawlessly dressed in a dark blue uniform, he had always reminded her of a very charismatic movie character.

"Your mother's already gone. She asked me to wait and to drive you over. She will drive you back. Are you ready?"

Exasperated, Jasmine held her tongue about her mother leaving without her. Charles was a friendly old man who had always minded his business and treated their family with kindness. He had been with Billard since *always*, it seemed. He was also an excellent driver.

"*Good morning*, Charles," she said, as she climbed into the back seat. "Thanks for coming."

He nodded, tipping his hat. Starting the car up, he steered them in the direction of the highway. They were well on their way before he spoke again.

"I'll bet you don't even remember the first time I drove you, do you?"

She smiled, not really being interested in reminiscing, but deciding to humor this man who appeared to be in his usual good spirits. He and her father were close friends, once. She was certain that he was missing him almost as much as she.

"No. When was that?"

"Well, it's been awhile. You were about *thirteen*, I believe. Your daddy bought a brand new, light blue Thunderbird, and he asked me to pick you up from school on my way from town. You were so *excited!* Even more than him, I believe."

She remembered, and said so.

"Yes, me and your father was good friends. When we were boys, we would play cards and fish on our days off. I'm gonna miss that old *geezer,* " he said, slapping his knee.

"When we was boys, if we got tired of hanging out, we'd just hang out some more." The man laughed gleefully, but this conversation was making her uncomfortable. She missed her father.

"Yes, we're all missing him."

He nodded. Silent, now. Hopefully he realized that she really didn't want to discuss it.

"Mind if I turn on the radio?" He asked. She said that would be fine.

Christmas music played for a time, relaxing her a bit. But all she could think about was this meeting, and what would be discussed. There was no doubt in her mind who was behind that fire last night, considering whose car she was sitting in. Always one to take matters into his own hands and *then* call a meeting, she seethed.

She'd had enough of this! This was her last meeting, her last everything. LaRetha could do what she wanted with her inheritance. She had a life to get back to, and that didn't include all the *lowlifes* that this endeavor was bringing her way.

The music ended and a news report came on.

"A farm in eastern Lovely, Kentucky, belonging to a LaRetha Watson Greer, is lying in ruin after an early morning fire that has destroyed the house, the barn and the garage. Our volunteer firefighters worked throughout the morning to extinguish the blaze."

Jasmine chuckled, involuntarily. Catching the odd glimpse the man cast from his rear view mirror. She looked away.

"Presently, police are trying to identify the remains of a body found in the rubble, burned beyond recognition..."

"Turn that up!" She exclaimed, leaning forward on her back seat.

"...It is believed to be the burned body of a woman who was in the house when the fire started. It's not yet determined whether the body found in the fire is that of LaRetha Greer, the owner. Or whether the body was burned before or after they were murdered, with the fire being set to destroy the evidence."

Jasmine gasped.

"Again, no positive identification of the body has been made, just yet. Further updates will be given as they occur. Now, back to our holiday music."

She sat back in disbelief, unable to speak. Aware that Charles was watching her very curiously, through his rear view mirror.

"Are you alright, Miss Jasmine? That was your cousin's house, wasn't it?"

"Stop the car, Charles!"

He did.

"I'll just be a minute. You don't have to get out."

Opening the car door, she slid out of the backseat, closed the door and leaned against it. She held her stomach, trying not to retch.

LaRetha Greer was dead! She couldn't believe it! This wasn't the plan! She had sworn that she would walk if anyone else got hurt. And now someone had killed her, and burned her in her own house.

And why hadn't Gerald called to tell her that LaRetha was back at home?

After a few minutes of steadying herself, she got back into the car.

"Can you get me there in a hurry, Charles? Thank you," she said, not waiting for a response. She reached for her phone, and quickly dialed Nell.

"I just heard the news," she whispered. "Was LaRetha in her house when it burned?" She asked, very aware that Charles was listening.

"I guess so," her mother said, sounding as surprised as she was. "I just heard it, myself. But, I thought you said she was out of town," she said, gushing on the phone.

"Listen, I *never...*" Jasmine stopped. Charles was being very quiet.

"How far away are you?" Her mother asked, understanding the situation.

"*Charles and I,*" she began, carefully, "have only been driving for about twenty minutes. Where are you?"

"I stopped by the shop to check on a few things."

"Mama, that shop will be just fine until after the holidays. It's not safe for you to be rambling around in there alone, anyway. You should have gotten one of the guys to go."

"Don't you worry. Just wait in the car until I get there. I'm locking the door, as we speak."

Hanging up, Jasmine glanced at Charles, who remained silent. She figured they must have been going seventy miles an hour.

"Can't you drive this thing any faster?"

Marilee gave the police her version of what happened and Laretta told them that someone had kidnapped her daughter. She was told not to jump to any conclusions. That is was possible her daughter had left willingly.

"She wouldn't have left without her coat and purse!" She exclaimed.

These might be two separate incidents, one of them said.

"Or maybe," she replied, sarcastically, "before she left, my daughter attacked Marilee!"

Since we're being stupid, she thought. The officer gave her an impatient look.

LaRetha could still show up at any minute, they insisted. She should just wait and call them once she was missing for over *24* hours.

She didn't think so! Time was of the essence and she really needed to speak with Douglas Davis. She called his office. To her dismay, he was out. His cell phone wasn't picking up, either. She left a message, asking him to call back, right away.

"You can take the rest of the day off, Marilee."

"But what about LaRetha? Do you want me to stay?" The woman was obviously shaken.

"No. I'll call if something happens."

She watched the woman leave and made sure every door and window was locked securely.

Where was LaRetha? She kept going over the past *24* hours in her mind, trying to think of who might be responsible. LaRetha had only talked to a couple of people from *Lovely,* since coming here. So, it had to be someone else…

Wait a minute! How in the world had this escaped her? She wondered. There was only one person that could be responsible for this. Someone LaRetha had just seen. *Gerald Greer!*

Remembering that his number would still be on her caller I.D., she dialed it back, hoping that he would answer. He picked up on the second ring.

"Hello?" He asked quietly.

"What have you done with my daughter?" She didn't care that she sounded almost hysterical. "I know you have her, Gerald. Let me speak to her, *now!"*

She heard a chuckle.

"What, do you have cameras around your place or something?"

"I *knew* you had something to do with this. Let me talk to her!"

"Sure, no problem," he said in a quiet voice. She heard the phone rustling as if being rubbed against his shirt. Then she heard him speaking and laughing, at once.

"Here, LaRetha. It's your *Mama,"* he said sarcastically. Then, speaking into the phone, in a more comical voice, he said, *"Oops!* Did I tell you she was here? I was mistaken. Try later. She might turn up."

The line went dead, and Laretta held the phone, in dismay. That idiot had LaRetha and he was planning to harm her. And what did he mean by *turn up?*

She called several times more. He didn't answer. He was playing games, but she couldn't let that stop her from trying to get through to him, and to LaRetha.

Laretta immediately drove to the police station. This time she told them that LaRetha's ex-husband was involved, repeating the conversation they'd just had and how LaRetha had just seen him the day before. If they weren't at his townhouse, she said, they would most likely be at that same apartment, only she didn't know where that was.

Finally, a car was sent to check out the townhouse. They would do all they could to find her, they said, but there was still the possibility that her daughter had gone willingly. She breathed a huge sigh of relief.

So then, who tied the housekeeper up in the pantry? She kept insisting. She *knew* her daughter, she said, and LaRetha would never *willingly* go anywhere with Gerald Greer!

Christmas Eve, and LaRetha was missing and Gerald was being sought for kidnapping her. Still upset, Laretta tried to calm herself, deciding that she would follow their advice and go home. LaRetha was coming home, soon. And she wanted to be there when she did.

Her chair was getting uncomfortable, and LaRetha was tired of waiting for Gerald to say something that made sense. His phone had rung, and he had gone into a back room to answer it, taking her keys with him.

But, she remembered something. Marilee often used that car, so her mother would sometimes leave a key under a floor mat inside it. Laretta kept spare keys, everywhere, much to her prior vexation. *It's dangerous,* she had warned. But right now, this could be the very thing that saved her life. *Please let it be there,* she thought.

Eyeing the front door from across the room, she could see that there was only one lock and a deadbolt to turn. If she moved quickly and quietly enough, she might get to it and out of the door before he even missed her. This might be her last chance, her *only* chance.

Slowly tipping to the door, she quietly turned the knob. It wasn't even locked! Slowly twisting the deadbolt, she jerked it open and slipped through, closing it behind her before running as fast as she could toward her mother's car. The doors weren't locked.

Thank you! She thought, sliding behind the wheel and reaching down to retrieve the spare key from beneath the mat. When she turned the key in the ignition, the engine made a beautiful sound. Speeding in reverse, she looked through the rear view mirror only once. Just in time to see an astounded Gerald chasing after her.

Eat my dust. She laughed with relief. Now to get home, again. She would deal with Gerald, later.

Jasmine dialed Atlanta on her cell phone, ignoring Charles' scrutiny in his rear view mirror.

"Hello?"

"It's Jasmine. Why didn't you call?"

Silence.

"Hello?" She was getting impatient now. *Nobody could be this dense.*

"LaRetha's *gone,*" Gerald finally said.

"So I heard. Why didn't you tell me she was back in *Lovely?* Surely you knew this?" She whispered.

"What?"

"It was such a simple thing, and you couldn't do it?" She murmured with great irritation.

"Hold up!" He said, pausing a moment. "Listen," he finally said. "She was here until a few minutes ago, but she managed to get by me when I was on the phone. She got away before I could stop her."

"What are you talking about? Are you saying you're in *Lovely?*"

"I'm *saying,* I'm in Atlanta, *LaRetha's* in Atlanta and Laretta is, too. What are *you* talking about?"

Even with the radio on, Charles appeared entirely interested, now, and made no move to conceal it. Hanging up, she figured Gerald just wasn't worth the risk.

Never send a boy to do a man's job, her brother Paul used to tease when he could do something better than one of his younger brothers. And what an imbecile Gerald was turning out to be! No wonder the woman had left him. Now, there was only one question weighing on her mind. *Who was the woman in the fire?*

"Thank Goodness!" Her mother said, greeting her with a big hug as soon as soon as she got out of the car. "I didn't know what had happened to you. I just got a call back from Douglas. He was saying something about a fire. At your house. In *Lovely.*"

Laretta was talking fast, and had barely gotten the words out before LaRetha ran past her inside and upstairs, with her following. She had to pack in a hurry. She had to go and see about her house.

She dialed the airline as she packed. The next flight was in four hours. *Four hours!* Well, there was nothing that she could do, but wait.

Hanging up, she continued to pull clothing from their hangers and dresser drawers. *Why did I even bother to unpack?* She thought. Her mother was watching with concern.

"LaRetha, slow down! I didn't get you back to lose you, now."

"My house! They burned my house?" She screamed with disbelief and anguish. "I have to go. My plane leaves at *four!*"

"LaRetha, stop! That plane's not going to leave any sooner, so sit down for a minute. Take a breath and just *think!* You don't know how glad I am to see you. I need to call the police station and tell them you got home, alright. But first, tell me what happened? What did Gerald do to you?"

"That man *kidnapped* me, right here in the driveway. I was sitting in the car and before I knew it, he had jumped in and told me to *drive.* I couldn't believe it."

"Where did you go?"

"To the same apartment that I followed him to, yesterday. He must have seen me and followed me back here, the *snake!*"

"Has he totally lost his mind? Did you know that he tied Marilee up and left her in the pantry? I found her in there."

"You're kidding! Where is she? Is she alright?"

"I sent her home. She'll be fine. He didn't hurt her, thank goodness. *But has he lost his mind?"*

"It sure seems that way."

"What did he want with you LaRetha? I was worried he had done something to you."

"He might've planned to, but as usual, he couldn't even get that right," LaRetha said. "I think he was going to tell me something. But a call came in, and I was able to get away from him." She still couldn't believe any of it.

"That must have been me," Laretta said.

"Thank goodness! Now, about my house…"

"But, what did he *say?*"

LaRetha seemed to grapple with words, before shaking her head. She couldn't repeat what he'd said about her father's death. Her mother would be devastated, and it probably wasn't even true.

"He never got a chance to tell me anything," she said. "I got away from him, first."

Dumping everything out of her purse to make sure she had everything, she then tossed the items back inside. Christmas Eve or not, she had to see what was going on at her house.

"How bad was the fire, Mama?" She asked, still very upset.

"I'm sorry, LaRetha. But the barn and garage are completely gone. The house is, too. But, it gets worse."

Laretta abruptly stopped talking and looked at her with a sad expression.

"What is it?"

"Douglas said someone was burned inside the house. Everybody thought it was you, until he set them straight."

LaRetha stopped packing, sitting back down on the bed, saying nothing for a minute.

"A body was inside my house? I don't believe this. I simply do not believe *this!*"

"It was a woman, and they don't know if she was killed by the fire or if she was already dead and brought there before the fire was set. They still haven't identified her. So, I don't think it's safe for you to even go back there. It's safer here, don't you think?"

"Maybe yesterday or this morning, I might have agreed with you. But not after the day I've had. I'm thinking that I don't have a lot of time," she said, thinking about the *30 days.* "If I don't go, it could only make matters worse, not better. Besides, I can't ignore this. This is….just too much!"

"It's too dangerous, honey. Besides, where will you stay?"

"In a hotel. I'll come back in a few days. I just need to see what's going on, first."

"Okay. I know you won't change your mind. So, just be careful, okay? Don't take any unnecessary risks."

"I won't," she said, carrying her bags into the hallway.

"Just stay in touch with me," her mother said, following her. "I'll call Douglas and tell him you're on the way, and get him to meet you at the airport."

"I drove to the airport. I can drive it back to town."

"But, you don't need to drive under these circumstances. You can always get your car, later."

"Okay," she said, blowing with exasperation. "But, I need to let Germaine know something's going on. I don't think that Gerald would harm him, but after this morning I can't be too sure of that."

"I'll call him. I'll probably have to leave a message."

"Good. Tell him to keep his distance from his dad for a while, would you? Until this is settled."

While Laretta was on the phone, LaRetha carried her bags, downstairs. She came back up as her mother was hanging up.

"Mama, I am so sorry about Christmas. Everything is ruined, now."

Laretta looked at her with amazement.

"Don't you worry. You've got other things to be concerned about, right now. Just promise you'll be back in a day or so. Or, if you have to stay, stay at Douglas' house. He just told me he's home for the holidays. You'll be safe there."

"I don't know, Mama. I've been having second thoughts about Douglas. I mean, I can't be sure that he's completely on our side. He seems on the up and up, but..."

"*Honey*. You're just upset about what Valerie told you, and I understand that. But, give the man a chance to explain. You can't be certain she was even telling the truth."

"I believe her. Why would she lie on herself? She wouldn't do that." She shook her head.

"Even so, you still should hear it from Douglas. He does owe you an explanation, if only for professional reasons. You need to know whose side he's on."

She nodded in agreement.

"But, I can tell you from the relief that I heard in his voice just now, he was really concerned about you," her mother added. "He was out at your place for most of the morning until he could find out what was going on, and he said he might go back, later on. But, look for him at the airport. He'll explain the rest, I'm sure."

"Why do you have so much faith in him, and so little in *Kellen?* We really don't know him, that well," LaRetha stated, solemnly.

"I didn't have *any* in Gerald, and look how that turned out," Laretta replied.

Before going downstairs for dinner, Laretta retrieved her phone messages and told LaRetha that Douglas wanted her to call him back, right way.

Serves him right, she thought. Out of curiosity, she dialed her house in *Lovely,* instead. Busy signals.

Her plane wouldn't leave for another three hours and her mother was insisting that she eat something. She conceded, and joined her for the spaghetti with turkey meatballs and toasted garlic bread. LaRetha poured glasses of sugarless iced tea.

"Here." Laretta put a plate in front of her. "Just sit down and relax a minute. You have plenty of time before you have to go."

Taking a sip, she gave a heavy sigh of frustration.

"You know, it might not be safe for you to be alone either, Mama. Gerald is still out there. And even if he wasn't, one of the others might be."

"What *others?*" Her mother asked,

LaRetha explained how Gerald had mentioned several times that there were *others* when he'd held her at the apartment.

"I can just guess who some of those *others* are," her mother exclaimed with anguish.

LaRetha could too. She ate a forkful of the tasty meal and bit into her garlic bread, hot from the oven.

"Thanks, so much," she murmured with her mouth full.

"You're welcome. I'm just glad that he didn't hurt you. He didn't, did he?"

"I would tell you if he had. I have no reason to protect Gerald. I might have hurt *him,* though. Still might, first chance I get."

Her mother laughed with relief. LaRetha finished her dinner, as a mental picture of her home going up in flames caused her to shake her head in disbelief. Laretta gave her a hug.

"Remember, as bad as it looks, this could have been much worse. Thankfully, you were here, and you're okay."

"Everyone keeps telling me that, but how much worse could it *be?*" She asked, stifling tears of frustration.

Laretta didn't answer and LaRetha figured she was probably wondering the same thing.

Changing into comfortable, stylish jeans and a soft gray sweater, LaRetha laid down to take a short nap. But first, she figured she should at least return Douglas' call. He answered on the first ring.

"LaRetha? Why have you kept me waiting? I've been expecting your call for over an hour," he growled.

"Nice to hear from you too, Douglas." She was calmed now by a full stomach and was determined to stay that way.

"I am so *mad* at you," he said, sounding every bit of it. "Why didn't you listen to what I was trying to tell you, this morning?"

"I think I already know what you were trying to tell me." If he thought he was going to ruffle her feathers any more, he was about to become angrier.

"I was trying to tell you about the fire. But, you're so *hot headed!* Laretta told me about Gerald. Are you alright?"

"Did you call because you were angry, or because you were worried?"

"Both. Now, are you alright?"

"*Apparently.*"

"So what is it that you're so angry about?" He finally asked.

"I think I'd better tell you when I get there. Can you pick me up from the airport?"

"I should say *no.*"

"But, you won't will you?"

"I don't have time to play this game. Look, I even talked to Kellen. Then Samira came by my office…"

I'll just bet, she thought, imagining the two of them in heated embrace on his office desk. She wasn't hearing everything that he was saying. She tried to focus.

"… and there's a lot that you need to know. It turns out that Kellen…well, I'll tell you that when you get here. But, your… your ex-husband has been involved in this, all along."

"I know that now."

"Well, there are other things we both need to know. Wait for me at the airport."

"Oh, Douglas?" She said, uneasily.

"Yes?"

"Did they find out who was burned in my house?"

He hesitated.

"Douglas?"

"Not yet."

She knew that she would have to get to *Lovely* to get answers.

It was evening when she arrived at the farm, and news reporters and spectators were everywhere. She gasped at the sight of it all.

"LaRetha, just stay in the car…," Douglas said, before getting out.

Ignoring him, she barely waited until they had stopped before jumping out. Stopping short at what was left of stone steps that led to nowhere, she stood before the black cinders that were the remainder of her home. Her hands flew to her mouth. She was mortified.

Everything was gone. Nothing was left; not one wall hanging, curtain or chair, even. This is what the *others* that Gerald spoke about had done. She could only stand there, in shock.

Warding off photographers and reporters, Douglas was at her side, and walked with her back to his car. She was heartbroken. This was her life and it was in ruins. Everything that she'd owned in the world had been in that house. *Everything.*

And when she thought of all that work! And unfortunately, aside from copies of important documents like insurance policies, tax papers and her Will, she hadn't kept any back-up disks off the premises. She would have to start all over, again.

Gone was the house that her father had built, and even worse, those things that couldn't be replaced - all those family memories, memorabilia from her travels, trophies of Germaine's and plaques from her writings. She gave a sudden outburst of anguish. Douglas put his arms around her shoulders.

"I know it looks bad. But, those things can be *replaced,* LaRetha. While you, on the other hand, were very lucky not to be here when this happened," he said, sounding angry at the thought.

Maybe I wasn't supposed to be home, she thought, as a reporter made his way over to them, with a cameraman following. Others came too, all of them barraging her with questions. Douglas quickly opened the door for her.

Miss Greer? Is this the first time you've seen your home since it burned?

It must be a terrible shock for you, coming home to find all your possessions in ruins. Do you know what might have caused the fire?

Do you know the person found in the ashes? Or why they were inside your home when you were away?

How is this related to the shooting incident here, just a month ago?"

"Miss Greer! Miss Greer!" She didn't have time to answer as Douglas quickly closed her car door and got in on the other side.

"Do you want to address them?" He asked.

She shook her head.

"Do you want *me* to?"

Slowly, she nodded. Something needed to be said. *But what?* Douglas got back out of the car and was quickly surrounded. She lowered her window to hear.

"Miss Greer has been out of town. She is very surprised and dismayed at what has occurred here, today. She hasn't any information just yet, about who was killed in this fire. Therefore, she is not ready to make any statements at this time."

A suited gentleman, gray haired with a rounded waistline, approached. He and Douglas exchanged a few words before he came to her side of the car.

"You're going to have to answer some questions at the police station. I can act as your attorney, until… well, if you want me to."

She nodded. It seemed that Douglas had all the business that he could handle, dealing with her. The suited man came over to her side of the car, and she could smell the combined scent of cigar and cinders on his clothing.

"Mrs. LaRetha Greer?"

She nodded.

"I'm going to meet you two at the station. We have a few questions for you." He repeated.

She nodded again, and Douglas said that he would drive her.

"I guess I wasn't arrested because I'm not a suspect?" She asked, blowing her nose on a tissue he gave her, while leaning helplessly against the door.

"No. Obviously, you couldn't have caused the fire if you were out of town. I'm sure they've already verified that."

Once again, the interrogation at the station was long and repetitious.

What possible connection could there be between the fire and the previous shootings? What did she know about the woman that was found in her home? What was this about a kidnapping? How was her financial position?

As if she would burn her own place to the ground! Indeed!

She had no idea what the connection might be, she said. And her financial position was just fine. And, she had no knowledge of anyone being inside her home while she was away. Whoever this person was, they had entered the house without her permission.

Douglas had warned her to answer very carefully. He intervened a couple of times, defending her responses and her right not to answer particular questions.

She wasn't getting off easy, she realized. Her move to *Lovely* was being linked to all the recent crimes, and with a few she hadn't known about. Those had nothing to do with her, she said.

"Isn't it a fact that Cecelia Watson was your stepmother? When did you last speak with her?" The interrogator asked rather callously.

Puzzled, she looked from Douglas to the woman questioning her, then back at Douglas. Uncertain of what was being asked, she felt a sudden surge of fear. She looked at Douglas again, but his eyes were avoiding her own.

"Why are you asking me about Cecelia?"

"It's been confirmed. It was her body that was found in the fire."

LaRetha looked at Douglas with disbelief. His expression told her it was true, and how sorry he was.

"But," she said, closing her eyes, the words suddenly being hard to say. "She moved to New Jersey. It couldn't have been her."

"It appears that she took a flight back here, late last night. Her remains have already been identified by her dental records. Her sons just left an hour ago. We're certain that it was her body in that fire."

She couldn't speak. Douglas was beside her immediately, allowing her to cry into his chest. He held his hand up to them, begging off from more questioning.

"Clearly you can see that my client had no prior knowledge of this," he said. "This whole ordeal has been a bit much for her. So if you have no more questions, or if you think they can wait a day or so, I'll take her home, now."

"Home?" The man asked.

"She'll be at my house until other arrangements are made. You can reach her there," Douglas said firmly.

Watching her closely as she quietly sobbed, the woman interrogator nodded and the man opened the door for them.

"I'm very sorry, Miss Greer," he said. "We thought you knew."

Waking up on Douglas's den sofa, LaRetha couldn't remember walking back to the car or coming inside. He had offered to take her to the emergency room, but she had remembered the sedatives in her suitcase. *And would he mind taking her to a hotel, please?*

He had flatly refused, saying she didn't need to be alone. And besides, he had promised her mother. She was going home with him.

Home. There was no such place for her, now. She would have to start all over again. Regroup, rebuild, re-establish, or just give them what they wanted and move away, altogether. The thought left her feeling crushed.

Inhaling now, she could smell a holiday mixture of scented candles and incense. Christmas hymns played quietly throughout the room and probably the rest of the house. She closed her eyes, smiling. Douglas had given her something and it was working. After allowing herself to float for a moment over the soft jazzy melodies, she remembered and a tear escaped her.

It wasn't supposed to come to this. And she wasn't supposed to be here – not like this. Not under these circumstances. But the grogginess she felt wouldn't let her concentrate on that. She closed her eyes again, giving in to the overwhelming peacefulness. And after a moment all her troubles disappeared as she fell into a deep sleep.

Jasmine arrived and Nell was there, waiting. And now what was left of the group was complete; Bob Billard, George Foreman, James Reeves from the local bank, Elton Gray from the hardware store, Greg Hogan from the automotive shop, her mother and herself.

They were all there, looking anxious and impatient.

"First of all," Billard began, "let me catch you two up to speed. It's been confirmed. The woman in the fire was *not* LaRetha Greer."

The two of them sighed with relief.

"Police have confirmed that it was *Cecelia Watson.*"

Nell gasped.

"*Oh my goodness!*" Jasmine exclaimed.

"Where is this going to end?" Nell asked, angrily. "We all made a promise that no more deaths would be tied to this business."

"That's right!" Jasmine agreed. "And nobody said anything to us about a *body,*" she exclaimed.

"How am I supposed to sleep at night, knowing that four people are dead, already?" Nell intervened. "Who can trust anybody, anymore?"

Jasmine nodded, shivering at how gruesomely this woman had died. *Killed and then burned!* And what if she wasn't even dead at the time of the fire? What a slow, torturous death! The type of death that no one deserved.

"Listen," said Foreman, the voice of reason and the one most likely to go along, "This will be my last meeting. We've gone too far. I didn't mind keeping an eye on the woman, but I'm no killer and I don't associate with killers," he said.

"*Right!*" Nell said, heatedly. "So, somebody in here has gone too far. Cecelia is *dead!* Would somebody, *anybody* mind explaining how that happened and why?"

"Looks like some of us did what needed to be done," Hogan said. "Nothing else was working and the buyers are almost ready to pull out. I guess some of us just did what we had to do."

Both Nell and Jasmine looked at him, appalled.

"*Hush,* Hogan. Talk about something that you know about," Billard snapped.

"Well, that's all the answer I need," Jasmine said. "In case none of you have noticed, I've lost a father *and* a brother. This has never been worth *one* life, and certainly not theirs. *So don't you dare talk to me about doing what needed to be done!*"

Nell agreed, wiping her eyes with a tissue. But, unlike her, Jasmine wasn't worried about Billard, at this point. Still, he spoke up.

"We're sorry for both your losses, Arnell. Jasmine. We regret that it happened and I personally intend to find out why. But wasn't that your cousin's truck that your father was in?"

But Jasmine wasn't listening.

"Daddy told us to walk away," she groaned. "That's exactly what we should have done."

"But *people,* let's not panic. That's just not the answer," Billard said. "Since none of us seem to know anything," he said, looking from Nell to Jasmine, "we have to figure that there's somebody else out there with the same interests as us."

"Now," he continued, "if this someone knows about us, then we also know that this *somebody* is a threat. And like me, I'm sure that none of you want to take the blame or go to jail for this, am I right?"

Several of the men agreed while Foreman remained silent. Nell and her daughter said nothing, as well.

Jasmine wasn't buying this innocent act, for a minute. But what should she do? She wondered. Her father had always protected them when he was alive. It wasn't until now that she realized how much.

There was never any discussion about setting *fires* and causing *death* when he was here. But they were in way over their heads, now. And neither she nor Nell was any match for these dangerous, greedy men with their outdated sexist attitudes and 'stop at nothing' mentalities. And none of them were any match for Billard.

"Like you all," the big man continued, "I'm about ready to just walk away and let whole this thing blow over. But first, we find out who's really behind this before they go any further," he said, looking again at Jasmine, "and then get them out of our way, fast. That'll clear all of us. And, if nothing else comes of this, we can at least go back to living our regular lives without any threat of harm, or of being exposed."

"Well, *finally,* somebody's come to their senses," said Elton Gray, a man who called himself a hard nosed redneck. Wealthy by unexpected inheritance, he was very proud of it. She'd been surprised to learn that her father was even in business with the man.

"That's promising, at least," he continued. "Look, I gotta get going. My kids'll be looking for big things in the morning. I have to play Santa. Somebody fill me in later, *won't cha?*" He asked, casually.

Billard nodded. "We're done here. We don't need to meet for very long. There's too much scrutiny taking place right now, as it is. You all find out as much about that fire as you can, and get back to me."

Everyone agreed and they began to disband. Billard followed as Foreman, Hogan, Reeves and Grey quickly left as if on cue. Turning back, he approached her as they were putting on their coats.

"I understand there was a meeting between our little Samira and Davis the other day. You mind telling me what that was all about?"

Jasmine and Nell exchanged puzzled looks.

"It's news to me. I'll certainly ask her about it," Jasmine said.

"You do that! You brought that woman in here…"

"And she's done everything we've asked her to," she defended. "It couldn't have been anything serious. They did date once, you know? But, I'll get back to you, for sure."

"Tell you what. Let's not wait for you to get back with me. Ask her right now."

Hesitantly, she looked to her mother, who nodded her consent. Dialing the number on her cell phone, she waited only a few seconds before Samira answered. Billard pressed *speaker phone.*

"Samira?" She asked.

"Yes?"

"*Jasmine*. A question has come up about you meeting with Douglas, recently. You never mentioned it. What was that about?"

"Oh," the woman said, "I was trying to find out what he knew about the shooting. But, his secretary wouldn't let me in his office. I couldn't get anything. You know he's representing Kellen."

The three exchanged equally disbelieving glances.

"I managed to get documents for you all before, remember?"

"Yeah, yeah," Billard interrupted. "But I tell you one thing, *girlie*. You had better not be playing your ends against the middle. Don't you let your personal feelings and your little anxieties cost us this deal," he said. "Because what costs me will surely cost you!"

Not waiting for Samira's response, Jasmine said she would call her later and hang up. Billard walked them to the door. Pulling her back by her elbow, he leaned toward her ear, his sour breath causing her to recoil.

"You'd better talk to that friend of yours, you hear? That girl's going to be *big trouble*. And I'm not having it. Know what I mean?"

"Don't worry about it." She nodded. "Trouble for you is trouble for us, too. And I'm not having it, either. *Goodnight*, Bob."

After consoling Jasmine and promising that she would think of something, Nell dropped her off at home to help Bernice with the grandchildren. It was Christmas Eve and her family hadn't wanted her to spend the holiday alone. The children had been excited all day that they would awaken in the morning at Grandmama's house and open all their presents. But first, to get them into bed.

Alone now, she blew a huge sigh of frustration. Jasmine had reason to be nervous. Their drama was far from over. Everybody was afraid to say it, but Bob Billard was *totally* out of control. The man was *crazy*. And with so many crimes taking place, and her husband being gone, she was at a loss at what to do about it.

Verry had tried to keep her uninvolved. She should have listened to him. But with his failing health, she'd thought her intervention was necessary. She'd always known that some things he'd done couldn't exactly be called *right*, but there was never a deal where everyone didn't benefit, even if they were initially unwilling. And now, she was beginning to understand what the other side felt like. And she, along with her daughter, were in it knee deep.

Cecelia was dead, and it was probably her friendship with Billard that had led to it. The woman should have just settled for her insurance money and stayed gone. Or had she forgotten all the trouble she'd left behind?

Billard had always considered that farm a 'sure thing', and had pressured the woman for years to get *Watson* to sell part of it to him. He had courted that situation, incessantly, and Nell believed he'd even taken a liking to Cecelia. And just when he'd said he had her cooperation, *Watson* had fallen ill and wasn't expected to recover. And considering all the money she had coming once he died, she wouldn't even discuss it, after that.

At least then, the woman had enough sense to take her money and leave town. So, there remained the one question: *Who, if not Billard, had gotten her to come back?*

They said that LaRetha was in Atlanta when it happened, so she couldn't have been expecting her stepmother's visit. And if LaRetha didn't let her into the house, who did? Surely she didn't break in? It had to be Billard, promising her something just as he had the others.

Reporters were saying that she had possibly been killed some-place else, and burned to get rid of evidence. And now that *she* was dead, Nell was thinking twice about Billard's suggestion that she continue pursuing the farm in Therell's name.

Creating that fake document naming himself as *Watson's* son had been an insane idea anyway, she thought. Nothing about that situation had gone as planned. *Verry* had already warned them that it was too risky. He'd pleaded with them to back off and see what the meeting with LaRetha and the attorneys would produce.

It was a fool-proof plan. Until they learned that Therell was under investigation for setting that other farm fire and for the death of that federal agent. He'd been suspended already from his job, and being found a fraud would do nothing to help that situation. So, he'd panicked, applying more pressure to Kellen than he should have. *And now...*

She should never have allowed their children to get involved. But *Verry* had assured her that nothing would ever touch them. That he could protect them all and keep them out of harm's way. And that once their debts were cleared, this education and their children's expertise would come in handy when running the 'family busi-nesses'. It had seemed like a good idea, at the time.

What in the world were we thinking, tossing them into the fire like that? She asked herself now, in anguish. This dream of theirs was coming at too great a price. She had always wanted all her children, and their children, to live privileged lives, and they had. But, it was evident that they were also sadly lacking in certain areas, such as in relationships.

Like Therell, Jasmine lived as if she didn't need anybody. And unfortunately, no one ever stayed around for long. Nell doubted that either of them had ever really been in love.

Despite her personal woes, however, when it came to business, the girl was *ruthless;* following in her father's footsteps, for sure. She was articulate, creative, intuitive and loyal to her purpose, which was to become independently wealthy by the time she was *forty*. This deal would have put her well on the way.

But impatience had taken its toll. *Verry* had done his best, but they had all tired of waiting. She felt she'd been waiting on him all of their married lives; waiting for him to get his act together and stop drinking and gambling, waiting for him to become faithful, waiting for his business to increase. Then, waiting just to *wait*.

They'd gotten through the drinking years, the incessant womanizing, those bad business dealings that had kept him on the move, and finally, the gambling. But not without a price. Because what the kids had seen, they had emulated; Bernice with her ever-growing bunch and no need for a steady man, and Dave with the wild San Francisco lifestyle he never spoke of and they no longer asked. Thankfully, Paul and their younger boys had wisely chosen more academic paths, going to college in other states and working white-collar jobs. Fortunately, they had managed to keep them uninvolved.

But then there was Therell who, like Jasmine, always had bigger dreams than pockets. And although his department hadn't found anything yet, they knew he was involved. He might have even gone to prison for it, eventually. She couldn't decide which fate was worse.

Billard had been *livid* when he found out Therell had killed the agent who had surprised him at the scene of the fire. He'd told them they had better get that son of theirs under control. But Therell, he'd said, was in this one all by himself.

Such monsters they had become. And as much as they had always detested and distrusted Billard, they had become worse than him - allowing themselves to depend on him for their bread and butter, and to be bribed at a price they could ill afford. It had brought out the worst in all of them. And she didn't know how they would recuperate from this one, or if they ever would.

Therell had been *their* son, long before *Verry* had confessed his mistakes. He'd never been *Watson's* child to her, anyway. And despite his problems, she had always been proud to call him *son*.

She wouldn't allow *Verry* to tell Therell the truth. *What good would it do to rock the boat?* Aurelia had been her greatest concern; until she realized the girl was truly out of the picture. Besides, *Watson* was providing for the boy, financially. And considering that farm business, he'd owed them.

Because of that, they had never legally adopted the boy. And as he got older, they just never found a reason to bring it up. He had always been *their* son. And that was enough, at the time.

It saddened her now to know that she had allowed Therell to go to his grave believing he'd been unwanted and unloved by *Watson*, the man he'd always thought was his true father. But she had never expected him to die before they did. Then Therell's death, compounded with the group's other worries had contributed greatly to her husband's poor health, she believed. And to his death.

Douglas Davis. He was onto them, and probably could have shut them down a long time ago. And now, he probably would.

He hadn't known about Samira, until too late. Or that the party that a major client of his was suing was one of Billard's silent partners. Davis had built an air-tight case. But being caught between Samira's womanly wiles and Billard's secrets, he hadn't stood a chance. His client had accepted money, off the record, and the case was a lost cause.

But, Douglas was no fool. In anger, he'd told *Verry* that whatever they had gained from their wicked deceptions would cost them far more. And she had to believe that some of the things happening to her own family were because of what they'd done, to him and others like him.

Douglas' career had truly been smiled upon by somebody. Coming up at a time when African Americans had a difficult enough time getting a job at the local market, he had followed his determined father's footsteps and was considered a powerful force in the legal community. So, it was a frightening day when he'd realized what they had done.

Nell had waited for the bomb to drop, and it had. Valerie had been like a daughter to her; well educated, from a wealthy family, and very much in love with Paul. And despite her initial misgivings, she remembered how the girl had turned out to be exactly as Jasmine had predicted; *just what her brother needed.*

The woman had challenged him in ways he'd never been challenged. Always the loner and the bookworm, it had take Paul some time to mature into the marriage, but he had. Valerie had validated him; encouraging and supporting his dreams, as far fetched as they were. And, in turn, he had become successful and happy, and he still worshipped the ground that she walked on. Together, they had made quite a dynamic team. *Until Douglas Davis.*

Her son was devastated when he found out, calling them in the middle of the night while Valerie slept in the next room, and crying – something he'd rarely done, even as a child. He said they had argued, and she'd admitted to being unfaithful, and who with. And if her son ever trusted the girl again, *she* sure hadn't. But, having weathered enough marital storms of their own, she and *Verry* had encouraged him to work through it. They had also promised never to mention it to the rest of the family. But the kids had known something was up. He would have to tell them, she'd said.

Carole's house was in sight, now. Her sister-in-law had promised to wrap and label all of the grandkids' presents. She would just have to check to make sure that Carole's grandkids weren't getting more than their fair share.

She wondered how LaRetha was feeling right now. She could only imagine her devastation at finding everything that she'd worked for, burned to the ground. And worse, to find her stepmother's body lying in the ruins. She slowly shook her head, in dismay.

But, like her mother, LaRetha always seemed to snap back. The girl seemed destined to be successful, *in spite of it all*. Even with all of her troubles, she was still beautiful, wealthy, and a successful writer. And she definitely had more than her share of men to choose from; Kellen Kincaid and now Douglas. Or why else would he have brought her to that funeral?

Nell recalled disliking Laretta for so many years – hating her, almost. Mostly for all the attention her husband had given her relationship with *Watson,* back in the day. And the trouble he went through to try and destroy it. She had sometimes wondered if he hadn't wanted to marry the woman, instead.

It took a long time, but after raising eight children and dealing with her own demons, she'd finally realized that her hatred had only harmed herself. And that it would eventually be her own destruction, and that of her entire family, if she didn't just let it go. No one could change the past. And besides, while well aware of their disdain for her, that Laretta Watson hadn't missed a beat.

If only she could take it all back. Reverse time to before Cecelia and Therell's death; before LaRetha had even moved here. Before *Watson* died and before *Verry* had concocted all those stories about Laretta. To before they had conned Douglas Davis. So that she could stop it.

Who could say things wouldn't have worked out better? That her husband and son wouldn't still be alive, and her daughter, happily married to the man she'd always loved? So very much would be different, if only she could take it all back.

But, it was too late for that now. She looked up from sitting in the driveway to see her sister-in-law's head bob up and down as she peered outside through fogged windows. Maybe she should have been more like Carole; happy with living a simple life, and content to just *be*.

But, that was never her style. She didn't know if LaRetha would ever sell the farm to them, at this point. Right now, she had bigger worries. There would be questions about Cecelia's death. People were frightened now, thinking that the farm fires were starting, again. There was talk of organizing and bringing in more investigators, which would endanger them all. She had threatened to walk, and she would. But not before she handled one last matter.

Billard was making some really bad moves, totally disregarding their opinions. But, if he was ever linked to Paul Straiter, Cecelia, or even her own husband's death, they would all go down. Patting the purse beside her she found her husband's gun right where she'd put it earlier. She had little choice right now. *Bob Billard must go!*

16

LaRetha awakened in an unfamiliar room, lying on a beautiful walnut sleigh bed, covered by blankets and resting on the most comfortable mattress she'd ever slept on. Sitting up, it took a moment to remember where she was, or why she was there.

She took her time showering and getting dressed, before sliding her feet into a pair of white house shoes, pinning her hair up in a loose bun, applying a little makeup and splashing on her favorite perfume. She went downstairs.

Douglas was already there, very comfortably in sweat pants and a thick sweater, pouring over a stack of documents on his dining room table. Looking up as she entered, he smiled.

"Merry Christmas!" He said, cheerily.

He stacked the papers and set them aside. "So, this is what LaRetha Greer looks like early in the morning."

"Sorry, I know it ain't pretty," she said, modestly.

"No. It's better than that," He smiled again and she could kick herself for actually blushing.

"Hungry? Mrs. Starks left enough food for an army, so help yourself. There's a full platter warming in the oven."

"Thanks," she said, retrieving it and filling a plate with pancakes and eggs. Douglas poured a glass of orange juice and handed it to her. But he wasn't having juice, she observed.

"It's a little early to be drinking, isn't it?" She asked, sipping her juice.

"Eat your breakfast." He avoided her question.

"And Merry Christmas to you, too," she said, raising her glass as if in toast and drinking from it. He stood up, patting her shoulder as he passed.

"Going somewhere?" She asked.

"I'll be right back. I have something for you."

She waited in suspense until he returned with a huge box, beautifully wrapped in silver paper with a huge white bow.

"You shouldn't have."

"I didn't. Marva did a few weeks ago, with my instructions," he said, chuckling. Inside the box was a beautiful crystal vase, with a card. She read it.

Beautiful things for a beautiful person. Enjoy it! Douglas.

She smiled.

"I take it that you like it?"

"I do! Thank Marva for me, will you?" She teased, not mentioning her gift for him that was still under her mother's tree. She had hoped to surprise him.

"Sure. So, how did you sleep?"

"Like a baby. That sedative did me good."

"I'll bet."

She remembered her question from earlier.

"Douglas, I want to ask you something. If you don't think it's any of my business, you don't have to answer."

"So ask. If it's truly none of your business, I'll let you know. How about that?"

"Deal."

"Well?" He said, waiting.

"What happened between you and Valerie Watson?"

He looked at her and frowned.

"What does that have to do with you?" He was annoyed.

"I don't know. Maybe nothing, maybe everything. But like I said, you don't have to answer if you don't want to." She got up to look in his cupboard. *"Got any cinnamon?"*

"In the cabinet above your head." His voice had lowered to almost a whisper. He was upset. She was sorry for that, but if he was seeing her cousin's wife, or worse - in love with the woman, she deserved to know.

He sat quietly for a moment before calmly gathering his papers and glass, and walking out of the room. Her heart fell. She hadn't meant to alienate him this way. Just to maintain trust and honesty between them. Surely, he could understand that.

She finished her breakfast, alone. Then washed and stacked her plate with the others. Looking around and satisfied that everything was in order, she proceeded upstairs to shower and change.

"Hello Mama! Merry Christmas to you," she said into her cell phone.

Laretta sounded happy to hear from her. What had happened? How was the property? She tried to answer all of her questions.

"I'm going to need all my insurance papers from you. I'll have to replace everything; the house, my computer, all of my belongings."

"Oh, dear. I was afraid of that. I'm so sorry, baby. Well, they're here. Did they say who the woman was?"

"Yes. They're pretty sure. Brace yourself because you simply will not believe it."

"So it was someone I know?"

She couldn't answer for a moment. With the sedatives wearing off, images of the woman as she'd last seen her were suddenly flooding her memory.

"It was Cecelia." She blurted.

There was a long pause before Laretta finally responded.

"What was she doing back there, in that house, in the first place?" She demanded, sounding very upset.

"That remains to be discovered. But, I'll call you a little later with the details once I get them. What're you doing this morning, by the way?"

"Sipping eggnog and opening presents from myself and from the family. I haven't opened the one from you, yet. I'm saving that for when you come back to Atlanta."

"Go ahead and open it, if you like, It's just one of a few things that I have for you. That one's a personal item."

She thought about the cute leopard print lounging gown. And that gorgeous dress suit that was still in her suitcase. She wanted to see her mother's face when she opened that one.

"You're gonna love it," she told her mother.

"You always give such nice gifts, so I'm sure I will."

"Mama, did you ever catch up with Germaine, and give him my message?"

"I left him a message, but I haven't talked to him yet. I'll call him this morning. I can tell him to call you."

So much for spending time with him, she thought. So far, all her plans were falling through. And this was supposed to be a happy holiday?

"Well, now those plans are ruined. No house, no reunion with my son. Nothing."

"Not at all! We'll keep him in our prayers. Everything will be fine. I'm sure of it."

"Save some of the presents so we can open them on New Year's," she said. She didn't want her mother worrying about not seeing her, again.

"That would be great! So, how's Douglas treating you?"

"Fine. He's a really good host."

"*Hmmm*," her mother said. "I guess I don't have to worry about you."

"Not at all. And how is Marilee?"

"She's shaken up a bit, but back to her normal self."

LaRetha was happy to hear it. She made a mental note to call and express her concern. Then, she remembered how angry Douglas was with her. And looking around this beautifully furnished bedroom, she felt even more displaced.

But it was Christmas! And everything about this house said so. Only she wasn't feeling the spirit, yet. But, it was early, still. And since she couldn't do anything about her house at the moment, she should try and put those problems aside and make the most of the day.

Douglas was in the den, watching a holiday special on television. Quietly, she sat at the opposite end of the sofa. He barely looked away from the screen, but nodded his acknowledgement of her.

From where she sat, she could see out of a nearby window onto the patio and lake, just beyond. She could imagine spending cozy evenings out there on the dock, just watching the boats come and go. *How fortunate he was to live here.*

This room was cozy enough, with long and beautiful burgundy and ivory colored drapes, beige carpeting and expensive rugs. And its very comfortable furniture. Christmas decorations adorned the room, their lights twinkling every now and then. A fire flamed lazily in the fireplace. And the mantel was filled with decorative candles, holly and family photos that intrigued her, but that she didn't ask about.

Finally, she turned to face Douglas. Without even looking her way, he used the remote control to turn off the television.

"So, you want to know about me and Valerie?" He asked calmly.

"Yes, I do." She was relieved

He turned to face her, studying her for a moment.

"And why do you care about my *torrid little affairs?*"

"Because, they all seem to be with people I know, or that I'm related to. And I'd rather know the truth than to wonder about it."

"Then let's make another deal. Tell me all about Kellen and your relationship with him. Tell me what happened with Gerald yesterday. And I'll tell you all about my stupid little rendezvous with your cousin's *wife.*"

"*Kellen?* There's nothing to tell, really. We met through my son and his younger brother. They were best friends so we became friends as well. But, there is nothing serious going on, there."

His blank expression said he didn't believe her.

"Let me explain," she added, seeing his disbelief. "Before I came here, he and I were becoming very close. But, he knew when I moved that I wasn't going to pursue it. He understood, although he didn't exactly agree. Then, after the incident with Paul Straiter, he came here to show his support. He did propose, but I didn't accept. And that's that."

"*And now?* I mean, if you two were once *lovers,*" he said slowly while watching her expression, "and you saw the need to leave him behind, why do you still feel the need to just be friends?"

"Because, he is a friend," she said, solemnly. "But for… different reasons, it's always been an awkward situation for me. Still, I think it was good of him to come here like he did."

Douglas frowned. She continued.

"As for *Gerald,* I hadn't spoken with him since we divorced. But yesterday, out of the blue, he tied up the housekeeper at my mother's, and jumped into my car. He forced me to drive to an apartment. Then, we just sat there like he was waiting for something, or somebody. But nothing happened."

Douglas looked relieved.

"Laretta called, looking for me and that distracted him long enough for me to get away. I remembered the spare key that she keeps under her car mat. Or, who knows what might have happened?"

Douglas listened intently. She continued.

"I don't know why Gerald did that, but it certainly wasn't for my protection, although he did tell me something yesterday that I couldn't possibly repeat to my mother."

She took a deep breath and exhaled.

"He told me that my father had been *murdered,*" she said, and he stared at her in disbelief.

"*By whom?*"

"He never got to that. I got away from him, first."

"And you believe him?"

"*No,*" she said, closing her eyes and shaking her head. "I think he was just trying to shake me up before he hit me with his real reason for kidnapping me. I just don't like him very much for saying it."

"How terrible for you."

Douglas extended his hand to her and after a moment's hesitation, she gave him hers. He pulled her to him and she found his arms very comforting as he hugged her, tightly.

"Your father was a *good* man, LaRetha. Don't let anybody tell you otherwise. He was hard, but he had to be. He worked hard. Nobody gave him a thing. What you have now? What he gave you is rightfully yours. No one can deny that."

"You've never said that to me before."

"I needed to remain impartial and I didn't know you well. And I admit, I wasn't sure just what your involvement was in all this."

"And now?" She asked.

"You are everything I thought you'd be and more. I think you're a lot like *Watson* – strong willed, driven and determined. *Good traits,* is what my father called them. I admire that in you."

"I never considered myself as all that. Either way, it didn't make either of us very popular."

"Someone once said that 'greatness is always rejected'. I believe that to be true."

"I'm anything but *great!*" She offered, frowning.

"Not to me. Somebody wanted you kidnapped, so that means you're something to them, too. But, did Gerald say anything else about how that supposedly happened to your father, or why?"

"No, he didn't. But, I know it's not true. My father was *ill,* not murdered. Besides, Cecelia would have said so. But, now, with her gone, I honestly don't know what in the world to think. I feel like I'm sitting in a den of disaster here, and I can't find my way out of it. Things couldn't possibly be any worse."

"You know Douglas," she continued, "even if he was every bit as hard and difficult as they say he was, he was only trying to protect what was rightfully his. How can people be so judgmental of that.?"

"Your uncle and the others have always blamed him for the way he took over that land," he said. "And now they're blaming you."

"And how do you think that was?"

"They needed money. *Verry* had debt that he couldn't pay, and a house that he couldn't afford, at the time. On top of that, he had a gambling addiction. And because everybody wanted money, your father bought them out. It was all fair and above board. The only hitch is that if you were to sell, they would have first right to purchase. But under certain conditions, of course."

"I know. I learned that at the reading of my father's Will. But, you never told me all that, either."

"I wasn't your attorney. It would have come up at that meeting with Therell, if we'd had one. But, so much has happened, and I haven't seen you much, since the funeral…"

She remembered the meeting that never happened.

"The problem with these folks, *your* folks, is they want it all. They had the money he paid them, and it seemed to have helped them. But now, they want more."

She nodded.

"My father told me this case was going to land on my desk, one day. That this would go on and on, until someone ended it. I think he meant someone like you."

"I didn't come here for this."

"How do you know you didn't?" He asked. "You were destined for this. Your father was strong, but you're stronger in a lot of ways. You're more educated, younger, healthier, and you've also got his history to guide you."

She contemplated this. Shook her head.

"I don't believe what Gerald said for a minute," he continued. "But we can't just discount it. You just have to make up your mind how far you're willing to go to resolve this. Just tell me what you want to do."

"You know I want this finished. I'm sure there are a lot of other people who do, too."

He nodded.

"I've lost my father, my uncle, a cousin and now, my *stepmother*? That's *unheard* of. I don't care what we have to do. Something has to be done before someone else dies. Can you help me?"

"I think so. You can do this, LaRetha. And I have no doubt that you will. So yes, I'll help you."

"So, you're really on my side?"

"*Who else's*? This thing has been right in front of our faces, all along, except until now, no one's made the connection between these fires and your family, and the people who're backing them. And no one would press charges when they did find something."

"But in this case, *Kincaid's* case, a lot of things are going to be brought to light. That's why I feel this was just meant to be."

"But," he continued, looking her directly in the eyes, "before I get into it, I have to know that I have your complete trust and cooperation. No matter what happens, we remain a team. No more doubting me or my intentions. *Deal?*"

"You haven't even made good on our first deal, yet." She smiled.

"Which deal was that?" He looked puzzled.

"You were going to tell me about you and Valerie."

"Okay. If you think you're ready to hear it, I'll tell you."

After he told her everything, LaRetha simply said, *okay then,* was quiet for a few moments and then got up and left the room. Minutes later she reappeared, saying that she needed to get her car from the airport, and would he drive her?

Douglas suggested that she borrow his new Mercedes, instead. They would get her car, later. He also gave her a key to the front door and the code to the security alarm. Then, she was gone.

It was Christmas Day, and she'd found some place else to be besides there, with him. But, he wasn't her man, so why was he concerned? She did say that she would phone him after a while. And having no other plans, he wondered what he was supposed to do with the rest of the day?

Spending the day with another woman friend was not the answer. They needed to work things out, somehow. He felt terrible, asking for her complete trust and then telling her this about himself. Would she ever trust him, now?

He couldn't believe this recent escapade with her ex-husband, Gerald Greer, and how, before the fire was even completely out on her home, she'd barely escaped the man's clutches in some mad kidnapping plot.

Could this get any *crazier?* First, there were invasions, shootings and burnings. And now, *kidnapping!* Douglas couldn't remember ever seeing so much disaster around one person.

Laretta was convinced that by coming back to *Lovely,* LaRetha was in even more danger than before. She wanted him to look out for her. He'd said he would, *if* she would allow it. He decided not to share his sentiment that all of this had to be for a reason.

Unfortunately, he was sworn to secrecy where Kincaid was concerned, or he would have told LaRetha what the man had said about Gerald's involvement before she'd left town. And even the details about her *precious* Kellen Kincaid. But, she had left so suddenly, leaving him no choice but to try and get her back here, first. He had never suspected that Atlanta would be dangerous for her, too.

Her opinion of him mattered. More than he wanted it to. But, she had wanted answers so he'd given them to her. But, with this latest revelation, he doubted she would ever share his feelings, or want to be in any type of relationship with him.

Valerie Watson! It shouldn't have surprised him that this terrible secret would raise its ugly head once again, and after so much time. He had tried to forget it, remembering that period as one of the lowest in his entire life. But, here it was again. And the timing couldn't have been worse.

They had met at the uncle's house over two years ago, right after he'd started up with Samira, who had insisted that they attend that family's annual barbecue, together. He'd noticed the woman, as beautiful as she was, but was very much into his date at the time and not into married women, ever.

He was full of himself in those days, he had to admit. And there had been no shortage of women for him, although he'd later resigned to keeping the women of *Lovely* out of his black book. But, apparently, back then this ego was easily recognizable. Because after Samira had betrayed him in the worse way, Valerie had called.

In light of this family's unforgivable betrayal, his first reaction had been to seek revenge, and he'd set out to get it. Apparently, Paul and his wife were having troubles back at home in *L.A.* She had needed *advisement,* she'd said. They'd arranged to meet on her next visit to *Lovely.* And right away, she made no bones about telling him that she was interested in him.

Foolishly, he had only briefly hesitated. And afterwards, he'd even been rather proud of himself, numbing his guilty feelings by saying that they had deserved it. But, he'd learned, this woman had as much a vengeful nature as he, considering she'd felt compelled to tell her husband, who had told his mother, who then told their father.

He figured that Paul must have hurt her very badly. Being a chip off his father's block, that wasn't doubtful. Still, two wrongs never made right, and he realized now that he'd had no right to interfere.

As an attorney, he knew the devastation that infidelity could do to a marriage, and a family. But he'd only been thinking about himself – seeing this as his grand opportunity to avenge their deception. But then, he'd been ashamed, and angry with himself for once again falling into a trap with one of *their* women. Not only that, but for giving that family yet another hold on him with this exhibition of his own lack of character. Quite the opposite of what he should have set out to accomplish.

He had also soon learned that acts carried out in anger or vengeance tended to destroy the perpetrator more than the prey, considering his conscious had whipped him like no man ever could. He had really grown up behind that incident, realizing that even he could fall, and that at some point, he would have to account for his own actions.

And so here he was, staring penance in the face. About to lose the woman he was fast falling in love with, because of this very stupid thing. Over time, and at the old man's insistence, they had made peace. The couple had worked things out and he guessed that his living long distance from them had helped. And until he'd met LaRetha, he had taken his lesson lightly, gently declining the family's numerous social invitations that followed.

He knew it all seemed quite bizarre to her, and probably to anyone from anyplace other than *Lovely*. But, they were a small community, and in many ways, needed one another. Besides, he had always been told by his own father that, given the right amount of power, this family would be dangerous. His father had kept an eye on them, and so would he.

Twice he had been with Valerie, and it was over, with no further expectations on either end. But, looking into LaRetha's eyes, seeing her disappointment in him when he'd told her, had revived all the shame that he'd tried to forget. She'd felt she deserved an answer, and she did - for the sake of the case, if nothing else. And so, he had given it to her.

He would take it all back if he could, he told her. It was a long time before he would regain his self-respect. And, when ruling out further personal involvement with anyone or anything even remotely related to those people, their friends or their associates, and certainly with another married woman, he had ruled out half the women in *Lovely*. And that had been fine with him. *Until now.*

After he told LaRetha everything, she left. Her disappointed expression saying he had let her down.

"I'll be out for a while," she said, not meeting his gaze. "Need anything?"

"No, but thanks" he told her, watching as she whisked out of the front door, and hating himself the entire time.

Leaving Douglas downstairs, LaRetha placed a call to Vera. The woman picked up, immediately.

"Merry Christmas!" The woman answered.

"Merry Christmas, Vera! It's LaRetha Greer. How're you doing?"

"Just fine, *girl,* and you?" She sounded cheery.

"Great. Look, I know it's a holiday…"

"Best time to call. I heard about your house. I am *so* sorry. I… I don't even know what to say. Are you alright?"

"I'll be fine. But, can I come over and talk with you? I understand if you're busy. I don't want to interrupt your festivities, being it's a family holiday and everything."

"Girl, ain't nothing going on around here, just me and a few relatives exchanging gifts, later on today. We did all our celebrating last night at service. *Come on over.* I'll give you directions."

"You sure?"

"Don't I sound sure? I've been trying to get you over here for the longest. So, just write this down."

LaRetha wrote down the address. Slipping on her shoes, she found Douglas and told him she needed to get her car. As she had hoped, he offered his, instead. She could think of nothing more to say. She just hadn't expected to feel so let down.

Maybe a little air would clear her thoughts, she'd figured. She had to admit, pulling that Mercedes out of the garage felt nice. As cold as it was, she lowered her front windows a bit, allowing the frosty air to greet her warm face. She needed a friend right now. And a new one would do just as well.

Douglas! Just hearing how he'd been with Valerie had somehow cut deep. She couldn't even deny it to herself any longer; she was falling for this man, and despite the tragedies at hand, had actually looked forward to seeing him, yesterday.

It was there the entire time, her attraction for him. Something about the way he looked at her made her insides melt a little bit more every time she was with him, and his overtures a lot harder to resist. Earlier, she had practically fallen into his arms, she thought, a bit ashamedly. She had to admit the truth; that this was no mere infatuation going on between them. Their chemistry and compatibility was real, even if it wasn't perfect.

Douglas had practically *everything* going for him; looks, success, wealth, intelligence and despite his past relationship issues, *sensitivity*. He understood her father's and her dilemma with his relatives because he knew its history. And, because of his past relationships, he also understood about her involvement with Kellen. And considering that both were important to Kellen's case, what more could she ask for, right now?

Still, if she were asked a few days ago about what, if anything, she would change about him, she would've wanted to see a stronger spiritual side, and for him to stop drinking so much. But now, that list was growing.

Valerie? And he'd had the nerve to show up at their house for the holiday party!

He wanted her trust, but she was beginning to wonder what was really going on around here? Why had they invited him, really? Who was it that killed Paul Straiter at the hospital? Who had killed Cecelia and set that fire? And just how deeply rooted in all of it was *Douglas Davis?*

If anyone could fill her in on the details, it might be *Vera*.

She rang the bell only once before the door opened and Vera appeared, dressed in a lovely gold sweater and brown pants. She practically yanked her inside, giving her a warm hug before showing her where to hang her coat.

LaRetha followed her into the lovely ranch-styled home with its spacious living room, brightened by two huge bay windows with long beige curtains pulled back. A tall lighted Christmas tree with presents underneath, graced one corner. And she couldn't help but admire the finely embroidered detail of the off-white contemporary sofa and two contrasting black and beige overstuffed chairs of African print.

Beautiful African art was everywhere. A huge engraved table made of ivory with glass inserts was centered between the chairs. Various sized rugs with black and ivory patterns were scattered about. Colorful African prints hang on the wall, and shelf after shelf was filled with various pieces of exquisite African art.

"I can tell that you don't have small children," she kidded. "This is very nice. I really like it!"

"Thanks," Vera said as she took her coat and hang it on a rack, nearby. "But, I would trade this fine furniture for some dirty-faced little brats, *any day of the week.* Since my husband died, I just stopped thinking about it. I guess you could say that I've married the mission and adopted all the homeless people. Believe me, my life is full."

"I believe you," she said. "I'm sorry about your husband."

"Thanks. Can I offer you something to drink, or to eat? I have…"

"No, no. Don't trouble yourself. I just had breakfast."

"I was so sorry to hear about your house, LaRetha," she said once again. "And when I heard you could have been burned inside, I was *terrified,*" she said, her face showing it. "Then, they said you were out of town, thank goodness! That was terrible! How are you making out?"

"Oh, Vera!" She said, shaking her head and fighting the urge to break down into tears. "My moving here was probably the *biggest* mistake I could have made, although everyone is telling me different."

Vera patted her hand, sympathetically.

"If you had told me a year ago that any of this might happen when I got here, I wouldn't have believed you. I've lost my father, his brother, *his* son, and now Cecelia. I still can't believe that was her in that fire. I don't even know why she was in my house!"

"My goodness! Wasn't she there to see you?"

"No. I haven't talked to Cecelia since just after my father's funeral. And I haven't been able to reach her. I guess she never got the messages that I left for her. I still don't know why Paul Straiter broke into my house, and now *this!* No one can explain it!"

"Did anyone else have keys to your house?"

"I changed my locks, so no! Not even Kellen, when he got here. But, the police are sure. They have dental records, and Thomas and Andrew identified her body."

"How terrible. This is puzzling."

"To say the least." Accepting a tissue, she dabbed at her teary eyes.

"So, what do you plan to do, now?"

"Well, I was planning to stay for Kellen's trial. After that, I don't know. It's hard for me to walk away from this, and even harder for me to stay."

"Well, sometimes walking away is what you have to do, although I agree that this might not be one of those times."

"*Right.* I mean, I look at all of this and I've tried to connect these incidents, somehow. And then I realize that the only connection is *me!* Except, I have no idea how to stop it."

"Well, it might appear that way, but there has to be an explanation. These people aren't out here hurting themselves. What about Douglas? I understand he's Kellen's attorney, now. Does he have any ideas about this?"

"Just what he's being told by the police, and by Kellen. With the trial pending, he's been sworn to secrecy, so I can't rely on what he tells me. I have to find out for myself."

Vera nodded and LaRetha decided not to ask about Douglas and Paul's wife. Chances were, she wouldn't know.

"He won't even tell you the reason?"

"We believe that my inheritance is at the center of this."

"Well, it makes sense. There's been confusion about that farm ever since I was a child," Vera said. "I remember how people would always speculate on who would end up with it. I heard your father got it, fair and square, but that the family wasn't happy about it."

"You've heard right," she said. "*Watson* bought everybody out to help them with their financial problems. And now, with him gone, they want to pretend that never happened. It took him years to cover the loans for the money he paid them. And now, they expect me to just hand it over. If I had known this, I wouldn't have come here."

"But, this might have happened anyway, even if you didn't. Even, Cecelia..."

"But not in *my* house!" She exclaimed. "And not with me in the middle of it."

"I understand," Vera said. "So, where are you staying now?"

"I'm with... I mean, I'm staying..."

"I didn't mean to pry."

"No," she said, smiling. "I'm at Douglas' place for a few days. But keep that under your hat, won't you?"

"*Really?*" Vera asked, wide-eyed with disbelief.

"Yes, and stop looking at me that way. I'm *staying,* not living there. And I'm not sleeping with him."

"*Shoot,* I don't know if I could do it. That's too much temptation."

"Girl, watch what you're saying. I came over here to be *rightly* influenced." She laughed.

"I'm telling you, that man is *super fine,*" Vera exclaimed. "So how did that come about? I know he's your boyfriend's..." her voice faltered. "Maybe I have this all wrong. I'll think I'll fix some hot cocoa and wash down this foot in my mouth," she teased.

"You're fine. Kellen is my good friend, not my lover. Douglas is his attorney, and he's also become a good friend of mine. He's insisting that I stay there because it's safe. I know it looks bad, but that's all it is."

"*Uh huh,*" Vera said from the kitchen. "And now I understand why you turned down *my* invitation," she laughed.

"*Vera!* His offer came at the right time, I guess. Besides, I wouldn't put you in the middle of this. Until I know what or why this trouble really is, I want to involve as few people as possible."

"*Girl,*" Vera returned with two steaming cups, with small marshmallows floating atop. LaRetha was careful not to spill hers as Vera blew the dark liquid and took a sip. "These people don't want me *or* my land, they want yours."

"True," she said, feeling no way reassured. "And I needed a break from it. I had to get out of the house today to clear my head and figure some things out. I was hoping you could help me."

"Sure. What is it?"

"Well, for starters, it's Douglas. How well do you know him?"

"Well, we were schoolmates. We never dated, but he did go out with a few girls from school. He broke a lot of hearts before he left for college. I remember him being engaged once, but I didn't know her. As far as I know, he's never been married. And word is, he won't date local women. I hear it's because he had a bad experience with that cousin of yours."

"I think you mean my cousin's *friend*."

"Oh? Who is she?"

"*Samira Neely*. And she's sort of a hidden thorn in my side. They work together. And, it looks like every man I know, she's been with."

"Is she following you around or what?" She asked, sipping her cocoa.

"That's what my mother asked me," she said. "It sure feels that way. But, can I ask you something else? It's about my father and Cecelia. And about the farm. I was wondering what blanks you could fill in for me."

Vera looked into her cup then at her.

"LaRetha, I make a point to stay out of other people's business. And, I definitely don't want to say anything that's going to create more confusion. Or worse, cause you any unnecessary pain."

"I'm *asking*, Vera. It's important that I know, so tell me."

"Well, okay. All I've heard is that Cecelia was in cahoots with people who wanted that land. She tried for years to get her name on that deed, but your father wouldn't do it. So, when he died.... well you know how people assume things."

LaRetha nodded, sadly. Frowned.

"All of that was just *hearsay*. And that's all I know. But, she must have loved the man," she added. "I don't know many women who would come here with small children and live a life *that hard,* unless they were in love."

"Did they seem happy to you? My father and Cecelia?" LaRetha asked, wondering how it had appeared from the outside.

"*I* think she worshipped the man. Now, what that attorney of hers was able to get her to do, I don't know. It's said that they were pretty close."

"*What attorney?*"

"*Bob Billard*. Who else? The defender of every criminal from here to Chicago, and usually he's behind some very scandalous stuff. I heard that he was really courting Cecelia for awhile. It was said that she would visit his office and meet him places for lunch, sometimes. But, that could've been legitimate business. Besides, your father was sick when he died, wasn't he? Billard couldn't have done that."

LaRetha nodded, listening. Thinking. *Why did Gerald lie?*

"You know *haters,*" Vera continued, studying her disturbed expression. "Your father broke a few hearts in his day, too. And besides, she was a *white* woman married to an African American. That disturbed a lot of people back in the day."

"It's just so puzzling. Every time I think I'm getting to the bottom of this, it just goes that much deeper. Bob Billard wanted the land, too? No wonder my father didn't like him, or so my uncle said," LaRetha sighed.

"Sorry. I hate being the constant bearer of bad news."

"Your story's not the worst I've heard. But I know my father wasn't murdered. They might have planned to, but that didn't happen."

"This thing goes generations deep, doesn't it?" Vera said, finishing her cocoa.

"So I'm starting to realize. It was never about me. I'm just the one caught in the middle."

"That's right. It's been this way since forever," Vera said, reaching over to pat her hand, sympathetically. "But, that's why your being here is a good thing. You seem to want to get to the bottom of this. Usually, people look the other way in matters like this, to protect their own name and interests."

"It's not something I planned, believe me," LaRetha said, half jokingly.

"But you're asking questions, and that's a good thing. This mess has got to stop, and no one else in this town is willing or able to do anything about it."

LaRetha drank her cocoa and listened.

"People here in *Lovely* have lost a lot; their homes, businesses, their farms. They've been scared not to tell the truth, and threatened when they do."

LaRetha straightened, listening.

"I just think that we're all so beaten down, spiritually, sometimes we think that if we take it to church and pray over it, something *divine* will fall on us and just fix it. Now, don't get me wrong, I don't move unless I pray. But, some *work* has got to go into it too, right?"

"I mean, at times we might feel compelled to just stand still and wait on God. But if we're led to do something, or to *not* do something, then what good was the prayer if we're not obedient?" Vera continued. "And then we don't feel blessed."

"These people have been controlling this town, long enough," Vera continued, emphatically. "Making us believe that even collectively, we don't amount to much. But without us, what are *they*?"

"*Exactly!*" LaRetha responded.

"Thing is, all of our angry people are gone. There's a lot of talk, but no action. But, we're people who came out of slavery, *doggonit!* If our ancestors had stopped trying, we would still be enslaved, today. And we have far more resources to work with than they had."

"But, so does our enemy," LaRetha said. "That's why we need to exercise the advantages that our faith gives us. To realize our individual *and* collective power and stop hating those of us who do. We *do* matter."

"I totally agree," Vera said. Looking strangely keyed up.

LaRetha was finding this conversation refreshing. At least Vera was willing to discuss the matter. And apparently the woman had a lot to say.

"We're slaves to our employers, because we've lost our farms and few of us know anything else," the woman continued. "We're slaves to creditors who ask for too much collateral or charge us way too much interest on our loans, knowing it's just a matter of time before they shut us down."

Having heard about this from her father, LaRetha agreed.

"We haven't even begun to claim our spiritual inheritance. So, as the system goes, only a few of us prosper and the rest of us fall to ruin. And we're okay with that as long as it's not our week to fall. And then they call that *good business?*"

"You're right," LaRetha said. "There is always someone prospering from other people's losses. But, these aren't just *today* losses, they're generational. They start in our homes and extend to business, our churches and everyone in them."

"And since when did we start serving politicians in our churches?" Vera asked. "I can't tell you how tired I get of having them show up our at church for votes and support. Especially the ones who don't come any other time, and who don't respond to our concerns."

"Here, here," LaRetha agreed.

"I know I'm just one woman with a lot of opinions, LaRetha," Vera said. "I'm sometimes accused of being a bit *obsessed,"* she said, smiling. "But I believe every prayer goes a long way. We have to commit ourselves to this cause, just like your father and mine did, and Douglas' father. Now *they* were true leaders. Those men knew no fear. They trusted God and stood together until something was done."

"You're right," LaRetha said. "Even with so many advances in education and technology, our more educated men are less likely to fight because they feel they have too much to lose."

"Right," Vera agreed. "But even if they weren't the most educated men, they weren't ignorant. With nothing but faith and courage, they spoke the truth and they knew when to do it."

"Isn't *that* something?" She agreed.

"We need more people like that in *Lovely,"* Vera nodded. "People like them. People like you."

The woman stood and took their cups into the kitchen. Apparently she wanted her to mull that over. LaRetha could see where this was going.

"Well, I didn't come here to be a leader of any kind. That land is important to me, but so is my peace of mind."

"Yes, but you must know that with all that land and peace, comes a certain responsibility in this town. It's a given. *Like it or not.*"

"*Maybe.* But I'm not a leader or an advocate. I'm not my father."

"No. But, you're in a perfect position to bring change, if you wanted," Vera continued, not to be dissuaded. "You own your own land. You appear to be well off to me, so no one here can control your finances. They can't run you out of business, or have your employer fire you for some trumped up reason. They can't take your house because it's paid for, and not even your land. The only thing they *can* do is aggravate you until you want to sell. I admire you for not giving in to that."

She contemplated all this. And she thought she had troubles. How terrible for these people!

"Even better, you're a writer with outside resources – a newspaper. And that can bring attention to the problems that none of the local papers are willing to report. You can get the ball rolling."

LaRetha sighed, thinking about the story for Mac Henry. She might need to write that article, after all.

"Okay, let's say I take this big strong stance for the people, but they never support it. What then? What you have to understand is that I have a family to be concerned about. I'm losing them, one after the other, and it's *frightening.* I can't wake up tomorrow and find out that another relative has been killed, or *burned.*"

Vera grimaced and nodded. She understood.

"It's not time for this, yet," LaRetha said. "I have other things to resolve, first. But I'm hoping that Kellen's trial will bring closure for some of us. And I'll gladly help wherever I can. Right now, I wouldn't know where to start. And even if I did, I'm not sure that it's what *I'm* called to do."

"I think it is. But, you have to do what you're led to do, when you're led to do it. I understand that. But, I'm here if you need me and I'll be praying for your entire family. It is a sad thing, this is."

"Yes, it is. It's bad enough that I've had to shoot a man. I never thought I could do that."

"I know. Paul Straiter used to come to our mission, you know?"

LaRetha's startled eyes met Vera's.

"You had to defend yourself. He left you no choice. But, when you know someone *personally,* you have to wonder why they would do something that's so far out of character."

"He volunteered for us, a lot," Vera continued. "There was some misfortune with a business he owned, and he lost his family in a car accident, a long time ago. He didn't say much about it, but he was always helping people. I was shocked to hear that he'd broken in and attacked you."

"They said he was a wanderer," LaRetha said. "That he'd done this before. The man had a record."

Vera shook her head.

"I think someone put him up to breaking into your place. Possibly made him do it. It just wasn't like him, otherwise."

"Anything is possible," she mused. "But, when he kicked my door in and rushed at me, I was sure that he was going to kill me."

"And you did exactly what I would have done, if it were me."

LaRetha nodded, feeling a bit comforted.

"I just thought you should know that he wasn't what they said. He was simply a man struggling to get back on his feet. Unfortunately, there are always people willing to use that for their own benefit. *Poor man.*"

Poor man, indeed, she thought. This conversation was beginning to bother her.

"I guess you had to be there, Vera. I've never been so scared in my life. I didn't know who he was or what he wanted. He didn't say anything, but just charged at me. The man was determined," she said.

Frowning, Vera seemed suddenly aware of her offense. LaRetha waved it off. *No harm done.* Seeing the time, she stood and put on her coat.

"I have to get going. I need to get the car back to Douglas. Thank you, for the talk, Vera. You've helped me a lot."

"*Anytime,* girl," she said, giving her a sincere hug. "Don't hesitate to call me for *anything*. I'm always either here, at church, or at the mission. And if you like, you can join me and my family for dinner. We start at *three.*" She smiled.

"Thanks, you're kind to offer. But, I wouldn't interfere. I think I'll share dinner with my host, if he doesn't have other plans."

"I can't say I blame you," Vera said, with a wink. She laughed at her insistence that there was more to the story. *Was there?*

"But there is something else. Do you know of any homes for rent around here? I'm looking for a place,"

Vera contemplated for a moment. Then smiled.

"Come to think of it, I do. There's a really nice house at the end of this street that's for rent. The owner is out of town but his number is on the sign in the yard," she said, pointing her in the opposite direction from which she'd come. "I think he's ready to unload it, so he might even sell it to you."

"Thanks, Vera."

"Sure. But if you change you mind about staying over, by all means *call me*. I have plenty of room. And it wouldn't be an imposition, at all."

"Thanks for the nice offer. I'll definitely keep it in mind. Merry Christmas, again. And you can call me anytime, too."

She left Vera's feeling even more certain that there was a lot more work to be done.

Douglas was on the phone as soon as LaRetha left. The death count was up to *four*, now, not including what had been implied about *Watson*. And she could easily become number five, depending on what her ex-husband and the rest had planned for her.

Someone at the station answered. He asked for Nelson Dials. The man was usually one of the first on the scene of a crime, and the one most likely to close a case. Nearing retirement age and having no close family in town, he'd once mentioned that he often worked on holidays. Sure enough, his extension rang only once before he answered.

"What can you tell me about *Cecelia Watson's* case?" Douglas asked.

"Almost nothing," the detective said. "Except, somebody killed her before they burned her body in that house. Why? Have you heard anything different?"

It was probably no secret in town that LaRetha was staying with him, for the time being.

"*Nothing.* Miss Greer was as surprised as anyone that her stepmother was found inside her house when she was supposed to be in New Jersey. Does anybody know what brought her here?"

"Well, her sons came and left rather quickly, yesterday. They didn't know why she was here, either. She was supposed to meet them in New York, for the holidays. Apparently she had a change of plans. We're still trying to find out how she got out there from the airport. And why she didn't tell her family she was coming."

"Looks like Cecelia Watson might have known things that someone thought she shouldn't have."

Dials was aware of the previous murders, and was undoubtedly working hard on those cases, as well. You never knew who he was watching or when. Adept in his profession, he was one to be reckoned with. They held a mutual respect for one another.

"Tell me something, Davis. Now, you and I go way back. We ran around together, swam in the same muddy creeks. Even chased some of the same girls."

Douglas remembered.

"What do you really know about this *LaRetha Greer?* It's obvious that you have some close kind of relationship with the woman. But, do you really know why she came to this town? And why she insists on staying even after everything that's happened?"

"Dials, I'm telling you, man, LaRetha Greer is not the culprit, here. She suspects, like I do, that the people behind recent attempts to take her land are behind this murder and arson, as well. Obviously, they'll stop at nothing."

"Really? Well, I know that family has been feuding over it for years. But, what would make it worth four lives to have it?

"Aside from the obvious value of it, I wish I knew. But, I'm keeping her under close watch until her friend's trial is over. With so many people dying around her, I'm almost certain she could be targeted, next."

"*Yeah?* Well, sounds like a good idea, for a lot of reasons. Just keep your eyes open. I don't want to wake up in the morning and hear bad news about you."

"You won't."

"Good. Just be careful. And how's that gorgeous sister of yours? Does she ever ask about me? We dated in high school, you know?"

"I do and *no,* she doesn't. But, I'm calling her later. Should I tell her husband you asked?"

"Not at all." They shared a laugh.

"Take care and Merry Christmas, Dials."

"Merry Christmas, buddy."

Hanging up, Douglas thought about how easily the two of them talked without ever revealing much of anything. Tricks of their trades, he guessed.

The hall clock chimed. *2:15pm,* and she was still out. Well, he had a few things to do, as well. Getting his coat, he looked around, and sighed. In spite of her troubles, this could have been the personal time they needed to become closer. But the battle wasn't over yet, he vowed. Turning the lock, he closed the door tightly behind him, feeling hopeful.

LaRetha was concerned to find Douglas gone and the security alarm off when she got back, and so she began a careful look around the house. Once satisfied that she was alone, she relaxed.

It was Christmas Day, and she could almost picture Douglas and Candace as small children, getting out of bed early to look beneath the living room tree, remembering days when she and Germaine had done the same.

So, the man had made mistakes, she thought. Not the type she'd make, that sleeping with a married person, but he was clearly sorry about it and what right did she have to judge him? She had to remember that theirs was a *business* relationship, she thought, and to stay *out* of his personal business.

With Douglas gone, she figured this was a perfect time to explore in the kitchen and see what Mrs. Starks had left for today's dinner. She wasn't disappointed. She decided to set a table for them.

Finished now, she admired the table before deciding to change into something more festive. A pair of off-white pants went well with a soft brown sweater with tiny gold beating around the neckline and sleeves. And a new pair of brown heels.

After combing her hair down, she selected chandelier earrings and added only a little makeup. Then, the doorbell rang.

She wondered who it could be, before remembering her last surprise visitor. Looking out through a sheer curtain, she brightened instantly.

Exclaiming aloud, she could hardly get the door open in time because standing on the other side of the door, looking taller than before, and sheepishly handsome, was *Germaine.* And he wasn't alone. Her mother and Tori smiled from behind him, each of them carrying large gift bags.

"I don't believe it!" She exclaimed, opening the door. "All my prayers are answered, now!"

Reaching out to her grown up son, she saw the uncertainty on his face disappear, replaced by a broadening smile. She felt silly for tearing up as she embraced him, but too happy and relieved to care. He wiped at a tear on his cheek as well, hugging her back.

"*Well, I'm going inside,*" her mother said, with her usual after-travel irritation. "It's cold out here." They all followed.

"Mama, you remember Tori. She's my fiancée, now."

Turning to see the face of the pretty girl, partly hidden under a sporty cap and auburn curls, she opened her arms to Tori, as well.

"I remember. Hello, Tori." She gave the girl a friendly hug.

The girl spoke, smiling bashfully.

"I've been worried about you, son. Come inside. Both of you."

They did.

"Where have you been for so long?" She asked, punching him hard on the arm.

"*Owww.*" He said, laughing. "I guess that's better than a whipping."

"You've got one of those coming, too," she said, taking their coats and scarves and hanging them on a nearly hook on the wall. "Douglas isn't here, but he should be back soon." Or so she hoped, she thought.

She urged them into the living room. Germaine whistled. The ladies commented with approval.

"And I thought *I* had it going on," Laretta laughed.

"Wow! Is this man a lawyer, for real?" Germaine asked.

"He'd better be," she laughed.

"I know that's right. For my money, anyway," Laretta agreed.

Germaine and Tori put their gift bags near the living room tree.

"I brought everything you left at my house," her mother said. "I figured we could open them here."

She thanked her mother, and showed her where to leave the gifts, before helping them get comfortable in the den.

"Now, Germaine. You really have some explaining to do. *Why haven't I heard from you?* I worried, so much.."

He shook his head.

"Sorry, Mama. But, Daddy said you were engaged, so I figured…" His voice faltered. "He said your religion wouldn't allow you to have anything to do with me and Tori if we weren't married. I knew you were mad and everything…"

"What? All of that is pure nonsense! I was only disappointed, son. There's a big difference."

"Well, he said it was true, and well… I guess I shouldn't have believed him. Forgive me?"

LaRetha gave him a look of utter disbelief, then hugged him.

"I'm your *mother*, Germaine, and you know me better than that. I am not engaged, and won't be, any time soon. And even if I were, why would I exclude you?"

"Oh." He said. She decided to discuss this with him, later.

"That man's got nerve. And he blames *me* for the divorce."

"Well, LaRetha, you know better than any of us how convincing that husband of yours can be," her mother mused, and she grimaced. "He had the boy acting like he was *motherless*."

"*Ex*-husband," she corrected. "I don't know what he's told you, but I've missed you, son." She went over to give him another hug. "And I'm glad you're here. And don't *ever* do that again."

"I know it!" Tori said. "He's been moping around for the longest. Wanting to call and *scared* to call. I couldn't take it, anymore."

"Me, either," he said and LaRetha smiled.

"So, you know all about Kellen?" She asked.

"Yeah. And I'm sorry about your house. And *Grandma CeCe,*" he said, his eyes tearing.

She gave him a consoling hug, having forgotten that he used to call Cecelia that, sometimes. His memories of her were fond ones. He would miss her.

"Mr. Greer asked Germaine to come to *Lovely* with him," the girl said, interrupting her thoughts. And LaRetha looked at her son, wide-eyed, considering the terrible possibilities.

"I told him about your message," Tori continued. "I didn't think it was a good idea," she said, ignoring the hard look he was giving her.

LaRetha looked at this girl again, but with different eyes. She might be a good influence on him, after all.

"Did he say why he was coming here? Does he know that you're here?" She asked him.

"I don't know why. And we hadn't planned to come yet, so he doesn't even know I'm here."

She breathed a sigh, of relief.

"Well, you're all here, safe and sound, now. So, just make yourselves comfortable while I finish up in the kitchen. I'll call Douglas to see how long he'll be."

Germaine and Tori talked quietly in the den. Laretta followed her into the kitchen.

"So, you're cooking for him, now?" She asked, gnawing on celery.

"No. His housekeeper did this. I haven't lifted a finger since I've been here. He won't let me."

"Girl, you'd better marry him, *fast.*"

LaRetha grimaced.

"Who says? I like being single. Just like you, I don't have to take care of anybody but myself, for a change. Besides, I resent the insinuation that *I* can't be a whole person without a man around. I don't need anybody taking care of me. Not even *Douglas!*"

"I know you, LaRetha. You used to *love* being married. Although why, is beyond me."

"And I *love* being single. I don't need a man to complete me."

"But, what if he just *does?*" Her mother asked, mischievously.

She shrugged. She had other things to think about. Like why Gerald was coming to *Lovely,* and what to expect once he got there.

"So, what's happening with Kellen's case?" Her mother asked, helping her set new places in the formal dining room.

"Well, it comes up in a few weeks and I don't know how prepared Douglas is. I think my being here is a big distraction for him…"

"I'll just bet," Laretta murmured, cutting a small piece of turkey and eating it.

"I haven't mentioned it to him, yet. But, I'm thinking about renting a house in town until this is over. I can't have people thinking I'm influencing him by *sleeping* with him. It would hurt Kellen's case."

"Well, it might not look good, but you do have to think safety, first."

"I am. I'll be safe in town."

"Douglas is going to hit the ceiling." Her mother said, chewing still.

"That's another problem. He thinks he can concentrate on this case and protect me, at the same time. He wouldn't even take me to get my car, today. I think he's over reacting."

"Well, I wouldn't make *that* assumption," her mother said. "But, I can assure you that Douglas has been an attorney long enough to know what's required to win a case. Besides, like I told you before, he's going to get Kellen released, just to get him out of his way with you. "

"I just don't want to mislead or disappoint him," she said, ignoring her mother's last comment. "I'm keeping my distance, as best I can. But he's not making it easy."

"And you?"

"What about me?"

"You know who you're talking to, right? As your mother, I would say that you seem to be falling for him too, with this setting of the table, and waiting dinner for him. Am I right?"

LaRetha gave her mother an impatient look, then smiled.

"I hate to admit it, and if you repeat it, I'll deny I ever said it. But I think so," she admitted. "And this is the first time I've said so. When I think about it, the man has *everything,* almost."

"*Almost?*"

She finished setting extra plates.

"Well, I give him credit for one thing," Laretta said. "He's determined if nothing else, which would make him an excellent attorney. You're lucky that he's on your side."

"I know I am."

She filled a tray with glasses of iced tea. Laretta grabbed two of them and led the way into the den. Germaine was poking at the dwindling fire, chatting about their ride up.

"Germaine did most of the driving," Tori said, proudly. "He drives much better than me."

LaRetha smiled, slowly shaking her head at her son, who beamed, proudly. Her mother gave her a long dry look of amusement, before reaching for a magazine on a nearby rack.

"*Good Housekeeping?*" She queried. LaRetha laughed.

"I think it came from his office. His assistant must have ordered them," she defended.

"Whatever turns him on," Laretta shrugged, flipping the pages.

They laughed at this. As they caught up with old news and current, LaRetha felt her cares fading. She had her entire family here, and she couldn't have asked for a better Christmas present.

Douglas thought about staying away and letting her have the house to herself for a time, then decided against it. He should be there with her. They shouldn't take any unnecessary risks.

He saw the champagne colored jeep with a Georgia tag, parked in his driveway. Fearing the worst, he hurried toward the house, just as LaRetha threw the door open and waited on the porch.

"Is something wrong?" He asked, searching her face for a sign of trouble. But, as he got closer, he realized that she was smiling.

"What is it?" He asked, anxiously.

"My son is here, Douglas. My son and his fiancé, and Laretta are here. Come on, inside. I want to introduce you."

"I guess I will," he said, thinking how he'd only been gone a short time, and already his house was being invaded.   But his concerns for his house were quickly dispelled once he saw them all sitting in the den and smiling at him.

"Good evening. How's everybody doing?" He asked.

"*Just fine. Okay. Hello.*" Everyone responded.

"How's everything going, Douglas?" Laretta asked.

"Very well. The trial is coming up. And Kellen is surviving alright. I'm sorry about LaRetha's stepmother, though. Very sorry," he said, noticing how Germaine's smile fell as he remembered.

"So am I. That was a terrible ordeal, wasn't it?"

"Yes. But police are investigating. They'll find something, I'm sure."

"Then, we can eulogize her, soon. Once they release her remains," LaRetha said, sadly.

Douglas noticed everyone's dampened spirits.

"But, hey!" LaRetha exclaimed. "This is a holiday and we're all here, together. It's okay to enjoy the day, you know? We can all be sad, later."

Douglas smiled, appreciating her effort to cheer them all up when she'd been so upset before. It seemed to work, because Laretta was on her feet, instantly.

"That's right. Besides, I haven't eaten since *six o'clock* this morning, so forgive me while I give in to all the delectable temptations in the next room. Won't you all join me?" She asked, already halfway gone.

Germaine and Tori followed. LaRetha held back until they were all out of earshot.

"Douglas," she said. "I hope you don't mind my setting the table for *five*. I had already set places for the two of us when they came and…"

"LaRetha, you don't even have to ask. My home is your home. And I'm as glad to see them as you are. *Almost,*" he added, as she beamed.

She looked radiant. So happy, in comparison to last night and earlier, today. His heart went out to her, and he hoped she had an inkling of how he felt about her.

Dinner was excellent. Mrs. Starks had bought a huge fried turkey and baked a hen, with several vegetable dishes, and a delicious dressing and giblet gravy. They also had buttered yeast rolls and sweet corn muffins, and their choice of tea, lemonade or soda. Germaine and Tori chose lemonade, and the rest of them, sweet tea.

After saying grace, they all dove in, exclaiming over how great everything was, with LaRetha, Laretta and Germaine debating over who could cook best; Marilee or Mrs. Starks. They declared it a tie.

"Just give my compliments to the chef," Germaine stated, rubbing his stomach. Tori agreed, laughing. He thought they looked vibrantly happy, together.

"Well," Douglas said, looking into several covered dishes on his counter. "If anyone wants dessert, there's strawberry cake, chocolate mousse, pound cake *and* homemade chocolate chip cookies. It looks like my housekeeper was expecting you, after all," he said, smiling at Germaine who, aside from Laretta, was the only one interested at the moment.

"I'll clear the table," the girl said. "Germaine can help me."

"Well, it's good that you told him now," Laretta laughed. "After dessert would've been too late,"

"Oh, he can eat like that and it doesn't even bother him. I have to watch my weight, though." She looked suddenly embarrassed at her near revelation of their close living situation. LaRetha frowned and Douglas withheld a smile.

"You and me both," LaRetha finally said, and the girl smiled. "But, I won't even count these calories. Besides," she whispered, "we can always exercise, tomorrow."

Her mother laughed first, then Douglas. LaRetha playfully swiped at his head with a cloth napkin. Pushing back from the table, he left the young couple fussing over how to load the dishwasher.

"Don't go too far. We're opening presents in a minute! We have something for you." Laretta said to him.

Douglas went into the den and listened fondly to all the chatter in the next room. This was so much better than dinner with a woman he barely knew or a half-cooked unseasoned meal with some temporary lover. Looking upward, he said a silent *thank you*. For his home, his life, and especially for his lovely LaRetha.

After clean up, Douglas went with them into the living room. LaRetha insisted that they follow tradition, and each give a thoughtful remark on how blessed they were, and why, before exchanging gifts. Despite their encouragement, he declined to participate in that one. Then, they exchanged gifts. And he enjoyed observing them.

Tori was delighted over a sweater and matching tote bag from the two women. Germaine was happy about the CD's and clothing, which accounted for the larger boxes. His grandmother gave him a sweater and cologne set, and seemed enthralled at the outfit she gave her. Tori also gave her a gold embossed photo album.

Germaine gave his mother two boxes containing a beautiful gold necklace and matching earrings, which she put on right away, placing her own inside the boxes. She made a big deal of unwrapping a larger box and was pleasantly surprised to find six crystal goblets, inside.

"How nice. Who really selected these?" She whispered to Germaine, slightly taken aback.

"I did," he said. "You can use them in your next house," he said, quietly.

Glancing at him, she smiled, before leaving the room and returning with the crystal vase that he had given her, earlier. They were a matched set. Everyone exclaimed over the coincidence, as did he. Of course, Laretta saw it as a sign of some sort.

She thanked her mother for a designer purse and two matching pairs of shoes. Then, Laretta passed him a box, surprising him. And he handed her one, in return. He had tried to be prepared for anything.

His gift from Laretta was a very nice crystal paperweight and pen set. Hers was a nice sterling silver picture frame. She said she liked it.

Lastly, he opened LaRetha's gifts, thanking her with a hug. He pretended to hide the designer tie and cologne from Germaine. Overall, everyone was pleased. Although for him, just seeing them all so happy together was enough.

As mother and daughter talked in the kitchen, Douglas sat reading in the den while Germaine quietly watched television, checking him out, from time to time, he noticed. After a while, he put down his newspaper.

"So, you're the man who's been looking after my mother?" Germaine asked, seriously.

"I guess... I... ah, yes, I suppose so." It seemed odd that her son would think she needed *looking after.*

"My father told me that. How is she really doing?"

"Let's talk in the living room," he suggested, concerned that the others were coming their way and might overhear. Germaine followed.

"I'll be right back," he said, before going into the kitchen and taking LaRetha aside. He didn't miss Laretta's raised brow.

"Your son wants to have a talk with me. How do you feel about that?"

"It's alright with me." She nodded.

"That's fine. I wanted to be sure. I didn't know how much he knew, already."

"Tell him whatever he needs to know. Just avoid the details, would you? I can talk with him, later."

"Sure thing." He turned to leave the kitchen.

"Douglas?"

He turned around.

"Thanks."

He smiled as he walked away, feeling he might have a part to play in this family, after all.

"You got a nice *crib,* man. I like it."

"Yeah? Thanks." He poured himself a drink. "I don't suppose you drink."

"Not around my mother," he said seriously, and Douglas laughed.

"Well, *my* mother's not here," he said, kidding and feeling sad.

Sitting down across from the young man, he could appreciate his stylish dreads, nice sweater and designer jeans. Germaine was young, but still a man. He would treat him as such.

"So, do you think Mama's out of danger, now?"

"I'm still concerned about your mother. What do you know about what's been happening, here?"

"Just what my grandmother told me last night. I can't believe Dad didn't tell me about all this." The boy looked angry, then relaxed. "But, I guess he's got his own problems. So, what's got you worried?" He asked.

"Well, what I'm about to say might not be too flattering where your father's concerned. Do you want me to go on?"

"If he won't tell me, then you have to, don't you? He can't get mad about that. He can't get mad about anything."

Douglas nodded, feeling comfortable enough to proceed. He told Germaine about the events leading to this day; from her home invasion to the shooting, and then the fire that had destroyed her home and that had possibly taken his grandmother's life.

Unfortunately, he said, it was Germaine's father who concerned him the most, right now. The boy nodded, looking ashamed and painfully disappointed.

Douglas learned that Germaine had talked to his father the day before about coming with him to *Lovely*. Luckily, he had declined the offer to tag along. It angered him, however, that Gerald Greer would say the things about LaRetha that he had.

"I don't know your father, Germaine. But, I know your mother fairly well, and it's too bad that he would portray her in such a bad light. I'm sure you can tell that she loved seeing you here. I haven't seen her smile this much, the entire time I've known her."

He grinned and Douglas could see how much he looked like his mother.

"And I love my mother. But, what is her relationship with you?"

"I'm just a good friend who would one day love to be much more. But, at her wishes, this is where it stands for right now."

They were quiet for a minute. He finished his drink and decided he'd had enough. He rinsed his glass and placed it behind the bar.

"Do you *love* my mother?"

"*What?*" He asked, absently.

"I think you heard me," the boy said, then tried to smile. "My grandmother thinks that you might." He was serious again.

"If I did, would that be a problem for you?"

"What about Kellen?"

"That's her decision. Whatever she decides, I'll accept. I'm going to represent Kellen Kincaid to the best of my ability. But, I've been honest with LaRetha from the start. I can't help but hope that she chooses me."

The boy was quiet for a moment. Then, looking him directly in the eyes, he nodded. And Douglas sensed that was all the approval that he needed.

17

LaRetha was finally going to sell. Gerald could hardly believe it. Jasmine had called with the news and he'd told her he was driving in, right away. She would have someone to meet him, she'd said. He could follow them to her location and they were supposed to settle up, this afternoon. Gerald made the necessary call. Afterward, he breathed easier.

"Oh, and by the way," Jasmine had said. "Samira is here. She says she can't wait to see you."

LaRetha had finally come to her senses! That fire must have been the last straw for her, and she wasn't wasting any more time. And now, the group was crediting him for helping push her toward the decision. They wanted to compensate him, now. Yeah, *right!*

He arrived in *Lovely* and at the designated place a half hour early. With the sun going down and the tall brush blocking the view from the main road, this spot would do just fine. He dialed Jasmine and left a message on her voice mail. Then, he waited.

Sitting in the solitude of his car, he thought about how cold and quiet it was out here, beneath this overcast sky. And how different tomorrow would be, if all went well. He would collect that finder's fee, he'd been told. He'd said that it was about time for her to come to her senses.

Checking his watch, he couldn't belief only a half hour had passed. Still, he was getting antsy.

Where were they? He was ready to get this over with. Besides, Jasmine said that Samira wanted to see him. Likewise, he thought.

She was his kind of people – daring, exciting and uninhibited. And someone he could hang with, were circumstances different.

But, he'd made a decision. Kellen Kincaid was right. He *was* a fool! But even a fool could change. He would see this through, for LaRetha and for Germaine. And hopefully it would improve his life, as well.

Keep it quick and simple. Still, despite assurances that he'd be safe out here alone, he had come prepared for the worst. It was early still, but the dark sky made it appear much later than it was. This made him uneasy.

He reached overhead and removed the light cover. Unscrewing the small bulb, he placed it in the glove compartment. Replacing the dome, he thought about his real protection, and felt for it on the side of his seat. His street sense told him that he shouldn't take any chances with these country folks. And he always trusted that.

They killed their own, for goodness sakes! He rubbed his thumb across the gun he'd brought along. It was fully loaded. *Just in case!*

Headlights were approaching from behind him, now. The driver pulled just ahead of him, parking about two hundred feet away. It had to be Jasmine's man, he thought.

Finally! These people were as slow as *molasses!*

Parked on the opposite side of the road from him, the driver got out and slammed his door closed. Gerald didn't close his all the way, but stood next to his car, waiting for instructions.

Gerald waited as the man approached, dressed tightly in a thick coat, wearing heavy black boots and carrying a large flashlight. The bib on his cap was pulled low on his face.

"*Are you Greer? Gerald Greer?*" His voice was hard and gruff.

"Yes. That's me."

"Well, they're waiting for you."

The stranger walked a bit closer and stopped about fifty feet away. Gerald still couldn't see his face. But, like him, the man seemed anxious to get this show on the road. He thought about Samira, again.

"I'll just follow you." He turned to get back into his car.

"Don't worry about it," the man said.

"*Huh?*" Gerald looked back just as a shot was fired, hitting him in his left arm. Another rang out and missed. Still, he doubled over, intentionally falling to the ground. The man was running toward him now. Using his boots to kick against the icy ground, he easily slid underneath the car, then out on the other side.

Holding his arm tightly, he managed to dig his heels into the ice and push with enough force to pull himself up, using the side mirror. Opening the passenger door, he dove inside, reaching his gun just as the shooter came to that side of the car. He would have to do something, and *fast*.

It was dark now, and very quiet. But he could feel the man's presence nearby. *Patience,* he told himself. With the gun poised and ready to shoot, he waited.

Suddenly, the shooter was standing right over him. Gerald fired.

One shot. The man slumped. Gerald slid out across leather seats. The man raised his arm and Gerald fired another shot, then another.

Down he went with a heavy thud. Pushing him away from the door, Gerald slammed it shut and slid back beneath the steering wheel. Starting the engine, he quickly backed away and made a quick U-turn, heading out of the brush the same way he'd come in, only much faster this time. He was able to make out the writing on the side of the tow truck as he sped past.

Hogan's Garage.

He had been set up, he thought. And all arrows pointed at *Jasmine.*

Germaine made the announcement that he wanted to visit Kellen. LaRetha was skeptical and Douglas was dead set against it.

"But, I have questions I need to ask," Germaine persisted. "I think he owes me an explanation. Don't you?" He asked his mother.

LaRetha spoke to Douglas about it, privately.

"It could be good for him," he said. "Give him the closure he needs." Still she wasn't sure

"Now, you know better than I do, what's going on, Douglas," she replied. "Now, I'm not trying to put my son in danger, so considering what you already know, what do you really think?"

"Kellen can't hurt him in there. Not physically, anyway. But stay close to him. I don't want Kellen influencing him to help him, in any way."

She nodded.

"As a matter of fact, I'll drive you. Then, if you need me, I'll be right around the corner. Visiting hours end in two hours. We would have to leave now."

"Okay, Germaine," she said to her son, who was waiting in the den for her answer. "We'll go. But I have to be there every minute. And remember, you can ask questions, but you may not like the answers you get. He's in jail for *murder.* I wouldn't expect him to be too sociable."

He nodded, contemplated this.

"I still don't think it's a good idea, *but...*"

"But Mama," he said. "This might be my last chance to talk to him and to get the truth. I'd rather hear that from him."

She sighed. She knew how he felt about Kellen. How close they'd always been. She had even shared the sentiments, once. Either way, he was entitled to an explanation.

"Okay, let's get Mama and Tori settled in. We've got two hours."

Satisfied, he and Douglas proceeded to carry the luggage upstairs, with Douglas showing each guest to their bedroom. He rejoined LaRetha downstairs. They waited for Germaine.

"So, how was your afternoon?" He asked, looking worried.

"Fine. Thanks for loaning me the car," she replied. "Right now, I'm just wondering if this is the right thing to do. But, if I don't let him go, and Kellen is convicted, I think he might hold it against me from now on. He deserves answers, doesn't he?"

"I suppose he does. We all do," Douglas said.

The ride was quick and peppered with only short conversation. Germaine was starting college in spring, he said, majoring in graphics design. He was working full-time in the mailroom of a catalog company near the downtown campus. They would allow him to work part-time when school started. She was elated.

"Sounds like a great start to me," Douglas said. "My first job was in a hardware store."

"*Really?*" Germaine asked, and she could tell he really admired Douglas. "Well, I plan to be like you man; rich and successful, successful and *rich*." LaRetha scowled at him and he laughed. "It's true."

"Of course, as long as it's *legit,*" she teased. "But seriously, money isn't everything. Live right and it'll come to you, because if you don't you'll never keep any of it. Remember that. My father told me that." Germaine knew all of her concerns about not getting caught up in the wrong activities for temporary gain.

"I guess my dad proved that," he said, glumly.

"Well, I'm disappointed in Gerald, too. I don't know how he's mixed up in this mess, but remember, whatever mistakes he's made, they're *his* mistakes, not yours. You can do something entirely different with your life," she said, with some exasperation.

"I know. But I still can't believe what he did to you. And Marilee! He's an *outlaw!*" He was clearly upset.

"I know. Thankfully, no one was hurt. I guess that wasn't in the plan."

Ignoring Douglas' raised eyebrow, she looked out of the window, instead. Her efforts to keep her son connected to his father were making her look pretty crazy right now, she guessed.

"You don't have to cover for him, Mama," her son said, reproachfully. "He's blaming you for the divorce and everything," he said, surprising her. She'd thought that he blamed her, too.

"I don't doubt it. I don't know what's happened to him, but he's in deep trouble so keep your distance. For awhile, anyway. I don't want you being drug into the middle of this."

He nodded sadly. She wished she could ease his disappointment.

They finally reached the jail. Douglas waited in the lobby, as promised. She and Germaine followed an officer into the visiting area. They had a half hour, they were told.

They only had to wait a few minutes before Kellen emerged. His surprised expression upon seeing her quickly changed to embarrassment when he saw Germaine. He picked up the phone, as did Germaine. She sat close to him so that she could hear.

"*What's up?*" Kellen asked, putting on a bold face. Touching the glass with a fist that Germaine met against the glass with his.

"So, how's everything?" Kellen asked.

"*I'm good,*" Germaine said, sadly. "How are *you* doing?"

"I'm surviving, what can I say?" Kellen, though smiling, was unsettled. He was ashamed.

"I hear from Kadero a lot," Germaine said. "I told him you had trouble, out here. He said he's coming as soon as he can."

"Thanks for looking out, man," Kellen said, his smile dropping only a little. "So, I guess you're visiting for the holidays?"

"Yeah, I came to see my mom. You were right. She never said all that stuff my dad told me. I'm glad I came."

"I'm glad, too," she said, causing them both to smile.

"So, is it just you? You came alone?" Kellen was prolonging the idle talk. She sensed his uneasiness at what would inevitably come.

"Grandma and Tori came. They're still at Douglas' house."

Kellen's questioning eyes met her unapologetic ones. He looked back at Germaine. Nodded.

"My mom wasn't sure I should come here, but I wanted to ask you for myself. *What happened,* man? How did you end up in jail?"

Germaine's directness seemed to throw Kellen a bit, his eyes squinting at his young friend, then at her.

"Stuff happens, *G,*" he shrugged. "I'll tell you all about it when I get out of here. Hopefully that'll be soon."

"I guess things change, huh?" Germaine asked, sounding almost unforgiving. She frowned.

"I guess so," Kellen said less friendly this time, as well.

"You even look different," Germaine's disappointment was evident. "They say you shot my mama's cousin. What did he do to you?"

"*Germaine!*" She exclaimed. But her son sat expressionless as he leaned forward in his chair, staring right into Kellen's eyes.

"Why did you do it? Did somebody pay you to do it? And to come out here? Because if they did, it looks like *you're* the one who got shafted."

"Germaine," she touched his arm. "Stop it. That's not helping," she whispered.

"It's helping *me*," he responded, before looking back at an angry looking Kellen. "You were my best friends, you and Kadero. And my mother trusted you. What *happened*, man?"

"Did Douglas put you two up to this?" Kellen was looking at them both, suspiciously. "Why are you coming at me like this?"

She shook her head. Germaine waited for his answer. Kellen looked away, then back at her son.

"Well, Germaine. We don't all have the luxury of running away and showing up a year later like nothing happened. You're the last one to be pointing fingers, man. I was there for your mother when you and Gerald should've been. See, if you'd been the son she thought you were, I wouldn't have had to come. None of this would've happened."

LaRetha was shocked! She took the phone from Germaine.

"Don't *even* blame my son for what you've done, Kellen," she said, heatedly. "He didn't put that gun in your hand. Take responsibility for your own actions, for once." She handed the phone back to her son. "Germaine, we should go."

"Mama, I want to talk to Kellen, alone," Germaine said.

"That's out of the question. We told you that."

Kellen pointed at her.

"Am I wrong for caring about you, LaRetha? Why are you two punishing me? Why won't you just try and support me...?"

"We're *here*, Kellen. What else can we do? You haven't made it easy to help you."

"I tried to protect your mother, Germaine. I never would've hurt her, and you know that." He looked desperate to be understood.

"I want to believe that, man. But, Dad said..."

"I hate to be the one to break it to you, but *he's* the dangerous one, not me."

"Germaine, let's just finish this and go," she intervened.

"So, you're saying you were trying to protect my mother and you ended up shooting somebody?" Germaine persisted. "You were just trying to protect her, and that's all?" Germaine asked, much to Kellen's apparent chagrin.

"Something like that," he snarled.

"I would thank you man, but I don't believe you. You've been lying to her this whole time."

"Oh, did your father tell you that, too? Did he tell you he wanted me to help him steal from her, but I refused?"

Germaine sharply inhaled and LaRetha looked at him with utter surprise.

"He did that. But I would never hurt your mother, Germaine. You know that."

"Well then, what's in it for you?"

Kellen said nothing.

"Why won't you answer me, then?"

"Germaine, just leave it alone," Kellen finally exclaimed with irritation. "You don't know what you're talking about. You don't know anything."

Germaine had stood up. He was just as angry, now.

"For what you tried to do to my mom, I hope you get everything that you deserve."

"You don't have any idea what you're talking about. You need to talk to your *dad*. Find out how in the heck he knows so much."

"Why? You're both the same. You're both *liars*. That much I know. If you ever get out of here, you'd better stay away from my mom, or you'll have me to answer to."

"Are you *threatening* me?" Kellen asked, giving a pretentious laugh. "Well, check you out."

"Let's *go*, Germaine," she urged, standing up. He did, too.

"No threats. Just a *promise*."

"Or, what?"

LaRetha took the phone.

"I expected better from you," she said, calmly. "Germaine has a right to be upset. You gave him the reason."

He shook his head, apologetically.

"That wasn't my intention. But, the truth is the truth, LaRetha."

"Well, whatever happens at your trial," she said, "just remember that you put yourself behind these bars." Angrily, she hang up the phone.

Kellen looked as if he wanted to say he was sorry but she didn't wait for it. Following Germaine to the door, she looked back. Kellen was watching them leave with sadness in his eyes. She could see his regret. Could almost feel him wishing he could change things. But, it was far too late.

Her son was right. Kellen and Gerald were one in the same; willing to do anything for self gain. And now she knew why her ex-husband was involved. They had both planned to deceive her. Together. This made it a lot harder to be in Kellen's corner.

Germaine was quiet all the way home. Probably feeling as confused as she, as to why this had to happen, she figured. But, he'd seen it for himself, now. Maybe he could put it behind him and begin healing from the pain his father had caused, and from the terrible loss of a very good friend.

None of them said much on the way back. Germaine retreated into the bedroom as soon as they got back to Douglas' house, and Douglas went into the living room. To get a drink, she imagined.

Deciding to talk to him about Gerald in the morning, she said goodnight and retired, as well. She had just showered and put on her gown when her mother tapped on the door

"Come in," she said.

She was sitting on the bed wearing a favorite midnight blue silk gown and matching robe. Her mother smiled upon seeing her and sat down on the bed across from her.

"Now *that's* what you should wear if you want this man."

"Not that, again? I'm still trying to be rid of the other two men in my life."

"Well, Douglas seems happy to have you here. He looks kind of lonely, to me. Who spends Christmas by themselves?"

"Lots of people, I'm sure. Besides, there had to be somebody that he could have spent the day with. He's just being hospitable," LaRetha said.

"And that says a lot. You two seem comfortable, together."

"Douglas is alright. He just drinks a lot."

"Really? I didn't know that. Besides, bad habits can be broken. Just give the man a reason to do it."

Laretta was right, she thought. Except for today, Douglas did seem a little lonely.

Laretta stretched out on one side of the bed, looking comfortable and relaxed in beige lounging pants and matching top, and ready to further annoy her about her love life.

"In spite of everything, you look happy. He's good for you."

"My divorce was good for me. *He* has nothing to do with it."

"*Humph!* You know, it was your son's suggestion that we come here, today,"

LaRetha smiled. Combing her damp hair into a ball on top of her head, she pinned it into place.

"I believe it! You should have seen him with Kellen, tonight. He raked him over the coals!"

"Yes, he can be a bit like me when he wants to be," her mother said, proudly. "Have you heard anything from Gerald?"

"Nothing yet. And it scares me that he could just run up on us, at any time. But Douglas knows he's coming, so I'm not too worried."

"Isn't it nice to feel protected?" Her mother smiled.

"I'm not sure that I am. Until Gerald's caught up with, none of us are. Kellen claims he tried to pay him to help take the farm from me."

"You're kidding! Just how well do they know one another?"

"I don't even know. But, I'm really not all that surprised at Gerald. I guess he thought Kellen would cave in like he must have."

"Poor dear!"

"Now, do you see why I'm in no hurry to marry, again? Who can you trust, these days? "

"Very few. I'm surprised that Germaine wanted to see Kellen, though."

"They were friends and he needed closure. Otherwise, I never would have allowed it. But, my child is strong. And he's sensible. I didn't want him to feel responsible for any of this."

"Good thinking," Laretta said as LaRetha rubbed a makeup removing cream onto her face with a tissue and wiped it off.

"Speaking of *trust...* " she said. "When a man like Douglas lives alone and seems content with it, you have to wonder about him. Do you think he could be *gay?*"

LaRetha stopped to stare at her.

"You know, a lot of these prosperous men have *secrets,*" Laretta added, looking questioningly around the lavishly furnished bedroom and back at her.

"No, I don't believe he's *gay,* Mama," she said, shaking her head with disbelief. "Happily single, *yes*. But not gay. But I'll be sure to ask him."

"I know I would," her mother said, shrugging.

"I hear he doesn't date the local women. Maybe he's just being really discreet. Not that there's anybody left, anyway."

Laretta's made a wide-eyed comical expression.

"Supposedly, he had his heart broken," LaRetha continued. "If that's the case, I don't blame him. People around here know far too much about one another, as it is."

"So, I guess they're going crazy right now, trying to figure you and him out."

"That's why I'm moving out. I told you about the mission? Well, Vera, the director? She told me about a house on her street that's for rent. I drove by it, today. It's a really nice two story with a good sized yard and two-car garage. There's one fireplace and a large deck in back. And a shed. The backyard is fenced in, too."

"I know you're kidding!"

"Oh, Mama. I'm tired and sleepy, and we can talk about it, tomorrow. Okay?" She wasn't going to argue an unnecessary point. It was her decision, after all.

"We sure will." Laretta walked to the door. "Sleep tight. I'll wake you for breakfast."

I doubt that! She thought, as her mother closed the door.

LaRetha turned out the lights before saying her prayers. She gave thanks for her family's safe delivery. Then, for protection, strength and direction in all areas of her life, and in the lives of her family and friends. Then, for a favorable and just resolution to Kellen's case. Lastly, she asked forgiveness of her sins, and gave thanks for all of her many blessings.

Sliding down between the cozy, cool cotton sheets, she smiled with satisfaction. Despite her concerns about Gerald, *today was a good day*. And a holiday well spent with all the people she loved.

It was very late on Christmas night. Certain that everyone was asleep, Douglas walked quietly from his room to hers. He hoped she was there, alone. *How embarrassing if Laretta were to answer, instead.*

She answered on the second knock, looking tousled and confused.

"Is something wrong, Douglas?"

He could only stare at her for a moment, being quite taken aback by her beauty, while immersed in those dark dreamy eyes that appeared a bit unfocused, as he had obviously roused her from a deep sleep.

Douglas saw the way her soft blue gown molded to her curvaceous figure underneath a partially fastened robe. She looked beautiful and womanly and timeless. And he longed for her.

She belongs in this house, he thought, forgetting for a minute that she was watching him, as well.

"I just wanted to talk to you for a minute, LaRetha." His voice sounded as unaffected by her appearance as he had hoped.

She slowly held up a finger and the door closed, then reopened a few moments later.

"Come on in. Sit down. I'll just be a minute."

He sat in a comfortable cushioned chair near the window. Crossing one long muscular leg comfortably over his knee, he waited. Looking around, he took in the sloppily made bed and the stack of neatly folded clothing that lay atop a suitcase in the corner.

The aroma of various bath oils and perfume still hang in the air. And he was intrigued by the various toiletries, all neatly lined across the mirrored dresser. It all seemed so fitting for her.

Water was running in the sink on the other side of the bathroom door, now. There was splashing, as she washed her face.

Was she brushing her teeth? Finally, the door opened and she emerged, looking even more beautiful to him than before.

"Sorry, but I had to wake up, first. What is this about?"

She tied her robe tightly around her and sat at the edge of the bed as he began.

"I wanted to ask you about your visit with Kincaid, today. How did that go?"

She gave him the details. He nodded when she finished.

"So, now you know the truth. That Gerald wasn't trying to protect you from anything. And you probably know Kincaid's reason for being here, as well." He couldn't say anything more than that.

"Nothing surprises me about him, anymore," she said, sadly. "I'm just glad Germaine had a chance to glimpse what's been going on, these past weeks. Now, I won't worry as much," she said.

"Well, I think it was a generous thing that you did for your son, today. Or should I say, *yesterday,*" he said, looking at the clock. *12:55.*

"I know it wasn't easy for you," he continued. "But you allowed him to see the truth. Now, he can sort through his feelings about what's been happening here. And he's much better protected now. Both of you are."

"Thanks for saying that, Douglas. I felt good about it. But I did wonder if I wouldn't regret it, one day."

"Well, your son is nobody's *wimp*. He's definitely got a mind of his own."

She beamed and Douglas was pleased that his opinion mattered to her. He stood to leave.

"I want to thank *you,* Douglas, for being so kind to my family, today. We all really appreciate what you've done. I know you're probably feeling a bit put out, with them showing up like they did."

"No, I'm not," he told her with sincerity. "Your mother's always a joy. And I see a lot of you in your son. I gather you've worked out your differences?"

She nodded and he remembered she hadn't shared that with him. But that Laretta had, over the phone.

"Let's hope so," she said, smiling and letting him off the hook. "Seeing him at that front door made this the best Christmas that I could have asked for. He thinks a lot of you, too."

"Well," he said, feeling truly surprised. "It's good having them here and seeing you so happy."

"Well the silliness gets worse," she laughed.

He stood up and she did the same.

"Thanks for stopping in. I always like talking to you. But you already know that," she said, softly.

His heart leapt. *Could it be that she felt the same for him, after all?*

"Douglas, I can't stay here forever…"

And why not? He wanted to say, but didn't interrupt.

"I might have found a place. It's a rental house, here in town. I'm thinking about moving there, if it works out."

Speechless, he burrowed his brows into a frown.

"Why? You can stay here for as long as you need to."

"That's the thing," she said. "I feel bad enough that I've needed so much from you. That's just not who I am. I'm an independent person, accustomed to taking care of myself. I don't want to overstay my welcome. And, when I leave, I don't want to feel I've taken advantage of you in any way."

"LaRetha," he said, standing beside her, now. "I'm not trying to control you. That's not me, either. But, you already know that you're more to me than a client. I would rather you stayed here until it's safer for you to leave." He hated not saying how he truly felt.

She nodded.

"I know you're independent, and I totally respect that," he continued. "So, whatever you think I've done for you, I did it because I *wanted* to. Because I care, and that's all."

"Well, when this is over, I don't want you to have regrets where I'm concerned. You're doing so much."

"It's nothing. I didn't have any other plans for the holiday, and I enjoy having you here, *period*. Normally, I would've gone to my sister's house in Chicago, but my workload prevented that, this year. So, I would've spent Christmas day in this big old house, alone. That wouldn't have been near as much fun as this."

He walked to the door.

"Oh, and for the record. I'm not intimidated by strong women."

His eyes stayed on hers. She didn't look away.

"I've been looking for someone like you for a long time, *Miss LaRetha Watson Greer*. So, neither you, nor any of your crazy cousins are going to scare me off, that easily. Alright?"

She looked astonished at his confession. Speechless. Satisfied, he turned to door to leave. There were no secrets between them, now.

"One more thing," he said, hesitating.

"What?" She asked, barely audibly. Apparently still in shock from his last comment.

"The housekeeper's gone until next week. Can I trouble you to help me make breakfast in the morning?"

"Of course," she said, sounding relieved. "I'll meet you in the kitchen at *eight*," she said. She still hadn't moved from where she stood when he closed the door.

Smiling victoriously, he stepped into the hallway, just vaguely aware that another door was softly closing across the hall.

Laretta, he thought. He chuckled to himself and went down the hallway toward his bedroom.

She was already in the kitchen when Douglas came down. He started a pot of coffee.

"Everybody's still asleep?" He asked.

"Yep! The whole lazy bunch!"

"So, what do you need for me to do?"

"I was about to ask you that," she kidded and he made a sour face.

They worked easily together, frying sausage and bacon, scrambling eggs and occasionally stirring a pot of buttery grits. There would be croissants and coffee. Juice for whoever wanted it. He had jelly *and* jam, he teased seductively, causing her to blush, involuntarily. And she wasn't surprised when he left the kitchen for the living room. Douglas wanted a drink.

She felt the urge to follow him, and watched him from the hallway as his back was turned. What made him *need* that? She wondered. After a moment, she left, and could hear him rinsing his glass, and stacking it back behind the bar. She hoped that would be his last for the day.

Breakfast was appreciated by everyone. Laretta was barking instructions and the young girl was working diligently to appease her.

"*That used to be my job,*" LaRetha whispered to Douglas, as he watched with concealed amusement.

Laretta asked where the cream was.

"I think your plate is getting cold, Tori," LaRetha said. "Mama, the cream is right behind you on the buffet. If you turn around, you can almost *touch* it."

Laretta grimaced in her direction, and Douglas chuckled. Germaine was oblivious to anything that wasn't on his plate.

Before he excused himself to go upstairs to work in his office, Douglas insisted she accept the keys to his Range Rover. The sun was out, today. They should go for a drive. A strip that they called the Holiday Mall would open until *one* this year, he said.

Excitedly, Laretta took control as usual, saying she would direct them to her most memorable places, of course. Her birth home had long been bought by old friends of her folks. Still, it was *home,* she said. She wanted to see it again. Everyone understood.

Traffic was surprisingly busy. The cold weather had lifted for a minute, so everyone dressed in light jackets. The tour was short but lively, finally leading them to the strip mall, where they split up. She and Laretta would meet Germaine and Tori in two hours, they agreed. From there, they would go for lunch.

The stores were surprisingly full, and LaRetha quickly realized that this was a tradition for these people; shopping the day after Christmas, showing off visiting relatives and exchanging stories and humor.

An elderly woman approached her and asked for help matching a comforter with a set of curtains. Once satisfied, she thanked LaRetha, just before another woman asked her to watch the toddler seated in her shopping cart for a moment until she could run to the back of the store and get something. LaRetha's puzzled look didn't stop her for a second.

"It'll only take a moment," the tired looking woman said, and she was off.

"It's a little late to be starting over, isn't it?" Her mother said, laughing at her plight. The woman returned and thanked her. LaRetha could only shake her head.

"Let's get out of here before I have to set up an errand service."

Their next stop was at a boutique. Laretta fell right into the rack of expensive sale items. Fortunately, she'd packed a lot of clothing for her trip to Atlanta. She only needed more shoes. She found several pair.

Lastly, they entered a furniture store. There was so much of it, that it was almost overwhelming. Thinking about her rental house, LaRetha jotted down items she would need, if everything worked out.

"We also have same day delivery," the smiling saleslady said, showing them rooms and rooms of nice pieces on display. They were having a *40% off* sale. LaRetha liked quite a few things.

"I think we're late," LaRetha said, and they went out to find Germaine and Tori waiting on the sidewalk, laughing and talking with people they couldn't have known, she thought. Apparently, they were making new friends.

"Is *anybody* hungry besides me?" LaRetha asked as she unlocked the car door and they all loaded their packages inside.

They were. She drove them to the *Burger Box*. Once everyone had ordered burgers, onion rings and shakes, they found an empty booth in the busy restaurant. Their conversation was lively and fun, the food was very tasty, and time passed much too quickly.

"It's getting late and we're imposing," her mother said. "We're heading out first thing in the morning, you know?"

"I can assure you that you're not imposing," she responded. "I'm having a ball, and Douglas likes having you here, too. It keeps me out of his hair while he works."

"I doubt he even minds," her mother said. "But your son has to be back at work, day after tomorrow, and I can't impose, forever."

"But, I can come back," her son volunteered. "We can drive up for New Year's Eve."

"Son, as much as I want you to come, that long drive could be dangerous on a holiday. Besides, I'm moving and I'm not sure if I'll have it all together, by then. I might even come to Atlanta for a few days. So, let's play that by ear, okay?"

She didn't want to say she was worried for his safety.

"But, it's no problem. We take road trips all the time," Tori said.

LaRetha smiled at the wide-eyed young woman, remembering how it was for her and Gerald at that age; so in love, with no earthly idea of how it would end. Never expecting to divorce.

"I'd like to know what plans the two of you have. You're engaged, but when's the wedding?"

"I knew that was coming," Germaine murmured.

"Then you should already have an answer." She retorted. Tori shifted nervously.

"Well, we've talked about it. We plan to get married after I graduate." He spoke quickly, making it clear that he didn't want to discuss it.

"Why wait? You're living together. What difference would it make if you were married before then?" She asked, innocently, watching with interest as both their eyes widened with fear. Her mother snickered.

"Well, we're kinda *young*," Tori said, shyly.

"But, you live together!" Admittedly, she liked making them squirm.

"Mama," Germaine started.

"I'm just *saying*, Germaine. You already know that I don't want that for you. And even if you think it's none of my business, it is."

"How so?" Her mother asked, looking humored.

"Because," she said, going into her playful mode. "You'll want to spend a few years of marriage together before you start having my grandchildren," she said, and Germaine looked stricken.

"You know," she continued, "to really enjoy each other, save some money, buy your first home. So that when the children come, you'll *both* be ready for them, financially, emotionally and other-wise."

Tori nodded thoughtfully as Germaine frowned. She winked at her mother when they weren't looking, and saw her suppressing a gigantic laugh.

"But really, whatever you do in life, always put the Provider, first. And do everything in a way that can be blessed. *Why cheat yourselves?"* She asked, and Laretta nodded, thoughtfully.

"But Mama," her son said, and she felt a reproach coming on. "you and Daddy didn't last."

Her mother gave her a *now you're done for,* expression that she ignored.

"It takes *two* people and a lot of work to maintain any relation-ship, Germaine. Nobody marries knowing they'll be divorced. But, where is it written that yours won't work just because mine didn't? We're different people and these are different times. It totally depends on the individuals."

"I don't mean to be disrespectful," the girl said. "But, aren't you and Mr. Davis… *you know?"*

"No, sweetie. Nothing of the kind is going on there."

"Really?" The girl looked totally surprised, which amused Laretta even more.

LaRetha sat back and gave the girl a questioning look.

"People can do that, you know? Now, anybody for refills? These shakes are delicious! I'm taking one back with me."

Germaine was up and at the counter before Tori could decline.

"Nope. No more excess pounds for me this week," Laretta said. "And you might want to reconsider."

"Love me, love my hips," she said, blowing a breath of intolerance at her mother. Tori giggled.

"I'm glad you came," she said, noticing Tori's embarrassment at her earlier reproach and hugging her shoulders. "You two obviously care a lot for each other. I wasn't happy about the way things happened, but I've had my say. I just want you to make *good* decisions."

"Yes, ma'am," Tori whispered. And her mother gave her a grateful smile.

They were well on the way back to Douglas' house when Germaine questioned her.

"So, Mama. You asked about our plans. What about yours? When do you plan to rebuild?"

"I've thought about that. I think I might do something different with the land, this time around."

"Like what?" He was leaning forward, now.

"Well, to build something that would make us a lot of money and help this town in the process."

"Here, here," Laretta said, approvingly.

"The farm's a bit far out and I don't think I want to be that isolated, again. I might even consider moving back to Atlanta, once the trial is over. Nothing's certain, just yet."

She saw no reason to wait until making this disclosure. Still, it surprised even her.

"What?" They all said, in unison.

"You're coming back to Atlanta?" Germaine was wide-eyed. *"Cool!* But, I thought... What about *Douglas?"*

"Douglas will be fine. I haven't told him yet, so keep it under your belts. I'll talk with him about it when the time is right."

Everyone agreed to her terms, although Germaine looked disappointed. But, she didn't want him becoming too attached to Douglas, or to any man who might be in her life, again. And that would be very easy right now, considering his differences with his father. But, nothing was certain with her and Douglas. Only time would tell.

To break the monotony of their suddenly quiet drive, Laretta started singing to an *oldies* music station. Germaine and Tori joined in, singing and rapping different lyrics from the remakes, or just creating some. Laretta thought they sounded pretty good. LaRetha took the long route to prolong their fun. No one minded.

The house was quiet when they arrived, and she discovered that Douglas wasn't there. *He's gone,* she announced. Unable to hide her disappointment.

"Well, I plan to watch a little TV in the den for awhile," Laretta said. "He's got a good DVD collection. Anybody want to join me?"

Germaine did. Tori went to take a nap. It was just after *four* and LaRetha was more interested in knowing where Douglas was.

He's gone to see another woman, she decided. But, she remembered their conversation from the night before. And with all her drama, she found it hard to believe that he really wanted to be with her.

She went upstairs too, leaving her mother and son to their movies and conversations in the den.

"Good night, Mama. Sleep tight." Her son hurried to the top of the staircase to give her a tight hug.

"Funny, I used to tell you that," she said. "Goodnight, baby."

"And, thanks for being so nice to Tori," he whispered.

"She's a nice girl. Take her future seriously. Do right by her."

Once upstairs, LaRetha waited until she could no longer hear Tori moving around, before allowing curiosity to get the better of her. Slipping down the hallway to Douglas' room, she quietly closed his door, locking it behind her. She found the wall switch that turned on a nearby lamp.

So this is Douglas, she thought, allowing her eyes to wander around. She noticed that the walls were all painted in deep shades of teal and brown. There was a brick fireplace in a far corner of the room. And a solid colored comforter with coordinating pillows and sheets helped give it a romantic feel. She quickly dismissed thoughts of what she would change to make it more feminine.

Feeling deliciously sneaky, she went to a desk by the window, where a large scrapbook lay closed. She sat down to look at it. Various papers were stuffed inside; certificates, diplomas, several Certificates of Achievements for his father, himself and Candace.

Turning the plastic covered pages, she saw more letters of commendation to the three of them, ticket stubs from traveling, movies and event parking. And several old menus from what must have been some great spots, back in the day.

There were postcards, mostly from their father to their mother from places he must have traveled. There were a few more recent ones from different women to Douglas. She didn't recognize any of their names. And then, lots of photos. She really wanted to organize it all, but decided against it.

There were old photos of the mother and father from when they first married, she guessed. In one of them, they were standing outside their house, beside an old car, and smiling. In each photo, they were dressed very tastefully. The mother, beautiful and petite, smiled much like Douglas. With her thick auburn hair perfectly coiffed and shining under a bright sun, she looked very happy, and very much pregnant.

Beside her stood a tall, very handsome and distinguished looking man, dressed in a suit with a long coat. In his hand was a watch, its gold chain hanging down, probably from his pants pocket, and where his coat was pulled back. *Jive chains,* she remembered her father used to call them. The man wore glasses and had a thick moustache. *Definitely Douglas Davis, senior,* she thought. There was no mistaking the similarities. The two made a very handsome couple.

Other pictures were of a small and slightly buck-toothed little boy. And then a teen-aged Douglas with a pretty little girl wearing long thick ponytails. They seemed so contented, she thought. So secure. And it only reminded her of just how precious your family truly was.

There was a black and white photo of Douglas' elementary school class. *Third grade,* it read. A tall, slim and nerdy looking Douglas was on the second row and surprisingly, Vera was in the background. This picture reminded her of old classmates that she'd lost contact with over the years.

A door opened and closed, downstairs. Quickly closing the album, she put it back in its place. Hurriedly, she switched off the lamp and slipped out of the bedroom, closing his door just as his footsteps sounded on the lower landing. She made it safely to her bedroom, smiling satisfactorily that she hadn't been caught.

Still, she listened as his steps came closer to her door, before retreating quietly down the hall. She let out a jagged breath.

Turning on the bathroom shower, she retrieved her gown and carried it into the bath. Her family was leaving early in the morning. And she had no idea what she would do once they were gone.

The house was quiet and dark. Douglas flipped a switch that threw a warm yellow light into the downstairs hallway, before going to pour himself a drink. He had just spent the last four hours at his office in town, where he could better focus on the task at hand. It was great having company at the house. And it wasn't that she bothered him in any way. But, admittedly, with LaRetha around, he wanted to do anything but work.

While they were out exploring, he had spent time scanning some files and shredding others, reading over briefs and preparing his opening statement for Kincaid's trial. That part had been easy, until thoughts of the woman staying at his house had crept in, totally taking his mind off his work.

LaRetha! Contagiously kind, caring and everything he wanted and needed in a woman. Finally placing the last folder on top of the stack to the left of him, he'd realized it was getting late and was sure that she was wondering where he was.

But, he had needed a few more minutes; time to wallow in the pleasantries of these new memories and the prospect of more. Looking at the family photograph on his office wall, he had thought about the last Christmas he had shared with both of his parents and his little sister. He was *eleven,* then. Those holidays celebrated after his mother died were nice but never the same. And now, with his father gone...

Holidays did this to him. While he was very appreciative of having such a good life, he often longed to regain old feelings of happiness and good cheer, again. Then, he'd called Candace.

"Hey, Sis," he'd said, smiling into the phone. "How's everybody?"

"Everybody's just great. We still wish you had made it up, this year. But, we understand that schedule of yours. I told Dade it must have been because of a woman. So, how's your holiday going?"

"Great! Much better than I'd expected," he said, teasingly. She caught his meaning.

"*Ooobh!* So, *Big Brother,* it sounds like somebody's in *love!*"

"I think so, Candace. And I can't even help it."

"That's *wonderful.* Tell me about her."

He began to describe her; her beauty and her heart.

"You mean, isn't she that same woman that's gotten *Lovely* in a stir? The one with the intruder... whose boyfriend shot her cousin or something like that? *Douglas, do you know what you're doing?*"

"No, not at all," he had sighed.

"Well, then it must be love."

"The closest I've ever been to it," he said, smiling happily into the phone.

"I can hear it. Well, take care, dear brother. I can't wait to meet her."

"I can't, either. You're going to love her as much as I do. She's *wonderful.* She has a grown son – *almost* grown. She and her mother are very close. She really loves her family, and she'll be crazy about you and Dade, and the kids."

"Well, you're the biggest kid I know, so that must be true. By the way, my kids are still trying to get to the bottom of that gift box you sent. It'll take them a year, at least."

"Good, that should keep *'em* busy," he had teased. He loved her three children and she knew it.

They had laughed and talked a bit longer before saying *'I love you's,* and hanging up.

Afterward, leaning back in his chair with his eyes closed, he had recalled how yesterday and today had been so full of pleasant surprises. It was nothing short of amazing, the way the right woman could come along and change a man's existence, entirely. And without hardly trying.

She was the other side of *him*, LaRetha was. She was *people*, being from *Lovely*, as well. But not so much that she had those country, conniving ways he'd come to dislike in the women he'd always attracted.

She was educated and industrious, sure of herself with a mind of her own. She challenged him, and he loved the way she didn't agree with him just to be in his good graces. Or to take advantage, like other women had. Her spirit was certainly refreshing and it was giving him a whole new outlook on life.

And now, back at his house and standing outside the bedroom she was sleeping in, he was tempted to knock. To awaken her so she would get up and talk to him. But she was probably sound asleep. He decided not to bother her.

Kellen Kincaid didn't know what he had, he thought as he went into his own bedroom. But, so it goes with these younger men who put themselves before their women. Or men who, like Gerald Greer, thought that weakening a woman's will, would keep her in her place. Or so her mother had said.

After twenty years of him, it was no wonder she held men at bay. Everyone except for Kincaid, that was. And he still couldn't figure out what, if anything, was happening there.

His father had once said that a happy and fulfilled woman was the greatest blessing a man could ever have. And he did intend to have LaRetha - as his wife. Whatever happened at that trial, the time was drawing near when LaRetha Greer would become *Mrs. LaRetha Davis*. And he planned to make her a very happy woman.

Man, I've really done it, now! Kellen thought, as he lay in his cell. Now, LaRetha *and* Germaine were angry with him, and at the worst possible time. But Germaine's questions had angered him. And although he'd wanted to tell him everything, he couldn't.

How could he explain his involvement with people who had done the things they had? With people who had hired a man to scare her off, then burned his mother's house, killing his grandmother?

He had wanted to say something that the boy might understand, except, every time he'd opened his mouth, only stupid things had come out. And he had managed to alienate the only people caring about him, right now. But he needed LaRetha, now more than ever. And not just for this case. He needed to know that she was still in his life.

But, that was just one side of the nightmare. Not only had Samira made him a proposition, and then Gerald, but so had *Mac Henry*. And by being in jail, that agreement would be impossible to uphold.

"LaRetha is just too close to this story," the man had said after making a lucrative offer, not realizing that he was the third person to do so.

"Still, it's a bit risky," he'd responded to his boss. "What if she finds out? It would cost us our friendship. She wouldn't write for you again, knowing this. How would I explain all of that to her?"

"You don't have to explain, anything. Not until after your story is published. Until then, we've never had this conversation."

He had shaken his head.

"Of course, it's *your* decision. But, personal feelings aside, put your heart into this story and see what happens. She can still write whatever she wants about the issue. What could it hurt?"

LaRetha would never trust him, again. But, he'd known that might happen whether he'd taken the assignment or not. Especially now that he had foolishly revealed his reason for coming to *Lovely*, in the first place.

So, with yet another check practically in the mail, but for a story this time, he had packed up the rental car and driven the distance - all the while, hoping he would never regret this. And already, he did.

He had come with two goals in mind; to make good on the money with both sources, and to protect her in the interim. But, how could he do that now, when he couldn't shower or go outside without permission?

He'd read about the fire that had killed Cecelia. How terrible that was! And he couldn't help but think that, had she been in town, LaRetha could have been in that fire, as well. Thankfully, she wasn't.

He wondered what she was doing now. Christmas Day was past, and he really wished he could have it back; to see Germaine all over again and make him understand, but without getting angry, this time. But what good would the same bad news do, *twice?*

When he closed his eyes, he could imagine them together again – him and LaRetha. Her kisses, her hugs and that sweet perfume that stayed with him long after she had gone.

But that thought was quickly chased away by a vision of Douglas Davis hurrying in and luring her away with his money and fancy cars, with Samira in the background, laughing at his distress.

Who was he kidding? She wasn't waiting for him, any longer. Obviously, her entire family was rallying around Douglas, now. And even after the trial, her life would go on. She would eventually put him out of her mind, entirely. He would just be a very bad memory. He cringed at the thought.

"Hey, Chief" he yelled. The guard took his time coming over.
"*Yeah?"*

"I need to make a phone call. Just one call, man. It's urgent."

He needed to ask her to come and visit him again, except *alone* this time. She should know how much he loved her. Maybe then she wouldn't get involved with Davis. He only needed her to remember *Atlanta...*

"You know the rules. No calls at this hour. It'll have to wait until tomorrow."

Man! He exclaimed, falling back onto his cot, punching the atmosphere with his feet in anguish.

I'm sorry, LaRetha. I love you. Wait for me, baby. Please. Wait for me.

Germaine awakened to the smell of toast, eggs and coffee. Jumping into yesterday's clothing, he tiptoed to Tori's room. She was still asleep.

"Wake up, sleepy head," he said, pulling her covers back. "We're leaving early so we've only got an hour to get downstairs and eat. I smell breakfast, so get up." He opened the blinds, allowing bright sunshine inside.

"Wow! This place is *tight!* Did you see the boats?" He looked across the back yard to the lake.

"*Go away*, Germaine," she said, protesting by pulling the covers high over her head. He laughed, snatching them back down, again.

Finally, she sat up. Looking around the room, she was as confused as he was when he'd first awakened.

"What are you doing in here? You know your mama and Miss Laretta would have a flying *fit*."

"I just came to wake you up. Remember what Grandma said. We have to be on the road by *ten*. It's already after eight."

"Which means you're in here much too early. Go on down. I'll be there in a minute. Just don't let your folks see you coming out of my room," she said, sleepily.

"You know I love you, don't you?"

"*Whatever.*"

He watched her attempt to sleep and shook his head. Then he leaned to her and whispered.

"Thanks for talking me into coming," he whispered. "And, for coming with me," he said, kissing the top of her head.

"I had to do something to keep you from leaving with your old *crazy daddy*."

He playfully bopped her head. "Come on, get up. I don't want to keep them waiting."

"Sure," she said, before dropping her head back onto a pillow. Giving up, he left her and moved quietly back across the hall and into his own sleeping quarters. After changing into a new pair of jeans and a shirt, his mother's present to him, he went downstairs to see what was good on the table.

Douglas was already downstairs, mixing a batch of eggs with milk and seasonings when LaRetha finally got there.

"Good morning early bird," she said. Tossing her head back and closing her eyes, she embraced the smell of real country sausage that he had already prepared. "It smells great in here. I guess I taught you well."

She was startled to open her eyes and find Douglas watching her from where he worked at the stove. It caused her to pause and then smile.

"I guess you did," he laughed.

"You must be *starving,*" she said with a yawn.

"Why do you say that?"

"Because, you're looking at me like I'm a well-done pork chop."

"You look beautiful, as usual." He smiled, shyly.

"Flattery will get you..." She stopped short, pouring a glass of apple juice but seeing his raised brow. "It's just a figure of speech."

She looked into the refrigerator to retrieve a few things.

"Careful about those *figures,*" he said, his eyes exploring hers. "Besides, are you here to help or to supervise?"

"The *latter*. I'll scramble some eggs while you warm the croissants."

"Sure, boss," he teased.

"I have got to stop eating like this."

"There is a spa in town, you know? He teased. "I go four times a week. I could show you around, sometime."

"Humph!" She said, and he laughed.

"Well, a good breakfast never hurt anybody." He spread light butter onto wheat toast.

"*Right*. Besides, I don't have to eat everything on my plate, do I?"

He laughed, again. "I used to eat a lot. Now, I have other addictions, I guess."

"You're not addicted. You just need other things to do, is all."

He stopped spreading the butter and walked over to her, raising her chin with his finger. Forcing her to look him in the eyes.

"Like what *things?*"

She laughed and winked, just before Laretta and Germaine entered the kitchen. Tori dragged in a few minutes later, and they all sat down. This time, to enjoy their last meal together, for a while. Afterward, Germaine and Tori cleared the table, as they talked in the den.

"As soon as they're done, they can load the car," Laretta said.

"I'll help with that," Douglas responded, as Germaine and Tori finally joined them.

"You don't have to," LaRetha said.

"I don't mind."

"Thanks, Douglas," Germaine grinned, and they began carrying bags from the foyer, outside.

LaRetha turned to hug her mother.

"Thank you for bringing them, Mama. It's been so good having you here. I haven't had time to worry about anything."

"I know, dear, but are you sure that you won't come with us?" Her eyes were pleading.

"No. But I'll let you know as soon as I'm moved, and everything. Hopefully that house is still available."

"You can't be serious about that!?" Her mother exclaimed. "You'll only be an easy target for whomever…"

"Well, I can't stay here, forever. If this leaks out, it could cause a problem for Douglas. I have to rent, some place."

"You *need* to come *home*. Or stay here until it's safe."

"I can't keep imposing. It's misleading to everybody," she whispered. "Including Douglas."

"Now I'm confused. Do you like the man or not?"

She didn't respond.

"I already know he's not going to approve of this. Wait just a minute." Her mother walked to the front door.

"*Douglas!* Can you come here for a minute?"

"Sure Laretta. In a second," he said, struggling to fit another bag into the back of the jeep.

"Mama, w*hy are you doing this?"* She whispered, angrily. "Don't you think I know what's best for me?" She asked, with a look of impatience.

"Not right now, you don't. You're under a lot of pressure and apparently the word *danger* isn't sinking in with you."

Douglas came inside, looked questioningly from one of them to the other. Laretta repeated her plans and he gave her the same response as before.

"LaRetha, you have to stay here where it's safe. I can get 24-hour surveillance. You have alarms here, and even my neighbors can look out. But, in town, especially *alone* – well, there's nothing that I could do to protect you. You should reconsider."

"But, Douglas, once this hits the press it'll be a media circus, right there on your front yard. Besides, I'll be renting so the house doesn't even have to be in my name. No one will know."

"Girl, I was born in this town," Laretta said. "They'll know as soon as you start moving in. Listen to the man."

She shook her head. She had barely escaped two controlling men and wasn't about to be crippled with other people's fears and lack of faith. Her mother acted as if Douglas owned her. This distressed her.

"Douglas, talk to her, won't you?" Her mother asked, frantically.

"*Mama!*" She exclaimed and Laretta looked at her with concern. "I know you think the sun rises and sets on Douglas' opinions," she said. "But this is *my* life, so *I'll* decide where I'll go and when. Not *you*, and not *Douglas!*"

"Excuse us for a minute, Laretta," Douglas said, pulling her into the hallway out of earshot.

"Why do you insist on being so stubborn?" He asked. "Can't we talk about this, later? To try and come up with something else?"

"Like what?" She remained unmoved.

"I don't know yet, but you're upsetting your mother."

"I know. She shouldn't leave here like that. We can talk later."

"LaRetha." Douglas pulled her back as she started to leave. "I'd rather talk about *us*. We can't keep dodging the subject. "

"That's not what I'm doing."

"I think it is. You can't seriously expect to have a relationship with Kincaid after all this? After what you know and the way he acted with you, yesterday?"

"Douglas, you're being very unfair," she said, her concerned gaze holding his. *Who said Kellen was the only reason I haven't chosen you?* She thought, amazed at his presumptuousness.

"*No!*" He exclaimed, causing her to frown and step back. "No," he said, much quieter, this time. "I'm not the one being unfair. *You* are. You need to decide, once and for all. I won't keep waiting."

"Waiting for *what*? And who asked you to? I never told you to stop seeing people. I'm just here temporarily. But I've been straight with you about that, from the start."

"Right," he said, angrily. "Well, let me be straight with *you!*"

She watched him incredulously as he stepped toward her, stopping within whispering distance.

"I won't be made a fool of when this trial starts. I won't be embarrassed by not knowing where we stand. Either you're at least *considering* a relationship, or else…"

"Or else, *what?*" She whispered, throwing her hands up, in anger. "You have no right to pressure me this way. I knew this would happen but you kept assuring me that it wouldn't. I can't answer you, right now. Why don't you understand that?"

"I just meant…"

"I *know* what you meant. You've said what you meant, and frankly I'm tired of hearing it."

She saw Douglas' expression change. He was angry. The fire in his eyes startled her. Raising a finger, he hesitated before speaking.

"*Then, do whatever you want, LaRetha!* I can't please you enough. I can't protect you enough. You have none of the answers, and all of them."

She stared at him, indignantly.

"If you want to move into town and put your own life at risk, after everything that's happened, then just go right ahead. I won't try to stop you. If you want to die out there, then so be it. Help yourself. Because frankly, *I've* had enough!"

She watched as he turned away and walked angrily into the foyer, where he went to retrieve his coat.

"Douglas?" Her voice was barely audible as she followed him into the foyer, but it caused him to stop and look at her. Except, she could only turn away. Walking quickly past her startled mother, she went upstairs and into her bedroom where she closed the door, shutting them all out.

They expected too much from her. They wanted to control her world, and it just wasn't realistic. Everything was a risk, these days. They might even be in danger for visiting her. She wouldn't keep putting them in that situation. Not after what had happened, already.

She couldn't go back with them to Atlanta, right now. Not after the fire and what happened to Cecelia. That could have been her in the house. Or what if her mother had answered the door instead of Marilee? What would Gerald have done to her? And why couldn't they see that she needed to stay in *Lovely*, at least until this was resolved? She couldn't bear to lose another person in her family.

And Douglas! She'd been expecting that conversation. He was in so deep that it made sense that he would be concerned about his reputation in this town. He wanted an answer, but to what? They'd never even been on a normal date! Had never had a conversation that wasn't about some crime or Kellen's upcoming trial. And now *she* was wondering if he wasn't trying to take advantage of *her*.

She wasn't looking for another relationship, but this one was being forced on her, it seemed. But if she *was* looking, she would want a man who loved her, and not just the idea of protecting her. And she wanted to bring her whole self to him. But she certainly didn't want anyone dictating her every move, thought or idea.

She splashed cold water on her face, realizing that this was not acceptable for her life. And she would never resolve this by trying to be what everybody else wanted. Leaving this house was the absolute right thing to do. Now, to find the right way to do it.

She started downstairs, and could hear her mother and Douglas talking quietly. Germaine and Tori were waiting in the den. She would say goodbye, get through this, and beyond it. *Somehow.*

But she already knew that she couldn't give Douglas the fairytale relationship that he wanted. She couldn't *be* what he wanted. And considering his concern for his *image*, it would be dead wrong to wring a relationship out of his pity, or to expect him to sacrifice his life's work by committing to her and possibly alienating the entire town. This place was his everything – past, present and future. But there was no future here for her.

She sucked in a sigh of regret, and went to find her mother.

Douglas waited with the others for LaRetha to come downstairs, and shortly afterward, she had, looking a little tired and red-eyed.

"Are you alright, Mama?" Her son seemed so concerned for her, Douglas noticed.

"I'm fine," she said, smiling and giving him a quick hug.

He didn't seem convinced.

"I'll be back in Atlanta, soon," she said, taking his arm into her own. "So, just be patient with me. It's all going to work out."

Hearing this, Douglas was taken aback. He hadn't known about this, and the news hit his chest like a hammer.

Disappointed and suddenly unsure of what to say, he accepted their goodbye hugs and left them. He went to his bedroom, upstairs.

When was this decided? He wondered. But, he realized, there was a group of people downstairs who had a bond that he didn't share. She had announced her decision. And apparently the others already knew because only he had been surprised to hear it.

The woman wants out of here. Now he understood that little speech of hers about not wanting him to feel *used*.

He had dreaded this day. This was supposed to have been their time to get to know one another. For him to show her what he and this town could offer her. But, after what he'd said, she must really hate him now because she was making it crystal clear that she couldn't wait to get away from him.

He sat down on the edge of the bed, back and shoulders taut, unable to relax. This was the *Valerie* thing resurfacing. His past had truly turned her against him. Those smiles and hugs had been for her family, not him. *How could he not have seen that?* He shook his head in disbelief.

He missed his mother and father – and those holidays that they'd all shared in this very home, as a loving family. And he wanted that, again. He was getting older and tired of the same old switcheroo dating games. More than that, he couldn't even envision having a happy future if she wasn't in it. His problem was getting her to see it the same way.

She was a smart woman, spiritual and intelligent, and so sure about a lot of things. But, somehow his feelings were escaping her. She didn't trust him anymore, and that bothered him.

He could hear them, downstairs. And he was tempted to join them, again. But no, it didn't matter, he thought. If she chose him, he would see them again. If not, then it wouldn't matter at all.

But he couldn't give up. He had to make the little time they had before the trial count in his favor.

It wasn't over until it was over, he thought, slapping his thighs with finality and getting up. There was still time, and he still had plenty of motivation to make this happen. And he would.

Douglas heard her go into her room, and decided not to bother her. He had work to do, so he went into his office and closed the door. It was another three hours before he looked at the clock, again. Looking out, he could see small flakes of snow falling, and the ice breaking and falling from the roof just beyond his window. Nothing else stirred.

What could she be doing?

Shutting off his computer, he put away his files, locking the drawers before turning off the lights and closing the door behind him. Once downstairs, he checked to make sure that the doors and window were secured, before venturing into the empty living room.

Just one drink, he thought, before changing his mind. He didn't need a drink. He only needed something else to do, just as LaRetha had said. Still, it took some doing to pass it up. His drinking had become serious. More serious than he'd realized before she'd come.

Hearing the television playing in the den, he went in there. She wasn't there or in any other room in the house. He panicked.

"LaRetha!" He called out.

He hurried through the hallway, before catching a glimpse of someone standing outside, on the patio. Wrapped in a thick wool blanket, she was staring out over the lake. He grabbed a jacket and went out to her.

"What are you doing out here? You'll freeze to death."

She said nothing, so he pulled her close to him, wrapping her inside his jacket before throwing the blanket around them both, allowing the heat to emanate from his body to warm her cold one. He wanted to pull her closer but didn't want to offend her. She didn't seem to notice the cold.

"It's so beautiful out here," she said, quietly. "I could stay out here for days."

"It is nice, isn't it?"

They were quiet for a moment, looking down and across the lake where holiday lights twinkled colorfully in the distance. Then, he felt her shiver. He looked down at her and she tried to smile at him through unshed tears brimming at her lids.

"I miss them, already," she said, softly. The tears were falling, now. Blinking slowly, she tried unsuccessfully to stop them.

Uncertain if she was speaking of the family who'd just left, or the ones she had recently lost through tragedy, he felt he had no choice but to comfort her.

Pulling her tighter to him, he allowed her to sob quietly into his chest. After a moment, it seemed only natural to kiss her on the cheek. Her tears were salty and warm, and the tighter he held her, the longer he smelled that wonderful fragrance she wore. And he couldn't think of a thing to say. Being totally drawn in by her sorrow, he said nothing, figuring she was due this cry.

"It's going to be fine, LaRetha. I know I keep telling you that. You just have to believe it."

She held onto him tighter and he was in no hurry to let go, now. He understood her loneliness. The pain of losing loved ones for reasons you didn't understand. Of being so often misunderstood, and also being angry with no relief until finally being able to let go.

He had handled a lot of things, badly. He'd been irresponsible with relationships and with his drinking. He'd made her feel responsible for his own behavior. His heart had once been crushed by deception and lies, and admittedly, he still hadn't gotten over it. But, that wasn't her fault, either.

She was quiet, now. Lost in the moment, he ran his fingers through her hair before nudging her head back so that he could look at her. Slowly, he lowered his face to hers. He rubbed his cheek against her colder one and she sighed. And without apology or hesitation, he kissed her.

She didn't pull away that time, but kissed him back. Then, just as he felt her responding to him, she pulled away and looked up at him. Studied him. That made him smile.

"What are we doing?"

"Something wonderful and long overdue," he said.

"I think I owe you another apology," she finally said.

"You don't," he said. "I was wrong for what I said to you, earlier. You were right. You never asked me to put my life on hold. And I never really did it. To tell you the truth, in spite of everything, my life is much better now than before I met you. I had no right to make that accusation."

"I didn't want you to be angry with me for taking my time. I wanted to be sure. Whatever happens…"

"*Sssshh*," he said, putting his finger to her lips. She owed him nothing. Certainly not an apology. "Tell me when you're ready. When it's time. Not before."

He wanted to say it. *I love you*. But, the words wouldn't come. It wasn't their time and considering her reasons to distrust him, she probably wouldn't believe it, anyway. But, when the right time came, *if* it came, he knew he'd say it, instantly.

"I just want to close a few chapters and reclaim my life," she continued. "I can't give what I don't feel I have to give. But, I understand if you have to… if you move on. I can't expect you to wait…"

"No expectations on either of us, okay? Let's just enjoy what we have right now. Tomorrow will take care of itself."

"Yes. It will, won't it?

After standing together for a while longer, she smiled up at him.

"I think I'll go upstairs for awhile," she said, almost breathlessly.

He hugged her, again.

"I think I'll go inside, now," she repeated.

"I might as well, too. Just try and get some rest."

"You too," she said. They went inside. She closed the door behind them before facing him, again.

"Oh, Douglas. I'll need to go to the airport, tomorrow morning. I have things to take care of. But I'll need to get my car, first. I understand if you're too busy to drive me. I could get a cab."

"Of course I will. But, can I make a slight suggestion? That when you go out, you don't ever go, alone? I can drive you any place you need to go. My office is closed until after New Year's. It's just a safety measure."

"I'm sure I'll be okay. But, I'll keep that in mind." Then she was gone.

He smiled when he really felt like shaking sense into her.

Whatever would he do if he lost her, now? Then it occurred to him that LaRetha Greer never conceded that easily. *She's finally beginning to trust me,* he thought, and his heart was glad.

Going into the den, he picked up the phone. Someone needed to know about *Lovely's* expected visitor. He phoned Dials. And as predicted, he was in.

18

Samira was tiring of watching the hotel room walls. Nell wasn't talking to her about anything, anymore. Jasmine was back and forth, from here to Ohio, and only said for her to stay put. But she didn't trust it.

It was after Christmas, but aside from one strip mall, most of the local boutiques were closed until after New Year's Day, which was five days away. Then, Kellen's trial would start a week later. She had already been subpoenaed.

Just below her hotel window, people were moving excitedly back and forth through the town's ice and snow. She wondered where they were going, and what their Christmas had been like. She had spent hers in here, for the most part, having driven in early Christmas morning after getting a call from Jasmine that it was important for her to do so. Then, hearing the good news that the Greer woman had finally agreed to sell, she had no choice but to wait here until she got her money.

At least this was a nice cozy room in a plush inn. Sadly though, there had been no one for her to share it with. She stood in front of the mirror. Still youthful looking by at least ten or fifteen years, her cocoa brown skin was flawless and smooth, her round faced enhanced by large dark heavily lashed eyes that were made up to disguise the slight signs of aging there. And with regular touch-ups of her weave and twice monthly trips to get her nails done, she had it all together, and she knew it.

She dressed well, lived well, and carried herself with style. She'd traveled with important people and lived amongst the rich and influential, their affluent lifestyles being her work. She had a lot going for herself. Yet, she thought, here she was, taking instructions from a couple of women who could have learned a few tricks from her.

An impending gray and cloudy sky was daunting on her holiday spirit. She had hoped to spend this time at home with family and friends. After a good financial year, she had presents to give. If her family's usual holiday stinginess and brokenness held true, there would be little *exchange,* but more *giving.* Still, she looked forward to seeing them and being away from here. But that would have to wait, she guessed.

She had done well, working for Jasmine and the group – recently buying her first house and purchasing a new *Jag.* And, between the office job and the work she preferred to do, she was finally earning her net worth. And now that she'd completed her last mission with these country folks, she was ready to leave and forget that she was ever involved. It didn't matter what Jasmine said or that she was expected to appear in court. As far as she was concerned, it was time to bail.

They'd told her she was worrying too much. *Nothing would touch her,* they'd said. But, she was nobody's fool. Jasmine was scared to death and so was Nell. And so was that old man, *Verry,* before they'd found him dead. This wasn't going well for any of them, it seemed. And with so many bodies turning up, and in ways that even the group couldn't explain, her street-wise instincts told her that it was just a matter of time before Old Man Death came *a-tippin'* 'round her door.

She'd never been on an assignment where anybody was killed, before. She'd experienced enough of that in her old neighborhood in New York, where she'd been romantically involved with one of the biggest criminals in the area. From him, she had learned to make the most of her assets, to take care of herself in any situation, and to always get her money. She had also learned that nothing good lasted forever, considering the way he'd been shot down with his body being tossed into a dumpster. She'd wasted no time getting out of town, and planned to stay away for a very long while.

With all her bags packed and sitting in the closet, ready for a hasty departure, she stopped and poured a glass of wine before settling down into a comfortable chair near the window so that she could continue watching the activities, below. She looked at her watch. *3:30pm,* and still no word from Jasmine, and she had promised to provide her final payment, this afternoon.

She hated the way the woman treated her. She couldn't help how she was, being so much like other women in her family - too pretty for her own good and always wanting things the easy way although it had never *been* easy for her – until now. And that wasn't until she had learned to use the people who were always trying to use her.

"I taught her everything she knows," the aunt who'd raised her used to say, usually laughing as she poured herself another shot of cognac, her stinking cigarette smoke only escaping the small apartment when the front door was opened.

She had been with different men for as long as she could remember. And it was nobody's fault that she had chosen this life, she figured. As long as it worked for her, she would live it. When it no longer did, she would just stop.

And that wasn't long in coming, she thought, sipping from her glass. She had seen how these people lived. How they raised their children. Why shouldn't she want some of that?

She could still get an education. Get married. Have some kids. Besides, the things she once did freely were beginning to feel degrading to her. She was tiring of being a puppet to people with no class just because they had money. But, quitting would require change, and change was a scary thing.

She had known Therell for only a short time when he'd suggested she work for Jasmine. At that time, she'd been vulnerable. Just having moved to the area, she had already met a man and then been put out of a condo by a wife she hadn't even known existed. So, being broken in spirit and finances, she'd been open for about anything. And that was the crack in the door that had let the devil in.

But, hanging out with Jasmine had proven beneficial. She liked the receptionist part. It was nice to have a legitimate title, for once. But, there were other terms she'd had to meet. Terms that proved far more lucrative. She had come to learn that, with Jasmine, there were always other terms.

Jasmine had always been generous because she was good at what she did. At first, she'd found it odd that a woman would run her business this way. She had never met or worked for a *madam,* before - certainly not one in the professional world. But, this was easy. And she was made for it.

There had been so many perks; an expense account, free concert tickets, free plane tickets and hotel rooms wherever she had to fly to get the job done. And then there were the men. *Humph,* compared to most of her dates, Douglas Davis had been one of the shoddy ones.

Everything had worked out great, until recently. On the very day after *Verry's* death, Jasmine had suddenly cut her off. No more expense accounts or use of the company car, until this was settled, she'd said. Nell had ordered it. Except she'd been caught financially unprepared. So, despite her recent decision to just quit, she couldn't just yet. And so, here she was.

Her greatest unease came with knowing how much Jasmine truly disliked her, despite telling people they were good friends. She knew the woman envied the effortless manner in which she'd floated in and out of relationships with the various men they set her up with; particularly Therell and Douglas. *But wasn't that what they'd hired her for?*

Therell Watson had been a man to be reckoned with. They had met at a bar and just hit it off. Handsome, rugged and tough, and gentle at the same time, he was the one who had made it all possible, and he was her favorite of all of them. Like her New York man, he'd had a terrible temper. But she could handle him and soon they had fallen into a secret relationship, unbeknownst to Jasmine.

He hadn't cared about what she did for a living, saying it didn't matter. He had protected her, treated her like a *person,* making sure that she always had what she needed, and that she was always compensated, as promised. They were happy whenever they could be together. And she would always miss him.

Now, she had to deal with that old fossil Nell on her own. There would be no more money until the deal actually closed, the old crow had said.

But how was she supposed to live? She'd asked. So, Jasmine had promised to pay her something, now. Unaware that she planned to use it to begin a new life. They could fight their own family battles, she thought.

Evidently, that recent fire at LaRetha's house had prompted her to sell the land and she'd been happy to hear it. She probably needed the cash just to get Kellen out of jail. Douglas' services didn't come cheaply, either.

Although Therell had been her true love, she was going to miss them all. Gerald, for being so creative about taking her places and figuring things out. And Kellen too, although she'd been sure that they were solid, until he had chosen LaRetha over her. But she wouldn't have married either of them; they would never be the faithful type. Still, they'd respected and appreciated the fact that there'd been no games to play with her.

And then there was Douglas. She could certainly understand LaRetha's attraction to the man. He was the whole package; good looking, rich, a great lover, and totally unpretentious.

He was also serious about his role in *Lovely.* He was kind of a renegade good guy, except unlike the other two, Douglas could back his game up. He was everything Gerald and Kellen hoped to be. And although a bit tame for her tastes, he was the man she would never get, now that he knew her true occupation. But she guessed that came with the territory.

"Don't go falling in love, Samira. This is *strictly business.* Once you finish the job, you move on. We have other plans for Douglas."

Jasmine was angry and embarrassed that her mother had unintentionally revealed her secret – this thing she had for Douglas. Admittedly, this had made conquering him all the sweeter.

But, she had begun to feel badly about it, especially after he'd mentioned the word *marriage*. He wanted a family someday, he'd said. A child to carry on the family legacy. And suddenly, she was sorry that she'd ever agreed to it. It would have been easier to do this to someone she hadn't liked.

But, the man must have learned something from them. He was less full of himself but definitely surer, now. And far less trusting and tolerant of certain things. He wasn't going to have her or anyone else getting near that *LaRetha* woman either, or interfering with his case. She respected that.

From what she could tell, Douglas was really in love, now. And she was jealous. That LaRetha Greer could be with any man on her list. But it was said that she was living with Douglas, so most likely she was sharing his bed as well. So as far as she was concerned, that innocent acting Miss LaRetha Greer was *working it*. And she was really the one calling all the shots, whether she realized it or not.

Douglas had finally made their meeting, and gotten the information she'd wanted him to have before she *skipped*. In spite of that subpoena, these folks would be hard-pressed to find her after today. She had new friends that she could visit in Spain, and she never planned to resurface again. Not until all of these crazy people were put away – Jasmine included. And she doubted that would ever happen.

Jasmine was really late, now. And, unfortunately, there was no one else for her to call on. She did tell her to stay away from Gerald. That once he found out what she stood to get, he would want an equal share, and that would only be trouble for her.

She picked up the wine bottle. *Empty.* Since Jasmine was late anyway, she would just leave a note and make a quick trip to a store down the block.

Back in a minute – wait for me! She wrote. Closing the door, she slipped the note inside it and hurried down the hallway to the elevator. This wouldn't take long, she thought. Then Jasmine would come and her troubles would finally be over.

Gerald had spent Christmas day, and the next, in the hospital emergency room. He walked out the next morning, fully medicated and carrying a prescription for pain pills. Asking directions, he finally found the jail.

Kellen wasn't at all sympathetic. But, seeing his predicament - his arm wrapped in a bandage inside a sling - he did look worried.

"It's about to go down, Kellen. And if you know where Douglas Davis lives, tell me. I need to talk to her before it's too late. I won't have her blood on my hands."

But Kellen had remained unmoved, telling him he was on his own. That he'd dug his own grave and he could go and lie in it.

"Don't you care about *LaRetha?*" He had implored.

"Of course, that's why I'm not telling you anything."

Frustrated, he had come here and was sitting at a traffic light, watching as a woman left the hotel and walked across the street to the parking deck.

Man, my timing is on these days! He thought, knowing he couldn't have planned it any better if he'd tried.

Even bundled up against cold weather, she still looked great - very warm and ready for *whatever*, which was basically her style. She had stolen, lied, deceived and slept with him and countless others to make a living. That group had used her to accomplish an end that would serve her well and that had nearly gotten him killed. And quite frankly, she owed him.

He whirled the car around the corner as she crossed, and followed her at a slow pace before pulling up beside her. Reaching across, he threw open the passenger door.

Get in!" He yelled, giving her a treacherous look.

One look at him and she appeared ready to run. But, he was prepared for that too, brandishing his handgun from beneath the coat he had slung over his injured shoulder. She saw the gun and walked over to the car.

"Get in, I said," he repeated.

"Gerald?" Samira smiled, her eyes darting around as though seeking an escape route. "What're you doing here, in *Lovely?*"

"I saw you crossing the street and figured I'd ask you that. Come on, get in," he said, much calmer this time, wanting to relax her. Make her think she had a choice.

Samira looked around one last time before sliding in beside him and slowly closing the door. She was as fashionable as ever in a soft black leather coat with a fur collar and matching cap, and in charcoal gray leather pants.

She could be a bit of sunshine on an otherwise screwed up day. *Until you got to know her,* he thought

"Where are we going?" She asked, fidgeting a bit, staring down at the gun lying in his lap, and still pointed in her direction.

"Off these streets to a safe place."

They rode in silence for a time, until he decided to put her at ease.

"Looks like you've been doing pretty well for yourself, Samira. Nice clothes. Staying in nice hotels and not spending a penny of your own money. Not a bad life, being a woman of the world, huh?"

She cast him an evil look. He laughed, and moved his left arm into a more comfortable position, making certain to keep it covered.

"I came to town, thinking I'd gotten some good news. They told me LaRetha had finally decided to sell. I wanted to be here for the celebration, and to get my money. But, I guess that was all a *lie.*"

She looked at him, oddly. Started to say something but didn't.

"So, why are *you* here? Let me guess. Your mission is complete and you came to get paid, too?"

She didn't comment, at first.

"Look, I don't need anything from you," he said. "You can talk to me."

"I need to get back to my hotel, Gerald. Jasmine will be there, any minute. She's bringing a package I've been waiting on."

"*Hah!* I wouldn't count on that if I were you. Just be glad you won't be there to collect it."

She frowned and looked away.

"I thought you were Jasmine's right hand woman. Don't they tell you everything?"

"They tell me the end they want to meet, and I help make it happen. Once they're satisfied, I get paid. That's it. I don't have to know everything."

He glanced at her as he drove. It was very possible that Samira was destined to meet the same fate that had been intended for him. And she didn't even have a clue.

"Look, how much do you trust Jasmine and her mother, really?"

"*Enough!*"

But he had already sensed her distrust of Nell. And from the things Jasmine had implied, he didn't think the woman or her mother cared for the girl. He didn't trust any of them. Not after what he'd seen and been told. He straightened to better conceal his arm, apprehensive about his fate and about the body he'd left in the snow.

"You look nice," he whispered. "You smell nice, too."

No use frightening her and making this harder than it had to be. Usually, he could count on having a good time with her. But she was expendable like him, now. They had more important worries.

"Thank you," she said, sounding sincerely flattered. "So do you. I like this *Shaft* look. I guess Atlanta's still agreeing with you, too?"

He nodded, slowing for a red light. He noticed that she had one hand on the door handle, ready to make an escape.

"We need to talk, Samira. I'm not sure how much time we have, so I'll just get right to it. I want my share of this money and I know you do, too. Am I right?"

She nodded.

"Only, I don't think we'll ever see it. Everything's gone crazy. I haven't talked with Jasmine, yet. But, things ain't happening the way they say they are. And if my suspicions are correct, plans are already into play to do away with the loose ends. Get my meaning?"

"Just what is your meaning?" She asked with slight arrogance.

"Meaning, loose ends like *us*. We're the two people putting them in the most danger. We have the least to lose by telling some things, and we're the ones most likely to do it if we had to. At least in their minds. We're *outsiders*. And probably the next targets."

"Targets? How do know this? Who told you things aren't going the way they say?"

"Now," he continued. "I'm told that Bob Billard is the man in charge. Have you even met him, yet?"

She nodded.

"I haven't. Somebody is scared. *Heck,* they're not even being loyal to each other, right now. They don't think they can trust us, anymore."

She looked at him for a moment, then down at his gun.

"It's not loaded," he lied, sliding it down beside his seat. Instantly, she relaxed. He'd read her correctly, though. She might just go along with him, after all. Samira was anything but a fool. And right now, she was probably scared to death. If so, his mission was practically accomplished.

"I think we should just talk to Jasmine and find out what's going on," she said, reaching for her cell phone.

"Put that down! *Are you crazy?* These folks mean business. The year is almost up. And I don't believe for a minute that LaRetha wants to sell any part of that land to them."

"But, why would she lie about that? We just need to talk to her. She won't know where I am if I call on my cell phone."

"Put it away. We've been *set up,* Samira. We're on the other side, now."

"But, why would you think that?" She asked, shaking her head. "I did my part. I'm not involved in the other stuff."

"*Now you are.* We both are. And if we don't stick together, I bet we'll both be dead by Monday."

She absorbed this for a moment.

"Maybe it's not that bad. We could talk to them. Let them know we won't cause any trouble. We could walk away right now, if we wanted. We may have to give up the money, but at least we'd be free of them and this dreary little town. They'll listen to that."

"I wouldn't be so sure of that, Samira." Gerald moved his coat aside to expose his bandaged arm. "This is what they call *talking*. Is this the conversation you want to have?"

"Who did this to you?" She looked horrified.

"Jasmine! *Who else?* She said she was sending somebody to meet me. But when I got there, *Rifleman* showed up, instead."

He slowed the car. Looking at her scared expression, he knew what she was thinking.

"Running isn't going to help. We'll be found by them sooner or later, or the courts, which is the same as them. We have to do something else."

"Did you kill him?" Her voice was almost inaudible.

"What do you think?"

"*No*, Gerald," she exclaimed. "Hasn't there been enough of that? Why did I ever..." She leaned against the door with her elbow, pushing long locks of hair from her face.

"It was either him or me, so guess who?" He tried to sound regretful, but really he was just happy to still be alive.

"Look, I don't know where you're driving us, but..," Samira rattled.

"Well, while I was lying on my hospital bed, wondering what to do next, I had to ask myself, who was in the middle of all this. Who is it that's pulling everybody's strings? Who is it that masterminded this whole thing from the beginning? And I mean from the *very* beginning. Not just when you and I got involved."

"Billard?"

"Well yes, him. But I'm thinking of somebody just as dangerous to us both, but who's smart enough to stay in the background with the hard stuff. Somebody who's got everybody fooled."

"Jasmine?"

"No. But, I think we should pay *Nell* a visit, don't you?"

LaRetha was upstairs reading her bible. She could hear Douglas moving about; up and down the stairs, but wasn't curious enough to see what he was doing. Admittedly, it had been a nice few days staying here with him.

If only things were different, she thought. Douglas' life was nice and neat. And safe. But, hers hadn't been for some time. And she still wasn't sure that she could risk falling in love, again. Love hadn't served her well over the past few years.

She'd made a lot of mistakes; like staying with Gerald for too long, for one. And if she had just remained *friends* with Kellen and never been intimate with him, and stayed true to her beliefs, he would never have believed they had a chance to be together and followed her here. And he wouldn't have even considered deceiving her into selling. Things would have happened differently. Therell would still be alive and Kellen wouldn't be in jail, right now.

Somewhere down the line, both he and Gerald had turned against her. They had conspired with her father's people the entire time, which was worse than reprehensible. And now, because of her associations with them, people were dead and everyone else's lives were forever changed. Even if this was their own doing, she would always feel greatly responsible.

It was early evening so she decided to place the call. It was a long distance number. She remembered from the *For Sale* sign that the owner was Thaddeus McGuire. A man answered.

"Hello, Mr. McGuire, please."

"Speaking."

"Hello, this is LaRetha Greer. I'm calling because I see that you have a house for rent on North Waldorf Avenue in *Lovely*. Is it still available?"

"Why yes, ma'am. It sure is. What's your name, again?"

"Greer. LaRetha Greer."

"I'm not sure I know any *Greer's*. Are you from *Lovely?*"

"I haven't lived here for very long," she said, before deciding that too many details might do more harm than good. "I'm interested in renting that house. Is it still available? Can I look at it?"

"Well, it is available," he said, proceeding to give her the details on the handsomely renovated home.

According to him, there was a large living room with a fireplace, a small study, a combination dining area and mid-sized kitchen with an eat-in area, on the first floor. There were two bedrooms upstairs and a small landing that could be used for a sitting area or a pull-out couch, he said.

There was a half bath downstairs, and two full baths, upstairs. And a laundry room. Someone kept the yard up for him, and garbage pick-up was Tuesdays and Fridays.

It sounded perfect, she told him.

"I can only do a *one year* lease though," he said. "Otherwise, it wouldn't benefit me to rent it after all the work I've put into the house."

Considering the modest lease, she agreed to it. Then asked if she could look at it, right away. She could.

They hang up and he called back, ten minutes later. His business associate would meet her at the house at *five*. Just two hours away. He was bringing a rental agreement. If she liked the house, she could sign it and mail it back to him with a list of references, a security deposit and first month's rent, he said. And, she could move in, right away.

Rent was due again on February *first,* he emphasized. That wouldn't be a problem, she assured him, before hanging up. She started downstairs. *Now where was Douglas?*

He was in the living room, reading from a very thick folder. He looked up as she entered and his eyes quickly appraised her.

"You're up, again? Great!" He said, happily. "I thought I'd have to spend the evening, alone. Join me. How about some eggnog?"

"No thanks!" She said, frowning distastefully. He laughed. "Besides, I wasn't asleep. I was making some calls. I need to go out in an hour. Could I bother you again for your keys?"

She hated to ask, but without a car, what choice did she have?

"I can drive you," he said with suspicious eyes.

She took a deep breath before speaking.

"Douglas, this is ridiculous. I'm beginning to feel like a prisoner, here. I know you don't want me to move out, and I appreciate your concern. But I've already arranged to see a house in town."

"Okay, LaRetha. I think I understand, but I can't say that I agree with what you're doing. It's not safe, but you know this."

"It's just temporary."

"So I've heard." He looked very disappointed before attempting a smile.

"Okay, I'll tell you what. Let's have dinner, first. Then, I'll drive you. Okay?"

"Whatever!" She exclaimed, figuring there was no use in arguing. Actually, she was glad that he was going. She didn't need any more drama or surprises, she thought.

"But, I think I'll be satisfied with a leftover turkey sandwich. You want one?" She asked, going into the kitchen.

He mimicked her earlier expression of distaste.

"Sure, why not? I'll take one."

He propped on a barstool and watched as she warmed a plate of turkey, then prepared sandwiches with fresh bread, mayonnaise, lettuce and tomato. After filling two glasses with iced tea, she slid his plate and glass across the counter to him.

"You're pretty handy around the house, huh?"

"I have to be. Unfortunately, I can't hire a housekeeper like you and my mother can."

"If you lived here, you wouldn't need to."

"But," she bit into her sandwich and chewed. He waited. "I don't live here." He bit into his sandwich, moaning his satisfaction.

They ate silently, smiling at one another from time to time, their smiles turning to huge grins, and finally, their grins to laughter.

"You *are* silly, aren't you?" He asked.

"That much we have that in common," she teased.

They finished eating and cleared everything away.

"Okay, now we go," she said.

"Whatever you say, but I've been thinking," he said. "If you want to rent a house, then certainly you should. But, you could still stay here, just until the trial is over. With Gerald running around, and considering *he* is the very least of our worries right now, it would be less risky for you. And I wouldn't have to worry about you all the time. How about it? Just for a while?" Those wonderful eyes were pleading.

"And *here*," he quickly asserted, "you would be safe. You'll have all the conveniences of home and business and I won't be in your way. The rental house would be there if you just *have* to go or need some space. How about it?"

Totally aware of the chemistry they were exchanging between them, she slowly gave in.

"I think... you're just wonderful for caring so much."

"Yes, I am," he said. And suddenly she didn't mind his being so protective.

What's happening to me? She asked herself as they were driving toward the house. But something was happening to the both of them. Douglas hadn't had a drink all evening.

First thing tomorrow morning, they would get her car. In the meantime, she needed another computer. She had to do a lot of work, all over again. But, that was alright. She was just thankful that she could.

Then she thought about something that Douglas had said as he'd helped her into her coat.

"You look so good in this house," he'd said.

She had smiled, thinking that she *felt* good in this house, too.

Douglas drove her, as promised, then headed to town, leaving her at her new computer, which she'd purchased at the Holiday Mall. She would work from the house, for a while. Fortunately, Mrs. Starks could stay until *1:30,* and then he would be home, again. Their arrangement would work out, just fine.

Kincaid had called from the jail. There were unexpected developments. Gerald had paid him a visit on yesterday.

"The man was bandaged up," he said. "He said he'd been in the hospital because somebody had shot him. He wouldn't say who had done it. But he looked like he was on some heavy medication. I think he left the hospital because he was *scared.*"

"Oh, yeah? What else did he say?"

"He said it was time for their *showdown.* I don't know what they've got planned, but their time is about up. LaRetha had better be careful. Anything could happen, now."

"So, what did you tell him?" He'd asked.

"I didn't tell him where she was, but he did ask where you lived. And if he hooks up with Samira or Jasmine, he'll find that out, soon enough."

Kincaid spoke as if LaRetha's staying with him wasn't disheartening to him. Douglas knew better.

"Thank you for the warning. We'll be on the lookout."

Kincaid was silent, and Douglas could sense his resentment, even over the phone.

"Well, take care of her," the younger man said. "Or when I get out, you'll have to answer to me. Understand?"

"I hear you," he'd replied, fully respecting his concern.

"What is it?" LaRetha asked when he rushed home before noon.

"Sit down. We need to talk."

After listening for moment, she reacted.

"*I wish he would come here and try something!*" She walked to the window and looked out as if planning something.

"We were expecting this, right? So, whatever his intentions are, we have to be ready for him."

"I agree, but there's no need for any more violence," he said. And instantly he regretted saying it. "What I meant was, we have to protect ourselves…"

"*Look*, Douglas. My ex-husband has come all the way here to deal with *me*. And if he's been shot like Kellen says, it only means that he's out of time which means that *I'm* out of time, too."

"I get that, but maybe we can get him to talk to us. Offer to help him in exchange for what he knows. Whatever he's here to resolve, he can't do it without you. And this could really help Kincaid's case."

"Maybe, but I don't intend to be used as *bait!* Not even for Kellen's sake. I can't believe you're even suggesting it."

"Okay. Not a good idea. But, wait here. By the way, what kind of car does he drive?"

"He has a black Dodge truck and a white Monte Carlo with some kind of grey design on the side and fancy wheels. You'll know it when you see it."

"Good."

He talked to someone on the phone in another room. Afterwards, he went into the kitchen to tell Mrs. Starks to be extra careful when she left for home.

"I understand, Douglas," the woman said. "If it concerns you, it must be something important. Besides, I'm not anxious to meet any angry *ex-husbands!* You just be careful."

He waited until she had left safely, and returned to find LaRetha still looking out of the den window.

"I called an investigator friend of mine," he said. "He says they need to question Gerald about a shooting incident. They're looking for him as we speak."

His phone rang before she could respond.

"All you have to do is sit tight. I'm meeting with Kincaid later this afternoon."

"And what do I use for protection while you're gone?"

Douglas looked around the room, which baffled her, before retrieving a baseball bat from the hall closet.

"How about this?"

"You must be kidding!"

"It's safer. *You're* safer," He sighed.

"Well, if it's only for an hour, this will do, alright." She took the bat, weighed it in her hand and playfully swung at him. He ducked just in time. "Yeah, this will do just fine."

"I wonder about you sometimes," he said, going to answer the ringing phone.

"Douglas?"

"Yes, baby."

"I like the sound of that," she said, smiling. And his heart brightened at this rare admission of her feelings for him.

"Thanks for going with me to look at the house, yesterday."

"No problem. I think it's a nice place, and a good deal. I'm glad you got it. It suits you."

She smiled, happily.

"But I have to run," he said. "Set the alarms and call me if anything out of the ordinary happens. I'll be back as soon as I can."

She thanked him, again. And remembering what had happened to Cecelia, he prayed that he was doing the right thing by leaving her.

Billard frowned. He still hadn't gotten confirmation that the job was done. And now was not the time for slip-ups.

"*Where is he?*" He asked, pacing the floor.

Reeves looked irritated, as did Elton Gray.

"Calm down. It shouldn't be much longer. Even if he drove, he should be here, soon."

Billard frowned. He wasn't concerned about Gerald Greer, but the man he'd sent to meet him. He'd known that Greer would come for the money, although he hadn't earned any.

"Well, he'd better hurry, before I send someone looking."

"You always panic too quick and move too soon," Reeves said in his usual drawl. "Let's just wait, and see what happens."

Billard shot him an angry look.

"Right," Elton Gray continued. "So we can be done with him and start planning our next course of action so that this new investigation won't end up on *our* doorstep."

"Well, don't expect too much from Greer," Billard replied.

These guys didn't know that Greer was coming under false pretenses. That he'd had absolutely no intention of paying the man. That would only make them suspicious about receiving their own cuts.

Nor did they know that he'd told Jasmine, who'd told Greer and Samira, that he was ready to sell. They would know better. But Greer wasn't going to make it here anyway, so he had no worries. Besides, better he cover himself on all sides, he thought. It was an excellent plan. He chuckled to himself. Now, if only Hogan would confirm.

"Well, hopefully he can find LaRetha and reason with her. If not, then..." Elton looked annoyed.

"*Then what?*" Billard growled. "You're crazy if you think I'm walking away, now. We've only got four more days, and we can't hold the buyers off, forever. It's either *now or never!*" He sputtered, as he looked at this man who served him no more purpose, other than to further split money that was unearned.

Foreman hadn't shown up, just like he said. But, he hadn't kept an eye on her, either. Jasmine had failed at getting Greer to hold LaRetha in Atlanta. All these fools were letting him down! And they wondered why things were happening without their knowledge.

Things were different when *Verilous* was alive. With him as a middleman, he could keep his distance from all of them. And at least then, he could get things done.

But now, with that old man gone, he'd just have to make the most of the situation, at least until he got his money. But, he couldn't afford to lose his cool. He still needed these people; for their cover and their silence.

"Look, you two go on home. I'll call you if something comes up."

Reeves looked relieved. He and Elton left and he locked the door firmly behind them, thinking how, having been a widower for ten years now, few things inspired him anymore. Aside from eating out almost every meal, he only had a few hobbies; like boating and fishing. But, the older he got, those trips were getting harder on his arthritis.

But what did motivate him was *money*. Money, money and *more* money. Winning cases to get money, and counting his money. Investing money and taking people's money. Watching money grow. It used to drive his wife crazy. She had called it an insatiable lust.

That farm deal had been his greatest challenge for the longest time. He'd been able to get about everybody in that family under his control, except *Watson*. And now, except for his daughter, LaRetha!

Verilous had been easy. The man had ideas he couldn't finance and debts he couldn't pay, well over *a hundred thousand dollars worth* –a fortune back then. So he had worked diligently for him, as had his wife. And he had done well by them, in return, putting unheard of sums of cash right into their hands. So when it came to the farm, they'd wanted that badly enough to include him in the deal.

The wife was determined to pay every penny of what she thought was owed to him. Except, that debt had been canceled by a credit life policy he'd kept on the old man, from years ago. It was too bad they'd never bothered to read their contract, he thought. In the meantime, they would get their hands on this nice chunk of property. Then he would come calling to collect in full, and it would all be his.

Nobody wanted that land more than him. But unlike them, he had no plans to sell it, right away, and didn't care if they didn't like it. He would do as he pleased with it.

Old man *Watson* had guardedly it very closely. But why he would leave it to a daughter who didn't know the first thing to do with it, rather than share at least some of it with his brothers and sisters had made no sense, *at first.* And now he figured that it was the same as when people left their fortune to pets rather than relatives. They'd been shown no love in life, so they gave none in death.

Watson had never liked him either, and told him so. And he had respected him for that. Like him, the man was also the type to shoot first and ask questions later. Just like that daughter of his.

Tired of waiting now, he drove the eight miles out of town to the spot where Gerald was to go. Aside from a splattering of blood on the ground and deep tire tracks from the tow truck, there was nothing. He kicked snow over the blood stains to cover them.

But, where was Hogan? And why hadn't he called to say that the job was done? He was fast becoming just like *Straiter.* You try to give somebody a job…

Paul Straiter had let them down and he had been forced to take care of him. Hogan had handled that for him, too. He'd said it would be easy to slip inside the hospital, and back out again, undiscovered. And he had been paid well for it. This should have been *easy.* Billard phoned Nell as he sped away.

"The man is down, but I can't find anybody," he grunted.

"I know. Gerald and Samira came by here a half-hour ago. I didn't answer the door."

"Gerald? Gerald came there? So whose blood was that on the ground?"

"*Our guy's!* That's who," she said in a low tone. Her family was home. "He's the one who got ambushed!"

They hastily agreed to meet back at his house as soon as Jasmine returned. Any place else was too risky.

He had grown to like Nell. But, she was useless to him, now. It was just a matter of time before she folded. That daughter of hers was loyal, but she'd been slipping too. Allowing that tramp friend of hers to think she was a partner was stupid, to say the least. Those little mistakes were going to cost her and her mother.

Hogan was shot and quite possibly the fifth body, now. Too bad for *Verilous.* His had been an accident. They hadn't expected the man to keep that truck. Those brakes were fixed to scare his niece, not even to kill anybody. But, there wasn't much he could have done if she'd ended up dead instead, was there?

Now, with this latest development, he just had to accept the fact that he might never see that money or the land. Well, he thought, at least he would be well rid of *them.*

But, somebody would have to take the blame for this almost perfect plan that had backfired. Kellen Kincaid would go to jail for Therell's shooting. But with Gerald still around, and possibly shooting his mouth off, that blame would very likely fall back onto the group. This mess needed to be cleaned up before he went anywhere, he thought.

He had planned to retire, anyway. But right now, there were people to silence. Like Gerald, Nell and those girls. He would do what he had to do, he figured. *Just like he'd done with Cecelia.*

Cecelia had lied to him. Double crossed him. Five years ago, she'd promised to get *Watson* to deed part of that property over to her, but then changed her mind. Then, she'd learned that he was chronically ill and soon to die, and apparently decided that something was better than nothing. She'd never said a word, but just strung him along, gotten her money and *ran*. Some people still thought she'd killed him. But he knew better.

That woman had *loved* that colored man immensely, much to his own dismay. She wouldn't have done it. It was the mixed marriage and the fact that he'd acquired so much wealth in his lifetime that had inspired such talk around town. But she was faithful, as far as he knew, having stood more to gain by *not* doing it. And then, there had been that matter of the *Will*.

He believed that *Watson* had loved Cecelia, too. But when it came to business, the man trusted no one. According to Cecelia, he'd had her sign a prenuptial agreement, stating that if he ever died of unnatural or even suspicious causes, *everything* would go to his daughter. Otherwise, the farm would still go to the girl, but the wife and those boys he'd adopted would be entitled to something. Cecelia could continue to live there until death or for as long as she liked, except she could never sell it, rent it or borrow against it. And, if she outlived LaRetha, the daughter's rights would go to her only son, Germaine.

He had thought the whole thing was bizarre for most people, just not the Watson's. The man had either been suspicious of the woman, or of her associations with people like him. He'd wondered why she even signed it, but then guessed that love did that to some people. Or rather, desperation. But, years into the marriage, Cecelia had become concerned. And she'd sworn it was all Laretta's doing.

"It's unfair that I had to sign that agreement. I think it's his ex-wife's doing. She never liked me, you know? I think he's been keeping her up for years. But what about *my* boys?" She'd asked him.

He knew the woman she spoke of. Laretta Watson was once a real fireball, and the first colored girl to ever give him a black eye, back in elementary school. It had seemed fitting that she and *Watson* would get together, and not surprising that they would end up, apart.

Laretta had done well for herself, he'd heard. And the daughter had lived pretty high with that dunce, Gerald Greer, as well. And now, considering all the insurance policies her uncle had claimed she had on her father, she was now a very wealthy woman.

He guessed it was possible, what Cecelia had said. But, he doubted Nell's claims that the woman had wanted anything to do with that broken down and busted husband of hers, back in the day.

Cecelia had rarely kept in touch with him, over the years. But she'd called a few weeks before Thanksgiving, saying Therell Watson had been trying to reach her, and asked if he knew why. Always distrustful of that family, she had loved the girl, however. And she had wondered if he wouldn't check in with LaRetha –*find out if she was in trouble*. He figured that time and distance had weakened the old broad's memory of him. And he didn't know why she wouldn't call LaRetha for herself. But, seeing that open window of opportunity, he had said that he would help.

By this time she'd had reason to be concerned. Therell was out of control and taking no direction from anyone, not even his father. After learning this, Billard had sworn to himself that if someone else didn't hurt that man, he would.

But Kellen Kincaid had done it. And it was of no surprise to him. Therell Watson's kind of smarts and insanity always was a dangerous combination. And as fearful as people had been of him, it made sense that he'd been hurt by someone least expected to do it.

Cecelia shouldn't have come back here. But, when he'd told her that LaRetha was considering selling, and wanted to speak to her about sharing a portion with her sons, she'd taken the first plane in.

She's looking forward to seeing you again, he'd lied, figuring correctly that she wouldn't verify it. While that would have been the sensible thing, the woman clearly wasn't always that. But she was predictable.

They would meet at the farm, he'd told her. And this was only right, he'd assured her. She deserved more, he'd said, figuring she'd probably gone through whatever money she'd left with.

He would represent her interests however she wanted him to, he'd offered. And she would be back on a plane in no time, but leaving as a woman who'd just made herself, her sons and grandchildren, very wealthy.

Apparently, the woman had no idea that both Therell and *Verilous* were dead, at this point. But, she wouldn't have to worry about running into *them*, he'd said. Which wasn't a lie. Cecelia had thought that she had everything to gain by coming, and considering her stepdaughter's generous nature, believed every word he had said.

So, they had met at the airport. She was carrying a big bag of gifts. But what she didn't know when she'd called to say that she was waiting at the airport was that, just hours earlier, LaRetha Watson had boarded a plane to Atlanta.

She wasn't even suspicious when they'd driven up. The house had been partly lit, so his story that she was inside waiting for them was believable.

They had rung the doorbell, and he had almost felt sorry for this woman who stood there, eagerly anticipating a reunion of sorts with her stepdaughter. To have come to *Lovely* so quickly, he imagined she must have only had happy thoughts all the way here. Still, this had to be done.

Ringing again, she called out to LaRetha. *Nothing.*

"Maybe something's happened," he said, sounding concerned. "She does live alone, doesn't she? I'll go around back and see," he'd said, trying to sound concerned.

He had disappeared for a few minutes, then returned.

"I don't see anything. Maybe she got the date mixed up. I'm just worried that one of them got to her before us. I'll need to break in. *Stand back!*"

He'd kicked the door in. She had hurried past him, anxiously looking for her precious LaRetha, so certain someone had done the woman in.

He'd been amazed when he threw on the bright lights and saw what the woman had done with the place. It was nothing short of a work of art, the way she'd combined colors, textures and designs. And that kitchen! He would have liked that design for his own.

He had pretended to look for LaRetha. Walking throughout the house, he had called out for the woman, to no apparent avail. But, if Cecelia had been slow to begin with, it didn't take long for her to finally get the picture.

"What have you done with LaRetha?" She looked worried, almost terrified. She started backing toward the front door. *Pitiful.*

"The question is, *what am I going to do to you?*" He'd responded. "There is a matter of an upcoming trial and a subpoena. And you're not testifying!"

"What trial?" She'd had no clue. That was even better. He mentioned the case against Kellen Kincaid. Her eyes had widened in fear.

"But, you said..." *Then,* she had started to scream.

The entire deed had taken less than a half hour; striking her until she stopped screaming, binding her with electrical tape and setting the fire. But first, he'd taken his time in searching the house, and found a large collection of computer disks. Taking them with plans to review them later, he had then set the fire, and two others in the barn and the garage.

It was almost daybreak when someone finally discovered the body amongst the ruins, all bound and burned. He felt badly for Cecelia. But she never should have married that colored man in the first place, he reasoned.

After moving his truck and clearing his tracks, he had taken the long road home, confident now that she wouldn't be testifying. But, fires had always been his specialty, he thought. And now, back at home again, he waited anxiously for the women to arrive.

Nell and Jasmine waited in Billard's basement den, as usual.

"What is he doing?" Jasmine whispered to her mother, who sat quietly beside her. The man had just taken their coats, telling them to wait downstairs until he returned.

"I don't know. And I don't like it, either."

"I think we made a mistake, coming here. Did you see how he looked? All *demented,* and like he hasn't bathed in *days.*"

Her mother nodded.

"And where is everyone else? Or is anybody else left?" She said, anxiously. "I went to get Samira, but she never showed. Mama, I don't know about you, but with LaRetha finally agreeing to sell, I don't want us getting caught up in anything *crazy!* Just by association, we've got as much to lose as Bob does."

"*Sssshh?*" Nell listened, and reached inside her purse. Her husband's gun was still there.

"Jasmine, from the way things are going, I don't believe she's ready to sell. I think it's just another one of Billard's plans to get everyone in town and get rid of us, one by one. We can't trust him, now. There's no telling *what* he's planning to do!"

"So, why did we even come? This man is *insane.* And we're going to end up either dead or *under* the jail, fooling around with him. We always knew how he was, but look, here we are, anyway! And it's our fault."

"No, baby, it's mine. And I'm so sorry about that. I was hoping we could break away, clean. I shouldn't have brought you into this. But, I thought I was helping you. Helping the family!"

"Helping, Mama? When has any of this ever been for *me?* You've trusted him more than you do anyone. Why is that?"

"I just wanted you kids to have a good life," Nell said, wiping the corner of one eye with a tissue.

"I *had* a good life, before this. So did you. But we can't keep hurting people and saying it's because *we* want to have a good life. We've lost Daddy and Therell, and who knows what we've just done to Gerald and Samira, leading them here based on what Billard said? I can't even begin to ask forgiveness for this." Jasmine started to cry.

"I'm sorry, baby. I really am. I wish I could change it."

"Well, you can't! Daddy would've never gone along with this..."

"Your daddy started this. Don't you forget that!" Her mother snapped, her eyes flaring with anger.

Then, a door slammed shut and there was bumping. They looked at one another. Nothing happened for a moment. But then, the one window in the basement went dark. And there was the sound of electrical drilling against the outer walls.

"*What's that?*" Jasmine shrieked. They both ran to the door. Nell twisted the knob, but it wouldn't turn.

"He's bolting it. He's nailing it shut!" Nell said with dismay.

"*Billard! Billard!* What're you doing?" Jasmine called, but got no answer. The nailing continued.

"Oh, this fool has really lost his mind, now." Nell said. She looked around the room. "Here, help me break this window so we can get out of here."

Jasmine grabbed a single chair and the two of them tossed it against the window. It didn't give. They tried again, succeeding only in cracking the glass and breaking the chair. They could hear another board being nailed from the outside. Jasmine was wide-mouthed with dismay.

"Wait!" Jasmine ran up the basement stairs, and tried to open the door that led inside the house. It was locked, as well.

"Bob?" Nell called out as calmly and sternly as she could. "You can't keep us in here, forever. You have to let us out of here."

"*My cell phone!*" Jasmine reached for hers, but found the outer pocket of her purse was empty. Nell's was charging in the car.

"He stole my phone when I came in. I never even noticed. I should have noticed," Jasmine said, sounding as panicked as she felt. "What is he planning to do..?"

"What does it look like, Jasmine?" Her mother cried, frantically. "He's going to burn us up like he did Cecelia. We've got to get out of here. *Think,* Jasmine!"

Just then, they heard a sloshing sound hitting the building. There was no question what it was. Saying nothing, Nell ran to the part of the wall that the sound had come from and pounded her fist against it. She tried the door knob, again.

How could her mother have gotten them into this? Jasmine was beside herself, and wondering if she really knew Nell, at all.

"You'd better not do this! Billard!" Nell screamed. "You can't kill us like this!"

The two of them began screaming and beating against the door as the sloshing sound continued, until they could hear it no more.

"He's going to burn the whole house down."

"Not with me in it, he won't." Nell kicked the entry door. Jasmine tried to help. But the door was nailed shut, by now.

"We have to do something," Jasmine said, hastily.

They pounded on the window until it finally broke. But it was already bolted closed and not even a beam of sunlight shone through. Then, there was a great *whooshing* sound, and within minutes, the wall was in flames and smoke was pouring in through every possibly opening in the window and door. They backed up, watching in dismay.

"Here," Nell said. "We don't have much air left," she coughed. "Let's push this sofa against the window, and see if it'll give. Help me."

Raising each end, they struggled to lift the small settee and ram it into the window as hard as they could. It only gave a little. Not enough to give them hope.

"Here. I'll stand on it. Give me something heavy."

Nell handed Jasmine an iron lamp, which she rammed against the wood with all her might. Finally, it gave. But instead of fresh air, a smoldering fire licked through the opening from outside, setting the curtains ablaze and singeing her face as she fell away from it. Within moments, the entire window was ablaze, and all the two women could do was watch.

19

The phone rang and Douglas wasn't surprised to learn that Gerald had been seen in town with Samira. He joined her for an omelet and coffee at the kitchen table.

"Who was that on the phone?" She inquired.

"Our investigator. Gerald is in town. He's with Samira…"

"Now, why doesn't that surprise me?"

"They've been holed up at a hotel for hours. It's just a matter of time before he's arrested for your kidnapping. They're keeping me posted."

"How much is this investigator costing me?"

"Just a few bills and a nice steak dinner, once this is all over with. And I'm paying for it. Hopefully, that day won't be too far away."

"Well, if Gerald is in town and hanging out with Samira, it's just a matter of time before the stuff hits the fan," she sighed.

"*Right,*" he exclaimed. "And he's already been shot, so apparently whoever he came to see wasn't too happy to see him. But, hiding out won't help him. If we know where they are, it's just a matter of time before someone else knows, too."

She looked away, and he realized her concern for her ex-husband. As far as he was concerned, the man was no better than Kincaid. But they'd been a family, once. And he was her son's father. He guessed that divorcing someone didn't always mean no longer caring about them. Still, it made him a little jealous.

Finally, she looked at him.

"That house is beautiful, isn't it? It wouldn't have taken much to get settled in, there," she said, wistfully.

Her statement stunned him. LaRetha was losing hope. Still unafraid, she was giving up - accepting the fact that she might not survive this.

He was speechless. He couldn't allow this. She would survive, and the right people would be held accountable, *if it killed him!*

"Whatever's supposed to happen," she said, washing her plate and glass in the sink, "it's already started. The month is over. The *thirty days*, remember? I imagine it's getting pretty hectic for Gerald and Samira. And all of them are probably racing around to see who'll succeed first at getting me to sell. I can't believe all of this could happen over property rights."

"Not rights, *greed*. And Gerald's heavily involved," Douglas said. "Kidnapping is no small offense. And even while that was going on, someone was here in *Lovely*, murdering Cecelia and burning your house. That's quite a conspiracy."

"That's not even *human!*"

"I agree."

"But you know? Don't think I'm crazy, but I wonder if Gerald wasn't just trying to save me, somehow," she mused.

He doubted it, but said nothing. The truth would come out soon enough.

"You know, Gerald was a lot of things when we divorced, but nothing like this and never to the point of hurting someone. Certainly not me. He was really a hard working, caring husband, for a long time."

He thought about how that would make sense, if he wasn't hiding out with *Samira*.

"But," she continued, "I guess money changes people. He thinks I owe him something, but I don't."

"I know what you mean, LaRetha," he said. "There'll always be people who will try and prosper at other people's expense, regardless of who suffers."

"But, Gerald didn't need any of this. This had to go deeper than money. I think he might resent the fact that I don't need him for anything. Thank goodness for that!"

"Whatever's going on with him," he said, "I doubt that he's here just to sleep with Samira. He's probably part of some plan to keep us from going to court, too. I hear its payday, and he still hasn't finished his job."

"That would explain the poorly planned kidnapping," she stated. "That deadline and Kellen's court date are upsetting a lot of people, I imagine. It's probably the reason they murdered Cecelia. They couldn't trust her testimony. I just wonder what she knew."

She sat down, wiping at a tear before going to the kitchen counter to put away dishes. She didn't want him to see her crying, he thought. *Didn't she know that it was her sensitivity that he loved most about her?*

She sniffled softly and he went over and gave her a tight hug.

"LaRetha, baby. I know it hurts."

"She was like a mother to me. When I was a child, she did everything she could to make me happy. She loved acting and poetry. Did you know she was the reason I got into journalism?"

He shook his head.

"She was just a good person. If I had just known..."

"*You* didn't kill anybody, LaRetha. Certainly not Cecelia."

"If she'd only called me back. We could have talked and..."

"You called her about this?"

"Several times, she never called back. I don't even know if she got my messages. I should have kept trying."

"At least you tried, baby. She should have called you back. It's not your fault."

"It is if I don't do something. What if I just call a meeting with them? With Jasmine and Nell, and Billard, and the rest of them?"

"No! It's too late for that. It's much too dangerous, now."

"But, I have to do *something*," she insisted.

"Not that! Their time is running out. So, just wait. They'll come to us. I promise you that. I'm sure they all know where you are, right now. It's just a matter of time. It's better that we wait for them."

He waited until she appeared convinced, then sighed with relief.

"But, Douglas, even if Gerald knows I'm here, I'm not worried. He would've already hurt me if he'd planned to."

"But what if he has to hurt you now, to save *himself?* It's a different game here in *Lovely.* Besides, don't you ever worry about your own well-being?" He asked, almost angrily.

"It's not over, so don't let your guard down, just yet. If anything happened to you, Laretta and Germaine would never forgive me, and I'd have to duel Kincaid to his death. Worse, I would never forgive myself."

"Besides," he said, tilting her face so he could kiss her cheek. "I have big plans for us. And, I fully intend to see them through."

She looked at him, thoughtfully.

"We do have a lot to talk about," she agreed. This pleased him.

"Yes. And I know you plan to go back to Atlanta, but let's give this a chance. Let's give *us* one and not take any chances.

"I think I can manage that," she said, a teasing smile passing her lips. And he was drawn to her. Kissed her. Held her for a moment.

"So, can you at least tell me who Kellen says is behind all this?" She asked.

He released her, the moment lost, for now.

"Well, it's no big secret, I suppose. Not now, anyway. But, you have to promise me; no articles on this story before the trial ends," he said.

"I promise." She understood his concern.

"It's not hard to figure out, at this point. Your entire family, Samira, Kellen, and evidently Gerald, have all been working for Bob Billard, this whole time. Even Nell is in the middle of it…"

"*No!*"

"It's true. I've had a man on this for awhile. The same man who's watching Gerald and Samira, right now. A group of them have been meeting at Bob's house for some kind of investment group. I guess you needed to know this. In case…" he paused.

"Nothing's going to happen to you, baby," she said, smiling. "Or to me. But, Douglas?'

"Yes?"

"Had you no idea before, that your law partner was spearheading this the entire time?"

"Not until I talked with Kincaid. It's the main reason that I closed the office. I've wiped my office clean of anything I thought he might use to his benefit."

"That explains why he was so against my fighting Therell for the farm. But, if you know this about him, why..?"

"Why did I stay in practice with him? *First of all*, this was all news to me. I've known this man for most of my life. He always used to seem a bit shady, even back then. But, I *knew* him, his hard work and achievements. He's always had strange ideas, but I thought I knew his boundaries."

She nodded.

"Besides, he always respected me and our clients. He's helped a lot of people in his career. I just never thought he would take this kind of a risk."

He shook his head.

"And *secondly,* I have an obligation to the people of this town to finish what's been started here. Sometimes I take cases for little to no money, just to prevent farmers and laborers from being run out of business, or denied work because they won't sell what they own. But, those people will only go so far. They have few resources, and I can't protect them, forever."

She nodded, appreciating this.

"Somebody has to make sure that this town isn't drained dry, and keep an eye on people like Bob. The heavy hitters, you know. So, when my father died, I just took over that role. I stayed close, suspecting the worse, and I was right."

She nodded.

"I'm not judging you, Douglas. I just thought the meaning of the word *partner* was that both people had similar ideologies and stood for the same things. Or, why be partners?"

"It was the only way. The closest I could get to him."

"I understand that much," she continued, "but just knowing how he was ruining so many people, especially *our* people... Forgive me, Douglas. I mean no disrespect. I guess I just don't understand."

He contemplated this.

"You understand better than you think," he responded. "My father faced animosity every time he made an unpopular decision, and so did yours. But, aside from the law, which didn't protect them, there were no rule books to follow and little education when it came to dealing with those people in positions of power who'd rather see them dead than see them succeed. They did the best they could, and that was enough."

She nodded. Listened.

"Both of them stood for something, and they left something in both of us that makes us want to stay and fight when the sensible thing would have been to pack up and leave a long time ago. So, what I'm saying is, if you can answer those questions for yourself, then you've answered them for me."

"But, it's not the same thing and you know it," she responded. "My fighting to keep the farm and your *fronting* for some old blowhard racist *puke* are two entirely different things."

"I was never *fronting!* But *I* made the decision to stay, same as you," he replied, heatedly. "The man is finally about to be exposed. Give me some credit, won't you? I've worked hard for this town."

"Sure, and all it took was the death of half my family, the loss of my home and everything I've invested in it, Kellen going to jail, and now, me being in danger of losing my life, for you to finally get to this point."

He stared at her in disbelief. *She blamed him for that?*

"*I am only one man, LaRetha!*" He walked away to keep from shaking her, silly. "And I can only do so much, alone. Unfortunately, until now, no one was willing to fight. And I mean, *no one!*"

"Until now?" She challenged and he calmed himself before speaking, again.

"It's *timing*, LaRetha. Change takes time. I didn't plan this. I hate this. But, if I have to use this bad situation to make good, then so be it. You of all people should understand that."

She nodded, saying nothing else. She just didn't know how badly he'd wanted out, he thought, and many times came close to leaving. But something always compelled him to stay. And now, he only wanted her to understand that they were one and the same – cut from the same cloth. But, she didn't look convinced.

"We have to understand one another's positions. If not, then I guess this has all been an incredible waste of time, our pulling together to help your *friend!*" He gave her a look of indifference.

Surprised at his reply, LaRetha's eyes narrowed. She started to leave the room.

"LaRetha, I didn't mean that," he said. "I'm just feeling very frustrated right now. I knew these people, too. Your uncle, Cecelia, and the rest. If I had known just two years ago what I know right now, I would have made sure that things happened differently. But, I wasn't expecting it. I wasn't even expecting *you*."

This, she seemed to understand. But, he needed to be certain. They needed to be united; now, if never before.

She studied him. Leaned back against the counter and studied him.

"Neither was I. But I understand, okay?"

He smiled, uncertainly.

"You know, I spoke to Vera Canter about all this."

"When?" He asked.

"I saw her on Christmas Day."

"Oh?"

"She told me a few things that surprised me. First, that *Paul Straiter* was no common criminal. Just a man down on his luck, and probably being manipulated to do what he did. I'm not even certain the man was there to kill me. He could have been warning me…"

"And kicking your door in to do it?" He asked, incredulously.

"I know. It's silly. But she made me think about it, and…"

"*LaRetha!* The last thing you need to do is to start entertaining opinions. We only need the *facts*. Besides, Vera might be a nice person, but she's very attached to the people she serves over there. How kind he was to her makes no difference in this case."

"I'm sorry. You're right. I just can't believe I ever thought I could do something positive in this town. The only thing I've done is to prove that my coming here was a terrible mistake - for me and everyone around me."

"LaRetha, stop it! I was born in *Lovely* and I know the people here, personally. What's so special about you that you should've known what the rest of us didn't?"

She didn't respond. He hated it when she beat herself up, like this.

"Are we in good shape for the trial, Douglas?"

"*Excellent shape*. After everything that's happened, it'll be a lot easier to get those charges dropped. All the witnesses' stories are consistent. My only concern is that no one claims to have seen the actual confrontation, yet. And the whereabouts of your uncle's gun. I still don't know."

She nodded.

"But," he said, "by the same token, no one can say the struggle didn't occur. And that's in our favor. So, stop worrying."

"I'll try." She sighed, giving him a hug that he wasn't expecting.

He said fine, glad to see her back to her normal self. Then, he noticed her standing suddenly still, blinking her eyes and staring at the back door.

"Douglas, there's somebody outside your door," she whispered.

"What?" He quickly turned to see.

"*Look!*"

She pointed to the back door that was just beyond the kitchen. Sure enough, there was the shadow of a person leaning against it as if trying to peer inside. Douglas switched off the bright overhead lights, making their visitor's outline appear even more obvious against the pale yellow curtains. Still, they didn't move.

And now, they were turning the doorknob, trying to get inside.

LaRetha stood there, shocked. But, Douglas reacted quickly.

"Go upstairs and lock yourself in your bedroom. If I'm not there in ten minutes, call *911.*"

"Are you sure?" she asked.

"Do it, now!" He whispered intensely. Reaching to open a drawer, he retrieved a long knife and handed it to her. Getting another, he wielded it upward as he stood against a wall and stepped slowly toward the door. It rocked her into a different state of realization. He could be in danger!

"No! I won't leave you." She was ready to confront them. She followed him.

"Then *hide!* Hurry, before they leave," he said, waving her back.

She did as he said, going around the corner to stand near the stairway. For the next few minutes, she heard nothing.

"Douglas?" She whispered.

Still nothing. Crouching down, she could hear his back door opening, then what sounded like a rush of voices, and the door slamming closed. It was definitely Gerald. She listened closely.

"I know she's here. Where is she? We need to talk to her."

"Not like this, you won't!" Douglas fired back. "You're crazy to even come here. You know you're wanted for kidnapping."

"Don't you worry about that," Gerald growled. "Now, you can either deal with us, or you can deal with the others, and I can guarantee you, they won't be doing much talking. So, will you call her in here, or do we all have to go and get her?"

"Forget it. She's not here."

"I don't believe him," the woman said. *Samira?*

"You're lying!" Gerald fired. "We heard you talking. Hold this," he must have said to the woman. "I wouldn't move if I were you, Douglas. She'll use it if she has to."

Hearing his footsteps coming in her direction, LaRetha stepped into the doorway of the kitchen.

"None of this is necessary, Gerald. Tell her to put that gun down, and I'll talk to you," she said, as calmly as possible.

They all looked at her as she stood watching her ex-husband with his lover and co-conspirator, who was holding a gun on Douglas. Gerald had one arm in a bandage and sling.

"*Careful*, LaRetha. You can't trust either of them!" Douglas said.

"Don't worry, Douglas" she said, "Gerald won't hurt anybody."

She only wished she could believe what she'd just said. She faced her ex-husband, feeling all of the anger she'd suppressed for so long. Gerald looked from one of them to the other and chuckled.

"Oh, so I see what this is. Here I thought he was helping your other man out, and turns out he's helped himself to even more than that."

"Not true, Gerald," LaRetha retorted, angrily. "And tell your *woman* to get that gun out of his face. I won't talk to you, like this."

"You'll talk to us," Gerald said, starting toward her, *"any way I say!"*

LaRetha stepped forward. He stopped. She kept walking closer.

"Did you come here to kill me, Gerald? Is that it? You missed your chance to do it in Atlanta, so you're here to finish the job? How much is my dead body worth to you? As much as my uncle's? How about my stepmother's?"

"Back up, LaRetha. I don't want to hurt you."

"Why are you even here? What's your interest in all this madness? You assaulted Marilee. You and your friends have killed people. You've burned my house down. Kidnapped me. When is enough going to be enough, with you? What are they paying you?"

"I didn't have anything to do with those murders or your house. Samira and I came here to *talk*. We thought you two should know some things, and that maybe we could help one another out. We're having a slight... slight problem."

"What, the easy money ain't quite so easy any more?"

"Same old LaRetha. You know everything, don't you? We don't know anything."

"This was all your doing, remember? You'll go to jail for what you tried to do to me."

"I was only trying to keep them from getting to you, first."

"Sure you were." Still, she was oddly relieved to hear it.

"I had no intentions of hurting you. That's why they're not too happy with me, right now."

"So, I've heard." She said. She looked at the coat slung over his arm and saw blood dripping from his sleeve. Sliding the coat down, she could see his bandaged wounds. She could tell by his pained expression that it hurt, pretty badly.

"*Humph!*" Gerald's female companion snorted.

LaRetha turned to face her.

"So, I finally get a formal introduction to *Samira?* And why are *you* here?" She asked the woman who looked at her, then away.

"She's a loose end, like me." Gerald said. "All bets are off, right now. Billard's investors are getting restless and with Kellen's trial coming up, everything's gone haywire. We can't trust anybody in this town. So, we came to get protection - ours in exchange for yours."

"You're in no position to make *deals,* Gerald," Douglas said.

"That's right," LaRetha added. "You should have stayed in Atlanta and minded your own business," she added. "And now, after what you've done and tried to do, *you* want protection from *us?*"

"That's right. Besides, it's for your benefit and his. Especially if they get to you before the cops, do."

LaRetha grimaced at her ex-husband, before noticing that he was wavering now. Staggering forward, he reached toward her before his eyes rolled upward and he fell unconscious to the floor. Samira screamed and dropped Gerald's gun, rushing to his side. It slid across the floor and Douglas quickly picked it up.

When Gerald finally came to, he was lying on the floor with his one free hand and both feet tied behind him. He struggled against thick ropes that Douglas had gotten from his garage. Samira was tied to a chair, much the same way. Douglas handed Gerald's gun to LaRetha.

"Here. We don't know why they're really here, so don't hesitate to use it if necessary. And I mean that."

Douglas was right. The truth hadn't yet been told about these two.

"I've had enough of guns, Douglas." She pushed it back to him.

"You have no choice. Hold it on them!"

She took it, holding but not aiming it. She wouldn't shoot anyone, ever again. She watched as he lifted Gerald almost effortlessly, tying him to a chair next to Samira, who was trembling in fear, now. Maybe she wasn't such a tough girl, after all, LaRetha thought.

Leaning against the kitchen counter, she watched them until Douglas returned from upstairs. He had a small tape recorder, which he placed onto the kitchen table in front of them. Plugging it into the wall socket, he made certain that it was working properly, then eased back onto a nearby stool.

"Okay, Gerald. Start from the beginning," he said. "And don't leave anything out. And Samira, when he's done, you're next."

I guess I've gone and done it now, Billard thought. There would be no turning back. Too bad Gerald and Samira hadn't been in the house with those two. *Then,* it would be over.

Now, to catch that plane to Mexico. There was one waiting for him on a private airfield. From there, who knew? His house was gone. He had cleared out all his accounts three days ago. As for that farm deal, he'd finally accepted the fact that this might be a lost situation.

May the best man or woman, have it, he thought. *And all the misery that comes along with it.*

He could still hear the yells and screams coming from inside his basement. It had only taken minutes for that wood siding to light up. Those two had died of smoke inhalation if nothing else. And, even if anybody came to put the fire out, with all the rubble on top of them, no one would think to dig down into the basement for bodies. They wouldn't possibly get there soon enough to save them.

"Billard! You're crazy. You can't do this. You can't kill us like this," one of them had yelled.

Watch me, he'd thought, with a snort. He would've stayed and observed, but time didn't permit. So, after driving a few more nails in, he'd left just as the whole side wall had burst into flames.

Let the witches burn! He'd thought, laughing gleefully.

Douglas finished writing, turned off the recorder and picked up the phone to call the authorities. He noticed that LaRetha was sitting quietly, obviously grief stricken at hearing her uncle's plot in detail.

"Why would you ask Germaine here, with all this going on?" He heard her ask Gerald.

"I *thought* he would be safer with me," he said, apologetically.

"He could have been killed! Both of you! How could you even think about putting him in the middle of this mess?"

"I'm *sorry* about that. I couldn't leave him unguarded in Atlanta. But you know I wouldn't hurt Germaine."

"I can't even believe you."

"Germaine wouldn't have come, anyway," Samira piped in.

The room was silent. LaRetha was looking at the woman with disbelief. As she walked toward her, Samira's eyes widened in fear.

"What would *you* know about my son, Samira?"

"I'm just saying, he didn't like it when…"

"When what? When you were sleeping with Gerald while we were married? Or did you try to seduce him, too?"

"No! I didn't even know Gerald until we met at your father's funeral."

"And you would conduct your business at my father's funeral?"

The woman looked helplessly at Gerald, who said nothing.

"Where is everybody now, Gerald?" Douglas asked.

"I don't know. Jasmine was sending somebody to meet me out on Spree Road, except somebody sent a gunman, instead."

"So, who shot you, Gerald?" LaRetha asked, sarcastically.

"I don't know. I couldn't see him very well, but the tow truck came from *Hogan's Garage.*"

She and Douglas exchanged glances.

"You'd better be telling the truth," Douglas said.

"Man, why would I come here to lie?"

"Why would you come here, *period,* is what I want to know."

Gerald shook his head, disturbed at not being believed. Douglas left the room. He returned and pulled LaRetha out of earshot.

"The police are on the way. They've sent a car to Spree Road. They should call back, soon. But if this is all true, we can finally link Therell and your inheritance problems to Billard, and Billard to your uncle's death."

She knew she should have been relieved, but could only feel despondent over the sad truth; her uncle's death had been no accident. Douglas hugged her briefly, well aware of stares from the other two.

"Now, what was *Cecelia's* involvement in all this?" He asked Gerald, who quickly exchanged glances with Samira.

"Well?" Douglas persisted.

"I don't really know," Gerald said.

"I do," Samira piped up. "Jasmine told me."

Douglas switched the recorder back on.

Billard was almost at the airfield. As far as he knew, his house was in cinders, by now. The woman had made this easy for him, doing something no one did anymore – she'd left her keys in the ignition. So, with her car in his closed garage, no one would expect to find her or Jasmine there. The smoke would have alarmed the neighbors though, and someone might try to contact him. He turned his cell phone off. Their time was up, but his wasn't. He increased his speed.

It was always extremely cold in *Lovely* in winter. And despite recent sunshine, the snow had returned. The air was especially frigid, today, but sunshine was expected again, tomorrow.

He hadn't told anyone he was leaving. Not even his financiers, who'd said he had wasted too much time, trying to get LaRetha to come around. That he'd cost too many lives. But, they weren't the ones going down and had already said as much, adding that if anything else went wrong, by the time they finished with him, he'd wish he'd gone down in that fire with Cecelia.

He had planned for Kellen Kincaid to get the blame for that fire, but Therell had been in the middle, messing everything up. So, that hadn't worked out. Then, he had considered framing LaRetha for her stepmother's murder, but she'd suddenly left town. Besides, Douglas had been all in the way of that, providing an alibi for her, every second of every single day.

Now, regretfully, he was leaving behind a lot of hard work; lots of victories and almost as many losses. And all that work was summed up on the deeds and other papers locked in the briefcase on the seat beside him.

Right now, the underdogs were winning. But at least he could leave and start over. Some of the others hadn't been quite so lucky.

His biggest regret was having to leave it all with Douglas Davis. He had turned out to be a great attorney, after all, proving himself worthy of the opportunity his father had insisted they give him. The sister had left to practice in the big city - her own great luck. Still, the father and son duo had been very successful.

Like his father though, Davis had never been one to do anything too borderline. He had been way too concerned about people's expectations of him and this legacy his father had left behind.

Douglas, Sr. had helped pioneer the original investment group. But, since his death, things had changed; the climate, the town, the world, *everything*. The only thing that hadn't were the hard times people were having in *Lovely*. So, he'd had to change with the world, or risk going under, as well.

But where was the appreciation for all the *good* things he'd done? He had given the father a place at his firm when other whites in the area would only hire folks like him to cook and clean for them. Some had called him a fool. Others had walked away from him, completely. But he'd known the value of those rarely counted dollars, back in the day. And, that knowledge had paid off.

Because of his alliance with the Davis's, when the economy was particularly bad, he'd been able to persuade more than a few of the local farmers, white and colored, to trust him with their property concerns. Too bad for them, they had believed in him. Many of those deeds were in his briefcase, right now.

He'd managed to keep them unaware of his activities for the longest time. But, they couldn't complain. Their partnership had served both men, extremely well. With Douglas' current earnings, and the money and investments that his father had left him and his sister, he was set for life, whether he practiced law or not. With him leaving town, and once the sting of the disgrace was passed, Douglas would be even better off than before, considering all the business that would come trickling down to him - the new town hero. He'd make a fortune just cleaning up the mess that *he'd* made, Billard thought.

And now, here he was, preparing to spend the rest of his life on the run, while Douglas' pockets and prestige grew fatter and fatter with a career that was on an upswing. Not only that, but he would share that great future with the already wealthy and most irritating *LaRetha Greer!*

Now, he truly could not allow that, could he? He thought. Figuring he had one last score to settle, Billard turned his truck around.

LaRetha shook her head in disbelief at what Gerald and Samira were telling them.

"That's *exactly* what I'm saying," the woman said in response to Douglas' last question, eyeing him coolly, before turning her attentions to LaRetha, whom she eyed evilly.

"So, Cecelia was involved with Billard," she stated with disbelief. "But Billard had shared too many things with her, and when she didn't deliver my father's property, she had to leave town just to get away from him?"

"That's what Jasmine told me," the woman said, smugly. "Billard hated the fact that she married your father and allowed him to raise her kids. He was trying to use her..."

She stopped when she noticed LaRetha's angry expression.

"And what was your cut in this, Samira?"

The woman blinked a few times. Didn't reply.

"Same as mine," Gerald interceded. "*Fifty thousand.*"

Fifty thousand! LaRetha couldn't even imagine that.

"*He's lying,*" Samira finally said. "It was *twenty-five thousand.*" She flashed an evil look at Gerald. He scoffed.

"And you, Gerald?"

"The same," he shrugged.

"That much, *each?* Just to get me to sell?" LaRetha asked with disbelief. "What were they planning to do with the farm?"

"That's what I was trying to say in Atlanta," Gerald said. "They know people whose projects could make them *millions*. You could've gotten a piece of it, too. But, when you wouldn't sell, they were planning to take it, one way or the other."

"That's why I got involved, LaRetha. I didn't want to see you hurt over what you didn't know about, and they weren't going to tell you because you might have taken it all. This way, we all had something to gain, and I could be certain that they wouldn't bother you, anymore. I was trying to save your *life*."

"Don't flatter me with that crap," she sniffed. "Whatever you did was purely for greed. You're only saying this now because we're your last resort."

He frowned.

"You should have known better. What made either of you think they would pay you, anyway? She exclaimed. "Now look at you. Shot by the same people who hired you. How did they get you to come here, anyway? I know I never could."

"They said you'd changed your mind after the fire. That I would get paid when I got here," he said.

"They told me the same thing," Samira said. "But, I think Gerald was right when he said I was better off not showing up to receive it."

"So you believe that Jasmine would hurt you?" She asked Samira, incredulously. "She's some cousin and a worst kind of friend, isn't she?"

"I wonder if she knew the truth. She didn't sound like she was hiding anything."

"*Sure, she was!*" Gerald said. "That's Nell's child. She was probably setting you up the entire time, just like me."

"I don't know, Gerald," LaRetha said. "If Billard killed Cecelia on his own, chances are he planned that one on his own, too."

"Well, that's what I was told," Samira said. "Can I get something to drink?"

Exchanging irritated glances, both Douglas and LaRetha ignored her request.

"I don't understand why they thought I'd just let them take my farm away. It's not going to happen, she said, angrily.

"You don't *let* them do anything," Gerald grumbled. "That's why it's called *taking!* These folks in *Lovely* mean business. We're not very safe, right now. And neither are you." He said.

Jarring his arm, he winced with pain. LaRetha lifted it to get a better look.

"You really need to have that looked at," she said, aware that Samira and Douglas were observing them, together.

"I have pain pills in my coat pocket," Gerald said.

Retrieving those, she ran water from the spigot into a glass and placed two pills in his mouth. She held the glass as he drank the water, all under Samira's evil glare.

Don't worry about any reconciliations, she thought. If they weren't needed to testify, she believed she might have strangled them both.

"Give me the names of all the group members," Douglas said to Samira.

"I haven't met everybody..," Samira started.

"Now *that's* surprising," LaRetha interrupted.

"*But,*" Samira continued, rolling her eyes at LaRetha, "aside from Billard, there's Nell and Jasmine, Mr. Reeves the banker, Elton Gray who owns a hardware store. Howard Hogan and your uncle. Oh, and Mr. Foreman. But, I don't think he's that involved."

Mr. Foreman! LaRetha shook her head in disbelief. This plot ran deeper than she'd thought.

"Tell me, what was Laura Harvey's part in all this?" She asked, remembering her intended roommate.

"I've never heard of her," Samira defended.

"One more question, Gerald. And you only have one chance tell the truth. If I don't like your answer, I *promise* you..."

"No, LaRetha," he said without waiting on the question. "Nobody killed your father. Certainly not your stepmother. I said I was sure when I wasn't. I was wrong for lying to you."

"And what changed your mind since last week?"

"I talked to Samira and... Well, I wasn't sure. I was trying to keep you in Atlanta. I'm very sorry..."

"*Shut up!* You're not sorry, at all." With this, LaRetha almost forgot her vow to never use another gun. But it wasn't true. Cecelia hadn't been capable of such a thing, after all.

"I could really hurt you for lying to me about something like that."

Douglas took Gerald's gun from her trembling hands. Relieved, she walked out of the room. It was so hard, talking about this. Douglas followed.

"Are you going to be alright?"

"This is just *too much!*" She whispered vehemently.

"I know. But it's almost over. Just hold on, okay?"

She nodded. They turned their attentions back to the two, who were arguing, now.

Douglas' cell phone rang and he answered. Saying very little, he listened before hanging up.

"They found the spot," he said. "And blood on the ground. The tow truck was back at the garage, with a bullet hole in it and bloodstains. Turns out, somebody else was in the truck with our shooter," he said.

Gerald's head snapped up. LaRetha gave him a questioning look.

"Apparently, Hogan made it to the hospital. He's in intensive care. But, this man claims they were out there on a distress call, and that Gerald just opened fire on them. That he's only alive because Gerald didn't see him hiding inside the truck. The police are looking for Gerald."

Gerald looked at them curiously when they approached him.

"Is this true?" Douglas said.

Gerald's eyes widened as did Samira's.

"No, no, no. I know I've done some stupid things, but LaRetha, you know I'm no murderer! I defended myself. That's all I did!"

"Well, be glad the man didn't die," Douglas said.

"Gerald only protected himself," Samira said.

LaRetha took inventory of the woman in front of her. Looking tired and afraid, there was no glamour left to her now.

"You've been a busy girl, haven't you?"

Samira sniffed her indifference.

"You're just everywhere. But, tell me something. Were you ever in love with *any* of them?"

With tears brimming at her eyelids, the woman nodded.

"I loved *Therell!*" She blurted, as LaRetha watched with surprise. Gerald made a comical face and turned his head away.

"How could you, though? *Love him*, I mean? When the family was using you like that?"

"We were alike, Therell and me," Samira defended. "He looked out for me..." She stopped, choking up, now. Gerald gave her a look of intolerance.

"He was your *pimp*, so to speak?" LaRetha implored.

"No! Therell wanted to... to marry me, when this was all over. But, Kellen took that away," she said. "He took my future away from me. I don't care if he *rots* in that jail."

"But, Samira, you brought Kellen here," she said. "And you've already said that Therell had approached him, *twice* that you know of. Is he guilty for defending himself? You blame *him* for what's happened?"

"He killed Therell out of jealousy. Over me. Over everything."

"*Please!*" Gerald blurted. "They used you and you let them. That's all it was."

"And just how would you know this?" Samira hissed at him. "It's not like you could ever keep a woman."

Douglas and LaRetha watched with amusement.

"I kept *you* a couple of times."

Samira rolled her eyes.

"This is a real comedy act," LaRetha said and Douglas agreed.

"This show will be over, soon. *Thank goodness.*"

"You're not still going to turn us in, are you?" Samira asked, frantically. "But, I thought you were going to make a deal for us. For our protection. Can't you can do *something?*" She pleaded.

"I never said I would. Did you, Douglas?"

"*Uh uh*. Not me."

"You're mean you're really not going to help us? I know you could if you wanted to." The woman looked desperate, now.

LaRetha sat there, enjoying the moment.

"You should have known better than that when you came here. Did you really think you would get away with kidnapping and for being an accessory to murder? And more than one? What exactly did you *think* we were going to do?" She asked the woman.

"*Nothing. That's what!*" A familiar male voice spoke from the hallway, startling them all.

"Well, isn't this cozy?" Billard asked, stepping into the kitchen with a gun that he aimed at LaRetha. Douglas quickly turned Gerald's gun on Billard. The man appeared unperturbed.

"This is just what I needed before I left the country, for good."

Billard looked very haggard. His round pudgy face and hands were sweaty and dirty, as were his clothing. And he smelled of soot. He wiped at his face with his bare hand, managing only to smear the dirt even more.

Looking from her to Douglas, his face held a wicked grin, as if he'd stumbled upon a lost treasure. LaRetha's heart sank and Douglas looked suddenly at a loss. Billard smiled at her.

"How'd you get in here, Billard?" Douglas demanded.

"Not a problem. Somebody left the patio door unlocked."

LaRetha grimaced. She had forgotten.

"So, we meet again, Miss Watson. This will be our last time."

"Please don't get my hopes up," she retorted.

"It's good to see you, *Billard!*" Douglas said, distracting the man. "Welcome to the party. We were just talking about you."

"So I heard. I knew these two had big mouths. I never should've fooled with any of *'em.* None of you people can be trusted, as far as I'm concerned. My biggest mistake…"

"So, you're leaving the country, Billard? Why is that? Didn't *any* of your plans work out?" Douglas chided further, causing the man to turn beet red, his gun still on LaRetha.

"Oh, my plans are working out, just fine. Don't you worry about *that.*"

"And here you were, a fine attorney worth his sorry *over-weight* in gold, and you gave it all up, for what? What did you gain from all this killing, Billard?" Douglas sounded angry, now. "For killing Paul Straiter, her uncle and then Cecelia?"

LaRetha kept her eyes on Billard's gun, trying to think of something while Douglas' diverted the man's attention.

"I can't take all the credit. But they were all so stupid. They didn't know the first thing about negotiating…"

"Oh, so you negotiated them into being murdered?" He asked, angrily. "So, you like those deals where everybody else dies and you end up on a plane, going nowhere?"

Billard snorted and looked past both of them at the two frightened people that were tied to chairs in the kitchen. Gerald was struggling desperately to free himself, obviously concerned at being a helpless target.

"Oh, I'm going somewhere, but not before I settle a few things."

"Like what?" Douglas asked. "You can't settle anything here, Billard. If I were you, I'd go on and make that trip before the police got here. We've already called them."

"I've been here for thirty minutes, listening to these little blackbirds sing. If you had called the police, they would've been here, by now." The man sounded certain.

"*As for you!*" He continued, looking at LaRetha. "You've been the source of all my strife since the first day you came here," he said to her. "If you had just done like I told you and shared the land *Miss Greer,* none of this would have happened."

"And if it weren't for greedy people like you, waiting in the wings to snatch what doesn't belong to you, I might have," she responded. "But, why would I share my father's legacy with the likes of you? It's not like you have a claim on it."

Billard looked as if he wanted to pull the trigger and she drew a sharp breath.

"That farm belongs to me. You people call yourself *investors?* You just a bunch of cold blooded *murderers!*"

Billard stared at her as though her outburst had somehow immobilized him. She only hoped Douglas would find an opportunity to disarm the man, somehow.

"Why did you kill *Cecelia?* You called her here and for what? What did you tell her to get her to come, Billard?"

"The same as the rest of them. I wasn't the only one out for what I could get," he sneered. "If you want to blame somebody, you should start with that family of yours."

"You didn't have to kill her," she whispered, vehemently. "You'll pay for that."

Billard looked at her in disbelief.

"That woman *wanted* me," he laughed. "She came here because she thought you were going to give her something. And she probably would've done what I'm about to do to you right now to get it."

"You're a liar, Billard. You lured Cecelia here under false pretenses. That's why she came to my house."

"It was as good a place as any," he said and she really wished she had that gun, right now.

"Don't let him get to you," Douglas said. "He'll say anything at this point. He knows he's going to prison, right along with these two."

"No!" Samira wailed.

"Put the gun down so I don't have to shoot you," Douglas shouted.

"Douglas! My man! I had a lot of faith in you. You let me down, son. Your father would have been very disappointed."

"I have *never* been your son. And don't bring my father into this."

"You're just like your old man - too straight for your own good. But he was a good lawyer, too. It's just too bad that dead men can't testify in court."

Douglas' eyes glazed. He blinked repeatedly as if trying to clear his vision. LaRetha worried that he might pull the trigger on Billard and miss. She tried desperately to think of a diversion.

"What do you want from us, Billard? You don't need anything I've got." She stared him squarely in the eyes, this time.

"Oh, no? Well, you won't need it either, after today."

"*Shut up, Billard!*" Douglas yelled.

"To think that I let your father bring you into the firm. We raised you like a baby, and now you've destroyed everything that I've worked for, and everything I've done for you. He was a part of us, you know? How do you think you survived in this town? It was *me* they respected. Not you. Not your *daddy*," Billard said. "But you could've had everything if you'd played your cards right."

"I already have everything I want, except I got it, honestly. You can't take that away."

"I wouldn't be so sure of that…"

He quickly directed his aim at Douglas and a shot went off, sending Douglas spinning around and falling to the floor, his gun sliding fast across the room.

"*Douglas!*" Ignoring the man with the gun now, LaRetha ran to him and kneeled at his side. Trying to turn him over, she felt Billard standing over her, now. She looked him in the eyes.

"You know you've gone too far, Billard. There won't be any explaining this. If you don't leave now, it'll be too late!"

"I'll tell you when it's too late, *girlie!*" He said. "*Now, get up!*"

Grabbing her by the arm, he effortlessly yanked her from the floor and shoved her against a wall. She felt a terrific pain rip down her back as she bumped her head. It dazed her.

"You and your father, you're just alike. Stubborn and arrogant! Thinking you're better than the rest of them. Your father was no hero. If anything, he was a blemish on this town. *A disgrace!*"

LaRetha shook her head.

"Say it, Billard. He married white. And a man like you would only take that personally. But, that wasn't it, entirely. *You* wanted Cecelia, didn't you? You tried to use her against my father, but it didn't work. As soon as you thought you had her right where you wanted her, he died, she got the money and she left. *How inconvenient for you!*"

Billard turned redder than she thought possible.

"And now, you're angry because despite the fact that you've just about destroyed my entire family, not to mention half the families in this town, you don't have much of anything to show for it." She angrily replied.

She turned her attentions back to Douglas, who seemed to be in terrible pain. She wanted to help him from the floor but she knew that Billard would shoot her in a heartbeat. She stayed put.

"You're talking mighty big for a dead woman, Mrs. Greer."

"You'll pay for what you've done, Billard. Everybody in town will know, by morning. It's all over for you."

Turning his gun on her, now. His dirty face scowled.

"Oh really? It's just too bad none of you will live to see it…"

Just then a shot rang out and Billard looked startled. LaRetha moved away from him. Billard's body made an awkward turn and another shot went off, but missed. She managed to duck just as a third shot caught him squarely on his forehead. Slowly, he pitched forward, falling heavily onto the kitchen floor.

She quickly ran over and kicked his gun out of his hand. Nudging him hard with her foot, she saw that he wasn't moving.

"I think he's dead," Gerald said. He'd managed to free himself from the ropes and get the gun that Douglas had dropped on the floor just in time to stop Billard from fulfilling an obvious plan.

She ran over to Douglas, who was bleeding heavily from his side. He looked weak and didn't appear to be breathing.

"Help me with him!" She yelled to Gerald, who rushed over.

"Your attorney friend sure wasn't nobody's boy scout. That little slip knot saved our lives," he said, holding his arm and grimacing in his own pain.

"I'm glad of that!" She said. "Are you alright?" She grabbed a towel and pressed it against Douglas's side. Still, he didn't move.

"I'll live I think, but first things first." Gerald went to check Billard's pulse. "Yep, he's dead, alright." He came back to her. "But, how are *you?*"

She nodded, still trying to assist Douglas, who wasn't responding. Gerald began to check his vital signs.

"He's weak, but he's breathing. Go ahead and call an ambulance.

She dialed for the ambulance, once again. They were on the way, the dispatcher said. She returned to Douglas, uncertain of how to help him.

"I'm sorry, LaRetha, about all of this," Gerald said. "I had no idea it was this bad. And I can't begin to ask your forgiveness. I just hope you can, someday. *Forgive me,* I mean."

"You never should have gotten involved in this, Gerald. We both could have lost our lives today, and for what? Money? What about our son? Who would be here for him? Did you even think about that? There's no way I would have done this to you."

"But what about *Kellen?* You still care about him?"

"Forget about Kellen! Look at what you've done! If you had just warned me, all of this could have turned out differently. Some of those people could have been saved. But, once again you were only thinking of yourself." She could only feel contempt for him.

"But, everything I said is true," he said, sadly, and she almost regretted blaming him for so much. "I was concerned about you. That's why I kidnapped you. You don't believe me? You will, before it's over."

"I guess we'll have to wait and see what the judge believes. I don't want to hear anymore, right now. How is he?"

"Still breathing. We just have to keep him still until they get here."

Hearing this, she was thankful that he wasn't going to try to escape. She didn't think she had the strength to detain him.

Douglas moved, painfully.

"Douglas? How do you feel?"

"I'm alright," Douglas groaned. "But won't *somebody* call an ambulance?"

"I did that, already. But, press this towel against the wound until they get here."

"I guess it's a good thing he had a slow aim," Douglas said. He reached for his cell phone, but she took it away from him.

"Save your strength. They're on the way."

"So much for 'protecting and serving' on the holidays," Douglas said, wincing with pain, and she laughed with relief.

"Hey! What about me? Isn't somebody going to untie *me?*"

They all looked at Samira.

"I think you're safer where you are," Gerald said. "I know we are."

"And you should sit down, too," LaRetha told him.

"I'll be alright. It's just those pills making me *woozy.*"

"*LaRetha!*" It was Douglas. She went to him. "Stay away from him. He's *dangerous!*"

Both she and Gerald exchanged looks. She sighed with relief.

"I can see you were in good hands all along" Gerald told her.

Suddenly, there was a distinct *click,* and she realized that the recorder had been on the entire time.

What luck! She thought. Billard's confession was all on tape. She continued nursing both men's wounds until they heard sirens.

20

Two ambulances arrived for Douglas and Gerald. After LaRetha and Douglas explained everything, a police car took Samira away. She went quietly. The coroner was called for Bob Billard. She stayed behind to answer questions.

It was over an hour before everyone had gone. Relieved, she went upstairs to shower and change out of her blood-stained clothing before going to the hospital to check on Douglas.

"How are you feeling?" She asked. Douglas was out of surgery and he'd been sleeping for most of the night. She was glad to be there when he finally awakened. Sitting on his bed, she gently stroked his brow.

"*Fine.* Now that I know you're here," he said, woozily. She smiled.

"You've been asleep for hours. I'm glad it wasn't more serious." She examined his bandaged midsection.

"I am too," he said, moving uncomfortably. She adjusted his pillow. "So, what's happened since I've been in here?"

"The police are holding Gerald for the kidnapping, for the shooting, and for assaulting Marilee," she said. "Samira's being questioned, so who knows how that'll turn out. Hogan's still in intensive care. I still don't know if they'll charge Gerald for Billard's death, though."

"And how are *you?*" He asked, unable to keep his eyes open.

"I think we'll *both* live. But get some rest. I'll be here all night, in case you need me." Instinctively she leaned down to plant a soft kiss on his lips. He smiled, just before he fell asleep.

Morning came quickly, and LaRetha awakened to find Douglas miraculously sitting up already, watching the news. Seeing her awake, he nodded toward the television set and used his remote to raise the volume.

She sat up to see what was so intriguing. There was footage of a house fire. She straightened to listen.

"...the firemen have concluded that this was indeed arson. The true mystery is why the homeowner, Bob Billard, a respected and long time practicing attorney, was shot dead at another location just hours after this fire was set. And that strangely, the location of his shooting was the home of his long time business partner, Douglas Davis, Junior."

"Mr. Davis is being cared for at a local hospital. He will be questioned as soon as he is alert. Investigators are looking for a possible connection between the house fire and the shooting. Stay tuned for updates. Back to you, Langley!"

Douglas switched channels. This time, it was Douglas' house that was being filmed *live,* from the front lawn. There were people and police tape all over the place. It was the scene of chaos.

"Oh, no. Douglas! I expected that."

He shrugged and listened.

"We're standing outside the home of one of Lovely's long time practicing attorneys, Douglas Davis, Junior. Like his father before him, he's been practicing law here in Lovely for almost eighteen years..," the woman said.

"Twenty-one," Douglas said to the television screen.

"... Police believe that last night's shootings that left Bob Billard dead and Douglas Davis injured, are both tied to the fire that totally destroyed Billard's home that same evening. And that both incidents are also tied to the fire that burned the home of LaRetha Greer just five days ago, where a woman's body was found inside. The woman was identified as Cecelia Watson, LaRetha Greer's stepmother."

Hearing it, LaRetha could see why it was big news.

"Cecelia Watson had been bound and burned in that fire, but the reason is yet, unknown. It's said that LaRetha Greer was out of town at the time and is not a suspect."

Douglas flipped to another news channel.

"...Gerald Greer is being credited for saving the lives of his ex-wife, Attorney Douglas Davis, and an Ohio woman, who has been identified as Samira Neely. The twist is that at the same time, Gerald Greer was being sought by Atlanta police for recently kidnapping his ex-wife in Atlanta, just days before this incident."

Douglas switched channels to catch the story, again.

"...no question that the fire was set. Police are hoping for the full recovery of both Nell and Jasmine Watson, the mother and daughter

who were saved from the fire. Then, they expect to get details on what started the fire, in the first place."

'What!" Douglas said more than asked. She shook her head, in disbelief. He turned up the volume.

"I know, Mindy. It was just the mother and daughter's luck that a neighbor from across the street saw them going into the house, and later saw what appeared to be very suspicious activity going on outside the house. Then, she says she saw smoke coming from the rear of the house and quickly called the fire department. They were here within minutes."

Someone was pointing to where the women were said to have been pulled from beneath the rubble.

"...the doors and windows were nailed shut and the fire was started just outside the basement. That neighbor's haste in action has very well saved these women's lives. Both women are in the hospital at this time, in critical condition. They are both expected to survive. And both will be questioned later..."

Douglas quickly turned off the television and turned to her. His shocked expression mirrored hers.

"Did you hear that?" He asked. "Nell and Jasmine were inside Billard's house when a fire started. There's no question in my mind that he set it on purpose."

"Unbelievable! Do you know," she said, "that if Billard had succeeded, the death count would have been up to *eight people*, me included?" She asked. He shook his head, sadly.

At that moment the doctor entered. He gave her a cordial nod.

"Attorney Davis! How are you doing, today?"

"I've been better, but I'm fine now, thanks to you and your competent staff."

"You had quite an ordeal last night. I'm happy to see you recovering so well."

"Thanks, Doctor Landis. We both are."

The doctor smiled at her, now.

"Well, I'm glad to hear it. As for your condition..."

He went on to explain to Douglas the further care he would require; how often to change bandages, the medication he'd been prescribed, the rest he would need, afterward. Douglas insisted on leaving the hospital, right away.

"You just got out of surgery, Mr. Davis. You'll need to rest, today. I'll check on you in the morning. Then, we'll decide, okay?"

LaRetha could see that this confinement was irritating Douglas.

"I'll make sure he stays put, doctor," she said, smiling at Douglas' look of dismay.

"Good. *Tomorrow,* Mr. Davis. We'll see then."

"Sure, doctor. Whatever you say," he finally said.

She let out a sigh of relief. Laretta and Germaine should hear this from her. She called Atlanta.

Not wanting to be in the house alone, LaRetha spent the next night at a hotel. Douglas was able to leave the hospital, just two days after the shooting. Only to find his front lawn totally trashed, and his beautiful garden trampled by reporters and onlookers who had waited for him to return. They were all gone, now. She managed to help him inside, closing and securing the front door behind her. She set the alarm.

No wonder people hate reporters, she thought. After getting him settled into the den, she checked the house and found everything in tact. Douglas asked her to stay for awhile.

It only took a few minutes to create a makeshift bed for him on the large den sofa. After helping him take two pain pills, she made him comfortable before dropping into a chair across from him, suddenly feeling very tired.

"Are you hungry, Douglas? Can I get you something?" She went to look into his kitchen cabinets.

"How about ham and eggs?" He asked.

"How about something that's a little easier to digest? Like eggs and grits, or chicken soup and crackers?"

He frowned but acquiesced, deciding on soup. As he ate, she went in search of a mop and pail which she soon found. It took some scrubbing to remove all the blood stains from his kitchen floor, thinking as she did so how this was becoming an all too familiar task. After finally putting everything away, she went back to Douglas. He was awake.

"I don't know why you're doing so much. Mrs. Starks would have done that."

"You wouldn't want all that blood scaring the poor woman off, do you?"

"You don't know Mrs. Starks. The woman was once a body-guard. She teaches martial arts."

"You're kidding me!" *That petite little lady?* She thought.

"I couldn't hire some wimp to take care of me, could I?" He laughed.

"I would think that, until now, you didn't need anyone."

He smiled at this, watching as she stretched out on her chair.

"Thank you, Douglas, for saving my life."

"Did I? Well, it was my pleasure, although that ex-husband of yours saved us all. I might be crazy, but it's possible that he was telling us the truth when he said he came here because he was worried about you."

"Yeah? It's amazing how a gunshot in the arm has changed that man's entire focus. Sorry, no offense to you."

"None taken. I totally agree. It sure opened my eyes."

"Really?" She asked.

Douglas looked at her intently.

"Come, sit beside me."

He shifted on the sofa and waited until she was seated comfortably beside him.

"Well?" she said, waiting. He started slowly.

"Forgive me, but my wincing has nothing to do with what I'm about to say," he began and she laughed. "LaRetha, I have always prided myself on being a man in control. And because of that, I've always had a hard time knowing the difference between what I thought I wanted, and what was actually meant for me."

She nodded. Waited.

"It didn't take all of what happened yesterday for me to know how I feel about you, but it sure was the rude awakening that I needed."

He took her hand.

"I hate to think that something might have happened to you, without me ever telling you how I really feel. You already know how much I care about you."

"Douglas. I know you have good intentions," she said. "But, whatever you have to say should wait until you're feeling better."

"You don't think I know what I feel?" He asked, groggily now.

"I know you do."

"So, what you're saying is that you can't handle it, right now?"

"Not at all. But you promised that we'd wait until after everything was over..."

"But it almost was, just yesterday." He took her hands into his. "I can't wait another day to tell you that I love you, LaRetha. *I love you.* Now, I've said it. You can't make me take it back. You're just going to have to deal with it."

His eyes said that he was serious. But, what she couldn't tell him right now was that, in spite of the fact that she cared for him also, even felt she loved him, she still had concerns.

Could she ever commit to Douglas? To living in this town and being his wife? To a possible lifetime of what she'd just experienced? What about the things she wanted? Was it unreasonable of her to insist that he give her more time?

She was only just divorced and now her ex-husband, and her last lover, was in jail. She truly didn't feel that jumping into another marriage would improve her life, right now. And Douglas clearly wasn't considering a long-term casual relationship, or engagement.

"Douglas, I care for you, too. A great deal. But, there are so many things to consider. Like the trials. Our future plans and goals. What we would have to sacrifice."

"You know I love this town," he said. "And until all this happened, you did too. I think that, once all this is behind you, you could learn to love it again. We could accomplish a lot of things together, in *Lovely.*"

She considered this.

"Besides, I've been single this long for a reason. And I can't compromise by not sharing my life with the right woman. Whatever I need to do to make it work, I'm willing. We could do it together. You're always good at that. At making the best of things."

He pushed her hair back to see her face better.

"What's the real reason that you never married, Douglas?"

"My career, lack of good prospects, poor timing when I finally thought I'd found someone, and then, too much drama. *A lot of reasons*. Not to mention that I wasn't willing to just settle, or to take the time to find the right person, I guess."

He touched his hand to her face. She held it, thinking how this moment almost wasn't.

"But now, everything is just *right*," he continued. "The timing, the person, the way I feel about you. Forget these circumstances. They'll pass. But, I think you and I could last forever, don't you?" She smiled and he closed his eyes.

"You're tired and you should rest, Douglas. I hear you, okay? I know what you're saying to me. And the worst for us is over, I think. But, right now, you should concentrate on getting your strength back. So, let's just take it a day at a time."

He nodded and lay back against the pillows watching her until he was no longer able to fight the sleep that was overtaking him. She went to her chair to sleep, as well.

With Douglas recuperating at home, most of the culprits in the hospital or in jail, and her mother and son being safe and accounted for in Atlanta, nothing was preventing her from moving.

After loading her car with her bags and new computer, she left Douglas' house, unnoticed. Turning the key to the front door of the rental home, she realized how good it felt to have a place of her own, again.

The interior of the house was freshly painted with new carpeting in every room, so it looked very spacious, bright and inviting. Upstairs, she looked out of a front window, expecting to see only trees in the island, there. But there was a small park on the other side. *Wonderful!*

Because tomorrow was New Year's Eve, she wasn't sure if the furniture store she'd visited before was open, but she drove there anyway, and they were. *And,* if she ordered before noon, they might even deliver her furniture today, the saleslady said.

It took her all of the morning and afternoon to do it, but she managed to furnish both floors, and to buy a new washer and dryer. Those wouldn't be delivered until next week, they'd said. And now, with the gas, lights and phone service still on, she only had to call and switch the accounts to her name, paying the deposits by credit card.

Thumbing through a mail flyer from an electronics store, and decided to order the *42"* flat screen television that was on sale and a bookshelf CD player. Lastly, she called a local grocery store that advertised that it delivered.

By late evening, aside from the disarray of flattened cardboard boxes and packing foam, the house looked as if she'd been living there for weeks.

It's really feeling like a holiday, now, she thought, smiling to herself as she happily made the beds that the deliverymen had set up for her, upstairs. Then she rearranged all the furniture to give more space.

9:30pm. She was exhausted and considering what to have for dinner when her cell phone rang.

"Hey, girl! How are you?" It was Vera.

"I'm fine, Vera. It's good to hear from you."

"Same here. Listen, I saw delivery vans driving by my house, today. I'm so glad we're neighbors. I told a few people at the church and they're excited for you, too."

Oh no! She thought.

"Ah, Vera?" She started.

"Yes?"

"I was hoping to be discreet about staying here. At least until the trial is over."

"*Oh no!* I'm sorry. I should have thought of that. I can call them…"

"No, no. That's alright. In all the commotion, I forgot to tell you that I was even moving. I'm just concerned about being bombarded by the news media."

"I don't blame you. That's quite a story they've been running on television. You'll have to tell me all about it."

"Sure. Soon, at lunch, remember? So, what's going on?"

"I got a call from a reporter. Some guy from Atlanta, wanting a story. I hear he's called quite a few people."

Vera's grapevine would prove useful, after all.

"I know you turned him down," she said.

"I sure did. But not until I got his name and information."

"Who was it?"

Vera told her. *Louis Cantrell!* That figures, she thought. Mac Henry was still trying to get his story.

"I know him," she said. "Thanks for telling me."

So, Mac was tired of waiting. But he'd asked too much of her. This was fast becoming her town, now. Besides, he had enough news to cover in Atlanta. *Why didn't he just butt out?*

After having a simple dinner of baked fish and hash browns, she decided to turn in. But first, to check on Douglas, again.

He answered the phone, still sounding very groggy.

"Hey beautiful. I was just thinking about you."

"Same here. Can I bring you anything before I turn in?"

"Just yourself," he laughed. "I thought you would stay with me for a few days. I really need you," he said, and she could almost see him smiling into the phone.

"I had to get my house together. I'm sorry. I should have stayed."

"It's okay. I know how excited you are about that house. How's it looking?"

"It's furnished now, and I just made dinner."

"Already? Well, if anyone could do it, you could. But, look, it's so late. Can you come over in the morning?"

"I can. And I can bring breakfast."

"Sounds great, but how about some real food, this time? They almost starved me in that hospital."

"I saw that. But, sleep tight. I'll see you in the morning."

They said goodnight. And that night, she was happy to sleep in her own bed.

Nell lay on her hospital bed, feeling little pain but a great deal of discomfort. She had just spoken to Bernice, who was still watching the kids at her house. The others would be here to see her, soon. Paul was catching the first possible flight.

She couldn't be happier that she was alive. And that her daughter had survived the terrible ordeal, as well. Heavily bandaged and taking as much pain medication as the nurses would allow, she sat up in bed, watching the story on the news, disbelieving the actual scene that was still being shown on the news.

She watched the broadcast and learned that Bob Billard was dead, Samira and Gerald were in jail, and Douglas Davis had suffered a gunshot wound but was expected to recover. And LaRetha had come out unscathed, as usual.

Listening to the news report, she couldn't stop the tears from running down her face, feeling angry that she wasn't able to wipe them away for the casts on both of her arms. She pressed a button. A few minutes later, a nurse appeared.

"Yes, Mrs. Watson. Are you alright?"

"How is my daughter?"

"Sleeping, but, she's going to be fine. In time, you'll both be back to your usual selves. It's amazing how you even came out of that alive! You must be giving thanks, every minute. I know I would."

The nurse extracted a tissue from the bed stand, nearby and gently wiped the tears from her bruised face.

Thanks, indeed! Were it not for her quick thinking and finding Billard's dead wife's oxygen machine in the basement closet, neither she nor her daughter would be alive!

But, from what she was hearing on the news reports, that *doofus*, Gerald Greer, was the hero of the hour. And LaRetha was still floating like a butterfly. Nobody should be that lucky. *It wasn't fair!*

But, there was nothing that she could do. Not until she recuperated. In the meantime, that woman had better be making plans to leave *Lovely*. Or she wouldn't be responsible for what happened, next.

Dressed comfortably in jeans, a sweater and her new winter boots, LaRetha drove to Douglas' house, carrying with her enough food for six people, she guessed. She would cook once she got there. She was prepared to spend the entire day, this time. It was New Year's Eve, after all, and she couldn't think of any place she'd rather be.

That man sure knew how to kiss! She hadn't thought of much else, since yesterday. Just the thought of that day they'd kissed on his deck gave her butterflies. And admittedly, the idea of being with Douglas was growing on her. Not just because he was *super fine,* as Vera said and she agreed, or even because of that certain chemistry that they had. But more than that, she'd just seen another side of this man. Douglas had put himself on the line in every way, risking life and limb to spare her own life! And if that wasn't saying *I love you,* then what was?

So they didn't agree on very much. Truthfully, they agreed on very little. But, being around him without having to think about Kellen the entire time, well, she was beginning to see what her mother already had. The two of them just made sense. If she had doubted that before, she didn't now.

Thoughts of him with Samira, and then with Valerie, were hard to brush aside. And she didn't quite understand some of the business decisions he'd made; like staying in practice with Billard, and associating with her uncle's family after all that had happened. But, the man had lived here all of his life, and she hadn't. So there would probably be a lot of things that she would never understand. But that shouldn't prevent her from loving him, would it?

All of that was in the past. And Douglas was quite possibly as lonely as her mother had said. And if she admitted it to herself, so was she. He had been great with her family. And they liked him. But he made that easy by always trying to make life better for the people around him, and that included her. If only he would do as he'd advised her, and think about what the drinking was doing to him.

According to her mother, Douglas was a *good* man. And even Gerald had commented on it, which had oddly seemed the ultimate confirmation. And now, she finally knew for herself what those words truly meant. And she agreed.

She called Laretta on the way to Douglas' house. No answer. She figured her mother was spending time with her mystery man, upstate. She decided to leave a message.

"Hey, Mama! Update. Douglas is out of the hospital and he's home, recuperating. I'm on my way there, now. I'll probably be there all day, maybe overnight. Anyway, I've moved into my house. It's furnished and everything. I believe I'm going to like it, there. Tell Germaine and Tori, hello, for me. I hope you all will have a great New Year's Day. Here's my number and address."

Next, she called Germaine and left a similar message for him, hoping she'd get to talk to him before the day ended.

Douglas was awake when she got there, somehow having managed to shower and shave, and change into clean clothing. He was watching her from the living room as she came inside.

"Tell me you didn't take those stairs without my help," she said.

"I couldn't meet my girl looking all dirty and funky, with stank breath, could I?"

"Humph!" There was no point in fussing, she thought. He'd do it, again, anyway.

"What did you bring me?" He asked, looking greedily into the containers she'd brought.

"I'm spoiling you, aren't I?"

She helped him into the kitchen, where she unpacked the food and began to cook. He watched, looking hungrily at the pancakes, ham with red-eye gravy, grits and scrambled eggs. She made coffee and they sat down to eat.

"Anything new happening, today?" She asked.

He nodded, chewing.

"Gerald is out on bond, but Samira's still in jail. Probably waiting on her partners in crime to get out of the hospital and bail her out. Kellen's trial won't be for two more weeks. I should be on my feet by then."

"Are you sure? Let me see your bandages."

She went to him and lifted his shirt. Aside from the distraction of his toned, muscular body, she saw that his bandages were changed and clean. She rubbed her hand lightly across them. He'd done a good job.

"Does it still hurt?"

When he didn't answer, she looked up to see him giving her a mischievous wink, chuckling as she pulled his shirt down and playfully rolled her eyes.

"How are Nell and Jasmine doing?" She asked.

"*Surviving.* They'll be called to testify."

"Aren't you worried?" She asked.

"About what?"

"That Kellen won't be acquitted. That he'll go to prison."

"I doubt that. But, it'll all depend on the testimony that's allowed in court, and the evidence, of course. We're well prepared, but you can never tell about these things. All I can say is, I have a good feeling he'll get off."

She nodded, and they ate in silence. He chewed and swallowed slowly as she poured him a glass of water.

"You're hurting. When was the last time you took something for pain?"

"Early this morning. I don't want another one, though. I don't want to fall asleep while you're here."

"If you take it, I promise I'll be here when you wake up. We'll celebrate the new year, together."

"Okay, but just one."

She cleared the kitchen and joined him back in the den. He adjusted his pillows to sit up and talk to her.

"To finish what I started, yesterday. I believe I poured my heart out to you, and you shut me up. Tell me now, LaRetha. How do you feel about us? About being here in *Lovely?* About being with me?"

"Right now, I just want us to celebrate the incoming New Year."

"But what happens in six months or a year from now, when your lease is up? Are you going back to Atlanta?"

"Douglas, you're asking me questions I can't even answer, yet."

"Okay, I won't pressure you. But, you know how I feel. I don't know why you're being so *commitment-phobic.*"

"Douglas, you just saw my ex-husband arrested, my ex-boyfriend put in jail for shooting my cousin, my uncle die from a heart attack, my house burned down, my stepmother killed and my aunt and cousin almost burned to death in a fire. Not to mention, both of us almost getting killed yesterday. And I'm sure I'll be blamed for all of it. So, do you *really* want me to answer that question, right now?"

"I guess not," he said, frowning.

"Good, because I'm really not ready to. So, get some rest, because tomorrow you're going dancing."

"Where?" He laughed.

"Right here. You and me," she said, softly. He hummed his consent.

"That sounds promising, at least. But, we've got a second chance, LaRetha. And I'm expecting nothing but good things for us, from here on out. So, come here."

He moved over and she sat beside him. She liked feeling the warmth of his body and his warm breath on her neck. The clean smell of his soap and cologne. The gentle way he moved her hair and the feel of his lips, as he placed soft kisses on her face. Sighing, he hugged her tightly.

"I don't care what you say. I'm not losing you, LaRetha."

They watched television that way for awhile and it wasn't long before the pills took effect and Douglas was falling asleep.

"You sure you'll be here when I wake up?" He asked.

"There's no other place I'd rather be."

"Hmmm," he murmured. And fell asleep.

Laretta drove to *Lovely* the day before the trial began, and came prepared to stay as long as she needed to.

"This is really nice, LaRetha. Once again, your decorating talents have turned plain into *fantastic!* "

Her daughter beamed at the compliment. It was true. The house was small but beautifully decorated, and very accommodating. She found her bedroom upstairs and unpacked, and then joined LaRetha in the living room, again.

"Has Douglas seen it?"

"Not yet. He's still recuperating."

"I know he's disappointed that you moved."

"Well, disappointment happens to the best of us."

"You two sure are taking it slow. Hasn't he proposed or *any-thing?*" She couldn't believe they were still playing *tag,* after everything they'd been through.

"He tried, but I won't let it get that far. It's too soon for me."

"So, there's nothing between you two, even after everything that's happened?"

"He told me that he loved me."

Now we're getting somewhere.

"And what did you say?" She asked her daughter, eagerly.

LaRetha shrugged and shook her head.

"Well, I think once Kellen's trial is over, you'll have a different answer," she told her, disappointed.

"Maybe so," LaRetha said.

And then, the thought of her daughter finally having all this behind her and starting again with Douglas made Laretta feel very hopeful.

Epilogue

The next few weeks would be hectic. The courthouse was crowded every day of the hearing. Cameras were forever in their faces, although LaRetha declined to answer any questions.

She and Laretta sat in the same section, everyday - just a few rows behind Kellen, who always sat looking straight ahead. He looked well but appeared very concerned. His life was on the line, after all.

LaRetha could only marvel at how well Douglas looked. He was still healing, but he walked with ease and seemed so completely within his element, in here. And so distinguished. Laretta must have noticed too, because she chucked her in her side the minute he would walk in.

He'd dressed so well, especially on that first day when he'd worn a perfectly tailored brown wool suit with matching shirt and striped tie. The man looked simply *divine*. Somehow, the atmosphere seemed to have changed when he entered the room. And by the time he began with his opening statement, LaRetha was totally transfixed.

The trial began slowly, and she nervously hated waiting for her turn to testify. But all bases were being covered as crime experts were called and pictures were provided, many of them being shown on a slide for everyone in the courtroom to see.

She shuddered as Therell's lifeless body was being displayed, and could hear variations of wailings from throughout the room. She diverted her eyes and saw Kellen drop his head for a moment. But neither Douglas or Laretta appeared to be affected, in the least.

It wasn't surprising that Nell and Jasmine would provide the most interesting testimonies. It was shocking, seeing them on that first day. With arms and legs bandaged, their faces and other exposed parts of their skin looking swollen and burned. And both would stop speaking to gasp for breath, from time to time. They appeared barely able to stand. LaRetha felt sad for them.

Live by the sword, die by it, her mother wrote on a note pad. She nodded.

The questioning was swift and detailed. Group members were named. Admission to involvement with some negotiations came easily from them. They both named Billard as the culprit for both her house fire and the one he'd set to kill them. And, for the murders of Paul Straiter and Cecelia Watson.

Normally calm and collected, they were very emotional when speaking about her uncle, and it saddened LaRetha to know that he'd been so unhappy just before his death. But it was when Therell's name was mentioned that Nell truly broke down.

Nell admitted to Samira's theory that her uncle was personally involved in hiring *Straiter* to just do odd jobs, which Douglas wouldn't accept, saying it had been for more than just that. That the man hadn't acted entirely on his own when he'd broken into LaRetha Greer's house.

"One can hardly say that a man who was hired to terrify an innocent woman so that she would leave this town and her inheritance behind, was acting *entirely on his own!*"

"But, it's all LaRetha's fault! She deliberately brought that man here to hurt Therell, so she could keep that farm. It doesn't belong to her. It belongs to my family."

Douglas had warned LaRetha not to take everything to heart. That she would have to ignore a few things that might be unkind or untrue. This, she figured, was one of those times. Because one thing was evident; both women held her responsible for most of what had happened - including the fires. Jasmine clearly stated that she'd wanted nothing to do with LaRetha, and that she felt sorry for the person who did, *including Douglas!*

"Just look at what happened to my brother, my father and her boyfriend!" She said, whereupon, Douglas came to her rescue, asking Jasmine how well she knew her.

"I *don't*," she said, vehemently, staring in LaRetha's direction. Laretta nudged her side. Seething, LaRetha didn't respond.

"Have you ever had a conversation with LaRetha Greer?"

"No. I didn't need to."

"But, you dislike your cousin. Why?" Douglas continued.

"Because! She took my father' attention, his affections, and then she took away his heart by causing Therell to die. But, that wasn't enough. She had to take my father's life, too! That was her truck that killed him - her and her father's. She did that on purpose. *She fixed those brakes!* The woman sobbed.

LaRetha gave her mother a horrified, questioning look. But Douglas wasn't done.

"So, you hold your first cousin, LaRetha Greer, responsible for the meetings, the planning, and the plots of this 'group' you belonged to, that was supposed to run her out of town?"

"I know nothing about a plot to do anything of the sort," Jasmine said. Douglas gave a pained laughed.

"Weren't you directly involved in this *investment group?*"

"I was an investor."

"And was this not the same investment group that Bob Billard participated in?"

"It was."

"The same Bob Billard who was responsible for the deaths of people like Paul Straiter and Cecelia Watson?"

"Yes."

"Objection, your honor!" The prosecution was standing now. "That is not the case we are trying here, today," he protested.

"Sustained," the judge said. "Careful, Mr. Davis," she warned. He nodded. Continued.

"Aren't you just a little angry that this same *group member* almost took your life, and that of your mother's? Where does your loyalty to this madness end, Jasmine!*"*

"Objection, your honor!" Her attorney repeated, vehemently. *"He's badgering the witness!"* The courtroom was totally disorderly, now. Again, it was sustained.

Douglas asked Jasmine if she knew if her feelings toward LaRetha were ever shared by Therell Watson. She boldly said that they were. Nell said the same.

"Tell us about Therell Watson and your relationship to him," Douglas later stated to Nell when it was her turn.

She appeared puzzled at first. Then, as if on cue and unable to stop herself, she began to describe this wonderful child that she'd been blessed to adopt. Urging further explanation, Douglas waited. She said nothing.

"Isn't it true that your *adopted* son had a medical condition. A condition that his doctor referred to as *bipolar?*"

Surprised by this revelation, she nodded before saying, *yes.*

"And isn't it true that he would often exhibit those symptoms? Many times becoming depressed, and then alternately flying into instant rages, even becoming violent, at little or no provocation from time to time?"

She nodded.

"Is that a yes, Mrs. Watson?"

"Yes."

"Wasn't your husband suffering from the same condition?"

"I think so."

"Was either man diagnosed?"

"Yes, my son."

"And isn't it true that Therell Watson *might* have inherited this condition from his father. His *real* birth father?"

She said nothing.

"Mrs. Watson?"

"Yes," she said, bursting into tears. The room was silent.

"And wasn't your husband, Verilous Watson, his birth father?"

Gasps were heard from the family's section of the room. The room became abuzz.

"And isn't it true that you kept this fact from Therell his entire life? That he went to his grave, not knowing that the man who raised him was really his birth father, and not *Vernell,* the man who'd supported him financially, for all those years?"

"Yes." She was barely audible. Someone in the room began to weep.

"And, that this was a big part of his reason for resenting LaRetha Watson for so many years? That he actually believed that he was entitled to part of that land? That it was his birthright? Isn't it true that you allowed this man whom you loved so much, the man you raised as your son, that *Therell Vernell Watson* lived his entire life, believing a lie?"

"Yes," she sobbed. "He never knew that he was really my husband's son. And I'll never forgive myself for not telling him."

It took a minute to quiet everyone, particularly the family that was there to support Nell. Bernice ran from the courtroom. One of the brothers followed her.

Nell admitted to intentionally passing Therell off as *Watson's* son, partly because of his financial support. And miraculously, she also admitted to helping Therell create that phony document in order to get more money.

Laretta looked at LaRetha, giving her an *I told you so,* expression.

Isn't it true that Greg Hogan was your husband's friend and a member of the 'group' in question, and to which you both belonged? Douglas implored, further.

"Yes, it is."

"And that your husband was personally involved with planning Paul Straiter's invasion of Miss Greer's home here in Lovely?"

"Well, it was never supposed to…"

"Yes or no, Mrs. Watson."

"Yes," she whispered.

"Thank you. I have no further questions for this witness, your honor."

Witnesses from the party were called, and LaRetha listened to account after account of what they said happened at the party the night of Therell's shooting. All could confirm that Kellen spent much of the time with Samira, that night. But none had overheard any arguments, they said.

It amazed LaRetha that Douglas could remain so composed whenever his name was mentioned. He had no secrets, it seemed.

The members of the 'group' were called. While admittedly belonging to the investment group, neither of them claimed any knowledge of wrong-doings, saying those must have been Bob Billard's practices. They all had the same story.

Foreman, Reeves and Gray claimed to have only made a few small investments with the company, and each provided documented proof. Nothing more was going on, they said. They knew of no burnings or murders.

Douglas presented documents pertaining to the fires and other questionable transactions, and several were signed by each of them. He persisted with his line of questioning.

What did they do for Billard and how could they have no knowledge when they were clearly involved?

"We invested in a few rental properties here and there. We helped out when he needed our business services. Mostly, we was buying up properties that folks couldn't afford to keep."

"But, did you ever strong-arm any of those people? Force them, or forcibly *encourage* them to sell or just to abandon their properties by burning them out?"

"*No way,*" they all said. We always did business, fair and square. Everyone who sold to us, wanted to. We never did none of that," they all said, innocently.

"Greg Hogan is the auto-mechanic, is that right?"

They'd all agreed.

"It's been verified that he was the person who'd fixed those brakes on LaRetha Greer's car, and who shot Gerald Greer in an attempt to kill him. What do you know about that?"

None of them knew anything.

"You mean, one of your *group* can die from having his vehicle rigged by another one of you, and none of you are willing to talk about it?"

"Like I said," Reeves spat out, angrily. "Whatever crimes they did, it was always Billard and him. Hogan was his triggerman. Not me, not Foreman and not Gray!"

"So, then you *were* aware that there was wrong doing?"

The man stopped. Said nothing. Looked as if he wanted to kick himself in the head. And even LaRetha couldn't believe he had incriminated himself this way.

LaRetha was finally called during the second week. And although, she found it hard to look at Kellen, she had no trouble admitting her initial feelings for him, and their relationship in Atlanta.

She told of her life in Atlanta, and in *Lovely*, before the incidents occurred. About how she hadn't learned of her mother's differences with the family until after Therell's shooting.

Then, she described how she and Kellen had first met, his relationship to her and Germaine, and to Gerald. And even her lack of one with her ex-husband, when she was asked. She explained that Kellen had come to *Lovely*, totally unexpectedly, and that she hadn't asked or encouraged him.

Under cross-examination, LaRetha vehemently denied the prosecution's theory that she had come to *Lovely* with malice toward her own family, and that she had enticed Kellen into coming to help fight her inheritance battles.

She explained how she had learned about the family feuds much later, and how no one, neither her mother or her father, had never mentioned Therell. The reason clearly being that neither believed he was *Watson's* son.

But, if I could change things, I would, she said.

"How so, Mrs. Greer?" The prosecuting attorney asked.

"It's *Miss,* and I don't know how. But, if I could, obviously I would."

Didn't she feel that family was entitled to part of the land? He asked.

No, she said, emphatically. By this time, Douglas had already presented proof to Nell and Jasmine that her father's purchase of the family land had been done, quite fairly and to their great advantage, money wise. She mentioned this.

When asked about her relationship with Douglas, she said he'd been a good friend, a legal advisor to her and to Kellen Kincaid. She was then told to detail her kidnapping and the shooting incident at her uncle's and then the one that had left Bob Billard dead. She did, in detail.

But wasn't it true that she had managed to somehow manipulate an already bad situation to her advantage? Or how else could she have survived all of this when so many others hadn't? She took great offense to this line of questioning and said so.

"Clearly, I had no control over who was killed, or any of that. This was no *manipulation,* as you put it. I couldn't have predicted this, even if I did have some idea what was going on when I came here, which I didn't. But I am a praying woman and I believe that's why I have survived. I'm not sorry for that."

"But, you do admit that the outcome is somewhat bizarre?"

Objection, your honor!" Douglas appeared very irritated at this.

"Sustained."

She easily answered the questions that followed, explaining how she'd never suspecting any association between Kellen and Therell, nor any of them with Gerald. And when asked to describe that day of Therell's shooting from the beginning, she did so, saying first that she and Kellen had been together all day, on the farm.

The prosecution asked if either of them had any prior experience with using guns. She said that she had, and first described hunting with rifles as a child with her father and brothers, just for sport. But, being taught how to safely use a gun, she'd never expected to hurt anyone.

Urged to continue, she took a deep breath, and described her and Kellen's walk around the farm, and then their early target practice. This information stirred surprise in the entire courtroom.

"You practiced *shooting*, Miss Greer?" To which she unfalteringly replied, yes.

"And where are those guns, now?" The short, balding man asked.

She explained how the police had taken her father's gun and hadn't returned it, and how she'd gotten rid of her own, before her house was burned.

"What other guns have you had in your possession, *Miss Greer*?"

She thought of her uncle's gun.

"I had one of my uncle's, but it disappeared."

"When did he give it to you?"

"The same night that Paul Straiter broke into my house and after the police took my gun away. He said he couldn't in good conscious leave me without one. He never knew about the other guns."

"Are we to believe that after your uncle hand-picked this man to break into your house, that he would provide a gun for your safety, as well? That doesn't sound like a man who's hired someone to scare or to harm his niece." He implored. "It appears to me that he was protecting you, after all."

"He gave me the gun. And I *didn't* shoot Paul Straiter for breaking in. It was after he lunged at me as if he were going to kill me. I had warned him that I had a gun, but he kept coming at me. It looked as if he was going to attack me. I was afraid. When he didn't stop, I pulled the trigger."

The room was quiet.

"So, it's established that you shot the man with your father's old gun. But, who do you think made that gun of your uncle's disappear? He probed.

"I didn't miss it at first. When I did, I asked Kellen. He told me he'd had it in the car, but that he had no idea where it was at the time of the shooting."

"*When* did he misplace it?"

"I don't know, exactly."

"Take a guess."

"Sometime between our gun practice and that same night, at the party."

"He took it to your aunt and uncle's house for the party?"

She said he had told her as much, but that she knew nothing of its present whereabouts. This raised murmuring in the courtroom, Douglas asked for a recess. It was late, and the hearings would resume in the morning, the judge said.

"Why didn't you tell me all this, before? *Target practice*, LaRetha? I knew about the one gun missing from your house. But *three?*" He looked very angry.

"I'm sorry, Douglas. I had hoped that Kellen would mention it, and when he didn't, I guess I hoped it wouldn't matter."

"What *matters* is that you would keep this from me. Kellen has only admitted to taking *your* gun, and that someone took his jacket with the gun in it. Have you asked *anyone* about it?"

"No. That one belonged to my uncle. No one's mentioned it."

"Well, now we have to explain why you felt the need for target practice if neither of you expected to use a gun, that night. That was supposed to be the furthest thing from his mind when he was at that party. Knowing he was preparing to use one really hurts our defense," he explained. She understood.

"But, it was *my* need for target practice, not his. He didn't suggest it. He didn't know why I asked him outside, and he didn't want to practice with me," she explained.

"Kellen has experienced a lot of heartache over guns," she continued to explain. "He's advocated against them for years. He's done seminars, he's written a lot of articles... He only said he would practice if it meant protecting me. But we never once discussed taking it to the party. It must have been an impulsive decision on his part."

"Some of that information might help," Douglas said, although he still didn't look convinced. "But how did he find your gun in the first place? Did you ever know?"

"He must have found it in the living room drawer. I didn't even think to move it when he came."

"Or, he saw you put it away, after *target practice*," he frowned. She knew he was greatly concerned.

"I'm sorry I didn't tell you, Douglas. I guess I knew it would cause a problem. But, I couldn't lie about it. I believe Kellen is innocent and now, everybody knows that he was defending himself."

"Some people might. We already know it was Therell's gun that killed him. What I'll need now is to convince the jury that the man is truly harmless, after all. I'll need for you to get some of those articles Kincaid wrote and anything else that you can find, relating to his advocacy against guns. Fax them to me. And warn me if you think of something else we haven't discussed."

"Fine. Thanks, Douglas."

"All in a day's work," he said.

LaRetha hoped that her testimony hadn't destroyed Kellen's credibility and Douglas' defense.

Back on the stand the next day, she explained Kellen's hatred of guns and his hesitation at using one. He had resented being put in the position of having to practice in order for her to feel safe, she said. He wasn't even a good shot, and he'd given it up rather quickly.

Douglas used Kellen's newspaper articles as evidence, and his speaking itinerary and notes as proof that he'd advocated *against* guns, for no reason other than his own personal desire to promote gun control. He was convincing, she felt.

Finally, LaRetha breathed easier, feeling relieved and praying that the impending disaster had been undone.

She watched as Douglas easily glided through each testimony, exposing lie after lie where the group was concerned - exhibiting document after document, proving his case against Billard and her uncle, and against Therell. The circumstances of the federal agent's death was under investigation, he said. And Therell's investigation had begun prior to the time of his death.

With so many former complaints against Billard and his 'group', that had gone unheeded, but that were now being allowed as evidence, it appeared as if the entire group was on trial. There were large checks to be explained. Equipment rentals and bombing chemicals found in Elton Gray's barn. The list went on and on.

Finally, Samira was called, having come directly from jail. Everything on her taped confession was confirmed. Aside from her job at Jasmine's public relations company in Ohio, she said, she was also an *independent contractor* - a statement that caused the entire courtroom to erupt into laughter. Apparently, her reputation preceded her, LaRetha thought. She had little to say that LaRetha didn't already know. It was Gerald's testimony that caught her completely off guard.

"How long have you been cooperating with Lovely's police department in the case of Therell Watson?"

LaRetha believed the entire courtroom had gone into shock, including her mother and herself. News people bustled about, several leaving the courtroom in a rush. The judge ordered them to quiet down or they would have to clear the courtroom. Douglas repeated his question.

"They called me the first time a week after her uncle died." He looked squarely at LaRetha, who could only stare back at him, in shock. His eyes said, *I told you so.*

"Why did they contact you, in particular?"

"Because, he was being investigated for murdering an agent here. When it was discovered that he and his family were after LaRetha's land, they contacted me to see if I would help."

"And had you been in contact with any of the Watson family, or their business associates prior to this?"

"Yes, I had."

He explained that Jasmine and Samira had called him, and ashamedly admitted that he'd even considered it and contacted Kellen Kincaid about helping him to change LaRetha's mind.

"So, what changed your mind, Mr. Greer?"

"Honestly? Something Kincaid had said. He told me what a fool I was for losing her in the first place. And he was right. I couldn't believe how low I was stooping for that money. But, it was cool, until I started hearing about those shootings. Then, I realized the danger she was in. So, I backed off from Jasmine and Samira. And when the police contacted me, I decided to get involved."

"Did you tell anyone about your involvement with the case?"

"No. And it was hard, but nobody knew who was doing what for whom, anyway, so I did what they said. I didn't tell anybody."

"Not even LaRetha Greer, your ex-wife?"

"No, sir."

"So, who planned for you to kidnap your wife?"

"That was my own bad idea. That went too far – I know that now. I never intended to hurt her mother's housekeeper. That wasn't part of the plan. I tried to quiet her because LaRetha was leaving the house, and I had to stop her. I felt her life depended on it."

"So, you were willing to commit an assault, in order to save your ex-wife?"

"I didn't plan to assault her. She panicked and bumped her head. I only tied her up. She bumped her head when she struggled with me. She was conscious when I left her. I know it was stupid. But like I said, that was not intentional. Remember, I wasn't trained for this."

His explanation was weak, to say the least. But, Douglas had known all along. *Gerald had been trying to save her, just like he said*.

She looked over at Laretta, and *could have bought her with a dime*, as the saying went, judging by the shock on her face. She could only laugh to herself, in disbelief. And from the look on Samira's face, even she hadn't known.

"So, you came to this town and put your life on the line to save your *ex-wife?* And you were merely trying to *subdue* the house-keeper?"

"I still care about LaRetha," he said on the stand. "And after being the kind of husband that I was, I owed it to her to do what I did. I never intended to hurt her, or anyone, for that matter. I just needed a way to talk to her, where she would listen. But I couldn't figure out how to do it without interfering with the police. I would never intentionally hurt a woman. And I never meant to hurt the house-keeper."

He admitted that her relationship with Kincaid had bothered him at first. A lot. But that he never believed she was seeing Kellen while they were married. He felt that she deserved to be happy. So did their son.

Finally, Kellen was also allowed to testify, his biggest revelation being that he'd accepted offers from both Jasmine *and* Mac Henry. The news floored her. Like her cousins, Mac had promised Kellen money. But for a story, with the possibility of a promotion, a book deal and other perks on the job.

The rest of Kellen's testimony was pretty clear-cut. He spoke very calmly, and he appeared very remorseful. He talked about his past distant relationship with his parents, and how she and Germaine had been like family to him and Kadero. Then, when the prosecutor persisted in knowing just how involved they had been, he told how she'd helped him out as a friend; getting him a job, helping to look out for his brother. He admitted that they had been intimate, once. And he said that, although he'd pursued her, she'd told him her regrets about breaking her spiritual vows of celibacy. And about jeopardizing their friendship, that way. They hadn't continued the relationship, he said.

He told everything; about the *30 day* deadline, his relationships with Jasmine and Samira, and then admitted to having had two physical encounters with Therell, the last one leading to the shooting.

He was afraid of the man, he said. And because of his threats, he'd been concerned about what he might do to LaRetha, as well. He greatly regretted shooting Therell Watson, he said. He hated even more that he'd ever gotten involved.

"I was hurt and angry about LaRetha' leaving, just when we were getting close. She had shut me out, and wouldn't explain why, other than to say she wanted more than I could give her in a relationship."

He had sold her out, he said. Deceived her. Made her think his intentions were pure. But, although he'd meant it when he'd proposed to her, his first objective was to get out of the mess with her family.

"They're *crazy*," he said. "I never knew that. I'd never met Therell or her uncle before I came here, but if you ask me, they were *both* insane."

When asked about his target practice with LaRetha, he said that after Therell's threat, he'd only been concerned about their safety. He did take her uncle's gun without her knowledge and lost it along with his jacket as soon as he got to the party, and didn't think about it anymore until long after the shooting.

Therell wasn't supposed to be in town, or at the party, he said. And he'd hoped that going to the party would help them to resolve this. That it might create some form of harmony between LaRetha and her family.

"Why was that your responsibility, Mr. Kincaid?" Douglas asked.

"Because, I knew they wouldn't leave the matter alone until they got that land from her. They were desperate people, and willing to do *whatever,* just to have their way. I only wanted her to make up her mind to leave, and to get paid for her land. To just let them have it. *Buy it,* I mean. But, it was her decision. I never said this to her."

He talked about his articles and seminars on gun control, and commendations he'd received. LaRetha held her breath, hoping it would be convincing enough. It appeared to have been.

Lastly, Kellen explained his behavior at the party. He'd been angry with LaRetha for not being intimate with him since his arrival. And he'd set out to make her jealous. He had felt rejected.

Samira had made both of his drinks, that night. He had refused her offer to go into the back, *to talk,* and now he was certain she had spiked the drinks with something, preparing him to meet Therell, who had waited in the back room for him, all night.

"You said you spent the evening dancing with Samira Neely. Weren't you in fact engaged to Miss Greer?" the prosecutor asked.

"No. I proposed but she never accepted. I asked her to wear the ring until she changed her mind. Still, she never accepted."

"And you would have married her, knowing that you were here on false pretenses?"

"In a minute. I still love her. She knows that."

"Sure you do, Mr. Kincaid. And where is that ring, now?" The prosecutor asked.

"She has it. She doesn't wear it, but she has it."

"And, how did you pay for that ring?"

Kellen was silent for a moment.

"I paid for it with money I got from Jasmine Watson."

A whisper came over the courtroom. LaRetha squirmed.

"And what did giving her that ring really mean to you?"

"Until this, I thought it meant I still had a chance. Now, I'm not so sure."

The courtroom erupted into laughter.

"I would imagine you wouldn't be, Mr. Kincaid," the prosecutor said. And even with his back turned, she could sense Douglas' relief.

Well, now you know the truth, she thought. *I am not in love with Kellen Kincaid.*

After the first week of testimony, newspaper headlines focused on her, Kellen and Douglas.

Is Triggerman's Attorney Caught in This Love Triangle?

LaRetha steered clear of reading the newspapers, but Laretta didn't. She even managed to make light of them all, before threatening to respond to a few stories she didn't like. There would be plenty of time for that, LaRetha said. She just wanted to get through the trial.

For the next few days, the hardest testimony for her to listen to was her mother's, which was a saga of their family's history of feuding and lies. Her comments on *Verilous* brought Nell to her feet.

"Liar!" Nell stood up and said. "You wanted my husband! You've *always* wanted my husband. She had it all," she said to the jury. "The land *and* the money. And still she wanted my husband!"

The courtroom stirred noisily and the judge warned Nell to sit down and to remain quiet. The outburst shocked LaRetha. She'd never known that Nell had felt so much rage toward her mother. She had hidden it well.

Unruffled, Laretta continued to tell her story about Aurelia and Therell, the land sale and the greed that had forced distance between them all. About how her husband had gone to his grave with a broken heart because of his brother. Nell spoke out again and was removed from the courtroom, this time. LaRetha cried softly for her both her father and her uncle.

She was happy to see Vera and a few familiar faces from the church. Dressed sharply in business attire, Vera would give her a smile and a wink, every now and then. It did strengthen her, somehow.

With testimonies finally coming to an end, closing arguments were intense. The prosecution portrayed Kellen as a *money hungry playboy,* which even she couldn't deny. Kellen Kincaid was never in love with LaRetha Greer, he said. Instead, he'd slept with Samira Neely to seal a deal that they had paid him handsomely, for. And, he had betrayed LaRetha further by making a deal with the newspaper that she'd helped him become employed at, as well. The man knew nothing about gratitude or appreciation. People in love didn't do that.

In spite of his fear of Therell Watson, Kellen Kincaid had come to that party carrying a gun, because he had intended to get his money, at any costs. He could have warned Miss Greer of the conspiracy against her. He'd had all the time in the world, he said, considering he was living with her on the farm, at the time. Just like all the others, Kellen Kincaid could possibly have prevented the loss of several lives, had he been forthcoming and honest.

Instead, he'd come to *Lovely* to make sure that he got what he wanted. He had taken money that he had to make good on, had a second installment coming, as well as a very lucrative job offer, once he accomplished his goal of convincing her he loved her, thereby using her to get it.

The man had already rented out his townhouse and moved to *Lovely,* fully prepared to stay for as long as it took to make the deal happen. That didn't sound like a man in love. He was, instead, a man on a mission. A very dangerous mission, the man said.

"Kellen Kincaid had received *three* offers and accepted two of them," the prosecutor said. The man was a *menace* to Miss Greer, not a friend."

Kellen was guilty of first degree murder, he continued, because all of his actions had been entirely premeditated. He had come to that family gathering carrying a gun and he was fully prepared to shoot someone. That target practice was more intentional on his part than Miss Greer believed. Fortunately, he'd gotten too drunk to keep up with the gun. But, he did manage to get his hands on another one; the one belonging to Therell Watson.

Lastly, he said that Kellen was guilty because he could have taken his companion's advice and left the party long before the incident occurred. Except, he had stayed, thinking he still had that gun he'd brought, and feeling he was prepared to handle anything that might happen. And despite Therell's medical history, or violent history, *that night,* Kellen Kincaid was no victim, he said.

That was no normal family gathering for Kellen Kincaid, but a business meeting – a chance to confront Therell Watson. To be rid of the man once and for all, thereby leaving open the possibility of marrying LaRetha Watson and getting that property under his control before she did decide to sell it. This was why he never asked her about selling it, the Prosecutor said. He knew its value, and he wanted *in*.

So, under the guise of being drugged and afraid of the man, he had done what he'd come to the party to do. What he'd anticipated doing all along. *He had shot his girlfriend's cousin in cold blood.* Kellen was the perpetrator that night at the Watson family's party. And not Therell Watson!

The man was detailed and he was convincing. And by the time he was finished, it appeared to LaRetha that Kellen would be going to prison for a very long time.

Douglas gave his best closing argument, keeping in mind that winning the case would only be his *second* biggest reward, if LaRetha accepted his proposal.

He began with a description of a young man who, out of feelings of loneliness and abandonment when everyone else in his life had gone, had clung to this woman and her son, feeling they completed the family circle left void by parents who'd left him behind.

He did not deny Kincaid's deceptiveness, and pointed out every incidence. He had lied to LaRetha Greer, deceived her, and added insult to injury by giving her an engagement ring. He'd met her family, and pretended he didn't know anything about them, as had they. He'd spent the better part of the evening on the shooting in question, dancing with the woman who'd been sent to seduce and use him. He'd known this, but not knowing the full extent of their plan for him and LaRetha, he had even assented to it.

Kincaid was drugged that night by Samira Neely – a woman hired to enter into intimate relationships for the purpose of financial gain. *And,* he added, a woman who was acting on *Therell Watson's* behalf. Not Kincaid's. Foolishly, he'd fallen into her trap, thinking that it might make LaRetha Greer envious, and encourage her decision to accept the marital proposal he'd made, earlier that day.

That night, Samira Neely had been assigned to the task of weakening this man, and diminishing his sensibilities to prepare him for a plans already laid by a gun-toting and desperate Therell Watson, who had been acting on the blessings of his family, and the group's. The man had hidden in the bedroom, laying in wait for Kincaid that entire night.

Kellen Kincaid was a lot of things, Douglas said, but he was nobody's *cold blooded murderer.* While he would never win any *Man of The Year* awards, he was no criminal and had no criminal history.

He had been afraid that night. Therell was known to everyone as a dangerous man, and he had already made it clear to Kincaid on one other occasion that somebody was going to die, quite possibly him and Miss Greer. Therell Watson, a man known for his terrible temper and rage, was out of control when he attacked Kellen Kincaid. But Kellen had won the fight.

Kincaid had made a number of errors in judgment, he said. But, if anyone else were put into those circumstances, with a man holding a gun in your face, angry about generations of feuding that you had no control over but he thought you did, threatening your life for not the first, but the second time, then lunging at you with a gun as if intending to take your life at that very moment, *what would any of you have done?* He'd asked.

If you were lucky, or if your immune system was as strong as Kellen Kincaid's, you would have been sober enough to do what he had, and lived to tell about it. Otherwise, Therell Watson's mission would have been accomplished, and there's no telling who might have been next. Possibly LaRetha Greer.

This was not just a *family* issue, he said. It was the story of *Lovely. This* was a trial of the people. Of each person in their town, who had ever been approached to do something they hadn't wanted to do in order to save what they owned or to get something they needed Or who had lost something precious to them at the hands of greedy people, and other tormentors.

Kellen Kincaid was no *saint,* he'd said. Not by a long shot. But, everyone involved in this complex scheme of lies, deception and thievery had pulled that trigger, that night. And had he not defended himself, Kellen Kincaid would be dead, already. Unrightfully so.

Twisted? Yes it was. Kincaid had admittedly accepted the money. But, not once after coming to *Lovely,* had he ever tried to persuade Miss Greer to sell her land. He had been foolish to attend that party. But hasn't everyone gone somewhere, then had regrets after the fact?

Several people laughed in agreement.

The man had been set up, Douglas said. *Should he to go to prison for life for defending himself?*

It was time for the citizens of *Lovely* to place the blame where it should lie. To stand for what they knew was right. To decide if this man, just because he was an *outsider* by many people's terms, should pay for years and years of intimidation and terror that he'd had nothing to do with.

There was nothing to fear, now, he said. Despite the tragedy of this situation, it was a new day, and past time for a change; for this young man and for the town, in general.

"Consider your decision, carefully," he said to the jury. "This is not a matter of taking one life to avenge another. This is a matter of taking something that has been wrong for far too long, within this family and within this town, and making it right. This man deserves to live his life as a *free* man."

Finishing his statement, he happened to look up and into LaRetha's eyes. They showed gratitude and admiration. They showed his future. And for now, whatever the outcome, he was pleased.

After just four hours of deliberation, the jury ruled that Kellen had indeed acted in self-defense. He was found innocent of all charges. He was free to go.

Kellen jumped out of his chair and grabbed him, hugging him tightly.

"Thank you, man! Thank you, thank you!"

Douglas hugged him back, guessing that freedom had never felt so good for him. A man at his age, with so much ahead of him in life, didn't deserve to spend it behind bars for one stupid decision, or for someone else's part in it. If anything, his actions had brought a lot of terrible secrets to light, and freed this town from disaster that might have gone on for an eternity. Life would be different for everyone, now.

After the reading of the verdict, the judge commented that, unfortunately, *Bob Billard, Verilous Watson, Therell Watson* and *Paul Straiter* would not stand trial. *Cecelia Watson* would never testify about the horror she had experienced on her last day, alive. And *Greg Hogan* would stand trial only when he recovered, *if* he ever did.

"Still," she said, "the wrongdoers who have passed on will surely be judged in a higher court. Luckily," she said to Kellen, "you can still make changes in his life. And now, you have plenty of time to figure out how to do it."

Douglas had planned to embrace LaRetha after the trial, but Kincaid beat him to it. At his first opportunity, the man had unabashedly brushed past several congratulators to get to her. His embrace seemed to surprise her, as did his kiss on her cheek.

Laretta had accepted a hug as well, and seemed genuinely happy that he was a free man. He'd never considered the man's relationship with that family, but it occurred to him that Kincaid was once a big part of it.

Neither woman acknowledged him, so evidently his job was done, he thought. His services were no longer needed. And like Kincaid, he was *dismissed.*

It confused him for a moment. But then, he understood. And now that the show was over, he would politely bow out, like a man.

He was leaving the courtroom unnoticed by them, just as he overheard Kincaid asking LaRetha about her plans for the evening. He hesitated to hear her response, as did several others. Not realizing that he was holding his breath.

"Kellen, I'm glad this is finally over for you," she said, "and for all of us. I plan to spend the evening celebrating with my family. We can finally go on with our lives."

Than she had reached inside her purse, retrieving that beautiful diamond ring that had at first made him so fearful of losing her. She handed it to Kellen, who stood looking at her, open-mouthed.

"This belongs to you. I wish you well, and I hope you'll let this experience mean something positive for you, in the future. Have a great life, Kellen."

With that, she turned to her mother. "I think we can go now," she said in almost a whisper.

With the crowd gathering around her, Douglas was unable to get to her. Still, what she'd said had made him proud.

LaRetha and her mother left the courtroom amid snapping cameras and questions from the press. But they were stopped on the front steps of the courthouse by a flood of people that stood waiting for her; both reporters and townspeople. And finally, the big question was asked; *what were her plans for the future, for herself, her love life and for the farm?*

With the cameras rolling and the numerous microphones pointing in her direction, she realized that a speech was in order. She took a deep breath, feeling very unprepared for this *impromptu* press conference. But, they were expecting her to say something.

"When I first came to *Lovely,* it was with expectations of living a quiet, peaceful life."

Several people laughed and she smiled with a heavy heart.

"I knew a little of the town's history, but almost nothing about the on-going troubles at the farms. Not even my own."

"What has happened since then is still unbelievable to me. I have lost people that I loved and cared about. That pain will never go away."

There was a murmur. She continued.

"This is a good town filled with good people. I know because the tragedy of this situation had brought me to them. My roots are here. And no matter what's happened, this town will always be a part of me."

"Recently, when I was asking someone why any of this had to happen, well, they couldn't answer that. But they did say that with my inheritance has come a great responsibility. I agree with them."

So what are you going to do? And do you plan to marry Douglas Davis?

She looked around to see Douglas standing aside- watching and listening. And refusing to comment to those reporters close to him.

"You people are way ahead of me," she said and many of them laughed. "Right now, I just want to be of some help to all the people who've helped me. And, I'd like for this community to pay attention to what's happened here, and work together to make sure nothing like this ever happens again."

There was murmur of agreement.

"Since my father's day, there has been a lot of work done here. Still, I believe there is so much more that we can do. Our fathers and their fathers had faith greater than a mustard seed. And now, we can look around and see the benefits of that. But more change can come. And we all have something that we can contribute to that change."

So what do you plan to do about it?

"It's not what *I* plan to do. It's what do *we* plan to do. People in this town have worked much too hard to have generations of heritage uprooted and destroyed by greed and unfair practices. According to an old African proverb, *the destruction of a nation begins in the homes of its people.* It's only right that the *unification* of our community would begin the same."

That's right. That's true.

"I just want to say one more thing." She asked. They listened.

"I am so sorry for my family. For everyone who's been affected by the type of ruthless activity that we've heard and witnessed in this courtroom over the past weeks. I am saddened, just knowing that something like this could even occur in these United States, and certainly that it could happen with people in my own family."

"I know that all of them shared the same dream, once. It's our responsibility to make certain that their living and dying has not been in vain," she added, wiping away a tear. "I thank everyone who has supported me. Please pray for all of our healings. Thank you."

As she began to leave, she momentarily glanced over her shoulder and into the faces of two very angry looking women - Nell and Jasmine. But, Bernice was smiling now, as was Paul. And she couldn't repress a tearful smile of her own.

The months that followed were consumed with more arrests, hearings and testimonies. She was called to testify, several times. Thomas and Andrew were subpoenaed this time, and testified about their mother and father, and their relationship to everyone, as they remembered them. It was certainly an emotional time for all of them.

With Billard dead, naturally all fingers pointed in his direction. And after LaRetha's computer disk were found in the rubble of his house, it was clear that he'd killed Cecelia and burned her house, taking these with him.

It was also more than clear that the judge wanted the news reporters out of the city, as soon as possible. So, the trials were quick and sentencing was swift. For Nell, ten years in prison for fraud and conspiracy to commit murder, but with a possibility for parole. Jasmine received five years for conspiracy, as well.

Greg Hogan was finally well enough to testify and was charged with first degree murder of Paul Straiter, then second degree murder for contributing to her uncle's death, and again for attempting to kill Gerald, receiving a life sentence plus twenty years with no possibility of parole.

Samira was sentenced to two years in prison and five years probation for her involvement, as well. And for their involvement with those found guilty, but because none of the fires or deaths could be tied to any of them, Foreman, Reeves and Gray were given five years probation, each. And that was only because they had lied about knowing about the crimes.

It was spectacular, and everybody seemed to have an opinion on the matter, most of them saying it was all Bob Billard's doing. Television cameras emerged from popular television shows, and write-ups in national magazines dragged the story on longer than she'd hoped.

Comments were sought from the community about this trial's effects on the town. And now the townspeople were no longer shy about speaking. Most people were hopeful, or at least optimistic, they said. Others, skeptical but staying informed, just the same. More than that, she was on the hot seat with the townspeople to do as promised, and she would, with their help, she'd said in one local television interview.

The number of people who had offered their support was unbelievable to her. Douglas was right, it *had* been a trial of people, she realized. And as Vera had told her, this was something that could turn the entire town around. Like the others, she felt the excitement in the air. This was the commencement of the change they'd all been waiting for. And this time it was a good change, for everyone.

Upon hearing his *Not Guilty* verdict, Kellen had hugged Douglas. When he turned around. LaRetha's was the first face he saw. She'd been there every day; crying for him, testifying on his behalf, and looking very concerned.

Kadero hadn't been able to come, but their parents were there for most of the trial. He'd asked them to tell no one who they were, for their own protection. They had waited for him after the verdict was issued, but he'd wanted to see LaRetha, first.

"I'm expecting you to stay out of trouble, this time, Kellen," Laretta had said when he'd hugged her.

"You can count on that. Thank you, for everything," he had smiled with relief.

"It's LaRetha you have to thank," she'd quickly said. "She stuck with you, and believed in your innocence the entire time."

He'd hugged her, as well, thanking her. She'd also been happy. And for some reason, he'd felt hopeful. So, he asked her about her evening. He hadn't expected the response she gave him, although he should have. Still, it had floored him, and embarrassed him in front of people who appeared in agreement with her decision.

They were those church members and friends who'd been there everyday, waiting to congratulate her. And although he was a free man, once again, and certainly forever grateful to her, Laretta and Douglas, he realized that there would be no way to make this right with her.

Standing open-mouthed and defeated, he could only stare at the ring in his hand, and watch as she walked completely out of his life.

The first thing she did when she got home was shower and change into comfortable clothing. Remembering, she said a tearful prayer of thanks for the outcome. Whatever Kellen did in life, she truly wished him well. As for Gerald, she still couldn't get over *him*.

After a while, she dialed the phone and waited for an answer. Finally, she got one.

"Hello, LaRetha," he said, warmly.

"I was hoping you were home. Thank you, for a job well done. This town should be very proud of you."

"Well, thank you," Douglas said. "But, that's not the first case I've ever won."

"I'm sure. So, I take it that you're healing pretty well? You didn't seem to be in any pain during the trial."

"I wasn't. *Medications,* you know. It made it a bit harder for me to concentrate, but I pulled through."

"I never would have known it."

"Speaking of which," he said, "I think you made a very brave statement to the press. You've got a lot of people thinking about making changes, I'll bet. It was an excellent speech."

"Well, I wasn't planning to make one, but they put me on the spot."

"I know. I also heard you talking about working with the town to make things better. I have some project funding information that might interest you. You can start a committee to tackle those projects and be up and running in no time. Just remember not to take on too much at once. I'll help with the legalities, certainly."

"Thanks, Douglas. But, tell me, what are you doing later tonight? We're planning a celebration dinner. Want to come over? Or, we can come over there if you'd prefer."

"Well, I wouldn't want to intrude."

"What? Now, you know you're always welcome. Mama's expecting you."

"Will Kincaid be there?"

She smarted at this, disbelieving his attitude.

"You think I would invite him to my house after everything that's happened? Don't insult me."

"I didn't know. I don't know where he stands, or where I even stand with you, right now."

"Humph! No? Well, now I know exactly where I stand with you. Maybe dinner isn't such a grand idea. Sorry to intrude. Goodbye, Douglas!"

She hang up the phone before he could speak, again. *The nerve of him,* asking if Kellen was coming!

Her phone rang. She answered.

"LaRetha? I'm sorry. I just… I had hoped we would talk after the trial…"

"Douglas!" This time, she heard his disappointment and smiled at his need for her affirmation, finding it very endearing. "I am so sorry. I was just anxious to get out of there. I guess I figured we could always get together, later. *My bad,* as the kids say."

"Well, let's make some good of it. I am totally beat, so I think I'll take a rain check on dinner. What I really need is a long nap. How about breakfast tomorrow? My house? *10am?"*

"*Will Kincaid be there?"* She retorted.

"He'd better not be."

LaRetha heard clicking on the line.

"Someone's trying to reach me, LaRetha. Come in the morning, alright? Promise?"

"I promise."

They hang up. And she was excited the entire night about seeing Douglas, again.

He called very early the next day, to cancel their date.

"Something unexpected has come up," he said. "I'll have to get back with you, LaRetha. Forgive me?"

"Sure," she said, disappointed. "Another time, I guess."

They made another date on the following day, and again, he called early on the day of, and cancelled. This went on for three more broken dates, with Douglas choosing to leave messages on her home phone rather than to call her, directly. Finally, she realized that Douglas just wasn't interested in seeing her, again. And she felt like such a fool for not seeing it, before.

Laretta was sympathetic on the phone.

"He's just trying to heal, right now. He was still hurting at the trial, you know? He's got physical and probably some emotional things, going on. He's dealing with the losses, too. Not to mention losing a law partner that he's been with for years. He's running that law firm by himself, too. All that takes time."

Oh, and what am I? Some sort of painful reminder? I think he's seeing another woman. That trial has made him pretty popular, I'm sure. But he should have just been honest with me. I could handle that better than this *brush off,* he's giving me."

"You should talk to him," her mother advised.

But how? She wondered. Besides, Douglas was a grown man, and knew better than she what was going on in his life. She deserved an explanation, but she certainly wouldn't beg for one.

Days passed and finally she could focus on other, more positive things. Still, there was no denying the huge void in her heart, and her life, without having Douglas there.

Then, it occurred to her that there might have been something said at the trial that had turned him off. Maybe, hearing Kellen talk about their intimate relationship...

But, he'd been in several of those, and she wasn't holding it against *him*, she thought. Besides, this was a promising time for her – for them. There was nothing more to worry about and the future was brighter, for it.

Sill, she grieved her losses. Those family members she'd never see again. Then Gerald, who had been very lucky to walk away free and clear of all the charges, since neither Marilee nor the police pressed any charges. And now, he was more involved with his son, which pleased Germaine.

As for her, she no longer had Kellen as a best friend, nor Mac Henry as her mentor. And now, it appeared, that list also included Douglas.

She told herself that she couldn't worry about that. It was time to get her life back on track, and her career. Not to mention, to make good on her commitments to contribute to some of the causes, around town. There was plenty to do, if she sought it out. And everyone was being receptive and helpful.

With her job at Mac's paper being out of the question, initially she'd been concerned about finding other writing opportunities. She needn't have been. The offers had been pouring in ever since the trial had ended. That exposure with the press had done wonders for the demand for interviews and novels. The local paper had called and made an offer, and didn't care that she would only work freelance. They wanted her to start, right away. So, once again she had plenty of work and a nice comfortable home to work from.

Feeling good about her spiritual life again, and so thankful that the past situations were resolved, she made time for studying the Word - wanting her life to be all that it could be, and her efforts to be a blessing to others. She got involved with her mother's church, thinking it might not be a good idea to attend *Joyful Baptist* with her uncle's family, just yet. There was still the pain of their losses and hers. Vera was disappointed, but said she certainly understood.

What was most surprising was that her mother would attend with her, whenever she was in town. And that was becoming more and more often. Already she could see the change in Laretta's attitude toward the town. She was feeling a part of it, again.

She was enjoying *Lovely*, too. And the rental house was growing on her, so she decided to go ahead and buy it. Her news traveled fast. Some people thought that meant that she and Douglas were together. To which she would simply say, *no*. They weren't.

Still, with the church work, her study and community involvements, writing for the paper and making plans for use of her farmland, there was little time to worry about him. Although there were those nights when she had to wonder where he was and what he was doing. Why he wouldn't call, and if he even missed her. She would tell herself that she should just go over there and demand an explanation. She never did.

Two months passed quickly. And even after seeing Douglas in court for the subsequent hearings, and even having him cross-examine her on the witness stand, she still hadn't heard a word from him.

But she needed her friend, not to mention a good attorney to help her with all those projects he'd promised to start. The community work was supposed to be *their* project. Feeling hurt and dejected, she decided to just give him more time.

Another month passed and no word, yet. Still, she was determined not to call him, first. With so much news and local attention on their supposed relationship, everyone around her was puzzled at her refusal to even talk about Douglas. And her own disappointment was greater than she'd anticipated. Finally, feeling angry and fed up with his childish lack of consideration, she wrote him off, altogether.

She was lounging on her bed one evening, editing an article for the local paper when her cell phone rang. Seeing Douglas' name and number appear, she didn't pick up.

He can just leave a message, she thought. And he did. She dialed her voice mail. Douglas wanted to meet with her as soon as possible, he said.

The nerve! It's been three months and he wants to see me, now?"

She ignored that message and several that followed, having decided that being alone again wasn't a bad thing. She was meeting other people. Had even had a few friendly lunch dates - but nothing that she would allow to become serious.

After a few days, the calls stopped. And she concentrated instead on planning her next visit to Atlanta. She did miss them all. And now, moving back didn't seem like such a terrible idea.

But, she'd made commitments that she would see underway before making that decision. Their first project meetings had already been held, and the support had been tremendous. She'd been pleased, and quickly shared the credit with her very motivated committee of six people whom she'd only met since the hearings. Vera would help out whenever she had time, which was rare, considering all her responsibility at the mission. Still, they often collaborated on programs and ideas, and at least that much was working out well.

It was Saturday in April, and she needed to get to the printer's before they closed. As she was leaving, the doorbell rang. Hurriedly, she opened the door. It was Douglas.

"Oh, it's you. Hello," she said with little emotion.

"Can I come inside and talk to you?"

His expression was serious, but did little to move her. He looked very nice in casual blue pants and a striped blue and beige button-down shirt with an open collar But, despite his handsome smile, his immaculate appearance, or the apologetic expression on his face, she was hardly enthralled at seeing him.

"Sorry. I was on my way out." She stepped outside and turned to lock the door.

"Where are you going? I'll go with you."

"*Never mind.* What do you want?" She started around the house to the garage, wanting to kick herself for not leaving through the kitchen door.

"You're angry with me?"

She raised a brow. *Why was he surprised?*

"I don't even know you. The Douglas *I* know doesn't stand me up, four or five times in a row. And he doesn't run away for three months."

"I know I've cancelled a lot. But, you have to let me explain."

"Don't even worry about it, Douglas. If you can stay away for two or three months, two more years won't make a difference."

She raised her garage door.

"LaRetha, listen to me."

"Why should I?"

"I need you to listen to me. I have to explain."

"*Uh huh.*"

Douglas grabbed her arm, stopping her.

"LaRetha, I had to get past the trial and get myself together. It was hard for me, seeing all these people I knew dying and going through so much... It was *really* hard. And I was going crazy, trying to get my health back, and piece my practice back together and handle all the calls. I had to decide if I even wanted to."

"Most of all, I had to figure out if it was me you wanted, or if I hadn't just misread the situation based on what *I* wanted. That maybe you only saw me in a professional light. I was stupid for not telling you, but I wanted to give you some space."

"In the meantime," he said, "I had to ask myself if I was even ready to give you everything you wanted and that I wanted for you. I always thought I was alright the way that I was. But you pointed out things that made me stop and think. After a lot of self-examination, I saw a lot of things that I didn't like. So, I decided to unload some baggage of my own."

She nodded, attempting to get past him. He wouldn't let her pass.

"Douglas! I'm in a hurry. *Excuse me!*"

"*Listen to me.* This is important and I'm not leaving until you do."

She stopped and waited impatiently.

"Okay. For one, I had to stop drinking. I realized I was no longer drinking, casually. And that you didn't deserve an alcoholic any more than I deserved to be one. When I came to you, I wanted to be different than before. I had to admit I had a problem. So, I went to *AA* meetings. And I'm so glad I finally got the nerve to do it. Thanks to you."

"I'm very happy for you, really," she said. "But, even though all that's good news, I don't quite believe that's what kept you away for so long. I think you realized how you truly felt and changed your mind. You were concerned about people expecting so much from us when you weren't that serious to begin with. *That's* why you didn't want to see me."

He looked baffled and she walked around him.

"I can't believe you even feel that way. I've told you how I feel. *I love you*, LaRetha," he said, and it made her pause. "You know I love you. And other people have nothing to do with it," he insisted.

"But, those things you said about me needing something else to do, well you were right. I was lonely. I was hurt. I was hiding behind my work. I had given up on ever trusting a woman and falling in love, until I met you. You just don't know how happy you've made me."

"Sure I do. Happy enough to stay away for three months." She gave him an ill-humored look and opened her car door. He closed it.

"Listen to me! We're not kids and we know where we're going in life. We're already here. We've *survived*, LaRetha! And, if what you said at that courthouse was true, then you're *still* going to need me. And I'm still going to be here."

She shook her head, again. Angry now, he quickly reached into his pocket and extracted a small blue velvet box.

"LaRetha Watson, will you marry me?"

She stood stock still and looked at him strangely. Facing him head on now, she was prepared to challenge him.

So, you think you want me? She thought. *We'll see about that!*

"I'm sorry, Douglas. You're just not my type," she said, matter-of-factly.

He straightened and looked at her as if she'd hit him with something. She guessed that she had.

"LaRetha, I am *not* Gerald Greer or Kellen Kincaid. You can trust me. You can count on me."

"I don't think so. I wasn't looking for love either. But one thing I know is that the next man I get involved with will keep his word to me. He won't make a fool of me by showing the world he doesn't care. I've been there and done that, but no more."

He was speechless.

"Three months is a long time for someone who was pressuring me so much before the trial, but then disappeared as soon as I was free to make my decision. So, it doesn't matter what you say. That speaks volumes on its own."

"I told you what happened."

"It doesn't matter. It's too late. Move out of my way, Douglas," she said, softly.

"I see your problem," he said, angrily.

"And what would that be?" She demanded.

"You don't believe anyone can love you. And you don't believe I would sacrifice everything to be with you, but I will. You think I'm playing games. But I'm not. I would never do that to you."

She frowned.

"A woman in my life was the last thing I thought I needed, but, in you walked with your country beliefs and your city ways, and with all those strong convictions. And I wanted you. *All of you.*"

She gave him an impatient look. He continued.

"How could I not fall for you?" He asked, and she remembered asking herself the same thing about him.

"*I want what you have,*" he continued. "I want to share my life with a woman with firm beliefs, a woman who excites me and makes me want to be at my best, and with a woman who wants more than just money and position…"

"*Hold on, now!* I might be all that and some, but I'm not *that* different. After faith and family, money and position rate high on the list!"

He laughed at this. "See, you make me laugh. We have fun. We *connect.* I like you, as a person first. And I love your spirit. I love what you've brought into my life and into my home. And, more than that, I *miss* you like crazy."

"So, make your point. What do you want from me?" She said, caustically.

"I love you, and I need you."

"I can't take your secrecy, Douglas. I have to know *you,* and I can't do that if you won't let me see who you really are. You didn't have to hide your problems from me, or what you were doing to resolve them. You shut me out. And I can't handle that."

"But *this* is who I really am. Think you can deal with me?"

She opened the car door, again.

"Look, woman, I'm begging. And I'm not leaving until you give me the answer I want."

She frowned at him and wondered if that gunshot hadn't affected his reasoning. He couldn't possibly be serious.

"Look, they say this is supposed to be easy," he said, getting down on the concrete driveway onto knee. "But, if you say no, I'll never do it again. It'll ruin my life, and it'll be all your fault."

"Get up," she said, smiling. "You're ruining your pants."

"I asked you a question," he persisted, still on his knees. She sighed.

"But, how could you treat me like that and then just show up and propose?"

He shrugged, shaking his head in apology.

"You know what? I think you're as crazy as the rest of them. *No!* I won't marry you!"

She sat inside the car, and he determinedly pulled her out, again.

"I'm not going to ask you, again," he said, softly. With that, he planted a deep kiss on her and she felt she would totally lose her composure. Wanted to resist but couldn't. So she did the only thing that she could, and kissed him back. He pulled her tighter and she felt those crazy butterflies, again. He was strong and everywhere it seemed, and she melted in his arms.

After a moment, he released her.

"See, I can take care of you, LaRetha," he said. "I can make you happy."

He kissed her again, this time she answered but her reply was lost in the wind as her breath was totally taken away.

"Now, what were you trying to say?"

She was speechless, but he continued to wait, looking very serious, which made it even harder for her to speak. Finally, she could say the words.

"I said *yes*. Yes, Douglas. I love you and I will marry you."

"Say it, again," he whispered to her.

"I've said it *ten* times, already," she said, twisting the five-carat ring on her left hand.

"But sometimes when you say it, it sounds different from the other times," he said, snuggling up to her in their honeymoon suite in the Bahamas.

"Douglas Davis. *I love you.*"

"Baby, for a while I thought I'd never hear you say it," he said, pulling her close. "Did I tell you that you were the most beautiful bride I've ever seen?"

"Yes. And you were the most handsome groom. I can't believe I almost missed that day. What was *I* thinking?"

"You were angry and blinded to the *truth*, baby!" He exclaimed, making her laugh. "I had to marry you to keep you out of trouble," Douglas said.

"And I had to marry you to keep you from finding law partners that would want to shoot you!" She said, causing him to laugh.

Later, at the beach, they enjoyed lying back and lavishing in the sun and watching a group of kids volleying beach balls in the water. A year had passed since the trials had ended. They had talked about them, planned their futures, spent long days together, talked about any and everything that came to mind, and it had only brought them closer together.

And now, they could happily laugh about some of the past, while able to share the sad times, too. With a lot of prayer and the distancing of time, the pain slowly dwindled, bringing healing. And that left more room for the joy they brought to one another.

"Your mother and her girls really outdid themselves on planning that wedding. I haven't danced like that in years," he yawned, lazily.

"Neither have I," she said. "Mrs. Starks and Marilee really did a fabulous job on that reception, didn't they? But, the best part was when Germaine gave me away. He looked so handsome in that gray tuxedo. I think he gave his number to every girl, there. He's still talking about it."

"He's seeing his father?"

"Yes. And I'm glad. He's doing well in school, too. He wants to visit next week. He's bringing friends. They'll be *vacationing* at the house, or so they say."

"I think he likes those checks you've been sending him, too. But what happened to Tori?"

"They date, but they see other people. I think they've both had time to think about how serious they really want to be. As long as Germaine keeps those grades up and stays out of trouble, we have no problems. Otherwise, he can just support himself. Besides, I'm renting that house out, soon. So I guess he'll have to visit us at your house, next time."

"It's *our* house, now."

She smiled.

"Alright. We'll call it the *Davis Family House*. And that means keeping it available to Candace and Dade and the kids. Besides, if I ever leave, I can build my own," she teased.

"Don't play like that."

She laughed and kissed him lovingly. And together, they watched as the sun began to set.

"So much has happened. But you know, it's nothing less than a miracle the way our families have come together," she said. "Thomas and Andrew are writing me, now. Bernice is coming around. We don't want anything to happen to either of us, again."

"*You* brought it together, with your blind faith," he said, proudly.

"Well, I wasn't the only one praying. My mother's been helping me with that forgiveness thing, a lot."

"I think your mother's not so disenchanted with *Lovely,* any more."

"No, not after meeting David Penny at his grocery store. He's a nice man. I can just see my mother, dressed to the *nine's,* bagging in his store, talking about she's retired! Did I tell he gives me free groceries, sometimes?"

"You're supposed to let Mrs. Starks do the shopping," he said, nuzzling her face with his chin.

"She's retiring soon. Besides, anything for my man," she teased.

They embraced again, enjoying the moment.

"This year, we should invite Candace and Dade and the kids over for Christmas. What do you think?" She asked, cheerily.

"I think you have a good idea, there. But, it's barely summer. Can't that wait until later?"

"I guess," she smiled, feeling happier than she'd ever been.

"Come on, let's enjoy the water again before we get dinner," Douglas said, snapping the waistline of her red swimsuit. "I'm all for seafood."

"How can I say no to *seafood?*" She shoved him into the water before jumping in after him.

Grabbing her arms, he pulled her further out into deeper water, pushing her underneath and quickly pulling her up. She gasped for air. And he kissed her again.

"Douglas!" She said when she could finally talk.

"*I love you, Mrs. LaRetha Davis!* Don't you ever leave me. *Ever,*" he said, those beautiful eyes of his burning with intensity.

They frolicked in the water. And as the sun appeared to slowly sink behind their beautiful ocean, she was pleased to see the glow of love in his eyes, and the expectations that she held for the two of them reflected there as well. It was truly a new season. A beautiful one.

"*I love you, too,* she thought. *And I can't wait to spend the best of my life with you.*

Book Club Discussion Questions...

1. Did Laretta and *Watson* play a part in LaRetha and Gerald's divorce? How so or why not? How do you think this affected her relationship with Gerald? With Germaine?

2. Was Germaine's separation from his mother really necessary for him? What could either of them have done differently to prevent it?

3. Do you agree with LaRetha that her intimacy with Kellen, which was a breach of her vow of celibacy, was the true cause of his deceit?

4. How justifiable was it that Laretta did not tell LaRetha about *Lovely,* before she moved there?

5. Should LaRetha have disapproved of Kellen's inquiry to Paul about a job?

6. Was the decision to not tell Therell about his true birth father a wise one at the time? How about later in his life?

7. Was Kellen's verdict an appropriate one? Why or why not? What about the others?

8. Was Mac Henry entitled to a story about LaRetha's hometown and her family problems there? Should he have asked LaRetha to write one? Or Kellen?

9. Was Kellen just being a professional journalist when he agreed to Mac Henry's proposal?

10. Do you think that LaRetha's move to *Lovely* was preordained, as Vera and Douglas suggested? Or was the outcome just a good ending to a bad decision?

11. Was LaRetha being unfair about keeping the land? And since the trials ended, should she feel obligated to share her inheritance with the family? Why or why not?

12. Should she have kept Kellen's diamond engagement ring?

13. What positive things should LaRetha use the farmland for?

14. Could you live in *Lovely*? Why or why not?

To write Faye Clark, the author, e-mail: fclarkbooks@comcast.net, or miss2busy@yahoo.com.